Three great Margaret Malcolm novels, all from Harlequin's Romance Library... an invitation to a world of love

Not Less than All... Rosamund fled from her stifling shallow existence with a ruthless domineering aunt and found sanctuary on a houseboat moored on a country canal. Into this peaceful setting came John Lindsay, who brought her love...and another kind of prison.(#1607)

The Lonely Road... Lucy Darwill liked being away from home, and her new job was wonderful. But Owen Vaughan, her employer's nephew, she could do without. She had to admit, however, that he'd helped her over the humiliation of being jilted and enabled her to face and enjoy life again!(#1728)

Cherish This Wayward Heart... Judith planned to get rid of Charles Saxilby. For six months she would have to tolerate his management of Windygates Farm—then she'd have the power to dismiss him. But, strangely, in that time, Judith would become woman enough to change her mind.(#1781)

**Another collection
of Romance favorites...
by a best-selling Harlequin author!**

In the pages of this specially selected
anthology are three delightfully
absorbing Romances—all by an
author whose vast readership all over
the world has shown her to be an
outstanding favorite.

For those of you who are missing
these love stories from your
Harlequin library shelf, or who wish
to collect great romance fiction by
favorite authors, these Harlequin
Romance anthologies are for you.

We're sure you'll enjoy each of the
engrossing and heartwarming stories
contained within. They're treasures
from our library... and we know
they'll become treasured additions
to yours!

The third anthology of
3 Harlequin Romances by

Margaret Malcolm

Harlequin Books

TORONTO • NEW YORK • LOS ANGELES • LONDON
AMSTERDAM • PARIS • SYDNEY • HAMBURG
STOCKHOLM • ATHENS • TOKYO • MILAN

Harlequin Romance anthology 72

Copyright © 1977 by Harlequin Enterprises Limited. Philippine copyright 1983.
Australian copyright 1983. All rights reserved. Except for use in any review, the
reproduction or utilization of this work in whole or in part in any form by any
electronic, mechanical or other means, now known or hereafter invented,
including xerography, photocopying and recording, or in any information storage or
retrieval system, is forbidden without the permission of the publisher, Harlequin
Enterprises Limited, 225 Duncan Mill Road, Don Mills, Ontario, Canada M3B 3K9.

All the characters in this book have no existence outside the imagination of the
author and have no relation whatsoever to anyone bearing the same name or
names. They are not even distantly inspired by any individual known or unknown
to the author, and all the incidents are pure invention.

These books by Margaret Malcolm were originally published as
follows:

NOT LESS THAN ALL
Copyright © 1972 by Margaret Malcolm
First published in 1972 by Mills & Boon Limited
Harlequin edition (#1607) published June 1972

THE LONELY ROAD
Copyright © 1965 by Margaret Malcolm
First published in 1965 by Mills & Boon Limited
Harlequin edition (#1728) published October 1973

CHERISH THIS WAYWARD HEART
Copyright © 1974 by Margaret Malcolm
First published in 1974 by Mills & Boon Limited
Harlequin edition (#1781) published May 1974

ISBN 0-373-20072-2

First edition published as Harlequin Omnibus in June 1977

Second printing March 1978
Third printing May 1983

Printed in Canada

Contents

Not Less than All 9

The Lonely Road 201

Cherish This Wayward Heart ...389

Not Less
than All

Rosamund Hastings and John Lindsay were both running away. And both were unwilling to discuss the lives they were fleeing.

All that mattered was the present...and their newly discovered love for each other.

But it wasn't quite that simple. For when the past, as it inevitably must, caught up with them, their love and trust were not sufficient. Would their past destroy their future?

CHAPTER ONE

HE couldn't believe his luck.

For weeks—it seemed more like months—he'd been looking for some quiet place where he could work undisturbed. He didn't care what sort of place—it could be a cottage or a bungalow or even a caravan. But it must be somewhere quiet. That was essential. But apparently impossible. Cottages which were once isolated were now either on a new arterial road or on the perimeter of an airport. Bungalows, he discovered, rarely came singly. More usually they were part of a development and were crowded against each other like hens in a battery. As for caravans—he shuddered at the memory of the camping sites he had visited. Hundreds of caravans stacked in neat rows and thousands of shouting, squalling children, to say nothing of transistor radios bawling without cessation.

And then, quite by chance, he saw the advertisement, not in an estate agency, but on a hand-printed card in the small crowded window of a general store where he had stopped to buy something for a picnic lunch.

The first time, he read it automatically as one does any single notice in a shop window. Then, as the penny dropped, he read it again incredulously, but with sudden surging hope.

"TO RENT for three months or longer by arrangement. Canal butty (i.e., living quarters, no machinery) permanently moored half a mile west of Yeoman's Lock.

ACCOMMODATION: well equipped galley, living room, sleeping accommodation for two in comfortable cabin. Extra bunk can be made in living room. Modern sanitation, Calor gas stove and refrigerator.
NOT SUITABLE FOR CHILDREN. No dogs, radio, television or musical instruments permitted.

A perfect haven for those who value isolation and peace.

Rent per month—"

But he didn't stop to read the last line. He must have it! Absolutely must, whatever the rent. It was surely the perfect answer!

He went into the shop, only to have to wait while the pleasantly plump woman in charge attended to two earlier customers, and exchanged all the local gossip.

At last it was his turn.

"That—that advertisement in your window." He was almost stammering in his eagerness. "Is it—is it still available?"

"Oh yes, sir," The woman looked at him curiously. "Would you be interested?"

"Very much indeed! It sounds just what I've been looking for. I'll take it!"

"What, without seeing it?" She gave him a doubtful look. Just what sort of a man was this, as young as he was—and good-looking—who wanted to hide himself away—and why? Didn't seem natural like—The doubt was so evident that there had to be an explanation.

"Yes, without seeing it. I'll take a chance. You see, I'm a writer, and I've been hunting for somewhere quiet where I can work undisturbed. This sounds ideal."

"Oh—a writer!" The woman's face cleared. "That's funny, now! It belongs to a writing gentleman, but he's gone abroad looking for some sort of colour for his next book."

"Local colour, I expect. Well, how about it?"

"Well, if you'll write down your name and address—and Mr. Thomas did say I was to ask for the first month's rent down—"

"Fair enough! Give me a piece of paper—"

But instead she produced a small black notebook which had evidently been prepared for just such an occasion as this, for, as she opened it at the first page, he saw that it was headed:

"Long-boat, *Seven Stars*."

"Now, sir, if you'll write your name and address, then

I'll put down each time you pay me. Would you like a pen, sir?"

But he had already taken his own pen from his pocket and wrote :

"John Lindsay,
31A Faber Street,
Bloomsbury, London, W.C.1."

Then, as she studied it carefully, he took out his wallet and counted out the necessary notes and added a few coins from his pocket.

With the payment entered in the little black book, he was the official tenant of the *Seven Stars*. He drew a breath of relief. But he wasn't allowed to seek his sanctuary yet. Boring though admittedly useful information was given with the key.

"It's Calor gas, sir, for both cooking and the fridge. If you go into the ironmonger's shop opposite, you can make arrangements for delivery of fresh supplies with Mr. Mangell. There's two containers on board, so what you do is let Mr. Mangell know as soon as you've emptied one. Then you never get caught without. He looks after the dynamo that does the electric light as well if it goes wrong. Then there's food, sir. If you care to give me an order, my son will bring it all down to you when he gets home from school."

"Thanks, Mrs.—?"

"Watchett, sir. My husband works up at the farm yonder—" with a jerk of the head.

"I see. Well, thank you very much, Mrs. Watchett, but I'll take supplies for a few days with me. After that—" He left the remark in the air, but in fact he'd made up his mind that he always would fetch and carry his own supplies. He didn't want a gangling schoolboy disturbing his peace !

It was only just as he was leaving that he remembered one important question.

"How near to the canal can I park my car?"

"Oh, quite near, sir. You go down the lane opposite and when you've passed a stile, you come to a field gate with an old barn just inside. You can park your car in the barn—but you have to pay Mr. Jobling, the farmer who owns it, for that. He only charges a pound a month. Then there's a small gate in the hedge and when you're through that, you're on the canal bank. Shall I tell Mr. Jobling you want to make use of the barn?"

"Yes, please. And now, food—"

A quarter of an hour he set off burdened with two heavily laden carrier bags. Mrs. Watchett watched him from the shop window as he got into his car and turned down the lane.

"Quite a nice gentleman, though a bit abrupt, p'raps. Looked as if he might have a bit of a temper, too, with that square chin and the frown creases between his dark eyebrows."

"I wonder what Miss Alice will make of him?" she pondered as she went back behind the counter. Then, with the vestige of a chuckle : "And I wonder what he'll make of Miss Alice?"

Incredibly, the advertisement had not exaggerated the amenities of the *Seven Stars*.

The galley *was* well equipped. It was also very conveniently arranged and spotlessly clean. The cabin *was* extremely comfortable, but it was, in fact, the sitting room which gave him the greatest satisfaction. To begin with, it was larger than he had anticipated. He thought that a second sleeping cabin had been sacrificed to achieve this. The fittings were plain and sensible, the two armchairs well sprung and upholstered. But best of all from John's point of view was the solid kitchen table set under a window which looked on to the off-side bank of the canal. The middle third of the table top was covered by a stout piece of felt marked with four small round indentations. With relief he recognised them as the unmistakable impressions left by a typewriter. So, notwithstanding the restrictions about noise, the sound of a typewriter was permissible. He thanked his stars that the boat's owner was also a writer, particularly as he had left behind him a small but useful selection of reference books—the Bible, two volumes of Milton and a complete Shakespeare, a good dictionary and an equally good

Thesaurus. John blessed the absent Mr. Thomas with considerable fervour. Anyone who couldn't write here simply hadn't anything to say!

Having inspected his quarters, he went out on deck and momentarily frowned. As far as it went the advertisement had told the exact truth—but not all of it. No reference had been made to the fact that the *Seven Stars* was not the only long-boat moored here. There were two others; the *Pride of London*, adjacent to the *Seven Stars* though with about a boat's length of water between them and beyond her, the *Rosebud*.

John's scowl deepened. Gone was his dream of absolute solitude. In fact, one or two people might be worse than a crowd if they happened to be of the gregarious type.

Still, presumably they, too, would be restricted about noise and might appreciate peace and quiet as much as he did. Moreover, on neither boat was there any sign of life. Perhaps, after all—

He turned his attention to his surroundings, and with these at least he could find no fault.

The canal, he knew, had not been used commercially for years, and there were evident signs not so much of neglect as of indulgence. On either side was a towpath backed by a hedge which had been allowed to take up far more space than would have been convenient in years past. In the main, it was of hawthorn. Falling petals drifted lazily like perfumed confetti on the slight, mild breeze. Then there were dog-roses, pale pink and white, whose delicate beauty surely warranted some more euphonious name.

At the base of the hedge spires of meadowsweet reared their creamy-white umbrellas and vied with purple loosestrife to delight the eye. Masses of forget-me-nots, the bluest John had ever seen, fringed the towpath, trailing down to the water and even drowning some of their blossoms in it.

And as the perfect complement to all this beauty, somewhere high up in the cloudless sky, a lark was throbbing out its heart—

John stood motionless, drinking it in, conscious of a

sense of peace and well-being within himself that he had not known he was capable of feeling.

"Good afternoon!"

Startled, he spun round so sharply that he almost stumbled.

A woman was standing on the near side bank. At a guess, she was perhaps in her middle forties—a sturdy woman and no beauty with her strongly featured face and short, straight black hair. She was regarding him with interest, even curiosity, and instantly that peace of spirit gave way to resentment against the person who had destroyed it.

"What do you want?" he asked harshly.

"Nothing, personally," she told him coolly. "But you left some of your property in Mrs. Watchett's shop and she asked me to give it to you so that you wouldn't worry that you'd lost it."

And she held out his note-case.

"Good lord!" John felt in his inner coat pocket and it was empty. "Yes, it's mine." He came towards her, crossed the narrow plank gangway—and belatedly remembered his manners. "Thanks," he said reluctantly. "Extremely careless of me. I'm very much obliged to both you and Mrs. Watchett."

"Not at all." She regarded him gravely. "And please, don't feel that you're under any obligation to me. I was coming down here anyway. I'm your next-door neighbour," with a jerk of her head towards the *Pride of London*.

"Oh yes?" Deliberately John made the two words sound as lacking in interest as possible. He could have cursed himself for having given her this opportunity to scrape acquaintance!

"Yes." There was amusement now in the dark eyes which had a shrewdly penetrating quality about them. "No need for alarm, Mr. Lindsay! Returning your wallet was a purely disinterested kindness with no strings attached. I value my own inviolability far too highly to want to trespass on yours—or anyone else's, for that matter!"

With a casual nod of farewell, she turned and walked back to her own craft with a confident, unhurried step which conveyed unmistakably her complete mental tranquillity.

And that was something John had completely lost in the engagement. He was fuming! An infuriating woman! In the space of a few minutes she had put him in her debt, had laughed at him—and had made him feel that he was behaving boorishly.

"Oh, confound the woman!" he muttered under his breath, and went into the galley to throw together the odds and ends of food he had collected for his first meal aboard. It was then he discovered that he had forgotten to buy any salt.

It took the best part of a week to master the essential mechanics of living on his own in the long-boat.

The first lesson he learned was the most important of all—what he didn't do himself wasn't done at all. And while, manlike, he could shut his eyes to a certain amount of dust here and there, other jobs, some of them none too pleasant, couldn't be neglected without penalty. At first it seemed a waste of time to heat water in order to wash up after each meal—far more sensible to save up and do the job once a day. But that, he discovered, only made it more difficult, especially where pots and pans were concerned. Besides, there were the flies—

He had not thought it necessary to make his bed properly each day. Surely just to plump up the pillows and heave the bedclothes more or less into position was sufficient—but that, he found, was not so. One or two restless nights convinced him of that. The bottom sheet became runkled up and the bedclothes wouldn't stay put—

Then there was the question of the water supply. True, there were adequate tanks on the craft and a stand-pipe reasonably near on the bank. But to fill the one from the other meant at least a dozen trips backwards and forwards carrying a couple of pails. It was both laborious and uncomfortable, for it required skill if one wanted to avoid spillage and consequent soaking of clothes and shoes. And the fact that his neighbour, with the aid of a sort of primitive milkmaid's yoke, performed the same task without difficulty, did nothing to decrease his sense of frustration.

It was all such a waste of time! For months past he'd had the bare framework of the play he intended to write clear and precise in his mind. All he had to do was clothe it in words. And words kept bubbling up into his consciousness—but always at the time when he was occupied with one of the wretchedly mundane jobs. Worse than that, by the time he was free to get them down on paper, the brilliance of inspiration had gone and what he wrote seemed second-rate and lacking in impact.

He was driven to working out a system. The household chores *must* take second place to his writing. There was only one way to make sure that they did. However disinclined he might feel, they must wait until he had already written himself out. Then inspiration was far less likely to visit him. He learned, from sheer necessity, that plates and pots and pans, if submerged in cold water, could safely wait without disaster.

But there was still shopping to do, and that meant observing other people's times. Thanks to the little refrigerator, he could, he had thought, cut down to a single trip a week—except for the question of milk. Even with a refrigerator, he doubted if it would keep that long. Besides, there wasn't room for more than a couple of pint bottles.

He almost wished he'd agreed to let Sid Watchett deliver whatever was necessary—but not quite. He'd seen Sid just once—and he *was* a gangling, goggled-eyed youth. Inquisitive, too, like his mother.

Besides, the fewer people who visited his retreat the better. To have a neighbour was bad enough, though he had to admit that, to use a favourite phrase of his old nannie, she did keep herself to herself. An artist, apparently, though whether amateur or professional he neither knew nor cared. At least her work absorbed her. He had seen her literally start inches from her little stool when a cow in a nearby field had given vent to a sudden bellow.

So, taking it by and large, life settled into a satisfactory rhythm and he found that he had not been mistaken. By sheer luck he had found ideal conditions for producing what, without vanity, he knew was good work. He had never been so happy in his life or so absorbed. But that was his trouble. It was all very well working out a system, but if one had reached a place where words were coiled up like a spring in one's brain, just waiting to be released, it was so easy to forget everything else.

That happened one day when, having got up early and without stopping even for breakfast, he had worked at white heat for hours on his first act of the play. Then, suddenly, he had remembered that he ought to get in supplies. He was out of tea, out of milk and very low on both bacon and eggs—his main standbys. And he'd got to see that chap Mangell about a new container of Calor gas.

He looked at his watch. Twelve o'clock—and, confound it, early closing day! He'd have to get off at once or go on very short commons until the next day. He pushed his chair back savagely, collected a carrier bag from the galley and went up on deck. That was when, for the first time, he realised that it was raining, not heavily, but with dreary persistence.

In a thoroughly bad temper he hunted out his mackintosh and set off. In an hour's time he returned in an even worse one. It hadn't seemed worth while getting the car out seeing that it was such a short distance that he had to go, but that had been a mistake. The rain had come on more heavily and, never a man to wear a hat if he could avoid it, his hair was soaked and streams of chilly water were running down inside his collar. Shivering, he planned to have a good stiff toddy when he got back and wished to goodness that, by the simple method of turning on taps, he could have a hot bath—and with a groan, remembered that he couldn't even have a cold one unless he filled the tank.

It was the last straw. He gained the comparative comfort of the galley, dumped the carrier bag and was just going to pick up the two pails when something caught his eye.

Last night he had worked so late that he had turned in without doing his day's washing up. He had dunked it in a bowl in the little sink and had left it. Now the bowl was empty and what had been in it, was dried and neatly stacked on the draining board. What was more—he sniffed experimentally—there was an unmistakable smell in the galley. Within the last hour someone had cooked bacon and eggs there.

Clearly he had entertained a visitor unawares. But who? Not his next-door neighbour whose name, he had been gratuitously told by Mrs. Watchett, was Miss Alice Coates, though she preferred to be known just as Miss Alice. No, not her. She might, just conceivably, have seen him go off and have been sufficiently curious to pry. She might, with that appalling sense of superiority possessed by so many females, have done his washing up for him. But she certainly wouldn't have cooked a meal for herself—

A tramp, then? No, he might have stolen food but certainly wouldn't have washed up. With a shrug, John temporarily dismissed the problem. The most important thing was to get himself into dry clothes. As for the water, that could wait. He'd enough for the day if he was careful.

He took off his mackintosh, hung it up where it could drip in safety and made for the cabin. Passing through the sitting room, he glanced at the table and saw to his relief that the papers on it were just as he had left them. Then he went into the cabin—and came abruptly to a dead stop, his jaw dropping.

There, lying on his bed, fast asleep, was a girl. Her fair hair was spread all over the pillow—*his* pillow—and she had pulled the coverlet roughly over herself.

For a moment John was too astounded to do anything but stare incredulously. Things like this just didn't happen—

But evidently they did, and indignation surged up. The cheek of it! To steal his food and then calmly to take possession of his bed!

He took a couple of quick strides and catching hold of her shoulder, shook it energetically.

"Wake up, Goldilocks!" he requested harshly. "The big bear has come home!"

Possibly that fitted in with her dreams, for without opening her eyes she made a petulant little movement as if to free herself from his grasp. So he shook her again.

"Wake up!" he ordered more loudly.

This time he got results. The girl's eyes opened. For a moment she lay still, half way between sleep and consciousness. Then, with a horrified gasp, she propped herself up on one elbow.

"Oh, my goodness!" she ejaculated. "This is the last thing I meant to happen! What must you think of me?"

John didn't answer immediately. Waking up, the girl had added still another shock to those she had already dealt him.

With fair hair like hers he would naturally have supposed, had he given the matter a thought, that her eyes would be blue. They weren't. They were green.

Then, because her pale cheeks were suddenly flooded with colour while her free hand clenched tightly, he realised that she was genuinely frightened at her predicament—or else she was a superb little actress. Well, he'd soon find out. And if she was scared, she had only herself to thank for that!

"Get up," he ordered harshly.

Obediently she turned back the cover and swung her legs on to the floor, scuffling her feet into the shabby sandals that he hadn't noticed until then.

She stood up—a tall girl and slim to the point of thinness. Her clothes, a creased and shapeless cotton dress topped by a woollen cardigan, were old and as shabby as the sandals. But she had recovered her poise by now. The green eyes met his unwaveringly.

"This way," he said curtly, and led the way to the day cabin. She followed meekly enough, but he took the precaution of placing himself between her and the door to the deck. "Sit down." And when she had done so, he sat down opposite her. "Now, if you'll be so good, may I have an explanation?"

"I truly didn't mean to go to sleep," she told him earnestly. "Only, when I'd made the bed, it looked so comfortable, and I was so tired—" her voice trailed away as if, even after her stolen rest, it was still almost too much effort to talk.

John's hands moved impatiently.

"Not just that. The whole business. Why did you come on board at all? And why did you steal my food?"

"Because I was hungry as well as tired," she explained, answering the second question first. She paused and then in a flurry of words: "I wouldn't have done it—honestly

I wouldn't—but I was *desperate*. You see, I had to stop—oh, hours ago—for petrol—"

"Oh, so you've got a car!" he interrupted. "Where is it?"

"In that field the other side of the hedge just by the old barn."

"Well, go on!"

"Well, when I decided to stop to have something to eat I couldn't find my purse. It wasn't in my handbag and it wasn't anywhere in the car. I suppose I must have dropped it at the garage."

There was a decided tremor in her voice, but John hardened his heart.

"Do you really expect me to believe that tarradiddle?" he asked sceptically.

"Why not?" Her head came up defiantly and John found her defiance far more attractive than her earlier pathos. "It was careless of me, I know, but things like that do happen if one has—has other things on one's mind—"

He looked at her sharply. She couldn't possibly know of his own carelessness in leaving his wallet on Mrs. Watchett's counter, but unknowingly she had got under his guard and much as he resented it, he had the honesty to admit to himself that he was hardly in a position to take her to task for a similar fault.

"So you came straight down here and helped yourself?" he suggested,

"Oh *no*!" she denied. "It wasn't like that at all. I didn't even know that there was a canal here, let alone boats. No, I simply turned down the lane because it looked quiet and I wanted to park somewhere and try to think what I could possibly do. You see, I started before breakfast—and I hadn't slept much and I knew it just wasn't safe for me to go on driving. So I drove into that field and hunted through everything I'd got with me to see if there was anything I could sell—and there wasn't. Then I saw the boats. I wondered if perhaps there might be someone who—who would help me, but there was no one about—" again that quaver in her voice. "So then—I—I took the law into my own hands. Oh, I know I shouldn't have done it, but truly, I was at the end of my tether and—and I did wash up and make the bed as a sort of payment—"

"H'm!" John considered. Yes, there was something, though not much, in that. "All right, we'll call it quits up to that point. But only on condition that you tell me the whole story. For instance, who are you? What's your name?"

She hesitated momentarily. Then—

"Rosamund Hastings."

He shook his head unbelievingly.

"Oh no—your real name, please!"

"But that is my real name," she insisted.

"I don't think so. You hesitated before you told me," he pointed out.

"I know I did. I was wondering if it would be a good idea if I made up a name. Then I decided that it might be inconvenient and too difficult to remember, anyway," she explained ingenuously. "So I told you my true one. Really I did."

Well, true or not, she'd stick to it, of course! He let it go.

"And where do you live?" he asked instead.

For answer she pressed her lips firmly together and shook her head vigorously.

"No? In other words, you're a runaway. Borstal?"

"Certainly not!" she denied indignantly.

John shrugged his shoulders.

"Sorry—but how could I know? After all, you *are* light-fingered, aren't you?"

"I don't suppose you'll believe it, but I've never done anything like that in my life before today," she told him earnestly.

"I'll have to take your word for it," he retorted ironically. "All right, not Borstal. Then where? From school?"

To his surprise, a change came over the serious little face. The lips curved in a provocative smile, the green eyes sparkled with amusement.

"How old do you think I am?"

He shrugged his shoulders.

"Fifteen—sixteen, perhaps."

"I'm twenty-three."

21

"I don't believe it," he retorted flatly.

The smile vanished and she sighed deeply.

"You haven't told me what your name is, but I know what it ought to be—Thomas! You seem utterly incapable of believing anything!"

"Now look here, young wonan—" he stood up, towering over her. "I've had enough of your impudence! What's more, I don't care whether you're telling me the truth or not. But one thing is very certain. Whether you're fifteen or twenty-three, you can't stay here! Is that clear?"

"But what shall I do?" she asked, her face starkly white. "Where shall I go?"

"That's for you to decide," he told her inexorably, "since you insist that you're of an age to run your own life!"

"But—" she began.

John interrupted her ruthlessly.

"Now listen, Rosamund Hastings, you're not getting easy money out of me! Understand? But what I will do is this—I'll pay the cost of a telephone call to anyone, a relative or friend, whom you believe will help you out of this jam—provided that I see and hear you make the call. Well?"

Again that stubborn look marred what was, he had to admit, quite an attractive face—if you happened to like a pink and white complexion, golden hair—and green eyes. For his part, he didn't.

"No," she said unequivocally.

"No?" He shrugged his shoulders. "Just as you like! But if that's your line, then off you go—at once!"

She stood up and without protest walked steadily to the cabin door. He watched her go in a mood partly of satisfaction that he was getting rid of her and partly of annoyance at having been forced into such an invidious position at all.

Suddenly an idea occurred to him.

"Wait a minute! It must have been raining when you got here, yet your clothes aren't wet. You must have had a coat or a mackintosh. Where is it?"

"In the galley on the hook on the inside of the door," she told him in a voice completely devoid of expression.

"Well, get it," he ordered grimly. "I don't want you to have any excuse for coming back!"

"You needn't worry, I wouldn't come back if I was dying!" she declared passionately, and dashed into the galley to emerge struggling into a mackintosh as unprepossessing as the rest of her clothes. "Would you like me to turn out the pockets in case I've stolen anything?" she demanded belligerently.

He ignored that, contenting himself with standing, arms folded, while she negotiated the narrow plank gangway. Then, involuntarily, he took a step towards her. The rain had made the wood slippery and just as she was about to step on to the bank, one foot skidded and she almost fell.

But John's intervention was unnecessary. At that precise moment Miss Coates emerged through the little gate in the hedge, unceremoniously dropped the parcels she was carrying and was in time to keep Rosamund from falling.

"That was a nearly!" she remarked cheerfully. Then, anxiously: "My dear, you're crying! Have you hurt yourself?"

"N-no," Rosamund stammered. Then she pulled herself together. "No, I'm quite all right, thank you very much."

"But you're not, my child," Miss Coates insisted. "Now, tell me what's wrong and we'll see what we can do about it!" And putting a protecting arm round the slim, shivering figure, she shot an unmistakably accusing look at John.

"Not what you're quite evidently thinking, madam," he was stung to retort. "I have not inveigled her here and I have not assaulted her! On the contrary, she came of her own free will and without my knowledge or consent. In addition, she had helped herself to some of my food, her excuse being a cock and bull story about having lost her purse! If you'll take my advice, you'll send her packing, as I've done!"

"But I'm not willing to take your advice," Miss Coates replied blandly. "Any more than you, I'm sure, would accept mine! Good afternoon, Mr. Lindsay. And now—" she smiled reassuringly at Rosamund, "let's go to my boat and share a cup of tea, shall we?"

John watched them go as they turned their backs on him and made for the *Pride of London*.

It would have been very natural if his principal feeling had been one of relief at having got rid of his incubus. But it was nothing of the sort. He was keenly aware of a sense of perplexity.

As Rosamund turned her back on him he was convinced that he'd seen her before, though where and when he had no idea. Oh, absurd! If that was so then surely he would have remembered her face, and he hadn't. But there was something about her walk—elegant to the degree that she seemed almost to float along, despite the roughness of the towpath. And the poise of her head—

No, he couldn't remember, and after all, what did it matter? Whether Miss Coates allowed herself to be imposed on by the girl or not, he would take good care that he wouldn't be further involved!

But it was vexing that several times that day—and afterwards—his thoughts turned involuntarily to the perplexing half-memory.

"Now, you sit down while I get tea, my dear," Miss Coates said cheerfully. "No, I don't need any help and you certainly need to relax! Sit down in one of the armchairs and try to think of nothing at all!"

Thankfully Rosamund sat down. That was easy enough, but to think of nothing—that was impossible! Too much had happened since she had started out so hopefully that morning.

She had laid her plans so carefully! Aunt Ruth, proprietress of one of London's most exclusive dress salons, had gone to Paris for a week, leaving Rosamund in charge and with urgent instructions to make absolutely sure that every dress they had designed and created for one of the biggest weddings of the season was absolutely perfect. In fact, everything went without a hitch, and in the evening Rosamund rang her aunt up at her hotel and reported to that effect.

"And I had quite a long talk afterwards at the reception with Mrs. Castleford," she went on to say. "You know, the wife of the American financier. They expect to be over here for three months and I think she was genuinely interested. In fact, she asked me to make an appointment for you to see her next week."

"Why me?" Ruth Hastings asked sharply. "Why not you, since you made the contact?"

"Because she's the sort of person that doesn't think she's getting her money's worth if she isn't looked after by the head of a firm," Rosamund explained, and instantly wondered if that didn't sound too glib.

But Ruth accepted it without question, gave a few details of her own activities since she had left home and then asked suddenly—almost suspiciously :

"What are you going to do tomorrow with the salon closed?"

"I've been thinking about taking a run into the country," Rosamund replied. "I could do with a breath of fresh air. It's stifling in London."

All of which had been absolutely true—but it wasn't the whole truth. She had said nothing about the shabby second-hand car she had bought or of the cheap clothes so different from the ones she usually wore. And most important of all, she had said nothing of her determination never to live or work with her aunt again. There was no point in doing so. She had tried so often to make her aunt understand how much she hated the life she was leading with all its cloying luxury, the over-heated, over-perfumed salon and the shallow, greedy women who patronised it, but without success. Aunt Ruth simply couldn't or wouldn't believe it.

To Ruth Hastings, her achievements in the world of fashion were all-satisfying. She revelled in success and the knowledge that she had fulfilled the ambitions which at one time had seemed so out of reach. She really enjoyed the work, too, and was completely blind to the fact that not all people are made in the same way. Of course Rosamund must feel as she did, and into the bargain, think herself lucky to benefit by someone else's efforts instead of having to drudge through all those years of alternate hope and despair.

Rosamund sighed. You couldn't convince a person like that that you *wanted* to make a personal effort, wanted, most desperately, to do your own thing even if you weren't quite sure what that was.

So, in the end, she'd decided that there was only one

thing to do—go away and stay away until Aunt Ruth had to accept her decision.

The most important thing, of course, was to avoid a confrontation, and in order to do that, she had gone to extreme lengths. She had drawn quite a large sum of money from her bank account, sufficient to last long enough not to need to draw any more until Aunt Ruth was convinced. Even though it was most unlikely that the bank would divulge to her aunt where a cheque had been drawn, she wasn't going to take even that small risk!

And now all her plans were wrecked by her own stupid carelessness. Without money what could she do except crawl back abjectly, convinced of her own stupidity and probably never again finding the courage to make the break.

She was not sorry when Miss Coates came back with an attractively laid tea-tray. For a little while she could try to forget her troubles and respond to the kindness that she was receiving.

Over the teacups Miss Coates did her best to put her visitor at her ease. She described life on the long boat with enthusiasm and not a little humour, poking fun at herself for the mistakes she had made at first. To her own surprise, Rosamund found herself compelled to smile and even laugh once or twice.

It was not until the tray was carried back to the galley and between them the washing up was done that her hostess asked what Rosamund had realised must be the inevitable question.

"Now, my dear, will you tell me all that you care to about yourself?"

Put that way, Rosamund found it easier to explain what had happened than she had when John Lindsay had crossed-questioned her. She was franker, too.

"Mr. Lindsay accused me of being a runaway. He thought—" she smiled faintly, "that it might be from Borstal—"

"How stupid of him," Miss Coates said unflatteringly. "Quite apart from anything else, he had only to look at your hands. I doubt very much if a Borstal girl would have such beautifully manicured nails as you have!"

"Oh!" Rosamund gave a little start and looked frightened. "I didn't think of that—how stupid of me!"

Miss Coates made no comment, but she stored the remark up for future consideration since she felt that it could be interpreted in more than one way.

"Go on, dear," she encouraged.

Rosamund drew a long breath.

"He was wrong about Borstal or that I had run away from school. But he *was* right about me being a runaway." She paused, looking doubtfully at Miss Coates.

"But you don't want to tell me why or from what?" Miss Coates suggested. "Now listen to me, Rosamund. All of us need to escape from something or somebody at some time or other in our lives. Sometimes it's a wise thing to do, sometimes not. *I* think I'm wise in spending as much time as I can down here. You see, I don't like limelight very much and I detest being lionised—"

"Oh!" Rosamund leaned forward. "Why, of course, I should have remembered before. You're the artist who painted that lovely portrait of Her Majesty the Queen!"

"And a most enjoyable task that was!" Miss Coates nodded. "None the less, it had the effect of putting me in the public eye, which was advantageous in a financial sense, but—" she made a little grimace. "Perhaps it sounds rather affected, but to do decent work, one *has* to belong to oneself, and beyond a certain point too much publicity makes that impossible. So, except when I'm actually working on a portrait, I rusticate down here and paint watercolours of birds and water scenes. So far, though I've earned the name for being eccentric, no one has discovered my hideout—and I sincerely hope they never do!" And she looked gravely at Rosamund.

"No one ever will from me," she promised earnestly. "And thank you for trusting me, Miss Coates." She stopped short, feeling embarrassed.

"But though I've told you my secret, you'd still prefer not to tell me yours? All right, I accept that, but I would like you to answer one or two questions. For instance, are you married?"

"No, I'm not," Rosamund met her eyes squarely. "Nor have I done anything against the law. It's just that—" she paused and then took the plunge. "You run away from lots of people. I'm running away from one. Someone I both live and work with. I—I've already told her several times that I want to break away and make a fresh start on my own, only she doesn't understand—"

"Probably doesn't want to," Miss Coates suggested dryly. "I've met that sort. They see other people only as adjuncts to their own lives—most exhausting. Makes you feel absolutely drained of all personality."

"You *do* understand," Rosamund exclaimed gratefully. "But do you see that because it *is* just one person, I don't want to say who it is?"

"Yes, I see that," Miss Coates nodded, wondering whether the girl realised how much, in spite of her caution, she was actually giving away. "All the same, isn't there a possibility of quite reasonable enquiries being made, possibly by the police? After all, when an attractive girl just vanishes into the blue—"

"I left a letter which explained everything very clearly," Rosamund assured her. "And I don't think my— she would like the sort of publicity that an enquiry would bring—"

"Probably not," Miss Coates agreed. "Well, that's all right, then! Now, let's be practical. About your purse. Do you remember the name of the garage where you got your petrol and where it was?"

"I didn't notice the name and I'm not very sure of where it was. Marlborough was the last big town I'd gone through. It was some miles beyond that and it was on an open stretch of the road and on my side of it. Not very big, but very well run."

"Not, by any chance, by a very cheerful little man with a shock of red hair? It was! Oh, splendid! I often stop there myself. What's more, I'm pretty certain I've still got a bill somewhere for a small repair he did for me once. I'll hunt it out and then we'll go to the village and ring through. I'll go and hunt that bill at once—and there's a letter I want to write to my next-door neighbour. No, not Mr. Lindsay. On the other side, the *Rosebud*. His name is Robert Dexter. Another runaway, when he can manage it! I won't be long."

She went through to her sleeping cabin, found the bill without difficulty and then took a writing case from a

28

drawer. For several moments she sat, frowning thoughtfully. Then, rapidly, she wrote:

"Dear Rob,

I don't know if you're planning to come down here this weekend, but if you possibly can, please do.

Something has happened which I find both startling and astonishing and I want to know whether you agree with me.

I don't think you'll feel you've wasted your time, but I must warn you that if you think as I do, you will be in for a shock. But please don't show it—that's important.

I'm sorry to be so mysterious, but you must judge for yourself.

Yours,
Alice."

CHAPTER TWO

ROSAMUND waited anxiously while Miss Coates made the telephone call.

"Tom? Oh, good! Look, Tom, a young friend of mine—a fair-haired girl in a rather battered blue mini car—stopped at your garage this morning for petrol. She thinks she may have dropped her purse—she did?" Miss Coates made a thumbs-up sign to Rosamund, standing outside the telephone kiosk. "Splendid! Well, look, it's rather late now to come to collect it. Tomorrow? About lunch time? Right! What? Yes, we'd like that! Thank you very much, Tom."

She rang off and came out to join Rosamund, beaming all over her pleasant face.

"Yes, you did drop it there, just as you got back into the car. But Tom didn't see it until you'd started off, and though he shouted to you, you didn't hear. He's put it in his safe. I told him we'd pick it up tomorrow."

"O-oh!" Rosamund breathed a deep sigh of relief.

"Yes, you've been lucky," Miss Coates acknowledged. "Tom is as honest as the day. And his wife is a delightful girl—a first-class cook, too. Which reminds me, Tom asked me if we'd have a meal there as their guests and I said we would. All right?"

"Yes, of course," Rosamund's eyes sparkled. "You know, when I was there this morning there was something cooking which smelt quite heavenly—something with onions in it. It made my mouth water and I almost asked if I could have a meal there, only—" the sparkle faded, "I wanted to get on—"

"Well, we'll make up for it tomorrow," Miss Coates promised. "And now we'd better get back. It was fortunate for us that the rain stopped long enough for us to get here, but the clouds are blowing up again."

Neither of them spoke much on the way back, Rosamund because the sense of sheer relief obsessed her to the exclusion of everything else, Miss Coates because she was genuinely glad that Rosamund had been proved to have told the truth and far from displeased that her own perspicacity had assured her that it would be so.

When they reached the gate in the hedge leading to the canal, they had a brief glimpse of John. He was swabbing down the deck and might or might not have seen them, but certainly he let go of his mop and vanished inside with considerable speed.

Miss Coates gave an unregenerate little chuckle which made Rosamund turn and look enquiringly at her.

"Just I was thinking how pleasant it will be to inform that young man that I was right and he was wrong!"

"About me telling the truth?" Rosamund asked, and when Miss Coates grinned and nodded, she looked doubtful.

"But is it worth worrying about?" she asked. "I mean, it wasn't only a question of my purse. I did do other things that annoyed him. I took his food and went to sleep on his bed and even though he hadn't locked up, from his point of view—"

"Are you defending him, by any chance?" Miss Coates interrupted in surprise. "Because, if so, I consider that uncommonly generous of you. He behaved like the oaf I'd already found him to be."

"Yes—well, perhaps he did. But I've been wondering—he looks like somebody with a chip on his shoulder. So perhaps he's had good cause not to trust anybody. And in any case, he was quite right about one thing. It *was* impossible for me to stay here."

"True," Miss Coates agreed absently, her mind suddenly off at a tangent.

For the first time she was reminded that many a love story has begun with conflict between the two people concerned and that almost invariably innocent bystanders were apt to get caught up in the maelstrom. She sighed. She liked what she had seen of Rosamund and she had her own reasons for being resolved to stand by her. All the same, it seemed likely that this summer the tranquillity of mind which she was accustomed to find here might be difficult, if not actually impossible, to come by.

Robert Dexter arrived during Saturday morning. He was a man in his early fifties and despite the fact that he was wearing extremely informal clothes, Rosamund's first impression of him was one of essential spruceness. For one thing, old though they were, it was evident that his clothes had been personally tailored. His brown hair, only lightly flecked with white at the temples, was short and well brushed. He wore a small Vandyke beard trimmed with professional skill and his hand, when Miss Coates introduced them and he took Rosamund's in his, was warm and firm. In fact, she took an instant liking to him and as their eyes met she smiled with instinctive friendliness.

Dr. Rob—which was how Miss Coates had introduced him—smiled responsively and his grasp of her hand tightened very slightly.

"I'm very glad to meet you, my dear!" he told her, and the way in which he said it convinced her that it wasn't just an empty, conventional remark. He really meant it, and even in that brief space of time she knew that she had made a friend.

"Well?" Alice Coates demanded.

The sun was shining gloriously now and freshened by the rain earlier in the week, hedgerows and flowers were more beautiful than ever.

But the two old friends, sitting together on the deck of the *Rosebud*, were barely aware of their surroundings.

Rosamund, thinking that they might enjoy their own company better if she was not there, had made the excuse of shopping to go to the village. Almost immediately Miss Coates had left her own craft to visit Dr. Rob.

"The likeness is undeniable," he said slowly. "And of course, the eyes—" He paused. "Tell me what you know about her, Alice."

"Not very much," she acknowledged regretfully. "She's far from being communicative. But what I do know all fits in. For example, she tells me that she's twenty-three, and though I don't know exactly when her birthday is, any time during that year would make it possible."

"True enough," Dr. Rob acknowledged. "What else?"

"Only odds and ends that I've pieced together," Miss Coates explained. "But of course it's possible that, having already jumped to a conclusion, I'm *making* things fit that really don't. So check on my reasoning very carefully, Rob!"

"I don't know that I'm the best person to do that," he said a little wryly. "You see, I *want* your conclusions to be right! Still, go ahead."

"Well, after the initial shock of realising the likeness, I looked out for anything she said or did that was in any way revealing. She admitted to me that she had run away from—somebody, but even before that I had thought it more than probable. You see, these days, most girls use make-up. Rosamund doesn't. Yet her nails are most exquisitely manicured. Now, those two things contradict one another. Nails like that *go* with make-up—quite a lot of it, in my opinion. But to stop using it is the best disguise a woman can adopt. I'm quite sure that nobody who knows her with it would recognise her as she is at present."

"Not even with those eyes?" Dr. Rob suggested, shading his own eyes with his hand. "They're very unusual, you know."

"Yes," Miss Coates acknowledged. "They are, of course. But if I'm right about the make-up, then she would certainly use eye-shadow—probably green. But quite likely, just because green eyes are so unusual, most people, unless they were face to face with her, would conclude that her eyes were no more than greenish-blue, and that she was deliberately emphasising the green to make a gimmick out of the unusual. You see what I meant when I said I was trying to make things fit," she added wryly.

"Well, as a mere man, I don't feel I can criticise your reasoning. I'm frankly out of my depth. But your suspicions were at least confirmed by her own admission later. Let's go on from there."

"I'll try to remember as nearly word for word as I can," Miss Coates promised, and after a brief interval, with her eyes fixed unseeingly ahead of her, she delved back into the recent past.

Dr. Rob listened attentively, once or twice looking at her with keen, half-closed eyes as she made some point or other. "So we know that she's doing work that she doesn't enjoy and is both living with and working for a woman who can see no other point of view than her own."

"You're quicker on the uptake than anyone else I know, man or woman," Miss Coates declared appreciatively. "I suppose it comes from sorting the grain from the chaff when your patients tell you their symptoms! Anything else?"

"By the way in which Rosamund referred to the *wrong* sort of publicity, it surely means that there is a *right* sort. In other words, that good advertisement is essential to—whatever sort of activity is involved." He looked questioningly at his companion, who nodded without speaking. Clearly that was not the only conclusion she wanted him to draw.

Dr. Rob pursed his lips thoughtfully.

"Yes. You made a correction in repeating something Rosamund said. First of all, you reported her as having said that she didn't think *her*—and then altered it to *she*. Whose correction, Rosamund's or yours?"

"Hers."

"H'm! '*I don't think my*—' Now, what did she nearly say? It would fit in if it was some group name for a special type of relative, wouldn't it? I think we can dismiss the possibility of it being 'mother'. There is a certain sentiment about avoiding such criticism. So—an older sister, do you think?"

"Possibly," Miss Coates admitted, but without enthusiasm.

"But that doesn't fit into your pattern?" Dr. Rob smiled faintly. "Cousin? Or aunt?"

"It could be," Miss Coates said, still in that non-committal way.

"But you're still determined not to put ideas into my head?" Dr. Rob touched her hand gently. "You're a woman in a thousand, Alice. In such circumstances most members of your sex would resent me doing any thinking of my own, because a woman's intuition is never at fault!"

"It isn't very often," Miss Coates said dryly. "Well, what next?"

"Well, next, my dear, is that you're withholding a vital piece of information, aren't you?"

"Am I?"

"Oh yes, that is if you know it. What's the child's surname?"

"Hastings," Miss Coates said briefly.

Dr. Rob stood up and walked to the side of the boat. His back was towards Miss Coates, but she could see that he was gripping the rail so tightly that his knuckles stood out white. Her eyes very tender, she waited in silence for him to speak.

"So it would seem to be possible that your little waif is—my daughter!" he said at length in a deeply moved voice.

"That's how it seems to me," Miss Coates said unsteadily. "Of course, it's not absolutely conclusive—"

"It's sufficiently conclusive to warrant me making enquiries," Dr. Rob asserted grimly. "And that I intend to do without delay!" And for emphasis, he lifted one hand and brought it down resoundingly on the rail.

"You mean—you'll question Rosamund?"

He thought that over for a moment, then turned and came back to his chair.

"No, not in the first instance. I want the child to get to know me better and, if possible, to like me before she's told—if, indeed, there's anything to tell. I've got to face it, Alice, there may not be. Which is another reason for saying nothing to Rosamund at this juncture."

"Yes," Miss Coates nodded. "All the same, Rob, in your heart of hearts you do more than hope it's true, don't you? You think it very likely is!"

"Yes, I do," he said slowly. "There's too much coincidence otherwise. Besides, this could be history repeating itself!"

He slumped in his chair, his hands in his pockets, deep in thought. Miss Coates waited patiently, wondering if he was going to take her into his confidence, and made up her mind that much as she longed to know just what he meant, if he preferred not to, she would respect his reticence. But suddenly, and to her, surprisingly, he said:

"How long have we known one another, Alice?"

"Since we were children. We've always been good friends."

"Yes, always," he agreed. "And yet I've never told you much about my married life, have I?"

"Not very much," she replied evenly. "But then our work lay in such different spheres. It was almost inevitable that we should drift apart. But I did meet Celia, you know. We met by chance in Regent Street, and you introduced us. I've never forgotten what she looked like—I remember thinking that I'd never seen a lovelier face and that I'd love to paint it. In fact, when I got back to my studio, I did a painting of her from memory. I still have it."

But she didn't tell him just why she had painted it—to be a reminder of her own folly. Even now, after so many years, she felt that agonising pang when she had seen the lovely girl he had fallen in love with. No wonder, once he had met her, he had forgotten his old friend's plain face! No, not forgotten. They were still the best of friends—but Celia was still enshrined in his heart.

"I'd like to see it some time, if you'd let me," Dr. Rob said quietly. "Particularly now, to make a comparison." He was silent for a moment, then, almost as if he was thinking aloud: "She was very lovely—and very young and inexperienced. As for me, I was a bumptious young cub!"

"Rob, you were never that!" Miss Coates disclaimed indignantly.

"Oh yes, I was, my dear! I had an extremely good

opinion of myself. I'd got on very well and I put that down entirely to my own brilliance instead of realising that I had incredible luck. The right opening always seemed to turn up at just the right time for me—"

"Perhaps it did—but only because you were the right man!" she insisted.

Dr. Rob smiled rather wryly.

"You always were a partisan where your friends were concerned, weren't you? Well, we won't argue about that, though my mentality at the time played a large part in the break-up of our marriage."

"It did break up?" This was news to Miss Coates. "I knew, of course, that you were in America when she died, but I had imagined that you were there only temporarily—that you thought you'd gain useful experience—"

"You were quite right. But that wasn't the only reason." He leaned forward, his hands dangling loosely between his knees. "The break was already imminent before I left and I, in my high and mighty way, thought that a temporary separation might bring Celia to her senses. But I'd reckoned without her sister—"

"Ruth Hastings," Miss Coates supplied quietly.

He looked at her sharply.

"So you knew that! How?"

"Because even then she was making quite a name for herself in the world of fashion," Miss Coates explained. "Not my world, of course—I've never met her. But very certainly an increasingly important person to more than one of my women clients. That's the worst of painting women. They will chatter so when one wants to concentrate," she added in parenthesis.

"Poor Alice!" Dr. Rob said absently. "But if you've never met her, you wouldn't appreciate what a dominant personality she had. She was, and I suppose still is, a brilliantly clever woman at her job. In addition, she and I had one thing in common—we were both ruthlessly ambitious! In an incredibly short time she progressed from being a very humble worker employed by a London couturier to being his chief designer—there was even talk of a partnership to come, so Celia told me. She, at that time, was modelling for the same firm and I gathered that quite a lot of Ruth's success was due to the fact that Celia displayed her creations to such advantage."

"I can well understand that," Miss Coates said gently.

"Yes, indeed. But Ruth never gave credit to anyone else, even a close relative, although subsequent events proved that she knew it well enough." He paused and sighed. "You know, Alice, it's one of the tragedies of life that something in a woman that attracts a man may, after marriage, be the very thing that irritates him."

"I don't think that's an exclusively male failing," Miss Coates told him. "I've known cases—still, that's by the way. Go on, Rob!"

"Celia was lovely enough to turn any man's head. She had in addition a look of exquisite fragility that made an irresistible appeal— Rosamund has that same look, though I hope that in her case—"

"That she has something of you in her as well?" Miss Coates supplied gently as he paused. "Don't worry, Rob, she has! Courage—and spirit. She's already shown that."

"Courage and spirit," he repeated. "Yes, that's what was lacking in Celia, poor child! She had to have someone to lean on, and inevitably Ruth made capital of that. But she overdid it. She not only overworked Celia, she dominated her to the point where she couldn't call her soul her own, and though Celia was really unhappy, she was quite helpless. That was where I came charging into the picture!" He laughed bitterly. "In my arrogance, I saw myself as a knight errant! *I* would rescue Celia from her bondage. We would get married and then Ruth would have to be more reasonable! I wouldn't listen to Celia's doubts. We were going to get married and that was that! She gave in—good lord, there wasn't much to choose between Ruth and me when it came to bullying the poor little soul. But I, of course, did it from the highest of motives! Well, we were married very quietly one morning, had lunch together and then went off to our different jobs. When I got back to my uninspiring lodgings, Celia was already there—in floods of tears. You see we—or rather I—had assumed that Ruth would appreciate that she hadn't sole claim on Celia now and would be less demanding. It hadn't occurred to me that she'd sack Celia out of hand. But that's what happened, and there we were, entirely dependent on what I earned as a houseman—which wasn't much for two to live on! It was a pretty bleak outlook."

"But surely Celia could have got a similar job elsewhere?" Miss Coates suggested, barely hiding her indignation.

"No. Ruth had seen to that. Celia had a contract which stipulated that she mustn't work for any other similar firm in London, and since I was based on London, what was there to do about it? If she worked somewhere else, we might just as well not have been married! As regards any other type of work—Ruth had taken care that she simply hadn't any abilities which would have made that possible. So there we were, hard up, living in squalid circumstances and rapidly becoming disillusioned, the pair of us. Quite apart from my determination to get on—doubled now that I had Celia to provide for—my work *was* demanding. Not only did I have to be away from home for long hours but there was also the fact that I could get caught up in an emergency. It's like that in a hospital and one has no choice but to get on with it. But it was all new to Celia. She felt neglected and she was bored beyond words. There wasn't enough money to spare for outings and there she was stuck in those ghastly lodgings with nothing to do. Small wonder that she felt I'd let her down. Not, of course, that I admitted it. I told her that she ought to have known what marrying a doctor meant—and that I'd no choice but to work hard in the hope of promotion since I'd got her to provide for as well as myself. She cried, poor child, and that made me impatient. I said a lot more things that I've bitterly regretted since."

He fell silent and Miss Coates stared straight ahead of her. She couldn't bear to see that regret that was even now, she knew, written on his kindly face.

"Then one day when I came home she was tremendously excited and gay. Ruth had been to see her. There was a big dress show coming off the next day and the model who had taken Celia's place had gone down with appendicitis. Would Celia take her place—but of course, only temporarily. There was no promise of future work—Ruth was too clever not to make that clear! But I saw it for what it was—the thin end of the wedge that she intended to drive between Celia and me. I told her that and she shrugged her shoulders. I'd blamed her for being a burden on me and so how could I object now that she had got a chance of earning some money?"

"Which, of course, was unanswerable," Miss Coates commented. "And naturally, there were more offers of work?"

"Oh yes. Occasionally at first but with increasing frequency. Then I had the offer of this post in America. I was determined to take it—and to take Celia with me, but she refused, point blank. She simply didn't trust me. I'd let her down once, how did she know that I wouldn't do it again? Suppose something went wrong in America? We argued—quarrelled, and in the end I gave my ultimatum. She could come or not as she chose, but either way I intended going to America."

"But still she wouldn't?"

"No, she wouldn't. I might have persuaded her, but not with Ruth in the background, frightening her—and offering her the old job back again. So that was the end of it. She went back to live with Ruth and a month or so later I left England. I went to see her the night before and asked

her for the last time to change her mind—she could have followed me over there. But it was no good." He sighed heavily. "That was the last time we saw one another, and though I wrote several times, she never replied."

Silence fell between them. Then Miss Coates said slowly:

"Yes, I do see what you mean, Rob, about the possibility of history repeating itself. Substitute Rosamund for Celia in what you've told me and it fits perfectly—except that Rosamund isn't married. She told me so herself."

"I'm glad of that. It puts me in a stronger position for dealing with Ruth," Dr. Rob said grimly.

"Yes, I suppose so." Miss Coates frowned consideringly. "Rob, how did you hear of Celia's death?"

"From Ruth. And there was no doubt but that it was the truth. She enclosed the certificate."

"Did she!" Miss Coates sat suddenly erect. "Rob, what was the cause—"

"Not childbirth," Dr. Rob had no difficulty in reading

39

her thoughts. "Influenza—there was a lot about just then."

"But that doesn't mean that she couldn't have had a child," Miss Coates argued eagerly. "But surely she'd have let you know, either before or after Rosamund was born!"

"She may have done, but if so, I never received the letter. There again, Ruth may have intercepted it." Dr. Rob stood up and paced up and down the deck. "What I must discover is how the child was registered at birth— also, more than likely, by Ruth. Was it under her correct name, if she is my daughter? Or under Ruth's? After all, Rosamund gives her name as Hastings. Ruth may have said that she was her own illegitimate child—"

"Yes, that's a possibility, I suppose," Miss Coates admitted. "Even so, there's Rosamund's likeness to Celia, particularly her eyes. That would want some explaining because, as stepsisters, there was no tie of common blood between Celia and Ruth."

"Yes, there's that," Dr. Rob agreed. "Then, speaking from memory, I think Celia died at a private address. I can verify that when I get back to town. It's important, of course, because in all probability, Rosamund was born in the same district, though not necessarily at the same address. That will help to limit the scope of the search. That, and the date of her birthday."

"I'll find that out somehow," Miss Coates promised, and stood up. "She's just coming through the gate, Rob," she warned. "Pull yourself together, my dear, or she'll guess that something has happened—and we don't want her to be afraid it's about her and take flight!"

"No, indeed!" Dr. Rob agreed fervently, as he, too, watched the approach of the slender figure. He slipped his hand under his companion's arm and pressed it gently. "I shall never cease to be thankful that she's fallen into your kind hands, Alice!"

Without speaking, Miss Coates returned the pressure.

Then, acknowledging Rosamund's blithe wave of the hand, they went smilingly to meet her.

Rosamund dangled her bare feet over the bank opposite the *Pride of London*, and decided that she had never been so blissfully happy in her life before or known such peace of mind. Even the erratic tapping of John's typewriter so near at hand didn't worry her. Why should it? He, presumably, was enjoying what he was doing and in her present frame of mind Rosamund was prepared to extend toleration, if not liking, towards any of her fellow beings who contrived to live their lives as it suited them—that was, so long as they didn't hurt anyone else in doing so.

Her smooth forehead puckered. *She* was living her own life, but in doing so she was certainly upsetting Aunt Ruth. She was truly sorry about that, but how could she avoid it? Just supposing she had not run away, what hope of compromise could there have been? Aunt Ruth's attitude where the Salon was concerned was so very definitely: *"All or nothing!"* Rosamund knew only too well that no matter how forcefully she had stated her case or how glibly Aunt Ruth had promised that things should be different and agree to make fewer demands on her in future, that state of affairs wouldn't have lasted. Sooner or later, enthusiasm would have run away with her aunt and they would have been back where they were before.

She was quite sure of that, for she knew beyond doubt that even after reading that letter which had been very difficult to write, so plain-spoken was it, Aunt Ruth still didn't blame herself for what had happened.

Her aunt had not written to her, of course. That was impossible since no one connected with her old life knew where she was. But Ruth had contrived to send her a message, none the less. Every possible day since she had read the letter she had put an appeal in the personal column of the *Daily Telegraph*. It read:

"Rosamund darling, come back to me! All forgiven, no recriminations, R.H."

Perhaps the appeal in the first part of the message might have made Rosamund weaken. But the last sentence was an unmistakable warning. There would be a prodigal's welcome for her and however little Ruth might actually say, in her heart, she would blame Rosamund, not herself for what had happened.

So there it was. You might regret causing distress to

41

someone else, but when you were convinced that what you had done was both right and necessary, you had to go through with it.

The week that she had spent with Miss Coates—or Miss Alice as she preferred to be called—had only served to strengthen that belief. It would hardly be possible to live in closer companionship with a person than in the comparatively restricted confines of the boat. Yet never once had Rosamund felt any sense of intrusion of her own personality. Nor, in addition, had she felt any uncomfortable obligation for the hospitality which had been so freely given.

You could hardly have two people less alike than Miss Alice and Aunt Ruth, and yet they had some things in common. Each did work which they loved and did it with great skill. And in each case, they were dependent on the approval of other people for their success. But there the likeness ended. Of course, Miss Alice didn't need anyone to help her do her work, whereas Aunt Ruth did. But it was something which went deeper than that. Something in the basic nature of the two women, though just what it was, Rosamund couldn't decide. The nearest she could get to it was that Miss Alice was essentially a *giver*, while Aunt Ruth was a *taker*.

All the same, one mustn't accept too much generosity when it seemed most unlikely that there would ever be any opportunity of making a return in kind. Of course, there was the question of the domestic chores which Rosamund had taken over, but that was only a very small thing, particularly as, though she was in a position to pay for her keep, Miss Alice refused point blank to allow her to do any such thing.

"Nonsense, child," she had said emphatically when Rosamund had broached the matter. "You're doing the jobs for me which I frankly dislike, and because of that, I've more time to do the work I enjoy—and for which, by the way, I shall be paid!"

Which Rosamund knew was true, yet it didn't altogether satisfy her.

"Miss Alice, why are you being so good to me?" she asked wonderingly.

Miss Alice looked up from her little sketch block and smiled.

"For a variety of reasons, my dear. At first, because you were in distress and it seemed to me that I could and should help you. Then, because I've grown fond of you. And finally—" she paused to concentrate on her delicate brushwork. "Finally," she said deliberately, "because you remind me of—someone I once knew."

"Do I? Had she got peculiar eyes like I have?" Rosamund asked with interest.

"Your eyes aren't peculiar, my dear. Just rather unusual," Miss Alice told her firmly.

And it was not until now that Rosamund realised that her question had remained unanswered, but of course, it wasn't of any real importance.

But she had let her thoughts slide away from making plans for her future, and really, it was too glorious a day to think of anything except *here* and *now*. She wriggled a little nearer the edge of the canal bank and dabbled her feet in the warm water. A brilliant Red Admiral butterfly settled momentarily near to her hand, and a kingfisher flashed like a living jewel from one side of the canal to the other. It was heaven! She could have stayed here for hours, but the chiming of the church clock in the village reminded her that it was time for tea. Regretfully she stood up, walked up to the lock and crossed the canal by the narrow bridge which was part of the lock gates.

She was smiling with the sheer joy of being alive on such a day as she passed the *Seven Stars* and it was only at the last moment that she saw John had left his typing and was now on deck.

It was rather an embarrassing situation for Rosamund. She had only seen him at a distance since the day when he had so unceremoniously bundled her off his boat and she had no idea whether Miss Alice had carried out her intention of telling him that the purse had been recovered.

The smile faded from her face. His back was towards her, so it might be possible to pass without him seeing her. She hoped that it would be. It would save any further chance of unpleasantness.

But she was unlucky. More than once during the day the pollen-laden summer air had made her sneeze. It did

43

so again with no warning whatever just as she came up to the *Seven Stars*. It wasn't a very loud sneeze, but it was enough to make John turn sharply. What was more, when he saw who it was, he came across his gangway and stood blocking her way along the path.

Rosamund stood still. She knew quite well that it would be impossible to dodge past him. There simply wasn't room, and John would certainly stay just where he was until he had said whatever was in his mind. All her earlier happiness evaporated. Was he still angry with her and was he going to make more trouble? She didn't want him to. She wanted to be friends with everybody in this little paradise into which she had strayed. But while it took only one person to pick a quarrel, it took two to make a friendship.

She waited in silence for him to speak, her grave eyes on his face—and then saw with relief that though he, too, looked very serious, he didn't look angry.

"I—I'm glad we've met, Miss Hastings," he announced with a diffidence which Rosamund found more surprising than anger would have been. "I—I owe you an apology. You see, I've been informed that you told me the truth about your purse—"

"Oh, please!" Rosamund said quickly, finding to her own surprise that though she was glad he knew she hadn't lied to him, it gave her no pleasure at all for him to have to eat humble pie. "I've realised since that you weren't to blame for thinking what you did. It must have sounded a most unlikely story."

"It shouldn't have done to me," John insisted, evidently determined to make a good job of it. "Not seeing that only a few days earlier, I left my wallet in the village general store!"

"Oh—I don't know," Rosamund said consideringly, her fair head on one side. "It must have seemed just too much of a coincidence, almost as if I might have heard of that—Mrs. Watchett *is* such a chatterbox—and decided that I might as well try it on!"

"You know, you're heaping coals of fire on my head," he told her wryly. "Because, until this moment, such an idea hadn't occurred to me. No, I was just flaming angry—"

44

"At having other people's problems thrust upon you when you'd just got everything nicely settled so that you could get on with your work in peace?" Rosamund suggested as he paused.

"That was just it," he replied eagerly. "Although—" dubiously, "put into so many words it sounds rather egotistic, doesn't it?"

"Not if it's a question of—of self-preservation," Rosamund said with so much conviction that John, she saw, looked at her with very lively interest.

"You know, that sounds as if you know what you're talking about—as if you've experienced the same sort of thing yourself!"

"Does it?" Rosamund asked lightly. "Well, I suppose everyone does at some time or other! And please, don't worry any more. After all, there was no harm done."

"But no thanks to me," John pointed out grimly. "What would you have done if Miss Coates hadn't happened to come along just at that moment?"

Involuntarily Rosamund shivered and though she did not realise it, there was a strained look in her face which spoke for itself. It was a question that she had more than once asked herself—

"I honestly don't know," she confessed.

"No, and nor do I. A pretty girl on her own with no money—I could at least have given you a pound or two without being so infernally cocksure and superior!"

He was angry now—but with himself—a very different state of affairs from the way he had been at their first meeting.

"Well, I'm glad you didn't lend me any money," Rosamund declared stoutly. "I shouldn't have got to know Miss Alice—or Dr. Rob—and they are such dears!"

"I thought he looked rather pleasant," John acknowledged, "but she's something of a dragon, isn't she?"

"Is she?" Rosamund suddenly dimpled. "I wonder what makes you think that?"

"My guilty conscience, I expect," John admitted wryly.

Rosamund laughed. She couldn't help it. He looked so like a small boy caught scrumping apples. Then her face grew serious.

"Actually, she's the most tender-hearted person I've ever met," she said softly. "And I can never repay her for the way she's taken me under her wing. But that, you see, is the very reason why—"

"Why she had it in for me," John finished. "She thinks of me as a wolf who threatened her ewe lamb!"

"Well, perhaps," Rosamund conceded. Then, as she heard the church clock strike the quarter hour: "Goodness, I must rush! I'm going to be late making tea as it is." She hesitated and then took the plunge. "Mr. Lindsay, won't you have tea with us so that you can get to know Miss Alice properly?"

"Shall I be welcome?" John asked doubtfully.

"Oh yes," Rosamund told him serenely. "She much prefers living at peace with people, and if you come with me, she'll know that everything is all right." The mischief danced in her eyes again. "I can promise you that the dragon won't breathe fire at you."

"In that case, I'd like to come," John said simply, and clearly meant it, although he would have been hard put to explain how it came about that his original intention of keeping his neighbours at arm's length now seemed both short-sighted and unnecessary.

Miss Alice didn't breathe fire when she saw him approaching, but she was surprised. She had already appreciated that though Rosamund had plenty of spirit, she was none the less essentially gentle by nature. That being so, no doubt she'd be able to forgive this young man for his harsh treatment of her, but surely they wouldn't be on the friendly terms they obviously were without his co-operation.

However, neither of them gave any explanation of the new state of affairs and Miss Alice had no intention of asking any questions. None the less, when Rosamund had left them to get the tea, she surveyed the unexpected guest with an artist's shrewd eyes.

Now that his face was not marred by that angry expression, she saw that he was really quite good-looking though not conventionally handsome. His features were good—clean-cut and well proportioned. His chin was, perhaps, rather noticeably strong, but his mouth was sensitive. It made rather a pleasant combination, she thought. And he looked you straight in the eyes.

"Do sit down, Mr. Lindsay," she said pleasantly.

For a moment or two there was silence. Then their eyes met and they both smiled. With relief John knew that there was no need for explanations or apologies. This was a fresh start.

Rosamund came back to find them deep in conversation.

"And you're finding this a good place for working?" Miss Alice was saying.

"First class," John replied enthusiastically. "Though that doesn't mean I haven't struck snags—"

"Yes?" Miss Alice encouraged.

"Yes. You see, I've had my plot in mind for months. But when it came to turning it into people, I knew that there was something wrong. The result just wasn't convincing. At first I thought I'd have to change my plot to suit my characters. Then, this afternoon, I realised that it was the other way round. I'd been so in love with my plot that I hadn't given sufficient thought to just what sort of people would behave and react in a realistic way in such circumstances. They just didn't come off the paper!"

"So?"

"Heroic measures! I'll have to re-write everything I've done." He sounded surprisingly cheerful in the circumstances. "The girl in particular—"

At that moment Rosamund came out with the laden tea-tray and as John jumped up to take it from her, something in his expression made Miss Alice wonder.

She had more than once visited the *Seven Stars* the previous year when Charles Thomas had been working there and now she visualised the layout of the day cabin.

The table at which John must almost certainly work was just under the big window that overlooked the canal bank. Rosamund had been sitting on the bank most of the afternoon.

Was there any connection between those two facts and his new conception of the girl of his play?

If so, Rosamund would naturally be entirely unaware of the influence she had had. But John?

Had it seemed to him to be a matter of inner vision—or

had he known that he was drawing from life? Even more important than that, if he had realised it, had it been personally significant to him?

Miss Alice gave herself a mental shake. Really, she was behaving like a hen with one chick! For all that she knew, the girl of the play might be a thoroughly undesirable character and not in the least like Rosamund. In any case, young people of today felt themselves to be completely competent to manage their own affairs! She must remember that!

She gave her entire attention to pouring out the tea. None the less, it was impossible not be aware that they seemed to have a lot to say to one another—

How could she help wondering *if* anything came of it, would it simplify life for Rosamund or complicate it still further?

And what would Rob feel about it?

CHAPTER THREE

"MISS ALICE, I'm getting *fat*!"

Miss Alice looked up into the pretty, dismayed face and smiled reassuringly.

"Not exactly fat, dear. You'd have a long way to go to get to that state! But I think you have put on a little weight—and very well it becomes you! When we first met you looked as if a puff of wind would blow you away."

"Yes, but, Miss Alice, one simply can't afford to be fat in my—" Rosamund stopped short. She had so very nearly said more than was wise, even where Miss Alice was concerned. That final word had been *job*, and there were only a comparatively few occupations to which the remark really applied. The stage, perhaps, or film acting. But certainly the world of fashion doesn't tolerate bulges! "I mean," she went on hurriedly, "if I'm not careful, none of my clothes will fit me, and think how expensive that will be!"

It sounded very lame to her own ears, but Miss Alice accepted it without comment.

"I'll have to take more exercise—and not eat so much," Rosamund lamented. "And it's awful to confess, but I do enjoy my food so much!"

"Not awful in the least," Miss Alice told her briskly. "Just natural, particularly at your age. In fact, to most people, eating is one of the natural pleasures of life. It needs to be since it's essential to life and health. Think how awful it would be if we found it so disagreeable that we had to force ourselves to eat! But you know, I wouldn't have said that you have a very big appetite. In fact, I would go so far as to say that if, before you came here, you ate less than you do now, then you weren't having enough. Or, of course," she added thoughtfully, "it could be that the circumstances in which you eat now are different—"

"What do you mean?"

Rosamund was conscious of the sharpness of her voice and knew that once again she had been incautious. She waited breathlessly for Miss Alice's reply.

"Simply, my dear, that you're living in much healthier conditions than it's possible to in London with its over-crowding and its polluted air. And our meals here are very leisurely and regular affairs. I expect that you, like most girls who work, had only a limited time to gobble down anything so long as it was quick to eat. Or even that you went without anything at midday if you wanted to do any shopping."

Unconsciously Rosamund drew a sigh of relief. It was all in such general terms that it could apply to any girl—

"Yes, that happens sometimes," she admitted. But not because she wanted to do any shopping. Because Aunt Ruth lost all sense of time and the need to eat if work was pressing. And she expected everyone else to show the same devotion. That sort of situation had been happening with increasing frequency lately. Indeed, it was one reason why—but Miss Alice, she suddenly realised, had evidently said something more for she was waiting expectantly.

"I was woolgathering, I'm afraid," Rosamund confessed. "Would you mind saying it again?"

"It wasn't all that important. Just that I'm going into

Bath this morning and I wondered if you'd like to come too?"

Rosamund considered.

"I would love to see Bath, some time," she said at length. "I've never been there yet—in fact, I've hardly been anywhere. But there are several things I really ought to do."

"Not housework?" Miss Alice asked quickly. "I don't want you to feel tied down, dear, particularly on a lovely day like this!"

Rosamund smiled at her with very real affection.

"I don't feel tied in the least," she said earnestly. "In fact, I've never felt freer in my life. But no, it isn't housework. It's just that I must look through my clothes to see if I can let them out a little. This waistband is really uncomfortably tight. And then I thought I'd go for a good long walk. That ought to help!"

"So it might," Miss Alice agreed placidly.

"All the same, I don't mind housework," Rosamund went on reflectively. "Oh, I know, some of it's dull and even disagreeable at times and you have to do the same thing over and over again. All the same, it does turn a house into a home, doesn't it?"

"If you don't overdo it," Miss Alice suggested dryly. "A woman who is over-houseproud is a menace to both the comfort and happiness of her entire family!"

"Yes, I expect so," Rosamund agreed, and then, hardly realising that she was speaking her thoughts aloud, she went on dreamily: "It must be wonderful to have one's own home and family—"

"And a husband?" Miss Alice teased gently.

"Well—yes. Only not just as a means to get a home of my own. I don't want to marry anyone unless—unless he matters so much that it wouldn't matter if we had to live in one room or in a palace!"

Miss Alice laughed.

"I wouldn't be surprised if you didn't find that there are problems in either. But you've got the right idea and you'll make out all right. He's going to be a lucky man, Rosamund!"

"But there isn't anybody—I mean, I was just talking in general terms," Rosamund explained in alarm.

"Of course. So was I," Miss Alice said absently as she checked through the contents of her handbag and made a few additions to it. "Now, is there anything you want me to buy for you in Bath? Cosmetics—anything like that?"

"No, thank you," Rosamund said so definitely that, seeing Miss Alice's slightly quizzical expression, she added hurriedly: "I suppose it does seem a bit odd that I don't use make-up, but it seems so out of place here—"

"Yes, I suppose it does, really," Miss Alice agreed. "Well, I think that's all. I'll be off now."

Rosamund watched her go with a sense of relief of which she felt ashamed. It didn't seem right to feel one must be on one's guard with anyone who had been so incredibly kind to her as Miss Alice had been, and yet she felt she must be. Miss Alice never asked inquisitive questions, but Rosamund knew that more than once she had been perilously near to giving more information about herself than she had meant to—almost as if she had been deliberately lured on to thin ice.

"But that's nonsense!" she told herself sturdily as she watched Miss Alice pause to exchange a few words with John. "She's far too nice a person to do that sort of thing. It's me! I don't think I'm really a deceitful sort of person and I just forget to be careful. I wish I felt I could tell Miss Alice everything. I would if only I wasn't such a coward! But I'm still too much afraid of Aunt Ruth to risk the possibility of anybody linking me up with her! If she suddenly turned up here and told me I'd got to go back with her—" She drew a long, shuddering breath at the thought and something of the brightness of the day vanished.

She went into her cabin and began, aimlessly, to turn over the clothes she had brought with her. They weren't very inspiring and she quickly saw that, being off the peg and cheap at that, they had been cut from the minimum amount of material and that the seams and turnings would allow for no letting out. She bundled them all back into the wardrobe-cupboard with a little sigh. Just for a moment she felt that it would be fun to wear the sort of clothes she used to—

But the sigh turned into a chuckle. All those immaculately tailored trouser-suits, the delicate materials of

51

dresses and negligées—why, besides looking out of place here, they wouldn't last five minutes! A few grassy stains on dungarees or easily washed frocks didn't matter, nor did brambles and briars do much harm to her bare legs that wouldn't heal in a few days, but Aunt Ruth's exquisite creations—!

All the same, something prompted her to study her face far more closely than usual in the rather spotty mirror. She'd never really liked using the heavy make-up Aunt Ruth insisted on, but now she felt that just a little, perhaps—

It was then, for the first time, that she realised how brown her skin was compared with what it had been and that the natural colour in her face and particularly lips was brighter than it used to be. Perhaps, after all, she didn't need make-up!

Anyway, John didn't seem to think so, for when she walked past the *Seven Stars* his greeting was extremely flattering even if he sounded slightly surprised.

"Hallo, you're looking remarkably attractive this morning, Rosamund! What's happened? Been left a fortune?"

"No, just I feel absolutely fit and flourishing," she told him gaily. "Partly because it's such a lovely day and also because I'm afraid Miss Alice is right—I am all the better for having put on some weight, even though all my clothes are getting tight!"

John inspected her critically.

"You don't look like a heavyweight to me even so," he remarked. "Just—" his hands moved expressively, "pleasantly curvaceous!" and he laughed. "Now I've made you blush—I didn't think girls could, nowadays! Come and have some coffee?" he added coaxingly. "Just to show you're not cross with me!"

"I'm not cross, truly," Rosamund told him. "But I really mustn't have extras like that or I shall get *huge*! Actually, I'm going for a good long walk—and I've brought just two apples with me—that's going to be my lunch!"

John groaned.

"Sooner you than me! I like my grub! Well, I hope you enjoy yourself! If you come back in a fainting condition, I'll cook you—bacon and eggs!"

She flashed a reproachful look at him and then asked impulsively:

"Why don't you come too? You don't get very much exercise—"

"Not get exercise!" He was really quite indignant. "What do you call humping buckets of water and doing housework and cooking and washing-up and going shopping—besides— " he ran his fingers through his hair until it stood on end, a note of irritation crept into his voice— "I simply must get down to that damned play! It's holding out on me!"

Rosamund didn't answer immediately. John rarely talked about his work and she wasn't sure what was the right thing to say. Ought one to be sympathetic or en-encouraging—either, she thought, might be rather irritating.

"You see," John went on bleakly, "it's too long! And I can't boil what I want to say down to the length it will have to be—at least, not without leaving out what I feel are some of the best lines I've written! Oh well, there it is! My problem, not yours! Off you go and enjoy yourself."

"I wish I could help," Rosamund said wistfully.

John looked at her curiously.

"Bless you, poppet, I believe you mean that!" He sounded as if he was really touched. "But I'm afraid it's a one-man job—and I'm the man! So off you go before I'm tempted to down tools and come with you!" He blew her an airy kiss and vanished into the day cabin.

There was a happy little smile on Rosamund's lips as she began her walk. What a different sort of person John had turned out to be from what she had thought he was when they had first met! Even the fact that he was in trouble with his writing didn't make him turn into that scowling, unfriendly person that he had been then.

Not for the first time she wondered not only what had brought about the change but why he had been like that at all. There had been something very wrong, though just what she had no means of knowing, for John was as reticent about himself as she was about herself. Not that it really worried her. John, she was quite certain, was thoroughly nice. She simply couldn't imagine him doing anything underhand or dishonest. So, as long as he was happier now, why worry? So she didn't—at least, not about that. Only about John's present problem. If only she could help him over that!

Deep in thought, she walked along the path up to Yeoman's Lock, crossed the bridge and paused to pass the time of day with the lock-keeper's wife, a plump, cheerful woman, busy kneading a batch of bread-dough.

"Going for a walk, are you, miss? And a very nice day for it, too! But you didn't ought to be alone, not a pretty lady like you! Isn't there a nice gentleman somewhere to keep you from being lonely?"

It was said in such a friendly way that it was impossible for Rosamund to take offence even though a knowing jerk of the head in the direction of the long-boats made it clear that the speaker had John in mind.

"Oh, I shan't be lonely, Mrs Bunce. I've got a lot to think about—" she said cheerfully, but that didn't satisfy Mrs. Bunce.

"You don't want to do too much thinking, not at your age," she disapproved. "What you ought to be doing is having a good time while you can! It doesn't last long, you know. Once you get married and the children come—" she shook her head, but looked so contented that Rosamund laughed.

"Well, you don't look as if you've found it too depressing," she commented.

"Ah, but then I've always had to work hard," Mrs. Bunce explained. "Right from a girl. Mother died and I was the eldest of five—but you, miss—" she shook her head reproachfully. "If you don't mind me saying so, you don't look as if you could stand up to much in the way of hard work!"

This was so obviously another feeler for information that Rosamund decided it would be wiser not to linger.

"Oh, I'm stronger than I look," she said lightly. "And now I really must get on with my walk or I'll have no time left!"

"Drop in on your way back and I'll have a hot loaf ready for you," Mrs. Bunce offered cordially.

Though the mere thought of hot home-made bread made Rosamund's mouth water, she was on the point of explaining that she was trying to lose weight when it occurred to her that John would certainly enjoy the treat, and accepted the offer gratefully.

An hour and a half later she was back at the Lock, very hungry and very tired. The apples she had taken with her didn't even take the edge off her appetite and she hadn't taken into consideration that she wasn't used to walking any distance. It was rather disturbing. Perhaps, after all, Mrs. Bunce had been right and she wasn't as strong as she had thought, though goodness knew, she'd worked hard enough until now! Aunt Ruth had seen to that! But of course, it had been a very different sort of work.

"A hot-house plant, that's what I was," she thought regretfully. "Too used to going even the shortest distance by car! Well, I'll just have to get into training, that's all, because I'm not going to miss half the fun in life because I'm so feeble!"

There was no sign of John when she reached the *Seven Stars*, but with Mrs. Bunce's lovely crusty loaf as an excuse, she crossed the gangplank and went in search of him. He was in the day cabin, sitting at the table. It was covered with sheets of paper and John, looking thoroughly gloomy, was stirring them up with one hand as if he was in despair of finding anything worth keeping among them.

"Hallo." He looked up, but there was no welcome either in his face or in the way he spoke. "Back again?"

"Yes," Rosamund said briskly, determined not to be put out by his lack of enthusiasm. "And I've brought this—" she put the loaf down on the table. "I'm being absolutely crazy after what I said about losing weight, but I'm *starving*, and I'm going to have some of it to eat now for my lunch! Will you go shares so that I don't have a chance of eating too much?"

"I don't honestly think I want—" he paused and gave his whole attention to the loaf. "It looks and smells good, doesn't it?"

Ten minutes later they were sitting companionably side by side on deck, eating hunks of bread—John had insisted that you didn't cut slices off a loaf like that. You just pulled pieces off. Then you put lashings of butter on and topped up with cheese.

With amusement that had an odd thread of tenderness in it, Rosamund found that she needn't have worried about putting on weight because, though he didn't seem to realise it, John was greedily tucking into the lion's share. And for the first time in her life she discovered how satisfying it is to see a man enjoying his food, particularly when one has been the means of providing it. And, of course, when one happens to be—interested in the man concerned.

They finished the meal with coffee, talking in a desultory way for a time, and then fell silent until suddenly John said bitterly :

"It's no damn good, Rosamund! I might as well tear up everything I've written! Going through it this morning, I realised that it's not only too long. There are far too many characters. It's clumsy, unwieldy—utterly impossible !"

Rosamund leaned forward and disentangled a stem of grass from the buckle of her sandal with quite unnecessary care and without looking at him, she asked tentatively :

"John, what made you decide to be a playwright?"

He shrugged his shoulders.

"An exaggerated opinion of my own cleverness, I suppose"

"No, I didn't mean what made you decide that it should be a *play*?"

"Because I—here, what are you getting at?" he demanded suspiciously.

Rosamund hugged her knees and rested her chin on them.

"Did you see Frederick Dane's play 'Guessing Game' last winter?"

"As a matter of fact, I did. But what's that got to do with it?" John asked impatiently.

"It might have quite a lot," she answered seriously. "So please, John, tell me what you thought of it."

"Oh—I don't know." He frowned as if making an effort to remember. "Yes, I do. It hung together all right and yet by the end of the first act I began to feel—" he paused, the frown deepening.

"Yes?" Rosamund urged encouragingly.

"As if—somehow or other, I had missed something vital," he said slowly. "Something that would have made the situation—and the cast—seem real. As it was, they were only two-dimensional."

"Yes," Rosamund agreed eagerly. "That was just how I felt! And it made me wonder if the book from which the play was written was as wonderful as I'd thought. So I read it again. And it still was."

She felt rather than saw that John had grown very still and tense and she waited, holding her breath.

"What are you trying to tell me, Rosamund?" he asked at last in a queer, strained way.

"Just that I don't think a really first-class book will of a necessity make an equally good play." Purposely she spoke slowly, deliberately, so that he had time to realise that every word she said was important. "There's so much more *room* in a book than there is in a play, isn't there, because there isn't the same time limit. And when I real 'Guessing Game' again. I discovered that what they'd done was just to use the *bones* of the plot, highlighting the essential points. But, to me, what they had left out was what made the book live," she explained earnestly.

"Do you mean you think that I—" he began slowly, and stopped short.

"It's cheek of me to suggest it, seeing that I don't know a thing about it," she said diffidently. "But do you think perhaps it's possible that really it's a book, not a play, that you've got in your mind?"

It was so long before he answered that Rosamund was convinced that he thought she was not only cheeky but stupid.

Suddenly he stood up and pulled her to her feet. For a moment they stood face to face, their hands still linked. Then he bent his tall head and very gently kissed her on her soft pink mouth.

"Bless you, Rosamund!" he said huskily, and without another word, turned and strode into the day cabin.

Rosamund watched him go, her fingers gently touching the lips he had just kissed. Then, feeling as if it must all be a dream, she took the coffee cups into the galley and cleared up the debris of their meal. When everything was done to her satisfaction, she went out on deck again and tiptoed to the door of the day cabin. She need not have been cautious. John was far beyond the state where extraneous noises could disturb him. Already he had reduced his scattered manuscript to a neat pile, and with occasional references to it, he was writing, writing, writing as if his life depended on it.

Perhaps it did, Rosamund thought—that creative part of him which, denied, would mean that he wouldn't be able to live his life to the full. And that, she thought passionately, was what she wanted most for him—fulfilment and, wonder of wonders, she had already played a part, however small, in helping him to achieve that.

Contentment filled her—a contentment of a sort so deep rooted that, inexperienced as she was where men were concerned, she knew instinctively could mean only one thing. She loved John. And she always would.

"No, no luck at all," Dr. Rob confirmed glumly. "Not even though you were able to let me know the date of her birth. How did you manage to get that, by the way? You didn't ask her outright, did you?"

"No, you asked me not to, so I resorted to devious means. You know, Rob," she added wryly, "I'm getting all too good at that sort of thing! I think I must have a naturally criminal mind."

"Most women have," Dr. Rob told her matter-of-factly. "They're convinced that the means are justified by the end—if it benefits someone near and dear to them."

And to whom did that refer? Miss Alice wondered. To Rosamund or to himself? She had no intention of asking.

"Well, be that as it may, I needed to make an application for a new passport and I took care to fill in the form in front of Rosamund. I made some stupid remark about my age—that when one gets to a certain age one ought to be excused from revealing it and that I did my best to forget my birthdays now. Then I said something about that not being the case where she was concerned and wondered if her birthday was sufficiently near at hand for us to have a party. And she told me when it was. July the twenty-third, as I told you."

"There was no hesitation in telling you?" Dr. Rob asked quickly.

"None whatever. But later on, after I'd rung you up to give you the date, she told me something that I found very interesting. She's never had a passport, Rob. Never been out of the country, in fact."

"In other words, has had no need to produce her birth certificate on that account," Dr. Rob said reflectively.

"Or, I think, on any other," Miss Alice suggested. "You see, I've watched carefully and I'm quite sure that the name Dexter means nothing personal to her as, surely, it would do if she knew that it and not Hastings is her true name."

"Yes, seems sound reasoning," Dr. Rob agreed. "Which suggests that Ruth has taken care she doesn't see her birth certificate because she was registered as Rosamund Dexter—"

"And *is* your daughter."

"It's a bit more evidence to support its probability," Dr. Rob said judicially. "But still not proof. And that I feel I must have before I claim Rosamund!" He beat his hand emphatically on the wooden arm of his deck chair.

"Just what have you done so far?" Miss Alice asked.

"Made a thorough nuisance of myself at Somerset House," Dr. Rob told her grimly. "I've had them search every district near to the address where Celia died, with no result at all. Which makes it clear that Rosamund was born outside that area. But where, where? Think what it means in London alone. It's like hunting for a needle in a haystack!"

Miss Alice was silent. Personally she had come to the conclusion that Rob might be mistaken in deciding not to take Rosamund into his confidence, but the decision was for him to make, not her.

"It's terribly discouraging," she said at length.

"It is, indeed," Dr. Rob agreed grimly. "So discouraging that I decided to make a more definite approach."

"You mean—tell Rosamund?"

"No, not that. Tackle Ruth herself."

"Oh, Rob!" It was impossible for Miss Alice to hide her dismay.

"Not wise, you think? Perhaps not, but in the circumstances, inevitable. In fact, I felt that so very strongly that I went to see her yesterday."

"And—?" eagerly.

"I might have saved myself the trouble. I was told that Ruth has had a nervous breakdown, is in a nursing home and is allowed no visitors."

Miss Alice looked at him sharply.

"It might be true, you know. She must be a very busy woman and not as young as she was. Besides, to a woman of her type, Rosamund's defiance must have come as a very real shock. All the same," she added shrewdly, "you don't believe it, do you?"

Dr. Rob shrugged his shoulders.

"It may as you say, be true. But on the other hand, she must be perfectly well aware that she has put up the one type of obstacle between us which I can't possibly override. It wouldn't be ethical."

"But that means you think she knows that you and Rosamund—No, that's impossible, Rob! How can she possibly connect you with Rosamund's disappearance?"

"I don't say that she can. But I do say that since she has never let me know of Rosamund's existence, she must always have been afraid that we might meet by accident—as, indeed, we have. So now, isn't it at least possible that she's wondering if that has happened and decided to manoeuvre herself into a position where I can't get at her to ask awkward questions?"

She didn't answer and after a moment he went on :

"I know what you're thinking, Alice. That even if she didn't really connect Rosamund's disappearance with me, she certainly will do so now! She'll feel that it's surely too great a coincidence that I turned up demanding to see her at this particular time. I'm afraid that's true." He stirred restlessly in his chair. "Yet is it such a very big risk? No one but my secretary knows where I am when I come down here and she also knows that the job wouldn't last five minutes if she gave me away! Still, just to make sure, after this weekend, I'm not coming down here for a bit. Indeed, I shan't be able to. I've had an invitation to lecture in America and frankly, I can't refuse it. It's not only that it's an honour, but I'd give offence to some very good friends."

"How long will you be away?" Miss Alice asked, her heart sinking uncontrollably. She had a conviction that the next few weeks were going to prove very important in the lives of the man beside her and the girl who had come so suddenly and unexpectedly into their lives.

"I'll be back in three weeks," Dr. Rob told her, and

frowned. "It means, of course, that I won't be able to make any more enquiries—but apart from that, will it really make much difference in the long run—that is, if you are staying on down here and will let her stay with you?"

"Yes, to both questions," Miss Alice said slowly. "But you must remember, Rob, that whatever Rosamund may choose to do, I've no authority over her at all."

He looked at her sharply.

"You've got something particular in mind, haven't you?" he asked.

"Yes, I have, Miss Alice said unwillingly. "Though I don't like telling tales out of school. It's simply that she and John Lindsay—" she indicated the *Seven Stars* with a jerk of her head—"have got very friendly this last week."

"No more than that?"

"At this stage, no, I don't think so." Miss Alice chose her words with considerable care. "But there's something about Rosamund—a sparkle a—a sort of inner light which might mean she's falling in love with him. It's difficult to explain just what I mean, but you must judge for yourself. They went into Bath together, but they'll be back for tea."

"H'm!" Dr. Rob's frown was almost a scowl. "What's your opinion of the young man, Alice?"

"I like him," she said unhesitatingly. "I think he's got a temper and is capable of being very moody—in fact, I know he is. On the other hand, he strikes me as being both clean and honest. But really I don't know a great deal about him. In fact, Rob, he's as reticent about his past as Rosamund is about hers!"

"Is he, indeed!" Dr. Rob exclaimed grimly, and then laughed. "You know, Alice," he said wryly, "Rosamund being reticent about her past simply seems to be natural and reasonable in the circumstances. But where this young man's concerned, I'm inclined to jump to the conclusion that he's got something shady to hide. In fact, with very little encouragement, I could play the heavy father to perfection! Perhaps it's just as well that I'm going away for a time. I might be tempted to interfere and precipitate something that otherwise might never happen. All the same—" his voice grew very tender—"keep an eye on my girl for me, Alice!"

"I'll do that," she promised gruffly, near to tears.

The warm summer days flitted past, one much like the other and, to Rosamund, all quite perfect. Every night, before sleep engulfed her, she would live over again the day that had just passed. The pearly morning when, disturbed by the clamouring bird song, she had gone out on deck to breathe the chilly, sweet-scented air. The simple, everyday tasks that she performed so effortlessly because she was so preoccupied thinking of the exquisite magic that had come into her life. And that, of course, meant that she was thinking of John. She knew now beyond all doubt that she loved him, and she was daring to hope that he was beginning to love her.

He sought her company, talked much more freely about his book with frequent references to the part she had played in finding the solution to his earlier problems. All that would have been wonderful by itself, but there was much more to it than that. The little silences that fell between them had a significance at once sweet and disturbing. The way he looked at her when he didn't think she was noticing and the way in which his hand so often touched hers. Surely all that added up to one thing—he loved her even if, as yet, he didn't realise it. But soon he would, and in the meantime she was content to wait in her world of dreams and hopes.

Only one thing troubled her. Sooner or later she would have to tell him more about herself—in fact, in view of his obvious interest in her, it surprised her that he had not already begun to ask questions, and oddly enough it didn't occur to her, as it had done to Miss Alice, that John himself was extremely reticent about *his* past.

Her concern was not whether John would be able to understand her genuine desire to get away from the hot-house existence of the past. It was the sort of life which, she was quite sure, would be repugnant to anyone of John's simple tastes. None the less, the fact remained that she had been used to luxurious surroundings such as, she knew, he couldn't offer her. He had been quite frank about that.

"I'm living on the small income I get from money which my mother left me," he had explained. "I plan to make out on that until—*if*—I sell my book."

"You will," Rosamund told him with serene conviction.

He gave her an enquiring look.

"What makes you say that so positively?"

"It's rather difficult to explain," she confessed. "But I think you—tell me, John, sometimes when you read through what you've written, do you just *know* it's good— and you can hardly believe that you've written it?"

"Yes! Even to the point of hardly being able to remember that I did write it! The old subconscious, I suppose. But how did you know?"

"It shows in your face—a sort of satisfied but awestruck look. I'm explaining very badly," she apologised, seeing how startled he looked.

"No, you're not, my dear! You're making me understand just how well *you* understand. It's as if you've read my thoughts! Tell me more about myself."

"Certainly not!" she refused mischievously. "You might get too vain—"

The colour surged up into her cheeks as she realised what John would read into that, and panic-stricken, she turned and fled. John didn't follow her, but as she reached the sanctuary of the *Pride of London* she couldn't resist the temptation to look back. John was standing just where she had left him. He was smiling and as she watched, he lifted his hand and blew her a kiss. For a moment Rosamund hesitated. Then she made a similar gesture and spent the rest of the day in such a bemused frame of mind that Miss Alice gave up any attempt at conversation. She understood what that head-in-the-clouds state meant. Rosamund *was* in love with John.

Miss Alice sighed. Perhaps it would be all right. Very often the two people most intimately concerned were the best judges of that despite the doubts of older folk. None the less, her promise to Dr. Rob to look after Rosamund for him was, if not a burden certainly a very real anxiety.

During the next week, Miss Alice had to go to London to see a prospective client. She was considerably put out about it.

"Wasting this lovely weather going to town," she grumbled. "It will be hot and smelly and extremely tiring."

"Do you *have* to go?" Rosamund asked sympathetically.

"I'm afraid so. You see, the lady in question is regarded as a great beauty, but that isn't enough, you know, to guarantee that there is anything I can really paint! Oh, one can make a charming map of perfect features, of course, but that's not the same as painting a portrait that *lives*. So I owe it to her and to myself to make sure that I can get something out of her. If I don't feel I can, thank goodness I've got to the stage where I can afford to turn work down if I think it's necessary. And since I've already got grave doubts in this case, I've no choice but to find out, face to face."

"She won't like it if you do refuse," Rosamund commented. "I mean, people who are very, very beautiful so often do expect to have their own way, don't they?"

"They do," Miss Alice agreed drily, not very much surprised at Rosamund's appreciation of such a situation. She could well imagine that the child had come across many such women in her aunt's salon! "Now, I expect to be home in the late afternoon—I certainly intend to get away as early as I can. Are you sure you'll be all right? John won't be here either for part of the day, you know, so you'll be all alone."

"Of course I'll be all right," Rosamund assured her confidently. "And John won't be away so very long—only an hour or so, he thinks. He's going into Bath to get his signature witnessed on some papers, that's all."

She didn't sound in the least curious as to what the papers were, Miss Alice noticed. Of course, they might simply be that John had told her already, but somehow Miss Alice didn't think so. It was, she thought, far more likely that it simply didn't occur to Rosamund to question anything John did or said. Which was natural enough when one was in love, but whether it was wise or not was another question.

As soon as both Miss Alice and John had left, Rosamund became very busy. She had made up her mind that this was an ideal opportunity for doing various jobs without making a nuisance of herself. Neither Miss Alice nor John seemed to think it necessary to do more in the way of cleaning than to flick round with a duster and mop the bits of floor that showed. Rosamund had different ideas.

She worked quickly because she knew that John would be back just as soon as possible and her plans took in the cleaning of the *Seven Stars* as well as of the *Pride of London*. She did John's boat first because she wanted to make sure that she had finished before he got back. That way, although he was sure to tell her that she shouldn't have done it, it would be too late to argue!

However, he still hadn't arrived by the time she had finished, so she returned to the *Pride of London* and set to work, though without the same enthusiasm. It was an extremely hot day, the sun, by now, was high in the sky and there wasn't a breath of wind. Rosamund decided that she had taken on rather too much and catching sight of herself in a mirror, saw that unless she wanted John to see her looking an absolute sketch, she'd have to leave the rest for another day. There were smears of dirt on her face, her hair, damp with the heat, was sticking to her head in streaky strands and how she wanted a bath, or at least a shower!

But she had only got as far as putting away her cleaning materials when she heard footsteps outside on the deck.

"Is that you, John?" she called out, wishing devoutly that she'd stopped work a quarter of an hour earlier. "I won't be long—I'm just tidying up—"

But John didn't answer, though he must have heard her, and after a moment or two, convinced that something must be wrong, she went out to investigate.

And there was, indeed, something very wrong. For it wasn't John. It was her aunt, Ruth Hastings, who stood within a few feet of her.

CHAPTER FOUR

WHITE-FACED, Rosamund stared incredulously at her aunt.

"How did you—how did you—?" she stammered.

"Find out where you were?" Ruth smiled derisively. "Oh, that was quite simple!"

That wasn't true, but she was convinced that the more she could impress upon Rosamund that she had not only been stupid to run away but also far from clever in covering her tracks, the easier it would be to regain her hold over the girl. But she had no intention of telling Rosamund just how she came to be here. That would mean telling her something which she sincerely hoped Rosamund hadn't already found out.

It had not needed Dr. Rob's attempt to see her to suggest to Ruth that he might be involved in Rosamund's disappearance, for it never occurred to her that she would take the risk of leaving the security she had always known if she hadn't some definite haven available.

But if, by chance, Rosamund had met her father, and as Ruth had always feared, he had appreciated the significance of her striking likeness to his dead wife, then there was the answer ! And the most likely one.

But it hadn't been quite as straightforward as that. Ruth felt it was reasonable to assume that if Rosamund had gone to her father, then she would no longer be in London. Much as she detested Dr. Rob, she didn't underrate his brain. He'd be quick to realise that she wouldn't let Rosamund go without a struggle and so he would bundle the hysterical little fool out of the way to some place or other where she couldn't be easily found.

But that might be anywhere ! It would be like looking for a needle in a bundle of hay ! Or would it? Ruth had always been on the alert at any chance mention of Dr. Rob's name. Now she recalled a conversation between two of her clients which she had overheard. It was to the effect that he had some retreat out of London to which he went as often as possible at weekends. Just where it was was apparently a jealously guarded secret for which the two women had a simple, and to them, an obvious solution.

"A woman," they agreed with meaningful nods of their heads. "Someone he can't acknowledge publicly—"

Ruth didn't care what the reason was for the secretiveness. All she cared about was *where*? She acted promptly. Apparently Dr. Rob rarely had a professional appointment after lunch on Friday. She would have him watched and followed.

And she was lucky. The weekend when Miss Alice had

summoned Dr. Rob was the first occasion on which her watchdog was on duty. His report gave Ruth all the information she needed for it even included an unmistakable description of Rosamund.

That she had had to delay her visit until now had been annoying but unavoidable. Her doctor had insisted that the cause of the periodic bouts of pain she was experiencing must be investigated at once. Annoyed, as only a person who has never known bad health can be in such circumstances, Ruth had agreed to go into a nursing home. The verdict—she had insisted on being told the absolute truth—was unequivocal. The condition of her heart was such that, at the best, she could not expect to live much more than a year—and then only if she lived a quieter, less demanding life. But she had little use for life on those terms and she ignored the warning.

"Easy?" Rosamund repeated, and shook her head emphatically. "No, it couldn't have been. I didn't tell anyone where I was coming. I didn't even know myself until—" she stopped short, deciding that the less she told her aunt the better. "So how *did* you find me?"

"Does that really matter?" Ruth asked with a shrug.

Ruth would have given a lot to know how that unfinished sentence was to have finished, but she had no intention of asking. Even in these few minutes she had discovered that there was a radical change in Rosamund. She had been startled, but she hadn't been scared by Ruth's unexpected appearance. That was clear from the mulish obstinacy of her expression and the defensive way in which she stood blocking the doorway.

Ruth sank down in one of the deck chairs. She was tired and that wretched pain was beginning to make itself felt, but not for anything in the world would she have confessed to either. One didn't dominate people by parading one's own frailties.

"What matters," she went on dogmatically, "is that I *am* here and that you are coming back to London with me!"

"No," Rosamund contradicted quietly but very firmly.

Ruth regarded her thoughtfully. She sounded completely sure of herself. There must be someone backing her in her rebellion. An idea occurred to her.

"This man, John," she said curiously. "Are you living with him?"

The bright, angry colour flamed to Rosamund's face, but she knew that she must not lose her temper. That would only give Aunt Ruth the advantage.

"No," she denied briefly.

Ruth believed her. Rosamund, she knew, was not naturally a liar. Besides, she had complete faith in her own ability to detect a lie.

"No? Then who are you staying with?"

"With an artist—a lady—" Once again Rosamund left her sentence unfinished and shook her head. "No, Aunt Ruth, I'm not going to tell you anything else. What I do is my own affair, and though I'm sorry if it annoys you, I've got to make you understand that it's not your concern at all. Please do accept that—and the fact that in no circumstances will I ever come back to work for you or live with you! That's finished completely."

Almost Ruth gave up. Despite Rosamund's almost uncanny resemblance to her mother, there was something of her father in her, too. His obstinacy, his inability to see anything except from his own point of view—

Her father! Had Rosamund and Dr. Rob discovered one another? Surely, if they had, Rosamund would have been told the whole story and would have used it to justify herself. But she hadn't and Ruth was puzzled. Rob simply couldn't have missed the likeness.

And, of course, he hadn't, but he wanted to make quite sure of his facts before he claimed his daughter. That was why he had tried to see her—and how lucky she had been that his visit had coincided with her stay in the nursing home!

But in that case one had to accept it that Rosamund coming to this out-of-the-way spot where she was bound to meet her father was sheer coincidence, and that Ruth found disconcerting. It was as if a stronger force than herself was playing a part! She discarded the idea impatiently.

"Now, don't waste any more time," she ordered imperiously. "Get your things together—"

"No!" Rosamund squared her shoulders and met her aunt's eyes squarely. "You've got to understand, Aunt

Ruth, that I'm not coming either now or at any other time!"

Suddenly the pain took command and it was all that Ruth could do to keep from crying out. Strangely, it didn't occur to her that if she had, if Rosamund knew, she would almost certainly have given in out of sheer pity. But at least it could be said for Ruth that she was as hard to herself as she was to anyone over whom she had authority. For a moment or two her hands gripped the arms of the chair until her knuckles were white. Then, as the pain receded a little, she spoke in almost her usual manner.

"You must be crazy!" she announced with conviction. "With me you've got prospects that most girls would give their eyes to have! I—I won't be able to keep on indefinitely, and then you will take over the Salon."

"But I don't want to, Aunt Ruth," Rosamund insisted earnestly. "I know it means a great deal to you, but it doesn't to me."

"But why not, Rosamund?" For the first time there was something like a plea in Ruth's voice.

Rosamund hesitated and then shook her head. She knew only too well why she had to make this stand and she had tried more than once to explain to her aunt, though always without success. That, she felt, might be because, however strongly one may feel, it is never easy to tell someone that they themselves are to blame for your actions. Now she must tell the brutal truth or, once again, fail to be convincing.

"Go on," Ruth said ironically. "Don't trouble to spare my feelings!"

"I don't find—" Rosamund began, and started again. "To me, it isn't a satisfying job. It's all so artifical and—and shallow. And so are so many of our—of your clients."

"They pay well," Ruth commented laconically.

"I think that's just it," Rosamund said eagerly. "They've got lots of money and they think that's everything. Oh, I know what you're going to say—" as Ruth's lips parted. "That there are very few things that money can't buy. But I think the things it can't buy are the most important ones."

"Such as?"

"Love, loyalty, common honesty," Rosamund explained diffidently, well aware that she was making no impression whatever. "Aunt Ruth, you *do* know what I mean! You know as well as I do how vain and silly so many of the women who come to the Salon are! And I'm so tired of having to flatter and fawn on people like that as if they were something special and wonderful! It's—it's degrading!"

"What a shocking little prig you are, Rosamund!" Ruth exclaimed irritably. "Let me tell you, my dear, if it wasn't for these women whom you despise so, you would have had to go without a lot of the things you've taken for granted all these years!"

"I know," Rosamund admitted distastefully.

Ruth's eyes narrowed. This was going to be more difficult than she had expected. But not impossible, of course.

"And that is all?" she asked indifferently.

"No," Rosamund said slowly. "There are other reasons. One is that I want to be myself. I can't go on making the Salon my whole life. I want to be free at least sometimes to have interests of my own." She paused. "That's one thing. The other—"

"Yes?" Ruth encouraged drily.

"The other is—"

"Well?" impatiently.

"Oh, Aunt Ruth, you must surely know!" Rosamund protested. "The Salon is such an unhappy place! Behind the scenes, I mean. Everybody grumbles and quarrels and gets upset—don't you realise that I've been spending half my time to help people and smooth things over! And I can't stand any more of it! I simply can't!"

Ruth didn't reply. She knew just how much truth there was in what Rosamund said, and though even to herself she wouldn't admit that her own aggressive, domineering manner was at the bottom of the troubles, she did acknowledge that Rosamund had got a knack of soothing frayed nerves and keeping the peace. That, in fact, was one of her biggest reasons for determining to take Rosamund back with her.

"So you see, Aunt Ruth, I *can't* come back with you,"

Rosamund went on, her face tense at the mere thought of doing such a thing. "I truly think I should be ill if I did! And now—if you'd like it, I'll get you a cup of tea, and then you must go, please."

Ruth stood up.

"Tea!" she almost spat the word at Rosamund. "Do you think I'll accept even a cup of tea at your hands after this? I've more pride than that! No, if that's how you feel, you're no use to me! With all these high-falutin' notions of yours you'd be more trouble than you'd be worth! I've no wish to have my clients upset by your offensiveness, and that's what would happen, sooner or later. So just consider this—if you don't promise to behave and come with me now, you don't come at all! I've finished with you! Is that clear?"

"Quite clear," Rosamund said steadily, thankful that at last her aunt understood that she must accept the situation.

But Ruth hadn't finished yet. Deliberately she looked Rosamund over from head to foot; a look that took in tousled hair and smudged face, bare suntanned legs and work-stained hands. A look that made Rosamund feel as if something in her had withered and left her defenceless.

"You arrant little fool!" Ruth said, the very softness of her voice making it all the more venomous. "I can almost find it in my heart to be sorry for you—but not quite! Your hypocrisy revolts me too much for that!"

"I'm not a hypocrite," Rosamund was stung into protesting.

"No? Then how would you describe someone who doesn't practise what they preach?" Ruth said contemptuously. "All this talk of yours about loyalty and honesty—it means absolutely nothing! It's no more than an excuse for your selfishness—"

Rosamund's heart sank. She had been too quick to imagine that she'd won the battle. She should have known that Aunt Ruth didn't give up so easily! What was more, what was coming now was going to be more difficult to combat than anything that had gone before. Instinctively Rosamund braced herself and deliberately took the war into the enemy's country.

"As your employee I've always been completely loyal to your interests, Aunt Ruth," she said steadily. "Though, as you know quite well, I've wanted to stop working for you for some time. Even so, perhaps I should have given you formal notice that I was leaving—or else have forfeited a month's salary. But as you haven't paid me yet for the last two months, I don't really think you have much cause for complaint on that score!"

Inwardly Ruth raged at being put in the wrong in this way and knowing that there was little if anything that she could say in her own defence, promptly changed her tactics.

"I consider that a very debatable statement," she declared with a dismissive gesture of her hand. "What I was thinking of is our personal relationship. I wonder—" she paused and seemed to consider what she was about to say very carefully. Then, with added emphasis, she went on : "Yes, I do indeed wonder, Rosamund, if you realise just how much you have cost me in happiness as well as in money!"

Rosamund, out of her depth, stared at her aunt dumbly. She had never known just how it had come about that Aunt Ruth was her guardian, for the few questions she had found the courage to ask were invariably ignored. Now, it appeared, she was going to be told—

"Your mother died when you were only a few months old," went on the cold, relentless voice. "She died completely penniless. I had the choice of putting you into a Home or looking after you myself. Like a fool, that was what I did. It wasn't easy. At that time I was earning only a small salary. I'd never been able to afford more than just about the bare necessities of life. Now I had to provide for you as well. Not just ordinary expenses, I mean. I had to pay someone to look after you so that I could work. I soon found that I couldn't make ends meet. So I worked harder. I took on an evening job as well as my day's work—"

The short, staccato sentences beat like hail on Rosamund's brain and by their very brevity, brought conviction. She swallowed convulsively, unable to speak, waiting for what was still to come. And Ruth, quick to see that she was making an impression, invented a story on the spur of the moment which, she was sure, would tip the scales in her favour.

"Then I met a man who wanted me to marry him. But, as his wife, I'd have to travel all over the world with him, never staying more than a few months in any one place. So I refused him. Not on my own account. I'd have enjoyed that sort of life. But for *your* sake, Rosamund. You needed a settled home and I decided that it was my duty—" Momentarily her face was convulsed with an expression which was an extraordinary mixture of bitterness and triumph. "So I gave up my chance of happiness."

"I—I'm very sorry, Aunt Ruth," Rosamund whispered. "I had no idea—"

"I didn't want you to have," Ruth told her bleakly. "I made the decision, not you. But I had thought that the natural affection you would surely have for me would make a sufficiently strong bond between us to repay me for what I had sacrificed. However—" she shrugged her shoulders in a fatalistic gesture— "it seems that I was wrong!"

Rosamund felt as if actual prison bars were closing round her. Her hands came up in an instinctively defensive movement as if to hold them off. Then she asked the question which she had never before found the courage to ask.

"My—my father?" she spoke the unfamiliar word with difficulty. "Am I—am I illegitimate?"

For the briefest moment Ruth hesitated. Then she shook her head.

"No. Your parents were married. But that made no difference. Your father deserted your mother less than a year after they were married. I believe he went abroad—certainly she never heard from him again."

"But he knew about me coming?" Rosamund whispered.

"To my certain knowledge, your mother wrote several times to tell him of your birth. I know that because I posted the letters myself."

"I—see." Rosamund's hands dropped limply to her sides. "Is—is he still alive?"

So Rob hadn't told her that he was her father!

"So far as I know he is," she shrugged indifferently. "But I haven't set eyes on him since he left your mother."

She held her breath. Had she worn Rosamund's resistance down to breaking point or were there to be any more awkward questions?

Apparently not. Rosamund's whole body seemed to sag and her wide eyes held the haunted look of a bird mesmerised by a snake.

"Well?" Ruth asked. "Now that you know the truth, are you going to repay the debt you owe me or do you prefer to admit that you *are* a wretched little hypocrite? It's up to you!"

"I—I—" Rosamund moistened her dry lips with the tip of her tongue.

"Rosamund! Hi, Rosamund, where are you?"

At the sound of John's voice hailing her blithely from the towpath, Rosamund came to life. She darted across the little deck and the narrow gangplank, straight into John's arms, and as they closed protectingly round her, she clung to him, sobbing like a frightened child.

"Darling, darling, what is it?" he asked urgently, and then, realising that she was beyond speech, his arms tightened. "Listen, Rosamund, listen! Whatever is wrong, you're safe now! I'll see to that! But try to tell me—"

Rosamund was still shaking violently, but she made a valiant attempt to control herself.

"My—my aunt," she whispered. "She—she's been trying to make me go back to London with her—and I can't, John, I can't!"

"Then you shan't, sweetheart," John told her matter-of-factly. "Come along and we'll tell her so!"

But Ruth had followed Rosamund and now, from the slight advantage of the gangplank, she looked down at them, her calm apparently unruffled.

"For your own sake, young man, I really do advise you not to interfere," she said coolly. "Rosamund is a very naughty girl, you know!"

Rosamund felt John stiffen.

"No, madam, I know nothing of the sort," he retorted coldly. "And please don't trouble further to convince me that you're right. It won't get you anywhere."

Ruth sighed and shook her head.

"How persuasive a pretty face can be!" she mocked. "Even when it could do with a good wash! Now, do be sensible! I know my niece better—" and bit her lip as she saw John's face harden. Stupid of her to make the mistake of trying to ridicule him in his own eyes! Clearly he had far too good an opinion of himself for that to produce results. "I don't think you understand the situation, Mr.—?"

"John Lindsay," John supplied automatically.

Ruth bent her head graciously.

"Mr. Lindsay. Thank you. As I was saying, I don't think you understand the situation. Rosamund has behaved very foolishly and inconsiderately. Indeed, most people would say that I'm being extremely silly in giving her another chance. However, that's just what I am doing! I'm willing to overlook—"

"No!" Rosamund said breathlessly. "No, no!"

Ruth felt a sudden stab of pain. Her air of patience, so deliberately assumed, snapped abruptly.

"Oh, for heaven's sake, Rosamund, stop this nonsense! Of course you're coming back with me—*now*!"

"No," John told her very quietly. "She's doing nothing of the sort. Rosamund is of age. Consequently she has the right to make her own decisions. That is definite and final!"

Ruth glared at him.

"If you don't stop interfering—" she threatened.

"But I have every right to interfere," John assured her a convincingly vibrant note in his voice. "Rosamund and I are engaged. Now do you understand? We're going to be married!"

Ruth had gone, but not before she had fired a parting shot. To Rosamund she enlarged on her earlier threat.

"From now on, no matter what sort of trouble you get yourself into, don't expect that I'm going to help you out! Do you understand? I've finished with you!"

To John she spoke with pitying contempt.

"You don't, of course, know what you're taking on, Mr. Lindsay. Well, you'll find out! Because Rosamund won't remain satisfied with love in a cottage—or on a barge—for very long. She'll soon be whining for the comfort and luxury she's always been used to when the initial glamour wears off, as it always does. A pity you're not a rich man, you know. If you were, your marriage could well be a success. As it is—" she shook her head. "Not a chance! Not, of course, that in your present besotted state you believe that. But remember, you have been warned!"

Over Rosamund's bent head John watched Ruth walk slowly along the towpath to vanish through the gate in the hedge. There was a peculiar expression in his eyes, part apprehension, but to a far greater degree of determination. But when Rosamund lifted her head from his shoulder, she saw nothing but kindness and strength there.

Tentatively she sought to free herself and instantly John let her go.

"Well, that's that!" he announced cheerfully, and then, as Rosamund didn't reply, he went on matter-of-factly: "I suggest that we indulge ourselves in Miss Alice's inevitable panaceas for all ills—a cup of tea! After that we'll talk things over."

Suddenly tongue-tied now that she and John were alone, Rosamund nodded in silence and ran quickly up the gangplank.

"I'll just tidy up first—" she said breathlessly, and hurried to her cabin.

Quickly she washed her face and hands, combed her hair and then stood hesitating over the choice of a dress. Not that there was a very large or inspiring selection. But there was one dress, a bluish-green which she knew suited her fair colouring better than anything else she had. Usually she kept it for special occasions—well, wasn't this a *very* special occasion? Of all times, didn't she want to look her very best?

She slipped into the dress, slid her feet into more attractive sandals and then, all ready to face up to John, she suddenly lost her self-confidence.

John had told Aunt Ruth that they were going to be married, but had he really meant it? Wasn't it much more likely that he had said it on the spur of the moment because he realised that it was the one argument which would checkmate Aunt Ruth?

She drew a deep breath. She knew that she loved John, but not that he loved her, and just because he'd come to her rescue so unhesitatingly didn't mean that she had any right to keep him to his word. She'd got to make him understand that—it was only fair.

She walked through to the galley and found John already there, just about to pour boiling water into the teapot. He looked up with a grin as she came in.

"I'm quite domesticated, these days," he remarked proudly. "Pop up on to the deck and I'll bring the tray."

Rosamund understood. That light, easy manner was, she felt sure, meant to put her at her ease, but it had the reverse effect. To her it meant just one thing—that without embarrassing her by putting it into words, John was telling her that there was nothing for her to worry about—that nothing that had happened need be taken seriously.

They drank their tea in a silence which seemed to Rosamund to grow more oppressive with every passing moment, yet it was beyond her power to break it. But John, though not exactly scowling, certainly looked worried. Supposing that he had already guessed that she loved him ! She *must* take the initiative—

"Another cup?" John asked abruptly, and when she refused : "Then shall we talk things over?" he suggested.

"John—" She saw that he looked taken aback at her urgency and it needed all her courage to go on. "Before you say anything, I want to tell you that I—I think it was quite wonderful of you to come to my rescue the way you did, but of course, I quite understand—"

"Just what do you understand?" John asked grimly.

"Why, that you—you only said—what you did to stop Aunt Ruth—"

"Now, let's get this straight," John insisted. "Do you mean that you think I said that we were going to get married simply to get the better of that objectionable aunt of yours?"

"Yes," Rosamund said miserably. Then, with suddenly upflung head : "Yes, of course," she told him resolutely.

In one swift, decisive movement John stood up, scooped her from her chair and held her so close that she could feel the pounding of his heart. His lips sought and captured hers with ruthless, passionate fervour.

"You little idiot, does that suggest that I was pretending?" he demanded savagely. "Does it? Or this—?"

Again his mouth claimed hers, and stirred to the very depths of her being, Rosamund knew that her dreams had come true. John loved her! She need not be afraid to show her own love—

Time stood still for them—

"And now," John said at last in a voice shaken with feeling, "will you kindly tell me why you did your best to scare the daylights out of me? Do you know you almost convinced me that—you didn't care?"

"Did I?" Looking up into his adoring eyes, her own glinted with mischief. "Well, it didn't seem to—to—"

"To cramp my style?" John suggested wryly. "Don't you understand, Rosamund, I was desperate! You seemed to be slipped away from me and I—" he left the sentence unfinished, but his lips sought hers again, not in passion now but as if he was seeking reassurance and comfort.

And in that brief moment of time it seemed to Rosamund that she was given a complete and awe-inspiring understanding of what love between a man and a woman can and should be. It was not simply a matter of romance, wonderful though that was. It was something much deeper and more enduring than that. It was the sharing of life in every respect, the desire to stand between the loved one and pain or danger. It was the knowledge that two imperfect human beings can make mistakes and yet forgive and start afresh. And perhaps, most important of all, it meant that there are times when even the strongest natures are vulnerable and need to know that they do not stand alone.

With utter conviction that this was one of those times, she put a hand on either side of John's face.

"John, my own dear, I love you so much," she said with passionate tenderness. "Now—and always. Believe that, for it's the truth."

And gently she laid her soft lips against his.

When Miss Alice returned she was, as she had anticipated, hot, tired and frankly, in none too good a temper. None the less, absorbed though she was in her own discomforts, she was quick to guess what had happened. True, John and Rosamund were simply sitting side by side on the deck, but before they had noticed her, she had realised how deeply absorbed they were in their conversation and as she got nearer and they jumped to their feet to greet her, she saw the unmistakable, glowing happiness in their faces.

"It's happened," she told herself helplessly. "They've told one another—this really is the last straw! What on earth do I do now? Oh, Rob, how I wish you were here!"

"Dear Miss Alice, you do look tired," Rosamund said sympathetically. "Do sit down while I get you some tea. Everything's ready so it won't take a minute!"

"Thank you, I'll get it for myself," Miss Alice said gruffly, and turned her back on them, ashamed at her apparent ungraciousness, but feeling that she must have a few minutes to herself to think over this new situation.

When she had gone, John and Rosamund looked at one another in consternation.

"I've never seen her like this before," Rosamund whispered, anxious not to be overheard. "What can be the matter?"

"She's pretty shrewd. I imagine she guessed about us," John frowned as he spoke.

"But how can she have done?" Rosamund protested. "I mean, we were only talking—"

John's expression softened as he put a finger under her chin and tipped her face up.

"Yes, my love, just talking. But possibly you don't realise that your eyes are like stars, and there's a sort of radiance—"

For a moment they forgot Miss Alice and then John said uneasily :

"All the same, supposing she did guess, why should it have upset her, as it evidently did? I mean, why should she object? And in any case, what business is it of hers?"

"None, really," Rosamund admitted. "Only she's been very good to me and I think she's really fond of me as I am of her. I think, perhaps, she feels sort of responsible for me—"

"Well, if she does, while I'm sure she'd be much more pleasant about it than your aunt was, she still mustn't be allowed to interfere," John started forcefully. "Rosamund, you won't let her, will you?"

"No, John," she promised gravely. "Neither Miss Alice nor anyone else."

"Good!" He spoke emphatically, yet his expression was one of preoccupation. "You know, Rosamund, I think it might be a good idea if we—"

At that moment Miss Alice returned and it was clear that she had regained her usual poise.

"Sorry I was so shrewish," she said cheerfully. "But I really was feeling at the end of my tether."

"Yes, of course," Rosamund began, and then, as John took her hand in his, she looked at him enquiringly.

"I think we'd both like Miss Alice to be the first to hear our news, wouldn't we, Rosamund?" And when Rosamund nodded, he turned smilingly to Miss Alice. "Rosamund has promised to marry me, Miss Alice! Will you give us your good wishes?"

Miss Alice looked from one face to the other. How happy they looked and how confident! Well, that was only right, of course. To start their life together full of doubts and fears would be both unnatural and disastrous. Yet she herself could not feel entirely at ease. Had they really had time to know each other? And wasn't that important, too?

Besides there was very definitely a protectiveness in John's manner towards Rosamund which made her feel instinctively that something had happened during her absence—something unexpected and possibly alarming—which might have precipitated matters. Or was she imagining things? Wasn't it only natural for a young man who was deeply in love to want to cherish the girl who had promised to entrust her life to him?

"I do, indeed, wish you both every happiness!" she said with a sincerity all the more genuine because of her unexpressed doubts. "Now, and for the rest of your lives!"

She kissed Rosamund affectionately, patted John's shoulder in a friendly way and then remarked that if they didn't mind, she'd like to have a little rest before it was time to think about the evening meal.

A little smile played round Rosamund's lips as she watched her go.

"What a pet she is!" she murmured softly.

"What?" John asked in a preoccupied way.

"Well, perhaps she does want a rest, but I think she was being tactful because she must know that we'd rather be alone!"

"Yes, I suppose so," John agreed, but something in the way he said it made Rosamund look at him quickly.

"What is it, John?" she asked anxiously.

He hesitated for a moment. Then he laid a hand on either of her shoulders.

"Rosamund!" He spoke tensely, imperatively. "You do trust me, don't you?"

"Yes, John," Rosamund said unhesitatingly.

"Then—" his grasp of her shoulders increased to almost painful intensity— "will you marry me at once—without telling anyone, even Miss Alice?"

CHAPTER FIVE

"BUT can we do that?" Rosamund asked. "I thought one had to wait quite a long time—weeks—before it was possible to get married."

"So it is, if it's a matter of having banns read," John explained. "But it's also possible to be married by licence and then there's only a very short delay—a matter of a few days, I think. But I'll have to go to London to find out the exact details. But if it is possible—will you, Rosamund?"

"Of course!" she said unhesitatingly.

John took her arm in his arms and as he looked down into her candid trusting eyes, a little muscle flickered at the corner of his mouth.

"Bless you, darling," he whispered fervently. "I swear you shan't regret it!"

"Of course I shan't," Rosamund said confidently.

"And—and I'm so glad you've suggested it, John. I shall feel so much safer, married to you!"

"Yes, that's just it," John agreed. "Once we're married, nobody and nothing can ever come between us!"

"That's how I want it to be," Rosamund sighed contentedly. "Actually, I think Aunt Ruth must realise by now that there's nothing she can do, but once we're married I shan't even have to worry that she might still try. I shall just hide behind you, John, and feel perfectly safe."

"I hope you'll always be able to say that!"

Rosamund's happiness was suddenly dimmed. There had been something disturbingly sombre about the way in which John had said that. It was as if, despite his determination, he wasn't entirely confident.

"John, it's not only because of Aunt Ruth that you're worried, is it?" she asked gently. "Because you don't have to be, you know. I mean, I think Miss Alice might try to persuade us to wait because she feels we haven't known each other long enough—"

"Has she said so?" John asked sharply.

"No, she hasn't," Rosamund admitted. "But all the same, I do think she feels like that—"

"You're quite sure you're not just assuming that because really you yourself feel it's true?" John asked searchingly.

Unconsciously Rosamund squared her shoulders as if to resist a threat she could sense but not understand.

"I'm quite sure, John," she said simply. "To me, all that matters is that we know we love one another. We'll have the whole of our lives to discover the rest, and I'm not frightened of the prospect. It sounds like—like heaven!"

With a queer, strangled exclamation, John caught her to him.

"You wonderful girl!" he said fervently, and then, as she smiled tremulously up at him: "That's why I've got the jitters! I can't believe my luck! You're so wonderful that the mere thought of ever losing you—"

She felt his body shudder against hers and knew that his fear went even deeper than she had at first thought. There *was* something—but it was for John to tell her if he wanted to. If not, then she would just keep on loving and trusting him until his fear left him—

"You're not going to lose me, John, I promise," she vowed.

To her relief, the black mood seemed to fall from John like a discarded cloak. His thoughts turned to the practical aspects of the situation.

"Tomorrow—" he began, and stopped short, looking over his shoulder at the door through which Miss Alice had gone. "Rosamund, walk with me up to the *Seven Stars*. I'd rather not risk any chances of being overheard—"

"That's better," he said a few minutes later when they reached his boat. "Now then, tomorrow I'll go up to town and make enquiries about the licence. I think there may be some residential qualifications required about at least one of us, but in all probability I can comply with them. Then I'll phone you—oh, damn it, I can't, of course. Well, in that case, I'll give you a number and you can phone me there at some definite time. All right?"

"Yes, I'll go into Bath to do some shopping," Rosamund planned. "And it will sound convincing because it's true."

"Convincing?" he repeated sharply. "To whom? Miss Alice again? But, darling, we've decided, haven't we, that it isn't really her business."

"I know, John," Rosamund agreed quickly. "But don't you see, whether it is or not, there's far less chance of her asking awkward questions if I volunteer a reason before she has time to ask them?"

"Something in that," John admitted. "On the same principle, I'd better give a reason for going to Town. And as it happens, it will also be a perfectly true one. Rosamund, I've had what may turn out to be very good news. I didn't tell you in case nothing came of it—but I sent my first chapter to a firm of London publishers last week together with a short précis of the rest of the book. And this morning there was a letter waiting for me at the Shop from them. They want me to go and see them to discuss it—hey, steady on! You almost had me off my feet!"

For Rosamund had flung herself into his arms and was hugging him with shameless delight.

"Oh, *John*!" she was bubbling over with enthusiasm. "How wonderful! How absolutely wonderful!"

"Well, it may be," he admitted cautiously, though he returned her embrace with fervour. "But we mustn't build too much on it yet. There may be snags. All the same—" he drew a deep, satisfied breath— "what a day! To know that you're going to marry me and that there's at least a chance for the book—"

"I'm glad you put the two events in their right order," Rosamund said demurely.

John gave her a little shake.

"You vain little minx!" he said with mock severity. "All the same, I'm willing to pander to your vanity still further! I admit that in any case I would have been pleased about the book. That's no more than natural. But cross my heart, Rosamund, it's sharing the news with *you* and knowing what it may mean to us—" he finished his sentence with his lips on hers.

A little later, Rosamund decided that she must go back to the *Pride of London* to prepare the evening meal.

"Will you have it with us?" she asked as, reluctantly, John let her go.

He considered.

"No, I don't think I will, if you don't mind. Actually, I want to read through what I've already written so that it's fresh in my mind. Particularly the précis. I'm not altogether satisfied with it. There are several situations that need expanding and it might be a good idea if I were to give them a bit more thought so that I can come up with the answers to any questions that might be asked. Provided, of course, that I can concentrate to that degree!" He touched her bright hair with gentle fingers. "You're a considerable distraction, sweetheart, as well as an inspiration!"

Rosamund laughed softly.

"That sounds rather a contradictory statement! And I'm not quite sure which I prefer to be! But I do know one thing for sure—I mustn't get between you and your work because it *is* you and I don't want you to be any different. No, John darling, let me go now," as his arms reached out for her again. "I shan't be very far away, you know!"

He watched her go, and once again he was struck by the familiar elegance of her walk as he had been on the day that they met. And again he was convinced that he *had* seen her before in different circumstances somewhere, but again, for the life of him, he could not remember where.

Oh well, one of these days they must compare notes and see if it was possible that they had met.

In the meantime he really must get down to work.

Fleetingly, as he sat down at his work table, it occurred to him that neither Rosamund nor her aunt had given any hint as to what their work was. A little bit odd, perhaps—

Oh well—he dismissed it with a shrug of the shoulders—it wasn't of any importance since, for Rosamund, that was all past history. He began to re-read what he had already written and was quickly absorbed in the world of his own invention.

Miss Alice heard the news of John's summons by his possible publisher with a generous enthusiasm that made Rosamund feel rather guilty.

"You see, it isn't only that I appreciate what this could mean to your joint future, but also because it always delights me when someone with a creative gift receives the encouragement that makes all the hard slogging they've done seem so very well worth while! I know. I went through it myself. And though John's gift and mine are totally different, they have this in common—we both do creative work. Something we spin out of our entrails as a spider does its web. Do you understand what that means, Rosamund?"

"That it's part of you," Rosamund said seriously. "And so you've *got* to do it because, if you don't, it would be like making a perfectly well person being made to live the life of an invalid. You wouldn't be *whole*."

"Yes, that's just it," Miss Alice agreed, but she wondered a little. Was what Rosamund had just said the outcome of an understanding deeper than one would expect from a young girl who was outside the charmed circle to which John with his writing and she with her painting belonged? Or was it just the repetition of what

85

John himself had already explained? A little of both, perhaps, but at any rate, the child did understand, which augured well for their future together. She realised that Rosamund was speaking again and gave her all her attention, though the topic had now changed to a less important one.

"I'm thinking of going into Bath tomorrow," Rosamund said so casually that, again, Miss Alice wondered a little. Wasn't it just *too* casual?

"Oh yes?"

"Yes. It's an opportunity, while John's away, to do a few odd bits of shopping and I thought I might have my hair shampooed. It's getting a bit dry with all this sunshine. Of course—" Rosamund felt that she was gabbling a bit now and that it all sounded artificial, but she ploughed on—"I may not be able to find a hairdresser with any free time, but I'll just have to take a chance."

"Quite," Miss Alice said equably. "In other words, you don't really know how long you'll be."

"No, I don't," Rosamund only just suppressed a sigh of relief at the easy acceptance of her announcement. "But I'll start off as early as I can so that I'm not too late back. Is there anything you want me to get for you while I'm there?"

"I don't think so, dear. In any case, you'll have your hands full getting through everything you want to yourself, won't you?"

Rosamund looked at her quickly. It was the most natural remark in the world and yet some quality in the way in which Miss Alice had spoken suggested that she suspected there was something more to the trip than a mild shopping spree.

"Or else it's that I feel mean at deceiving her," Rosamund wondered uncomfortably. "I wish I could explain—but it just isn't possible—and it isn't as if we're doing anything *wrong*—"

Having reassured herself on that point, she went to the galley and began preparations for the meal which, fortunately, was a simple one, for she only gave half her mind to her work.

But how could she help that when John was occupying all her heart and a large part of her thoughts? The incredible wonder of it! He loved her. And that wasn't all. He trusted her. He must do, for the beastly things Aunt Ruth had said about her hadn't made any impression at all on him! How *heavenly* life was—and it was going to be even better, for in a few days' time she would be John's wife! Happiness bubbled up in her and she began to sing softly to herself for the sheer joy of living.

Miss Alice heard the blithe little song and momentarily the tears sprang to her eyes. It was such a young sound and so confident—indeed, with all her heart she *did* wish them well, particularly this girl that she had taken under her wing. For her, she wanted happiness and security—all the good things of life. And much as she liked John, she wasn't entirely sure that Rosamund had made a wise choice—

She pulled herself up with a jerk.

"I'm an old fool," she told herself severely. "I'm being possessive, that's the trouble! I don't want her to fly away yet and so I'm inventing reasons why it would be better that she didn't. But it's no use. Once people grow up, they have to take their chance and there's nothing one can do about it. Thank goodness, there's no talk about them getting married yet! That really *would* have worried me!"

"Yes, we can fit you in this morning, madam," the receptionist told Rosamund. "One of our ladies had to make a last-minute cancellation, but I'm afraid it's not for another hour and a half—?"

"That will do beautifully," Rosamund assured her. "It will give me time to do some shopping."

"And your name, madam?"

"Hastings. Oh, will you tell the assistant who will be looking after me that my hair is very dry so that she'll know what sort of shampoo to give me?"

"Certainly, Miss Hastings. At eleven-thirty, then," the receptionist smiled, and Rosamund went out into the sunny street feeling that this was quite evidently going to be her lucky day.

The feeling was intensified a little later when she found just the dress she was looking for. One couldn't really say that it looked particularly like a wedding dress, yet its white simplicity struck a note which seemed just right to

Rosamund. She smiled as she looked at her reflection. John, she thought, would like it, though Aunt Ruth, if she were to see it, would probably dismiss it as a rag!

The thought of her aunt made Rosamund remember all the fashionable weddings which the Salon had dressed—the silks and laces, the embroidery—the yards and yards of tulle and the way in which even the plainest girls seemed to blossom into something like beauty in their bridal finery.

Yet she had no envy for any of them, for after all, none of them had married John! She bought another two dresses, one blue, the other green, cotton. Just the thing for a honeymoon on a barge! She completed her purchases with a pair of white shoes with silvery buckles and then went back to the hairdressers.

The assistant who looked after her did her job well, but she was something of a chatterbox and Rosamund wasn't sorry when she was left to herself under the drier. Content to let her thoughts drift happily, the time passed quickly and with ample time to spare before she rang John up, she stopped for a thoroughly feminine lunch of a poached egg, fruit salad and coffee. Then the Abbey clock struck the hour and it was time to phone John. She dialled the number he had given her and his voice answered immediately.

"Rosamund darling!" There was a lilt in the way he said it which told its own story. Everything was all right! So she was not surprised when he went on: "It's all set! No difficulty at all. I've got the licence and we can be married in any church we like right way!"

"Oh, John!" Rosamund was half laughing, half crying with happiness. "How wonderful!"

"Isn't it?" he agreed. "So—when, darling?"

"Whenever you say," she told him unhesitatingly.

"Bless you!" There was a caress in his voice and her heart swelled with tenderness. "Then how about Thursday?"

"Perfect!" she sparkled.

"And where?" he went on.

"I don't mind, John. Just so long as we do get married!"

"We'll do that all right," he assured her confidently. "Now, how do you like this idea—I'll be home tomorrow and then, on Thursday morning, we'll start off very early and drive until we find a nice old village church we like the look of. Then we'll rustle up the Rector and persuade him to do the job—"

"Persuade?" Rosamund said quickly.

"Well, it's going to be very short notice—he may have other engagements," John explained.

"Yes, of course. I hadn't thought of that." She hesitated momentarily. "John, what are we going to do about Miss Alice? I mean, we can't just vanish without giving her some explanation, can we?"

"No, I suppose not," he admitted reluctantly. "But we did decide that we wouldn't tell anybody, didn't we? And anyhow, we'll be coming back the same day—look, I tell you what, we'll tell her that we're going off for an all-day picnic and not to worry if we're late getting back. How's that?"

"Yes," Rosamund agreed, relieved. "And we'll have a picnic and that will make it true!"

John laughed softly.

"You're a truthful little soul, aren't you?" he said, and then, with sudden earnestness: "You don't know how much that means to me, Rosamund! Don't ever change, will you?"

"No, I won't," she promised seriously. "Oh, John, I am happy!"

"So am I!" And then, rather ruefully: "But I'll be even happier if my interview this afternoon is satisfactory."

"It will be," Rosamund assured him serenely. "I'm quite, quite sure it will be. Don't you realise, our star is in the ascendant? Nothing *can* go wrong!"

"Hey, keep your fingers crossed when you say that!" John advised, and Rosamund was not quite sure whether his alarm was genuine or pretence. "You don't want the gods to be jealous, do you?"

She laughed confidently.

"That's just superstition," she scoffed. "You'll see—and now I must ring off, John. Somebody is waiting for the phone. Goodbye, darling. I'll be thinking of you all the time and wishing you luck!"

"That should do the trick if anything will!" John said gratefully. " 'Bye now, darling! See you tomorrow!"

There was a little smile on Rosamund's face as she left the telephone box. It was so wonderful to feel that John relied on her and turned to her for reassurance. And equally wonderful, that for the rest of their lives, she would have John to rely on.

She walked to the car park where she had left her car and putting her purchases carefully on to the back seat, began her homeward journey. When she reached the village, she stopped outside the shop and went inside to ask Mrs. Watchett if there were any letters for Miss Alice.

Mrs. Watchett, engaged in cutting up a side of bacon into joints, wiped her hands on her voluminous apron and reached behind herself to the shelf where letters to be called for were put until they were claimed.

"Two, miss." She inspected first one and then the other so earnestly that Rosamund began to wonder if she had X-ray eyes and was able to read the letters through the envelopes without opening them. Then, reluctantly, she doled them out to Rosamund. "And one for you, miss," she added unexpectedly, reaching to the little shelf again.

"For me!" Rosamund was too much surprised to hide the fact, and Mrs. Watchett's eagle eyes raked her mercilessly.

"Miss Rosamund Hastings," she pronounced. "That's you, isn't it?"

"Oh yes," Rosamund confirmed, her heart sinking. She knew that it could only be from Aunt Ruth because no one else knew where she was, and a glance at the neat, angular handwriting told her that she was right.

"Nothing wrong, is there, miss?" Mrs. Watchett asked, agog with curiosity. "You look quite pale."

"I always do when it's very hot," Rosamund said mechanically. "Thank you, Mrs. Watchett!" And made her escape.

She drove down the lane and turned into Joblings' field. There, in the lee of the old barn, she picked up her letter from the seat beside her, but even then she couldn't find the courage immediately to open it. Then, with sudden resolution, she tore the envelope open and took the letter out. After all, no matter how unpleasant she might be, what real harm could Aunt Ruth do now?

She began to read :

"Dear Rosamund,

"Clearly, you're not such a fool as I thought you were. In fact, I congratulate you on a campaign very cleverly planned and skilfully executed."

Rosamund paused, frowning. What on earth was Aunt Ruth talking about? A campaign? It didn't make sense. She read on :

"However, a word of warning. Your young man, tired of the sort of popularity which his money brought him (particularly among his girl-friends) vanished from his usual haunts a few weeks ago. Just how you managed to run him to ground I don't know, but to represent yourself as a damsel in distress while keeping your knowledge as to his identity to yourself was really clever. I'd be proud to have thought of it myself."

Rosamund shook her head impatiently. Really, Aunt Ruth must be crazy! But, horribly fascinated, she read on :

"And here I would like to say that I bear you no grudge for having represented me as the bad fairy. Your act was quite brilliant——he didn't have a chance!

"But that warning I spoke of——no man likes to know that he's been made a fool of by a woman, so take care that your knight errant never discovers how clever you've been. He wouldn't forgive you, believe me! And if, at times, you find it boring to keep on playing the beggar maid to his King Cophetua, remember that there are and always will be plenty of women only too eager to step into your shoes!

"Every good wish for your future success.

Ruth Hastings."

"P.S. Of course, you'll come to me to be dressed."

Rosamund folded the letter with hands that would shake, despite her conviction that Aunt Ruth had made the whole thing up just to create trouble.

John, wealthy, and herself a fortune-hunter! What utter rubbish! It wasn't worth another thought.

Then, as she put the letter back into its envelope, she saw that there was a slip of paper still in it which she had previously missed.

She took it out and caught her breath.

It was a photograph, obviously cut from the pages of a glossy society periodical, of a young man incredibly like John. For a moment the picture blurred dizzily. Then, forcing her eyes into focus, she read the caption below it.

It *was* John.

"John Lindsay, only son of the late Gordon Lindsay. Mr. Lindsay, whose tragic death occurred recently when piloting his Pippet IV plane, was, of course, a financier of international repute. John ('Johnny' to his friends), a popular young man with a gift for enjoying himself, is, needless to say, regarded as one of the most eligible bachelors of the day."

"No!" Rosamund whispered through dry lips. *"No!"*

She couldn't think clearly.

John—her John—wasn't a poor man with a purpose in life as he'd led her to believe. He was rich. He had so much money that he didn't need to work. He was the masculine version of the shallow, idle women who patronised her aunt's salon—a playboy.

And he had lied to her. Deliberately misled her. Why, why, *why?*

The word hammered relentlessly in her brain. There must be a reason—

She turned again to the letter.

"—tired of the sort of popularity which his money brought him—"

Yes, that must surely be the answer. And how understandable that made everything! Why, there might even have been a girl to whom he had been attracted only to find that she was interested not in him but in his money. Certainly Aunt Ruth more than hinted at that.

Small wonder if he had been disillusioned and had sought sanctuary in a different world where he could be a different person. Small wonder, too, that he had deliberately given the impression of being a comparatively poor man or that, at first, he had been so suspicious and unfriendly. He simply couldn't believe in basic decencies like sincerity or integrity.

But he did now. He believed in her love for him.

Her forehead puckered in perplexity. Her first impulse was that she must assure him that she didn't want to be rich. That she, too, had run away from a life as superficial and unsatisfying as his own had been.

If John had been immediately available that, she knew, was what she would have done. But he wasn't here and he wouldn't be until tomorrow. Inevitably, she began to question whether impulse was her best guide.

Of only one thing could she be absolutely certain. The criterion which must guide her decisions was that she must do whatever was best for John. And that could surely only mean that his new-found faith in humanity and himself mustn't be destroyed, least of all by her.

Again she consulted the letter.

"No man likes to know that he's been made a fool of by a woman."

Well, she hadn't made a fool of John. She did truly love him and money didn't enter into it—except from the point of view that she'd rather they didn't have too much of it.

But would John credit that? Would he be able to? Wasn't it too big a risk for her to take?

She drew a deep breath and made up her mind. She would say nothing at all about the letter, either now or in the future, even though she would so desperately prefer to have no secrets from John. But honestly, what satisfactory alternative was there? Trying to put herself in John's place, she decided that there wasn't.

Very well, then, she would destroy the letter and say nothing about it. But even so, she could see that there were dangers in such a course.

For one thing, there was Aunt Ruth. Supposing she was ever able to convince John that he had been a victim of, to use her own words, a skilfully executed campaign? Unconsciously, Rosamund shook her head. That was unlikely in view of that very typical P.S. Aunt Ruth saw her chance to make something out of the situation and she didn't hesitate to make use of it. It was something unpleasantly like blackmail, but at least Rosamund could be quite sure that she would never risk imperilling the possibility of making money!

The other, far greater and more personal danger lay in herself. Every instinct she had, everything in her nature, made her want to be absolutely honest with John. But when, sooner or later, he told her of his wealth, she would have to act a lie—and keep on acting it. She'd have to seem convincingly surprised, and she didn't trust her own histrionic capabilities sufficiently to be sure that she could carry it off. And that would spell disaster.

But as quickly as it had returned, the temptation faded. *Her* mind would be at ease if she told the truth, but how about John's?

Vividly there returned to her mind that moment of understanding which she had had on the day when John had told her of his love—that love wasn't only a question of romance. It was, among other things, the desire to stand between the person you loved and pain or danger. John was still too vulnerable, too sensitive for her to risk endangering his newly found self-confidence.

Her mind finally made up, she rummaged in her handbag for a flat packet of matches. Then she got out of the car, tore the letter and its envelope into shreds and set fire to them.

John's photograph? She hesitated, unable to bring herself to destroying that. She tore the caption carefully off and added that to the little blaze. She waited until nothing but black ash remained, and even that she stamped into further nothingness.

The photograph she put into her handbag.

They drove for over an hour before they found just the right church. They saw it from a high level road and simultaneously they exclaimed: "That's it!"

It was old and weathered and it had a look of permanence that delighted them both. And it was tucked into a green valley beside a sparkling little river. Perfect!

What was unmistakably the Rectory stood just by the church. It was large and square and just a little bit shabby and it was set in a garden which was obviously someone's pride and joy. Flowers and shrubs burgeoned as if they liked growing there.

94

"It looks just like a Rectory ought to look," Rosamund remarked contentedly. "I'm sure the Rector will be just right, too!"

But it was actually the Rector's wife whom they saw first. She was kneeling beside a border that she was weeding and she, too, had that indefinable air of gentle shabbiness. She wore a big, floppy-brimmed hat which had seen better days and a big hessian apron. Like a true gardener her earth-stained hands were bare of gloves.

She looked up with a smile as Rosamund and John came towards her.

"I'm afraid my husband is out at present," she told them. "Can I do anything for you?"

"Well, actually, we want to get married," John explained, smiling in response.

"How nice!" The Rector's wife beamed at them and got to her feet with so obvious an effort that John put out a helping hand which she accepted gratefully. "Thank you so much. It's this wretched arthritis, you know. I get stuck in one position and then I creak like a rusty gate when I try to move. That's better!" She straightened up. "Now then, you want to get married. Well, I don't suppose my husband will be long. He's over at the church with his warden."

"Splendid!" John said heartily. "Then, if you don't mind coming with us, the Rector can marry us and you and the warden can be the witnesses!"

"Oh, but, my dears, it's not as easy as all that!" the Rector's wife said sympathetically. "It takes time, you know. Banns have to be read—"

"Not for us!" John declared triumphantly. "We've got a licence."

The troubled look faded and the kind old face beamed again.

"Have you? How exciting! Francis will be interested. Usually it's banns here, you know, and sometimes it's just a little bit embarrassing. The girls will giggle so! Only nerves, of course, but sometimes it makes one wonder if they realise what a tremendous step they're contemplating. Now, will you sit on that garden seat—it's quite clean—or come into the house while I make myself presentable? You'll stay out here? Right! I won't keep you waiting long."

She was as good as her word. In a very short time she was with them again wearing a different dress, old but well polished shoes and with her hair tidy and her hands clean.

"Now, my dear, if you'll just zip up my top six inches," she requested, turning her back to Rosamund. "I never can manage to do it myself. That's it! Now, come along—"

The church was as right inside as it was out. Its pews were carved and were mellow with age and elbow grease. The memorial tablets and the two big family tombs spoke of the many generations who had brought their joys and sorrows here. And the altar flowers were fresh—

"I'm so glad—I did them again this morning," the Rector's wife whispered. "That's what's so nice about the summer—we're never short of flowers to bring here."

They found the Rector in the vestry. He was a tall, scholarly-looking man whose face had the benign expression of a medieval saint and, like his wife, he too beamed when he heard why they had come to him.

"Yes, indeed, I will marry you," he agreed, and studied the licence which John handed him with almost boyish enthusiasm. "How very interesting! It's a long time since I saw one of these—quite ten years, I should think. You remember, my dear. That very nice couple who arrived in the middle of a snowstorm."

"Yes, I remember." The Rector's wife nodded. "They wanted a quiet wedding because they thought people might be amused at them falling in love so late in life. Actually, they needn't have worried. Most people are really very kind. They don't laugh when they see real happiness!"

"Indeed, no," the Rector agreed. "Now, I'll call Budge—"

And so they were married in the quiet church, with sun pouring through the windows and the birds singing outside—

"To love, cherish and to obey—"

The old, familiar words took on a new and vital meaning. This was for always—

Out in the sunshine again, they said good-bye to the kindly couple, refusing an invitation to stay for lunch, but promising to come back and see them quite soon. Then they were on the open road again, very silent and perhaps a little shy of each other. But as Rosamund's right hand cradled her left one with its bright new ring, John laid his hand over both of hers and no words were necessary.

They found the ideal spot to stop for their picnic, high on a hillside with miles of unspoilt countryside surrounding them. The crusty new bread and cheese they had bought at a village shop was sheer ambrosia as the canned, rather warm drinks were so much nectar—life was wonderful! They could not tear themselves away from that enchanted spot.

Then, reluctantly, they knew it was time to turn back. They made sure that they had left no litter and went back to the car. John opened the door for Rosamund, but just as she was getting in, her foot turned on a loose stone. She made a grab at the door frame to save herself from falling—and dropped her handbag.

It flew open as it hit the ground and its contents were scattered far and wide.

"Golly, why you women carry all this junk about I can't think!" John announced, as he began to pick up the bits and pieces. "Anybody would think you—"

Abruptly, he left his remark unfinished and stood erect. He was staring at a small piece of paper that he had picked up.

Then he looked at Rosamund and her heart froze, for his eyes, bleak and hostile, were the eyes of a stranger.

CHAPTER SIX

"SO you knew all the time!"

"No, John, no, *no*! It wasn't like that at all!" Rosamund heard the rising note of hysteria and struggled for self-control. She faced John squarely. "I didn't know until the day you were in town," she insisted—and read cynical disbelief in his stony eyes.

"Really? Then why didn't you say anything about it to me when I got back?"

"Isn't it rather—why have you never told me?" she suggested sadly. "Didn't you trust me?"

"If I didn't—" John began, and stopped short. "All right, go on! Let's hear your version, but I warn you, you'd better make it convincing!"

She knew that she was battling against tremendous odds—that John, in the past, had been so badly hurt that now he was already condemning her out of hand. John who, such a short time back—she swallowed convulsively.

"Well, go on!" the harsh voice ordered.

"Aunt Ruth wrote to me. She enclosed the cutting—"

"Which I recognise as having been taken from a periodical that was published nearly six months ago!" John commented ironically. "Are you trying to tell me that since she paid her visit, she just happened—by pure chance, of course—to come across it? Oh no, Rosamund, you'll have to do better than that!"

"If I were lying to you, I'd probably have thought up a more convincing story," Rosamund retorted spiritedly. "But this happens to be the truth, so there's nothing I can do to make it more plausible!"

A muscle flickered faintly at the corner of John's mouth and Rosamund felt a momentary hope. Had she made an impression, however slight, on his impregnable mistrust? But if so, he gave no further indication of it. Simply, he waited in silence for her to go on.

"She said some pretty beastly things," Rosamund ploughed on desperately. "She, of course, assumed that I already knew—"

"Why 'of course'?" John asked in an abstracted way as if it wasn't really of much importance.

"Because she's got that sort of mind. It just wouldn't occur to her that there could be any other explanation. She thinks people will do anything for money—"

"I appear to have done her an injustice," John commented. "She evidently has a very sound knowledge of the world and its ways!"

Momentarily Rosamund sagged against the car, her eyes closed.

"John, what's the use?" she asked hopelessly. "It doesn't matter what I say. In your heart you've condemned me already."

He gave no sign of having heard, but stood there, rock-like, so close yet miles away—

In desperation, she tried again.

"What really matters is why I didn't tell you, isn't it? It was because I felt I understood why it could hurt you so. You see, long before I had Aunt Ruth's letter, I'd realised that—that something had happened which—which made you want to make a fresh start—"

"How could you know that?" he demanded sharply. "I said nothing—"

"No, that was just it," Rosamund explained eagerly. "Except for referring once to your mother, you never spoke of yourself or your family—nothing."

"Nor, for that matter, have you told me much about yourself," he reminded her.

"I know," Rosamund nodded. "And that was why I felt I understood. I didn't want to talk about my past, either. I just wanted to forget it. You see, I ran away from Aunt Ruth because I couldn't bear the life I was living with her. I didn't only live with her. I worked with her as well. I could never be myself—"

"Your aunt—" John interrupted with a faint gleam of interest. "Just what is her job—and yours?"

"She runs a very exclusive dress salon," Rosamund told him. "And she was training me to take her place later on."

"Ah, now I remember!" he exclaimed. "I was sure I'd seen you somewhere before! I got dragged to a dress show and you were modelling some of the clothes. I didn't remember your face—it was the way you walked that stayed in my mind."

"Yes, I did some modelling," Rosamund agreed. "But not lately. I've been understudying Aunt Ruth—seeing clients and helping them make their choice."

"It doesn't sound very onerous," John remarked with a shrug.

"It can, in fact, be very tiring, particularly with clients who can't make up their minds. But it wasn't just that. It was—oh, the whole atmosphere! The triviality of it all— the sort of women I had to deal with—greedy and shallow—"

"And rich?" John suggested drily. "I suppose, in fact, you were jealous of them!"

"No." She shook her head. "Not that. Just—exhausted by it. All I wanted was to get away from it all and make a fresh start. I tried to make Aunt Ruth understand, but it wasn't any good, so in the end I just walked out."

"And what's the moral of this pathetic little tale?" John asked sardonically.

"Just that—because of the way I had felt, I guessed that for some reason or other, you'd felt the same way," she explained. Then, with sudden impatience, she caught him by the arm and shook it.

"Oh, John, don't shut your mind against me! Please, please believe me!"

He looked at her with lacklustre eyes.

"You know, I almost might—but for one thing," he said slowly.

"What?" Rosamund asked eagerly.

"There's altogether too much coincidence about the whole thing!"

"Coincidence?" Rosamund repeated. "But coincidences do happen!"

"Oh, to be sure they do," he agreed. "But when they come as thick and fast as all this—well, really, you can hardly wonder if my credulity is strained to breaking point!"

"What coincidence?" Rosamund challenged.

"Oh, must we? All right, if you insist! Coincidence number one—" he ticked off on one finger. "You just *happened* to choose *my* boat for your opening gambit although there were two others to choose from—"

"Yours was nearest to the gate," Rosamund reminded him.

"So it was! All right, we'll let that go. However, number two—you tell me that you ran away from your aunt, by which I presume you mean me to understand that you didn't tell her where you were going. Right? Then how do you explain that she found you with apparently little difficulty?"

"I don't know," Rosamund admitted flatly. "I asked her, but she wouldn't tell me."

"But to me it's perfectly understandable," John told her, his lips curling derisively. "Your aunt's visit was all

100

part of the scheme—a put-up job. The idea was to convince me that you were in trouble."

Something snapped in Rosamund's mind.

"I think Aunt Ruth put it rather better in her letter," she said in a brittle voice. "*She* referred to me as a damsel in distress and you as a knight errant!"

Again the muscle twitched at John's mouth.

"Ah yes, that letter! It should make interesting reading! Let me see it—it might even convince me that you're telling the truth!"

"I can't," Rosamund said miserably. "I burnt it."

"What a pity!" John mocked. "Your one piece of evidence—and you destroy it!"

"John, stop it! Stop it at once and listen to me!" In sheer desperation, Rosamund stamped her foot in its pretty silver-buckled shoe.

Her peremptoriness startled him, for she saw that though his eyes were still hostile, she had at least gained his whole attention.

Time seemed to stand still and to Rosamund it seemd as though her brain had stopped working as well. What could she say to him that she hadn't already said—what was there left that would convince him?

Then, as if she was listening to someone else speaking, she heard her own voice saying very clearly and deliberately as one might speak to a little child or a sick person:

"John, I'm not going to defend myself any more, because it's no good—it only makes you doubt me all the more. I'm just going to tell you one thing. I married you because I loved you. For no other reason. And I shall go on loving you, whether you can believe it or not. That's all!"

She turned away blindly from him and got into the car to sit very still, staring straight in front of her.

For what seemed like an eternity John stood motionless. Then with a sudden, violent movement, he tore the photograph he still held into fragments and flung them from him. Then, grim-faced, he walked round to his side of the car, got in and started up.

It was a silent journey and if John drove with a sort of determined recklessness, Rosamund was hardly aware of it. She had a strange sensation of utter emptiness as if all thought, all feeling, had been blotted out. She wasn't herself any more. She was just the hollow husk of a girl who, so short a time ago, had experienced the fullness of life.

And John? She had no idea what his thoughts were and, strangely, little curiosity. She knew now that what she had previously only partly sensed was true. Before he had ever met her, some experience had so poisoned his mind that he had lost faith in *himself*. That was the real trouble and that was why he couldn't believe that her love for him was genuine. Nor could it be otherwise until, somehow, the poison was expelled. And that was something that John must do for himself. There was no way in which she could help—except, of course, to go on loving him—

Quite suddenly she was stirred from the grey mist that enveloped her.

"John, aren't we going in the wrong direction?" she asked warningly. "Too far south?"

"We would be—if we were going back to the *Seven Stars*," he agreed. "But we're not."

"Not going—" she faltered uncertainly.

"No. You see, I seem to remember that, not so very long ago, I promised to endow you with all my worldly goods—"

"Oh, John!" she protested despairingly.

"So," he went on as if she hadn't spoken, "why shouldn't I start doing that right away? We're going to Lindacres which, in case you've forgotten, is the house that my father built in Hampshire some ten years ago. You'll like it, I'm sure. It's built in the grand style—practically every bedroom has its own bathroom, there's a ballroom, two swimming pools, one under cover, and magnificent gardens and hothouses. Father used to use it for his really big parties—"

He went on talking, but what he said made no impression on Rosamund. One thought only echoed and re-echoed in her numbed brain.

She had failed, utterly, hopelessly. Failed to regain John's trust, failed even to persuade him to give her a chance and so failed in her battle to give their marriage any hope of fulfilment.

"You're not very enthusiastic!" John's reproachful

voice cut through her nightmare. "Would you perhaps rather go up to my—sorry, *our*—London flat? Or the villa at Cannes? Or perhaps a cruise? That might take a little time to organise, but it wouldn't really matter, would it? You could spend the time buying clothes—"

Rosamund's hands, clenched together in her lap, turned white at the knuckles, but she didn't speak. She'd said she wasn't going to try to defend herself any more and somehow or other was going to stick to that. She mustn't let him goad her into argument—

"Or perhaps," went on the mocking voice of the stranger who had been John, "you'd prefer that we went back to the *Seven Stars*? In the hope of convincing me that you really do prefer the simple life, you know!"

In her mind's eye, Rosamund saw a picture of the *Seven Stars* and its setting—the tranquil water, the flowery hedges and the birds singing in a blue sky. But even more vividly she recalled the peace and happiness of the place and the friendliness she had been shown there.

Her hand moved in sharp protest.

"No! Not there. Not now!"

"No? Just as you like. Then we'll make it Lindacres, shall we?"

"I don't think, really, it matters where we go," Rosamund told him quietly. "I leave it to you."

John didn't answer, but his foot came down more heavily on the accelerator. He drove for the best part of an hour and then, for no apparent reason, stopped on the crest of a hill. Rosamund, roused from her apathy, turned to look at him questioningly.

John pointed down to the valley.

"As a sentimentalist, I thought you'd like to have your first glimpse of your new home," he explained. "Charming, isn't it? So simple and homelike!"

It was surely the least apt description of Lindacres that there could be!

Glaringly white in the bright sunshine, it sprawled incongruously in grounds that were outstandingly beautiful. It was angular, clumsy and pretentious. To Rosamund it also looked oddly self-conscious as if it knew that it didn't really belong in that delightful setting.

"No, I'd hardly call it charming," she said consideringly. "I think functional is the word I'd use to describe it. Built for a special purpose and probably quite satisfactory from that point of view. As to it being homelike—it could be, of course, because being a home doesn't depend on any particular building but on the people who live in it."

John laughed shortly.

"You're right about it being functional. But if you can turn that soap-works into a home, I'll—" he left the sentence unfinished to go on in a puzzled way: "What the deuce is going on down there? There's a coach just drawn up at the front door and another one following it. And they're both full of people—children—masses of them!"

"Could it be a fête of some sort?" Rosamund speculated without much interest. "Do you lend the grounds for that sort of thing?"

"I think so, sometimes, though I can't say I know much about it. But it can't be that. It's too late in the day for people, particularly children, to be arriving for a thing like that. Besides, there'd surely be marquees or tents if it was a fête. There always are. Oh, confound it, perhaps, after all, we'd better go up to town—"

"No, we can't do that," Rosamund declared decisively. "If it isn't a fête, then it must be an emergency of some sort, and we must see if we can help."

John, startled not only by her earnestness but also by her evident concern, looked at her sharply, and then without comment started the car up again.

When they reached the wide open gates of Lindacres it became clear that Rosamund was right—there was some sort of emergency, for a policeman was posted there. John pulled up as he came towards them.

"What's up?" John demanded.

"A fire at the Greystoke Orphanage and they're bringing the kids here," the policeman explained briefly. "I must ask you to move on, sir, you're blocking the entry. No, you can't go in!" he laid a heavy hand on the side of the car as if to detain it by force. "It's not a peepshow, you know!"

"Don't be a fool, man." John said crisply. "It happens to be my property! I'm John Lindsay."

"Sorry, sir," the constable apologised, taking his hand away. "I didn't know. I'm new in this district—"

John accepted the explanation with a nod and continued along the well-kept drive. On either side of them were immaculately kept lawns that were broken at intervals with glowing flower beds and low-growing shrubs. It was, perhaps, rather formal, but none the less very beautiful, yet neither John nor Rosamund had a look to spare for them. They were motivated by a common urge to get to the house as quickly as possible.

A little spark of hope flamed in Rosamund's heart.

"At least we're sharing something," she exulted. "Perhaps—"

But after that, she had no time to think of anything but the contretemps into which they had so suddenly and unexpectedly become involved.

Pandemonium reigned! Children, both boys and girls, milled in and out of the house, completely out of control, shouting and screaming with excitement. There didn't seem to be anyone in charge of them.

"This won't do!" John declared wrathfully. "I don't mind coming to the rescue, but I'm damned if I'll stand—there *must* be someone in charge! Follow close behind me, Rosamund, and we'll see if we can wade through these brats—"

He succeeded in clearing a way into the huge hall, but here the commotion, if possible, was even worse. The children, most of them sitting disconsolately on the floor, were younger than those they had already encountered and they were frightened and unhappy. Most of them were sobbing uncontrollably and several had flung themselves face down in a state of near-hysteria. And still there seemed to be no one in charge.

Grim-faced, John made his way to the preposterously ostentatious staircase at the foot of which was an outsize metal gong. Seizing the stick, he began to beat an imperative and noisy tattoo on the gong.

The effect was instantaneous and dramatic. As if by magic the hubbub stopped and even the older children crowded silently in from the garden to see what it was all about. Even more, two startled women shot out of a room which opened off the hall. One was elderly. Her grey hair was dishevelled and her distracted air gave the impression of a hen that is convinced someone is going to rob her nest. The other was very much younger, at the outside not more than twenty-two or three. She had a pretty little face that looked as if it was made for smiling, but at the moment it was preternaturally serious and concerned.

"Well, really!" the older woman snorted indignantly, her hand on her heart. "As if we haven't enough to put up with already—"

"Are you in charge of the children, madam?" John demanded, ruthlessly cutting across the fluttering complaints.

"Yes, I am!" The elderly voice assumed a rather incongruous note of authority. "And whoever you are, I must really ask you not to make a nuisance of yourself. Everything is difficult enough—"

"And will become rather more difficult still if you don't even try to keep these little hooligans in order! Because unless you do, I'm going to turn the whole lot of you out, lock, stock and barrel! And if you question my authority for saying that, the answer is that this is my house and you are here without my permission!"

It was brutal, but it was effective. The mouth of the older woman opened and shut like that of a stranded fish, and if there was the hint of a grin on the younger one's lips, she quickly suppressed it.

But now, Rosamund saw, John was at a loss to know what the next step was—and small wonder. This was essentially a woman's problem.

"Is there a housekeeper?" she murmured, and saw the relief in John's face as he nodded. "If you'll send for her, I think she and I might put our heads together—"

He accepted the suggestion without comment and was about to go off in search of the housekeeper when a dignified presence made itself felt at the top of the staircase. In her trim black dress and immaculate white collar and cuffs, to say nothing of her air of authority, this could only be a housekeeper of the most competent type.

"Really, Miss Fletcher, I should have thought—" she began coldly, saw John—and they had another near-hysterical female on their hands. "Mr. John!" she exclaimed in dismay. "I had no idea—of course, if I had, I'd never have agreed—though the children had to go somewhere and both the Rector and the doctor thought—"

"All right, Mrs. Brickwell," John interrupted briskly. "I fully appreciate that this is the only house for miles around big enough to cope with the situation. My dear—" he turned formally to Rosamund, "this is our housekeeper, Mrs. Brickwell. Mrs. Brickwell, my wife."

If the housekeeper had been startled by John's unexpected arrival, she was completely flabbergasted by his announcement. Her mouth was slightly open and she breathed heavily as she came slowly down the stairs.

Rosamund had a strange sensation of change in herself. She was not the cool, businesslike self that she had been in London. Nor the self she had become when she had gained her freedom and happiness. Nor even the brokenhearted self of the last few hours. She had become a blend of all three.

Here was a practical problem to be tackled, but she would do it for love, not money. And her own grief should help her to understand other people's distress. Mrs. Brickwell, she reasoned rapidly, had been forced by circumstances into an extremely invidious position, and now, because of John's sudden appearance, had been caught in the very act of having assumed an authority which was not hers. Nor, it was clear, had John's acceptance of the situation entirely reassured her.

It was more than a possibility, too, that there was at least a degree of antagonism between the housekeeper and Miss Fletcher. Each, used to giving orders, would resent the presence of the other and would be convinced of her own superior claim to having the last word.

It was the sort of situation which had more than once occurred in the Salon, and there was only one way out of such an impasse. A third person whose authority neither contestant would dispute must take command. And she knew quite well who that person was at this moment. Not John because, as a man, he would be at a disadvantage dealing with two women. Herself.

And so, by the time Mrs. Brickwell reached the hall, Rosamund was there to greet her.

"How do you do, Mrs. Brickwell?" she asked, holding

out her hand. "I'm so glad we've arrived in time to be of help!"

Rosamund had been careful to speak pleasantly, but she had also taken care to speak with confidence. One had to at times like this, even if one was shaking in one's shoes. People didn't, in her experience, accept authority unless it was made clear to them that one took it for granted that they would. And to her relief, Mrs. Brickwell proved to be no exception to the rule.

"Indeed, madam, you could not have arrived at a more opportune moment," she declared with a baleful glance in Miss Fletcher's direction. "Really, we're all at sixes and sevens. I hardly know which way to turn—"

"A very difficult situation," Rosamund agreed briskly. "And naturally, the children are alarmed and excited. Fire is a terrifying thing."

"Yes, indeed, madam," Mrs. Brickwell answered meekly, evidently realising that she had been firmly told that allowances must be made, but in such a way that she had not lost face. "I expect you'd like to know what arrangements have already been made—"

"Yes, we would, wouldn't we, John?"

She turned to him and saw a look on his face that she had never seen there before. The grimness had gone, though there was no suggestion of amiability. Simply, it was an intent, preoccupied look as if his own thoughts were of more absorbing interest than the chaos around him.

"John—!" she gave his elbow a gentle nudge.

"Oh yes! Of course! Arrangements." He came back to earth with a start. "The children will have to spend the night here, I suppose—"

"Will you discuss just what's to be done with Mrs. Brickwell?" Rosamund suggested. "I want to have a word with Miss Fletcher—something must be done to amuse those children! How many are there, Mrs. Brickwell?"

"About fifty, so I've been given to understand."

"Good lord, only fifty!" John ejaculated feelingly. "I'd have said nearer five hundred! Yes, by all means try to organise them a bit, Rosamund. Absurd to have sent even fifty with only two adults in charge!"

Rosamund made her way over to where Miss Fletcher,

with singular incompetence, was trying to quieten the children nearest to her, some of whom were still in tears, though others had got over their fears sufficiently to have become obstreperous. But while Miss Fletcher was really quite hopeless, Rosamund noticed that the younger woman was making a better job of it, though clearly she realised how inadequate an effort it was, for she smiled ruefully at Rosamund.

"If only we could get them all into the garden where there's more room," she said under her breath. "But—" and she glanced significantly at Miss Fletcher.

Rosamund nodded encouragingly, but she didn't stop. It was Miss Fletcher whom she had to persuade and cajole and, as a last resort, coerce. But it wasn't going to be easy. Miss Fletcher was probably only too well aware of her own incompetence and would all the more resent—and possibly fear—having her authority undermined.

"I am Mrs. Lindsay," Rosamund explained, and added sympathetically: "*What* a responsibility for you, Miss Fletcher!"

"I don't mind responsibility," Miss Fletcher insisted in an aggrieved voice. "If only I could get some co-operation!" And she in her turn shot a malevolent look across the hall! Yes, decidedly, there had already been trouble between her and Mrs. Brickwell!

"Yes, indeed, we must all pull together in an emergency like this," Rosamund said briskly. "I think, if you'd give me some idea of just what has happened so far, and what damage has been done at the Orphanage—" she suggested, hoping that Miss Fletcher would feel that here, at last, was someone who was willing to be genuinely co-operative—by which, of course, she meant helpful without being self-assertive.

It appeared that the fire had started in the kitchen of the Orphanage—an old brick building with timber floors and staircase—and had got a good hold before, by chance, it was discovered since the last evening meal had been served and the clearing up done.

"And it spread with such terrifying speed," Miss Fletcher explained agitatedly. "We had only just time to get the little ones—who, of course, were in bed—out before the staircase was involved." She shuddered. "It's terrible to think what might have happened—"

"How thankful you must be that it didn't," Rosamund interjected fervently. "Now, I gather that the kitchen will be completely out of action. Is there any hope of beds and bedding being salvaged?"

There appeared to be some doubt about that, at least as regarded the dormitories above the kitchen. For the others, on the far side of the house, there appeared to be some hope. Indeed, Miss Fletcher explained, the men had gone back in the coaches to see what they could get.

"Which men?" Rosamund asked.

"Two of our resident masters and another who lives in the village. And two of the outside staff here," Miss Fletcher explained. "And really," with a glance at her wrist watch, "they are taking their time about it!"

"It's probably not an easy job if the staircase has gone," Rosamund suggested. "But I don't suppose they'll be long now. In the meantime—" she glanced round the cluttered hall and decided that she'd allowed Miss Flecher sufficient rope—"you'll be anxious to have the children safely out of the way before they start carrying things through. Otherwise, some of them might get hurt. I expect you'd prefer them to be out in the garden, wouldn't you, Miss Fletcher?"

And with only a token bleat that the grounds were so large that the little ones might get lost, Miss Fletcher agreed that that was what she'd like—but of course, she hadn't liked to suggest it.

"The last thing I want is for us to be a nuisance to you," she explained virtuously.

It was nearly midnight when John and Rosamund finally got rid of the last of their guests. Tim Ferris and Owen Weeks, the two masters in charge of the boys, had gratefully accepted the offer of a late-night drink and had shown a disinclination to leave the sitting room for their rather spartan quarters in the gymnasium. And even when they had gone, there were still things to discuss.

"I'll go and see Matron or the Headmistress or whatever she calls herself tomorrow," John announced pouring himself out another modest drink. "Also I want to see for myself what the damage is before I meet the Governors."

"Yes, I suppose so," Rosamund agreed, twisting her own half full glass so that the light glinted on the facets of the cutting. "If it's really bad, will you let them stay on here?"

"It might be the simplest solution," John said thoughtfully. "For them, at any rate. It *is* the only place for miles around that can accommodate fifty children and the staff and still leave rooms available for classes."

"Classrooms," Rosamund repeated. "That would mean emptying the rooms of their furniture—is there room to store it?"

"Enough, I should think," John said consideringly. "Although if they're going to stay long, the boys won't be able to sleep in the gym. They'll want to put that to its proper use."

"Yes, of course," Rosamund agreed absently.

John glanced enquiringly at her.

"Tired?" he asked quite kindly.

"I am, rather," she admitted, and that was very true, but not so much physically, she could have added, as mentally. She felt as if she had lived a lifetime in a single day. So much had happened and it was all so—she groped for the right word—so *disjointed*. She felt as an actress might if she had to play one act from 'Romeo and Juliet' followed immediately by a second one from 'Othello' and the third—no, no play ever written could possibly contain an act even remotely resembling events since they had reached Lindacres!

It was all so completely unreal! And not the least fantastic aspect of it all was the way in which she and John had worked together to bring order out of chaos. How was it possible that two people, head over heels in love and on their wedding day, no less, could first meet with such bitter disillusion and then, all personal emotion put aside, could work together like—well, like two partners in a business enterprise? That it was an impersonal relationship, born of the emergency, she knew quite well, but they had trusted and relied on one another—

And that was the most incredible fact of all. John, who had made it so clear earlier in the day that he had lost all his faith in her, had asked her advice and accepted her decisions without question as they dealt with the problems of this extraordinary situation. Was it just force of necessity that had compelled him to turn to her or—was it something that went deeper than that though he didn't realise it?

She couldn't tell and she certainly couldn't ask. She had told John that she had married him because she loved him and that she would go on loving him. There was no more for her to say. The rest lay in John's hands.

The clock struck midnight and he stood up.

"I don't think there's anything more we can do to-night," he remarked. "You and Mrs. Brickwell have fixed up about food supplies for tomorrow. Some of their domestic staff will come over first thing to lend a hand—that seems to be the lot. No, there's one thing I forgot to tell you. The Press put in an appearance while you were coping with the food situation."

"Oh!" Rosamund exclaimed in dismay.

"Yes," John agreed grimly. "They thought they'd come to report on a simple human interest story—and stumbled on a scoop! We're news, Rosamund! Front page at that!"

"Yes, I suppose so," Rosamund agreed faintly. "What—what did you tell them?"

John shrugged his shoulders.

"Simply that, not wanting the fuss of a big wedding, we'd got married very quietly. I managed to choke them off seeing you, but of course, I had to co-operate to some degree, otherwise they'd have decided that there was a mystery about it and been on the trail like bloodhounds on a scent! Not that I think it was much use. I had to give them your name, of course, and one of them knew you. So, more than likely, they'll look up your aunt—and heaven knows what she'll tell them!"

"*I* know," Rosamund told him wearily. "She'll tell them that she knew all about it and thoroughly approved. She'll make it sound like the romance of the year—" she caught her breath in a little sob.

"Rosamund—!"

"Oh, but of course she will!" Rosamund declared reck-lessly. "Don't you see? You're rich. I'm your wife. She sells expensive clothes. She won't risk a word of criticism!

As a matter of fact, she said in her letter that she'd expect me to come to her for my clothes. It was to be the price of not letting you know that, as she believed, I'd known all along—"

Silence fell between them. A silence that seemed to intensify as the moments ticked past. A silence that neither of them could break.

It became unbearable. Suddenly Rosamund jumped to her feet.

"I—I think I'll turn in now," she said in a high-pitched, breathless voice. "I really am tired—"

"By all means."

John walked over to the cocktail cabinet and put his empty glass down with exaggerated care, his back towards her.

"I hope Mrs. Brickwell has fitted you up with everything you need?" he went on with studied politeness.

"Oh yes, thank you." Rosamund did her best to echo that impersonal tone.

John opened the door for her.

"Good night, Rosamund."

"Good night," she responded, her head in the air so that he wouldn't guess how near she was to tears.

The door was closed quietly but firmly behind her.

CHAPTER SEVEN

MRS. BRICKWELL had a sense of the fitness of things. No matter how drastic the emergency, from the very first she had put her foot down in one respect. While she had her strength, no one was going to be put in the principal suite of the house.

"It's not suitable—beautiful rooms like that!" she had declared adamantly.

And how right she had proved to be! Really, she felt, with Mr. John and his new wife turning up so unexpectedly, it really looked as if she had been *guided*!

So John and Rosamund were duly installed in the suite—two connecting bedrooms, two bathrooms and a small sitting-room which, within a very short time, was to become the hub of the house.

Rosamund was half awakened early on the morning after their arrival at Lindacres by the sound of a door shutting near at hand. For several moments she lay still, bewildered by her unfamiliar surroundings. Then memory flooded back and she buried her face in her pillow.

It couldn't be true! Two people as much in love as she and John had surely been couldn't become so terribly estranged within a few hours of being married! It didn't make sense.

And then, on top of that, all the crazy events that had followed! They had been pitchforked into a state of affairs that one would hardly expect to encounter once in a lifetime. And it had to happen on that particular day! And yet perhaps it had been just as well that it did. John and she had to forget their own differences in order to take a firm grip on a situation that was completely out of hand. To them had fallen the task not only of dealing with practical problems, but also with very personal ones, particularly where conflicting claims to authority had arisen.

By the end of the day, they had dealt with everything even if only on a temporary basis, and Rosamund for one had felt utterly exhausted as a result. Exhausted and oddly empty of all emotion. Too much had happened in too short a time. It was as if a careless photographer had taken several exposures on the same negative. The result was blurred—meaningless.

But now—she sat up in bed, hugging her knees—here was a new day to be faced. What would it bring? Could it bring anything except more confusion and more heartache? And if it did, could she find the courage and the wisdom to deal with it?

She had told John that she loved him and that she would go on loving him. That had been nothing less than the absolute truth—but how could she prove it to him?

She pondered deeply, unable to find a simple solution to such a complex problem. Then, from nowhere, it seemed, a quotation came into her mind.

> *"To thine own self be true,*
> *And it must follow, as the night the day,*
> *Thou canst not then be false to any man."*

114

"Yes, that's it!" she told herself, unconscious that she spoke aloud. "I've got to be absolutely honest. That means I've got to be *myself* as I really am, no pretence because it seems as if it might be expedient—that would be cheating John—and myself. And surely, what he must want to know for sure is that I *am* the girl he believed me to be when he asked me to marry him!" She sighed deeply. "But it won't always be easy—and it won't be quick—"

A light tap on the door interrupted her thoughts. John?

But in answer to her summons, Mrs. Brickwell came in carrying a small tray.

"Good morning, madam," she said briskly. "I've brought your tea myself because I thought it might be advisable if we discussed one or two things—"

"Good morning, Mrs. Brickwell," Rosamund said pleasantly though with a sinking heart. Problems so early! Still, better get it over. "By all means tell me what's wrong."

"Not exactly wrong, madam," Mrs. Brickwell explained rather diffidently as she handed over the tray. "It's—well, it's about clothes. I mean, seeing that you and Mr. John hadn't planned to stay here and consequently brought no luggage I thought perhaps you might prefer to wear something—a little different—"

"How very kind and thoughtful of you, Mrs. Brickwell," Rosamund said with very real gratitude. "And have you found something that will do?"

"It's been a bit difficult, madam," Mrs. Brickwell explained. "You see, you're rather tall and very slim—in fact," apologetically. "All I could find was a blue nylon button-through overall. It's a very nice one and quite new—"

"That will do splendidly," Rosamund told her serenely. "Of course, if we decide to stay on for a time, and I think Mr. John may feel that it's necessary, then I must see about getting my own clothes—" she stopped short.

But that meant going back to the canal—to the place where John and she had been so happy. How could she bear to do that? How *could* she! She swallowed the lump in her throat.

"Or else perhaps I could buy a few things more or less locally?"

"Well, you could," Mrs. Brickwell admitted doubtfully. "But if you don't mind me pointing it out, madam, I think you're going to be very busy today."

"I think so, too," Rosamund agreed. "There are bound to be a lot more decisions to be made. But—" she gave Mrs. Brickwell a quick, enquiring look—"I think you've got something particular in mind, haven't you, Mrs. Brickwell. What is it?"

"Well, actually, it's Cook," Mrs. Brickwell explained. "You see, as we understand it, the cook from the Orphanage is coming over here to work. And while that's only fair to Cook, seeing that she can hardly be expected to cope with all the extra work, you know what they say about two women working in one kitchen!"

"I do, indeed," Rosamund said feelingly. She considered for a moment. "Do you know anything about the Orphanage cook? I mean, is she younger than our cook?"

"Oh yes, madam, considerably, I'd say. And of course, only experienced in what you might call institution cooking—which is very different from the standard here!"

"I expect so," Rosamund agreed reflectively. "Well, perhaps Cook would like to discuss the matter with me? She may have a solution to the difficulty. Ask her to come and see me after breakfast. In the little sitting room here, please. There's less likelihood of us being disturbed. Will you ask her to do that?"

"Certainly, madam." There was an unmistakable note of respect in Mrs. Brickwell's voice. Really, young though she was and, so far as one could judge from what the newspapers said, not particularly *anybody,* Mr. John's wife certainly knew how to handle domestic problems! And she was to have further confirmation of this within a few moments. For, just as she was leaving the room, she turned with a vexed click of the tongue.

"I'm sorry, madam. I almost forgot to give you a message from Mr. John. He has gone over to the Orphanage to see just what the extent of the damage is and he said not to wait breakfast as he wasn't sure how long he'd be."

"I see," Rosamund said composedly. "Thank you, Mrs. Brickwell. But in future, if ever you have a message for me from Mr. John, will you please make a practice of delivering it at the first opportunity?"

"Yes, madam," said a subdued Mrs. Brickwell. "I'm sorry—"

Rosamund smiled her acceptance of the apology and Mrs. Brickwell went resolving that when she gave Cook the message, she would also tell her not to try anything on because the new Mrs. Lindsay wouldn't stand for any nonsense. Pleasant and sympathetic, yes, but a lady who knew her own mind and wasn't afraid to speak it. And quite right, too!

It was almost noon before John returned. Rosamund had spent much of the morning in the little sitting room to which she had taken quite a liking. It was obviously planned to be a woman's room, for the furniture, mostly really old, was elegant rather than sturdy. The armchairs and the seats of the smaller chairs were upholstered in soft green satin with a design in roses and satin bows on it. The curtains, though plain, toned with the green of the chairs and the polished floor had a few good rugs on it. There were two walnut occasional tables, a walnut-framed mirror and a workmanlike little desk. On this were two telephones, one presumably the house phone.

Rosamund had her breakfast there—a very simple one, but beautifully served. Newspapers had been brought up with the tray and she glanced at two with a growing feeling of distaste. Aunt Ruth had been interviewed and she had said much as Rosamund had expected she would—it didn't make reassuring reading. Then she had been visited, briefly, by Dr. Milward who had come to make sure that none of the children had suffered any harm, and for a longer period by Cook, a big, raw-boned Scotswoman who made the little room seem even smaller.

When John arrived, Rosamund was writing to Miss Alice.

"They told me you were here," he remarked casually.

"Yes. I thought it was a good idea to keep out of everybody's way as far possible until you had a chance to make any decisions. And I've found the room useful for interviewing people I really had to see—Dr. Milward and Cook. I hope you don't mind me taking possession of it like this?"

"Very sensible." John sat down in one of the armchairs, his long legs stretched out straight, his hands thrust into his trouser pockets. "It's essentially a woman's room, as you've probably realised. Bound to be. My mother planned and furnished it. She said she had to have one room where she didn't rattle about like the last pea in a pod. It rather vexed my father. You see—" there was a dry note in his voice—"he liked everything to be on a grandiose scale!"

"I see," Rosamund said, non-committally, as she thought.

He looked at her curiously.

"I gather you agree with my mother," he commented. "Don't you like the house?"

"I think that the grounds—what I've seen of them—are outstandingly beautiful," Rosamund told him. "But the house—"

"Yes?" He evidently meant to have a direct reply to his question.

"You referred to it as a soap-works," she reminded him. "I don't agree with you there. To me, it suggests a hotel. A very good hotel—but not by any stretch of the imagination a home." She deliberately changed the topic of conversation. "How did you get on at the Orphanage? Is it very badly damaged?"

"Just about gutted," John replied crisply. "And small wonder! The place should have been condemned as dangerous years ago, and to have had masses of children living there when the fire risk was so high was utterly infamous! How the devil it comes about that there were no casualties, I don't understand. Well, there's one consolation. The damage is so bad that they'll have to rebuild now, and a good job, too! But of course it will take time—"

"So you will let them stay on here?" It could have been a question or a statement. John took it as the former.

"Nothing else for it. I met Sir George Parks over there—he's one of the Governors—and he told me that one of the difficulties about rebuilding was the problem of where to put the children during that time. Well, I'm prepared to consider the possibility of them staying here for, say, a year. But I'm not willing simply to hand over, leaving them to their own devices—not after the chaos of last night. They'd wreck the place through sheer inefficiency. And though apparently neither of us like it, I see no reason why I should allow that. But it will mean that we have to stay here for a time until we're satisfied that it's properly organised. Will you mind?"

"No."

John accepted her brief reply without comment, and when he spoke again, it was of a different matter.

"You said you'd had visits from Milward and Cook. I suppose Milward's was simply a courtesy visit, but Cook—I imagine she was on the warpath! There's going to be trouble in the kitchen, mark my words!"

"I don't think so," Rosamund told him serenely.

John's brows lifted.

"You don't? You don't know Cook! Superb at her job, but a tartar if ever there was one!"

"Is she? I found her very co-operative."

John stared unbelievingly at her.

"Did you, indeed!" he ejaculated. "And just what form did her co-operation take?"

"She told me that there are two kitchens—the big one that was used when there was a big house-party, and a smaller one for when there wasn't."

"Yes, that's true," John acknowledged. "But—"

"And she suggested that they should use the big one while she had the smaller one," Rosamund explained.

"*She* suggested that? Oh, come, that's just not on! Why, even if she doesn't always use it, the big kitchen is the pride of her life! She'd never give it up without a terrific struggle. Now tell me, just what really happened!"

"Why not ask Cook?" Rosamund suggested coolly with a significance which was not lost on John. As clearly as if she had spoken the words, she was telling him that if he didn't believe her, he could easily check her statement. It was up to him.

John thrust his fingers through his hair in a familiar, boyish way that caught at Rosamund's heart. So many times in the past she had seen him make that gesture when he was puzzled or in any way put out. Then, it had usually been accompanied with a rueful grin—but he was not smiling now.

"I expressed myself badly." From the stiff way in which he spoke it was clear that he found even so inadequate an apology difficult to make. "But knowing Cook, I anticipated that you must have found her difficult to deal with. Consequently, I shall be interested to know what led up to her making the suggestion."

"Nothing very much," Rosamund said frankly. "I told her that we fully appreciated what a difficult situation it was and that we would be very glad if she could suggest a solution. So then she told me about there being two kitchens, which, of course, I didn't know before."

"I see—but are you absolutely sure you didn't get it wrong way round—that she intends to stick to the big kitchen?"

"Quite sure," Rosamund said confidently. "Because she did make one proviso—that she hoped she wouldn't be expected to cater for big dinner parties with only a small kitchen to work in but that she'd do her best if we wanted to entertain a few friends."

"To which, I suppose, you replied that if anybody could manage it, she could?" John suggested drily.

"Oh no," Rosamund answered composedly. "It's probably true, but I haven't known her long enough to know from personal experience, so it would have been rather insulting. As if I thought she was the sort of person who couldn't tell genuine appreciation from when someone was trying to curry favour with her."

"I see," John commented. "You seem to have taken her measure pretty accurately!"

Rosamund didn't answer. Did John mean that he thought she had acted with sincerity or did he think that she had simply been rather unpleasantly shrewd? She didn't know and she couldn't bring herself to ask.

After a moment or so John stood up.

"I'd better go and clean myself up for lunch," he remarked. "And I can do with it, seeing that I missed breakfast. Or is there anything else—?"

"Only you spoke of Dr. Milward's being a courtesy visit. Well, it was, for the most part. But he did tell me he's rather worried about Miss Fletcher."

"Oh?" John said without much interest. "What's wrong with her—other than that she's an infuriating old twitter-pate?"

"She's apparently had a grumbling appendix for some time and he's afraid it may be coming to a head. But she won't do anything about it—not even let him make a proper examination."

"Stupid old idiot," John said unsympathetically. "Why the deuce not? Can't Milward scare her into being sensible?"

"Apparently not."

"Well, where do you come in, anyhow?"

"Dr. Milward thinks there's some reason that she won't tell him why she's so scared, and he thought perhaps I might persuade her to tell me," Rosamund explained.

"Now look here, Rosamund, you can't take everybody's problems on your shoulders!" John protested. "If you do, you'll be regarded as Public Relations Officer to the whole shooting-match!"

"Well, why not?" Rosamund demanded, stung to sudden defiance. "Do you think I want to have time to sit and twiddle my thumbs and—think? Believe me, that's the last thing I want to do!"

Deliberately she turned her back on him and picked up her pen. John accepted the dismissal without comment. She heard him close the door behind him and she blinked back the tears she had been too proud to let him see.

"I'm desperately sorry, Rob," Miss Alice said heavily. "I've let you down badly."

"No, you haven't, my dear!"

They were sitting opposite one another at the table of the *Pride of London's* cabin, and he put out a hand to grip hers as it lay inert before her.

"There's nothing you could have done. I shouldn't have gone away, no matter how important it seemed that I should. Though, to be quite honest, I don't think I could have done anything either."

For several moments neither of them spoke. Then Dr. Rob picked up one of the newspapers that lay on the table and frowned at it.

"You know, Alice, there's something that puzzles me.

Neither you nor I like this marriage. But why? I mean, on the face of it, what is there to dislike? Other, I mean than that we feel rather hurt at having been left out. But that's unreasonable. After all, they had every right to make their own decision—"

"Oh, but it goes deeper than that, Rob," Miss Alice said quickly. "Much, much deeper."

"Yes, but why?" Dr. Rob asked impatiently. "You tell me that they're very much in love with one another. Then, from a worldly point of view, Rosamund has done very well for herself. In addition, Ruth must know that she's met her Waterloo now."

"Has she?"

Dr. Rob looked at her sharply.

"You don't agree? Why not?"

"Because I can't see Ruth missing an opportunity like this," Miss Alice explained. "Don't you see, Rob, that as the wife of a very wealthy man, Rosamund could be a very valuable client? No, Ruth will do everything in her power to prevent there being a breach."

"But can she do that?" Dr. Rob frowned. "I mean, from the very little Rosamund did tell you, and what we've been able to read between the lines, won't she seize the opportunity for making a clean break with her aunt?"

"If she can."

In her turn, Miss Alice picked up a newspaper and studied it.

"I don't like the sound of what Ruth told the reporters. About Rosamund not knowing how well off John is."

"You don't believe it? Why not? Simply because Ruth said it?"

"Partly," Miss Alice admitted. "But what I wondered was, true or false, why does she lay such emphasis on it? She does, you know. It's not just coincidence that every report features that aspect."

"H'm," Dr. Rob pondered. "Well, there's one reason you can dismiss out of hand. It wasn't because Ruth is a romantic at heart and believes in true love! There's nothing sentimental about Ruth!"

"Then there must have been another reason why she took such a definite line," Miss Alice insisted. "And there's only one I can think of that fits—I don't think it was because she believes it but because she's convinced that it's what Rosamund wants John to believe!"

"Do you mean to say that after all, you don't think Rosamund married for love?" Dr. Rob asked sharply. "That she married him for his money?"

"Of course I don't mean that," Miss Alice denied indignantly. "And you ought to be ashamed of yourself for even suggesting such a thing! Rosamund just isn't the mercenary type. I've no doubt about that! But I'm equally sure that John didn't tell her he's well off."

Dr. Rob scowled.

"That sounds rather unpleasant to me," he remarked distastefully. "Deceitful—underhanded—"

"Rubbish!" Miss Alice declared robustly. "If it were the other way round, if he'd pretended to be rich when he wasn't, then you'd have reason for criticism. But that isn't the way of it at all. You know, Rob, you and I are inclined to look at this purely from Rosamund's point of view. But how about John's? That young man is what is vulgarly described as a catch. And while I don't believe that Rosamund would have married him for his money, I'm afraid there are lots of girls who would. And then, how about friends? How could he ever be sure that they really cared for *him*? Pretty humiliating and disillusioning for a young man to believe that, without his money, nobody would be interested in him."

"I grant you that," Dr. Rob admitted grudgingly. "But even so—"

"Wait a minute, Rob, let me finish. You and I come here for relaxation—to escape from the pressures of our normal lives. We live simply, well below the standard we could easily afford. Are we being deceitful because we don't go about trumpeting how much money we earn? Of course not! And nor was John. He came here for the same reasons that we do. Not perhaps exactly the same, but near enough. And it didn't occur to us to ask questions. Why should it?"

"All right, you've made your point," Dr. Rob admitted. "It wasn't our business. But not telling us and not telling the girl he wanted to marry are two very different things. Surely she had a right to know! What was he afraid of?"

"Himself, I think," Miss Alice said simply. "Just

imagine, Rob, how marvellous it must have seemed to him to know, absolutely for certain, that Rosamund really loved *him*! Oh, can't you see? Perhaps it was foolish, but I do feel that in the circumstances, it was natural. Besides—" she added reflectively, "just imagine how difficult it would have been for him to broach the subject! Rosamund is very sweet. She's also very sound. She's got her priorities right, and what's more, she's willing to fight for them. And unless John is an utter fool, he must surely realise that. So how could he, in effect, tell her that it didn't really matter she was quite happy to share love in a cottage with him because he's got lashings of money? Of course he couldn't!"

"He's told her since," Dr. Rob commented, picking up a single sheet of notepaper that lay among the newspapers and reading from it.

"Dear Miss Alice,
John and I decided that to avoid any fuss, we would get married very quietly at once. But we hadn't expected things to turn out quite the way they did.

"We had fully intended coming back to the Seven Stars after our wedding, but John took me to see Lindacres and as I expect you will have seen from the newspapers, we had no sooner arrived than we became involved in an emergency and simply had to stay to get things sorted out.

"To make everything more difficult, reporters came to Lindacres because of the children being there and when they heard of our marriage they made a big story of it.

"Will you forgive us for having caused you anxiety and for not having taken you into our confidence? If we could have told anyone of our plans it would have been you, but for family reasons, this just wasn't possible.

"I shall never be able to thank you enough for your kindness to me.

Yours affectionately
Rosamund Lindsay"

"Yes," Miss Alice agreed judicially, "he must have told her. Judging by the picture in the papers, Lindacres is the sort of place that only a very rich man could afford to run. I wonder if he told her spontaneously or whether—"

124

she paused and shook her head. "To my way of thinking, Rob, there's something missing in that letter!"

"Is there? It seems to me to cover everything."

"I don't agree. For one thing, she makes no mention of them coming back here sooner or later, as would surely be natural, particularly as there's quite a lot of their gear here."

"That's true." Dr. Rob glanced down at the letter again. "There's a suggestion of finality about the way she finishes off—as if it really is 'good-bye'."

"Exactly! And then there's this—the two of them, very much in love, have just got married. Wouldn't you have expected there to have been some reference to how happy they are?"

"I suppose you would," Dr. Rob agreed. "So what you're saying, Alice, is that you think something has gone wrong?"

"If I'm right in the conclusions I've drawn from the letter, then yes, I'm afraid that's what I do think!"

"H'm—of course, one can't help jumping to the conclusion that if that is so, then in some way this money question is at the bottom of it." Dr. Rob pondered. "Do you think the reporters let the cat out of the bag and Rosamund was hurt—no, that won't do. They were already at Lindacres before the Press turned up." Again he considered. "She speaks of wanting to avoid fuss. That could simply mean that they didn't want the publicity that they ran right into. On the other hand, she also refers to family reasons. Well, John, one gathers, isn't afflicted with relatives. But Rosamund—" he shook his head.

"Ruth?"

Dr. Rob nodded.

"I can't for the life of me see how she was involved at that stage," he confessed. "But I'm convinced that she was. There's something about this whole business that strongly suggests she had more than a finger in the pie!"

"But even if she did, does that matter now so long as Rosamund is happy?" Miss Alice demurred.

"But is she? Do you really think so? No," as Miss Alice shook her head. "And neither do I! But I grant you, I haven't, as things stand, the right to find out. So—" his face grew grim—"I shall do the only other thing possible—I shall go and see Ruth and get at least some of the truth out of her."

"But can you? I mean, until now, I thought you didn't feel that it would be any good to try direct methods of that sort. What's made you change your mind?"

"Partly it's the result of sheer desperation," Dr. Rob acknowledged. "There's still no result from my enquiries about Rosamund having been registered at birth as Dexter—nor, for that matter, as Hastings. But there is something that Ruth will find difficult to lie about—something that, like a fool, I've forgotten until very recently. Ruth is Rosamund's aunt. Rosamund's surname is—or rather, was—said to be Hastings. But since Celia and Ruth had no brother, that can't be true! And that Ruth will have to admit. It gives me something of an advantage, even if only a slight one."

"When will you go?"

"Tomorrow."

"Well, I wish you luck, Rob!" Miss Alice sighed as she began to fold up the newspapers.

"Meaning that you think I'll need it?" Dr. Rob suggested grimly. "So do I."

Within twenty-four hours of her arrival at Lindacres, Rosamund's problem about clothes had been solved in a totally unexpected and far from welcome way.

All her London clothes were delivered, beautifully packed and obviously sent at Ruth Hastings' orders, though no message had accompanied them.

Now, a fortnight later, as she stood in front of her open wardrobe, Rosamund surveyed the beautiful clothes hanging there with mixed feelings.

There was no doubt about it, she would have been in a quandary without them, particularly at this moment. John had invited Sir George Parks to dine with them so that they could finalise arrangements for the renting of Lindacres by the Orphanage authorities. It would be an informal affair, but none the less, she needed to dress the part of the mistress of Lindacres as she could not have done without these dresses to choose from.

But though John had made no comment when they had

arrived, Rosamund felt sure that he took it for granted the clothes had been sent at her request. The inference which he drew from that was only too clear—he assumed that she and her aunt were not only still on friendly terms, but also that they certainly had been in collusion right from the start. And, helplessly, Rosamund was beginning to feel that she could hardly blame him for his scepticism. Conclusive evidence, as it appeared, had piled up so against her the interview which Aunt Ruth had given the Press had added considerably to it. And to counter it, all she had was her own bare word. What was more, the longer they remained in this strange state of armed neutrality, the more difficult it would become to make any real contact with one another.

Somehow, she was convinced, that barrier of silence between them must be broken down, but how, she had no idea, since she still felt that John and not herself must make the first move.

However, there was no time to brood on that now. She had thought she had left plenty of time to dress for dinner, but at the last moment Miss Fletcher had come to see her and had rambled on at great length with complaints about the sleeping arrangements. She was used to having a room of her own. She didn't think it suitable that she should have to share a dormitory with the children. She hadn't had a good night's sleep since coming to Lindacres—

Rosamund let her run on, not so much listening to the complaints, repeated over and over again, as making use of the opportunity to study Miss Fletcher. Very quickly she decided that Dr. Milward was right—there was something wrong with her visitor. Physically, she was a bad colour and far too thin. That, of course, might be due to the grumbling appendix. But there were other signs of trouble as well. The nervous twitch of her mouth, the restlessness of her hands and the way in which her eyes fell so quickly from one's own. She was in a state of considerable nervous tension. That might be apprehension at the possibility of an operation—but it might not.

Whichever it was, a glance at her watch told Rosamund that she had no time to try to find out now. She terminated the interview by standing up, leaving Miss Fletcher no choice but to do the same.

"Of course, Miss Fletcher, we must remember that in an emergency arrangements can't always be perfect," she pointed out. "And what final decisions will be made must, I think, depend largely on how long you are all going to be here. But that, as I'm sure you will appreciate, does not depend on me. However, Sir George Parks is dining with us tonight. I may have an opportunity of discussing your complaint with him—"

"Oh, please, don't do that!" Miss Fletcher said agitatedly, positively cringing. "The last thing I want to do is to make difficulties."

"I see," Rosamund said slowly and, indeed, she thought she did. Miss Fletcher, she was reasonably sure, was afraid of losing her job, and that fitted in with her refusal to go to hospital. "Well, thank you for letting me know how you feel, Miss Fletcher. And now, if you'll excuse me, I really am short of time—"

Miss Fletcher scuttled away and Rosamund went to her bedroom.

Twenty minutes later she joined John and Sir George showing no signs whatever of having hurried through her preparations.

She was wearing a gauzy silk dress of an unusual shade of green. It sparkled subtly with a hint of gold thread and the huge, bat-wing sleeves fluttered attractively with every movement of her arms. For the rest, it was very plain, moulded to her slim body with flattering emphasis. She had no time to do much about make-up or hair, though the sophistication of the dress would have warranted it. Her hair, which John was used to seeing loose, she had gathered into the nape of her neck, fastening it with a big Victorian tortoiseshell clip. It was a severe style, but it revealed the delicacy of her features to perfection. All in all, she looked charming, poised and essentially feminine. And she knew it—the sudden, startled look in John's eyes and the flattering appreciation in Sir George's left her in no possible doubt.

John made the introduction and as Rosamund offered her hand to their guest, she smiled disarmingly.

"I must apologise, Sir George, for not being here to

greet you," she said with the charming deference of a young woman to a considerably older man. "I was delayed by a slight domestic problem."

"Please don't apologise, Mrs. Lindsay," Sir George said warmly. "After all that you have already done to help us, you and your husband, I feel that it is an imposition to add to your burden by coming here to dine. But there is a lot to be decided and it is vital that an early decision should be made about the suitability of this house for any protracted period."

"Yes, indeed," Rosamund murmured. "A sherry, please, John," she turned her head to say as he walked over to the the cocktail cabinet. She turned back to Sir George who was eagerly waiting to resume their conversation.

"You spoke of a domestic problem, Mrs. Lindsay. I hope it really was a slight one—and that none of our people caused it?"

Rosamund smiled reassuringly.

"It really was just a trifle, Sir George, and as for your people—they're being most co-operative, I do assure you!" And if that was stretching the truth a little where Miss Fletcher was concerned, she had no intention of telling tales out of school. "Of course there are bound to be some adjustments to be made, but I'm sure that won't take long!"

"If that is so, then I'm quite sure, from what I have heard, that it will, in no small part, be due to your charming self!"

The compliment was rather too fulsome for Rosamund's taste, and as John handed her the glass of sherry, she saw from his expression that he hadn't liked it either.

She made up her mind that as far as possible, for the rest of the evening she would keep in the background or even, once dinner was over, that she would leave the two men to discuss the situation on their own. But this proved to be impossible. Sir George laid such stress on the value of a woman's point of view that she had no choice but to stay, and since he referred to her constantly, to give her opinions.

Fortunately, in the majority of cases, they happened to be the same as John's. None the less, as the evening wore on, she took matters into her own hands, explaining that she had several letters to write which must catch the early post in the morning—would Sir George excuse her?

A few more compliments—thanks for the perfect dinner and the valuable help she had given—an apology for having detained her so long—and she was free. But once the door had closed behind her, Rosamund hesitated. There were some letters she had to write, but they weren't really as important as all that—an overpowering desire to escape from the house, if only briefly, took possession of her and she surrendered to it before she had time for second thoughts.

Letting herself out by way of a side door, she walked swiftly to the open swimming pool. By day she had felt that its garish modernity was in doubtful taste, but now, in the gentle light of the moon, it was transformed. Dim purple shadows softened the angular lines of the low buildings which surrounded that pool and the still, dark water was spangled with stars.

Rosamund found a chaise-longue and with a little sigh of relief relaxed at full length on it. She lay perfectly still, gazing straight up at the heavens, and for a while she lost herself in the remote beauty, conscious only of a sense of being a part, however small, of it all.

Then, abruptly, the spell was broken. She swung her feet to the ground at the sound of approaching footsteps. It was John.

"Well," he drawled, "our visitor has gone at last! He evidently didn't feel it was worth staying once you had withdrawn your charming presence!"

Rosamund didn't answer. John was not only very angry, he was trying to goad her to a hot retort.

"And small wonder, of course," he went on ironically. "Since you were out to charm, weren't you? Both by your manner and your appearance! Enough to make any man lose his head! You know—" he regarded her critically, his head on one side—"you're an extremely beautiful woman, Rosamund. Far more beautiful than I had realised. But then, of course, I've never seen you in your fine feathers before, have I? You pay for dressing, my dear!"

Rosamund stood up. Her hands were clenched to her sides. She was almost at breaking point, yet somehow she must maintain her self-control. Otherwise there would be a complete breach between them.

"I'm tired," she said quietly. "And I shall need to get up early tomorrow——"

She turned to leave him, but his hand shot out, swinging her round to face him.

"Wait!" he commanded menacingly. "I've something more to say!" He surveyed her from head to foot with hot, possessive eyes. "Yes, quite lovely enough to make a man lose his head! Rosamund——" his hands were gripping her shoulders now with painful force—"we can't go on like this! Do you understand?"

Rosamund stood very still, neither responding to his grasp nor shrinking from it.

"Then what do you suggest we should do?" she asked almost inaudibly.

"Do?" John repeated harshly. "Well, for one thing, I suggest that you should remember something you seem to have forgotten—that you *are* my wife!"

CHAPTER EIGHT

DESPERATELY Rosamund tried to free herself, but there was no escape from the merciless arms that crushed her as John's lips sought hers in a kiss that held neither tenderness nor love. A kiss that made something in her shrivel and die.

This was not the John she had fallen in love with. This was a man who believed that everybody had their price and that money could buy anything, everything. And there was no appeal from that conviction. It was an ingrained part of his nature and the man she had believed him to be had never existed except in her own silly dreams.

Then, so suddenly that she stumbled, she was free. For a moment John stood rigid, staring blindly at her white, quivering face. Then his lips parted.

"I wish to heaven we'd not got married!" he told her

131

with a vehemence so intense that it had the quality of a physical blow.

He turned sharply away, leaving Rosamund to a silence from which all peace and tranquillity had been wrenched. In its place was the silence of utter despair.

At first, when John's footsteps had died away, she sat motionless on the chaise-longue, too numbed to think coherently. Then, vaguely aware that she was shivering violently, she made her way slowly back to the house and gained the sanctuary of her own room. For a while she listened, but heard no sound to tell her if John was in his room or whether, indeed, he had returned to the house at all.

Mechanically she undressed and got into bed to lie wide-eyed and rigid, unable to sleep, unable to feel—

Then, slowly, agonisingly, feeling returned.

John had said he wished they'd not got married. The words hammered relentlessly in her brain. And then she realised that she was speaking aloud, just as if he was there and she was answering him :

"And so do I!"

It was true! If they had never met, if, in her blind adoration of John, she had never known such happiness, then she would never have experienced the bitter disillusion that was hers now.

She lashed herself with bitter scorn. What a fool she had been—what a naïve, credulous little fool with her schoolgirl hero-worship and her belief that love conquered everything! She had been so sure that John was everything that was fine and true and all the time—she closed her eyes as if to shut out the memory, but it was useless. She knew John now as he really was and with that came understanding. There was only one thing for her to do. She must leave him—for good. What else was there to do when their marriage was such a mockery? All her dreams were shattered—and it was John who had destroyed them.

Until now she had found excuses for his lack of faith in her. The evidence had looked black against her. And quite likely, before they had met, there had been people to whom his money had meant more than his friendship. Because of that, she had made up her mind that, however difficult it might be, he should always find a loyalty and a love in her which would restore his faith in himself and his fellow beings. Now she knew that to have imagined such a thing to be possible was just one more foolish dream.

But there would be no more dreams. On that she was determined. From now on, she would accept only reality, however unpleasant it might be. Dreams were part of the past on which she would shut the door, never to open it again.

Not that she could ever again be the heart-happy girl of those few weeks which had followed the day when she had freed herself from the bondage which her aunt had imposed on her. She could put John out of her life in the sense that she would never see him again, but always his shadow would darken the future. Never again would she trust or believe in any human being alive! John had imbued her with his own lack of faith and always she would doubt her own judgement. She would even discredit her own motives—

She slept at last as dawn was filtering through the curtains to wake when her morning tea was brought in. And her first thought was simply a repetition of her decision of the night before :

"I will leave Lindacres today!"

And nothing should be allowed to stand in her way.

Then she saw that propped up against the teacup was a letter addressed to her in John's handwriting.

Her face hardened as she picked it up and held it, unopened, in her hand. Since nothing John could say would make her change her mind, what was the point in reading it? Then, with a shrug, she slit it open. It would make no difference, but she might as well know what he had to say—

Her eyes widened as she read. Without preamble, John had written :

"After my discussion with Sir George last night, it is necessary for me to go to London to consult my solicitor on various points that emerged.

"I expect to be away about a week and I shall be grateful if you will take over in my absence on the clear

133

understanding that you have entire authority to make
whatever decisions you may feel are necessary.
                    John."

Her hand shook as she laid the letter down on the quilt.
Her first reaction was one of resentment. After what had
happened last night, after what he had said, what right
had he to take her compliance for granted like this? Even
his use of the word "grateful" didn't mollify her. It was
nothing more than a form of words carefully chosen to
mask the fact that in reality he was giving an order. Sheer
expediency, that was all.

She was quite sure of that. John saw everything from
one point of view only—his own. To the feelings of others
he was completely insensible unless he had to take them
into consideration in order to get what he wanted. From
such a man one could expect neither compassion nor
kindliness. And certainly not love as she had dreamed
it could be. Well, one thing was very sure. Never
again would he be able to hoodwink her in that way
and never, never again would she allow herself to
dream! It made one too painfully vulnerable.

As for John's request—no, she would not accede to
it. If she were truly his wife—even if she had been a
paid employee—she would have done her best to stand
in for him. But she was neither. She owed John no
duty whatever. And so she would carry out her plan
to leave Lindacres today—for good.

Abruptly the house phone bell rang in the sitting
room. Rosamund tried to ignore it, but it kept on
persistently and at last, simply to silence it, she slid
out of bed and answered it.

An agitated male voice answered her.

"Tim Ferris speaking, Mrs. Lindsay. I'm terribly
sorry to bother you, but there's a flap on and we
don't—"

"Mr. Ferris, please understand that I'm not responsible for your problems," Rosamund interrupted firmly.
"You really must deal with them yourself—"

"This isn't quite like that, Mrs. Lindsay," Tim interrupted in his turn. "Miss Fletcher has been taken

ill—very ill, we think, and she absolutely refuses to allow us to send for the doctor!"

It was exasperating, but knowing as much as she did about Miss Fletcher's health, it was impossible to stand by and do nothing.

"If she's really ill, of course the doctor must see her, whether she's agreeable or not," Rosamund answered crisply. "I'll get through to him myself. But first tell me what's wrong."

Obviously thankful to have her co-operation, Tim gave the necessary information and Rosamund grimaced sympathetically at his vivid description. It certainly sounded as if Miss Fletcher was very ill indeed.

"I see. Very well, I'll get on to Dr. Milward at once," she promised. "In the meantime, try to keep her as quiet as possible and don't on any account give her any stimulants!"

"Right!" Tim promised, and rang off.

Dr. Milward answered the telephone himself and swore fluently at the news.

"Sorry, Mrs. Lindsay, but my feelings got the better of me! This is just what I've been warning the silly old girl could happen. I'll be right over."

For a moment or two Rosamund hesitated. Surely, in summoning the doctor she had done all that could be expected of her. It was for him to issue the orders now.

And yet how could she leave it at that? To be old and ill and frightened—and, perhaps even worse, to be one of those unfortunates who don't inspire affection—it didn't bear thinking of.

Hurriedly she put on her dressing gown and slippers and ran downstairs to be met in the hall by Tim.

"He's on his way," she said briefly in reply to his enquiring look. "Where's Miss Fletcher?"

"In the staff sitting room—we got her there out of the way of the kids—" Tim explained, but found that he was talking to Rosamund's retreating back.

She walked swiftly into the pleasant room that had been set aside for the use of the Orphanage staff's use.

Only two people were there, Miss Fletcher and Mrs. Brickwell.

As Rosamund came in, Mrs. Brickwell caught her eye and shook her head with gloomy foreboding. Miss Fletcher, she was quite sure, was not going to recover.

Miss Fletcher wasn't even aware that Rosamund was there. She was sitting crouched in an armchair, her head lolling against one of its wings. Her eyes were closed, but little moans fluttered feebly through her livid lips. Her thin hands were clutching with claw-like tenacity to the arms of the chair. There was no doubt about it, Miss Fletcher was a very sick woman.

Rosamund dropped on her knees beside her and took one of those frightened hands in her own warm grasp.

"Miss Fletcher!" She spoke quietly but very clearly. "I want you to try to understand what I'm going to say. There's nothing for you to worry about. You must believe that. Dr. Milward is on his way here and he'll know what to do to help you—"

The closed eyes opened momentarily and there was stark fear in them.

"Not—operation," Miss Fletcher moaned. "Only—only indigestion!"

"We'll let Dr. Milward decide that," Rosamund said with gentle firmness. "He'll know best. And I don't think that the idea of an operation is what's really worrying you, is it? It's afterwards that frightens you, isn't it?"

The only answer was two tears that forced themselves out from under the closed lids and trickled unheeded down Miss Fletcher's parchment-like cheeks.

"Yes, I thought so! But there's no need for you to be afraid of that." Rosamund tightened her grasp and raised her voice a little. "Because you're not going to lose your job! Or, if you decide you don't want to go on working, then there'll be enough money found for you to live in comfort. You must believe that, Miss Fletcher, because it's true! I promise you it's true!"

For a moment there was no response and Rosamund was afraid that Miss Fletcher was too near unconsciouness to have understood her. Then she opened her eyes again and the burning gratitude in them told Rosamund that she had guessed correctly.

"That's all right, then!" Rosamund said, and then, looking over her shoulder, she added thankfully: "And now here's Dr. Milward!"

She stood up, still holding Miss Fletcher's hand in hers. Indeed, she could not have released herself without using considerable force, which she was reluctant to do. She glanced enquiringly at Dr. Milward, who nodded approvingly.

"Stay just like that, if you don't mind, Mrs. Lindsay," he said quietly. "Now, Miss Fletcher—"

He bent over his patient and made a brief examination, asked her a few questions to which a simple "yes" or "no" was sufficient answer. Then he stood erect.

"No doubt about it," he said under his breath to Rosamund. "Absolutely typical! Now, Miss Fletcher, I'm going to take you along to the hospital and we'll put this trouble of yours right before you can say Jack Robinson! But first of all, I'm going to give you a little jab that will ease the pain for you. Will you roll back her sleeve, please, Mrs. Lindsay?"

Rosamund did so as Dr. Milward prepared the syringe. The injection was given and after a moment or so the doctor gave a satisfied grunt.

"That'll hold her for a bit," he said softly as they looked down at the unconscious woman. "Poor old soul, she's been an absolute idiot, but you can't help feeling sorry for her."

"No, you can't," Rosamund agreed. "Dr. Milward, will she be able to stand the operation?"

"She's got to," he replied grimly. "It's that or—" he left the sentence unfinished, but Rosamund had no difficulty in finishing it for herself. "As a matter of fact, physically, she's in reasonably good shape. Her heart's above average for her age. It's her mental condition that worries me. I don't mean she's off her head or anything like that, but she's the sort that can scare herself to death when she ought to recover."

"She won't," Rosamund assured him positively.

Dr. Milward looked at her with considerable interest.

"You sound very sure of that," he remarked. "May I ask why?"

Briefly Rosamund told him of her promise and its effect and he nodded understandingly.

"I see. Yes, of course. I should have known that for myself. Well, that gives her an excellent chance. Now, if I may use the telephone—I alerted the hospital before I left home, but I must confirm that she is coming in. They promised to hold an ambulance for half an hour unless there was any other emergency call. Stay with her till I come back, will you, Mrs. Lindsay? I won't be long."

He was back in very short time looking considerably relieved.

"Everything laid on," he said with satisfaction. "Twenty minutes at the outside. I'll stay with her if you want to—" he stopped tactfully, but Rosamund flushed as she remembered that she was still in her dressing gown.

"My goodness, yes!" she exclaimed ruefully. Her hand went up to her hair. "I must look an absolute mess! I'd only been awake a few minutes when they called me down."

Dr. Milward grinned in a friendly way.

"You look, if you don't mind me saying so, about sixteen in that rig," he told her. "And yet—" he put a hand on her shoulder and turned her to face the light—"you also look very strained and tense. Anything wrong, Mrs. Lindsay?"

"Well, of course there is," Rosamund said quickly, pointing to Miss Fletcher. "Isn't an upset like this enough—" Her voice trailed away as she saw him shake his head.

"No, I don't think so—you're too sensible to let a thing like this get you down. Besides, whatever's troubling you is of longer standing than just the last half hour or so."

Rosamund shrugged her shoulders.

"Then in all probability it's just that you've not seen me without make-up before," she suggested. "All women look hags when they are only wearing their natural faces, you know!"

"But you hardly use any make-up," Dr. Milward persisted. "I remember noticing that the first time I saw you. No, all right, Mrs. Lindsay—" as he felt her shoulder move restlessly under his hand, "I'm not going to probe. All I'm going to say is that young though you are, unrelieved tension could work havoc with you as it has with Miss Fletcher, even if not in the same way. No, there's one other thing. If there's any way in which I can help, let me know. I've got the habit of keeping any confidences that are given to me!"

"I'm sure you have," Rosamund said gratefully. "But truly, there's nothing—"

It had been on the tip of her tongue to say "*nothing that you or anybody else can do*," but she left the sentence incomplete. Fortunately Dr. Milward didn't seem to realise that, and she made her escape.

Ten minutes later, rather breathless, she was downstairs again in time to see the still unconscious Miss Fletcher off in the ambulance. Dr. Milward went with her saying that he'd got someone to run him back to Lindacres later so that he could collect his car.

Rosamund went slowly back into the house and was met in the hall by Mrs. Brickwell.

"Young Mr. Ferris asked me to give you a message, madam," she announced. "He asked me to say that two of the non-resident mistresses are coming in half an hour earlier than usual to ease matters."

"Oh, good!" Rosamund said fervently. Evidently Tim had taken her earlier warning to heart and was settling problems on his own.

"Also, madam—" there was a note of conscious virtue in Mrs. Brickwell's voice—"I have personally been giving assistance supervising the children at breakfast—"

"Splendid, Mrs. Brickwell!" Rosamund spoke with all the enthusiasm of which she was capable. "I don't know what we'd do without you!"

She went upstairs, free at last to consider her own affairs. But no, she wasn't! She'd made a promise to Miss Fletcher and it was a promise that she must see would be substantiated. She considered for a moment and then went to the sitting room. She looked up Sir George Parks' number and with a little grimace of distaste, got through to him.

"Mrs. Lindsay speaking, Sir George," she began briskly, but was immediately interrupted.

"How delightful to be rung up so early in the morning by such a charming neighbour! And what can I do for Mrs. Lindsay this bright and smiling morning?" he asked with that same overdone flattery which had annoyed her so the previous evening.

She wished she could slam down the telephone in protest, but she mustn't offend him if it could be helped because she knew that in him lay the best chance of keeping her promise to Miss Fletcher. None the less—

"For me, personally, nothing," she told him. "But for Miss Fletcher, quite a lot, I hope!"

"Miss Fletcher? Who's she?" Sir George asked blandly. "I don't know anyone—oh, you mean Miss Fletcher at the Orphanage! Well, what's the matter with her?"

Briefly Rosamund explained and heard Sir George click his tongue with impatience.

"How extremely troublesome of her! Really, to choose a time like this—"

"That's just the point, Sir George," Rosamund said crisply. Really, the man was impossible! "This trouble has been looming for some time, as Dr. Milward will confirm. But Miss Fletcher has been afraid to do anything about it in case her absence meant that she lost her job."

"Well, of course, we have been considering the advisability of replacing Miss Fletcher with someone younger and more able," Sir George admitted. "We have, however, as you may not be aware, already stretched a point in keeping her on several years beyond normal retiring age."

"But that's just it, Sir George," Rosamund said earnestly. "Miss Fletcher felt that she *must* stay on if she possibly could because otherwise, she'd starve!"

"Oh come, Mrs. Lindsay!" Sir George was taken aback by her bluntness and also put out by it. "I really can't believe it's as bad as all that!"

"I'm afraid it's more than likely to be," Rosamund insisted. "You see, so far as I've been able to discover, she has no relative with whom she could live. So even the most modest rent would be a terrible strain on her resources. It would mean going short of food and warmth—"

"Now really, Mrs. Lindsay, don't you think you're exaggerating?" Sir George suggested, very much on the defensive. "I think your kind heart is running away with you. After all, other people manage."

"Yes, but usually one finds that they have other resources—relatives who help, or perhaps a little nest egg. Or even a pension from their employers. Of course, if Miss Fletcher knew that she would be getting a pension from you, it would make all the difference in the world—" she paused hopefully.

"I'm afraid there's nothing like that, Mrs. Lindsay," Sir George said stiffly. "I don't say we wouldn't like there to be, but our funds are limited and overheads are increasing all the time—"

"Oh dear!" Rosamund said regretfully. "I had so hoped that *you* would be able to help!"

Sir George didn't answer immediately and when he did speak again it was in a far more conciliatory way.

"Now, you mustn't misunderstand me, Mrs. Lindsay," he began ingratiatingly. "I'm not a hard man, believe me! But my fellow Governors and I have the responsibility of handling money that isn't our own. Consequently, we have to be realistic. And that, as I'm sure you will see, means putting the needs of the children first."

He paused as if he expected her to agree with him, and Rosamund realised that he had, rather cleverly, taken the wind out of her sails since one could hardly argue that the children shouldn't be put first. At a loss how to answer, she said nothing at all, realising only too well that she had been over-optimistic in making that promise to Miss Fletcher, at least as far as Sir George was concerned. And, surprisingly, her silence had far more effect than any answer could have had, for Sir George ploughed on with, surely, a growing note of anxiety in his voice:

"However, appreciating, as I do—as we all do—all that you and your husband have done to help us in our recent dilemma, I should not like you to feel that we are not grateful! And since you make a personal matter of Miss Fletcher's case, I'll do all I can. Mind, I'm not making any promises at this juncture, but I will go so far as to say that if, after thorough investigation, your anxiety on her account is felt to be justified, then we will see if anything can be done! Now, does that satisfy you, Mrs. Lindsay?"

"Yes, indeed," Rosamund said earnestly. "It's most reassuring because I'm quite sure that you wouldn't go as far as that unless you, too, intended to make a personal matter of it—and if that's so, then I'm quite sure something will come of it! For you must, I'm convinced, have a great deal of influence where the other Governors are concerned!"

It was the sort of compliment that Sir George himself might have paid, and Rosamund hadn't found it pleasant to use such tactics, but certainly they were successful. Sir George positively purred!

"Well, dear lady, I mustn't boast, but you may be right, and I will certainly exert it to the utmost in view of your confidence in me. One does like to live up to the expectations of one's friends—I hope I may call you that?"

"Of course," Rosamund murmured.

"Delightful! And fellow conspirators as well, of course.' This shall be our little secret—we will form a Miss Fletcher Benevolent Appeal, shall we?" Sir George paused expectantly.

"What an amusing idea!" Rosamund said lightly. "I *knew* I could rely on you, Sir George!"

"I will let you know how matters progress," he promised expectantly.

"I shall be most interested to hear," Rosamund said cordially. "But of course, the really important thing is to let Miss Fletcher know as soon as possible if it's good news. It would, I'm sure, facilitate her recovery from her operation."

"Yes, of course," Sir George agreed without much interest. "I will take immediate steps—"

"Thank you *so* much!" Rosamund said earnestly. "Then I won't waste any more of your time, Sir George. Good-bye!" and rang off before he had time to say more.

For a moment or two she sat still at the desk, her elbows on its polished surface, her face buried in her hands.

She was reasonably sure that Miss Fletcher's future was now assured—Sir George would see to that. For one thing, his change in manner could only mean that it had suddenly occurred to him how dependent he and his fellow Governors were on the good will of John and, in hardly a lesser degree, herself. Indeed he had almost said as much. And then appealing to him in the way she had done had pandered to his vanity. He would just hate to admit that he hadn't got the influence necessary to sway the Board!

She gave an impatient little sigh. Was John right! Had everybody got their price? Was expediency always the controlling factor? It certainly seemed like it nowadays, so why not run with the herd? Why put oneself at a disadvantage by believing in such old-fashioned things as disinterested kindness and generosity? It simply didn't pay! Much more sensible and far less painful to accept that as fact and harden one's own heart.

Her thoughts were interrupted by the arrival of a maid with her breakfast tray.

"Cook asked me to say that she's that sorry it's so late, madam, but somehow, with all the upset, the kitchen got sort of out of routine—" she apologised.

"It's all right," Rosamund said mechanically. "I'm only just ready for it. Thank you, Rose."

There were, she saw, two letters lying on the tray, but she left them unopened until she had poured out her coffee and drunk half of it. Then, leaving the food untasted, she turned her attention to the letters. The first she opened was from her bank manager, acknowledging her request that her account should now be in her married name. The second—she flinched as she saw the familiar handwriting—was from her aunt. It was very much to the point.

"It may come as a surprise to you to know that financially, I'm in very low water. Why? The usual reasons—ever-increasing overheads and less money being spent on luxuries.

"None the less, I'm confident that I can make out if I can keep going for another year. Unfortunately, I can't find anyone to agree with me—and who also has the capital to back me.

"So, naturally, I turn to you! You are now the wife of a very rich man to whom the ten thousand pounds I want is a mere trifle. In all probability, he has by now settled a pleasant amount on you, but whether he has or not, I want ten thousand and I mean to have it by fair means or foul.

"Understand, Rosamund, I mean that, and you'll be a fool to turn me down.

Ruth Hastings."*

Rosamund didn't hesitate. Of course she couldn't do as her aunt wished, threats or no threats. She pushed the breakfast tray to one side and wrote a brief reply.

"What you ask is out of the question. Please understand that this is final.

> *Rosamund Lindsay."*

She put the letter into an envelope, sealed and addressed it and then hesitated uncertainly with it balanced on the palm of her hand. It wasn't that she was afraid of her aunt's threats—she had already done so much harm that it was difficult to see what more she could do. But it was clear that she intended to make an issue of it, and that being so, it was doubtful if she would accept such a curt dismissal of her request.

There was, in fact, only one way in which to convince her—by explaining just why it was out of the question. And that Rosamund shrank from doing in writing, unreasonable though that was. Her determination to leave John was an admission that her marriage was in ruins and that it was beyond her ability to rebuild it, even if she wanted to. And yet—there was such a finality about the written word—

"I'll go and see her," she decided. "Tell her that I can't help her, let her make all the threats she likes and then explain why. It won't be easy, but it will put an end to it once and for all."

Having made up her mind, Rosamund wasted no time. She consulted a time-table, arranged to be taken by car to the nearest station and that done, changed into clothes more suitable for London. Finally she rang through to Mrs. Brickwell, explaining that she had to go to Town on business but she would be back in time for dinner.

"I think that's all—" she thought as she replaced the house phone. "Gloves, handbag, money—yes, that's everything." Then she caught sight of the letter she had written still lying on the desk. "I'll take it with me," she decided. "In case I can't get hold of Aunt Ruth."

It was as well she did take it, for her aunt was at neither the flat nor at the Salon. She had, it appeared, flown to Paris the previous evening and was not expected back until the following morning.

Rosamund left her letter at the flat with instructions to the hall porter to see that it was delivered immediately Miss Hastings returned. Then, with nothing left to do, she left the block of flats and wandered aimlessly along the busy, noisy street.

How incredible, she thought idly, that at one time not so very long ago this had been part of the familiar background of her life that she had accepted without question.

"But never again!" she decided. "Whatever happens, I'll never live in London again—never! It's intolerable."

The thought brought to her mind the need to decide just what she was going to do. In no circumstances, once she had left him, would she accept any money from John. Anything else was out of the question. She had enough money of her own saved which would tide her over for some time, but ultimately she must find work. Work as different as possible from that which she had previously done—it might not be easy—

Her thoughts were interrupted by the realisation that someone was obstructing her way. Automatically she stepped to one side, but came to a halt at the sound of a familiar voice.

"Rosamund, my dear, how very nice to have met you!" said Dr. Rob.

With a little gasp, Rosamund looked up into the pleasant, smiling face. There was no reproach there, no suggestion that he regarded anything that had happened as being in the least out of the ordinary. Reassured, Rosamund pulled herself together.

"How amazing that we should have happened to meet," she said lightly, "for I'm only up in Town for a few hours."

"Then perhaps we may regard the coincidence as a special dispensation of Providence," Dr. Rob suggested just as lightly, "and make the most of it! Have you lunched yet?"

"No, I haven't," Rosamund admitted reluctantly, realising what was coming and how she could possibly excuse herself. "But—"

"No?" Dr. Rob interrupted gaily. "Then perhaps my luck is in! Will you indulge an old fogey who doesn't often have the opportunity of entertaining a pretty girl by having it with me?"

It was impossible to refuse, for, without waiting for her

to reply, Dr. Rob had slipped his arm through hers and had hailed a passing taxi.

He took her to his club for lunch—a solid Victorian building which had a reassuring air of permanency about it. It was also very quiet and peaceful, and as he led Rosamund through the entry hall to the restaurant, he had the satisfaction of seeing that she relaxed a little—but only a little. Clearly, there was something very far wrong and he was determined to do his best to find out what it was—but not immediately. He must lead up to it gradually—gain her confidence.

"Now," he said cheerfully as they sat down at a table, "I don't know how you feel about it, but as far as I'm concerned, a light meal is preferable this weather. Does that suit you?"

"Yes, please," Rosamund said, pulling off her gloves. "As a matter of fact, I had rather a late breakfast."

"Oh? Did you sleep in?" Dr. Rob asked casually.

"No, nothing like that. Just there was an upset. One of the Orphanage staff had to be rushed off to hospital for an emergency operation," Rosamund explained, thinking with surprise how long ago all that seemed. "She'd had a grumbling appendix for some time and it came to a head suddenly."

"I see. But, Rosamund, how did you get involved in that? I mean, surely some other member of the staff could have dealt with the situation?"

"I expect they would have done if they'd been at the Orphanage," Rosamund said quickly. "But they haven't been very long at Lindacres, you know. And it takes time to get settled—"

"Also—" he looked at her thoughtfully, "I have an idea that you're the sort of person to whom other people turn in an emergency," he suggested quizzically. "Partly because you keep your head—and partly because they know that they can rely on your kind heart coming to the rescue?"

At that moment the waiter brought the iced melon Dr. Rob had ordered and she was able to avoid replying immediately, and to her relief, when Dr. Rob next spoke, it was on some entirely different and trivial subject.

For the rest of the meal he very skilfully maintained an

almost one-sided conversation about nothing in particular until, over their coffee, he said suddenly :

"I don't know if you're aware of it, but Miss Alice is in town at present. Would you like me to take you to see her?"

"Oh!" Rosamund shrank back a little and her coffee cup clattered slightly as she set it down in its saucer. "I—I'm not sure that Miss Alice would want to see me. You see I—it must seem to her that after all her kindness I treated her rather shabbily—though, honestly, I couldn't help it, Dr. Rob!"

Her eyes—so like another pair of eyes that he remembered—pleaded with him to leave it at that, and almost he was tempted to do so. The child was so near to breaking point that even the slightest extra pressure might be the last straw. And yet—he drew a deep breath.

"Rosamund, my child—" he spoke very gently and laid his hand momentarily over hers, "I'm not a doctor for nothing, you know! I can see, only too well, that you're in trouble. Won't you tell me what it is? I might be able to help."

"No, nobody can do that," Rosamund told him dully. "I—I can't talk about it. And anyway, it isn't fair to burden someone who is—"

"Who is practically a stranger?" he suggested, finishing her uncompleted sentence for her.

"That sounds ungracious when you're so kind," Rosamund admitted. "But yes, something like that."

"I see." Dr. Rob nodded, his fingers tapping a little tattoo on the tablecloth. "Well, if that's how it is, I'll do no more than ask you one question which, of course, you don't have to answer if you don't want to—"

He paused. Rosamund had stiffened defensively and her eyes were full of apprehension. But he had gone too far to draw back now.

"It's quite a simple question," he assured her. "Just this—will you tell me what your mother's name was?"

"Oh!" Rosamund almost laughed with relief. She had expected something very different from this! "Celia. Celia Elizabeth Hastings. But—but why do you want to know?"

For answer, Dr. Rob took his wallet from his pocket

and extracted a folded paper from it which he handed to her in silence.

Wonderingly, Rosamund unfolded it and saw that it was a marriage certificate. She read it once—and a second time—with a growing sense of amazement.

"But—but—" she stammered, her eyes still on the certificate.

"Yes," Dr. Rob said deliberately. "The certificate of the marriage of Celia Elizabeth Hastings and Robert Irwin Dexter. *My* marriage certificate—and your mother's. Now do you understand why your happiness means so much to me—*daughter*?"

CHAPTER NINE

ROSAMUND sat beside Dr Rob, her hand held comfortably in his. When they had left his club, he had brought her to his Harley Street flat and now, though she was still dazed at the discovery that she had a father, she was beginning to believe that it was true.

But there was much that they had to explain to one another. Dr. Rob told his story first, and he did not spare himself.

"Looking back, I realise what a thoroughly objectionable young man I was," he said wryly. "Cocksure of my own abilities, ambitious and singularly unappreciative of any other point of view than my own!"

Rosamund caught her breath at the description and Dr. Rob paused to look at her enquiringly, but she shook her head.

"No—nothing. Please go on."

"Well, to sum up in one word, I was arrogant beyond belief. I was quite sure that I could solve all the world's problems with one hand tied behind my back. And it was when I was at the callow stage of my development that I met your mother." He stared straight ahead as if he was gazing into the past and his voice softened as he went on: "She was quite lovely—like a fragile flower." He paused momentarily and then went on slowly as if he was choosing his words with great care. "And, like a flower, she needed support to withstand the storms of life. That she had always had from her sister Ruth. It's odd," he remarked parenthetically, "how often you find those two strains in the same family—the dominant type and the dependent. And, to be honest, I don't know what Celia would have done without Ruth. And so it worked out quite well for a time. But Ruth's ambition matched my own. She was beginning to make her name as a designer and she meant to miss no opportunities. Admittedly, she drove herself to incredible lengths—but she also drove Celia, who was her leading model, to a point beyond endurance."

"I know!" Rosamund said quickly. "She did the same to me. It makes you feel like a bird beating its wings against the bars of a cage that's too small anyhow!"

"Exactly," Dr. Rob agreed. "But you, my dear, had the strength to get out of the cage by your own efforts. My poor little Celia hadn't. And that was where I, in my arrogance, took command! I insisted that we should get married at once. Then I would have the right to defend her from Ruth's demands. At first, Celia wouldn't agree. She was by no means sure that I was right in thinking that Ruth would accept the fact that she no longer had exclusive claims on her devotion and would consequently be less demanding. But I over-persuaded her and we were married. And immediately it was clear that Celia had been right and I completely wrong. As soon as she heard what we'd done, Ruth sacked her!"

"Oh no!" Rosamund exclaimed incredulously. "Surely even she—her own sister—"

"That made no difference," Dr. Rob said grimly. "It may even have made matters worse in Ruth's eyes. So there we were, entirely dependent on what I earned—which wasn't very much—with Ruth taking care that Celia didn't get another job. As a result, we had to live in near squalor with little or no prospect of any improvement in the near future. I worked as hard as I knew how to, but that meant I was away for very long hours and Celia, poor child, was lonely and bored, particularly as there was no money to spend on entertainment of any sort. Inevitably, we both became disillusioned and being young, we each blamed the other for things having gone wrong."

He sighed and Rosamund gave his hand a sympathetic little squeeze which seemed to encourage him to go on.

"Just what would have happened if we'd been left to ourselves, I've often wondered. But of course, we weren't. Ruth hadn't finished with us yet—and she held the trump cards. She came to see Celia when I wasn't there and offered her work for a few days in an emergency. That, of course, was just the beginning. Every now and again, Ruth would offer her work and she would accept it. Then, out of the blue, I had the offer of a post in America. It was a wonderful chance for a young man, one which could make all the difference to my future career. I went home, very cock-a-hoop, and told Celia that all our troubles were over, we were leaving for America in a month's time. To my astonishment, she told me bluntly that I could go if I liked, but she wasn't coming with me. I'd let her down once and for all she knew I might do the same again. We quarrelled half the night—and then she admitted that Ruth had already offered her her old job. I knew it was hopeless then. A month later I left for America—alone. Celia and I never saw each other again. I wrote several times and I sent money to her, but I never had a reply. Yes, my dear?" as Rosamund made a convulsive little movement.

"Aunt Ruth told me that my mother wrote several times to you to tell you of my birth," Rosamund told him shakily.

"Letters which, I've no doubt, Ruth undertook to post," Dr. Rob suggested grimly, and when Rosamund nodded : "And never did, of course, though I've no proof of that—" he looked at her questioningly.

"You don't need to prove it, not to me," Rosamund said firmly. "Not only because I know Aunt Ruth, but because—I believe it because you say so !"

"Bless you for that, child !" Dr. Rob said, deeply moved. "It's the most wonderful thing you could possibly tell me !" He was silent for a while. Then, with an effort, he went on : "I had one letter—from Ruth, nearly a year later. It simply said that your mother had died of influenza and enclosed the certificate. Still nothing about you. And that, I concluded, was the end of a sad little story—until, by chance, you suddenly turned up at Yeoman's Reach. It *was* by chance, wasn't it?" he paused to ask.

"Yes, just chance," Rosamund confirmed gravely. "But *I* can't prove that!"

"You don't have to, my dear. Not to me! Well, Alice, bless her, realised how like your mother you are, even to the colour of your eyes. She sent for me and we put two and two together with the result that we concluded that you might well be my daughter, particularly as you gave your name as Hastings. That, and other odds and ends you let out—like never having been out of the country, which could mean that you'd never seen your birth certificate as you'd have had to do if you applied for a passport." He looked at her enquiringly.

"No, I've never seen it," she confirmed.

"Didn't it occur to you to wonder how it came about that your surname was the same as your mother's maiden name?" Dr. Rob asked. "Or did Ruth tell you that you were illegitimate?"

"She didn't tell me so, but when I grew up I assumed that was the case, particularly as she never spoke of my father. And though by the time I—I married John, she told me that I was legitimate, it didn't occur to me that the fact held any significance as regards my surname. I've become so accustomed to accept it as being Hastings, you see."

Dr. Rob drew a deep breath.

"Ruth is, in many ways, an extremely clever woman," he commented grimly. "Particularly when it comes to getting her own way. Sometimes I find myself wondering if, perhaps, she even convinces herself that she's telling the truth! Well, that's my story, my dear. Now tell me yours."

Rosamund didn't reply, and after a moment Dr. Rob put his arm round her shoulders and gave her an encouraging hug. At first there was no response. Then suddenly Rosamund turned and buried her face on his shoulder.

"There isn't really much to tell," she said in a muffled voice.

"Well, tell me what little there is," Dr. Rob coaxed. "Perhaps two heads will be better than one."

"There's nothing anybody can do," Rosamund said

dully. "It's too late! You see, John thinks I married him for his money and—"

"What!" Dr. Rob almost shouted. "The damned young fool!"

"No, he's not really," Rosamund denied tonelessly. "I don't see how he can believe anything else—there's so much evidence—"

Dr. Rob scowled portentously.

"Is Ruth mixed up in this?" he demanded. "She is? Then, my dear, I want you to tell me the whole story, please. I've a feeling that this time she may have overreached herself! So tell me, Rosamund."

So, haltingly and occasionally interrupted by a pertinent question from Dr. Rob, Rosamund told him all that had happened—or almost all. She couldn't bring herself to tell him of that humiliating kiss—

At last it was finished and Rosamund stole a timid glance at him as he sat pondering and frowning.

"H'm, it doesn't help us much, does it? I'd hoped you'd be telling me something that would at least help to give us the whip hand over Ruth, but it seems that her luck still holds. We're just where we were—"

"Not quite," Rosamund suggested softly. "We've found each other—"

"So we have," Dr. Rob agreed, his expression softening momentarily. "And of course, that's something Ruth doesn't know—though I'm pretty certain she suspected we had much earlier—as we might well have done if I hadn't felt it advisable to make absolutely sure that you are my daughter before I spoke of it to you, and if I hadn't gone to America—America seems to be my jinx, doesn't it? That's the second time I've played into Ruth's hands by going there."

"What I don't understand is how Aunt Ruth found out where I was," Rosamund remarked. "I literally hadn't told a soul where I was going—how could I, I didn't know myself!"

"Well, one can only guess at that," Dr. Rob admitted. "But it seems to me more than likely that it was just one more case of Ruth's luck holding. You see, it probably never occurred to her that you'd have the courage to go off into the blue as you did with no haven in sight. And so it wouldn't be surprising if she assumed that you'd found out I was your father and had come to me. If she had *me* watched and followed, she could easily find out where my week-end retreat was and the rest followed. By incredible chance, her guess turned out to be right though her reasoning had been wrong." He paused, frowning. "Do you remember if you said anything that would tell her that though we had almost certainly met, you knew nothing of our relationship?"

"I'm not too sure—" Rosamund hesitated, trying to remember. "Yes, I did, I asked her if I was illegitimate. that was when she told me that you'd—you'd—"

"Deserted your mother?" Dr. Rob finished grimly. "Yes, of course, that told her that I'd said nothing so far—fool that I was!"

"Please don't blame yourself," Rosamund begged gently. "How could you have known?"

"I ought to have learned that where Ruth is concerned, one shouldn't take chances, however well intentioned," Dr. Rob replied morosely.

They sat in silence for several moments. Then, suddenly, Dr. Rob asked a question.

"Rosamund, why did you come up to Town today? You said that John was already up here. Was it to meet him?"

"Oh *no*!" Rosamund said quickly. "I came to see Aunt Ruth—"

"To see Ruth!" he stared at her in amazement. "But my dear child, why on earth—?"

"Because I had a letter from her this morning—" Rosamund began.

"A letter? You didn't tell me that!" Dr. Rob ejaculated. "What did she say? Have you got it with you?"

"No, I left it at Lindacres," Rosamund explained. "But I can tell you just what she said—" And as nearly as she could, she repeated the contents of the letter while Dr. Rob listened spellbound.

"And what did you tell her?" he asked with a softness which somehow made the question all the more urgent.

"I didn't see her. She's in Paris. so I left the letter I'd written before I decided that I would probably make more impression on her if I told her face to face—"

"And just what did you say in that letter?" Dr. Rob asked without raising his voice.

"I told her in so many words that it was out of the question to do as she asked."

Dr. Rob brought his hand down with a resounding thwack on the arm of the settee.

"That's it!" he exclaimed triumphantly. "That's what we wanted! Now we've got her! My dear, don't you see? If Ruth is desperate for money, she'll do anything to get it—even to the point of telling the truth!"

"But you don't understand," Rosamund said desperately. "I *meant* it. I haven't got the money to give her and I can't—I *won't* ask John for it! How can I when—" she bit her lip, unable to complete her sentence.

"I'm not suggesting that John should come into this at all," Dr. Rob said bluntly. He didn't add that, in the circumstances, he couldn't see John paying up even if he was approached. No need to hurt the child still further. "This is *my* job! If she gets any money at all, it will be mine! Is that clear?"

"Yes, but why should you—"

"Oh, for a variety of reasons. To begin with, I want to get things straightened out for you. That's the best reason of all. Then to clear myself beyond all doubt in your eyes of the neglect of which Ruth accused me. And finally—" his lips twisted in an unmirthful grin, "I must admit that it would give me tremendous satisfaction to get the better of Ruth at last! Yes, it's my job all right! But it wants thinking out carefully. There mustn't be any mistakes—"

His voice trailed away to silence. Rosamund leaned back and closed her eyes. It was wonderful to have discovered that Dr. Rob was her father. Perhaps even more wonderful to know that he hadn't callously ignored her very existence all these years. But in other ways, nothing was altered, nor would it be. It wouldn't make any difference to the way John felt, or the way she did. Whatever Dr. Rob—she couldn't get used to calling him "Father" yet—might say about getting things straightened out for her, there was no future for John and her. It was too late for that.

She was roused from her apathy by Dr. Rob saying with satisfaction:

"Yes, I think I've got it. When did you say Ruth was expected back?"

"Tomorrow morning."

"So she'll have your letter then. You, of course, will have one from her the following morning—"

"Will I?" Rosamund asked doubtfully. "You don't think that, seeing I've said I won't help her, she'll just carry out her threat—whatever it is?"

"Oh no," Dr. Rob said positively. "Not if she wants money so badly. And if she once broadcasts whatever it is she's so sure you don't want known, then she's lost her hold over you and she could whistle for all the money you might have paid her to keep quiet."

"I see. But—" Rosamund shook her head—"I simply can't think what there can be that she feels she can use to blackmail me like this. Because it is blackmail, isn't it?"

"It's blackmail, all right," Dr. Rob said sternly. "And of course, she may be bluffing and really there's nothing at all. But somehow, I don't think that's so. Don't misunderstand me, Rosamund. It isn't that I imagine for a moment that you've done something you shouldn't have, but Ruth is no fool. *She* thinks she's got something. So we must find out what it is—in other words wait for her next letter. Until that comes, I shall stay out of it. But once it does come, you must let me know *at once*. Then I'll go and see her. Is that clear?"

"Yes, quite clear," Rosamund said with a little shiver. "Father, is it true, do you think? Will people do anything for money?"

"A great many will, no doubt. But certainly not everybody. *You* know that because you're one of those who won't."

"Sometimes I've wondered if that's true," she told him despondently. "Perhaps I've got my breaking point like other people—" She looked at her watch and gave a little exclamation. "As late as that! I'll have to go now if I'm to be back in time for dinner."

"Stay and have it with me," Dr. Rob suggested, but Rosamund shook her head.

"I'd like to, but I think it would be better if I go back at the time I said I would—in time for dinner. You see, I said I was coming to Town on business, but if I'm late, it would

155

look as if it was something more than that, and I just don't feel I can stand any more complications," she finished wearily.

Dr. Rob didn't argue.

"Right, my dear, if that's how you feel," he said, standing up. "There's just one other thing, though."

He went over to a small bureau, unlocked a drawer and took out a key which he handed to Rosamund.

"The key of this flat," he explained. "I want you to feel absolutely free to use it if ever and whenever you wish—and whether I'm here or not. Promise?"

Rosamund gave her promise and took the key. A few minutes later, she and Dr. Rob took a taxi to the station and he saw her off.

She reached Lindacres to find, to her relief, that nothing untoward had happened in her absence. Indeed, there was good news. Dr. Milward had phoned through to say that Miss Fletcher had stood the operation very well and that so far everything was going satisfactorily.

From John there was no message at all.

Just as Dr. Rob had predicted, on the next morning but one, a letter came from Ruth Hastings, even more malicious and to the point than the first one had been.

"*You little fool, do you think I don't mean what I say, or that I'd blackmail you—oh yes, I know what it is!—if I hadn't got very good cause to know in just how strong a position I am to make you do what I want?*

"*Why? I'll tell you, my dear!*

"*I gather you've always assumed that your surname is the same as your mother's maiden name because you are illegitimate. Well, that's not so. Your parents were married, but I let you be known as Hastings simply because it suited me. But legally it isn't your name and never was.*

"*Consequently, when you got married, you made a false declaration and as a result, your marriage was not a legal one. A pity, isn't it, after all the trouble you took to hook a wealthy man!*

"*Well, you know best, no doubt, whether or not he'd like to be free of you—my own belief is that he would.*

156

You see, I happened to see him dining at a London restaurant a few evenings ago, and believe me, the way he looked, it was very easy to see that your dear John is far from being a happy bridegroom. What have you done to disillusion him so soon, I wonder?

"*Still, disillusioned or not, it's up to you to get the money out of him. Do that and I'll hold my tongue. Refuse—and I will most certainly let your dear husband know that he's nothing of the sort! And then where will you be? Out in the cold, my dear, with all your efforts wasted!*

"*Wouldn't that be a pity?*

"*Ruth Hastings.*"

Rosamund let the letter fall on to the desk and sat staring blindly at it.

So this was what her aunt was so sure gave her the whip hand! Well, since she measured everyone by her own standards, that was no doubt natural enough. It would simply never occur to her that, in fact, by her own action she had destroyed any possible chance she might have had of obtaining the help she wanted.

For, shorn of its malice and cynicism, which was really of no importance, one fact stood out. Here, beyond all argument, was the way of escape from an intolerable state of affairs. She and John were not legally married. That lovely service—all the vows they had taken—meant nothing at all. They never had. How very fitting that seemed, Rosamund thought bitterly, in view of all that had happened since.

But it was pointless to dwell on that. Married or not, John's future and hers lay apart. They both knew it. All that had changed was that now, presumably, it wouldn't take so long to make the break. Indeed, she must take the first steps in making it at once.

She pushed her hair back from her face, unconscious of the nervous tenseness which prompted the action for it seemed to her that she was entirely cool and collected.

First of all, she must ring through to her father.

Dr. Rob himself answered her so promptly as to suggest that he had been waiting for her call.

"I've had another letter—" she began, and came to a

full stop. Her mouth felt constricted and dry. Somehow it seemed impossible to put it into words—

"Yes, my dear?" Dr. Rob encouraged.

Rosamund swallowed convulsively.

"She says—that John and I aren't really married," she said baldly.

"Not married! But, Rosamund, surely—" Clearly Dr. Rob was taken aback.

Rosamund laughed mirthlessly.

"Oh yes, we thought we were! But, you see, apparently, if you get married in a name that isn't your own, it isn't legal. And of course, that's what I did."

"But without realising—"

"I don't suppose that makes any difference."

"Perhaps not. All the same, I'm not too sure—look, Rosamund, this will have to be gone into properly. We can't just take Ruth's word for it, you know!"

Rosamund's heart gave a convulsive leap. Everything had seemed so settled—so simple. Now it seemed that there might be a doubt—

"But so long as we don't know for sure, you can't stay on at Lindacres, Rosamund," Dr. Rob went on firmly. "You appreciate that?"

"Yes," she agreed faintly. Odd that she had been so determined to leave Lindacres, and yet now that there was no alternative, she should feel almost reluctant—

"Of course, you'll have to let John know at once," Dr. Rob continued. "By letter I think would be best."

"Very well," Rosamund promised. "But I shall have to leave it here for him. I—I don't know where he's staying in town."

"No?" Dr. Rob spoke calmly as if there was nothing unusual in a husband leaving his wife in ignorance of his whereabouts in this way. "Well, the delay can't be helped, in that case. But make very sure, Rosamund, that he will have it as soon as he returns. And also, it's essential that you should tell him where you are."

"Is it?" Rosamund said doubtfully. "Very well, if you say so. But there's one thing you must know before I come to you, Father—"

"Yes, my dear?"

"If it's true—if we're not married—then nothing will

158

persuade me to get married to him. And if we *are* married, then there will have to be a divorce."

"My dear, it's early days to talk of divorce," Dr. Rob said gently. "You've hardly given yourselves time to get to know one another—"

"I know it must seem like that to you," Rosamund admitted wearily. "But really, the trouble is that we didn't give ourselves time *before* we were married. Afterwards, it was too late."

"Well, we'll have to find out the truth about the legality of your marriage before we think of the next step," Dr. Rob pointed out. "Now, when can I expect you? Today?"

"Yes, if you don't mind," Rosamund said eagerly. The last thing she wanted was to meet John face to face. "Some time this afternoon?"

"Excellent! Oh, bring both of your aunt's letters, will you? I shall go and see her this evening and with those for evidence, she can hardly deny what she's been up to! That reminds me, did she tell you your real name?"

"No—she just said it wasn't Hastings."

"Just like her," Dr. Rob commented. "Still holding on to what she thinks is a trump, even if a small one! Well, never mind, she'll soon know now how little value it is to her. I must go now, my dear, I've a patient due in a few minutes. I'll see you this afternoon, then. Good-bye, Rosamund."

"Good-bye," Rosamund repeated mechanically, and rang off.

She sat very still for several minutes. Now she had the most difficult task of all to do—write her letter to John. She made several false starts before, at last, she scribbled away desperately and put the letter into an envelope without reading it through. It would have to do because, after all, what was there to do but simply make a bald statement of the facts?

It was late when Dr. Rob returned to the flat. He looked tired and troubled as if he carried a heavy burden on his shoulders. Rosamund jumped to the obvious conclusion.

"She wouldn't—?"

Dr. Rob sat down wearily in an armchair and leaned his head on one hand.

"Oh, she admitted everything—in writing," he said heavily.

"Then—?" Rosamund asked uncertainly.

Dr. Rob didn't answer immediately. Then he said slowly :

"I never thought I'd say this, Rosamund, but I've come away with a feeling of admiration for Ruth ! Oh, not for what she's done—she's knowingly and without mercy sacrificed us all—first Celia and myself and then you and John—simply to suit herself. That is unforgivable. But none the less, she has very real courage which I, as a doctor, could not fail to recognise—and admire."

He paused and Rosamund waited in silence, puzzled at the turn events had taken.

"She has a very serious heart condition," he went on gravely. "So serious that the end may come at any time—"

"Oh no !" Rosamund exclaimed compassionately.

Dr. Rob looked at her curiously.

"So you can find it in your heart to pity her," he said gently. "I'm glad of that, Rosamund. Even though I know it makes you desperately vulnerable, I wouldn't have you hard-hearted !"

Rosamund shook her head. She hardly knew just what she did feel towards the woman who had contributed in such a large degree to the wrecking of her happiness, but she could at least recognise Ruth for what she was—a woman who, nearing the end of her life, stood utterly alone because she had never been able to command affection.

"Does she know?" she asked.

"Oh yes, she knows—she also knows that with care and rest she could hope to prolong her life for some time— though no one could say for how long. But she laughed— with quite genuine amusement—when I suggested that it would be wiser for her to retire. No, she intends to go out fighting and, for the life of me, Rosamund, I can't help but admire her courage !"

"Yes, I think I feel the same," Rosamund confessed thoughtfully. "All the same, it doesn't surprise me. When you come to think of it, she's never been afraid to take risks all her life!"

"True enough," Dr. Rob agreed. "Well, there it is. It's no excuse for her having tried to blackmail you, but if one *can* look at it through her eyes, she is genuinely desperate for money. She's in very low water—there's no doubt about that. She showed me her accountant's statement. There's also no doubt about it that, given a little time and sufficient money to tide her over, she'll get the Salon on its feet again. She convinced me of that—and I wasn't in a mood to be convinced, I need hardly say! She believes she can do it in a year and she intends to defy all the probabilities in an effort to do just that! Personally, I wouldn't say but what she may pull it off—from the point of view of her health, I mean," he added reflectively. "I've seen far too many people die when logically they should have survived and many, too, who have pulled through when there appeared to be no hope for them. It's a question of having guts—and something to live for. She has. It may not seem a very worth-while something to us, but to her that salon means everything."

"Yes, it does," Rosamund agreed. "Really, I suppose, that explains everything—" She pondered for a moment. "You know, Father, I feel I ought to offer to go back to her—"

"She wouldn't have you," Dr. Rob said bluntly. He had been afraid of a reaction of this sort from Rosamund and he was thankful that he could truthfully go on: "She made that quite clear. In fact, she sent you a message to the effect that she wanted neither help nor pity from you or anybody else. She said that she had always stood on her own feet and she preferred to do so now! No, my dear, there's nothing to be done beyond—" he stopped short.

"Beyond what you've already done," Rosamund said softly. "Because you've given her the money she wants, haven't you?"

"Yes, I have," Dr. Rob admitted. "Although, to my own surprise, I regard it less as being in payment for *this*—" he took several folded sheets of paper from his pocket, "than in the hope that she will live long enough to achieve her ambition. Strange, isn't it?"

161

"Not very. You say you're glad I'm not hardhearted, Father. Well, if I'm not, I think I owe that to something you've passed on to me!'"

"Do you?" Dr. Rob looked at her, smiling rather wryly. "I don't know, my dear. Nor do I know, if it's true, whether or not you should thank me for it. As I said, it makes one extremely vulnerable."

Rosamund didn't reply and after a moment Dr. Rob stood up and handed the folded sheets to her.

"It doesn't make very pleasant reading, but none the less, I think you should read it. It may well prove helpful to you in sorting out your own problems. Then tomorrow I'll let my solicitor have it to deal with." He hesitated momentarily. "As a matter of fact, Rosamund, I have already had a word with him on the telephone, and he told me that since you were married in the name by which you had been known all these years he is of the firm opinion that your marriage is legal."

"I—see," Rosamund said dully.

"Well—" Dr. Rob, understanding her need to be alone to face her problem, yawned and stretched his arms, "I think I'll turn in now. This has been quite a day, and I've got a busy one tomorrow. Everything satisfactory in your room?"

"Yes, thank you," Rosamund assured him.

"Splendid! Goodnight then, my dear." He hesitated and then, almost shyly, went on: "I'm glad that—at last—my roof is giving you shelter, Rosamund."

He bent to kiss her, gave her shoulder a gentle pat or two and left her.

Rosamund stood looking down at the sheets of paper she held. Then, without unfolding them, she laid them down on a table. After all, what was the good of reading what Aunt Ruth had said? Nothing anyone said or wrote could help, as her father had put it, sort out her problems. It was too late for that.

Three days later John came to the Harley Street flat. Rosamund answered his ring and when she opened the door and saw who it was, she fell back a pace or two.

"I—I asked you not to come here," she reminded him breathlessly.

"I know you did," he admitted. "But I felt it was necessary for us to meet. However, if you're alone, perhaps you'd prefer that I should come back some other time?"

He stood still, waiting for her reply. Rosamund, feeling that his consideration had put her at a disadvantage, gave him a quick, uncertain look.

How serious he seemed to be. How absolutely lacking his expression was of all emotion—as if he was keeping a very tight hold on himself. Well, she would show him that she could match his self-control—

"Since you're here, you may as well come in," she said with deliberate indifference, and led the way to the sitting room. "Do sit down," she added as impersonally as if they had just met for the first time.

But John preferred to stand—not very near to her, but so that he had a full view of her face. For an appreciable time, neither of them spoke. Then John said quietly:

"First of all, may we deal with the question of your maiden name since, as you will appreciate, it's something that must be cleared up as quickly as possible." And when Rosamund nodded, he went on: "Will you tell me a little more about it all? How you came to be called Hastings when your real name was—what was it, Rosamund? You didn't tell me that."

"Dexter," she told him reluctantly.

"Dexter!" John exclaimed. "do you mean that Dr. Rob—?"

"He's my father," Rosamund explained matter-of-factly. "And though I don't expect *you* to believe it, until this week, I had no idea that was so, any more than he had known, all these years, that he had a daughter."

"I see." John made no attempt to rise to the unmistakable taunt at his probable incredulity. "Will you tell me how that came about? Please understand, I'm not just asking out of curiosity, but because I *must* know since I'm as deeply involved in the matter as you are."

It was true, of course, so as briefly and clearly as possible, Rosamund told him the whole story. John listened in silence, but when it was finished, he drew a deep breath.

"And you say that your aunt had made a written statement of her share in it all?"

163

"Yes."

"Good! That's likely to be very helpful. I'll let my solicitor know and he'll tell us what the next step must be. He will, of course, need to see the statement."

"I suppose so."

Silence fell between them. Then, as if it took considerable effort to ask the question, John said:

"Rosamund, have you—or has Dr. Rob—made any enquiries about the legality of our marriage?"

Rosamund nodded and then, her head still bent, stared at the ring which John had put on her finger.

"In that case," he went on deliberately, "you know that beyond doubt—we are husband and wife?"

"Yes, I know that," Rosamund admitted in a voice completely devoid of emotion. "A pity, isn't it?"

CHAPTER TEN

"IS it?"

Rosamund looked up, startled. She had said that it was a pity that their marriage had been legal and John was questioning the statement.

"But of course it is." Deliberately she kept her voice steady, unemotional. "Since we both feel it was a mistake."

"Not as far as I'm concerned," John stated unequivocally.

Rosamund stared at him in amazement.

"But you said—"

"That I wished to heaven we hadn't got married," John nodded. "Yes, and I meant it! For the first time, you see, I realised—" he paused. "Look, Rosamund, though I admit that you've every justification for sending me packing, will you let me tell you all that led up to that—incident?"

"If you like," she shrugged indifferently.

"Thank you," he acknowledged gravely. "I'll cut it as short as I can, but I need to go back a bit—to a time before you and I met. My father was an extremely rich man and a very generous one. Too generous, perhaps, as far as I was concerned. There simply wasn't any need or incentive for me to work, so, as most young men in that situation would probably do, I devoted all my energies to having a good time. Then my father died and instead of having an allowance, however generous, I was a rich man in my own right."

"*'One of the most eligible bachelors of the day'*," Rosamund murmured.

"Just that," John agreed. "At first, though it may seem improbable to you, I didn't appreciate what that meant. And then something happened which drove the fact home beyond all doubt. There was a girl—I fell in love with her and I believed she cared for me. I was on the point of asking her to marry me when—I overheard a conversation between her and my best friend." He paused and then went on grimly: "I heard Viola admit that she loved him, but it was out of the question for them to think of getting married since he was a poor man without prospects and she—she was very frank about it—hankered for the fleshpots. So, she told him coolly, she intended marrying me because I could give her everything that she wanted. He took it badly—tried to persuade her to change her mind. When he found that was impossible, he told her that this was the end and that he hoped he never saw her again. And then she laughed and told him that there was no need for melodrama. It wasn't as if she loved me—he had no need to be jealous. They'd have to be very careful, of course, but—she didn't finish the sentence, but there was no mistaking her meaning. Though she would be married to me, they would be lovers. He turned the idea down flat—but she was very lovely and he was deeply in love, so—" John shrugged his shoulders. "Perhaps I ought to have told them then and there that I'd overheard them. But I didn't. I was too sick at heart. I simply went away and left them to draw their own conclusions." He drew a deep breath. "And while I'm not asking you to regard this as being an excuse for—all that has happened between you and me, I think perhaps you'll agree that I had some reason for becoming a misanthrope where money was concerned."

He looked at Rosamund enquiringly as if doubtful of her probable reactions.

"*Every* reason," Rosamund declared with a vehemence that surprised her.

"Thank you, that's generous of you," John said quietly. "Inevitably, of course, I lost faith in myself. I'd always realised that some of my circle were opportunists who regarded friendship—or what passed as that—as a means of feathering their own nests. But they didn't really matter. Those two did. I'd thought that they both, in different ways, really cared for me. I'd have sworn it! At first, I was too stunned to think very coherently. Then I began to ask myself what I'd ever done to merit love or loyalty, and the answer to that was—nothing! I'd played my way through life on the money my father had earned. I'd never made the least effort of my own— except for an odd bit of writing now and again and that only in a dilettante sort of way, although I had had the idea for a play in my mind for some time. Now I decided that I'd really get down to it. I'd go away, live on the money my mother had left me and see if I could make anything of myself. I hunted for somewhere quiet where I wasn't known and found the *Seven Stars*. It seemed ideal—then you turned up—"

Until now, Rosamund had listened in silence, sitting very still. Now she moved restlessly.

"John, please, is it any good going on? It can't get us anywhere, you know. I mean, you've filled in the details, but I'd guessed that it must be something like that when I read the caption under your picture. That was why I—" she checked herself hastily, but not before it was clear what she had been going to say.

"Why you said nothing to me about your discovery?"

"Yes," Rosamund admitted slowly. "I think, without actually putting it in words to myself, I knew then that it wasn't really *me* you'd fallen in love with. It was just that *I* was in love with *you* and not with your money."

"You're quite right." He spoke dispassionately, almost coldly, but he walked over to the window and stood with his back to her before he continued deliberately :

"There's nothing I can say which can justify me in my own eyes for what I did. Don't think I didn't find you attractive—I did. But your chief attraction to me was the fact that your love was disinterested. That boosted my ego tremendously. I felt that, after all, I did amount to something!"

"Don't!" Rosamund begged, flinching at the bitterness in his voice.

"Why not? I've got beyond the point where I'm willing to sail under false colours, even to get what I want. Besides, you've a right to know and to condemn me for that and for my refusal to believe you told me the truth."

"But I don't condemn you for that—I never did," Rosamund protested. "After all, it was only my bare word—"

"That should have been enough," John insisted sternly. "Even the little I knew of you should have told me that!" He paused. "Then—Lindacres. And in a breath, it seemed, you became a different person. Not the sweet, unworldly, trusting girl I thought I'd married. Nor the calculating gold-digger I afterwards believed you to be, but a loyal companion who stood by me in an emergency and to whom everybody turned for help, confident that you'd play fair and make the right decisions. Oh yes, that's true," as Rosamund made a little gesture of dissent. "Mrs. Brickwell, Cook, Miss Fletcher—they all looked to you for leadership because they knew they could trust you to be both practical and kind. And the same goes for Dr. Milward and young Ferris and Weeks. Even Sir George—" He paused and then repeated slowly: "Sir George. I suppose you didn't realise, Rosamund, that I was absolutely eaten up with jealousy that evening he dined with us?"

"But why? I didn't like his sort of compliments any more than you did."

"I wasn't in any mood to appreciate that," John confessed wryly. "You see, short though the time has been, it's been long enough for me to realise what a blind fool I was ever to have thought that money came into it. Over and over again you proved yourself to be loyal and sincere and—altogether desirable. Is it any wonder that *this* time, I fell in love with you—*you*, not just as a salve to my injured vanity, as a real person."

"No, John, *no*!" Rosamund's hands flew up as if to defend herself from an actual blow.

"It's true. Quite true," he said doggedly. "Though I've no way of proving it. Particularly seeing that—it's the fact that I tried to snatch what should only have been mine if it came as a gift from you that you can't forget or forgive, isn't it?"

She nodded silently, her lips pressed close together.

"Yes, of course it is. Before—all this trouble, your kisses had been so sweet, so generous that I knew mine were welcome to you. And so, when I felt you shrink away from me, I knew what I'd done—and I loathed myself. That was why I said we shouldn't have got married. In every possible way I'd betrayed your trust in me and, as a result, I'd lost you! If only I'd waited a little instead of rushing you into getting married so soon, I might have learned—"

Rosamund didn't reply. Everything he had said was true—there was nothing more for either of them to add. But John seemed to think differently.

"I told you that I had come to Town to see my solicitor about the Orphanage and Lindacres. That was perfectly true, but all that was settled in one comparatively short interview. For the rest of the time I was trying desperately to discover some way in which to repair the damage I'd done. I came back to Lindacres to beg you to give me a chance to do that, though I'd no right to expect that you would. When I got there, I found your letter waiting for me and I knew that my task would be doubly hard since you so clearly wanted to have nothing more to do with me." He paused as if expecting a reply, but when it didn't come, he went on haltingly: "So it comes to this—we are married. But you need never again be afraid that I'll try to snatch at the shadow. I want the substance of love, Rosamund. And I want you to have it as well. But I can only *tell* you that. Only time can prove to you that it's true. So that's what I'm asking you to do, give me time—will you do that? Because more than anything else in the world, I want you for my wife. So don't put me out of your life, for if you do—" He left the sentence unfinished, but the torment in his eyes completed it for him.

168

But Rosamund hardened her heart. John had hurt her too badly for her to be willing ever to trust him again. Why, he himself had said that he had no right to ask it of her.

She heard him speak again, very quietly yet with an emphasis which was convincing.

"If ever you come to me, it will have to be of your own free will, Rosamund!"

"Then it will be never!" Rosamund declared passionately.

"That may well be," John acknowledged gravely. "But those are my terms. I don't want you on any others!"

And without waiting for her reply, he turned and walked quickly out of the room. A moment later she heard the outer door close.

During the next two weeks Rosamund saw John twice— both times briefly at the solicitor's office and with Dr. Rob present as well. There were statements to be made and sworn and documents to be signed, but on each occasion, once the business was concluded and they reached the street, John had said a brief good-bye and had left them.

Both times Rosamund was left with a feeling of anti-climax. Despite John's insistence that she had no need to fear him, she *was* afraid. Afraid that despite all the dictates of common sense, he would somehow persuade her to surrender to him. How or why that was to come about, she did not stop to think. Simply, she had made up her mind that she would not retreat a single inch from the stand she had taken. The past was over and done with. The door to it was firmly shut and that was how it was going to remain.

So she told herself on each occasion when she set out with her father to meet John and deliberately braced herself to resist even the slightest move on his part towards reconciliation.

But he had not made any such attempt. His manner had been impersonal, businesslike and courteous—nothing more. There was nothing for her to resist, which made her feel rather foolish, though not entirely reassured. John *might* have accepted her refusal to give him the chance he asked for as definite and final—or he might be deliberately

169

putting her off her guard. But it really didn't matter which, she told herself firmly. Meeting John for the purpose of straightening out the tangle of her having been married in the wrong name was one thing. It was unavoidable. But to meet him on a social footing was a very different matter and a state of affairs which she could and would see never happened. So that, very definitely, was that. And John would have to realise it.

All the same, she wished she hadn't got so much time on her hands. For so many years she had been accustomed to working hard and though the time had come when she had desperately needed a holiday, the desire for relaxation had gone. What she wanted more than anything else was for time to pass as quickly as possible, and to work hard was, she was sure, the only way to bring that about.

She explained this to Dr. Rob, but though he agreed that she was right in principle, he was far from encouraging when it came to the questions of her putting precept into practice. In fact, he asked her point blank not to do so, and it was a request which, coming from him, she hadn't the heart to refuse.

He had been so good to her, but more than that, she was very much aware of the warmth of his feeling for her and the deep satisfaction which it gave him to look after the daughter he had only so recently known existed. Satisfaction—and something more. Peace of mind. Rosamund knew that he blamed himself to a large degree for the estrangement from her mother, and in caring for her, he felt he was making a belated atonement.

So she agreed to wait for a time before looking for work and turned her hand to whatever she could to occupy her mind. And here Dr. Rob helped. He introduced her to the big London teaching hospital at which he was a consultant and Rosamund quickly found herself involved in a variety of ways. She helped with the shop on wheels which did the rounds of all the wards, and with the hospital library as well. She wrote letters for patients who for one reason or another couldn't do it for themselves, and she did her best to amuse children bored by enforced inactivity. It was satisfying work, but it was too piecemeal to be entirely absorbing. However, it did suggest the possibility of training for some full-time hospital work, and she wondered if that was the reason why Dr. Rob had got her interested in it. If it was, he made no mention of the idea, evidently feeling that the decision must be entirely hers.

Nor was that the only evidence of his tact and understanding. Knowing just how much his weekends on the *Rosebud* meant to him, she had dreaded the possibility that he might take it for granted she would go with him on these trips. But that would have been something she would have had to refuse him. That brief interval of happiness when she had lived in a fool's paradise was too bitter a memory for her to want to recall it. However, the question didn't arise, for Dr. Rob suggested that, since she had seen so little even of her own country, they might do some exploring together. Thankfully, Rosamund agreed, and the first weekend they spent at a centuries-old hotel in Suffolk, which was almost as unknown to Dr. Rob as to her. She liked the tranquil, unspoilt countryside, and if the two of them didn't talk very much, they were none the less conscious of a sense of companionship.

The second weekend they spent at the home of some old friends of Dr. Rob's in the heart of Sussex, and though Rosamund didn't enjoy that so much, she admitted to herself that it was a good thing to meet people. It compelled one to forget one's own troubles.

Miss Alice felt old and tired and dispirited. Everything had gone wrong and so far as she could see there was nothing that could be done to put matters right. And such a short time ago everything had looked so promising. She knew, none better, just how much Rob regretted his share in the failure of his marriage. Then, at last, it had looked as if he was going to get some happiness out of it. She'd rejoiced wholeheartedly with him over Rosamund's unexpected arrival in his life, not least of all because she had been able to help there. But now much of his joy in the discovery that he had a daughter had been ruined by other people—by Rosamund herself, by John and, of course, by Ruth. She knew the whole story from Rob's letters and because it was his happiness which mattered most to her, she felt cross and impatient with the people who had stood in the way of its fulfilment.

171

"Bother them and their complexes and inhibitions," she muttered irritably. "Why should any of them expect that life should be arranged just to suit them? If they were less concerned with getting what they want out of it and thought more—my poor old Rob!"

In this brooding state of mind, even painting brought no solace. She found difficulty in concentrating and she was thoroughly dissatisfied with her watercolours of the canal scenes which had once provided such satisfying material.

"No life in 'em," she said disgustedly, and tore them up into fragments. "Might as well give up and go back to Town—"

But she stayed on, lonely and disconsolate and yet oddly reluctant to leave the *Pride of London*.

"Almost as if I felt that somehow or other I'll be able to help, just staying here," she mused wonderingly. "though for the life of me, I don't see how that can make sense! Oh well, I'd better make a cup of tea, I suppose!"

Drinking her tea, she made up her mind that she would stay just two more days. If nothing happened by then, she would admit defeat—

The very next day John turned up. Miss Alice, sitting idly on deck in the sunshine, saw him come through the gate in the hedge and caught her breath. Had she been right? Was there a purpose behind her decision to stay on here? It made one wonder—

As he reached the gangplank of the *Seven Stars* he saw her, hesitated and then walked slowly towards her.

"Good afternoon, Miss Alice."

She looked at him with unfriendly eyes.

"And what are you doing here?" she demanded.

"My tenure of the *Seven Stars* expires in a few days' time," he explained equably, ignoring her truculent manner, "and as I'm not proposing to renew it, I must clear out my gear."

"In that case, I'll pack Rosamund's clothes and you can take them as well," Miss Alice said briskly, watching intently for his reaction to that.

John frowned. He had been hoping that his visit might coincide with a time when Miss Alice happened to be away, but his luck was out.

172

"There's not much point in me doing that," he said coldly. "Rosamund, as you surely know, has left me and is living with her father."

"Yes, I do know," Miss Alice admitted tartly. "And I never heard such nonsense in all my life! Quarrelling before you've been married five minutes—you ought to be ashamed, the pair of you!"

Without replying, John turned deliberately and walked in the direction of his own boat, but Miss Alice hadn't finished with him.

"That's right, run away!" she called waspishly after him. "That's all you young folk ever do if you don't get your own way! No backbone, that's your trouble!"

John wheeled and came back. They confronted one another, two very angry people.

"You don't know what you're talking about," he declared loudly.

"No? Then suppose you tell me?" Miss Alice snapped, quite unperturbed by this irate young man who towered so threateningly above her. "And kindly don't shout at me! My hearing is perfectly good, I'm glad to say."

"I'm sorry," John said impatiently. "I shouldn't have spoken to you like that. But this is Rosamund's business and mine. I can't discuss it with you."

"No? Even though the minx is running circles round you and you haven't a notion what to do next?" Miss Alice said quizzically.

"I—" John began, and stopped short. "Look, Miss Alice, I'm sure you mean to be kind, but really—"

"Now, as I see it, this is the situation," Miss Alice said briskly just as if he hadn't spoken. "For some reason, you and Rosamund have, to use a nice, old-fashioned phrase, fallen out with one another. No, don't worry, I'm not asking you to tell me the reason for that, though, at a guess, I'd say it's something more than just your wretched money, isn't it?"

"Yes," John admitted curtly.

Miss Alice looked at him consideringly. Rob, not unnaturally, perhaps, blamed him rather than Rosamund for the estrangement, but she wasn't so sure. Usually there were faults on both sides, and anyway, she'd always found something likeable about John, despite his inclination to scowl so blackly—as he was doing now.

"I wonder how much you know about the way a woman's mind works?" she remarked meditatively.

John shrugged his shoulders and earned a nod of approval.

"Well, at least you know your own limitations," she commented drily. "Which is more than most men do!" She paused and then went on almost casually: "But even so, of course you know that the quickest way of persuading a woman to admit that she's wrong is to apologise for the offence as if you were the culprit."

"You may be quite right," John said distastefully. "But I'm not interested in double-dealing of that sort. In any case, it doesn't apply here."

Miss Alice made no comment, but a question was so obviously in her mind that John's annoyance mounted. He'd been a fool to rise to that gibe of hers—if he'd ignored it, she'd have been left high and dry. But now—wasn't the simplest thing to tell her the truth?

"The fault for what has happened lies with me alone," he told her harshly. "Rosamund is not in the least to blame."

Still Miss Alice said nothing. John scowled. Confound this inquisitive, interfering old woman—

"She is fully aware that I admit this and also that I greatly regret—" he left the sentence unfinished and went on doggedly: "You will have to accept the fact, as I have had to, that the decision rightly rests with Rosamund. I absolutely refuse to coerce her in any way and I most sincerely hope, Miss Alice, that neither you nor anyone else attempts to do so. Is that clear?"

"Oh yes, quite clear," Miss Alice assured him placidly. "Thank you for explaining. Of course, it's a pity, but there it is, these things happen and one has to accept the fact! But one can't help feeling that, the way things have turned out, it would really have been better if your marriage hadn't been legal, wouldn't it?"

Again John turned his back on her—but not before she had had a fleeting glimpse of the desolation too deep and bitter to share with anyone.

"Oh, poor boy, poor boy!" she thought compassionately. "He'd give anything—everything—he's got to get her back! I do wonder what—but really, that matters less now than the fact that he's played himself into an impossible position! It's all very fine and noble to say that he's to blame and he won't have her coerced, but what that means is that he's robbed himself of any chance of making good in his eyes because he won't go near her. I wonder—" her eyes narrowed in the way they did when she wanted to concentrate on one particularly important detail of a painting. "Yes—I think he asked Rosamund to give him a chance to do just that—and she refused," she decided. "So now, unless Rosamund makes a move, they'll drift further and further apart—and somehow, I doubt whether she will. Not with her upbringing!"

She frowned deeply, considering this. Ruth's fangs had been drawn as regards making any future trouble, but had the damage already been done? Despite the sophisticated background which Rosamund had known, it wouldn't be surprising if she was almost completely inexperienced in the ways of men. Of course, she must have met plenty, but one didn't need to be very perceptive to conclude, particularly when one remembered past history, that Ruth would see to it that the child never had a man friend. She was far too valuable an asset to Ruth for that to be allowed to happen! Which would inevitably mean that the child had no idea that the same man could, at times, be a blundering hobbledehoy and at others, far more vulnerable and sensitive than any woman could ever be.

Nor would Rosamund ever learn that this inherent contradictoriness is an infuriating, intriguing and—altogether lovable male characteristic which makes life for a woman worth living—if she really loves her man.

"Of course, she'd say she doesn't," Miss Alice sighed impatiently. "And so long as she sees nothing of him, she'll be able to convince herself that's true! Dear me, it's very difficult to think of anything—"

The telephone bell was ringing as Rosamund and her father came into the flat. They had been to the theatre and were rather late—a fact on which Dr. Rob commented on as he picked up the receiver.

"And I hope to goodness it isn't an emergency patient,"

175

he commented wryly. "I'm beginning to feel my years and I need a good night's sleep. Yes, Robert Dexter speaking," he said into the instrument. "Who? Mrs. Watchett at the shop! Yes, what's the trouble, Mrs. Watchett?"

His expression changed from one of mild vexation to one of extreme concern as he listened for several moments to Mrs. Watchett's voluble flow of speech which paused now and again, but only so briefly as to give him time to say : "Yes, yes, I understand—" at intervals.

Rosamund stood rigidly beside him, unable to guess what was wrong from the one-sided conversation, but feeling more and more tense and apprehensive. It was evidently something serious—

At last Mrs. Watchett came to a breathless halt and Dr. Rob was able to speak.

"Yes, I quite understand, Mrs. Watchett," he said briskly. "And I will make the necessary arrangements without fail. I'll also ring the hospital to see if they consider them satisfactory—have you got the number?" He scribbled it down on the nearby pad. "Yes, I've got that—what's that? Yes, I'll ring you as well when it's all fitted up. Either tonight or first thing tomorrow morning. Thank you very much for letting me know! Good night!"

He replaced the instrument but stood for a moment with one hand still on it, his lips pursed. Then he slowly paced up and down the pleasant room once or twice, deep in thought.

"Father—?"

He gave a little start as if he had suddenly realised Rosamund's presence and came to a halt facing her.

"Alice has had an accident," he said abruptly. "Dropped something heavy on her foot and has broken a couple of bones in her instep. She's in hospital now, but it was some time before she was found. If I've told her once, I've told her twenty times that she ought not to be alone on that damned boat with nobody within hail—"

"Oh, poor Miss Alice!" Rosamund exclaimed with a sympathy which was yet tinged with inexplicable relief. "I *am* sorry!"

"Are you?" Dr. Rob laid his hand on her shoulder. "How sorry?"

"I—I—" Rosamund stammered, guessing what was coming.

"I've realised, of course, that you haven't wanted to go back to the canal, and that's understandable enough," Dr. Rob said deliberately. "But now I'm asking you to forget your personal feelings and to go there to look after Alice."

"But if she's in hospital—" Rosamund demurred.

"They're keeping her in until the day after tomorrow," Dr. Rob said shortly. "And that's longer than it would be if she were younger. And these days there aren't enough beds or staff to waste them on people who don't need them. No, she can't stay there, but they want her to be in the neighbourhood so that she can keep in touch with them. So she'll be going back to the *Pride of London*. But she'll be in a plaster and that means she must not be alone—and it must be a woman that's with her, of course."

Rosamund didn't reply immediately. Then she asked :

"Father, who—who was it that found Miss Alice after the accident?"

"Young Sid Watchett. Fortunately it was his day for delivering her supplies, and for once, in a way he showed some sense. He ran back to the shop and his mother phoned for the ambulance."

So it hadn't been John—she had been half suspicious, but after all, he, no more than herself, would want to go back there. Even so, it would be hard enough, but there seemed no alternative—

"All right, I'll go," she promised. "Just when will she be back?"

"I'll get through to the hospital and find out," Dr. Rob said, going back to the telephone. "You'll need to go down the day before to get everything ready."

Rosamund stood on the deck of the *Pride of London*. She had come down from Town early that morning and now, in the late afternoon, with everything spick and span for Miss Alice's reception, she had time on her hands. And that was the last thing she wanted, for in these surroundings how could she help but recall those earlier days which she had spent here?

Never in all her life had she been so happy and

confident. She had been so sure that golden days for John and herself stretched ahead in a limitless procession. But instead of that, so soon, she had found disillusionment and heartbreak. And never again, she knew, would it be possible for her to experience such enchantment. It was the sort of thing which could only happen once.

In London, it had seemed possible to accept that and shut the door firmly on the past. Even those brief meetings with John at the solicitors' hadn't disturbed her very much because it had all seemed so impersonal, as if they were both different people from the ones they had been.

But now, here, it was different. Memory stirred and would not be stilled. All the little things, all the important ones that had gone to make up those halcyon days were as clear to her mind's eye as when they had actually happened from the moment when an irate John had shaken her to consciousness when she had dropped off to sleep in his cabin to the moment of culminating bliss when he had taken her into his arms and told her that he loved her.

She beat her hand on the boatrail in a mood of hopeless frustration. Would she, no matter how she tried to forget, always be at the mercy of these bitter-sweet memories of hers? Would they, all unbidden, suddenly possess her, as they were doing now, stronger than any resolution she might make to leave them in the past?

"They shan't, they shan't," she told herself passionately. "I must forget—I *must*! There's no alternative!"

But there was. She could give John the chance he asked for—let him persuade her—

"Never!" she declared as fiercely as if someone else, not herself, had made the suggestion. "It's finished, absolutely finished!"

She would stop thinking about John, now and for all time. And instead of moping out here like this, she would get herself a meal—

She turned to go into the galley, and at that moment, John came through the gate in the hedge.

CHAPTER ELEVEN

SO it was a trap! A trap to bring John and her together again. What was more, not only John himself was responsible for it. Her father and Miss Alice, people whom she believed she could trust and rely on, were as much involved as he was.

She said as much to John, but he denied it, not indignantly, but matter-of-factly and with a suggestion of the tolerance one would show to a child encountering a problem it could hardly be expected to understand. To Rosamund, he sounded insufferably patronising and self-confident.

"Nothing like that," he assured her.

"I don't believe it," Rosamund declared stubbornly.

"You mean you think it's a put-up job?" John suggested bluntly. "That Miss Alice didn't have an accident at all? That she and your father and I put our heads together to devise a plan which would trick you into coming here?"

"Yes, I do think that," Rosamund told him defiantly.

John shook his head.

"You're wrong. Oh, I grant you it would have been a most ingenious scheme, but there's one snag. The hospital. Do you honestly think that we could have persuaded the authorities to play our game if there had been nothing wrong with Miss Alice? Of course we couldn't!"

And that, she had to acknowledge, was undoubtedly true.

"Well, if it wasn't that—" she began impetuously, and stopped short.

"If it wasn't that—then what? If, as you believe, it was a put-up job, then there's only one alternative, you know. That it wasn't an accident at all. In other words, that it was done deliberately either by me or by Miss Alice, persuaded by me. Well? Does either sound very likely to you?"

"No," Rosamund admitted grudgingly. "All the same, can you deny that you came here because you knew I'd be here?"

"Oh yes, I can deny that," John said easily. "I came down here several days ago to clear my gear out of the

Seven Stars because my tenancy was on the point of expiring. Unfortunately, I had to go to Lindacres on the day that the accident happened, and so not only was I not here to lend a hand, but I neither knew about it or that you were here until I called in at the shop a short time back."

"Well, now that you do know, the least you can do is go away as quickly as possible," she insisted doggedly. "Surely you can see that!"

But John shook his head, his jaw set obstinately.

"No, Rosamund, I can't! The way I look at it is this—you've refused to give me a chance to redeem myself in your eyes, but fate or luck, whichever you like to call it, has played right into my hands and I intend to make the most of my opportunity!"

"But you said that you only wanted me to come back to you of my own free will," she reminded him indignantly.

"I still say that, and I mean it. It's because I feel it so strongly that I'm determined *you* shall have a chance!"

"A chance for what?" Rosamund asked scornfully. "To make a fool of myself all over again?"

"If you like to put it that way," John conceded. "But as I see it, a chance to discover just what it is that your will really wants if you give it the freedom to decide. No, let me finish!" There was a new authority in his manner which checked the furious words on Rosamund's lips. "I've hurt your pride badly. I know that. I also know that you believe I've killed your love for me. Well, I don't believe that! Oh, not because I'm such a terrific chap that I'm irresistible! Far from it. No, it's on you that I'm pinning my faith. I believe that because you're incapable of feeling a shallow emotion—the sort that can easily be destroyed—you do still love me—"

"No!" Rosamund disclaimed passionately. "You're wrong—quite wrong!"

"Perhaps. But I intend to find out for certain. Is that clear?"

"Quite," Rosamund told him stonily. "But you're wasting your time."

John regarded her with an intentness that made her feel

uneasy. It was as if he was striving to penetrate her very innermost thoughts.

"It couldn't be, I suppose," he said thoughtfully, "that you're taking this line because, though in your heart of hearts you want us to make a fresh start, just as I do, you're afraid to admit it?" And then, as she didn't reply, he went on deliberately : "You can't keep on running away from life, you know, Rosamund. Or if you do, you can't hope ever to be able to live at peace with yourself."

She looked at him with wide, startled eyes. Then, with a shake of her head, she turned away and John made no attempt to stop her. But he called after her :

"Let me know if there's any way in which I can lend a hand to help Miss Alice !"

Of course she wouldn't call on John for help! Rosamund was determined about that, and really she could not see that it would be necessary to do so. Between them, she and her father had surely thought of everything. She had brought a folding wheelchair down in the car with her, and Mr. Mangell, the ironmonger, had been rung up to see if he could possibly make up a timber ramp so that the chair could be run up and down the two steps from the living quarters to the deck without difficulty. He'd turned up trumps and had brought along not only the ramp but a couple of wooden chocks to keep the chair stationary when required.

Yes, that was all right. Then food. She'd checked that over and made a few useful additions. The Calor gas supply was adequate—the water tank was full. So, if John thought he was going to ingratiate himself by being useful, he'd made a big mistake ! She would be able to manage quite well without his assistance !

She cooked her meal, ate it, though with an indifferent appetite, and cleared up. Then she settled down to read the book she had brought with her. But very soon she found to her surprise that daylight was fading. She looked at her watch. Surely the sun was setting sooner than she remembered it doing before? Oh, but of course it was ! It was that much later in the year now.

She got up to light the lamp, but first she went to the door and peered out. It was all the darker because the moon was in its first quarter. There was a mist lying like a fleecy blanket over the fields and the whisper of an evening breeze stirred the reeds. It was really rather eerie to a town-bred girl. One couldn't help thinking about tramps or poachers—she'd be glad to have Miss Alice's company to-morrow, but in the meantime she'd just have to be sensible about it. Besides, if any marauder came prowling around, she had only to shout and John would come—

She was so angry with herself for thinking of such a thing that she forgot to feel scared any more.

"I'm terribly sorry, my dear, but I just can't manage it," Miss Alice said apologetically, almost in tears. "This plaster makes me so clumsy and I'm so dreadfully afraid of falling."

Everything had gone swimmingly until now. Rosamund had been a little worried lest the ramp might be rather too steep for her to have perfect control when wheeling the chair down it. But that proved to be quite satisfactory. What even Dr. Rob had not thought of was that Miss Alice might have difficulty in getting from the chair to her bed. But here she was, completely unable to make the transfer, even with Rosamund's help.

"How did you manage in hospital?" Rosamund asked anxiously.

"Oh, two nurses," Miss Alice explained. "And of course, they have the knack—oh, I do wish your father was here! He'd know just how to hoick me over!"

"And I'm afraid I don't," Rosamund admitted regretfully. "I'm sorry—"

"But it's not your fault, dear," Miss Alice said quickly. "It's just that I'm being difficult. Shall we try again?"

But by now Rosamund felt as apprehensive as Miss Alice did. She had had little or no nursing experience and Miss Alice was a sturdily built woman. A slip might cause incalculable damage.

"I think—I'd better go and ask John if he'll lend a hand," she said in a high, unnatural voice.

"Oh, do you think he'd mind?" Miss Alice said dubiously. "As a rule, men don't like to have anything to do with illness—"

"As a matter of fact, he offered yesterday to do anything he could to help you," Rosamund told her. "I'll go right away—"

Before she regretted her suggestion to the degree where she couldn't bring herself to make the request that was obviously so necessary—

She took a torch with her and John, evidently seeing its bobbing light, came to the top of the gangplank to meet her.

"Anything wrong?"

Briefly Rosamund explained, thankful that with the light of her torch shining in John's direction, he couldn't see her face clearly.

"Right!" John said briskly. "I'll come at once. Just let me get my torch for the return journey and I'll be with you."

But Rosamund didn't wait for him. She didn't fancy even the short walk with him along the narrow footpath.

"He's coming," she told Miss Alice rather breathlessly, and a moment or so later John looked up in the doorway.

Miss Alice held out her hand to him.

"This is good of you, John! I'm sorry to be such a nuisance."

"Not at all," he replied matter-of-factly. "Obviously the most practical solution. Now, let's study the situation— yes, I think I can scoop you up out of the chair and deposit you safely in bed if Rosamund steadies your plastered foot so that you don't feel the weight of it and it doesn't hit against anything. Ready, Rosamund?"

"Yes," she said briefly.

Between them Miss Alice was settled as comfortably as possible in bed, and unconsciously, Rosamund gave a sigh of relief.

"Splendid!" Miss Alice said gratefully. "But I think I'll read for a little till I get really drowsy, if you wouldn't mind getting my book, dear. I left it on the table."

Rosamund went to get it, but John didn't follow her. He stood looking down at Miss Alice, his expression enigmatic. For a moment their eyes met. John gave a little exclamation and then, impulsively, bent down—and kissed her. A moment later he was gone, but when Rosamund returned, Miss Alice was smiling contentedly.

"I think I shall sleep quite well tonight," she said confidently.

"Yes, I quite agree, Alice, everything is going very smoothly," Dr. Rob said. "All the same, the time is coming when you'll have to leave here—and before very long at that. Autumn's on the way—there's a distinct chill in the air of a morning. If you were normally active, it wouldn't matter too much, but you're not, and the next thing will be that you start getting aches and pains that may not be so easy to get rid of. You don't want that to happen, do you?"

"Of course not," Miss Alice admitted. "But it will be at least another month before the plaster can come off, and you know what they said at the hospital about keeping an eye on me—"

"And *you* know perfectly well that it can easily be arranged for the responsibility to be transferred to a London hospital. And that's what's going to happen," Dr. Rob told her firmly. "No, it's no good you sticking out your chin in that pugnacious way at me, my dear! I know what I'm talking about and you know I do. No matter what the circumstances, I can't have you taking any more risks."

Miss Alice was silent for a moment. Then she looked at him pleadingly.

"Give me another fortnight, Rob. Then I'll do anything you say."

"You will?" he looked at her keenly. "All right, on those terms—"

"Now I've let myself in for it," she said resignedly. "And obviously you've got something up your sleeve. Out with it, Rob, let me know the worst!"

"I don't want you to go to your flat," Dr. Rob explained bluntly. "I want you to stay at mine so that I can keep an eye on you!"

"But Rob, my dear, that will never do!" she objected, a suggestion of unsteadiness in her voice. "What about your professional reputation? Even with Rosamund to chaperone us—"

For a moment Dr. Rob hesitated. Then he took her hand in his.

"There'd be no possibility of gossip, nor for that matter, any need for a chaperone," he said gently, "if you could see your way to becoming my wife, Alice."

When Rosamund heard the news she wasn't surprised. Indeed, she had often wondered why two people, so obviously fond of one another and so admirably suited, hadn't got married long ago. None the less, her feelings were mixed. For her father and Miss Alice she was unfeignedly glad, but she couldn't help wondering just how their approaching marriage would affect her. It was true that they appeared to take it for granted that she would live with them and certainly the Harley Street flat was big enough to accommodate the three of them. But there were other considerations than those. Would she really fit in with their way of life or wouldn't they be happier on their own? That Miss Alice would never do anything to make her feel unwelcome Rosamund was quite sure. She was far too nice a person for that. All the same, the constant presence of a grown-up stepdaughter could become irksome at times, particularly if, as Rosamund knew was the case where she was concerned, she wasn't a happy person or one who had any real interests of her own.

That was the trouble. Her father and Miss Alice would feel obliged to include her in their activities—do their best to "take her out of herself". And that, she was sure, must inevitably restrict their freedom and might even mar their late-found happiness.

And then, from her own point of view, it would be a strain to live with people, however dear, who were always anxious on her behalf. It meant keeping up appearances, and that Rosamund knew would be extremely difficult in her present mood.

She was restless—restless and unsure of herself. She didn't know what she wanted—a fresh start, but one that wasn't haunted by memories? But that was impossible, as impossible as she still felt it to be that there could be any future for John and herself.

John. He was the stumbling block. Her forehead puckered at the thought of him. He had spoken of the chance that luck had given him, and of his intention to make the most of it. But he had done nothing to substantiate that threat. True, he was always available if he was needed in any way, and occasionally, particularly at the weekends when Dr. Rob came down, he would have tea with them. But that was all. He never sought her out, never tried to be alone with her and rarely spoke to her except when conversation was general. They might just have been newly met acquaintances instead of what they really were.

At first it hadn't seemed to make sense. Then, gradually, she realised what John was doing. He was giving her the onus of making the first step towards reconciliation.

"But I won't do it," she told herself mutinously. "It would be almost as if I was to blame if I did. And I wasn't, I wasn't! It was his fault. And why should I risk being hurt all over again? Oh, I shall be thankful when we've left here and he can't be always—always hovering in the background like a storm that may break at any moment! Well, it won't be long now!"

But before they did leave, several things were to happen. To begin with, Dr. Rob insisted that they should get married before he and Miss Alice left for London, and although she protested that nobody ever heard of a bride going to her wedding in an invalid chair, she gave in when he told her firmly that even if she'd been a stretcher case, they'd get married just as he planned.

But he did agree that it should be a very quiet wedding. In fact, he pointed out, there was no need for anyone but John and Rosamund to be present as the necessary witnesses.

Rosamund's heart sank at the prospect. How could she leave the past behind when everything—and sometimes she felt, everybody—conspired to remind her of it? The same words, the same vows that she and John had spoken such a short time ago—she couldn't refuse, of course, but surely John could? She keyed herself up to ask what was practically a favour of him, but John shook his head.

"Sorry, Rosamund, but that's out of the question. For one thing, it's the simplest arrangement and consequently, the best for Miss Alice. But apart from that, I've no wish or intention of hurting their feelings by refusing."

"Oh well, if that's how you feel about it, there's nothing more to be said!" she said frostily.

"But there is," John told her imperatively. "It's going to be *their* day. Nothing should be allowed to spoil it. So will you bury the hatchet for the occasion? Without prejudice, of course."

Rosamund hesitated. Put that way, it was difficult to refuse, as he was perfectly aware. So, though she had the uneasy feeling that he was forcing her hand, she agreed—but with mental reservations.

Rosamund came back from what would be her last visit to the shop to see a stranger pacing impatiently up and down the little deck of the *Seven Stars*. She wondered vaguely who he was, but after all, what business was it of hers? She turned along the towpath only to be hailed by the visitor.

"Hi, there! Any idea when Lindsay will be back?"

Rosamund glanced over her shoulder.

"Not the least," she said indifferently, and went on walking.

But she didn't escape as easily as that. The man not only followed her along the path, he somehow managed to get past her so that she could go no further. She felt uneasy. He looked quite respectable, but none the less, he was obviously worked up about something. And since her father had taken Miss Alice to the hospital for a last check-up, there was no one she could summon.

"Now, listen," the man said urgently. "I don't want to make a nuisance of myself, but I've *got* to see Lindsay. I've written half a dozen times, but he simply doesn't answer. And I'm getting worried. My name's Rutherford, by the way. I'm his publisher—or his would-be publisher, I should say," he added grimly.

"Oh, I see," Rosamund said with relief. "But I'm sorry, it doesn't make any difference. I've no idea how long Mr. Lindsay will be. I didn't even know he'd gone anywhere."

"Oh, confound it" There was unmistakable chagrin in Mr. Rutherford's voice. "That's torn it. I suppose he might not even be coming back at all today."

"I don't know," Rosamund told him firmly. "And now, if you'll excuse me—"

"Wait a minute!" He pondered, frowning. "Look here, do you live on one of the other boats?"

"On the *Pride of London*," Rosamund admitted, nodding in its direction. "But—"

"Well, surely, living in such a small community, you must all be on friendly terms—it would be intolerable not to be. So you must know something of one another's affairs. Surely you can tell me, for instance, if he's writing or not?"

"No, he isn't."

"Sure?"

"My father asked him the same question a few days ago," Rosamund explained. "And that was what Mr. Lindsay said."

And again she felt the unwelcome little stab that John's admission had caused her. He had said it with no show of emotion whatever, but perhaps, just because of that, it hadn't been difficult for her to appreciate why that creative gift of his had failed him. He simply hadn't the heart to write. And she knew why—

"Oh, damn!" Mr. Rutherford sighed gustily. "And all because he was fool enough to marry a twitter-pate of a woman who hadn't the sense to recognise genius when she met it!"

"Genius!" Rosamund repeated, too startled by his use of such a superlative description to give any thought to his unflattering description of herself.

"Downright genius—and I know what I'm talking about," Mr. Rutherford insisted didactically. "Generally speaking, a publisher doesn't hope for too much because he knows he won't get it anyhow. If you could see some of the drivel I get—that doesn't get into print, of course. No, what any publisher goes for is the reasonably sound book that will earn him—and the author, of course—a decent profit. But just now and again something so good turns up that one feels the age of miracles hasn't passed. Lindsay's is the first manuscript that's come my way about which I can say that for years. But it's incomplete. And now you tell me he's stopped writing!" He brooded for a while and then said suddenly: "This girl he married—she's not one of the set he used to run around with. Dropped out of that some time ago. D'you know anything about her? Did he meet her down here?"

"I really can't discuss Mr. Lindsay's affairs," Rosamund told him frigidly. "And now—"

"I think he must have done, you know," Mr. Rutherford went on broodingly. "Probably fell for her because he thought she didn't know about his money—he's extremely well off, you know—only to find that she'd known all along and kept quiet about it until she'd got him safely hooked—"

"It wasn't like that at all," Rosamund burst out furiously. "His money had nothing to do—" she stopped short, realising that Mr. Rutherford was looking at her intently through narrowed eyes.

"You seem to know a lot about it," he commented. "I suppose, by any chance, you don't happen to be the girl in question, do you?"

"Yes," Rosamund said briefly.

"Well, well, well! Quite a coincidence! Odd, though, because you don't look the nitwit, gold-digging type."

"I told you—"

"So you did," Mr. Rutherford nodded. "And as it happens, I believe you, though Lindsay may not have done. Was that it?" He paused expectantly.

"Mr. Rutherford, you really can't expect me—"

"No, I suppose I can't," he agreed with a sigh. "Well, never mind. It's the fact that matters, not the cause. You and he have parted brass rags—"

"Who told you that?" Rosamund interrupted. "John?"

"I told you, I haven't seen him or heard from him since our first meeting. And in any case, surely you know him better than that! He's not the sort to go about snivelling that he's been hurt—and he *has* been. Why else has he stopped writing? Any chance of you making it up? No?" as Rosamund shook her head. "Pity. All that lost talent—"

Silence fell between them. Then, squaring his shoulders, Mr. Rutherford returned to the attack.

"Look, my dear," he said kindly. "It's very clear that you've been hurt as well. But don't you think it's possible that there were faults on both sides? There almost always are, you know. And one has one's pride about being the first to apologise. I know. I've been through it. Most of us have, one way and another. But you, being a woman, haven't got the same stiff-necked attitude about admitting you were in the wrong that a man has. Make the first move, my dear. I don't think you'll regret it—"

He laid his hand gently on Rosamund's shoulder, but when she made no response, he said briskly :

"In that case, I can see nothing for it but to let John speak for himself! Here—" He dropped his hand from her shoulder and unzipped the briefcase he was carrying. "This is a copy of what he's written so far! Read it—and you'll have some idea of the man you've married!" He thrust the bundle of typescript into her arms and Rosamund stood aside to let him pass.

She herself walked slowly on to the *Pride of London* mooring, but once again Mr. Rutherford hailed her and she turned.

"Ever thought how intolerable it would be to live with someone who was absolutely perfect?" he asked pensively. "Somebody who never made a mistake? See what it would mean? You'd always have to be on your best behaviour— never dare to relax because if you put a foot wrong, you'd feel so small, so inferior by comparison! Intolerable, yes, that's the right word! Much better that we should all be imperfect beings!"

He lifted his hand in salutation and strolled along the towpath. Rosamund watched him until he vanished. Then she went slowly back to the *Pride of London*.

It was not until she went to bed that night that Rosamund was able to read the manuscript of John's book without fear of interruption. She drew the curtain close over the window so that the light would not show from outside. Then she punched up the pillows to form a comfortable back rest and got into bed.

The manuscript was lying on the table beside her, and for a moment she looked at it irresolutely. Mr. Rutherford had given it to her to read, but had she really any right to? John hadn't said she might, and without his permission, wasn't it very much like eavesdropping?

Then, as if she was compelled by a force stronger than

herself, she picked it up and turned back the cover. She began to read—

An hour later, when she had come to the end of the four chapters that John had written, she smoothed the last page with a hand that shook.

It hadn't needed Mr. Rutherford's opinion to convince her that John had written something exceptional. It shone in every word.

The characters came alive from the typescript pages— they seemed as real as if she had actually met them. And one wanted to know more about them. They *mattered.*

As for the plot, though there was no more than, perhaps a third or so of the book written, one was already aware of the threads which, each arrestingly interesting in itself, were later going to be woven into an absorbing, satisfying pattern—

But while all that was so clear and though Rosamund could well understand Mr. Rutherford's anxiety for John to finish the book, it was something else which held her enthralled.

There was a perceptiveness, a sensitiveness in the way in which it was written that, more than once, made Rosamund catch her breath. This wasn't just a commercial venture. Nor was it simply a brilliant brain-child. It was something that John had written with his heart's blood.

This was John, fulfilled and whole. The man she had fallen in love with but whom she had come to believe had no existence outside her own dreams.

And yet how could a man be less in stature than the characters he created? And how could he breathe life into them so convincingly if he didn't give them something of himself? She read through several passages again and knew that she was right. It was all here—the aspirations, the hopes, the failings that are part of every human being. And something more. The warmth and tenderness that make life worth while—

It was a long time before Rosamund went to sleep, and when she did, her hand was tucked under the pillow, resting on the manuscript which lay there.

Dr. Rob and Miss Alice were married late one afternoon. They had said nothing of their intentions to anyone but the vicar, but somehow the news had leaked out and there were half a dozen or so inveterate wedding-watchers in the church when they arrived. Dr. Rob pushed Miss Alice in her chair up the aisle and Rosamund and John followed, side by side, but apart so that not even their hands touched.

One could not say that this church was really very much like that other one. It was much newer for one thing, but all churches have similar features, and when the service began Rosamund, listening, was carried back in time.

And John? She stole a cautious glance at him, but he was gazing straight ahead, his face devoid of all expression.

Then it was all over. The register was signed and they went out into the churchyard. Good-byes were said and the two men helped Miss Alice into the big, comfortable car which Dr. Rob had brought down from London. Then they were off—

"Well, that's that," John remarked briskly. "Now, you'll be wanting to get off—"

The arrangement was that Rosamund should follow the newly married couple in the smaller car. Nobody had asked John what he intended to do and he had volunteered no information.

"Yes," Rosamund agreed matter-of-factly, "I must go. Can I give you a lift anywhere?"

"Thanks, no need for that," John told her. "I'm going back to the boat—I can walk."

"Just as you like, of course," Rosamund said carelessly. "I'm going back as well—for something I've forgotten. So—?"

"I'll walk," John said shortly, and set off.

Rosamund got into the car and a moment or so later she passed John in the lane. She parked in the field and was aboard the *Pride of London* when he appeared. He came straight to her.

"I'm rather glad you've come back, Rosamund" he said in a strained voice. "No, you needn't be afraid," as she looked at him with quick, apprehensive eyes. "It's just that it's given me an opportunity of saying something I've had to admit to myself must be said—"

Her eyes dropped and she waited in silence for him to go on.

"It's just this, Rosamund—you've convinced me beyond doubt that—we're finished. It's no good pretending anything else, is it?"

"No, it's no good pretending," Rosamund agreed pensively.

"So this is good-bye, Rosamund," he told her in an oddly mechanical way as if it was a lesson which he had forced himself to learn by heart. "It may take time for you to free yourself of me, but don't worry, I'll see to all the arrangements and you needn't be afraid that I'll ever make a nuisance of myself again to you. I've had my lesson—and loving you as I do, I know that the kindest thing I can do for you, in fact the only thing that may bring you happiness in the future, is to go out of your life entirely."

"I see," Rosamund murmured.

"I suppose—no, it's too much to ask you to forgive me," he said harshly. "All the same, I'd like you to believe that I am truly sorry—"

"Yes." It was little more than a whisper.

"So that's all. Good-bye—and bless you always!" And he turned to go.

"John!"

"Yes?" He stopped but didn't turn back.

"It's going to be a lovely evening—clear and a full moon," she remarked conversationally. "It's a pity to miss it, don't you think? I really feel like putting off going back to London—"

He came back to her then and stood over her threateningly, his hands clenching and unclenching.

"You'll go *now*," he told her savagely. "Otherwise I won't answer—"

"But, John, it was *you* who told me that it was time I stopped running away from life," she reminded him. "And I've come to the conclusion that you were right."

He stared at her incredulously, a muscle flickering at the corner of his mouth.

"Don't try me too high, Rosamund," he said sternly. "I'm only a very ordinary mortal—and there are limits—"

193

"Yes, I think there are," she told him gravely. "Limits to my own stupidity, John."

"What!" His hands shot out and he gripped her by the shoulders—but this time she didn't resist him. "Do you know what you're saying?"

"Yes, I know," she said, her voice vibrant with certainty. "I'm telling you that I know now that there can never be any happiness for me if—I ran away from you, John!" and slipping her arms round his neck, she lifted her face to his.

With a catch of his breath, he caught her in his arms and held her close. The lips that sought hers were passionate, demanding and yet unutterably tender. There was no escape from their searching eagerness, but she had no wish to escape. To his incredulous joy he felt her respond to him as he had never thought could happen again.

When at last his arms slackened round her it was only sufficient for him to look down into her wide, glowing eyes, even now anxious to make sure that it was true. What he saw must have satisfied him, for he held her close again.

"This is—for always!" he told her huskily, and felt her breath against his lips as she repeated : "Always!"

"But *why*?" John asked at length. "What made you change your mind?"

"Oh—" Rosamund said consideringly, twiddling her finger round a button of his jacket, "this and that! Actually—Mr. Rutherford."

"Rutherford?" John said sharply. "How does he come into it?"

"He came down here that day last week when you weren't here," Rosamund explained. "Simply bursting with rage and frustration because you'd stopped writing. He blamed me up hill and down dale for having got in the way of you finishing what he truly believes could be a masterpiece—"

"Now, listen to me, Rosamund," John said sternly, "I don't care a damn if that book would be the best-seller of all time, I won't have you sacrificing yourself—don't you understand, it's your happiness that matters to me, the book is nothing, *nothing* beside that !"

194

Rosamund sighed plaintively.

"Darling, don't jump to conclusions! You've got it the wrong way round. He gave me your manuscript to read because he said that if he couldn't convince me, *that* would."

"Well?"

"I think he was right, John," Rosamund said with conviction. "It is going to be a wonderful book. And I'm glad. But not exactly because it will be a success. It's because—I found you again in it—the you I thought I'd lost. But I hadn't. You were *there*, John!" Her voice lilted with gladness. "The *real* you—the you I loved. Nobody could write like that without being absolutely sincere about it. It was just as Mr. Rutherford said, it spoke for you. Now do you understand?"

"I'm beginning to," John said slowly. "And I don't know which I feel most—triumphant because you should feel like that or humble for—the same reason, I think! Do you understand?"

"I think so," Rosamund said, and gave a little bubbling chuckle which made John smile, though he looked a little puzzled.

"That was a very nice sound—and one that I haven't heard for all too long," he remarked. "But what prompted it just then?"

"Oh, something else Mr. Rutherford said," Rosamund explained. "As a parting shot, he asked me if I realised how dreadful it would be to live with someone who was absolutely perfect. It would mean, he said, that one's own faults stood out so glaringly. And I thought that seeing I can't always make up my mind about things quickly, perhaps it was a good thing that you can't either!"

"Our Mr. Rutherford seems to have talked rather a lot," John remarked tolerantly. "However, in the circumstances, I'll forgive him."

"That's nice of you!" Rosamund commented mischievously. "Personally, I've fallen for him in a big way!"

"Watch it!" John cautioned, half jocular, half serious. "Because I'm not standing for any rivals, Rosamund! You're mine! *Mine!* Understand?"

"That's how I want it to be," Rosamund said contentedly. "Yours! That's everything."

Later, they realised that they must let Dr. Rob and Miss Alice know their change of plans.

"Well, you go to the village and phone them," Rosamund suggested. "While I get us a meal—"

"Yes, I'll do that," John agreed reluctantly. "You'll still be here when I get back, won't you?"

"Yes, I'll be here," she promised seriously.

Half an hour later he was back again. *Rosebud* and the *Pride of London* were in darkness, but bright beams of light shone out from the uncurtained window of the *Seven Stars*.

John cleared the gangplank in two quick strides, confident of the welcome that awaited him.

THE LONELY ROAD

The Lonely Road

When Dick Corbett jilted her on the morning of their wedding day, Lucy courageously set out to build a life without him.

She found a pleasant job as a secretary to an author. And it was Owen Vaughan, her employer's nephew, who helped Lucy gather up the pieces of her shattered dream.

But Fate played cruel tricks. For among the first people Lucy met in her new life were Dick and his bride!

CHAPTER I

LUCY sat up in bed and crowed with sheer delight. The night before she had left her curtain wide open so that the moment she woke up she would be able to see just what sort of day it was. It was so very, very important that at least it should be dry because this was the most important day of her life—her wedding day.

At half past eleven that very morning she and Dick were to be married. And here, just as if it had been ordered along with the wedding cake and the champagne, was a perfect April day. The blue sky hadn't so much as a puffle of cloud in it and the sunshine poured in at the window. There was only one description for it—bride's weather.

Smiling contentedly, Lucy lay back on her pillows, her hands linked above her head. Gently she twisted the engagement ring that Dick had given her a year previously. To Lucy it was the most beautiful ring in the world, not because Dick had spent far more money on it than perhaps he ought to have done, but because it was the outward and visible sign of his love for her, just as the plain one he would give her in a few hours' time was the proof that their love would last for ever.

Dreamily she recalled the beginning of their love story. There had not, perhaps, been anything dramatic about it, but from the very beginning it had felt so *right*.

Fifteen months previously they had met at a wedding in the Surrey village where Lucy lived. They had not been among the principal characters, which was just as well, for it left them free of the duties which fall to a best man or a bridesmaid, and so they had been able to spend all their time together. And that was just what they wanted for, as Dick afterwards said,

"Even before we were introduced, I *knew!*" And Lucy, starry-eyed, had whispered that so had she.

Dick, a native of Sheffield, had intended going back early on Sunday, but he changed his plans. He would catch the latest possible train so that they could have as many hours together as possible.

It had been quite dreadful, saying goodbye that evening, but they wrote long letters to one another and had such protracted telephone conversations that Lucy's father had said they ought to get a reduced rate for quantity!

Of course, everybody who saw them together knew that they were in love, but though they had no doubts themselves, they decided not to announce their engagement until they had known each other a few months. Actually, it was Lucy's idea.

"I just couldn't *bear* it if there was a fuss," she had said earnestly. "It would—it would—well, of course, it wouldn't spoil everything. Nothing could. But all the same—"

At first Dick had not seen why there should be a fuss. He had a reasonably decent job with excellent prospects. He had a nice little sum of money in the bank, left to him by his parents, and it wasn't as if he was the rackety type. What more could anyone ask of a young man of twenty-seven?

"Oh, not *that* sort of thing," Lucy had replied.

"Then, for goodness' sake, what?"

"Just—we haven't known each other very long, and I think, perhaps, Mummy and Daddy might worry that we should change our minds."

Lucy was very fond of her parents and she was their only child, so she felt her attitude was not only natural but reasonable. Dick, left an orphan at an early age, didn't see it that way.

"*I* shan't change," he had declared emphatically.

"Nor shall I," Lucy had insisted as positively. "So

we're quite safe to wait—just a little while, aren't we ? And I'd rather we suggested it than be asked to."

And Dick, though he had grumbled a little, had given in, but he had stuck out that the engagement should not be longer than six months. In the end, that had turned out to be impossible. Dick had been transferred by his firm to a branch in Leicester, and as that had meant promotion and really hard work, he had been compelled to tell Lucy that it was out of the question for him to have time off for a honeymoon for some time to come—unless, of course, they got married but postponed their honeymoon ?

They talked it over, and in the end, decided to wait. It had been something of a heartbreak, particularly when the day they had originally planned as their wedding day came and passed just like any other day. But now all that was over. In another few hours—

Lucy slid out of bed and crossed the sun-warmed floor to her wardrobe. Almost holding her breath, she opened one of its doors and gazed at her wedding dress, still encased in its cover of protecting plastic. It was a very lovely dress, soft and lacy and thoroughly feminine. It had cost Lucy a lot of money, but in her mind's eye was a picture of Dick turning as she came up the aisle—and she knew that nothing but the best was good enough.

In an otherwise empty drawer of her dressing table was her veil and the little coronet of orange blossom she would wear—she looked at them and sighed with pure bliss. How lucky she was, she thought, that she had the sort of hair, honey-coloured and thick, that did just what one wanted it to without any bother. Other brides might have to worry about a last-minute set, but she didn't.

There were sounds of people moving about the house now. Collie, their nondescript dog who was anything but a collie, barked because he knew that the drawing of the bolt on the front door meant he was going to be taken out for his early morning walk. There was a gentle tinkle of china and Lucy slipped back into bed because, last night, Mrs. Darvill had told her that she should have her breakfast in bed, and would not listen to any protests. Darling Mummy, not too happy at losing her only child, but certainly not going to spoil this heavenly day with tears or reproaches.

A delicious smell of bacon and coffee wafted up from the kitchen. Lucy, suddenly discovering that she was hungry, plumped up the pillows behind her and waited in happy anticipation. A moment or two later her mother came in bearing a daintily laid tray which she set on Lucy's knees.

"There you are, darling. And what a lovely day you've got !" she said, kissing the happy face that was lifted to hers.

"M'm !" Lucy sniffed appreciatively. "This smells heavenly ! Has the postman come yet ?"

Mrs. Darvill laughed.

"You're surely not expecting a letter from Dick this morning ?" she asked. "Why, you'll be seeing him in just a little while !"

"Yes, I know," Lucy answered. "But you see, there wasn't one yesterday, and travelling down as late as he had to, it wasn't really possible to telephone—has he come, Mummy ?"

"Feel in my apron pocket," Mrs. Darvill said teasingly. "There might just be something !"

Lucy took out four letters from the pocket, and one was from Dick. She tucked that under her pillow and opened the others while her mother waited.

"A cheque from Aunt Millie," she announced. "A very generous one, too. And a letter from Mrs. Marchment saying that they're bringing their present with them because they had to order it and it didn't come in time to post. And—" she burst out laughing, "a very agitated note from Mr. Keane asking if I have any idea what has happened to the Pottinger and Pringle file ! Poor darling, he's always popping things into his own drawers and forgetting. I expect that's what it is this time !"

"Poor Mr. Keane, he'll miss you," Mrs. Darvill remarked. "After all, you were his secretary for three years, and the new girl must have a lot to learn."

"I'll ring her up before he gets to the office and tell her to look in his desk. He hates having to admit that he's absent-minded."

"Well, now get on with your breakfast," Mrs. Darvill suggested. "When you've read Dick's letter, of course !"

She went out of the room and Lucy opened the letter. It was not very long—

Then, without any warning, the world stood still. Lucy's world, at any rate. She stared at the lines of Dick's easy flowing hand—stared and felt her heart turn to ice, for what he had written was not capable of misinterpretation.

"I can't go through with it, Lucy. I thought I could, but there are some things stronger than common decency.

"I know I'm an utter swine, letting you down like this, particularly at the last moment, and there is only one thing I can say in extenuation—I'm doing you less of an injury by backing down than I would be if I married you. You deserve a better chap than I am.

"Forgive me if you can.

      Dick."

The sunny room was very silent and still. Then, with a strange conviction that she was somehow standing outside herself, controlling a situation that silly, happy Lucy Darvill could never have coped with, she folded the letter with hands that were quite steady, and slid it back into its envelope.

With the deliberate movements of an automaton she put the breakfast tray on the bedside table, got out of bed and put on her dressing gown and slippers. Then she went downstairs.

Passing the open drawing-room door she noticed the perfume of the flowers with which it was decorated, and caught a glimpse of the wedding cake's white elegance. But neither meant anything to her now. Hearing her parents' voices, she walked unwaveringly to the kitchen and stood framed in the doorway.

"Did I leave something off the tray?" Mrs. Darvill asked. And then, seeing her girl's frozen face: "Darling, what is it? Tell Mummy!"

"There—won't be any wedding." Lucy said in a toneless voice entirely devoid of feeling. "Dick—has changed his mind."

They stared at her, unable to take it in. Then, with a little cry, Mrs. Darvill put her arms round her, only to feel as if it was a wooden doll she held.

"Darling, there must be some mistake—" she insisted. "Dick would never—"

"You'd better read it," Lucy said listlessly, and took the letter out of her pocket.

They read it in silence, and when they had finished it, Mrs. Darvill was in tears and Mr. Darvill was muttering fiercely under his breath. It would have gone hard with Dick Corbett if he had turned up at that moment!

"I think it would be a good idea, Daddy, if you were to ring up the Rector at once," Lucy heard herself say in a matter-of-fact way. "Then he can let the organist and the choirmaster know."

"Yes," Mr. Darvill said heavily. "I'll do that."

"And then," Lucy went on, "telegrams or telephone messages to as many people as we can possibly manage—"

Beyond words, Mr. Darvill nodded and went out to

the telephone. They heard him ask for the Rectory number and then Mrs. Darvill pushed the kitchen door shut. Lucy went to the window and stood staring out at the garden, gay with the daffodils Mr. Darvill had been assiduously cultivating for this day.

"Did you—did you eat your breakfast?" Mrs. Darvill asked, thinking that surely one of the hardest things in life is to see your own child suffer and be unable to do anything to ease her pain.

Lucy shook her head.

"And by now, it's all cold and unappetising," Mrs. Darvill said briskly. "Well, you shall have a glass of milk instead. That will keep you going quite nicely."

Because it was too much trouble to protest, Lucy drank the milk. When she put down the empty glass Mrs. Darvill asked the question that had been in her mind since the moment Lucy had broken the news to them.

"Darling, what are you going to do?"

Lucy shrugged her shoulders. What did it matter what she did?

"I know, Lucy, but you must make up your mind. Would you like us to cancel our holiday—?"

Mr. and Mrs. Darvill, shrinking from the thought of the empty house, had decided to start their own holiday the following day.

"No, no, certainly not, Mummy," Lucy said so quickly that Mrs. Darvill flinched.

"Then would you like to come with us?"

Lucy hesitated.

"I'd like to go away," she said slowly. "But—but please do try to understand, I'd like to go alone—and be among strangers. They wouldn't know—"

"Yes, I see what you mean," Mrs. Darvill refused to allow herself to feel hurt. There was something in what the child said. "But you know, darling, we shall be rather anxious—"

207

"You needn't worry," Lucy said composedly. "I shan't do anything silly—and I shan't have time to mope because—I shall get a job. That's what I want," she added, almost under her breath. "To work hard—"

"But, darling, you can't just go into the blue and hope to find a job—" Mrs. Darvill protested. "Wouldn't it be better—?"

"You don't understand, Mummy," Lucy explained patiently. "I have a definite job in mind." She glanced at the alarm clock, ticking away on the table. "It's too early to do anything about it yet, but I should think by the time Daddy has finished telephoning—"

"Yes, but what is the job, dear—and where?" Mrs. Darvill asked anxiously.

"Mr. Keane has a sister who lives somewhere near Lyme Regis," Lucy explained. "She is an invalid—rheumatoid arthritis—and she wants a secretary-companion. He told me about it a week or so ago and asked me if I knew anyone suitable. If she hasn't found anyone—and if I can go today, I think it would be quite a good idea."

Mrs. Darvill turned away so that Lucy should not see the tears that sprang to her eyes. Instead of a honeymoon, a job with an elderly invalid woman who, more than likely, was difficult to get on with.

"Quite a good idea," she said briskly. "I'll tell your father."

* * *

No more than a few hours later Lucy left Waterloo for Lyme Regis.

Mr. Keane had been most helpful. He had accepted Lucy's statement that she was not, after all, going to be married with no other comment than an offer of her old job. This Lucy had refused gently but firmly, and had enquired whether his sister was still without a secretary-companion. It appeared that she was and that the matter was becoming increasingly urgent as Mrs. Mayberry was anxious to start a new book—she wrote historical novels—and because of her infirmity could not write or type for sustained periods.

Yes, Mr. Keane thought Lucy would do admirably for the job, and no, he could see no reason why she should not leave for Lyme that very day. He would telephone to his sister at once and then ring through to Lucy to tell her the result.

When, half an hour later, he spoke to Lucy again it was to tell her that his sister was delighted at the news, and suggested that she should travel by a train leaving Waterloo at one o'clock, and had promised to see that she was met the other end.

And then Mr. Keane had earned Lucy's undying gratitude. He wished her success in the venture, remarking in the most casual way that he had not told Mrs. Mayberry any of Lucy's private business. Simply that she wanted a change of work.

So here Lucy was, on her way to start a new life among strangers, her broken romance and everything connected with it left behind. On the rack above her head was a suitcase—not one of the glamorous new set that had been one of the wedding presents—and in it there was not a single garment that had formed part of her trousseau.

She was still in that strange, detached frame of mind, conscious less of any personal grief than of pity for the girl who had been Lucy Darvill—a quite sincere feeling, but not one having any connection with herself.

The journey would take about four hours or so, and though there was a restaurant car, Mrs. Darvill had realised that in her present mood Lucy was unlikely to bother about food, and had wisely insisted on packing a few sandwiches. Even these Lucy forgot until nearly half past two, when she ate them more because she did not want to risk collapsing with hunger as soon as she met her new employer than because she felt any need for food. Later, because the journey seemed interminable, she went along to the restaurant car for tea to help pass the time. And then, at last, the train drew into Lyme Regis station.

She got out of the train with her suitcase, and looked vaguely about her. A considerable number of other passengers had also left the train, quite a few of whom were being met, so that the platform was quite crowded. It was impossible to pick out anyone who had come to meet her, so Lucy waited until everyone else had gone—everyone else, that is, except a tall man in grey flannels and an open-necked shirt to whom Lucy took an instantaneous and unreasonable dislike. For one thing, she could not help feeling that the casual crimson cravat he was wearing had been especially chosen because the colour suited his dark handsomeness—oh yes, he was handsome, Lucy admitted grudgingly—and no doubt knew it. But besides that, he was scowling most unpleasantly as he came towards her.

"Miss Darvill ?" he asked coldly.

"Yes, I'm Lucy Darvill," she acknowledged with an upward inflection of her voice.

"I'm Mrs. Mayberry's nephew, Owen Vaughan," he told her, and then, picking up her case, he turned his back on her and began striding towards the exit. Lucy followed, vaguely wondering why he was in such a bad temper, but not really very much interested.

In the station courtyard stood an open sports car. Owen Vaughan dropped the case on the back seat and without a word held open the door for Lucy to get in. With a murmured "Thank you," she took her place and a moment later they were on their way.

The station lay to the back of the town and Owen Vaughan turned in the opposite direction from it. None the less they were on a busy main road, and more than once, with a deepening scowl, Owen had to drop to a crawl while the tangled traffic sorted itself out.

Neither of them spoke until Lucy, stirred from her apathy by his boorishness, remarked with a show of spirit that since it had obviously been a nuisance for him to have met her, wouldn't it have been possible for a car to have been hired?

Owen Vaughan laughed shortly.

"At the very last moment—on a Saturday in late April? My good girl, all the cars for miles around are booked up with wedding engagements. Except for June, April is one of the most popular months for weddings that there are, you know."

Involuntarily Lucy shrank a little in her seat, but she managed to say in quite a controlled voice:

"Yes, I suppose so. I hadn't thought of that. I'm sorry you were forced to come to my rescue, Mr. Vaughan."

Owen gave her a quick, puzzled look. Something in the way she had spoken had caused his anger to evaporate to a perplexing degree—but he was not entirely appeased.

"Why was there such a deuce of a hurry for you to come today?" he demanded.

"It suited Mrs. Mayberry—and it suited me," Lucy said coldly.

"I grant you it suits Aunt Louise." Owen admitted. "She's been like a cat on hot bricks for the last month, wanting to get on with her book. All the same, the suggestion came from *you*, via Uncle Stanley." He gave her another quick, searching look. "Well, I want to know why!"

Lucy did not reply, and after a moment Owen said very deliberately:

"I've always found secretiveness a most unpleasant

trait in anyone's character. To me it smacks of—under-handedness."

"Evidently you feel about that just as I do about unjustifiable inquisitiveness." Deliberately Lucy mimicked the way he had spoken. "To me it smacks of—bad manners."

For a moment there was silence. Then, as if he were faintly amused, Owen remarked:

"I see—mutual mistrust and dislike! Well, at least we know where we are, which is something, no doubt!"

For the rest of the trip there was no conversation.

•   •   •

Spindles, Mrs. Mayberry's home, lay well off the Uplyme Road. One reached it by twisting, turning lanes that led up and down sharp little hills to a five-barred gate which Owen jumped out and opened. This, presumably, was the drive to the house, although until they passed a small coppice there was no sign of any building.

Then, abruptly, one saw Spindles, mellow, elegant and strangely tranquil. Involuntarily Lucy gasped, not only because of its beauty, but because of its size. Spindles fell a lot short of being a stately mansion, but it was certainly a very large house—larger than any that had previously come into Lucy's life.

"Lovely, isn't it?" Owen remarked, evidently forgetting their recent clash in his own appreciation of the house. "I've always thought myself very lucky that it happened to be on the market just as I was able to buy it."

"You—bought it?" Lucy exclaimed. "But I thought —"

"That it belonged to Aunt Louise?" he finished with, again, that slightly amused smile. "Oh no, it's mine all right. But when Uncle Ben—her husband—died, I suggested that she should come and live here. There's plenty of room—she has a complete suite to herself—and the arrangement suits us both. She doesn't have to worry about household arrangements and I know, if I'm abroad as I often am, that the house isn't getting musty by being shut up."

"I see," Lucy said briefly. This was something for which she had not bargained, but perhaps he would be going abroad soon—

"I'm afraid not," he announced ironically, just as if she had spoken aloud. "As a matter of fact, I've only just got back from America. I shall be here for at least six months."

"How interesting," Lucy commented in a voice completely devoid of interest or any other feeling.

And was almost certain that Owen chuckled very quietly to himself.

• • •

If Lucy had taken an instant dislike to Owen, the reverse was the case when she met Mrs. Mayberry. She was waiting for them in her wheelchair on the sunny terrace, and although she made no attempt to get up to greet Lucy, her whole bearing expressed a welcome.

In her youth Louise Mayberry had been a beautiful woman, and even now in her middle fifties and marked by the indelible lines of constant pain, she caught and held attention.

Her hair was snowy white, cut short but thick and curly. Without the skilful make-up she so gallantly used her clear skin would have been entirely devoid of colour, but as it was, the hollows under her cheekbones hardly showed. Her mouth was both sensitive and strong, but it was her eyes that Lucy noticed most. They were big and dark and vital. The spirit that lived in the twisted body shone through them, refusing pity for itself though not lacking in sympathy with the troubles of others.

And now, as this tall, fair girl walked towards her, Louise Mayberry could not help wondering, though she was careful to suppress any signs of curiosity. That there was something wrong was obvious, even if there had not been that insistence to come here at once which had so clearly indicated a desire for escape. But there were more indications than that. Her new secretary companion's smile had a fixed quality about it, and it went no farther than the soft pink lips. The dark blue eyes were no more than dim, deep pools, entirely lacking in expression of any sort. Clearly the poor child had had a bad shock and it was as yet too recent for feeling to have returned. When it did—

Louise smiled and held out her hand.

"I can't tell you how welcome you are, my dear," she said warmly. "I'm just *itching* to get on with my book and I'd almost given up hope of ever finding someone suitable to help me."

Very gently Lucy took the proffered hand in hers. It was badly twisted and through its fragility she could feel the bones, slender as a bird's.

"I hope that I shall be able to do what you want," Lucy said sincerely. "It will be different from the work I did for Mr. Keane."

Instead of protesting that, of course she would—a remark which could only have been an insincerity since, so far, Lucy was a stranger to her, Louise simply nodded and turned to Owen, a silent listener to the conversation.

"Owen dear, will you take Miss Darvill indoors and ask Bertha to take her to her room? I am sure she would like a wash after what must have been a hot and tiring journey. Bertha is our guardian angel," she went on lightly to Lucy. "She looks after both of us— and sometimes she bullies us. That, of course, is natural where Owen is concerned—" she flashed him a mischievous look, "because she was once his nanny, and to a nanny, her charges never grow up."

"It still astounds me that she's ever given up asking it I've washed behind my ears and cleaned my nails," Owen put in with a gaiety which surprised Lucy. Evidently there was another side to his nature than the surly one she had so far encountered!

The house was cool and shady after the bright sunshine, and, in fact, Lucy stumbled because her eyes had not become adjusted to the difference in light. Instantly a strong hand shot out and steadied her.

"Careful!" Owen said warningly. "No need to hurry."

Quickly Lucy released herself, murmuring a word of apology, and then, to her relief, a woman in a severely plain blue dress, so obviously a one-time nanny that she must be Bertha, came into the hall from the back of the house.

"This is Miss Darvill, Bertha," Owen explained.

Bertha inclined her head graciously.

"I'm very glad to see you, miss," she announced. "Madam has been needing a young lady to help her, it has really worried her, not being able to get on with her work. This way, please, miss. Is that all your luggage? If you'll put it down, Mr. Owen, I'll get John to take it up."

"I'll tell him," Owen offered, and with a slight pursing of her lips, Bertha agreed to this.

Feeling that she was suddenly a child again, and that in some way it was her fault that she had not come here sooner, Lucy followed the sturdy figure up the thickly carpeted stairs and along a corridor.

"Here we are," Bertha announced, throwing open a door and standing back for Lucy to pass her.

It was a beautiful room, although Lucy was not in a frame of mind to appreciate it in detail. What she

215

did realise was that, short though the notice had been, every care had been taken to give those personal touches that mean so much. The windows were wide open so that the room was pleasantly fresh, there were flowers on the mantelpiece and dressing table, and a selection of books and magazines lay on the bedside table. Realising that Bertha was waiting expectantly, Lucy turned to her with a smile.

"How very nice you've had it made for me."

Bertha looked gratified, not only because this young lady evidently knew the proper way things ought to be done, but also because she realised that Bertha herself, though responsible, had actually given orders for the room to be prepared.

"And this is your bathroom, miss," she explained, opening another door. "I think that's all, but if there's anything you want, ring the bell and one of the maids will come. Ah, here's John with your case. Would you like to have it unpacked for you?"

"Thank you, I can see to that," Lucy told her, but Bertha still lingered.

"Dinner is at half past seven, miss," she announced. "And if you don't mind me telling you, dress isn't in the least formal when the family is alone. Just an ordinary summer dress would do nicely."

"I see." Lucy began to wish she would go, but she had realised by now that Bertha was a law unto herself. She came and went as she saw fit. "Thank you, Bertha."

And then, with a final comprehensive look round the room, Bertha did at last leave her.

It did not take Lucy very long to unpack, tidy herself and change. Then she was left wondering what she should do. There was still nearly an hour before dinner. Ought she to stay in her room until nearer the time for it, or should she go downstairs? A glance from her window which overlooked the terrace showed that there was no one there, so presumably both Mrs. Mayberry and Owen were making preparations for the evening. Lucy decided to go and sit outside until something happened.

She retraced her steps to the hall, but before she reached the door she was intercepted by Owen who appeared from one of the rooms. He had changed into a lightweight summer suit which had the effect of making him appear a taller and more imposing figure.

"My aunt is having a little rest," he told her. "Do come in, we usually have drinks before dinner. Can I get you something?"

The last thing Lucy wanted was a tête-à-tête with Owen, but it would be difficult to refuse his offer without appearing ungracious, so she asked for a sherry and followed him into the room.

While he got her drink, Lucy took a quick look round. It was an interesting room, for though it was extremely beautiful, it was evident that it was not only well loved but well used. Much of the furniture, she guessed, was antique and very valuable, but nothing had been chosen for that reason alone. Chairs and sofas were obviously there because they were comfortable to sit on, and there was plenty of room to move about unhindered by the presence of small, niggling pieces of furniture which Lucy had always disliked.

"I hope everything in your room is as you like it?" Owen asked her politely as he handed her a glass.

"Thank you, yes," Lucy told him. "There were even flowers there. I think that was marvellous, seeing what short notice your staff had that the room was needed."

She was, she knew, taking the war into the enemy's camp, but she felt that in doing so she was robbing Owen of an opportunity for saying something much like that himself. Owen, however, was apparently not in a combative mood.

"Bertha prides herself on those little feminine touches," he said gravely. "Personally, I bar flowers in my room. They always get in the way, and it's incredible how far the water in a small vase goes."

Lucy did not reply. She did not really hear what he said, for she had just noticed that beside her on the sofa where she was sitting was an evening paper. At first she had only glanced casually at it and then, incredibly, she realised that she was looking down at a photograph of Dick.

But it was not a photograph of Dick alone. Hanging on to his arm and looking up at him with adoring eyes was a pretty girl. And the caption, dancing before her eyes, read :

"Millionaire's Daughter Weds Father's Employee."

CHAPTER II

"Miss Darvill ! *Miss Darvill !*"

Someone was saying Lucy's name over and over again. The voice was both urgent and anxious, but to Lucy's ears it seemed no more than the buzzing of a fly—maddeningly persistent but entirely meaningless. She made an impatient little gesture with her hands to make it stop.

Then strong hands gripped her shoulders and shook her sharply.

"Miss Darvill, you must pull yourself together ! My aunt may be in at any moment and I cannot have her distressed by seeing you in this condition."

Because it needed more strength than she could find to resist that authoritative voice, Lucy allowed herself to be dragged from the dark swirling waters that had engulfed her, and opened her eyes. For a moment she did not know where she was. Then she realised that Owen Vaughan was standing over her, and memory returned. Dick, married to another girl—Lucy gave a little shuddering moan and closed her eyes again.

"None of that !" Owen said roughly. "You fainted, but you're all right now. Do you hear ? You're all right !"

Lucy moistened her dry lips.

"Yes—I'm—all right," she muttered with an effort. If only he would leave her alone !

But that Owen had no intention of doing.

"Excellent !" he approved bracingly. "Now drink some of this."

He put her glass into her hand and instinctively Lucy's fingers closed round its slender stem. But when she raised it to her lips, it chattered so against her lips that she could not drink. Owen's hand closed round hers, steadying it and forcing her to sip the wine.

After a moment she tried to push his hand away.

219

"No more," she whispered, but Owen was relentless.

"Every drop !" he insisted, and mechanically Lucy obeyed.

"That's better," he announced, setting the glass down. "And now, you will kindly tell me just what made you faint ?"

"Oh—" Desperately Lucy sought an explanation— any explanation but the true one. "Just the heat, I expect—and the journey—"

Owen drew up a chair and sat down facing her.

"Now I should have thought you were far too young and too healthy a girl to be knocked out by a comparatively short journey on a day that is really no more than pleasantly warm," he announced with detestable persistence. "Tell me, do you often keel over like this ? Because if so, I can't see you being much use to my aunt and I think the best thing you can do is to go straight back home first thing in the morning !"

"Oh, no !" In her alarm, Lucy sat up straight and faced him defiantly. "I can't do that !"

"No ? Why not ?" And when Lucy did not reply he went on : "Are you in trouble at home ? Have you run away ?"

"No, no—nothing like that," Lucy insisted. "Truly not."

"You mean, your parents know where you are ?" Lucy nodded.

"I see." Owen leaned back in his chair. "Yet, for some reason or other, you wanted to get away from your home in a considerable hurry, and you don't want to go back. Is that a fair statement of fact ?"

"Yes," Lucy admitted. What else was there to say ?

"I'm going to find out the reason for that, you know," Owen told her very softly.

"No," Lucy said desperately. "It—it's nothing of which I need be ashamed, but it isn't—"

"Isn't my business ?" Owen suggested, and now he

leaned forward very close to her. "But you see, I intend to make it my business! As I told you, I don't like secretiveness, and as I haven't told you but you may have realised for yourself, I am very fond of my aunt. That adds up to the fact that I don't intend to have her worried by your troubles, and so I intend to get to the bottom of them. Well?"

Lucy shook her head, her lips set in a straight line.

Owen glanced at his watch.

"Time is getting on," he remarked conversationally. "So, rather than waste time in convincing you that I mean exactly what I say, *I'll tell you* what happened today!"

"No!" Lucy cowered away from him. "You can't— you can't possibly know!"

"My dear girl, it's as plain as a pikestaff!" Owen said impatiently. "First of all, when Uncle Stanley rang through this morning he told Aunt Louise that you had been his confidential secretary until quite recently, and that he could thoroughly recommend you. Which means that you had not left in disgrace and also that you have had some time in which to look round for a job—you could even have suggested coming here some weeks ago. But no, it wasn't until today that you suddenly made up your mind you must leave home at once."

Lucy turned her head away. He was intolerable— and he was very clever, too.

"Now," he went on deliberately, "I can think of only one explanation that fits in with all that. You left my uncle's office because you intended to get married." He paused, but when Lucy made no reply he went on: "You do realise, don't you, that if you don't refute what I'm saying, it's as good as an admission?" Another pause. "Well, to continue. I think that you expected to be married today—and that at the last moment, your boy friend jilted you. Am I right?"

Lucy's hands flew up to cover her face. How could he—how could he! Didn't he realise that he was torturing her?

"What's more," the hateful voice went on deliberately, "I think that picture in the paper is of the young man in question, and that until you saw it you had a sneaking hope in your heart that it wasn't final because you had no idea that he was marrying another girl today instead of you!"

Lucy's hands dropped to her lap. What was the good of trying to deny it? He was too clever!

"You're quite right on all counts, Mr. Vaughan," she said listlessly. "And I think perhaps it would be better if I did leave tomorrow."

"Oh, I don't see that," Owen said judicially. "Not now that you've owned up. As you said, it's nothing of which you need be ashamed."

Not ashamed—but humiliated, hurt beyond endurance, needing only a hole in which to hide—

"You don't understand," she said hurriedly. "My whole reason for leaving home was that I wanted to be among strangers—people who didn't know—and now that you know—" she shrugged her shoulders helplessly.

"Yes, I see your point," he agreed. "I think I might feel the same in similar circumstances. Although—" he rubbed his hand thoughtfully over his chin, "perhaps not for quite the same reason."

"What do you mean?" Lucy demanded suspiciously.

"Well, what I am wondering is, are you simply running away from what has happened—refusing to face up to it? Or have you made up your mind to make a fresh start?"

"I don't know," Lucy admitted. "But one thing I do know—I don't want anybody's pity. And now that you know—"

"My good child, I don't pity you, I think you've had

222

an extremely fortunate escape," Owen told her bluntly. "Haven't you realised yet how lucky you are that this has happened *before* you were married ? It might have been afterwards !"

"Oh, no, no !" Lucy protested. "It couldn't—"

"Oh, yes, it could," he insisted. He picked the paper up and studied the photograph. "Of course, you never realised it, but that young man has a thoroughly weak face—his chin recedes and his eyes are too close together. He is the sort that will always take the line of least resistance—particularly when it pays him to !"

"How dare you !" Lucy stormed. "You don't know anything about him—"

"Do you ?"

He shot the two words at her, and Lucy flinched. She had thought she knew Dick as intimately as she knew herself—but now she knew that wasn't true.

Without comment, Owen turned back to the paper and began to read.

"Miss Gwenda Kelsall, only child of millionaire property owner Lawrence Kelsall, after her marriage today at Caxton Hall to Mr. Richard Corbett. Mr. Kelsall is at present in America and is unaware of his daughter's marriage, but this seemed to cause the young couple no misgivings since, as the bride confidently remarked: 'Daddy never says no if I really want something—and I certainly wanted—' "

Lucy snatched the paper from him and crumpled it fiercely in her hands.

"You're enjoying this, aren't you ?" she flared. "You like hurting people—you're cruel, sadistic—"

"Not at all," Owen said calmly. "I'm actually doing the kindest thing possible—making you realise that you've lost nothing worth having. That should enable you to get over your lovelornness in the shortest possible time—that, and the fact that you've surely got sufficient selfrespect not to allow yourself to give another thought to—a married man !''

"You mean, though we've only known each other a few hours you feel enough concern to go to all this trouble on my behalf ?" Lucy said scornfully.

"Naturally. We shall be living under the same roof for some time, and if I can sting you into showing some pride I shan't have to put up with seeing you mooning about like a rag doll with its stuffing running out !"

Lucy glared at him in speechless indignation. He was intolerable, absolutely intolerable, and she was completely at his mercy because, in his arrogance, he recognised none of the limitations which good manners or kindliness impose. He thought simply of his own comfort and convenience, no matter who suffered thereby.

"Oh, I admit that my motives aren't disinterested," he told her coolly, just as if he had read her thoughts. "But all the same, I've already done you quite a bit of good ! It's a far healthier state of affairs for you to have lost your temper with me than for you to be fainting all over the place. Why, you've even got quite an attractive colour in your cheeks." He regarded her with his head on one side. "And your eyes are positively sparkling. Temper suits you, my child !"

Lucy clenched her hands and made a terrific effort to speak calmly.

"You would be more accurate if you referred to my 'temper' as more than justifiable anger," she said. "Hasn't it occurred to you that you've poked and pried into my private affairs in an absolutely disgusting way —and that you've shown no consideration for my feelings—"

"I thought you said you didn't want pity ?" he interpolated.

"Nor do I," Lucy countered swiftly. "All I want is to be left alone—"

"We'd better get this straightened out," Owen announced firmly. "Without giving any warning that you were in a highly emotional—one might almost say distraught—condition, you inflict yourself upon people who have every right to assume that you are a perfectly normal, balanced young woman who is prepared to behave rationally and to work hard. In the circumstances, can you honestly blame me if I take what steps I deem fit to make sure that you do come up to that specification?"

"From your point of view, I suppose not," Lucy admitted grudgingly. "But I think someone wiser and kinder than you might have found another way—have *you* ever been really up against it, Mr. Vaughan?"

"No," he answered unhesitatingly, "I haven't. But that state of affairs can't be expected to continue indefinitely, of course. I shall meet my Waterloo sooner or later. And when I do—"

"You'll meet it like a hero!" Lucy finished mockingly. "I'm sure you will, Mr. Vaughan. Insensitive people get off fairly lightly, you know."

He regarded her thoughtfully. He had thought her a colourless, spineless personality, but really, there was more to her than he had imagined could possibly be the case.

"All right, we'll leave me out," he announced. "After all, what I might do in similar circumstances can only be guesswork. All the same, I do know something about suffering. Take my aunt, for instance. Not so very long ago she had a husband whom she adored and who adored her. What's more, they were really good friends—which is something different again. He died tragically and unexpectedly. Then, two or three years ago, this damned arthritis got a grip of her. It's hopeless and she knows it. She's never out of pain—

sometimes desperate pain. But as you will find out when you know her better, she has courage and endurance—I'd give all I've got to be able to do something for her—" he finished with sudden fury.

Lucy was startled. It was the first indication he had shown of having any feeling for others' suffering, and she felt at a disadvantage.

"Not quite such a brute as you thought?" he suggested ironically. "Disappointing, isn't it? But to continue—there's dear old Bertha. Years ago she was engaged to a boy she'd known all her life. They'd had to wait because he'd got an invalid mother to provide for and he hadn't got enough money to get married as well. Well, the war came, the old lady died and they were to be married on his next leave. But he never had it. He was killed. But does she moan? Never!"

"But there's a difference—" Lucy began stormily—and stopped short.

"Yes, there is, isn't there?" Owen said deliberately. "*They* can think of their men with pride and love. You—"

Lucy sprang to her feet.

"But that's just it—" and stopped short because Owen's expression had completely altered. It was as though, because at last he had made her admit the truth, he was satisfied. Satisfied, but something else as well. Some other emotion was there, but what it was she could not even guess.

Perhaps he would have told her, but he had no opportunity, for at that moment the door opened and Mrs. Mayberry, in her wheelchair, was pushed into the room by Bertha.

"I'm sorry I've kept you waiting," Mrs. Mayberry apologised. "But I had a sudden idea, and I just had to get it on to paper! Yes, just a small sherry, Owen, and then we'll go in to dinner."

To Lucy's relief, Mrs. Mayberry did not seem to

226

notice anything at all strained in the atmosphere. Had she seen the enquiring lift of her employer's eyebrows as she took her glass of sherry from her nephew she might not have felt so sure. On the other hand, the bland, completely noncommittal smile which was the only reply Owen gave might have reassured her.

* * *

To her surprise, Lucy ate quite a good dinner. That might have been because the food was very attractive and she had eaten little that day, or it might have been the consciousness that Owen was keeping a constant and critical watch on her. Whatever the reason, Lucy had to admit that she felt better for the meal.

After dinner Owen announced that he was going out for an hour or so, and Mrs. Mayberry took the opportunity to discuss business matters with Lucy.

First of all there was the question of salary, which had so far not been mentioned. The sum Mrs. Mayberry suggested was less than Lucy had been earning in Mr. Keane's office, but on the other hand, she would not have the expense of travelling up to town each day and she would be living in. Taking this into consideration, she accepted the offer unhesitatingly.

"And now, tell me about yourself," Mrs. Mayberry went on. "Or rather, your abilities. I think my brother said that your shorthand and typing speeds were quite good ?"

"Mr. Keane seemed to find them satisfactory," Lucy admitted. "Although he didn't dictate very quickly—and, of course, I became familiar with the legal terms he used."

"Yes, of course. I'm glad you brought that point up," Mrs. Mayberry told her. "You see, with historical novels, one must use phrasing suitable to the period, at least in dialogue, although I must say one does come across writers who appear to rely entirely upon illustrations to convey atmosphere. On the other hand, one cannot be too pedantic because that can be quite irritating to a reader. There is no doubt about it, you see, our ancestors did have what seems to us a most peculiar way of expressing themselves—almost unintelligible at times, in fact. You have only to read sixteenth-century letters—and it is the Tudor period with which I shall be dealing—to appreciate that. So, out of necessity, I have had to work out some sort of compromise, using a turn of phrase rather than unfamiliar words. None the less, one cannot entirely eliminate them, so while I have been without a secretary, I have worked out a glossary which will help you both to see what I'm driving at and to familiarise you with unfamiliar spelling. I'll give it to you tomorrow morning."

"Thank you," Lucy said gratefully. The last thing she wanted was for Mrs. Mayberry to be dissatisfied with her efforts, and it was reassuring to find that she would be working for a businesslike person.

"My story is of the extremely interesting and dangerous period just preceding Queen Mary's death and the succession of the Princess Elizabeth," Mrs. Mayberry went on in an eager way that showed clearly how much her work meant to her. "You see, no one quite knew what was going to happen. The Queen had quite seriously considered executing her half-sister. Up to the very last, she might have done so. If she had, there was a very real possibility that her husband, Philip of Spain, would have succeeded her. Indeed, that could happen in any case. If it had, then obviously those of the Catholic faith could have hoped to keep their posts. On the other hand, if Elizabeth succeeded, there was little doubt but that she would show favour to the Protestant faction. As you can see, it made for uncertainty—particularly among those who had no very strong convictions but wanted to be on the winning side."

"Yes, I see," Lucy said encouragingly, realising that Mrs. Mayberry was, as it were, setting the scene for the work they would do together.

"My heroine, though of a Catholic family, has actually Protestant leanings plus a very real sympathy for the Princess, a younger and much more attractive personality than the Queen. She—my heroine—is deeply in love with a handsome, brilliant man who is a time-server of the most cold-blooded sort. And that," Mrs. Mayberry finished with considerable relish, "gives me a situation which ought to produce plenty of conflict and heart-searching!"

Conflict and heart-searching! Involuntarily Lucy flinched and Mrs. Mayberry, looking at her downcast face, patted her hand reassuringly.

"It will come right in the end," she assured her cheerfully. "But how am I to spin out my seventy or eighty thousand words if I don't make life difficult for the principal characters?"

"Yes, of course," Lucy managed to smile, but to herself she added: "And, of course, it will be truer to life than if nothing went wrong!"

There was a little silence and then Mrs. Mayberry spoke again.

"There is just one more thing I want to say to you and then we will never speak of it again. As I believe my brother told you, I am bothered with rheumatoid arthritis. Fortunately for me—and those about me—there are times when I can forget about it. But not always. When that happens, I'm not fit company for anybody and so I keep to my own room. Bertha looks after me, but apart from her, all I ask is to be left alone. Do you understand?"

"Yes, and I'll remember," Lucy promised, and changed the subject as, she felt, Mrs. Mayberry would wish. "Would you mind, Mrs. Mayberry, if I ring my parents up to let them know I arrived safely? I would write, but they're flying to Jersey tomorrow."

"By all means, my dear. Put your call through in my study. You cross the hall to the door exactly opposite this one. You can't mistake it."

Lucy found her way without difficulty. The study turned out to be essentially a working room. Books lined two of the walls, there was a big double desk on which were two telephones and a covered typewriter. Except for the curtains and the carpet it was just like an office, with the only relief from austerity a big and beautifully arranged vase of flowers. Even this was placed well out of the way of anyone working at the desk although within range of their vision. Lucy sat down, and seeing that one was unmistakably a house phone, lifted the receiver of the other and asked for the number. Her mother answered.

"It's me—Lucy," Lucy said briskly. "I thought you'd like to know I got here safely and—and that everything is all right."

"Oh, darling, I'm so glad." Mrs. Darvill took her tone from Lucy and spoke with deliberate cheerfulness. "I was hoping you'd ring. Are you—are you alone?"

"Yes, in Mrs. Mayberry's study," Lucy explained.

"Well, darling, there's something—" Mrs. Darvill began, but Lucy interrupted her.

"If—if you mean the evening paper, I've seen it," she said quickly. "And—that's that, isn't it? There's nothing more to be said."

"Nothing at all, darling," Mrs. Darvill agreed with evident relief.

"And you got—everything tidied up?" Lucy asked hurriedly.

"Oh, yes, Aunt Millie came round and lent a hand. I was surprised how quickly we got through," Mrs. Darvill said, just as if cancelling a wedding and putting off nearly a hundred guests was an everyday occurrence.

"Oh, good, I'm glad," Lucy replied. "And tomorrow you're both off for a perfectly lovely holiday! Have a good time!"

"Yes, darling," Mrs. Darvill promised, but Lucy could hear the break in her voice. "Lucy, you're really quite sure——?"

"Quite sure, Mummy—and I really must ring off now," Lucy told her hurriedly. "Love to both of you!"

She rang off and her hands dropped limply into her lap. She had made as gallant an effort as possible to reassure her mother, but the utter finality of her own words echoed relentlessly in her brain.

There was nothing more to be said. Dick had gone out of her life—she would never see him again. Must try never even to think of him. But what did that leave? Just empty, aching *nothingness*.

Lucy buried her face in her hands. How could she go on? What was the point in trying to?

And then, from the hall, she heard the sound of Owen's voice. Instantly her head came up. Her heart was broken, but that was her business. At least she would not wear it on her sleeve to be jeered at.

．　．　．

In the weeks that followed Lucy realised over and over again how right she had been to leave home and come among strangers. At home everyone would have been sympathetic and would have made allowances for her so that she was constantly reminded of her loss. Here, there was nothing like that. Mrs. Mayberry had no idea that there was any reason for sympathy and Owen had no intention whatever of making allowances. In addition, she was so busy that sometimes, for hours at a time, she gave no thought to her own affairs. And when she did, it was only to dismiss them again as unimportant.

"I'm getting hard," she told herself in self-congratulation. "And a good thing too ! I was a silly, romantic little idiot—and nobody's ever going to have a chance of hurting me again like that !" And she set her pretty little round chin determinedly.

Sometimes, of course, it wasn't so easy. When, for instance, she went into Lyme Regis and saw happy young honeymoon couples strolling along hand in hand. Or when she saw anyone whose fair hair, or perhaps his walk, reminded her of Dick. But on the whole, she told herself that she was not doing too badly, and since Owen said nothing, he evidently thought so as well.

She enjoyed her work. Mrs. Mayberry had the gift of making her characters live, and Lucy became entranced with the way in which she spun the thread of her story through the exciting and moving personal incidents in it. Katherine, the heroine, was a darling. For Robert, the hero, she did not feel so much sympathy. He was handsome and romantic and daring, but she could not help feeling that there was something wrong. One day she realised what it was, and without stopping to think she said aloud :

"But he isn't strong at all. He's weak ! He's at the mercy of his own ambitions."

Far from resenting the criticism, Mrs. Mayberry looked pleased.

"If you realise that, then I'm doing my job," she remarked. "Does Katherine realise it ?"

"No," Lucy said slowly. "No. At least—if she does, she won't let herself."

"Better and better !" Mrs. Mayberry announced. "She's blindly in love, poor child, and that never did a woman any good yet."

Blindly in love—was that what she had been ? Lucy wondered. Ought she to have realised that there was

232

an inherent weakness in Dick's character? Owen had said she ought to have done, but surely, if one loved, one trusted as well?

"Read that last sentence, will you, my dear?" Mrs. Mayberry requested. "So that I can pick up the thread—"

* * *

Lucy found it very easy to slip into the simple ways of the household and little by little, she learned more about the people who composed it.

Mrs. Mayberry's husband had been a Professor of History at Cambridge University, and it was from him that she had acquired her interest in the subject.

"He really loved his work, and he had a gift for teaching," she told Lucy one day. "You see, to him, it wasn't a matter of dates and political events but *people* with much the same ideas and ambitions that we have, and whose influence on the course of events was largely the result of what they themselves were. And somehow, he could get into their skins so that you had the feeling he had met them just the day before—" She mused for a moment and then went on, "It was he who encouraged me to write my first book. It was after I had helped him with some rather tricky research about the period I am dealing with now. I was very dubious about my capabilities, but to my amazement, people liked my book. So I kept on—and I've been very thankful that I have. There's nothing like a really absorbing job for making life seem worth living."

"I think you're quite right," Lucy said with complete conviction. "I can't think of anything more worth while."

Mrs. Mayberry looked at her thoughtfully. She had

no intention of prying into Lucy's affairs, but wasn't it surprising that the child had completely missed the point? What she had said was that work made life *seem* worth living. In fact, it was no more than a deliberately cultivated illusion designed to take the place of simple human happiness. Worth a lot, but only second best. But she had no intention of telling Lucy that. If what she wanted was hard, interesting work, she should have it. One of these days she would no doubt find out for herself—

Most of what Lucy discovered about Owen was from Bertha, just as it was she who showed Lucy all over the house. Bertha, it was clear, found all her happiness in looking after Mrs. Mayberry and Owen— particularly Owen. She was never tired of talking about him.

"I had him from the month, miss," she explained. "And a more lovable baby you couldn't have found. And he's grown up into a fine man. Of course, there's some that call him hard, but they're the ones who don't know him the way I do !"

To that Lucy made no comment, but she listened with interest to Bertha's rather confused explanation of what Owen did for a living.

"Not that really he need do anything," Bertha explained. "He comes of a wealthy family, you see, but he was never one to enjoy idleness, and music has always been his hobby—he plays the piano very nicely, you know."

But he wasn't, it appeared, a professional pianist. As far as Lucy could make out, his interest lay in the encouragement and advancement of music in any of its forms. If, for instance, there was a festival of music anywhere in the world, you could be sure that Owen was in some way concerned in it. Quite likely, Lucy guessed, he had a financial interest in it, for Bertha went on proudly :

"And whatever he has dealings with is a success, you can be sure. He isn't only musical, you see, he's got a real business head. But there's more to it than that. There's many a young player or singer that owes their big chance to Mr. Owen. And most of them are successes, too, because he's got what they call a flair for picking them out. But of course, there's one particular one—you come along with me to Mr. Owen's room and I'll show you !"

And taking no notice of Lucy's protests that perhaps Mr. Vaughan would prefer that she didn't, Bertha led the way to the back of the house.

"This is the music room," she explained, opening the door. Real concerts there are here sometimes when Mr. Owen entertains some of his musical friends. But this is what I was going to show you."

She picked up a silver-framed portrait from the desk in the corner of the room and handed it to Lucy.

"There!" she said triumphantly.

Lucy gazed down at the portrait of a strikingly beautiful girl. She had masses of curling dark hair and enormous dark eyes, and she was smiling out of the frame right into the eyes of the beholder.

"Why, that's Marion Singleton!" Lucy exclaimed. "I've got most of her records at home. She has a most beautiful voice."

"That's right," Bertha agreed complacently. "And it was Mr. Owen who discovered her, as they say. She owes everything to him—and she doesn't mind admitting it." She took the picture from Lucy and regarded it approvingly. "A lovely young lady, in every way, and we do think—well, of course, it's not really for me to say, but there's no doubt about it, Mr. Owen is much more interested in her than he is in any of his other prodigies."

Lucy thought that Bertha probably meant protégés, but she did not say so. It was of such minor importance compared with Bertha's revelations.

Owen Vaughan deeply interested in music was astonishing enough, but Owen Vaughan in love—that was incredible!

CHAPTER III

Lucy had her first experience of what entertaining at Spindles meant when she had been there about a month.

One morning, instead of beginning to dictate to Lucy from the notes she had made the previous day, Mrs. Mayberry announced that they would be entertaining about eight people for the following weekend and she would be glad of Lucy's help in working out details.

"Owen wrote to them all last week," she explained, opening a filing folder which lay on the top of a small pile of papers. "And so far he has had five replies. I would like you to make two lists on the same sheet of paper, one of acceptances, one of queries. Ready?"

Lucy's eyes widened as the lists were dictated. Owen must be a very important person indeed, she realised, for surely few hosts could summon such a talented collection of guests as this! All were well-known personalities, some indeed were famous.

Among the men was an operatic singer of international renown, a conductor whose name was a household word and a judge who found relaxation with a violin.

"He could have been a top-ranking professional had he wished," Mrs. Mayberry commented in parenthesis. "But law is in his blood—his father and his grandfather were judges before him."

Marion Singleton headed the list of the women, and under her name was that of a brilliant actress whose recent one-woman show had been a scintillating success both in America and in this country.

Two other names, one of a man and one of a woman, went into the "query" list.

"Owen expects to hear from them today—they are only just back from a European tour," Mrs. Mayberry explained. "If they don't feel like making the effort so soon after that he will ask the Littleton twins—the brother and sister who play piano duets."

"But either way, won't you be a woman short, Mrs. Mayberry?" Lucy asked, looking up from her pad. "You've given me the names of four men, but only three women."

"Oh, no, that's taken care of," Mrs. Mayberry assured her. "*You* are to be the fourth woman."

"Oh, but I couldn't!" Lucy protested. "I should feel terrible! I mean, your guests are all so famous—wouldn't they feel affronted at having a mere secretary—?"

Mrs. Mayberry laughed softly.

"My dear child, you've evidently yet to learn that the more genuinely famous people are, the less they are concerned with their own importance! I have been told that is because it is so assured that they don't have to worry about it, but my conviction is that it is due to a far more attractive quality than that—a humility that comes when you know that you have a gift of God. In addition to that, all people who spend much of their lives in the public eye need to relax—and very often they do it in a way that would surprise and perhaps shock their devotees! Lord Manderville, the judge, for instance, has an absolute passion for Western novels and films. If there is one on television, we simply can't drag him away from it. Lisa Freyne likes to put on the oldest clothes she's got and spend her time helping Bence in the vegetable garden—no, you needn't be in the least bit worried, Lucy. You will feel perfectly at home with them and they with you."

"If you're sure—" Lucy still felt doubtful.

"Quite sure," Mrs. Mayberry said briskly. "And now, which bedrooms they are to have—"

From the file she took a sheet of paper which Lucy saw was a printed plan of the first floor of the house—evidently nothing was left to chance at Spindles!

"Lord Manderville in his usual room," she murmured, pencilling in his name. "Lisa *here*—she'll have a good view of the vegetable garden from the windows—she likes to see the results of her labours! Jeremy Trent—" her pencil hesitated and then wrote in the names. "Yes, that will do. I'll put Sinclair Forbes in the adjoining room and they can share a bathroom. That's the men. Now—Marion—" She frowned and tapped the list impatiently. "If only I knew whether it was to be the Champneys or the Littletons! One way I want a double room, the other way, two singles. Difficult!"

"Would it help if someone had my—had the room you've given me?" Lucy suggested diffidently. "I mean, it's such a lovely one—and with its own bathroom. Surely it's one you usually use for your guests?"

"Yes, it is," Mrs. Mayberry admitted. "Thank you for suggesting it, Lucy. Well then, if it's the Champneys, they can have the room just opposite yours, and if it's the Littletons, Celia can have that room and Robin can have yours. Then—" her pencil hovered uncertainly, "I'm afraid that means putting you in rather a dull little room without much of a view and without its own bathroom. Will you mind very much?"

"Not a bit," Lucy averred cheerfully.

"Of course," Mrs. Mayberry remarked, "some people would say that we are silly to give the staff so many of the good rooms, but after all, they are here all the time and we furnish theirs as bed-sitting rooms. Everybody needs somewhere comfortable where they can be alone if they want to, don't you think?"

"I think it's very thoughtful of you," Lucy said wholeheartedly. She had certainly been grateful that her room had afforded her that luxury.

"That's all, then," Mrs. Mayberry said with a sigh of relief.

"You haven't allocated a room for Miss Singleton," Lucy reminded her.

"Oh, Marion always has this room if it is possible." Mrs. Mayberry indicated it and Lucy saw that not only was it the largest of the single rooms, but also that in addition to a bathroom it also had a small sitting room opening off it. Clearly Marion Singleton was a very much favoured guest at Spindles!

"There!" Mrs. Mayberry sat back. "Now, if you will fill in the names in rather bold print—Bertha's eyesight isn't as good as it was, but she won't wear glasses —you can give it to her and she can have the rooms prepared. Now, is there anything else? Places at table. No, I can't see to that until we know just who is coming. Oh—yes, there is just one thing, dear. On these occasions, we dress for dinner. It's the only concession we make to convention. Nothing elaborate, though. A cocktail dress—?" There was an upward inflection in her voice which was an obvious question.

"I haven't anything suitable here," Lucy told her. "But—but I have at home."

"Good! Then can you have it sent—no, better than that. You've been a month away from home now, and I'm sure your parents would like to see you. Why not go home tomorrow, stay the night and return the following day?"

Lucy swallowed hard. She knew quite well that Mrs. Mayberry was right. Her parents, now home from their holiday, would like to see her, but facing up to them was going to be something of an ordeal. They wouldn't ask questions, and they wouldn't mention Dick—but she would know what was in their minds. Keeping up appearances would certainly be more difficult than it was here where no one concerned themselves with her affairs—even Owen had stopped watching her with that half cynical, half apprehensive look which suggested that he thought she was going to faint or burst into tears at any moment.

Then, too, the cocktail dress she had in mind had formed part of her trousseau. She could imagine just how tactfully her mother would refrain from remarking that it was really only sensible to use it—and the other clothes she had left behind. And yet that was the truth. It would be stupid to buy new clothes which she could not afford when all that she needed was ready to hand.

"Thank you very much, Mrs. Mayberry," she said steadily. "If you're sure you can spare me?"

"Yes, dear, of course I can. Now, if you catch the early train—no, wait a minute. If you put it off a day, Owen can drive you up. He's going to London anyhow and it will hardly take him out of his way at all. Yes, that's a far better plan. It will give you a lot more time with your parents than if you go by train. And he is returning the following day so he can pick you up—"

"Oh, but really, that's too much to ask of him," Lucy said hurriedly. "Really, it's quite all right for me to go by train!"

She had no wish whatsoever to spend several hours alone with Owen in the close confines of a car, but Mrs. Mayberry had already lifted the house telephone and was speaking to Owen.

"Yes, that's quite all right," she said a moment later. "He will be starting at half past nine the day after tomorrow, and he can pick you up the next day at eleven."

"Very well," Lucy said meekly because it was impossible to reject the offer without appearing ungracious. "I'll see to it that I'm ready on time so that I don't keep him waiting."

"Yes, perhaps you'd better," Mrs. Mayberry agreed. "If there is one thing that Owen is a bit difficult about it is punctuality!"

Lucy smiled a trifle wryly. *One* thing that he was

241

difficult about! Surely that was an understatement if ever there was one!

. . .

Lucy did not imagine for a moment that Owen could have really welcomed having her as a travelling companion. Like her, he had much more likely accepted the situation because there was really no way out, but at least he gave no sign of annoyance and even went so far as to produce sufficient small talk to avoid awkward silences. As a result, Lucy found it comparatively easy to do her share, and the journey passed with none of the embarrassment she had anticipated.

It passed far more quickly, too, than had seemed likely, although, despite the powerfulness of his car, Owen had kept his speed well within reasonable bounds. Involuntarily Lucy remembered some of the drives she had taken with Dick in the secondhand car he had run. Dick loved speed and invariably he flogged every last ounce of power out of the car until Lucy had felt as if her teeth were chattering in sympathy with its boneshaking vibration. Those trips had made her feel physically and mentally tired—but she had never had the heart to ask Dick to drive more slowly because he was so obviously enjoying himself. Except, of course, that he had so often mourned his inability to have a better car—

When they reached Lucy's home, secure in the knowledge that she had telephoned her mother the previous evening, she asked Owen if he would come in and meet her parents. She had not expected for a moment that he would want to, but to her asthonishment, he agreed readily. On the whole, Lucy was glad. In Owen's presence it would be impossible for their greeting to her to show any more than very normal emotion.

She was a little concerned, however, as to how Owen and her parents would get on together, but she need not have worried. Whatever his manners might be in his own home, as a guest they were exemplary and he showed a deference to a generation senior to his own in a way which took no account of wealth or social position.

He accepted Mrs. Darvill's offer of tea with what at least appeared to be genuine gratitude, and accompanied Mr. Darvill into the garden while Lucy went with her mother to the kitchen.

"It was very kind of Mr. Vaughan to bring you," Mrs. Darvill remarked, lighting the gas under the kettle. "In fact, he seems a very pleasant young man altogether."

"Yes, he does, doesn't he?" Lucy agreed discreetly, though privately she wondered if her mother would feel the same way about Owen if she knew just how different he could be.

"Now, if you'll just wheel the trolley in—oh, fill the milk jug first, will you? The tea won't be long."

It was a surprisingly pleasant little meal. Most of the conversation was provided by Owen and Mr. Darvill, but Owen, Lucy noticed with slightly reluctant approval, took good care to see that neither she nor her mother was entirely left out.

When he left, after shaking hands with his host and hostess, Owen turned to Lucy.

"Tomorrow, eleven sharp?" he asked pleasantly.

"Eleven sharp," Lucy agreed, and took his extended hand. The contact was brief, but it was long enough for Lucy to note that his was a firm grasp—she detested a flabby handshake, particularly from a man—and that it had an oddly sustaining quality about it.

Mr. Darvill saw their visitor off. When he came back to rejoin his wife and daughter, he was smiling.

"Nice young chap, that," he remarked, absently taking a left-over sandwich from the plate. "Seems to know all about roses, too."

"Does he?" Lucy was surprised. She had imagined that Owen's only interest in his extensive gardens was very secondhand. Certainly she had never seen him so much as snip off a dead flower.

"If you eat any more of those sandwiches, you'll be putting on weight again," Mrs. Darvill remarked, deftly whipping the plate out of her husband's reach. "Now, off you go out into the garden again while Lucy and I wash up."

This was it, Lucy thought wryly. An opportunity for a confidential chat if ever there was one! That was the last thing she wanted, and yet if nothing was said at all, she knew quite well that it would be such an unnatural state of affairs that the past would assume the nature of a barrier between her and her parents. She need not have worried. Mrs. Darvill dealt with the situation promptly and finally.

As soon as she and Lucy were alone together she took the bull by the horns.

"Now, Lucy, your father and I think you are absolutely right in feeling that there is nothing to be said over—what happened. We think, too, that you were quite right to go away, so there's nothing to be said about that, either, is there? And now, tell me about your work. Is it interesting?"

"Very," Lucy told her with convincing emphasis. "Much more interesting than working for Mr. Keane, nice though he was."

"And you get on well with Mrs. Mayberry?"

"Yes, I do. I like her very much indeed. And I think she likes me."

"Why shouldn't she, I'd like to know?" Mrs. Darvill was up in arms immediately.

Lucy laughed.

"You're something of a partisan, aren't you, Mummy? Still, it's nice to have it that way!" And she gave her mother a hug which both of them knew was really an expression of Lucy's gratitude for her parent's understanding. "But the important thing is that when two people get on well they can work together so much more smoothly."

"Do you ever do any work for Mr. Vaughan?" Mrs. Darvill asked.

"No, never," Lucy replied, wondering whether, after all, her mother had been shrewd enough to guess that Owen might well be a very difficult person for whom to work. "I don't see very much of him at all, really. Meals and odd times, that's all. He's a very busy man and he has a study of his own as well as an office in town."

In response to her mother's obvious interest Lucy explained what Owen's work was, and that gave her an opportunity of explaining just why she wanted a smart dress.

"Just fancy, Mummy. I shall be meeting some of the most interesting and famous people in the world," she went on with deliberate enthusiasm. "It's an opportunity that few people get. I think it's very, very kind of them to include me on—well, practically on equal terms with their guests."

"It certainly is," Mrs. Darvill agreed warmly. And then, the washing up done, she went on briskly: "And now, we'd better go up and see what dresses you want —I suppose you'll take more than just the cocktail dress?"

Why not? Lucy thought. Since she was making the plunge, why not make a complete job of it? It wouldn't really hurt more to break into her trousseau for half a dozen dresses than it did for one.

"Yes, I think I will," she agreed.

"Well, you go up then, dear, and I'll join you in a few moments. I just want a word with your father first."

Lucy went slowly upstairs to the familiar room—

and memory flooded back. Not just the memory of the shattering blow that had been dealt her here, but memory of trifling details which had seemed so important on the morning she had believed was her wedding day. The sun shining on the carpet, its warmth as she had pattered over to the wardrobe to look at her wedding dress—

Slowly she went over to the wardrobe and opened the door. The wedding dress had gone—well, of course, it would have done. Her mother would have seen to that. She wondered drearily what had happened to it—then she heard her mother's brisk footsteps on the stairs and quickly took the first dress that came to her hand from the wardrobe.

In the end, she decided to take the larger part of her clothes, although her one long evening dress she left hanging.

"I shan't need that," she remarked with an attempt at casualness.

"Well, I don't know, dear," Mrs. Darvill said doubtfully. "If you'd been asked, I'm pretty sure you would have said that you would have no opportunity of wearing the cocktail dress at Spindles—but you see, you have. And if Mrs. Mayberry and Mr. Vaughan are kind enough to regard you more as a friend than an employee, well, really, you don't know what you might want. And it might not be so convenient as it has been today for you to get it."

So that dress was packed as well, and Lucy had to admit that it was just as well that she was travelling back by car, for she could certainly not have managed to handle all her luggage herself had she gone by train.

The evening passed uneventfully. Lucy put on one or two of Marion Singleton's records, her father dealt in detail with the correspondence he was having with the local Council on the subject of a tree in the front garden which he wanted to have cut down and which they said must remain because it constituted a rural amenity—and then it was time for bed.

And if, involuntarily, Lucy remembered the last time she had gone to bed in this room, at least the following morning had so little in common with that other morning that she did not give it a thought. After a long spell of fine weather, it was raining with a sort of dreary persistence that suggested it had come to stay.

Promptly at eleven o'clock Owen arrived. While he was putting her cases into the car Lucy said a quick goodbye to her parents.

"I do hope this weather doesn't last over your party," she remarked as they started off.

"It won't," Owen said confidently. "I'm always lucky over weather."

And Lucy, who had, on the previous day, felt that perhaps Owen was rather nicer than she had thought, decided that her earlier impressions had been the correct ones. At least where she was concerned, he was a thoroughly irritating person.

Yet when they stopped for lunch, he really put himself out to be pleasant, though that in a way was equally irritating. Since if he chose he could be so charming, why did he have to be so beastly at others?

"I like your parents," he remarked with every appearance of sincerity.

"So do I," Lucy told him. "And I've known them longer than you have!"

Owen did not reply, and Lucy, feeling that he was waiting for her to say something more, ploughed on:

"It isn't only that they're *truly* good or that they mean so much to one another—important though that is. But, as well, I know I matter so much to both of them. I've always known that, but never so much as now."

"No?" Owen encouraged.

"No. You see," Lucy went on slowly, "because of

247

the way they feel about me, it hurts them terribly if—if I'm hurt. And they want to comfort me. Yet they accept my decision to leave them, and that—that there's nothing to be said about—it without question." She looked at Owen doubtfully, wondering why she had given him this confidence and how he would take it. He answered her briefly, and, astonishingly, paid her a compliment—the last thing she had thought would ever happen.

"They're very wise—and so are you." And promptly changed the conversation.

．　．　．

The days before the party passed quickly and busily. As the Littleton twins and not the Campneys were completing the number, Lucy had to turn out of her bedroom. Certainly it was not such a pleasant room to which she went, but on the other hand she had the pleasing feeling that Mrs. Mayberry would not have fallen in with her suggestion had she not regarded her as a friend from whom she could accept favours.

But the final proof of her acceptance in the home came from Bertha. On Friday morning, Bertha asked her if she would make a round of the bedrooms just to see that nothing had been forgotten.

"I'm sure there isn't, Bertha," Lucy smiled. "But I'd love to come all the same."

So each room was visited in turn, Bertha standing in the door while Lucy made a punctilious inspection. Everything was perfect. Mirrors and furniture gleamed with fresh polishing, bedcovers lay smooth and unwrinkled. There were flowers in vases which had clearly been chosen especially for the rooms they were in, and there were selections of magazines and books— Westerns where Lord Manderville was concerned. Lucy could not find reason for a single criticism until they came to Marion Singleton's room.

"Why, you haven't put any flowers here," she exclaimed.

"That's right, miss. Miss Marion doesn't like flowers —at least, not perfumed ones. So Mr. Owen always gets her some orchids."

There was no trace of criticism in Bertha's voice— but it was singularly devoid of any expression whatsoever, which did rather suggest that she did not sympathise with Marion's taste. That might, of course, be because to some people orchids suggest sophistication and even downright evil. Or it might be that Bertha felt a little hurt because her own efforts would not be appreciated. But it could surely not be that she disapproved of Owen going out of his way to please the girl of whom she herself had earlier spoken in such warm terms !

The inspection came to an end. Lucy congratulated Bertha on the thoroughness of her preparations, and went down to Mrs. Mayberry's study to finish off some work before the guests could be expected to arrive. Mrs. Mayberry called to her from the sitting room which opened off the study and which in its turn led to her bedroom.

"Yes, Mrs. Mayberry ?"

Mrs. Mayberry held out a sheet of paper.

"I've been arranging where we shall sit at dinner. It's too small a party to bother about place cards, but I thought you might like to see where you are. I've put you between Lord Manderville and Robin Littleton—they're both extremely easy to talk to, so you needn't feel in the least bit nervous." She gave a final glance at the diagram. "Thank goodness, though, that it's a round table. So much easier to arrange than a long one—Owen's idea. He doesn't like formality when he entertains here, and if he has to sit at the top of the table, he says he always feels cut off from everybody else."

"Yes, I see what you mean," Lucy acknowledged, but she could not help noticing that, informal or not, Marion had been given the place of honour on Owen's right.

"That's all then—except that before dinner we don't have any of the staff to help with the drinks. Owen sees to it, but he asked me if I thought you would mind lending a hand. I said I was sure you didn't. Is that all right?"

"Quite," Lucy said tranquilly, wondering whether she was being paid a compliment or whether Owen had rather cleverly chosen this way to make it clear that, after all, she was no more than an employee. "Just what am I to do?"

"Oh, just make sure that nobody has an empty glass and either catch Owen's eye or if he is busy, take the glass over to him yourself. Really, do just what you would in your own home if you were helping your father."

So it was a compliment! Lucy smiled and went back to her typewriter where she put in a solid morning's work, in the course of which she heard a car arrive and a little later Owen's and another man's voice out on the terrace. At lunch time she was introduced to Lord Manderville and found herself instantly attracted to him. Just how solemn and awe-inspiring he might be in his official capacity she had no idea, but here he was relaxed, charming and friendly, putting Lucy immediately at her ease. He put her slightly in mind of her father, possibly because of his age and his thick white hair, but also because of the lines of humour and kindliness so firmly etched round his eyes and mouth.

"He doesn't look like a judge," Lucy thought. "He's just as a favourite uncle ought to look!"

The rest of the guests arrived between lunch and dinner. Sinclair Forbes, the conductor, and Jeremy

Trent, the operatic star, arrived together as they had travelled by the same train and had been met at the station. Lisa Freyne came next in her own car, shortly followed by the Littleton twins on their own motor scooters and bubbling over with youthful exuberance because they had made such good time.

Marion was last of all. She arrived very late indeed, and more than once Mrs. Mayberry glanced at her watch with a little frown. Owen, however, appeared to be completely oblivious to her absence as, with Lucy's help, he supplied his guests with drinks.

Nor did he give any sign when the car arrived, but when she was announced a moment or so later, he turned and walked towards her—only to come to a sudden halt.

For, just inside the door, Marion had paused, poised and smiling, just as though she was on a concert stage and was waiting for the applause.

And she got, if not applause, something perhaps better. A sharp little indrawing of the breath from certainly three of the men present—and small wonder. Regally tall, slim and beautiful in a dark, almost Southern way, she was a woman to command attention and admiration anywhere.

She advanced gracefully towards Owen with both hands outstretched.

"I'm so sorry I'm late, Owen," she said, her deep, rich voice ringing through the room. "We had a little trouble with the car—"

"Too bad," Owen said easily. "Well, no drinks for you, my girl ! Say how do you do nicely to Aunt Louise and then off you go upstairs and change—and don't be too long about it !"

Marion laughed softly, carressingly.

"Darling, I adore it when you bully me," she declared as she walked gracefully over to Mrs. Mayberry.

251

"Dear Mrs. Mayberry, you'll forgive me, won't you, even if Owen won't?"

"Of course, Marion," Mrs. Mayberry said pleasantly.

But she did not smile, and when Marion had gone, she withdrew into a not very pleasant reverie.

In her own mind Mrs. Mayberry did not doubt that Marion had quite deliberately delayed her arrival until she was reasonably sure that the little house party would all be assembled in the drawing room for the express purpose of making that theatrical entry.

Well, perhaps one had to excuse that. Marion was young enough and success was still sufficiently new to have turned her head a little. But what disturbed Mrs. Mayberry was the girl's complete self-confidence. She had been quite sure that Owen would let her get away with an exhibition of bad manners which he would never have tolerated in anyone else.

Sure of herself—sure of Owen. That seemed to add up to just one thing—an understanding of some sort that sooner or later could lead to marriage.

Mrs. Mayberry tried to reassure herself by dwelling on the belief that whatever plans Marion might be making, it would be Owen who decided whether he asked her to marry him or not.

It was not an entirely satisfactory conclusion for, unlike Bertha, she was not at all sure that Owen was in love with the beautiful singer. Not, of course, that everyone felt love to be an essential ingredient of marriage. Some people seemed to get on quite well without it.

"But I do so want the very best for the boy," Mrs. Mayberry thought sadly. "Yet I can't help him. It's the sort of thing people have to work out for themselves—and stand by the results. Besides, Owen would resent interference even from me. It might even drive him—" she sighed deeply.

No, Owen might be heading for disaster, but there was nothing she could do about it except wait and hope.

MRS. MAYBERRY was quite right in thinking that Marion fully intended to marry Owen. Not that she was in love with him, although apart from his boringly serious outlook on life, she liked him well enough.

But despite her somewhat exotic appearance, Marion was essentially practical. She had every reason to be, since before Owen had set her feet on the path of fame she had known what it meant to count every penny.

She was one of a large family and her parents had not been able to afford to give her a specialised education of any sort—not, as Marion admitted in her franker moments, that she had sufficient brains to have taken advantage of it if they had. As a result she had never been able to command more than a very mediocre salary doing jobs which held no future at all.

To the possibility of earning a living by singing she had never given a thought. It was simply a useful little amateur talent which had enabled her to enjoy a limited loyal popularity. And then, on one never-to-be-forgotten Saturday evening at the conclusion of a charity concert, Owen, escorted by a greatly flurried producer, had come backstage to make her an astounding offer.

He had liked her voice. He thought it had possibilities. If she would come to his office the following Monday he would give her an audition.

Marion went—having first taken the precaution of ringing up the office where she worked to say that she would not be in as she had a bad headache. No use throwing away one job before getting another.

She had been greatly impressed by what, to her, was the magnificence of Owen's office, but not in the least overawed by it. After all, if he could afford such luxury he must be a successful man, and successful men don't make mistakes. Consequently, if he said her voice was good he knew what he was talking about.

All the same, she was completely taken aback at the offer he made when the audition was over. It was nothing less than that he was willing not only to pay for her voice to be properly trained but also to make her an allowance during that time so that she could give all her mind to her training.

Marion had blurted out one word:

"Why?"

"Because, I believe you have what could be a truly beautiful voice," he had explained patiently. "And because music of all sorts is not only my means of earning a livelihood. It is also my greatest interest in life."

"I still don't see why you should pay for me," Marion had told him suspiciously. In her experience there was no such thing as disinterested kindness—particularly where men were concerned. "What do you get out of it?"

"A very real satisfaction," Owen had told her promptly. And then, seeing how completely blank she looked: "Can't you understand that feeling as I do about music, I feel literally compelled to help anyone I can if I think they can add to the beauty of the world?"

No, she couldn't understand that. It went completely above her head. But slowly several things did dawn on her shrewd, calculating little mind.

He meant what he said. He must be very rich, and to use her own phrase, there were no strings to it. In fact, he made only one condition.

"You will work hard—very hard," he had told her sternly. "Otherwise—finish! And since I shall have regular reports from your instructors about your progress, it will be no use tying to pull wool over my eyes. Do you understand?"

"Yes," she had nodded. "That's fair enough. You're paying. But what happens when I'm trained?"

"That will depend largely on yourself." He had looked at her thoughtfully. A lovely voice—he knew he was not mistaken about that. But was there anything more? Had she got it in her to develop the warmth, the understanding, the personality that went to the making of a really great voice? Time alone could answer that, and in the meantime she was too young, too ignorant for it to be any use explaining. "I believe that at the least you will be able to earn a better living than you do now. In a year's time I will be able to judge whether there's more to it than that. Well?"

She had accepted, of course. And she had worked harder than she had ever done before in her life, partly because she knew he had meant what he said— laziness would mean the end of his interest in her—but also for another reason. Despite the fact that she later discovered she was far from being the only beginner whom he had helped, she could never disabuse her mind of the conviction that in her case there was more to it than that. After all, wasn't she beautiful —and wasn't he a man?

But though Owen turned out to be quite right about her voice, she had been forced to admit to herself that she had never really got any further with him. At least, not until she had made a name for herself. Not that she blamed him for that. Naturally a man in his position didn't want a nobody for a wife.

Well, she wasn't a nobody now—nobody could say she was. And that wasn't only due to her voice and her beauty. She had acquired poise, she knew how to behave in public and she was perfectly at home in houses far larger than Owen's—the owners of some of them had, in fact, wanted to marry her, but so far she had always refused.

The reason for that was simple. Marion wanted to eat her cake and have it. Accepting any one of the offers she had had would mean the end of her career —and why should she agree to that just when she was beginning to touch the really big money?

Now, with Owen, it would be quite different. He would never expect her to stop singing, admittedly not because of the money, but because of the way he felt about music. He'd be able to help her tremendously, too, not only because of all his professional interests but because of the background that an attractive home and a wealthy husband give a woman.

But there was more to it than that. A complete realist, Marion had taken to heart a lesson learned from other singers now past their prime—*a voice doesn't last for ever!* So marriage was an essential insurance against the time when her day was over, and marriage to Owen fulfilled all her ambitions—the continuation of her career and permanent security.

It did not occur to her to ask what Owen would get out of marriage to a wife who would spend long periods away from home, but then it never did occur to her to consider other people's points of view. She wasn't made that way. She knew what she wanted and she had every intention of getting it. And she was quite sure, so far as Owen was concerned, that there was no doubt whatever but that she would one day be his wife.

She did rather wish, though, that he would come to the point. Oh, he was charming and indulgent and she was made especially welcome when she visited Spindles—except by that appalling old woman who obviously saw the end of her rule when Owen brought a wife home. All the same—

Well, on this visit she was determined to bring matters to a head. Casually she had asked Owen who the other guests would be and had heard with considerable satisfaction that she need fear no competition from the other women. Celia Littleton was quite clever in her way, of course, and so was Lisa Freyne. But Celia was too young and Lisa too careless of her appearance to make any appeal to Owen. Then, just as Lucy had done, she realised that there must be another woman to make up the number and had asked Owen who she was.

"Oh, Lucy," he had said carelessly, and had gone on to explain just who Lucy was.

No danger there, Marion had thought complacently. Tall, thin and fair—no, even though Owen saw her every day, perhaps because he saw her every day, there was nothing to fear in that quarter—an opinion which she felt had been confirmed when she saw Lucy.

The men, on the other hand, might be very useful. Not Lord Manderville, of course. He was as old as the hills and he always gave her the feeling that he was looking right through her and out the other side. But the others—Jeremy Trent and Sinclair Forbes—yes, they were all right. Not that she had any intention of flirting with them or letting them flirt with her. Owen would only be disgusted by that. But that little gasp which the two men and young Robin had given when she had made her entry—how flattered they would be had they known it was for their benefit!— had told her all she needed to know. Without any relaxation from the part of a charming but regally aloof woman that she intended to play, Owen would see with his own eyes how desirable other men found her! And since he was anything but a fool, he would see to it that none of them got ahead of him!

Marion drew a deep breath of satisfaction. She was on the brink of a second and in a way greater success than her professional one had been!

Lucy found that Mrs. Mayberry had been quite right. It would be impossible to find two more pleasant or friendly people than Lord Manderville and Robin Littleton, for neighbours at dinner, though in totally different ways.

Robin, like his twin, was bubbling over with high spirits. He thought the world was a wonderful place and that all the people who occupied it were good sorts—especially Owen.

"He's absolutely terrific," he confided to Lucy. "He's always got an ear to the ground, you know, in search of new talent, not because he wants to make out of them, but in case there's anyone that needs a hand to make the grade. Well, Celia and I were both in our last year at the Academy and he heard us playing at one of the pupils' concerts—as solo turns, you know —and then he wrote to us, asking if we'd come and see him. Of course we did—and he was very blunt. He told us what we'd both realised— that though we both adore playing the piano and would hate doing anything else for our living, we just hadn't got it in us to make top grade. And then he said : 'And I'll tell you what I think is the reason for that. You're twins, and neither of you is quite complete without the other. Well, my advice to you is that you should cash in on that. Either play duets on the same piano or else use special arrangements for four hands on two pianos. I think you'll get somewhere then because you'll each give the other something you haven't got individually.' You know, we'd never thought of that, but he was right ! It works like a charm and we have the greatest fun ! And now, to top off everything else he's done for us, he's invited us here. That's a terrific compliment—people angle like anything to get an invitation, but they're the very ones that don't get it. I say, you must enjoy living here !" and he regarded her with frank envy.

"It's very nice," Lucy admitted, feeling that after Robin's eulogy her remark must sound singularly lame and inadequate. "Actually, I don't see a great deal of Mr. Vaughan—it's Mrs. Mayberry for whom I work."

"Well, I should think that's pretty interesting, too," Robin commented. "And anyway, there's something about the house—I don't know, but the moment you come into it, you feel it's *right*, somehow. People doing the jobs they want to, perhaps."

Then, realising that he had spent so much time talking that he was in danger of keeping the rest of the table waiting while he finished the course, he gave his attention to his plate, and Lucy turned to Lord Manderville.

And now, instead of listening to someone talking about themselves, she found herself being gently and brilliantly persuaded to talk of herself. Not that Lord Manderville asked direct questions, but one thing just seemed to lead naturally to another so that before very long he knew all about her likes and dislikes where books and painting and music were concerned.

"Not that I really know anything about them," she confessed, suddenly self-conscious at having expressed such definite opinions. "But then perhaps no one can know unless they themselves create something—"

Lord Manderville considered.

"I am not sure you are right over that," he told her. "You appear to me to have considerable natural taste —and as for not creating anything, have you never realised that you, the appreciative audience, are the real creators of all successful artists ? Oh, yes, that's true ! Without you, they simply would not exist."

"I think that's the nicest thing I've ever had said to me," Lucy told him happily. "You've made me feel so tremendously important and clever !"

And they laughed together like old friends.

The evening passed quickly, although to Lucy's surprise, neither then nor on the following day was there any suggestion that use should be made of the music room. She had taken it for granted that there would be some sort of informal concert, but instead, during the day everyone went their own way and both the evenings were spent in conversation, sometimes above Lucy's head, sometimes amusing, but always interesting. Only Marion Singleton seemed to take little part in it and Lucy, seeing her sitting quiet and, incredibly, rather out of things, found the courage to go and sit by her and tell her shyly how much she enjoyed her singing. Instantly Marion came to life.

"How quite charming of you, my dear," she said in that rich, warm voice. "How many times have you heard me sing?"

"Oh, I'm afraid I haven't been to any of your concerts," Lucy confessed, shamefaced. "But on radio and television—and I've got most of your records, I think."

"I'm making some new ones soon," Marion told her. "Would you like an autographed recording of a special favourite?"

"I'd love it!" Lucy said enthusiastically, and at that moment Owen drifted over to them.

"Now what are you two girls gossiping about?" he asked lightly. "The latest thing in hairstyles—or was it clothes?"

"We weren't gossiping at all," Lucy told him indignantly. "We were talking about Miss Singleton's records—and she has very kindly promised to let me have an autographed one."

"She's got a frightful memory," Owen remarked with a sidelong look at Marion which Lucy could not interpret. "But I'll keep her up to it—I believe in advertising!"

There was a brief silence which Lucy found embarrassing. Then Owen turned to her.

"Lucy, Aunt Louise is turning in now and she'd like to have a word with you first."

"There's nothing wrong, is there?" Lucy asked anxiously with a glance at her watch. "I thought, at dinner time, that she looked particularly well— better than she has ever since I came."

"Yes, she was thoroughly enjoying herself," Owen confirmed. "No, there's nothing wrong. But she wants to make sure that she is all right for tomorrow evening, so she's going to bed early tonight."

"Tomorrow night?" Lucy asked vaguely. "Is there something special about that?"

"Oh, I thought Aunt Louise would have told you. Yes, we always end up a week like this with a show —everybody doing a turn, including Aunt Louise. She wouldn't miss it for the world."

"Oh!" Lucy said breathlessly. "And can I be there? Can I listen?"

"Oh, yes, certainly you can be there, and certainly you can listen," Owen promised.

Lucy looked at him in a puzzled way. He had spoken in a way which had suggested that he was consumed with inward laughter, but as he evidently had no intention of telling her what the joke was, she shrugged her shoulders and went across the room to speak to Mrs. Mayberry.

*   *   *

The next morning such of the guests as did not go to church found some occupation out of doors, some walking, some simply lazing in the sunshine and in the case of Owen and Marion, riding.

Only Lucy felt that she could not treat the day as a holiday, for though she had been encouraged to feel part of the houseparty, she was none the less an employee and did not want to give the impression that she was taking too much for granted.

But when she heard the sound of horses' hooves on the gravel outside she was irresistibly drawn from her desk to the window. Owen and Marion had paused for a moment to speak to Mrs. Mayberry, and Lucy thought she had never seen such a handsome couple. They were so perfectly matched, both tall, so alike in colouring and each so completely self-assured.

Lucy turned away from the window with a little lump in her throat. This was an entirely new world into which she had strayed and despite the kindness she had received she knew she did not belong to it and never would. Tears stung her eyes as appreciation of her own inadequacy came home to her, and she envied these people from the bottom of her heart—not because of their wealth and position but because they were so completely at their ease, so able to make a success of life, so fearless.

And those were qualities which Lucy had lost and which she knew she would never possess again. How could she when once she had proved to be so blind, so stupidly trusting ? For the rest of her life, no matter what sort of appearance pride forced her to keep up, she would be assailed by doubts and fears—

She began to hammer away on the typewriter, forcing herself to concentrate on her notes until Robin strolled into the room and announced that Mrs. Mayberry had sent him to bring her out.

"She says it's against the rules to work on one of these weekends," he explained, and when Lucy began to protest he went on coaxingly : "Oh, do come out ! Celia and I have invented a new sort of croquet. You swop balls after each stroke, so the game is to leave your ball in as awkward a position as possible for the confounding of your opponent. It's great fun !"

So Lucy let herself be persuaded and was shortly

not only convulsed at Robin's antics but was also beating him hollow since, as she had never played the game before she was making such bad strokes that Robin could neither make them worse for her nor contrive to get through the right hoop and so score a point. It was just as Lucy, eyes tight shut, hit the ball so that it glanced off Robin's foot and went clean through the hoop that Owen and Marion returned.

They had walked round from the stables, and Marion paused in astonishment at the sight of Lucy convulsed with laughter while Robin, riding his mallet like a hobby-horse, protested that she'd only beaten him by a foul and appealed to Lord Manderville for a decision in his favour.

"Well, well, well," Marion said softly. "Robin seems to have worked a miracle. The little secretary girl looks positively animated!"

"So she did last night when she was telling you how much she liked your singing," Owen reminded her shortly.

Marion's eyes narrowed slightly. She was not particularly fond of riding, but she had been quite willing to accompany Owen because she was sure he had suggested it in order to make an ideal opportunity for coming to the point. And instead of that, he had spent almost all the time telling her about a winter festival that he was planning. Of course it was true that she would take a leading part in it, but that wasn't the point. And now he was really speaking quite sharply to her.

"Yes, bless her," she agreed sympathetically. "So she did—but terribly serious, all the same. And that was why I was so surprised—and pleased—to see her laughing like this. She's so serious, and at her age life ought to be fun, not frightfully real and earnest all the time!"

Owen made no comment since they had now reached the group on the terrace, but the slight frown had
cleared from his face and Marion gave a little sigh of
relief. That hurdle safely passed ! But she must remember in future—Owen was the sort of man who hated
to hear one woman criticise another simply on principle.

Or was it something more personal than that ? Was
it that he demanded absolute perfection as essential in
his future wife ? Or, disturbingly, was he sufficiently
interested in the little secretary to resent criticism of
her ?

Marion quickly made up her mind how she would
deal with that possibility.

. . .

The show, as Owen had called it, was at its height.
He himself had opened it by playing the "Entry of the
Gladiators" with considerable verve and brilliance.
That, it appeared, was traditional on these occasions,
partly as he had explained, in order to make it clear
that no mercy would be shown to any shirkers and
partly so that he was in a strong position to harry
them if they tried it on.

Sinclair Forbes who, as a conductor, had a comprehensive knowledge of most musical instruments, chose
to perform on a harmonica and brought the house
down with his rendering of "Three Blind Mice" with
variations, his long, lean face as serious and absorbed
as when he was conducting the orchestra he had made
famous.

Then the Littleton twins played a duet which began
with a slow, simple movement, but gradually both
tempo and embellishments increased until it was impossible to follow the flashing movements of their
hands. They concluded with a crashing chord and went
back to their seats.

After the twins came Lord Manderville. To Owen's

accompaniment he played Mendelssohn's "Overture to A Midsummer Night's Dream", and if his performance was not quite up to professional standards, Lucy had no fault to find with it and joined wholeheartedly in the applause which followed.

There was a little pause.

"Now you," Owen announced.

No one moved, and Lucy glanced round in surprise. Everyone else had seemed to know when it was their turn.

"You," Owen repeated. "Lucy!"

"Oh, no!" She shrank back in sheer horror.

"Oh, yes," Owen contradicted firmly. "I told you that we all perform. Now then, what's it going to be?"

"But—but I don't play the piano—or anything," Lucy explained breathlessly. "Truly I don't."

"Then you must sing," Owen told her inexorably. "Come along!"

He beckoned to her, looking at her through half-closed eyes, and before Lucy knew what had happened she found herself standing by the piano.

"As a concession, you may stand with your back to your audience," he announced. "That's it!"

But the concession, if it was that, meant that she was facing Owen himself as he sat down at the piano, and because his eyes never left her face, neither could she look away from his.

"Do you know the words of this song?" he asked, playing a few bars.

"Yes," Lucy whispered.

"Then here we go!"

And without any volition on her part, Lucy found herself singing, timidly at first and then with growing confidence.

"Maxwelton braes are bonnie,
    When early falls the dew—"

And so to the last verse :

"Like dew on the gowans lying
Is the fall o' her fairy feet,
An' like winds in summer sighing
Her voice is low and sweet.

Her voice is low and sweet
And she's a' the world to me;
And for bonnie Annie Laurie
I'd lay me doon an' dee."

There was a moment's silence as voice and music faded away—a silence that a professional could have told her meant far more than the applause which followed. She slipped back to her chair, blushing furiously, and found her hand gently taken by Lord Manderville.

"Thank you, my dear, that was delightful !"

"Oh, you're very kind," Lucy stammered. "But—"

"My dear, I'm not being kind, I'm being truthful," Lord Manderville said firmly. "I know, as of course you do, that your voice is not strong enough for you to take up singing professionally. None the less, just like the girl in your song, it's low and sweet—and very pure. It gave me great pleasure to listen to you—particularly as you sang that song. My wife used to sing it to me."

Lucy gave his hand a little squeeze of gratitude and sympathy and turned to watch Lisa Freyne give two short impersonations. But brilliant though she was, neither she nor the following turns made any real impression on Lucy.

She felt completely dazed—dazed and bewildered and strangely exultant.

She, ordinary, insignificant Lucy Darvill, had been accepted by these wonderful people as one of themselves ! Not that she overrated the measure of her success, for despite what Lord Manderville had said, she knew quite well that she had been judged by kinder standards than they set themselves. None the less, she need not feel an outsider any more, and the doubts and fears which had assailed her only that morning dwindled to insignificance. And the astonishing thing was that all that she owed to Owen—

Later that evening, when they were all in the drawing room he came over and sat down beside her.

"Forgiven me yet ?" he asked quizzically.

"Yes," Lucy said shyly. "In fact, there's nothing to forgive—except I—I wish you'd warned me—"

"Not likely !" Owen declared stoutly. "You'd have worried yourself sick—and had time to think up some plausible excuse !"

"But why were you so determined that I should take part ? Supposing—supposing I'd let you down ?" Her eyes widened at the mere thought of such a thing.

Owen smiled, but he chose only to answer her second question.

"I knew there was no danger of that, Lucy."

And left her to wonder just why he had been so confident and even more why he had thought it worth while to go to the trouble of bringing her out of her obscurity as he had done.

CHAPTER V

BY lunch time the next day all the guests had left,
though not all at the same time. Marion was the last
to go, but not before she, like the others, had said a
special goodbye to Lucy.

She came to the study, smiling and friendly, to
assure Lucy that she would not forget the autographed
record.

"Though Owen is quite right, I do forget things."
She hesitated, her lovely face troubled. "It's odd, isn't
it, that two people can be as deeply in love as he and
I are and yet see each other's faults so clearly."

Lucy was not surprised to hear it confirmed that
Owen and Marion were in love, but she felt it was
rather strange that she should be the recipient of such
a confidence.

"Perhaps it's better that way," she suggested awk-
wardly. "After all, no one is perfect, so what's the
good of being blind to faults, even if one is in love?"

Marion looked at her sharply. She had thought Lucy
too simple a type to possess such worldly wisdom and
wondered what lay behind it. However, to pursue that
line would side-track the conversation from the path
she firmly intended to take, so she let it go.

"I suppose you're right," she admitted. "But how
much nicer it would be if one could live in the clouds
all the time! Coming down to earth can be so very
painful." She sighed deeply. "As I found it to be last
night."

Lucy wished she could tell Marion that she would
much rather not listen to her confidences, but she
knew that she had not the finesse to do so without
giving offense, so she said nothing. But lack of encouragement had no effect.

"Owen was very naughty," Marion went on regretfully. "To make you sing, I mean. It was so incon-

siderate—but that's just it. Sometimes he is so thoughtless of other people's feelings. But you will forgive him, won't you—for my sake?"

"There's nothing to forgive," Lucy said quickly.

Marion could have boxed her ears. Really, the girl was too stupid for words!

"Oh, but my dear, there *is*," she insisted. "I only wish there wasn't, but sometimes Owen can't resist playing that Svengali trick of his—"

"I don't think I understand," Lucy told her discouragingly. "And really I think—"

"Oh, but surely you know the story of Svengali and Trilby?" Marion interrupted quickly. "The girl who could only sing when she was mesmerised?"

Yes, of course Lucy knew it, and against her will she remembered how compelling Owen's dark eyes had been—

"Of course, not really like Svengali," Marion went on. "It's more that he can make people do what he wants them to against their will. I've seen him do it several times and it always makes me shiver, especially as he finds it so amusing."

As he had found it amusing on Sunday evening when she had so innocently asked if she could be present at the "show".

"I tried to persuade him not to try it on you," Marion went on with a sigh. "But it was no use. He was so confident that he could compel you—"

Confident of his own powers, not of hers. That was why he had been so sure that she would not let him down—and why he had avoided explaining what had made him so determined—

"I've had to come to the conclusion that he can't help it," Marion went on softly, well content with the impression Lucy's silence told her she had achieved. "I think it must be some sort of childish exhibitionism, the result, perhaps, of living at such close quarters with an older and such a very strong personality—"

Lucy stood up suddenly.

"If you don't mind, I would really rather not listen to any criticisms of my employer," she said bluntly. "It seems to me disloyal."

"Oh, my dear, yes, of course," Marion said apologetically. "I should have been more thoughtful. But I'm so worried—"

Lucy did not reply, and Marion, realising that she had lost ground, went on wistfully :

"But you will forgive my poor Owen ?"

"There's no question of forgiveness," Lucy said with a dignity that surprised her almost as much as it did Marion. "I shall not give the matter another thought ! And now, if you will forgive me, Miss Singleton, I really must get on with my work."

With more apologies and an effusive farewell, Marion drifted out of the study.

Lucy sat very still.

So that was Owen ! Well, she might have known it ! Hadn't he, the very first day they had met, exerted a very similar sort of domination over her ? Stupidly, though she had resented it at the time, she had allowed herself to forget it—had allowed herself to get on practically friendly terms. But he had not forgotten— and it had amused him to show his power again, in front of an audience.

"He will never be able to do it again," she vowed. "I'll see to that !" And then, bitterly : "Of course, really I've only myself to thank. If I hadn't wanted to push myself in where I don't belong—well, that will never happen again, either. And now, for goodness' sake, get on with your work, girl ! At least you can make a reasonable success of that."

But as she fitted fresh paper into the machine, she suddenly paused.

Why had Marion talked so freely to her ? If, as she

said, Owen's trick of showing off distressed her wouldn't it be more natural not to want to talk about it to anyone, least of all to someone whom she must regard as a social inferior ? Indeed, unless she had some very good reason for being so frank, it seemed to Lucy that Marion had been guilty of disloyalty to the man whom she loved.

But what reason could there be ? Did she think it only right that Lucy should be warned in case Owen attempted such a thing again ? But wasn't that unlikely ? To a man with a mentality like Owen's, surely it would be poor sport to continue making a butt of the same victim, particularly one who had proved such easy game. Far more likely, Lucy thought, that he would look for fresh worlds to conquer, in which case, she was safe. But if she realised that, then Marion who had a far deeper knowledge of Owen ought to have realised it as well and so need have said nothing.

Lucy shook her head and got on with her job. It was all really too puzzling and too unpleasant to dwell upon. Much better to do as she had told Marion she intended—forget all about it.

* * * *

But that, Lucy found, was not easy. Safe or not, she intended taking no chances, and that meant she must be constantly on her guard.

As far as was possible without making it too obvious she avoided Owen, particularly on occasions when Mrs. Mayberry was not present. She was not sure whether he noticed this or not, but at least he made no comment. All the same, it was a relief when he went up to town for a few days and she could consequently relax her guard.

He came back sooner than he had anticipated, however, reporting that London was unendurable in the heat and that he had begged off from a very formal

271

reception because he could not face the thought of a stiff shirt and collar.

"I made what I thought was a convincing explanation to my host," he admitted with a grin, "but he wasn't taken in. He said he didn't blame me in the least and he'd get out of it himself if he'd got half a chance !"

Lucy, to whom the remark was addressed, made no reply. His early return had caught her at a disadvantage. It really was a very hot day and she had been grateful for Mrs. Mayberry's suggestion that they should both take the afternoon off. As a result, when Owen arrived, Lucy was sitting reading in the shade of a big tree and had no chance of escaping when he left the car on the gravel drive and strolled over to her. Worse than that, there was an empty deck chair beside her and as a matter of course he dropped down in it. Lucy greeted him briefly and without comment, but that did not prevent Owen from giving his explanation.

"Lord, it's good to be back," he went on, settling himself more comfortably in the chair. "I've been dreaming of what it would be like here all the way down, only to find it's even better than I'd thought possible. And that's in no small measure your doing, Lucy. You enhance the scene considerably in that blue outfit."

Lucy shrugged her shoulders and returned to her book. If he thought he was going to get round her by paying compliments—

"In fact," Owen went on lazily, "there's only one thing missing—a long, cool drink—"

Lucy jumped to her feet. It was annoying that he had interrupted her quiet afternoon, but at least here was a way of escape.

"I'll go and see about it," she offered.

272

Instantly Owen shot out a long arm and caught her by the wrist.

"No, don't do that! I've an idea that if you do, you'll send out one of the maids with it and not come back yourself—and I'm enjoying your company."

Deciding that it was wiser not to give in to the natural instinct to struggle, Lucy stood perfectly still.

"Will you please let go, Mr. Vaughan?" she said coldly.

"Certainly—if you'll sit down again," he promised, not relaxing his grip in the least. "How about it?"

"Don't you think you're being rather silly, Mr. Vaughan?" Lucy suggested. "If I want to go indoors, it really is my own business—"

"But you don't want to go," he said softly. "Or rather you didn't. I'm quite sure you'd planned to stay here—your book and a writing pad and a pen make that clear."

"I've changed my mind," Lucy told him shortly.

"Obviously—and the reason is equally obvious," Owen retorted coolly. "It's because I've turned up!"

"Then, if you realise that, don't you think it's rather bad-mannered of you to try to make me stay?" Lucy suggested.

"Very," Owen agreed. "But the trouble is, you've raised my curiosity to fever heat—and I want to know what it's all about."

"I don't know—" Lucy began, but he shook his head.

"I think you do," he insisted quietly. "But in case I'm wrong. I'll explain. Since last Monday—the day after the show—you've been dodging me as if I've got the plague and freezing me if you couldn't dodge. Now, if I let you go, you'll not come back. What's wrong, Lucy?"

She shook her head, determined not to explain.

"You're not afraid of me, are you?" he asked softly.

"Certainly not!" Lucy retorted indignantly.

"No? I'm glad to hear it—but it would be more convincing if you'd sit down again as I ask instead of running away!"

And since she knew that nothing she could say would convince him now that she would not be running away, Lucy sat down. Instantly Owen let go of her wrist.

"That's better!" he announced. "And now tell me, what have I done to annoy you?"

Lucy, sitting very erect, her hands clasped round her knees, merely shrugged her shoulders.

"Of course, I know why you disliked me so at first," Owen reflected. "I bullied you unmercifully, didn't I?"

"You were certainly very unpleasant."

"So I was," he agreed calmly. "But if you're honest, you'll admit that my bullying helped you to face up to things far better than any amount of sympathy would have done. Isn't that true?"

"Perhaps," Lucy said grudgingly. "But if you remember, at the time you said that if you could sting me into showing some sort of pride you wouldn't have to put up with seeing me mooning about like a rag doll with its stuffing running out! So you can't pretend that it was disinterested kindness on your part any more than—" she stopped short, but she had already said too much.

"Any more than—what?" Owen demanded, suddenly very alert. "No?" as Lucy set her mouth firmly. "You're not very co-operative, are you? Never mind, I expect I can find out. I think you were going to say: *any more than—something else—was disinterested*. And that 'something else' is what has upset you. Now what can it be? Not, of course, anything to do with my letting you in for singing? No, it couldn't have

274

been that because you assured me, I'm sure in all sincerity, that there was nothing to forgive me for on that score."

Lucy did not reply, but her expression must have betrayed her, for Owen sat up suddenly.

"D'you know, I believe, after all, it was that ! That means that between Sunday evening and—let's see—Monday lunch time ? About then, anyway, you changed your mind. You decided that I had done something beyond forgiveness, didn't you ? And since we hardly exchanged a word on Monday morning, so far as I remember, it must be on account of something that happened before then—yes, I'm sure it was that singing business ! Am I right, Lucy ? And if so, what was it ?"

Lucy hesitated. She knew quite well that Owen would not rest until he had got to the bottom of the puzzle, yet she could not bring herself to tell him the entire truth. That would mean bringing Marion Singleton into it, and that she was determined not to do. How could she ? Marion had confided in her, and though she had felt that was wrong—no, *because* she had felt it was wrong, it simply wasn't possible for her to make matters worse by breaking that confidence.

"I'm waiting, Lucy," Owen said softly.

"Very well, I'll tell you," Lucy agreed. "Do you remember, on Sunday night, I asked you why you had been so determined that I should sing ?"

"Did you ? Yes, I believe you did."

"But you didn't tell me," Lucy went on. "Do you remember that as well ?"

"Possibly. But *you* remember, don't you, that I had told you *everybody* performed ?"

"Yes, you did," Lucy admitted. "But I don't think it was unreasonable for me not to realise that included me. After all, everyone else was a professional—"

275

"Not Aunt Louise, not Manderville, not me," Owen murmured, his eyes half closed.

"Perhaps not—but all three of you have pretty high standards, and you're used to performing in front of an audience, even if it is made up of your friends."

"True," Owen admitted. "So—"

"So why were you so determined to risk making both me and yourself look silly?"

"No risk at all. There's something about your speaking voice that convinced me you could sing. And since you had the pleasure of hearing all the others, I didn't see why you shouldn't do your bit. Satisfied?"

"No," Lucy told him bluntly. "I think there was another reason than that!"

"Well, you tell me what it was," he suggested lazily.

"The evening before—Saturday—when I asked you if I could be there, you were amused," Lucy said accusingly. "I couldn't understand then, but afterwards—"

"Afterwards, you did?" he suggested. "And what were your conclusions?"

"I think," Lucy said deliberately, "that you were amused not only because you knew what you had planned to let me in for—and that I had no idea of it, but also because—" she paused, seeking the right words. "Because you enjoy making people do what you want—making them do better than they really can—"

"My good child!" Owen was wide awake now. "Do you mean you think I put on a sort of Syengali act—good lord, yes, you do! Well, of all the—"

"You never took your eyes off me once," Lucy accused him. "And—and I couldn't look away—"

"Couldn't you now? That's interesting." Owen stood up and looked down at her thoughtfully. "Well, my child, you've come to entirely the wrong conclusion."

"Then tell me what the right one is," Lucy suggested.

Owen hesitated. Then he shook his head.

"No—not yet. Perhaps not ever—though, if it gives you any satisfaction, I admit that my motive was not entirely disinterested. And now, I really must go in search of that drink !"

He strolled off, but after he had gone a few yards he turned and came back.

"Lucy, for your own sake, just because you have had one unhappy experience, don't persuade yourself that everyone is tarred with the same brush. It isn't true, and it will only make you unhappier to believe that it is."

Then, without waiting for her to reply, he retraced his steps in the direction of the house.

. . .

A few days later Mrs. Mayberry came to the study to speak to Lucy. She was smiling and she had a letter in her hand.

"It's from my brother Stanley—the Mr. Keane for whom you worked. Some time ago he asked us to spend some time with him in Monaco—he has a villa there and the plan was that we should visit him in June. It isn't, I understand, one of the really large villas, so I wrote to him asking if there would be room for you as well as Owen, Bertha and myself. And this morning I had his reply. There is !"

"Oh !" Lucy was too surprised for the moment to say anything else. "But why should I be included in your holiday arrangements, Mrs. Mayberry ? I mean, I've only been with you such a very short time—"

In fact, she was not at all sure that she liked the idea of being on holiday with Owen making up one of the party. Since their conversation in the garden he had made no further attempt to discuss the reason for his insistence and her resentment, but since he had said he had no intention of telling her the truth, at least not yet, that did not surprise her. But it did disturb her. In his own opinion he had had a good excuse for his inconsiderate behaviour. Then why not tell her ? His reticence puzzled Lucy, and for some reason that she could not understand, it made her feel supremely self-conscious in his presence. Fortunately her work and his kept them from seeing too much of one another, but on holiday—that could well be a different matter.

Mrs. Mayberry looked slightly surprised, probably because Lucy had not shown the delight she had expected at the prospect of such a delightful experience.

"Well, dear, it won't be entirely a holiday as far as you and I are concerned," she explained. "I shall want to continue working at my book, you see. I never like to make a long break when once I have started and it is going reasonably well."

"I see," Lucy said, brightening up.

"So I do hope you will feel you can come, Lucy, because I must have a secretary, if not you, then someone else—though I would very much prefer, of course, that it should be you."

It was kindly said, but it reminded Lucy gently that she was, after all, Mrs. Mayberry's employee and could really not refuse to go any more than Bertha could.

"In that case, yes, I'd like to come," she said. "It was only that—"

"I know, my dear. You are both independent and honest, and you did not like the idea of accepting something to which you did not feel you were entitled. Well, I respect your attitude, but really, that is not the situation at all."

Lucy felt rather uncomfortable at accepting praise which she did not feel she deserved, but there was really nothing she could say—unless she explained her real reason, and that, of course, was out of the question.

"Well then, let's get down to definite arrangements," Mrs. Mayberry went on briskly. "I expect you would

278

like to ask your parents if they are quite agreeable to you coming with us?"

"I would," Lucy answered. "Not because I think that they will object, but I think they'd like it if I did."

"Of course they would! Well then, telephone to them today. And then—a passport. Have you got one?"

"Oh, yes," Lucy said quickly, and paused. "I mean —no, I haven't."

Not unnaturally, Mrs. Mayberry looked puzzled, and Lucy was forced to explain.

"I—I did have one. But not in my name," she stumbled.

"But, my dear—!"

Lucy took a deep breath.

"I—was going to be married. And the passport was made out in my—in the name I should have had, and the Rector was to keep it until—until afterwards. But —but I didn't get married," she explained baldly.

"I see," Mrs. Mayberry accepted the explanation calmly and without comment. "Then I expect, in that case, that the Rector has dealt with the matter. Perhaps you could take it up with your father when you ring up?"

"Yes, I'll do that," Lucy promised, grateful that no unwelcome sympathy had been shown.

However, just as she was leaving the study, Mrs. Mayberry paused.

"Lucy, you weren't going to Monaco, were you?"

For a moment Lucy could not think what she meant.

"Going to—?" she said in a puzzled way. "Oh, I see. No. We—we were going to Spain."

And wondered that she could speak of that dream

honeymoon so calmly—so much as if it had all happened long, long ago, and had never been the concern of Lucy Darvill at all.

∗   ∗   ∗

After that, arrangements for the holiday went through smoothly and quickly. In the mood in which Lucy liked him best, Owen consulted her on the subject of making it as easy a trip as possible for Mrs. Mayberry.

"As you know, though walking is painful and she can't do too much of it, the worst possible thing is for her to sit in one position too long. So, as far as I can see, the best thing is to make the journey in as easy stages as possible with pauses between each stage. From here to the airport—"

"About a hundred and thirty miles—between three and four hours' driving. We must stop at least twice," Lucy pondered.

"Yes." Owen spread a map out on the desk. "I thought perhaps Salisbury for one."

"That's a busy town," Lucy said doubtfully. "It might not be possible to stop right in front of the hotel. What about Wilton or Winterslow? We stopped at both of those when we went to Devon last year. Either would be quite easy for Mrs. Mayberry, and neither is far from Salisbury. And for the next stop—" she frowned. "There doesn't seem to be anything at about the right distance. We bypass Basingstoke—Hook? I don't remember anything about it though I think it's only a small place. Couldn't you find out if there is an hotel there and phone to find out just how convenient it would be?"

"Good girl!" Owen sounded so genuinely grateful that Lucy was not annoyed. "Then, when we get to the airport, she can move about for a bit—I'll arrange for a chair for getting her along corridors and so on.

But there's nothing to be done once we get on the plane, and that means something over two hours. Too long. Oh, hell ! Y'know, I don't think she ought to attempt it."

"But she does so want to," Lucy sighed. "Look, Mr. Vaughan, if we go via Paris it will take longer in total, but isn't there a long stop there ? Or better still, couldn't you say that you have business in Paris and need to stop the night ? That would mean Mrs. Mayborry could have a proper night's rest without feeling that she was being a nuisance—and she does so hate to feel that."

"She does, indeed," Owen concurred. "Yes, that's the ticket ! Of course, there will have to be a genuine appointment, otherwise Aunt Louise will rumble it as easy as winking ! Well, I can arrange that. Then on to Nice the next day. I'm arranging to hire a car there —I don't like using a car with a right-hand drive on the Continent—and that can pick us up at Nice airport. Yes, that's about as good as we can manage, I think. What an admirable accomplice you make, Lucy !"

For a second his hand dropped lightly on her shoulder, but even as he turned to go he asked a question.

"How does it come about that you're so *au courant* with air routes and schedules ?"

"I looked them up," Lucy replied briefly, not thinking it necessary to add that actually, before deciding to go to Spain, she and Dick had considered honeymooning in the South of France and she had obtained the information then.

However, Owen appeared quite satisfied, for with no more than a nod he left the room, whistling cheerfully.

CHAPTER VI

DESPITE all their care and forethought, Mrs. Mayberry was tired to the point of exhaustion when they touched down at Nice airport. As a result, when they had passed through customs, Owen insisted on a wait in the lounge before making the final stage of the journey by road.

After having provided a brandy for Mrs. Mayberry and sirop for Lucy and Bertha, Owen left them to go in search of the car. When he returned, Mrs. Mayberry insisted that she felt considerably better and quite equal to continuing.

Lucy did not feel entirely convinced that this was so, but realised that the sooner Mrs. Mayberry reached her destination and was able to relax, the better it would be for her. Bertha, too, was anxious to reach Villa des Fleurs so that she could make her mistress "a cup of decent English tea—better than all these foreign drinks".

But though Lucy made no protest, her anxiety prevented her from appreciating her surroundings. As a result she had only a blurred impression of the exotic glitter of Nice, the winding road which led to Monaco, bounded on one side by the incredibly blue sea and on the other by steeply rising mountains. It was, in fact, a considerable relief when she realised that they had turned off the main road and were surely coming shortly to their journey's end.

At last they came to open double gates through which the car turned, and Lucy had the first glimpse of the villa which was to be her home for the next four weeks.

Perhaps, by some standards, it was not so very big or magnificent, but to Lucy it looked like something out of a fairy tale. Dazzlingly white where it was not smothered in the wine purple of bougainvillea, the Villa des

Fleurs lived up to its name. It was set in the most perfect garden Lucy had ever seen. Flower beds, breathtakingly vivid, dominated the scene. And as if that were not enough, flowering shrubs grew with a luxuriance that they can never attain in a colder climate. The eye rested almost gratefully on the deep green of trees which provided not only shade but an impressive background for the brilliance of the flowers. Lucy thought she caught the glimpse of blue water among the trees, but by this time the car had stopped and the door was opened for her to get out.

The villa was a long, low building, roofed in green tiles and having green shutters at the windows. Along its full length was a terrace protected from the heat of the sun by a green and white striped awning. As Lucy got out she saw that Mr. Keane—a very different Mr. Keane from the precise professional man for whom she had worked in London—had been waiting to welcome them and now he came to the car.

Naturally, the first concern was to help Mrs. Mayberry from the car and indoors, but now, in her pleasure at seeing her brother—and perhaps in relief that the journey was over—she seemed to gain both strength and mobility in an amazing way, and refused all but the minimum amount of assistance. Owen, however, had evidently no intention of allowing her to overtax herself further. After allowing the brother and sister a few minutes to greet one another, he coaxed his aunt into her chair and wheeled her indoors with Bertha trotting beside him. Mr. Keane turned to Lucy, who had been standing rather shyly in the background.

"I'm extremely glad to see you, my dear," he said pleasantly. "And I hope you will thoroughly enjoy yourself here."

"I'm sure I shall," Lucy said, grateful not only for his kindly welcome but because there was no hint, either in his manner or in the way he looked at her, that he was in the least bit curious as to how she had weathered the blow he knew she had received. She had been just a little bit afraid that, in all kindness, he might ask questions, but clearly that was not going to be so. "I think it was very, very kind of you to be willing for me to come."

Stanley Keane smiled. He had always liked this girl who had worked so well for him, believing her to be a particularly nice-natured person—sensitive, too. That was why, as soon as it had been suggested that she should come here, he had made up his mind that she should quickly be assured that the past was, as far as he was concerned, a permanently closed book. That he had been right in thinking that she was the last person who would want to snivel over her broken love story had been made perfectly clear by the gratitude she could not hide. Well, she was right, of course, and he sincerely hoped that one of these days she would find that the reward for her courage was that she had forgotten the young man who had treated her so scurvily and had fallen genuinely in love with a worthwhile man. But that wasn't the sort of thing you said to the person concerned. You just waited and hoped on their account.

"I was delighted when my sister wrote to me suggesting it," he told her. "And though I know you and she intend working, I'm sure there will be plenty of time for you to get about and see something of the place. I must admit that I'm too old now to enjoy racketing about and I spend most of my time in the garden here."

"I don't wonder," Lucy said warmly. "It's so very beautiful."

"Yes, it is," Mr. Keane agreed, and laughed softly. "You know, it was left to me by an old friend and client some years ago. When I heard about it, I admit I wasn't particularly pleased. I had no use for a villa on the Côte d'Azur, and it simply meant that I was faced with the bother of selling it. However, I decided to look at the place in order to get some sort of idea of the value of it—and that was my downfall! I fell in love with it and now nothing in the world would persuade me to sell it. One of these days I shall retire here," he added with considerable satisfaction. "And now, I expect you would like to see your room, but if you could spare me a moment or two first, I'd be obliged if you'd tell me what you think of my sister's condition."

He motioned her to a chair and Lucy sat down, her forehead puckered.

"It's rather difficult for me to say. You see, I haven't been with her for very long so that I can't really make useful comparisons. And then she's so very brave—but I think, judging by the way she has kept down to work, that it can't be as bad as it sometimes is. And then, a few weeks back, she and Mr. Vaughan entertained some people for the weekend, and that didn't seem to tire her too much. Of course, she rested quite a lot—"

Mr. Keane chuckled.

"One of those famous weekends ending up with a show and everybody doing a turn?" he asked. "I got let in for one of those once, and when my turn came, all I could think of was some not very respectable limericks! However, they went down very well! What did you do?"

"I—sang," Lucy admitted reluctantly, and then, in a burst of confidence: "It was rather dreadful, because I've never done such a thing before in front of people —and one of them was Miss Singleton!"

"Oh—yes, the singer. One of Owen's protégés—and a very successful one, I believe, though possessed by rather a troublesome sense of gratitude."

Lucy could not hide her surprise.

"But if Mr. Vaughan has done so much for her, isn't it natural—?" she suggested.

"No doubt," Mr. Keane agreed drily. "But the peculiar thing about gratitude is that it's something of a boomerang. If you have earned it, in time it can happen that you, and not the recipient of your help, become under an obligation—ah, here is Owen. Well, my boy, how is Louise now?"

"Not too bad, all things considered," Owen told him. "Bertha has made her a cup of tea—the old dear brought over all the necessary tackle in a small case she insisted on clinging to all the way with the result that Customs were convinced it must hold something very valuable and insisted on going through it with a fine tooth comb! I only hope they couldn't understand all the things she called them. Interfering young busybodies was the least of them !"

Mr. Keane laughed. Then Lucy suggested going to her room and left the two men alone. Mr. Keane looked at his nephew speculatively.

"You look almost as fagged as Louise does," he remarked.

Owen shrugged his shoulders.

"The last year has been pretty busy," he admitted noncommittally.

"H'm. And will I kindly mind my own business?" Mr. Keane suggested. "All right, I can take a hint."

"Good," Owen said laconically.

"All the same, there's one tip I'm going to give you," Mr. Keane announced.

"Well?"

"Be content to make haste slowly," Mr. Keane told him. "In fact, at present, simply marking time would be even better."

The eyes of the two men met and there was a certain grudging admiration in Owen's.

"You see too damn much," he complained disrespectfully.

Mr. Keane chuckled pleasurably. He was extremely fond of his nephew, but it would be against nature if, as the older generation, he did not get considerable satisfaction out of scoring a point off the younger.

* * *

Lucy's room was large and airy and very pleasant. She liked the sense of space which the simple furnishings gave it and saw with appreciation that flowers had been put in the room just as they always were at Spindles. The maid who had shown her to her room had asked if she would like help with her unpacking, and Lucy, in her rather schoolgirl French, had said that she could manage alone. The girl had smiled, but she looked rather disappointed. Perhaps, Lucy thought, she had been quite pleased at the advent of someone almost as young as herself in a home where everyone else was considerably older. So Lucy obligingly changed her mind—only to be treated to a eulogy on the subject of—Owen! Thérèse had apparently been bowled over at first sight.

"So handsome, so distinguished, so much a man of the world!" she said enthusiastically, abandoning her task of putting away Lucy's undies in order to roll her eyes up to heaven. "Mam'selle is very fortunate to have his constant companionship!"

"But I don't," Lucy assured her as emphatically as her command of French permitted. "I am Mrs. Mayberry's secretary, and I shall be working here just as I do in England."

But Thérèse was not in the least convinced.

"Ah—England, yes," she agreed disparagingly. "But here—it will be different! Mam'selle will see!"

And then, since there was nothing else to excuse her lingering, she left Lucy to think over what she had said.

And just what she did think, Lucy was not quite sure. Certainly she was annoyed at the girl's suggestion that romance could ever blossom between Owen and herself, but on the other hand, really it was so ludicrous as to be almost amusing. Finally, she shrugged her shoulders.

Thérèse would soon find out how mistaken she was!

But thinking of Owen had made her remember something else—Mr. Keane's extraordinary remark about Marion being possessed by rather a troublesome sense of gratitude and of it being a kind of boomerang which had put Owen under some sort of an obligation—

Lucy sat down in the gaily chintz-cushioned armchair. Troublesome—obligation—it simply didn't make sense. Owen and Marion were in love with one another. There simply couldn't be any question of Owen experiencing any embarrassment! Certainly, he had shown no evidence of it that Lucy had seen. Besides—

Lucy shook her head and finally came to what seemed to her the only conclusion. Mr. Keane was a dear. She had always been fond of him, and in his present friendly, relaxed mood, she thought she would come to like him still more. But that did not mean he might not have his own ideas about the suitability of the girl his nephew had chosen to be his wife. Certainly Lucy remembered that he had applauded her own decision to give up work when she got married. Yes, that might be it. Mr. Keane might think it would be better if Owen married someone who would devote all her time to him instead, in all probability, of giving much of it to her career.

"But whatever he thinks, there's nothing he can do about it," Lucy decided. "I can't see Owen letting anybody tell him what he ought to do—let alone doing what they want if it doesn't suit him!"

•   •   •

The next few days passed very placidly and, even Lucy admitted, happily. Mrs. Mayberry, eager though she had been to continue her book without delay, was so influenced by the beauty of the Villa des Fleurs and the holiday atmosphere that reigned that she was content to be idle. Which meant, of course, that Lucy had nothing to do either.

On the day of their arrival she had explored the grounds of the villa and had found to her delight that the glimpse of water she had noticed was a swimming pool complete with a diving board, and on the smooth tiled surround to the pool, cane chairs made comfortable with cushions covered in waterproof material.

She was gazing entranced at the limpid blue water, wondering whether she would be allowed to swim in it, when Owen startled her by speaking close to her. He had approached noiselessly over the smooth turf and was now standing beside her.

"So you've discovered my delight and joy," he remarked, gazing, as she had done, at the inviting pool. "I always come here as soon as I can manage it."

"I'm sorry," Lucy said stiffly. "I didn't realise—or I wouldn't have come—"

She turned to go, but he blocked her way.

"Don't be a duffer," he advised her amiably. "This pool happens to be Uncle Stanley's property, so I've no right whatever to claim exclusive use of it, as you'd realise if only you'd use those wits of yours."

"No right, perhaps," Lucy agreed. "But you may wish you had."

"Well, I don't," he retorted flatly. "And for heaven's sake, don't read something I don't mean into everything I say! It makes life so difficult. In fact—" he hesitated. "Lucy, will you do me a favour?"

"It depends what it is," she replied cautiously.

"Not taking any chances, are you?" Well, here it is in words of one syllable—while we're here, will you agree to a truce? I'd be most grateful if you could see your way to it."

Lucy was too surprised to answer. Owen begging a favour! It was so out of character as to be incredible.

"But why?" she asked dubiously.

"You do like chapter and verse, don't you?" he sighed resignedly. "All right, you shall have it. To begin with, it's my sincere hope that despite her determination to get on with her book, Aunt Louise will so enjoy Uncle Stanley's company that she'll let things slide—which would be a good thing. Don't you agree?"

"Yes, I think I do," Lucy agreed thoughtfully. "I think sometimes she drives herself to work because it keeps her mind off the pain she suffers."

"Exactly!" Owen agreed. "But none the less, that produces a sort of tenseness which doesn't really do her any good. Now if she can achieve the same result nattering happily to Uncle Stan, she'll relax. And nothing could be better for her than that."

"Yes, but I don't see—"

"Isn't it obvious?" Owen sounded surprised at her lack of comprehension. "If she doesn't work, nor do you. Now, if you're hanging about at a loose end because you can't stand the thought of spending an occasional odd hour in my company, she'll spot it immediately, because we're living at closer quarters here than at Spindles. And she'll start feeling she ought to get down to work for your sake. But if she sees you're enjoying yourself, or at least, appearing to, she won't worry. See?"

"Yes, I see what you mean," Lucy assured him. "But there's one thing I don't think you've realised. Mrs. Mayberry is a very kind person. If she thought I was enjoying myself, wouldn't she pretend she didn't want to work in order not so spoil my fun? And that would be dreadful because she does pay me to work."

"You needn't bother about that," Owen assured her confidently. "When the writing bug really bites my Aunt Louise, no other consideration is of the least importance! I don't say she'd actually yank you out of bed in order to get on with it, but precious near!"

It all sounded very convincing, yet Lucy hesitated. Might it not be just another of his clever tricks? Though she could not imagine what it might be, wasn't it possible that his real reason for suggesting a truce was something quite different—something he wasn't willing to admit? She looked at him doubtfully.

"You're quite right," he admitted. "It's one reason why —but not the only one." He hesitated. "I don't like begging for favours, least of all from you, Lucy, but the fact is I'm so damned tired that I can't face up to an atmosphere of intolerance and misunderstanding—"

If, more than once this afternoon, Owen had surprised her, now she was really startled. Owen tired out! It didn't seem possible, and yet when she looked closer she could see undeniable evidence that he was speaking the truth. There was a tenseness about the lines of his mouth and jaw, and his eyes were ineffably weary.

He smiled wryly at her.

"Makes me seem almost human, doesn't it?" he remarked. "Well, there it is, my dear. I'm completely at your mercy, because if you choose to fight, you'll win because I shan't even try to defend myself! So what's the verdict?"

For answer, Lucy simply held out her hand and Owen took it in a firm clasp.

"Thank you, Lucy," he said simply. "I'm truly grateful!"

"No," Lucy said quickly. "Don't be grateful, there's no need for that. But do be sensible—"

"All right, I'll do what I'm told," Owen promised with surprising meekness. "Though I can see you're going to bully me unmercifully. What's the treatment, Doctor?"

"I think you yourself probably know the answer to

that quite well," Lucy said severely. "Stop doing the things that have made you tired!"

"Out of the mouth of babes—" Owen marvelled. "But that's rather negative. No other suggestions?"

"Yes—only do the things you really want to! At least —" she added hurriedly as an amused gleam came into his eyes, "so long as that doesn't mean annoying other people. For instance, why not have a swim now—before dinner? You would enjoy it, wouldn't you?"

"That," Owen told her, "is sheer inspiration. Yes, I certainly should—particularly if you'll join me?"

Lucy hesitated. That, surely, was making rather much of what Owen himself had referred to merely as a truce. And yet—why not? It would be heaven to slip into that warm, unruffled water, to feel it rippling smoothly past as one swam—to forget the past, even momentarily, in a purely hedonistic delight—

"The waters of Lethe?" Owen suggested softly, his eyes on her expressive face. "Let's see how effective they are, shall we, Lucy?"

"Yes, let's," she said breathlessly.

* * *

Despite Owen's assurance that not only would it be better if Mrs. Mayberry did not work, but also that she would not want to, Lucy was not entirely reassured. However, as the days went by, it became more and more clear that he was right. Mrs. Mayberry was obviously happier and in better health than Lucy had yet seen her. She and Mr. Keane spent almost all their time together, talking, laughing and taking walks in the grounds. What was more, these walks were increasing in duration and distance and Mrs. Mayberry was sleeping better than she had done for years. As a result, Lucy felt she could enjoy herself with a clear conscience, and she was honest enough to admit that her truce with Owen contributed in no small degree to her pleasure.

For one thing it meant that with him she could go to places she could not have gone to alone, and for another, with the car practically at her disposal, she could go farther afield.

"Old Monaco first, and then Monte Carlo?" Owen suggested.

"Please," Lucy replied, adding hastily : "If it won't bore you—I suppose you know it all by heart, don't you?"

"Perhaps it would be more accurate to say by head than by heart," Owen said lightly. "Somehow one doesn't take much notice of places if one is on one's own. But now I shall see it afresh through your eyes. Come along !"

Perhaps because it was all so new to her, Lucy fell in love with everything she saw, whether it was the terracotta houses and villas of Monaco, dominated by the solid mass of the Palais Princier or the new, glittering buildings of Monte Carlo. She stood entranced in a cobbled square, its quaint houses like something out of a fairy tale—and yet she was just as enthralled by the prodigal display of such luxuries as she had never seen in the Boulevards, which surely existed solely for the benefit of multi-millionaires. At one moment her attention was caught by the flash of precious stones—bracelets, necklaces, tiaras, all rivalling one another in their chilly beauty, lace so fragile that one would be afraid to handle it, trinkets so delicious in shape and workmanship that one could hardly believe they were made by human hands—Lucy could hardly tear herself away.

"Do you wish you could afford to have this sort of thing?" Owen asked curiously with a comprehensive sweep of his hand.

"No, I don't," Lucy said unhesitatingly, turning to

him from the contemplation of an exquisite Fabergé trinket.

"No? I thought all women coveted thing like this."

Lucy shook her head.

"I love looking at them," she explained. "But if one could afford to buy them I suppose one could really afford to buy almost anything in the world?"

"More or less, no doubt," Owen agreed.

"Well, I think that would be dull," Lucy declared firmly. "Fancy never looking forward to having anything—never saving up for it! And fancy having so much that no one thing stood out—no, I don't envy that sort of person!"

"Wise child," Owen commented. "Then let's go and have a bathe, shall we?"

"In the sea?" Lucy asked with almost childish glee.

"In the sea," he promised.

Unused, at home, to swimming in anything but almost invariably chilly seas, the warm, tideless water was a revelation to Lucy. Side by side they swam out to an anchored raft, lay supine on it in utter contentment until Owen insisted that she had had sunshine enough for the time being and then swam back to change and sit for a while in the shade of the trees under which the beach nestled. They spoke but little, for Lucy was too entranced by the constantly moving scene—the speedboats flashing across the glassy blue water, the children, wearing the absolute minimum in the way of clothing playing with gaily coloured beach balls, the women, so many of them lovely enough to make Lucy sigh faintly, and wearing such glamorous beach costumes that it was clear they were never meant for swimming in—all these in turn caught and held her attention, and Owen, looking at her eager, alert face, was well content to sit silent.

"Well?" he asked at last. "Does it meet with your approval?"

"Oh, *yes!*" she told him ecstatically. "It's like something out of a book!"

"Not quite real?" he suggested.

"Not quite," she agreed. "Or else it's that I don't feel quite real. You see, it isn't *my* world."

"Nor mine," Owen concurred. "For a holiday, yes. But—" he shook his head. And then after an interval: "What is your world, Lucy?"

"I don't quite know," she admitted. "Not—what it used to be. And not this. But I haven't got any further yet than that."

"You've travelled a good distance already," he commented, and touched her hand lightly with his.

.   .   .   .

The next day he refused to tell her where he was taking her. All he would say was that if she imagined something utterly and entirely different from what they had seen the day before she would not be far out. Also that she had better bring a coat with her.

Guessing that the possible need of a coat meant that they were to take a mountain drive, Lucy was surprised and a little disappointed when Owen drove along the road by which they had arrived in Monaco and so to Nice. But once through the town he turned to the right along a road that ran by the side of a river. Almost immediately the road began to rise steeply and Lucy could see that they were heading for the mountains of the Alpes-Maritimes, but she asked no questions, for she knew they would not be answered.

But once she could not help exclaiming: "How beautiful!" to be answered by the one word: "Wait!" But Owen was smiling.

On they went, climbing all the time and always following the path that the rivers had worn during the centuries. They passed through wild, steep defiles cut through rock that was copper-coloured and which Owen told her were the Georges de la Vésuble. But names meant little to Lucy. She was intoxicated by the wild beauty and the fresh, wine-like air, beyond words, content just to look—

At St. Martin Vésuble he slowed down almost to a walking pace.

"Would you like to see the sanctuary of the Madonna at Fenestre—or the cascades at Boréon?" he asked doubtfully. "They're both worth seeing in their own way."

"Couldn't we do both?" Lucy suggested, and Owen laughed.

"It will mean we're a bit late for lunch," he warned her.

"Does that matter very much—on a day like this?" she asked, and again he laughed.

"Not really," he admitted.

So they saw first the charming sanctuary and then the wild, tumbling falls. After they had gazed their fill, Owen turned to the car, and Lucy made her first suggestion of the day—only to have it rejected.

"Couldn't we have lunch here?"

"No, not here." And then, as if he were anxious not to hurt her feelings : "You'll see why—when we get there."

So they went on, along a narrow valley, with mountains towering on either side until at last Owen said softly : "Here!" and stopped the car.

There was no need to ask why he had chosen this particular spot to stop. They were by the side of an enchanted lake, an emerald jewel set about with trees and with crimson rhododendrons beginning to show their colour.

They got out, but neither of them spoke. Neither consciously thought: "This is the most beautiful place in the world, I must not forget a single thing about it!"

because they knew that such utter loveliness never could be forgotten any more than one would ever be able to find words to describe it. But each knew that their delight was greater because it was shared—

But on the way home, in the middle of a long silence, Owen suddenly said:

"I've been there several times before, but always alone. I've not risked taking anyone else in case—"

"Yes?" Lucy encouraged gently.

"In case—they talked too much," he confessed, and grinned in a half shamed, half confiding way that once again left Lucy silent.

.　.　.　.　.

Just after breakfast, two days later, they were entertained by the arrival of an unusually large and luxurious yacht in the harbour.

"I think I know her," Mr. Keane remarked, picking up his binoculars and focusing them. "Yes—*La Mouette.* She's been in once or twice before. She did belong to an American, but I heard he'd sold her recently—I don't know to whom."

"Someone with a good lot of money, I should imagine." Owen remarked drily. "It comes expensive to run a tub of that sort!"

Mrs. Mayberry reproached him for his disparaging description, but to Lucy it had come as something of a relief. To her there was something overpowering, even threatening about such magnificence, and Owen's light dismissal of it seemed to break the spell.

Suddenly he turned to Lucy.

"Let's go into Nice and have a look at the old town," he suggested. "I've never had time to before and I believe it's worth a visit."

Lucy looked at Mrs. Mayberry for permission.

"Yes, of course, my dear. But, Owen, it's going to be a really hot day. Don't walk the child off her feet!"

"I won't," he promised. "And what's more, when we've done enough sightseeing, I'll take her to one of the hotels on the Promenade des Anglais and stand her a drink on the terrace. How's that?"

Lucy enjoyed seeing the old town, with its quaint buildings and its streets climbing, sometimes steeply, sometimes up wide, shallow steps, to the rocks behind. The flower market was not yet open, although it was a scene of bustling activity in preparation for the day's trade, but every window seemed to have a show of flowers and the many balconies were draped with vines and creepers. But charming though it all was, Lucy was not sorry when Owen suggested that they should go in search of the drink he had promised her, and drove first along the Quai des Etats-Unis and then the Promenade des Anglais.

The terrace of the hotel he chose was protected from the sunshine by a gaily striped awning and Lucy sank down gratefully in its shade.

"Something long and cold?" Owen suggested, and gave his order.

Despite the chatter all around them and the sound of traffic, their table became a pleasant little oasis of peace and contentment, but that state of affairs was not to last long. Lucy was less than half way through her drink when a man approached and laying a hand on Owen's shoulder, greeted him enthusiastically in French so rapid that Lucy had considerable difficulty in following what he was saying. She felt rather out of it because although Owen performed the necessary introduction punctiliously, the newcomer obviously regarded this chance meeting as a heaven-sent opportunity to talk business. What was more, despite an entire lack of encouragement on Owen's part, he made an insistent request that he should come to his room in the hotel—"but only for a moment!"— in order to see some documents he had there. In fact, he jumped to his feet, obviously expecting Owen to follow.

"This is a confounded nuisance," Owen remarked in an irritable undertone to Lucy. "The last thing I wanted was for it to get out that I'm in the locality, but Le Marquand is so insistent—and to be perfectly honest, he's too big a noise to offend. All the same—" he frowned. "Look, Lucy, would you mind if I leave you here for a few minutes? You see, that way I have an excuse for cutting it short that I wouldn't have if you came with me. I'll have a word with our waiter to keep an eye on you so that you're not annoyed—"

"Of course," Lucy said quickly. "I quite understand. And I'll be quite all right."

Still frowning, Owen hesitated momentarily and then strode off. Lucy sipped her drink slowly and pensively, hoping he wouldn't be too long. Then she became so lost in thought that she was startled when someone spoke her name.

"Lucy! What in the world are you doing here?"

It was Dick Corbett.

CHAPTER VII

"Dick!"

It couldn't be true, Lucy thought wildly. Coincidences like this didn't happen in real life. She and Dick had parted for all time—and yet here he was, sitting right opposite to her in the chair which Owen had so recently vacated!

"Lucy, what *are* you doing here?" Dick repeated urgently, and, it seemed to Lucy, uneasily. "It isn't because you knew—I mean, you're not hoping—"

Lucy was suddenly angrier than she had ever been in her life before.

"If you're insinuating that I knew you would be here and I hoped that we would meet, you're quite wrong," she said icily. "I'm here because my employer has need of my services here."

"Your employer—old Keane?" Dick looked surprised.

"No, not Mr. Keane. His sister. She is a novelist and I'm working as her secretary," Lucy explained shortly. "And now, Dick, I think you'd better go. We have nothing whatever to say to one another."

"I'm not so sure of that—"

His mood had changed. Instead of being perturbed by her unexpected presence, he now appeared reluctant to leave her, all the more because Lucy, uncomfortably aware that Owen might return at any moment, was giving him no encouragement whatever.

"I am—quite!"

Dick regarded her moodily. He knew perfectly well that he had treated this girl, who had given him her trust and love, in a shameful way. But he was not the sort of man who could tolerate being presented with an unflattering picture of himself. Somehow or other he had got to make her understand that it had not been his fault—

"I don't wonder you're sore," he said, calculatingly abject. "I treated you like an absolute heel—oh, yes, I did," deliberately misunderstanding Lucy's gesture of distaste. "And I'm damned sorry about it, Lucy. But the fact is—"

"Does mam'selle require—anything?" the waiter asked suavely at Lucy's elbow.

Remembering that Owen had said he would ask the waiter to keep an eye on her, Lucy knew that she had only got to say that Dick was annoying her for him to be requested to leave in no uncertain terms. But she could not bring herself to do it. Dick was hardly likely to accept such an ignominious rebuff without making a scene—Owen would become involved, and he would detest that, particularly if Monsieur le Marquand was present. Somehow, she must persuade Dick to go. She shook her head, but Dick took it on himself to make use of the man's presence.

"Yes, get me a double scotch on the rocks—and another of whatever that was," pointing to Lucy's glass.

"Dick—no!" Lucy said sharply. "I don't want it— and I wish you'd go."

She would have gone herself, only Owen would expect to find her here when he returned. She glanced at the door through which he had vanished, half hoping, half afraid that he might be coming back. There was no sign of him, and Dick was talking again, taking up the conversation at exactly the same point as he had dropped it.

"The fact is, I lost my head completely over Gwenda. It's no excuse, of course, but—well, it's flattering to a chap who's an absolute nobody if a girl like Gwenda makes a dead set at him. I mean, with her looks and her money, she could have taken her pick. But she made it clear how she felt about me and—well, I fell for it, hook, line and sinker—" he covered his eyes momentarily with his hand. "Honestly, Lucy, I didn't mean to let you down. It just sort of—happened."

Lucy did not reply. Stirring faintly in her mind was the memory of something Owen had said about Dick— yes, of course, it was when he had seen that wedding photograph in the evening paper.

He had said that Dick had a thoroughly weak face, that he was the sort who would always take the line of least resistance. She had been furious with Owen for that, but now Dick himself was making his own weakness an excuse for what he had done.

Realising that he was making no impression whatever, Dick ploughed even deeper into the mire.

"Of course I don't expect you to forgive me—why should you? But I'd like you to know that I realise now that I've made the most ghastly mistake of my life. You see, though Gwenda can be as sweet as honey when she gets her own way, she's been so spoilt all her life that if she meets with the least opposition, there's the deuce—"

"Dick, stop!" Lucy said peremptorily. "I won't listen! It's absolutely horrible of you to talk like that about your wife."

"Well, I only thought you'd like to know that if I played you a dirty trick, believe me, I'm paying for it," Dick said sulkily.

"Well, you're quite wrong. I don't want to hear anything about it. And if you don't go at once, Dick, I'll ask the waiter to make you!" Lucy said resolutely.

"Not until I've had my drink," Dick insisted obstinately. "Ah, here it is!"

"Now—at once!" Lucy said firmly, completely beyond caring now what result her insistence might have on him.

"Oh, very well!" He stood up, fumbled in his pocket and slapped down the few coins he drew from it on to the table. "Pay for it out of that—every sou I've got—and all I shall have until I eat humble pie and get back into Gwenda's good books ! Pretty grim for a man to be next door to a beggar when his wife is absolutely rolling in it, isn't it ?"

He laughed bitterly, leaving Lucy dismayed and sick at heart.

So that was Dick ! Disloyal to her, even more horribly disloyal to his wife.

"Mam'selle is feeling unwell ?" the waiter asked diffidently.

"Yes—no—I'm all right," Lucy said hurriedly. "But please take the drinks away—and the money as well."

"But mam'selle truly looks a little faint. Perhaps it would be a good thing to drink a little ?" the man suggested.

"No," Lucy said sharply. Not for anything would she accept anything from Dick ever again—even so small a thing as a fruit cordial. "Take them both away, please, at once."

With a shrug the man complied. He had done his best, but these English were not to be understood ! To waste two good drinks—and also to pay for them—incredible !

Lucy sat very still. She wished she could forget all about Dick and the things he had said, but it wasn't possible. How could it be when in a few brief moments she had been forced to realise that the Dick she had loved had never really existed ? If only he hadn't said those things about Gwenda ! And if only Gwenda were not so rich ! It had hurt terribly to believe that Dick's love for herself had been such a little thing that he could forget all about it and fall really in love with another girl, but now she knew that there was something much worse than that—or could be. Why had Dick married Gwenda ? For love—or for her money ? Despite the heat of the day Lucy shivered.

She had remembered that Owen had said Dick would always take the line of least resistance—but he had said something else as well : *"Particularly if it pays him to."*

And everything Dick had said confirmed the truth of that—his insistence that he had made a terrible mistake—his resentment that he was not able to spend his wife's money as freely as he wished—

"Sorry I've been so long."

Owen was back. Lucy stood up quickly, thankful that he had stayed away so long, even more thankful that now she could leave this horrible place.

"Le Marquand simply wouldn't stop talking—" Owen went on.

"It didn't matter," Lucy said dully. "There was—plenty to look at."

Owen looked at her intently, but though she appeared to be a totally different girl from the one he had left not really so very long ago, he did not comment on the fact.

"Would you like another drink ?" he asked. "Or shall we go straight back ?"

"Oh, straight back," Lucy said quickly. And then, realising that it must seem to him she was acting in a peculiar way, she added: "I've got rather a headache—"

"Have you ?" he said sympathetically, slipping his arm through hers. "Too much sunshine, perhaps. Well, come along. We'll be home in next to no time and then you can have a rest in a shaded room."

It was a very silent journey back to the Villa des Fleurs. The purring of the car and the breeze which their own movement produced lulled Lucy into a sort of stupor. Owen, presumably, was silent out of consideration for her far from fictitious headache. But it was he who first broke the silence.

"Lucy, if your head is better by the evening, will

you come with me to the Opera House ? There's an internationally famous ballet company visiting Monaco—they're doing Swan Lake tonight."

Lucy, only vaguely aware that he had spoken at all, looked at him dully.

"What did you say ?" she asked.

Owen repeated his request, and this time Lucy sat bolt upright.

"I—I—" she began, and to her horror, burst into tears.

Immediately Owen stopped the car at the side of the road. For a moment his fingers fiddled with the rim of the steering wheel. Then, very gently, he asked :

"Would you like to tell me ?"

"There—isn't very much to tell," Lucy said, her head turned away from him, so that he could not see her tearstained face. "Just that—when you were with Monsieur Le Marquand—Dick suddenly—turned up."

"I know," Owen said shortly. "I saw him. Actually, I wasn't so very long with Le Marquand, but just as I was coming out to rejoin you, I saw Corbett was with you—"

"Oh," Lucy exclaimed anxiously. "You—you didn't think that—that I knew he was here? That I had arranged to see him?"

"Not for a moment," Owen declared emphatically. "As a matter of fact, I was on the point of coming over with the express intention of kicking him into the middle of next week when I realised that you were doing just that—and far more efficiently than I could possibly have done!"

"I hope that I never see him again," Lucy said in a strangled voice. "It was—horrible. You see, I realised that all you had said about him was true—"

"Go on," Owen said quietly.

"I don't think I ever made excuses for Dick," Lucy obeyed, staring straight ahead. "But I did realise that people can quite genuinely change—even at the last moment."

"You mean, you believed that he was at least honest about having had a change of heart?"

"Yes," Lucy whispered. "That—hurt, but it wasn't as bad as—" she shook her head, unable to finish.

"Money?" Owen asked curtly.

Lucy did not answer, but her silence told Owen all he wanted to know.

"And he told *you* that ?" he exclaimed. "The young swine! I wish I'd interfered—"

"No," Lucy said painfully. "It's just as well that I should know not only that, but that he had such a poor opinion of me as to imagine that I would be gratified because—already—his marriage isn't the—the success he had thought it would be."

And that Owen found quite easy to interpret. Evidently young Corbett had met—and married—his match! The Kelsall girl might be genuinely in love with him, but she had no illusions about him. So she was keeping a tight hold on the moneybags—and serve him right! There could hardly be a more fitting punishment for such a man. And if Lucy, bless her, wasn't paltry enough to find pleasure in that state of affairs, he, Owen, was frankly delighted—and for more reasons than one. But he had no intention of telling Lucy that.

Instead, he dropped a hand lightly over Lucy's clasped ones.

"Lucy, would you say that you're—cured?"

Imperceptive of the almost diffident way in which he spoke, Lucy nodded.

"Yes, quite cured," she said sadly. "But—how I wish it hadn't been this way. It—it isn't pleasant to discover that someone—you thought the world of just couldn't ever really have existed—" her voice trailed away, and Owen's grip on her hands tightened.

"No, it isn't," he agreed. "And it also means that you have now got to face up to something new—lack of faith in your own judgment, and the fear that no one is trustworthy. What are you going to do about that, Lucy?"

Lucy gave him a crooked smile.

"It always seems to be your job to make me face up to my problems, doesn't it?" she remarked. "You must get rather tired of it!"

"Perhaps I do," he admitted. "But then, you see, it happens that I'm very much—" He paused briefly and then continued, "am very much of the opinion that you're someone who is well worth helping. And if it lies in my power to do that—but you haven't answered my question. What are you going to do?"

"Work as hard as I possibly can, I suppose," Lucy said after a moment's thought. "And try to get some sense of proportion. It sounds rather dreary, doesn't it?"

"So dreary that I think you might add—*and have as good a time as possible,*" Owen suggested cheerfully. "And that brings me back to what I said at the beginning of this conversation—will you come to the ballet with me tonight? Le Marquand has asked us to share his box, and though I can't promise you that royalty will be present, it is a gala performance."

"Us?" Lucy queried in surprise.

"Certainly—*us,*" Owen confirmed. "He referred to you as my charming little friend, and so that there should be no mistake who he meant, he buttoned up his fingers, snatched a kiss from his lips and dispatched it in your direction. Like this!"

His exaggerated imitation of Monsieur le Marquand's gesture amused Lucy sufficiently to make her laugh, but she still had a question to ask.

"But it will mean that you have to wear formal evening clothes. Won't you dislike that, on holiday?"

"Bless your kind little heart !" Owen sounded really touched by her thoughtfulness. "Well, I admit that the thought of a stiff collar isn't too pleasant, but it will be worth it—particularly if you haven't seen Swan Lake before ?"

"No, I haven't," Lucy told him.

"Good ! It's my favourite, and to share it with someone who has never seen it will be as satisfying as giving candy to a child ! And now we'd better make for home. It's getting late and we've still a longish way to go."

And then, for the first time, Lucy realised that they were not on the coast road but another one, still running roughly parallel with the sea but so high above it that the sea had become a tranquil turquoise plain, shimmering in the sunshine, and trees and houses were dolls' house size.

"Where are we ?" Lucy exclaimed.

"On the Grande Corniche—Napoleon's road, and before that, a Roman road. It's a longer way back, but I thought you might be glad of a bit of extra time— and it's cooler up here," Owen explained.

Lucy found it suddenly impossible to speak, but she laid her hand momentarily on his bare forearm, and as they started off again, Owen began to whistle an exceptionally cheerful little tune.

•   •   •

As Lucy got ready for the evening's outing she was aware of a growing sense of excitement which was considerably enhanced by the knowledge that Owen would have no need to feel ashamed of her appearance.

She had only worn her dress once before, and that had been during the previous year when she had been bridesmaid at a cousin's wedding. The soft, supple

308

material was the delicate lavender-blue of a delphinium and it suited Lucy's fair colouring to perfection. With it went long silver gloves and shoes. At the wedding she had also worn a short-sleeved bolero of the same material as the dress. Now she regarded this doubtfully.

She was quite sure that when she reached the Opera House a strapless evening dress would be entirely suitable, but would it perhaps be a good thing to wear the little bolero going and returning ? Surely one ought to have a cape or a stole or something ? She decided to ask Mrs. Mayberry and went in search of her.

Mrs. Mayberry was reading, but she instantly laid her book down and gave a little exclamation of pleasure.

"My dear, how absolutely charming—and how absolutely *you* ! But you look worried. Is anything wrong—and can I help ?"

Lucy explained her problem, and Mrs. Mayberry agreed that yes, most women probably would wear something over their shoulders on arriving and that the little bolero would be perfect.

"Though I can lend you a light-weight fur stole if you like," she offered.

"Thank you very much, but if you don't mind, I'd rather not borrow," Lucy said diffidently. "Particularly something valuable, so if you're quite sure it will do, I'll wear this."

Before Mrs. Mayberry could answer, Owen came into the room, minus his coat and with a white tie in his hand.

"I say, Aunt Louise—" he began, and stopped short, his eyes on Lucy. For a moment he said nothing, and Lucy felt her colour rising. Then, slipping his hand under hers, he raised it to his lips and gently kissed it. "You look quite lovely, Lucy. I shall be the envy of all the other men there! And now," his voice became abruptly matter-of-fact, "about this tie. I've already ruined two. Do you think you could possibly tie it for me, Aunt Louise?"

"My dear, I'll try, if you like," Mrs. Mayberry said doubtfully. "But I don't feel at all confident about the result. Do you know anything about tying this sort of tie, Lucy?"

"I—I usually tie Father's," Lucy answered. "I'll try, if you like, Mr. Vaughan."

But somehow, performing this little service for Owen was very different from doing the same thing for her father. Owen stood as still as a rock, yet she was supremely conscious of his nearness, of the warmth of his breath on her hair, and despite all her efforts to control them, her fingers would tremble. None the less, she produced a very creditable result, and Owen professed himself as being perfectly satisfied. Then he went off to put on his coat and returned a moment or two later carrying a spray of flowers in his hand.

"A reward for services rendered," he remarked. "If you will accept it?"

His offering was the most exquisite spray of orchids that Lucy had ever seen. Mounted on a background of delicate fern, each tiny pink flower was a jewel in its own right. Lucy exclaimed with delight.

"How very, very lovely!" she said warmly. "And—and—" with sudden, almost childlike glee, "how marvellous to be going to see Swan Lake *and* wear orchids for the first time on the same evening! Thank you more than I can possibly say, Mr. Vaughan!"

Smiling as if he found her thanks completely adequate, Owen pointed out that fixed to the back of the spray was a silver clip which would fix over the edge of her dress, holding it firmly without marking it.

"I'll show you," he offered, and with quick, deft fingers slipped the flowers in position. "How's that,

Aunt Louise ?" he asked, stepping back to observe the result.

"Quite perfect," Mrs. Mayberry approved. "I admire your choice wholeheartedly, Owen !"

"I'm glad of that," he remarked, and though he spoke in a perfectly ordinary voice, Lucy had the feeling that in some way they had exchanged a message having a deeper meaning than the ostensible one, but what it was, she had no idea. Not that she worried about it. Whatever it was, there was no unkindness in it.

Owen had arranged for a chauffeur to drive the car so that he would not have to concern himself with parking it. It was a short but magic drive to the Opera House. It was not yet dark, but already there was a velvety quality about the sky and the sea had taken on a darker, richer blue. Street lamps glowed like strings of diamonds and fairy lamps glinted like lesser jewels.

"It's like fairyland," Lucy breathed.

Owen could have told her that it was a fairyland backed by sound business sense which knew the value of glamour to the last sou, but he felt no wish to destroy her illusions. Rather, he himself saw it all with her eyes, and smiled as he recalled his remark that even wearing a stiff collar would be well worth while. How right he had been !

And if she felt she had driven through fairyland, then Lucy found the Opera House the fairy palace itself. To her, all the men appeared handsome—though none so handsome as her own escort, she thought complacently. And all the women were beautiful. Certainly all their gowns were, and though most of them wore wonderful jewellery, even tiaras in some cases, Lucy did not feel the least shadow of envy. *She* was wearing orchids for the first time.

They were conducted to Monsieur le Marquand's

box where he received them, paying Lucy a flattering compliment before introducing his wife, who exclaimed at Lucy's complexion.

"The perfect English rose type," she announced. "Or perhaps I may be allowed to say *American,* since our princess has the same colouring."

That was a compliment which completely took Lucy's breath away, and she could only stammer a few words of thanks. Then the le Marquands and Owen began to talk of matters about which she knew nothing and she was free to look about her and take in the magnificence of the scene. The seats and boxes were now almost all occupied, and massed together the effect of glittering jewels and dresses of all colours of the rainbow were breathtaking. And as if that were not enough, exquisitely arranged flowers were massed everywhere, their perfume filling the air with almost intoxicating sweetness. Though, as Owen had warned her would be the case, no royal personages were present, Lucy was breathless with excitement and anticipation.

Monsieur le Marquand, seeing her rapt expression, broke off his conversation with Owen to point out various celebrities, speaking of them in a friendly, casual way which made it clear that he, too, was one of them. Surreptitiously Lucy pinched herself to make sure that she was awake. It simply couldn't be that ordinary Lucy Darvill was playing her part in such a glamorous scene !

Then the orchestra filed into their places and there was a little anticipatory hush in the babble of conversation which had been rippling over the audience. Instruments were tuned and tested—a sound fascinating in itself. A brief silence, then the lights dimmed and the orchestra began to play the captivating overture to Swan Lake. And finally the curtain rose—

Lucy lost all sense of time. The music was familiar to her, but she had never seen the ballet performed before. In fact, her only knowledge of ballet at all was what she had seen on television, and delightful though that had been, there could be no comparison with this "live" performance. Now and again a little sigh passed her lips, and once or twice she half raised her hand to call Owen's attention to some particular delight. On one of these occasions he took her hand gently in his, but Lucy was too enthralled to notice, and as gently, he let it go.

At last it was all over. The lights came up and slowly the auditorium emptied.

The le Marquands suggested waiting a few moments until the crowds of people had dispersed a little, and Lucy, back again in a world of reality, thanked her host and hostess in her rather halting French for the delightful evening, adding an apology for the inadequacy of her thanks.

Monsieur le Marquand, bowing over her hand, smiled at her.

"Your thanks, little one, are in the dreams which still linger in your blue eyes! And they are more than adequate!"

They had to wait briefly before the car arrived at the door. Involuntarily Lucy shivered a little, for after the warmth of the Opera House, the night air struck chilly. Owen said nothing, but when they got into the car, he took a fur cape which Lucy recognised as one Mrs. Mayberry sometimes wore from the front seat and put it round her shoulders.

Snuggled in its soft cosiness, Lucy sat back, living over again what she had seen and heard. Bemused by the memory of so much beauty, she was startled when the car stopped.

"Is anything wrong?" she asked anxiously and then, in astonishment: "Why, we're home! It hardly took any time at all!"

Owen laughed softly as he helped her out.

"About the same as usual. But then time doesn't exist in a dream world, does it?"

"Perhaps not, but I've been very rude," Lucy said regretfully as they crossed the veranda and went into the villa. "I remembered to thank Monsieur le Marquand and his wife for inviting me, but really it's you I ought to thank for taking me. I do thank you, Owen, with all my heart! I shall never forget this evening!"

Owen took both her hands in his and gazed down into her flushed, upturned face.

"Nor shall I," he said softly.

There was a moment of silence that held a strange tenseness. Then, gently, Owen turned her round and propelled her in the direction of her room.

"It's late," he told her. "And young ladies who have visited fairyland need a good settling dose of sleep! Off you go—and pleasant dreams!"

Laughing, Lucy did as she was told, only to pause in front of her mirror, looking at her own reflection with dreamy eyes, to undress slowly and with frequent pauses, thinking again of this delight and that—

Slowly she got into bed and lay with her hands linked above her head. What a wonderful—what a perfect day it had been—

And was startled to remember that it was still the very same day as that on which she had seen Dick and he had been so horrible.

"I'd forgotten all about it," she thought in wonder. "It seems so long ago—and as if it doesn't really matter—"

She settled down to sleep and her last thought was

not of Dick but of Owen. She had called him by his first name, and he hadn't seemed to mind at all !

·   ·   ·

In the morning, when she went in to breakfast, Mr. Keane and Owen had already started.

"I'm so sorry I'm late," she apologised. "I'm afraid I slept in !"

Mr. Keane laughed and asked her what she expected would happen if she kept late hours.

"I hear you enjoyed yourself very much," he added.

"It was wonderful," Lucy sighed, something of her dreams still in her eyes. "So wonderful that I can hardly believe it happened to me !"

Both men laughed at her quaint phrasing, and then Mr. Keane gave a little exclamation.

"That reminds me, there's another treat in store for you—for all of us, except Louise who doesn't feel quite up to it."

"Oh ?" Owen looked up from helping himself to marmalade. "And what's that ?"

Mr. Keane pointed out of the window.

"That yacht—*La Mouette*. You know I told you it had changed hands ? Well, it turns out that the present owner of it happens to be an acquaintance of mine and he's asked us all to lunch with him on board. His name is Kelsall, by the way."

CHAPTER VIII

MR. KEANE'S announcement was followed by a silence that seemed to Lucy to be interminable. He, of course, had no idea of the predicament she was in, since he did not know that Dick had married Gwenda Kelsall. But Owen must know exactly what she was thinking.

Yesterday she had not asked Dick where he and his wife were staying, but since *La Mouette* belonged to Mr. Kelsall it was only reasonable to assume that they were with him. In that case, how could she, Lucy, possibly accept Mr. Kelsall's invitation? But it had already been accepted on her behalf, and to back out now meant giving a very good reason for doing so. That she had, of course, but it was hardly one she could give, certainly not to Mr. Kelsall, and only reluctantly to Mr. Keane, who would then be put in a very embarrassing position. The situation was made even worse by the fact that she, a mere employee at the Villa des Fleurs, had been very kindly included in the invitation.

"Kelsall?" Owen asked casually. "Is that the big-time property man?"

"That's right. I've come in contact with him over some of his deals, and though he's perhaps something of a rough diamond, he's a pleasant enough fellow at heart." And then, evidently realising that his announcement had not given rise to the enthusiasm he had anticipated, he asked anxiously: "I hope you don't mind me having let you in for a bit of lionising, Owen, but really, it was difficult to get out of it. He was rather insistent."

"Oh, that's all right," Owen said with a casualness that startled and disconcerted Lucy. "Just what is the drill?"

"He's sending a boat ashore to collect us at half past twelve," Mr. Keane explained, getting up from the table as he spoke. "Does that suit you?"

"We'll be ready," Owen promised, and with a nod, Mr. Keane went out of the room.

As the door shut behind him Lucy turned to Owen.

"But I can't possibly go, Mr. Vaughan!" she said imploringly.

"But, my dear, in the circumstances, what else can you do?" Owen asked gravely.

"I know," Lucy admitted, trying to speak calmly. "That is, not without explaining why I don't want to go. And I don't see how that can be done. Yet—"

"I do appreciate how you feel, Lucy," Owen agreed. "What's more, I feel the same way—on my own account as well as yours. I wish to goodness Uncle Stanley hadn't let us in for it, but he has—and the only way to get out of it would be by hurting his feelings. And I'm too fond of the old boy to want to do that."

"I know. So am I," Lucy sighed.

"So do you think we could prop each other up—put a good face on it and let him down lightly?"

Lucy hesitated.

"In one way, it doesn't matter whether I see Dick or not. I mean, it won't make any difference to how I feel—or rather, don't feel about him. But you do realise, don't you, that it will be a terribly awkward situation?"

"Yes, I appreciate that," Owen nodded.

Yet still Lucy was reluctant to commit herself. She could not help remembering that there had been a time when Owen had inveigled her into taking a definite line of action by giving her a reason for doing so which had at the time seemed convincing but which had turned out not to be his real motive. She

317

had forgotten that particular facet of his personality of late, but now she wondered—

She leaned towards him.

"You do believe that I am—what was it you said yesterday—'cured' of Dick?" she asked earnestly. "You don't think that he and I—put our heads together and contrived this meeting?"

Owen met her eyes unflinchingly.

"On my honour, such a thought never so much as entered my mind," he assured her.

Lucy sighed, though whether with relief or resignation she hardly knew.

"Very well, then, I'll see it through," she promised.

•   •   •

Quite deliberately Lucy chose a very simple dress and used only the minimum amount of make-up. She had no intention whatever of trying to shine at this lunch party or attract attention in any way. She was, after all, an employee out here to do a job of work, though it was sometimes difficult to remember that when everybody else seemed to forget it. But just because of that, it was all the more up to her not to push herself forward. And if that made her appear rather dull and uninteresting, well, so much the better on this occasion.

At the last moment she decided to wear a wide-brimmed hat which shaded her face, and as they left the villa, she slipped on a pair of dark glasses.

At the quay they found a little motor-boat bobbing gently up and down in charge of one of the crew of *La Mouette*. They took their places and a moment later were making the short trip to the beautiful white yacht.

An accommodation ladder had been lowered over her side and at the top of it a rather stout, middle-aged man stood waiting to greet them.

"Very pleased to see you all," he announced heartily. "Now, this will be Miss Darvill—"

"Mr. Kelsall," Mr. Keane murmured to Lucy.

She felt her hand enveloped in a firm, rather fleshy grasp, said a few words of appreciation for the invitation and quietly stepped to one side.

"And you," Mr. Kelsall went on, turning to Owen, "are the famous Owen Vaughan!"

Naturally, Owen made no comment at being described in such a way, but Lucy could sense a withdrawal in his manner. She realised what he had meant by saying he wished to goodness Mr. Keane had not let them in for this party. Evidently he had gone through similar experiences of blatant lionising before, and had realised what he would be likely to meet on this occasion.

Talking just rather too loudly, Mr. Kelsall now led them towards the sun deck where a group of people were chattering and laughing as they sipped their drinks. Altogether there were about half a dozen of them, but Dick was not among them, and for one hopeful moment Lucy wondered if, after all, he and his wife would not be present.

But almost at that moment the motor-boat, which had returned to the quayside, came back with three more passengers, two women and a man. And the man was Dick. One of the women wore a hat even bigger than Lucy's, as well as dark glasses. The other, hanging possessively on to Dick's arm, was unmistakably Gwenda.

Lucy held her breath as she came face to face with Dick's wife. She had, of course, seen that picture of her in the newspaper, but she was not prepared for what she now saw.

Gwenda Corbett had been born after her father's feet were firmly placed on the ladder of success. As a result, she had been brought up to believe, as he did, that if you pay top price you must of a necessity get the best. Unfortunately, rigid adherence to this formula was combined in Gwenda with a complete lack of taste. Everything about her, her clothes, her jewellery, her make-up and her hair style, while in the height of fashion, appeared exaggerated and unsuitable for a girl as young as she was, nor could they do anything to soften the essential hardness of her face. Appalled though Lucy had been at Dick's disloyalty to his wife it was impossible not to appreciate the significance of her thin lips and her coldly calculating eyes. In all her life Gwenda had never been denied anything she wanted and she had no intention whatever of allowing that state of affairs to alter.

And yet, as they shook hands and momentarily their eyes met, Lucy saw amusement in Gwenda's. Amusement—and triumph.

"She knows who I am," Lucy thought, panic-stricken. "She knew I was going to be invited—perhaps she even wanted me to be ! How utterly, utterly beastly ! Oh, I wish I hadn't come ! I ought not to have done, whatever Owen said !"

And now, Dick was shaking hands with her, mumbling some conventional remark. And Gwenda was more amused than ever because, from his expression, it was clear that Dick had not been told that Lucy would be here and had not the courage to admit that he knew her.

Then, to Lucy's intense relief, Mr. Kelsall took the centre of the stage.

"And now, I've got a surprise for you all," he announced loudly. "And an especially delightful one, I'm sure, for Mr. Vaughan," with a meaning glance in Owen's direction before turning to the other woman who had arrived with Dick and Gwenda. "Take off your disguise, my dear !"

With a soft, rich laugh that Lucy was almost sure

320

she recognised, the woman took off her hat and glasses. It was Marion Singleton !

There was a little chorus of surprise and pleasure from all the guests, but completely ignoring them, Marion turned to Owen.

"Well, aren't you pleased ?" she asked beguilingly.

Owen, rigid and showing no emotion whatever, had not joined in the general welcome. Now, as Marion held her hand out to him, he bowed over it formally.

"Naturally," he said coolly. "But I must admit, considerably surprised. I was under the impression that you were fulfilling a series of engagements in Germany."

"So I would be—if I hadn't had trouble with my throat," Marion explained with every sign of regret. "But I was ordered—on the best authority, believe me —not to sing for several weeks, so what could I do but cancel the engagements ?"

"Hard luck on you, my dear," Mr. Kelsall remarked, clearly a little put out at Owen's reception of his surprise. "And on the audiences who were to have heard you, but good luck for us !"

Marion turned to him.

"You've been so kind," she said warmly, and then to anyone who cared to listen : "Mr. Kelsall had asked me to join this party right from the beginning, but I had to refuse because of my engagements. Then, when I had this distressing news, I wondered if I might presume on Mr. Kelsall's kindness to suggest that I joined him here—"

"Delighted to have you, my dear," Mr. Kelsall declared gallantly. "And you can take it from me that now we've got you, we're going to take very good care of you, believe me !"

He put an arm round Marion's shoulders and drew her very slightly to him. Lucy's eyes fell. She did not want to look at Owen just then. It had been obvious that the pleasure he would otherwise have felt at Marion's presence had been offset by the knowledge that she should not have been free to come. No doubt his fears had been relieved in one way by Marion's explanation, but he could not possibly like Mr. Kelsall's over-familiar gesture. Owen, she thought sympathetically, was having an even worse time than she was.

"I want a drink," Gwenda announced with a slight querulousness which suggested she disliked another woman taking so much of the limelight. "Dick, mix me a Pimms, will you ? And do get the measurements right this time. The last one you did for me was horrible."

There was a little bustle, which did at least something to relieve the overcharged atmosphere, as all the newcomers were provided with drinks. Then the first bell for lunch was rung and the party broke up. Gwenda suggested that Lucy and Marion should come to her stateroom to prink before the meal.

"Of course, your cabin is all ready," she remarked to Marion. "But I'd like you to see my room. It's really something special."

It certainly was. In all her life Lucy had never seen such a lavishly fitted and furnished room. To begin with, its size was incredible, even for so large a yacht as this, but even more, its colour scheme of rose and gold was almost overpowering. The curtains, the drapery of the bed and the skirt of the kidney-shaped dressing table were of shimmering rose satin. Chairs were upholstered in rose and gold brocade, and wherever possible were loops and ties of gold cord and braid. The carpet, into which one's feet sank, was of a deeper shade of rose and the toilet articles on the dressing table were apparently of solid gold.

"Well ?" Gwenda asked Marion. "What do yo think of it ?"

"I think it's the most beautiful room I've ever seen," Marion said with every appearance of conviction.

322

"It ought to be," Gwenda commented complacently. "It cost enough." She turned to Lucy. "And you ?"

"I've never seen anything like it in my life," Lucy said truthfully, hoping that Gwenda would take the remark as a compliment.

Whether she did or not, it certainly amused her.

"I don't suppose you have," she commented. "I don't suppose you earn as much in a year as it cost to do this up as I wanted it ! Even Father made a fuss about it! "

The remark was in such appalling taste that really there could be no answer to it, and fortunately Gwenda did not seem to think one was necessary, for she asked Lucy shortly if she would like to wash and opened the door which led to the bathroom, hardly less lavish than the bedroom.

When she returned, Marion and Gwenda appeared to be deep in confidences.

"I'm afraid my poor Owen was rather put out at me turning up like this," Marion was saying regretfully. "You see, though we're quite crazy about one another, we don't quite agree over the importance of my career. He thinks I ought to keep on with it at least for a time, but I'd so much rather give it up and devote all my time to him—which I'm sure you will agree is only natural."

"Yes, of course it is," Gwenda agreed promptly. "Why should you work when he can afford to keep you in comfort ?"

"Oh, that isn't quite—" Marion began, when she realised that Lucy had rejoined them. With a slight but expressive shrug she went on : "But I mustn't bother you with my affairs. Only I do want you and your father to understand why he was a little bit— odd."

At the lunch table, to Lucy's relief, she had strangers sitting on either side of her. She might have been put next to Dick ! But her relief was short-lived. Evidently appreciating that she did not really fit into these surroundings, one of her neighbours became curious.

"You're one of Keane's guests, aren't you ?" he asked bluntly.

"Not exactly," Lucy explained coolly. "I came out here to work—as a secretary."

"Did you, though !" He glanced across at Owen and promptly jumped to the wrong conclusion. "I must say, one way and another, Vaughan does himself well !"

Lucy felt the indignant colour rising to her cheeks, but she kept her voice steady.

"I'm not Mr. Vaughan's secretary," she explained. "I work for his aunt, Mrs. Mayberry, who is also at the Villa des Fleurs."

"Oh. Oh, I see," he digested this for a moment. "All the same, she doesn't seem to drive you very hard, not if she doesn't mind you spending your time on a jaunt like this !"

"Mrs. Mayberry is unfortunately the victim of rheumatoid arthritis and is so not able to come on a 'jaunt' like this," Lucy could not keep a tinkle of ice out of her voice now. "I was invited simply to make the number up."

"Oh, was that it ?"

Mercifully, at that point he lost interest in the subject and turned to the girl on his other side. Lucy's other neighbour immediately claimed her, but to her relief, he was a fishing enthusiast and was more than content to describe his prowess at length with no other encouragement from her than an occasional : "How interesting !" or "Do tell me about that—it sounds wonderful !"

At last the meal was over. Lucy wondered how long they would be expected to stay, and noticed with relief that Mr. Keane was more than once glancing down at his watch. Evidently he would be as glad to get away as she would. As for Owen, evidently he had good-naturedly decided to make the best of the situation, for he was the centre of a little group who, having a "lion" in their midst, took it for granted that he would entertain them.

"And are all artistes temperamental?" a rather shrill voice asked.

"More or less, I suppose," Owen agreed carelessly.

"And which is Miss Singleton?" someone else asked. "More—or less?"

Owen glanced briefly in Marion's direction. She smiled lazily.

"Go on, tell them the truth," she said encouragingly.

"Miss Singleton is in a class entirely by herself," Owen said deliberately.

Just for a moment an odd expression flickered over Marion's face. Then she smiled right into Owen's eyes.

"Well, I suppose that's one way of putting it, darling," she commented, and laid her hand briefly on his arm.

Mr. Keane stood up suddenly.

"I think, Kelsall, if you don't mind, we must be getting along now," he said pleasantly. "Time is getting on and I'm expecting a telephone call through from London that I don't want to miss. Thank you very much for a most charming interlude—you must look us up some time at the Villa des Fleurs."

Whether his final remark was anything more than lip service to convention was impossible to tell, but Mr. Kelsall took it literally.

"I'd like that," he replied promptly. "We're not leaving here for a couple of days or so. Would to-morrow suit?"

"By all means," Mr. Keane replied. "Lunch? And

—" he looked vaguely round the chattering groups, "your young people, perhaps ?"

"Fine !" Mr. Kelsall agreed, clapping him on the shoulder. "And perhaps I'll have the pleasure of meeting your sister ? I can't say I've read any of her books—I'm not what you'd call a reading man, but I've a great admiration for those that can put their ideas down on paper. About the same time ?"

"Excellent," Mr. Keane said politely. "Lucy—?"

"I'm quite ready," she replied quickly. "Oh, I must get my hat. I left it in your room, Mrs. Corbett."

"Oh, just pop along and get it, will you ?" Gwenda said indifferently. "You know the way."

Lucy nodded and went in search of her hat, not sorry that Gwenda had not offered to accompany her. She found her way without difficulty, picked up her hat and was on her way back to the deck when a man's figure intercepted her. It was Dick.

"Look here, Lucy, I've got to see you somewhere—alone !" he said in a low voice with a glance over his shoulder.

"I've told you before, Dick, we have nothing at all to say to one another," Lucy said firmly. "Please stand out of the way."

He took no notice of the request.

"If we've nothing to say to one another, why did you come here today ?" he demanded doggedly. "You must have known I'd be here."

"I thought it more than likely," Lucy answered. "But unfortunately the invitation had already been accepted on my behalf, and I couldn't get out of it without giving a good reason why. You know what the reason would have been—one that I don't think you would like Mr. Kelsall to know, would you ?"

She despised herself for using what practically amounted to a threat, but this was no time for half measures. Dick had got to be convinced once and for

all that she meant what she said, and apparently she
had achieved her aim, for he seemed to shrink visibly.

"Good lord, Lucy, you wouldn't do that, would
you?" he asked in alarm. "There'd be the deuce—"

"I hope that I shall never need to," Lucy said significantly. "And now—"

He stood aside to let her pass, and then for a second
she paused.

"Yes?" Dick asked apprehensively.

It was on the tip of her tongue to ask him if he
realised that his wife had certainly known who she
was—if she had not, indeed, actually manoeuvred the
invitation. Then she changed her mind.

"No, nothing," she said, and hurried back to the
deck.

Gwenda looked at her suspiciously.

"It took you a long time, didn't it?" she remarked.
"Did you lose your way?"

"No," Lucy said crisply. "As he will no doubt tell
you, I met your husband as I was returning, and I
stopped for a moment to say goodbye to him."

Gwenda's eyes dropped, but not before Lucy had
seen the enmity in them.

•   •   •

No one spoke much on the way back to the Villa
des Fleurs, but later when they were alone, Owen
apologised unreservedly to Lucy.

"I was utterly wrong to persuade you to go," he
said. "Actually, Corbett himself didn't behave too
badly—certainly he had no idea you were coming. One
could tell that. But that wife of his—whew!" he
whistled expressively. "One must admit the young
man has feathered his nest nicely, but none the less,
I could almost find it in my heart to pity him!"

"Please!" Lucy begged. "It wasn't—nice. But it's
over now. It's better forgotten."

"You're right, of course," Owen agreed. "But before we do that, I'd like to tell you how much I admired the way you kept your end up. You kept the initiative in your own hands the whole time ! And if there is anything I can do to make up for what I let you in for—"

"There is," Lucy said quickly. "Tomorrow—could you possibly see to it that I have a really good excuse for not putting in an appearance—except at lunch, of course. That can't be helped. But apart from that ?"

"I'll see to that," Owen promised. "And I might say, Lucy, that I wish to goodness I could find an excuse for myself as well. I really must have a word with Uncle Stanley about making such peculiar friends. He's really not safe to be trusted out alone !"

They parted on that light note with, Lucy could not help noticing, no reference to Marion's presence. But then, of course, there was no reason why there should have been. He was probably anxious about her voice, but certainly he would have got over his first reaction to her presence. And either way, why should he take her into his confidence ?

• • •

Whether Owen was responsible for the decision or not, the following morning Mrs. Mayberry announced that she simply must get down to work again.

"Not that I want to," she admitted ruefully. "But if I don't make a start soon I shall forget all that I've said already, and that means going back to check rather tiresomely. So—in about an hour's time, Lucy?"

"Yes, of course, Mrs. Mayberry," Lucy said with alacrity. "Which room would you like me to work in ?"

"Oh !" Mrs. Mayberry glanced at her brother.

"You can have my study," Mr. Keane said good-humouredly. "Because if you intend to work on holiday, I don't ! You'll find a typewriter and paper and carbons

there, Lucy. If there is anything else you want, ~~let me~~
know."

They settled down to work soon after breakfast, and
despite Mrs. Mayberry's fear that she might have lost
the thread of her story, she dictated steadily almost
until lunch time from notes she had already made. This
made Lucy feel rather guilty as she knew that Mrs.
Mayberry must have been working since coming to
the villa while she had been free to enjoy herself. However, remembering what Owen had said about the
good it would do his aunt to relax, she made no reference to this. At least she could make up for lost time
by transcribing her shorthand during the afternoon,
which would give her every excuse to avoid the expected visitors.

At a quarter past twelve, Mrs. Mayberry looked at
her watch.

"Dear me, it's later than I had thought," she remarked. "I must go and tidy myself before Stanley's
visitors arrive. I'm not too fond of meeting strangers,
so come and support me as soon as they arrive, will
you, Lucy?"

It was said in all kindliness, of course, in order to
make it clear that though Lucy was now working, she
was to be included in the party. None the less, it was
a considerable relief, when she went out to the veranda,
to find that only Mr. Kelsall and Marion had come. He
was, in fact, just explaining the reason for that to Mr.
Keane.

"My daughter's not feeling too good," he announced
regretfully. "And her husband felt he'd better stay with
her. I hope you'll excuse them—and I'm sure Miss
Singleton will make up for their absence?"

There was a polite murmur of regret, and a welcome
for Marion. Owen attended to drinks for the guests
and then for the members of the house party. As he

handed a long frosted glass to Lucy he remarked in an undertone:

"Might have been worse !"

"Indeed, yes," she agreed. "All the same, thank you for persuading Mrs. Mayberry that it was time I started working again."

He grinned in a conspiratorial way and then went over to talk to Mr. Kelsall. A little later, they went in to lunch. This passed off without any awkward incidents occurring, possibly because Mr. Kelsall appeared to be in rather a subdued mood.

As soon as the meal was over, Lucy slipped quietly away and began typing. Consequently she had no idea that Mr. Kelsall had seized an opportunity of saying confidentially to Mrs. Mayberry :

"I'd be much obliged if you would spare me a few minutes of your time—somewhere where we could talk privately ?"

Slightly surprised, Mrs. Mayberry suggested that he should wheel her in her chair to her favourite spot in the garden in the shade of a big tree. Once there, she looked at him inquiringly. He came to the point without delay.

"I owe you an apology," he said abruptly. "Not so much because my young people haven't come, but the reason why they haven't. The fact is, there's nothing wrong with my daughter—except temper—but I wouldn't let her and her husband come. Not likely— not after yesterday." He sat with a hand on each knee, scowling deeply.

"Yesterday ?" Mrs. Mayberry echoed, puzzled.

He looked at her sharply.

"She didn't say anything about it ?"

"She ? Who ?"

"That nice little girl you've got working for you. No I can see she didn't. Well, the fact of the matter is, my daughter behaved very badly to her yesterday.

Apparently she knew all about Miss—what is it ?—Darvill ? Yes, well, Gwenda knew all that, and she deliberately persuaded me to ask her—"

"Mr. Kelsall, you're talking in conundrums," Mrs. Mayberry interrupted. "Why on earth should Lucy not have been included in your invitation ? She is a charming girl and—"

"Ah, I can see you don't know about it. Well, did you know that Miss Darvill was on the point of getting married when the man broke it off ?"

"Yes, I knew that," Mrs. Mayberry said reluctantly.

"Yes, but did you know this—the man that jilted her, on her wedding day, what's more, is now married to my daughter ? No ? Well, he is. Now do you see what I'm apologising for ?"

"Did Lucy know she would be meeting him ?" Mrs. Mayberry asked sharply.

"I don't know. But whether she did or not, she behaved just the way you would have liked her to. All the same, I'm worried."

Seeing that he had evidently made up his mind to unburden himself, Mrs. Mayberry decided that, on the whole, perhaps she had better hear the whole story, little as she wanted to. And after a moment he went on :

"I don't say my daughter's choice of a husband would have been mine, but to be honest, I don't know what sort I would have chosen for her. The fact is, I've spoiled her all her life. That means she'd never have knuckled down to the strong, arrogant type. And she'd have been bored by an intelligent man as much as he'd have been bored by her. So I suppose the only sort for her is the easygoing playboy. Not but what I'd thought there was more to him than that. He worked for me, you know. That's how he met Gwenda. I thought quite a lot of him—one of the younger men I'd got my eye on for promotion. But Gwenda's idea of a husband is that he shall be a playmate at her beck and call—"

"And he doesn't mind that?" Mrs. Mayberry asked distastefully, thinking that perhaps Lucy had a lucky escape.

"Not at first. Now—" he frowned, "I'm not so sure. He's entirely dependent on Gwenda for cash, you see, and I've a notion she keeps him pretty short. Natural enough, I suppose, from her point of view. But it could make for trouble, and that I don't want —won't have. I'm old-fashioned in some ways, and I don't want a divorce in my family. They're married— and they're going to stay that way."

"But can you enforce that?" Mrs. Mayberry asked gravely. "And if you could, would it be wise?"

"Wise or not, that's how it's going to be," Mr. Kelsall announced grimly. "And I can enforce it all right. As a matter of fact, I've always foreseen something like this—Gwenda falling for a young man without any money of his own. So though she's got some money of her own, mainly she's dependent on the allowance I make her, and the pair of them can't live the way they seem to regard as necessary without it. Gwenda will toe the line all right if she sees a danger of having to make out on less!"

"And the young man?"

"Corbett? Well, he's learned pretty quickly to enjoy having all the things money can buy, and he hasn't a penny piece of his own—spent all his savings on Gwenda when they first met. He hasn't got a job, either, and I certainly shouldn't give him his old one back—not if he left Gwenda."

"He might get another one," Mrs. Mayberry suggested.

"He might. Though, as I say, he likes living rich, and he couldn't hope to earn that much for a good many years to come."

"May I make a suggestion?" Mrs. Mayberry asked diffidently.

"Go ahead!"

"Have you considered the possibility of making Mr. Corbett a personal allowance? Not a big one," seeing Mr. Kelsall's frown, "but sufficient to allow him to feel he has a measure of independence. It might make a very real difference to the relationship between him and your daughter."

"It might, at that," Mr. Kelsall admitted. "I don't know but what I wouldn't do it, but for one thing."

Mrs. Mayberry waited in silence.

"That little girl, Miss Darvill. I wish to goodness she wasn't here!"

"Indeed?" Mrs. Mayberry said coldly. "Why?"

"Oh, no criticism of her! But it seems to me that a man who will let one girl down is quite likely to do the same thing to another girl. And if Gwenda has really got him on the raw, and he'd got money in his pocket, I wouldn't put it past him to make up to another woman just to score off her." He paused and then added deliberately: "And it seems to me that the stage is set for just such an act."

"I'm not going to pretend I don't know what you mean, because of course it's obvious. You think Lucy may still be in love with him." Mrs. Mayberry shook her head emphatically. "You're quite wrong, Mr. Kelsall."

"You sound very sure of that," Mr. Kelsall commented.

"Quite sure," Mrs. Mayberry assured him. "And for the best of all possible reasons."

"Oh? In love with someone else?" Mr. Kelsall said astutely. "Well, that's a load off my mind, anyhow. She seems a nice little thing—I wouldn't like her to be mixed up in anything shady."

"She won't be," Mrs. Mayberry insisted. "And now, Mr. Kelsall, I really think we must go back—"

"Yes, of course." He jumped to his feet and pushed the chair carefully back to the villa. And immediately both of them forgot what they had been discussing.

Marion, white-faced, her eyes closed, was lying back in a long chair. One of her shoes had been taken off and Owen was examining her swollen ankle.

"Miss Singleton has hurt her ankle," Mr. Keane explained somewhat unnecessarily, in a voice totally devoid of all expression. "It would seem advisable that she should see a doctor."

COMPLETE silence followed Mr. Keane's explanation. Then, wincing with pain, Marion apologised for being a nuisance.

"I can't think how I could have been so careless," she said forlornly. "My ankle just seemed to turn over. But I'm sure it will feel better soon—there's no need to worry about a doctor."

"Nonsense, my dear girl," Mrs. Mayberry told her briskly. "Of course a doctor must see it. Do you know of one, Stanley?"

"As a matter of fact I do," he said a trifle guiltily. "I got hold of the name and address of one when—er —when—"

"When you knew I was coming here," Mrs. Mayberry finished, smiling at him. "Very wise of you, Stanley, particularly as things have turned out. Well, you'd better ring him up."

"I doubt if my French—" Mr. Keane objected.

Owen stood erect.

"I'll go," he said shortly. "Is his name on your desk list, Uncle?"

"Yes—under D for Doctor," Mr. Keane explained. "Perhaps I'd better—"

But Owen was already striding into the villa and a moment or two later Lucy was startled by his abrupt entry into Mr. Keane's study.

"Marion has hurt her ankle," he explained briefly in answer to Lucy's anxious look. "It seems to be advisable for her to see a doctor."

He ruffled through the leaves of a small desk telephone list.

"Ah, here we are. Dr. Henri Lefevre—"

He lifted the telephone, asked for the number and in a few moments was speaking rapidly to someone.

After giving exact directions for reaching the villa, he rang off.

"That was lucky," he remarked feelingly. "He was just on the point of going out. He'll be here quite soon."

"Is it very bad ?" Lucy asked sympathetically.

"It appears to be paining her considerably," Owen told her. "I suppose you don't know anything about first aid for this sort of thing, do you, Lucy ?"

"Not really. All I know is what had to be done when I once hurt my own ankle," Lucy explained. "It had to be supported in the position I found most comfortable, and it was bandaged. Oh, yes—the bandages were kept wet with cold water. But it may be a different sort of injury in Miss Singleton's case, and that might be the wrong treatment."

"Yes, I suppose it might." Owen pondered. "Oh, well, as Lefevre is coming quite soon, perhaps it would be better to wait for his diagnosis."

He walked over to the door, but with his hand on the knob he turned.

"How did you come to hurt your ankle, Lucy ?" he asked. "High heels ?"

"No—playing tennis," she explained, surprised that he should bother to ask such a question just now.

"Oh, do you play tennis ?" he asked in a preoccupied way. "We must have a game some time."

"It wouldn't be much fun for you," Lucy warned him. "I'm only just out of the rabbit class !"

"I'll take you up on that !" he announced, smiling faintly. "I know from experience that you're inclined to underrate your abilities ! Well, I suppose I'd better get back to the scene of the catastrophe !"

He sauntered off. Lucy, wondering whether she ought to have asked if there was anything she could do to help, decided that if there had been, Owen would have mentioned it. So she got on with her work, though once or twice she paused, a rather puzzled expression on her face.

* * *

Dr. Lefevre was most emphatic. Miss Singleton must have rest, rest, and more rest. Above all, she must not attempt to walk until the swelling had gone down.

"How long will that take ?" Marion asked apprehensively.

The doctor shrugged his shoulders.

"A few days, no more, I hope. I will come and see you tomorrow—"

"But I shan't be here," Marion explained. "I don't *live* here."

"Miss Singleton is my guest—on my yacht," Mr. Kelsall spoke for the first time since the doctor's arrival. "*La Mouette.*"

"But this is difficult," Dr. Lefevre exclaimed. "*La Mouette*—a beautiful yacht, I have much admired her. None the less, it presents difficulties for Miss Singleton. To get aboard—it might do fresh injury."

"That's what I was thinking," Mr. Kelsall agreed. "Not that we wouldn't be only too willing to look after you, my dear," he added to Marion. "But—"

"And then, in a day or so, I would suggest an X-ray—" Dr. Lefevre went on. "One wishes to make sure—"

"Oh, *dear*!" Marion lamented. "Why was I so stupid ! Could I go to a nursing home or something ?"

Mrs. Mayberry took the law into her own hands.

"You had better stay here, Marion, until you are able to have your ankle X-rayed," she said briskly. "Then, according to how you are, you can go to the hospital or a nursing home in a car or an ambulance. If there is a bone broken, presumably you will have to have your ankle in plaster, and then, in a sense, you will be more mobile—we can discuss what's to be done then."

Dr. Lefevre looked relieved.

"That would be excellent, madame," he announced. "I will bandage the ankle—and this must be soaked in cold water and kept in this condition. Miss Singleton should rest, preferably in bed, with the injured ankle raised and with a cage or some other suitable article placed over so that there is no pressure from the bed-clothes. A mild sedative now, and a somewhat stronger one tonight—that is all that can be done for the time being."

"Are you sure it's all right for me to stay?" Marion asked Mrs. Mayberry anxiously. "I'll try to be as little bother as possible, but—"

"In the circumstances, it seems the best thing to do," Mrs. Mayberry replied. "Don't you agree, Stanley?"

"What?" Mr. Keane had evidently been deep in thought. "Oh, yes—can't see anything else for it."

"Yes, exactly," Mrs. Mayberry said rather hurriedly. "Now, Mr. Kelsall, if you don't mind me suggesting it, I think it would be a good idea if you were to go back to your yacht and have someone pack a case for Miss Singleton—she would naturally like to have her own things. I expect your daughter can suggest what is necessary—"

"Yes, yes, good idea," Mr. Kelsall agreed. "I'll bring it back myself—"

He bent over Marion, still reclining on the chair.

"I can't say how sorry I am about this, my dear," he said with a gentleness that surprised his hearers. "I hate to think of you being in pain—and I had been looking forward to your company."

"I'm terribly disappointed, too," Marion said softly. "But perhaps it will only be for a day or two."

"I shall certainly postpone leaving until then," Mr. Kelsall said firmly, and taking Marion's hand in his, he raised it to his lips with awkward gallantry. "Take care of yourself, little lady!"

"I will," she promised gratefully, and watched him with thoughtful, half closed eyes until he vanished from sight.

There was a brief silence. Then Mrs. Mayberry turned to Owen.

"If you will wheel me to my room, I can sit in another chair while you use this to take Marion to one of the guest rooms. I will send Bertha to help you."

"How good you are," Marion sighed. "Everyone is so kind when one is in trouble!"

"Who would not be kind to so beautiful and talented a young lady?" Dr. Lefevre inquired, and glanced at Owen for confirmation.

But Owen was already wheeling his aunt indoors and so did not notice the look.

*   *   *

Thérèse, the romantic-minded maid who had helped Lucy unpack when she had first arrived at the villa, was enchanted to hear that Marion was to stay and that she would be entrusted with her care.

"Such a beautiful young lady," she sighed happily. "And with such talent! Have you heard her sing, mam'-selle?"

"Yes, I have," said Lucy. "She has a wonderful voice."

"So pure, so true!" Thérèse lifted her eyes expressively. "It is no wonder that all the gentlemen are in love with her! But she, of course, has eyes in one direction only! Monsieur Owen—he is fortunate indeed! And then her clothes—her lingerie—but out of this world. All made by hand and so fine—but I must go. That is her bell."

It seemed to Lucy that the bell rang a great many times that day. Indeed, during the afternoon, it rang so persistently that it disturbed Lucy at work in the study. It was, she knew, Thérèse's afternoon off, and evidently no one else considered it their business to answer the bell. For a moment Lucy hesitated. Then as it continued to ring, she went to find out what was the matter.

She tapped on the door of Marion's room and an irritable voice answered. As Lucy went in she gave a little gasp. She knew that during the morning flowers from Mr. Kelsall had arrived for Marion, but she was not prepared for such a lavish display as this. The room looked like a florist's shop, and the perfume was almost overpowering.

"Oh, so you've decided to come at last—" Marion began, and stopped when she saw it was Lucy and not Thérèse who had answered her summons. "Where's that girl? I've been ringing for her for ages."

"It's her afternoon off," Lucy explained.

"Oh, it is, is it?" Marion said irritably. "And why wasn't anyone else told to answer my bell, I should like to know?"

"I'm afraid I can't tell you," Lucy said quietly. "I don't have anything to do with the household arrangements."

"Naturally!" Marion sounded surprised that Lucy should think it necessary to make such a remark. "Well, anyway, now that you're here, you'll do as well as anyone. I'm going to get up and I want some help."

"But, Miss Singleton, I understood that when the doctor called this morning he said—"

"He said I'd got to rest until the swelling went down. Well, it has. Look!" Marion thrust her foot out from under the light bedclothes, and certainly the swelling did seem to be considerably less. "Now stop making a fuss and get my clothes!"

Lucy was in a very unpleasant position. Marion was a guest here, though an unexpected one. Lucy herself was an employee. That meant she could hardly refuse

340

to do as Marion wished unless she took the rather petty line that acting as a lady's maid was not within the terms of her engagement. She decided to see if persuasion would not solve the difficulty.

"Miss Singleton, I do think you would be unwise to get up before the doctor has definitely said you can," she said earnestly. "And surely, if he had felt that it was all right for you to get up this afternoon, he would have said so this morning."

"Will you kindly stop arguing, and do as you're told?" Marion said rudely.

"I'm afraid I can't," Lucy said quietly. "You are asking me to take too great a responsibility, Miss Singleton, particularly as you've made it clear that your ankle isn't really better yet. It can't be, or you would not want assistance to get dressed.

Marion capitulated abruptly.

"Oh, very well," she said sulkily. "If you won't, you won't! But I'm bored, stuck here all on my own. Where is everybody?"

"Mrs. Mayberry and Bertha are both resting," Lucy explained. "Mrs. Mayberry had a bad night and Bertha was up looking after her."

"Oh?" Marion said indifferently. "And the men?"

"Mr. Keane went to see a friend in Menton this afternoon. Mr. Vaughan went out this morning after breakfast. I have no idea where to or when he will be back," Lucy told her. "And now, if you'll excuse me, Miss Singleton, I must get back to my work."

"And that's another thing," Marion said sourly. "That exasperating tap-tap-tap for hours at a time. Can't you do something else for a change?"

"I'm afraid not—unless my employer tells me to," Lucy said steadily.

Marion shrugged her shoulders.

"Determined not to lose your job, aren't you?" she suggested sardonically. "Well, if you ask me—"

Lucy fled. She reached the study and sat down at the desk, only to discover that her hands were shaking too much for her to resume work. She pushed the little machine away, rested her elbows on the desk and buried her face in her hands.

Really Marion had behaved outrageously, and even boredom and the pain she might still be feeling—though it could not be much—was no excuse. Lucy felt angry and unhappy. She knew that it was not for her to sit in judgment on the girl Owen was in love with, but how could she—how *could* she behave in such an ill-bred way? And could love be so blind that it would overlook such behaviour?

"Hullo, something wrong, Lucy?"

Lucy gave a little scream. Owen had come into the room by the open french window and was standing looking at her.

"You do manage to sneak up on me, don't you?" she said resentfully. "Can't I stop working for a single moment without—"

Owen sat down on the edge of the desk.

"Truce at an end?" he asked. "Because if so, I do think you might tell me why. What *has* upset you?"

"Oh, nothing," Lucy said wearily. "I'm being silly, that's all."

"I'm sure you are," Owen agreed. "Obviously you've got an attack of the mullygrubs and you're refusing to take the proper medicine for them."

"What *are* the mullygrubs?" Lucy asked, suddenly feeling much more cheerful.

"Oh, don't you know?" Owen looked surprised. "It's when something has upset you and for some reason or other you can't do anything about it. You get a feeling of repression and frustration which can only be relieved by screaming at the top of your voice. Or—" he added thoughtfully, "by heaving a brick through a plate glass window, according to some people. Everybody gets 'em at some time or other. I've had them all day."

"Oh!" Lucy could not repress a smile, though she wondered just what had caused the attack in his case. "And which are you going to do—scream, or try the brick cure? They've got some lovely plate glass windows in some of the shops in Monte Carlo!"

"Don't tempt me!" Owen pleaded, holding up his hand. "No, actually, I'm going to try another cure! I'm going to have a swim."

"Oh!" Lucy could not keep a note of envy out of her voice. Then, remembering that she had work to do, she added primly : "I hope the cure is effective."

"It won't be—if I have to undergo it alone," he announced. "You come too, Lucy!"

"I'd love to," she said frankly. "But I've got some work to finish, and besides—"

"Besides—?" he prompted.

"It doesn't seem quite fair—when Miss Singleton is stuck in bed. She's feeling rather bored, I think—" her voice trailed away before Owen's penetrating look.

"Oh, so that was it!" he remarked. "You were at the receiving end of Marion's sulks! Well, forget it."

"Mr. Vaughan, please!" Lucy protested uncomfortably.

"Now what have I done?" Owen asked plaintively.

Lucy twittered with her fingers on the typewriter keys, her eyes downcast so that she should not meet his.

"Well, just I think it's—rather disloyal of you to—to speak, like that of Miss Singleton to me—or to anyone else, seeing that you and she—" she glanced up appealingly at him. To her relief he did not look angry.

"I know what you mean, Lucy," he said gravely. "And I quite agree with you. If two people mean a lot to one another, they should be loyal to each other. But will you take it from me that in this case—" he hesitat-

343

ed— "I know just what I'm doing, and there's no question of any disloyalty?"

"If you say so," Lucy said doubtfully.

"I do say so," Owen was very emphatic. "And now, will you come down off that very moral high horse of yours and come out to the pool?"

"Yes," Lucy said recklessly. "I will!"

•   •   •

That evening Lucy had the unpleasant experience of overhearing a conversation that was not intended for her ears.

She was sitting at her bedroom window thinking over all that had happened during the day, and she was in a mood when starlight appealed so she had not put on the light.

Half dozing, half day-dreaming, she suddenly realised that two people had come out on to the veranda, one end of which terminated within a few feet of her window. They were talking in undertones, but all the same, she could recognise their voices.

For a moment she hesitated. Should she, by pulling her curtains and putting on the light, let them know that she was there? Or didn't it matter, seeing that she could not hear what they were saying?

Before she had decided, however, Mrs. Mayberry raised her voice slightly.

"Your trouble, Owen, is that you're a lot too kind hearted! This would never have happened if—" Lucy heard her say.

"Go on, rub it in," Owen, replied wryly.

"Well, it's true, my dear! You go out of your way to help people—"

"Never again!" Owen declared. "At least, not—"

He left the sentence unfinished, but evidently Mrs. Mayberry understood what he meant.

"I'm delighted to hear it," she announced. "But I

344

warn you, Owen, I'm not too sure that hints, however pointed, are going to be sufficient. You may have to make the situation clear in so many words—"

Lucy clapped her hands over her ears, horrified that she had listened so long. She had no idea what they were talking about, but that was not the point. She was eavesdropping, and that was a despicable thing to do. Very carefully she crept over to the door of her room, opened it silently and then closed it with a little crash, at the same time switching on her light. Then humming a little tune, she walked over to the window and rattled the curtains along their runners. Surely that would give the impression that she had just come into the room and they would never know that they had been overheard! And then she could put what she had heard out of her mind with an easy conscience.

But the day was not yet finished. A little later, as she was returning from her room after taking a shower, Marion's door suddenly opened, and Marion, hanging heavily on to the handle, beckoned to her.

"I want to talk to you," she announced imperatively.

"I'm rather tired," Lucy said truthfully. "Won't to-morrow morning do?"

"No, it won't," Marion snapped. "I want to talk to you now!"

With a shrug, Lucy complied, automatically giving Marion a supporting arm to get back to bed.

"Thanks," Marion said shortly, and looked at Lucy critically. "You know, I don't think you're a bad sort, at heart. But that doesn't stop you being an utter little fool!"

Lucy promptly moved in the direction of the door, but Marion called her back.

"All right, it wasn't particularly tactful of me to say that," she admitted. "But honestly, I'm worried on your account."

"Oh?" Lucy said sharply. "Why?"

"Because you're heading for a crash," Marion said calmly. "And if it's possible, I'd like to prevent that actually happening."

"I don't think you know enough about my affairs to be in a position to say that," Lucy said steadily.

"No? That's just where you're wrong," Marion announced calmly. "For instance, I know all about Dick Corbett and you."

"Who told you?" Lucy asked sharply.

"Owen, of course," Marion explained, arranging her pillows more comfortably. "You've got him really worried, you know."

"If, as you say, Mr. Vaughan told you that Dick and I were once engaged, then he must also have told you that there's no need to worry on that score," Lucy kept her voice even with difficulty. "That is over and done with—as Mr. Vaughan knows."

Marion laughed softly.

"Oh, my dear girl, he knows that all right!" she admitted. "But that's just the trouble. Having got Dick out of your system—somewhat quickly, I can't help feeling— you've become something of a menace to my poor Owen!"

"What do you mean?" Lucy stared at her blankly.

"Now look, don't play the innocent with me!" Marion urged impatiently. "It just isn't any good."

"I think you'd better explain—" Lucy suggested crisply.

Marion shrugged her shoulders.

"All right, if you want it that way! Well, Dick jilted you on your wedding day, didn't he? And that was the very day on which you came to Spindles. You were upset—quite naturally, of course. And Owen realised it, took you in hand and put some spirit into you. As a result, although you resented it at the time, you were ultimately very grateful to him. You're not going to deny that, are you?"

"I've no wish to," Lucy said coldly. "I have every reason to be grateful to Mr. Vaughan."

"Yes, I know. But gratitude can be a bit of a bore at times," Marion drawled. "Particularly when it turns to—love!"

Lucy caught her breath.

"You've no right—" she began hotly, but Marion ignored her protest.

"Now look, no woman seeing you when Owen is about could possibly mistake the signs! You hang on to every word he says, you make calf's eyes at him, and if you can't get him to yourself, you sulk—"

"It's not true!" Lucy insisted, nearly in tears.

"Oh, yes, it is," Marion insisted. "Of course, it's partly Owen's own fault. He's so absurdly kind—he's always doing good turns to people and it was inevitable that, one day, something like this would happen."

Lucy stared at her in sheer horror. It simply could not be coincidence that Marion had referred to Owen's kindness and its results in almost identical terms to those which Mrs. Mayberry had used not very much earlier. And now there was added point to that final remark which she had overheard:

"Hints—may not be sufficient. You may have to make the situation clear in so many words—"

They had been talking about her.

Lucy turned and stumbled from the room.

Lucy lay very still, her face half buried in her pillow. At first, when she had reached the haven of her own room, she had been too numbed by what Marion had said to think coherently.

Now that initial shock had passed, and odiously crude though Marion had been, Lucy knew that she had spoken nothing but the truth. She did love Owen.

Yet it was only today that she had realised it, and even then she had been reluctant to admit it to herself in so many words. It was so new a discovery, there was such a gossamer quality about it. Lucy had been reminded of that exquisite lace which she and Owen had seen in one of the Monte Carlo shops—so fragile that one would be afraid to handle it. Just like that. She had been content simply to exist in a haze of happiness that needed no words to explain it.

And now, that happiness was shattered into a thousand fragments. And, sick at heart, Lucy knew that she had only herself to thank for being in this predicament.

Looking back, she knew that from the very beginning Owen had been kind to her. At the time she had felt that he had been brutal, but for a long time now she had realised, as he had then, that it was an occasion for shock tactics. Anything else would have encouraged her to indulge in self-pity, perhaps indefinitely.

Yes, she had every cause to feel grateful. Grateful? What was it Mr. Keane had said about gratitude ?

"The peculiar thing about gratitude is that it is something of a boomerang. If you have earned it, in time it can happen that you, and not the recipient of your help, become under an obligation—"

An obligation to continue the kindness that is expected of you—that comes to be taken for granted, as Lucy felt she had done.

She remembered how many times since they had

come to Monaco he had gone out of his way to give her pleasure, and it seemed to her now that he had had no other course because she had perhaps dropped a hint or shown an eagerness—

This afternoon, for instance. When he had said he was going for a swim in the pool, she had not been able to hide the fact that she had envied him. So he had been pratically compelled to invite her to come as well. Oh, he had done it very charmingly, of course. But all the same—

Nor was that all. There had been an incident a little later, the memory of which scorched Lucy like flame.

On the way back to the villa after their swim, Lucy had stumbled. Instantly Owen had caught her in his arms, holding her up. To Lucy it seemed that time stood still. Then, releasing her, Owen had said lightly :

"Hey, steady on ! We don't want another sprained ankle!"

Nothing more than that. But Lucy knew that she had lingered in his arms just that moment longer than was strictly necessary.

Owen had known that, too, and he had realised just what it meant. That explained the determination he had expressed:

"Never again! At least, not—"

He had not finished the sentence, but no doubt he had in some way indicated the window of her room. Perhaps even, he had known that she was listening.

So there it was. She loved Owen. That was why what Dick had done had left no permanent scar.

Owen, on the other hand, felt no more than kindness towards her. And she had repaid him by causing him intolerable embarrassment.

With bitter self-scorn, she told herself that she was no better than Gwenda. She had allowed herself to fall in love with a man who owed his allegiance to another girl—perhaps not in any definite thought or words had she hoped that Owen might one day love her, but was that really true? If one loves, of course one hopes for love in return.

Lucy sat up suddenly, clasping her arms round her knees.

With painful clarity she realised that there was only one thing she could do for Owen. She must go right out of his life—and stay out.

At once. She must leave the Villa des Fleurs the very next day, even though it would inconvenience Mrs. Mayberry. But in view of what Lucy had overheard her say, it seemed probable that she would be so relieved to see the back of her troublesome secretary that she would regard any inconvenience involved as a small price to pay.

But there must be no hint of the real reason why she was going, Lucy thought feverishly. Somehow she must find an excuse which could be accepted without difficulty. That would not only mean that she could hold her own head high, but it would also save Owen from further embarrassment.

But how could one produce a convincing excuse just like that, at the drop of a hat? A few days earlier and she could have made out that it was Dick's presence. But that excuse had gone since it was most unlikely that she would see him again. And in any case, she had admitted to Owen that she was really indifferent where Dick was concerned. No, she must think of something else—

Still trying to solve the problem of what excuse she could possibly produce, Lucy at last fell asleep.

And with the morning came an excuse such as she had never dreamed of, and which sent her in search of Mrs. Mayberry, white-faced and almost in tears.

"My dear, what is it?" Mrs. Mayberry exclaimed as she came into the room.

Lucy held out an airmail letter which had just come in with the morning mail.

"If you'll read this," she said shakily. "It's from Mother."

Pulling the trembling girl down on to the edge of her bed, Mrs. Mayberry read the letter.

Mrs. Darvill had written to say that Mr. Darvill had had a heart attack. Not perhaps a very bad one, but none the less, one which the doctor had said must be treated with respect.

"Try not to worry, darling," Mrs. Darvill wrote. "Daddy is a strong man and a very sensible one. He will do just what he is told, and he is having the very best of attention at the hospital, rest assured of that. I will let you know every day how things are—"

"And not a word about wishing you were there to stand by her!" Mrs. Mayberry marvelled. "Mothers are wonderful people, Lucy!"

"I know," Lucy said with difficulty. "So are fathers. But I feel I should be there—"

"Of course you do, dear," Mrs. Mayberry said briskly. "I wonder whether you can get a flight today? Oh, dear, I do wish Owen hadn't gone out—and I've no very great faith in my brother's ability to make arrangements of this sort in French!"

"Quite likely there'll be someone who speaks English," Lucy said, her nerves steadied now that she could make definite plans. "And anyhow, I think I could manage—if I may telephone?"

"Of course—do just whatever is necessary," Mrs. Mayberry told her. "I'll send Bertha to your room to pack—"

Lucy got on the telephone and to her relief was told that there was a single seat on a flight leaving Nice in two hours' time. She reserved it, making a careful note of the time at which she must reach the airport in order to claim it, and went back to Mrs. Mayberry.

"Splendid, my dear," Mrs. Mayberry said kindly. "Now, money. Go to the top drawer of the chest over there and bring me a leather wallet you will find in it—"

"But really, Mrs. Mayberry, I think I've got enough —" Lucy protested.

"We'll make quite sure of that," Mrs. Mayberry insisted. "Get the wallet, please, dear."

She opened it and pulled out some notes. Some were foreign, some English.

"There, I think that will see you through, Lucy." And then, to Lucy's relief, she added: "We'll work out just what it represents in terms of your salary later on. Now, a car to get you to Nice—I'm afraid we shall have to hire one, as Owen has taken his. Telephone through to the same place from which he hired that. And use his name, then there won't be any hitch. Anything else you can think of?"

"If I could just have a sandwich or something before I leave," Lucy suggested. "Then I won't have to waste time once I start."

"Yes, certainly, a good idea. Yes, what is it, Bertha?"

"Just to say I've packed Miss Lucy's clothes, madam," Bertha explained. "And I'd like to say how sorry I am about your father, miss."

"Thank you, Bertha, that's very kind of you," Lucy replied gratefully. "And now I'll go and telephone about the car, Mrs. Mayberry."

"Oh—" Bertha looked slightly put out, "I'm afraid Miss Marion is on the telephone at the moment, miss."

"Oh, dear!" Mrs. Mayberry frowned slightly. "I hope she won't be long."

"I shouldn't think so, madam. It was a call from London—from Mr. Kelsall, I believe."

"In that case—no, I don't suppose it will be a very long one—although I must say that man seems to have no idea whatever about money—oh, well, I suppose he doesn't have to." She paused and then said curiously: "Where is Miss Marion taking the call, Bertha?"

"In the study, madam," Bertha explained. "I helped her along there."

"I see," Mrs. Mayberry said noncommittally. "We'll give her a few more minutes and then she will have to end the call."

But to Lucy's relief, there was no need for Marion to be interrupted, for shortly after she came out of the study and limped back to her bedroom. She was smiling in a satisfied sort of way. Mr. Kelsall had been very much upset because he had had to fly to London on business and could not hope to return for a couple of days.

"But when I do get back, the first thing I'm going to do is come and collect you, my dear," he had told her. "And in the meantime—well, you'll be getting some more flowers in the morning!"

On the whole, Marion felt thoroughly satisfied with life. Whatever the future might hold, it wasn't a bad thing to have a man as wealthy as Lawrence Kelsall— well, at least interested in her.

When, later in the day, she heard that Lucy had left Monaco, she felt that everything was playing into her hands.

Lucy arrived at Nice airport with time to spare, which meant that she had time to think, and that was something she did not want to do.

She was truly concerned on her father's account, and foolishly, felt rather guilty because his illness had provided her with the excuse she had so desperately needed. None the less, she could not put Owen out of her mind. It was a good thing that he was still out when she had left. It saved explanations, and more important than that, it saved the necessity for saying goodbye. It would have been terrible if she had said or done anything which had shown how agonising it was to know

353

that she would never see him again. But she had been spared that—and so had he, which mattered even more.

Vaguely she began to wonder what she would do when she reached home. For a little while, until as she hoped, her father's condition had definitely improved, she would stay with her mother. But after that—

To her surprise, Mrs. Mayberry had taken it for granted that sooner or later she would return, either to the Villa des Fleurs or to Spindles, and Lucy had promised that she would—if it were possible. But of course she never would. It was out of the question.

At last the announcement was made over the loudspeaker that passengers for her flight should now proceed to the plane. Gathering up her handbag and a few magazines she had bought, she joined the rest of the passengers at the barrier. A few moments later she was in her place in the plane. It was carrying practically a full complement of passengers. In fact, there was only one seat vacant, and that was beside Lucy's. It would be nice, she thought, if no one sat there—she did not feel like talking, and so often fellow passengers took it for granted that they must make conversation. But she was doomed to disappointment.

Almost at the last moment a belated passenger arrived, hurried along the gangway, and sat down beside Lucy. Inadvertently he sat on the edge of her coat and muttered a word of apology.

"It's all right," Lucy said politely. "It was my—" and stopped short.

The latecomer was—Dick Corbett.

. . . .

For a moment they stared at one another. Then, just as he had said on that other occasion when they had unexpectedly met in Nice, Dick exclaimed:

"Lucy, what in the world are you doing here?"

All the tension that had been building up since the previous day came to a head. Lucy turned on him.

"What do you mean, what am I doing here?" she demanded spiritedly. "What business is it of yours, and if it comes to that, what are *you* doing here?"

Dick, considerably taken aback by the challenge, left the last question unanswered.

"Well, it's only that it's rather a coincidence—" he said lamely.

"Coincidences do happen—unfortunately," Lucy told him shortly. "And one just has to put up with them. However, since you appear to think it may not, after all, be a coincidence that I'm travelling by the same plane as you are, I'd better tell you that I'm going home because my father is ill."

"Oh!" Dick, subdued by her bluntness, took several moments to realise that her announcement called for some comment. "I'm sorry about that, Lucy."

"Thank you." Lucy began to look at one of her magazines, and Dick took the hint that further conversation would not be welcome.

Half an hour must have passed, and then he said suddenly:

"I've left Gwenda."

The magazine dropped to Lucy's lap.

"You've *what?*" she demanded incredulously.

"Left Gwenda," he repeated. "Oh, I know, we've hardly been married any time, but I told you before how difficult she was—and things have got worse since you came to lunch that day on *La Mouette*."

"Since I appear to be involved in it, I suppose you'd better tell me what you mean," Lucy said resignedly. "Although I'd much rather not hear."

"Well, it was Gwenda who put the old man up to including you in the invitation," Dick explained. "I didn't know anything about it—"

"I realised that at the time," Lucy told him. "Well?"

355

"Well, the old man spotted that something was wrong, and he went for Gwenda until she owned up. There was a dickens of a row—he wouldn't let us come to lunch at the villa, and he told Gwenda just what he thought of her. She was furious—blamed me for everything. She said some things that—well, I lost my temper, too. A thoroughly edifying scene." He laughed mirthlessly. "This was after the old man had gone ashore to lunch with you, but it kept on at intervals ever since. Last night, I suddenly felt I couldn't stand it any more. So—" he shrugged his shoulders. "Here I am!"

Despite the repugnance which Lucy felt at having heard this squalid story, there was one point about it which aroused her curiosity.

"But I thought you said that she—that you had very little money to spend. How did you manage to pay your fare — and what are you going to live on?"

Dick chuckled triumphantly.

"Ah, that's something Gwenda didn't reckon on! Of course, when we started rowing, she clamped down tighter than ever on cash, but I'd got a bit in reserve that she didn't know about, and last night I went to the Casino, and struck lucky! That's what made me decide to leave her. Actually, I didn't go back to the yacht last night, and this morning I sent her a note by one of the fishermen saying that this was it, goodbye!"

"I see," Lucy said slowly.

"Do you blame me?" Dick asked hotly. "There are some things a chap can't swallow, and Gwenda's attitude of having bought me body and soul is one of them."

Lucy did not reply, and after a minute, Dick went on:

"Oh, I know, I asked for it! And for once, I'll tell you the absolute truth, Lucy. I told myself that I was in love with Gwenda—but I doubt if I'd have found it such an easy job if it hadn't been for her money. Lord, what a fool I was! Having to beg for every penny—"

"Dick, be quiet a minute, I want to think," Lucy told him authoritatively.

Dick subsided in his seat, his face gloomy. For the life of him he couldn't see that any thinking Lucy might do was going to help.

"Yes, I think I've got it sorted out now," Lucy said at length. "Until you got married you'd never been dependent on anyone else for money. You'd earned what you had and so you had the right to do what you liked with it."

"Well, of course," Dick agreed. "That's what I've been saying."

"Yes, but there's more to it than that," Lucy insisted. "Don't you see, Dick, if having a good time was all that mattered to you, you wouldn't mind having to eat humble pie. You'd think it was worth it, wouldn't you?"

"I suppose so," he admitted doubtfully. "But where does that get me?"

"Oh, don't be so dull!" Lucy said impatiently. "I'm trying to help you—though goodness knows why! Listen, Dick, and try to understand what I'm driving at. People like us aren't brought up to do nothing but enjoy themselves. It may be fun for a time, but not for always. I think, really and truly, you're bored with doing nothing because all your life you've had to work and you're missing it."

"Maybe," Dick did not sound enthusiastic. "But does it really make sense that I should work when—" he checked himself, seeing her expression of distaste. "Oh, I know, you don't think it's at all nice for a man to live on his wife's money. All the same.—"

"But, Dick," Lucy interrupted earnestly, "you're talking as if one only works for the sake of money—"

"Well, that's what most people work for, isn't it? You've got to live so you have to work."

"Yes, of course that's true," Lucy answered impatiently. "But there can be a lot more to it than that—if you really enjoy the work you do. That's why quite a lot of really rich people keep on working when they don't need to. I should say that Mr. Kelsall is one of them."

"Clever girl," Dick commented, considerably surprised at Lucy's shrewdness. "You're right. He gets a real kick out of pitting his brains against his rivals."

"Then why shouldn't you?" Lucy asked eagerly. "You've got brains, Dick, or you wouldn't have got on as you did."

"That may be true," Dick looked slightly more cheerful. "All the same, just how do I get a job now? I can't exactly ask my father-in-law for references, can I?"

"No, but you can tell him you're tired of doing nothing—and ask for your job back," Lucy retorted. "And I think that would appeal to him so much that you'd get it!"

"By jove, you've got something there!" Dick exclaimed, sitting erect. "Judging by one or two cracks he'd made about sons-in-law who—well, never mind that." He pondered for a moment. "There's more to this than that, you know. If I went after any old job, Gwenda would have something to say about it, but if her father agrees to taking me back, she can't object because she's dependent on him for a hefty allowance." He chuckled softly. "And I'll have some cash of my own—which means I'll also have some independence. That will shake my dear wife rigid!"

Lucy did not reply. She thought it was disgusting of Dick to speak like this of his wife, even though Gwenda had contributed her share to the trouble between them, but what was the good of saying so? She thought perhaps the suggestion she had made might help matters, but really and truly it was for Dick and Gwenda to solve their own problems.

Perhaps Dick had realised that for, deep in thought, he showed no further wish to discuss his affairs with her. She thought that he had even forgotten she was there and was thankful to be neglected. Dick and she had drifted so far apart now that they had really nothing to say to one another. Thank goodness that once they had gone their separate ways there was little probability that they would ever meet again.

Dick must have been thinking along the same lines for, once through Customs at London Airport, he suddenly turned to her, his hand outstretched.

"I don't suppose you and I are likely to see each other again, Lucy," he said diffidently. "But I would like to say that I think you've been an absolute brick—will you shake hands?"

"Yes, of course." She put her hand into his and gave it a brief, firm grip. "I wish you the very best of luck, Dick!"

He mumbled something, shamed by her generosity, but Lucy had already turned away and was making arrangements for her luggage to go on the bus to the terminal. Dick, apparently, made other arrangements, for she did not see him again.

* * * *

Mrs. Darvill hugged Lucy close.

"Darling, I couldn't ask you to come home—but I am thankful that you have!" she exclaimed.

"But I had to," Lucy protested. "How is Daddy?"

"They're very well satisfied with his progress," Mrs. Darvill replied thankfully. "Of course, it's going to be a slow business, but he's very patient, bless him! He's looking forward so much to seeing you."

"I ought never to have gone away," Lucy said contritely. "I ought to have been here to help when it happened."

"Nonsense, dear," Mrs. Darvill said briskly. "No one

could possibly know that this was going to happen—
and in any case, your father and I quite agreed with
you that going away was the wisest thing you could
possibly do."

It seemed to Lucy that there was an enquiry in her
mother's tone, and knowing what must be in her mind,
she answered the unspoken question.

"It *was* the best thing, Mummy," she said quietly.
"And there's no need for you to worry. I feel as if it
all happened to someone else, not me. And as if it was
all a long long time ago."

Mrs. Darvill looked relieved.

"In that case, darling, we'll just forget all about it.
And now, would you like a cup of tea ?"

"I'd love one," Lucy said, and followed her mother
to the kitchen.

"It was very kind of Mrs. Mayberry to let you come
at such short notice," Mrs. Darvill remarked as she
put the kettle on to boil. "It must be inconvenient for
her to be without you."

"I'm afraid it will be," Lucy agreed. "But as you
say, she is very kind. She simply took it for granted
that I must come."

"And she'll keep your job open for you ?" Mrs.
Darvill asked anxiously.

"Oh, yes," Lucy said casually, and changed the
subject.

Mrs. Darvill took the hint. Lucy did not want to
discuss the question of returning. Of course, the explanation for that might well be that she had already
made up her mind to stay with her parents. Well, they
couldn't have the child sacrificing herself like that, of
course, but somehow or other, Mrs. Darvill had the
feeling that there might be another reason why Lucy
would prefer not to go back. What that reason might
be she had no intention of asking, but one could not
help wondering—

Then the kettle began to boil and for the time being she gave the matter no further thought.

.   .   .

The next day, Lucy wrote to Mrs. Mayberry. She explained that although the specialist was quite satisfied with her father's progress, he had made it clear that it was out of the question for Mr. Darvill ever to work again.

"What he really meant, of course, was that the same thing could happen again at any time," Lucy explained. "And because of this, and because of the extra work that will fall on my mother's shoulders with my father always at home, I feel I ought not to leave them. I know my decision will cause you a great deal of inconvenience, and I am truly sorry for that, but I do hope you will understand—"

She sealed the envelope and took the letter to the post. Just for a moment, as she was going to drop it in, she held on to it. She couldn't do it! Never to see Owen again—she couldn't bear it.

But she had got to—for Owen's sake.

"He'll be thankful to know that he's seen the last of me," she thought bitterly. "And no wonder!"

Resolutely, she let go of the letter, turned her back on the pillar box and walked slowly home, her hands clenched deep in the pockets of her coat.

And that was the end of it all, she told herself firmly.

CHAPTER XI

MRS. MAYBERRY passed Lucy's letter to Owen and waited in silence while he read it.

"Just what you expected," he commented as he handed it back.

"Yes. As I told you, I felt her mind was made up before she left," Mrs. Mayberry confirmed.

Owen rubbed his hand thoughtfully along the line of his jawbone.

"Natural enough, really. She's extremely fond of her parents."

"Yes, she is," Mrs. Mayberry agreed. "But if that was how she felt, why shouldn't she have told me so before she left ? Or at least said that she thought it very likely that she would not be returning."

"Just exactly what did she say ?" Owen asked.

"I let her see that I assumed she would come back to work for me, either here or at Spindles," Mrs. Mayberry replied precisely. "And she promised that she would—if it was possible."

"H'm. Doesn't that come to the same thing—and that when she did reach home, she felt it wasn't possible ?" Owen suggested.

"Yes, it could have been that," Mrs. Mayberry agreed. "But for one thing." She hesitated momentarily as if choosing her words with considerable care. "Beyond all possible doubt Lucy was deeply distressed on her father's account. None the less, I got the impression—" she paused again, "that in some peculiar way she was experiencing a very definite relief. I can't be more precise than that, I'm afraid."

"I think what you mean is that, distressed though she was, she was thankful to have an excuse to clear out," Owen said harshly. "A genuine excuse that could not be questioned."

"Yes, I suppose that is what I mean," Mrs. Mayberry

admitted. "But just why she should want such an excuse, I've no idea. Do you think it could have been anything to do with that unspeakable young man ?"

"Corbett ?" No, I don't think so. Judging by what Lucy herself said, she had entirely got over any feeling for him."

"I'm not surprised. One way and another, she must have been completely disillusioned, poor child. Yet, in a girl as sensitive as Lucy, I would have expected disillusionment itself to have left a mark. Possibly a loss of trust in humanity in general, or perhaps a degree of hardness. But I didn't see any trace of anything like that in her. I would say, in fact, that since we all came here, she has been completely happy and carefree—?" she looked enquiringly at Owen.

"So she was—until that damned yacht arrived," Owen agreed grimly.

"And yet you don't associate any wish she may have had to get away with young Corbett ?"

Owen shook his head without comment.

"Of course," Mrs. Mayberry mused, "one does hear it said that nothing drives the memory of one man so completely out of a girl's mind as falling in love with another."

"Does one ?" Owen smiled faintly. "Do you think perhaps she's fallen in love with old Kelsall ?"

Mrs. Mayberry treated this remark with the disdainful scorn it deserved. Owen dropped his hand affectionately on his aunt's shoulder.

"No, you're right, it isn't a thing to joke about," he admitted penitently. "I think I was whistling to keep my courage up—and goodness knows, I need something that will do that !"

Mrs. Mayberry patted his hand understandingly.

"What are you going to do, Owen ?" she asked anxiously.

"Ultimately, go and see Lucy," he replied unhesitatingly. "But first I'm going to do something I should have done long ago, and see what reaction that produces. I think it might be rather revealing."

"Yes," Mrs. Mayberry agreed. "Yes, I think you're right, Owen. But you won't find it pleasant, you know."

"I'm not so sure of that," Owen told her grimly. "I think perhaps making a few facts very clear may afford me considerable satisfaction. But you can take my word for it, pleasant or not, I'm going through with it!"

.   .   .

Marion was reclining at her ease on the veranda. She was in a very pensive mood.

It was no good refusing to admit—to herself, at any rate—that things had not gone the way she had been so sure they would.

As she had seen it, her fortuitous accident, necessitating a stay of several days at the Villa des Fleurs, had meant that Owen would have a welcome opportunity of spending all his time in her company. But it hadn't worked out like that. In fact, she had hardly seen anything of him at all.

She nibbled her thumb, frowning thoughtfully. She had been furious that she had not had an invitation to stay at the villa until hospitality had been forced on Mr. Keane by her accident. And goodness knows, she'd angled hard enough to get one as soon as she had heard of Owen's plans.

But that was just it. Owen had been really stuffy when, almost in so many words, she had suggested that he could wangle an invitation for her. He had made it clear, in that irritatingly aloof way he could assume if he liked, that one didn't do that sort of thing.

At the time she had found an explanation for his attitude. Absurb though it sounded in reference to such a dynamic man as Owen, he was completely under the thumb of that wretched old aunt of his, though heaven alone knew why, seeing that he was quite well off himself. But the fact remained, and so did Marion's conviction that the old woman didn't like her, though she'd had the good sense not to show it too much. All the same, what was more likely than that she had got round her brother to leave out the girl she so disliked —or disapproved of as a wife for her precious nephew would perhaps have been more accurate. And in that case, quite likely Owen had had it made clear to him that she wasn't going to be asked and had consequently been considerably embarrassed when Marion herself had suggested it.

She'd been convinced that was it, and it needed very little self-persuasion to believe that he would have liked her to be with him. All the same, there was clearly nothing to be done about it—until Mr. Kelsall's invitation had come along.

She had met him at a charity concert at which she had been singing. He had asked for an introduction to her, and had told her how much he had enjoyed her singing. A day or so later, he had sent her flowers, and had followed that up with an invitation to lunch. Marion had been in two minds whether to accept it or not. She thought his company would probably bore her. Then, as she had nothing else to do, she finally accepted. And, on the whole, she had not been bored. For one thing, though she did not put it quite so bluntly when thinking over the occasion later, he had encouraged her to talk about herself. What was more, such information as he did impart concerning himself was both interesting and intriguing. For instance, he made no secret of the fact that he was a self-made man and rather proud of the fact. She could understand that. Wasn't she self-made as well ? Oh, of course, Owen had helped a bit, but she was the one who had really done all the work. And then Mr. Kelsall had spoken of the thrill he got out of getting the better of his rivals—she could understand that as well. But he had not gone into any details, any more than he had bragged at all about his wealth. But then he didn't need to—it was enough simply to demonstrate it. The absolutely first-class restaurant to which he had taken her for lunch, the obsequious service he received, his casual reference to the yacht he had recently bought—these were more than enough.

But he had taken care to give her one definite piece of information—that he was a widower of a good many years' standing. That appeared to be said very casually, but Marion had a shrewd idea that it had been said with definite intent.

They had seen quite a lot of one another whenever Mr. Kelsall happened to be in London—and that seemed to be with increasing frequency. And then had come the invitation to tour the Mediterranean in *La Mouette*. Marion could have cried with disappointment because of that wretched series of engagements in Germany. It would have been so perfect—she could have killed two birds with one stone. Of course they would stop at Monte Carlo. In fact, Mr. Kelsall had said that he intended doing so, and that he wanted to look up an acquaintance of his who had a villa there. When that acquaintance turned out to be no other than Mr. Keane, Marion decided that by hook or by crook, she must go too.

But just how she could manage it, she could not for the life of her imagine. Her agent attended to the terms of her contracts, but she knew that there was always a penalty clause in them which would apply if she broke one without sufficient reason. Owen would be put out, too, and that she dared not risk. Regretfully, she turned down Mr. Kelsall's invitation.

And then, just as *La Mouette* had begun her cruise, Marion woke one morning with a relaxed throat. She tried to sing a few notes and produced nothing but a harsh croak. She sent for her doctor, and he in turn advised consulting a specialist.

"I admit that in an ordinary case, I should suggest a few days in bed, confident that that would be all that was necessary. But in the case of an important lady like yourself whose voice means so much to the world —no, I cannot take any chances."

And the specialist had said the same thing, though he went further. No singing at all until she was completely better, and if possible, had had a holiday.

"But I can't," Marion had croaked. "I've got engagements that I must keep."

"The show must go on, eh?" the specialist had quoted. "I know. Well, all I can tell you is that this is not the first time I've met with this situation. On one occasion, my patient decided to ignore my warning."

"And what happened?" Marion whispered huskily.

"Her voice gave out—permanently. Now, Miss Singleton, I don't want that to happen with you."

"It mustn't," Marion said, genuinely panic-stricken. "I've got to earn my living!"

"Well then—" said the specialist gravely.

After that, it was simple. A cruise in the Mediterranean—just the thing! Joyfully Marion had a message wirelessed to *La Mouette* and received a prompt and enthusiastic reply. Her luck had held good. It had even been Mr. Kelsall's idea that they should surprise Owen about her being there at all. This was when he had told her that a party from the Villa des Fleurs was lunching with them that very day and she had admitted that she was just a little bit afraid that Owen might think she had made too much of her illness in order to be able to have this wonderful, wonderful holiday.

Mr. Kelsall had been indignant.

"Well, if he thinks anything like that, he'd better not say it in front of me!" he had declared. "And that's the way we'll make sure it is ! He shan't have a chance of seeing you in time to think up anything unpleasant to say—or in circumstances where he could, anyway. Now listen to me—"

Well, that had gone off all right, though Owen had been a bit put out. And, of course, she hadn't bargained with that girl—Lucy—being there, nor known anything about her and Dick Corbett until Gwenda had told her. Still, by and large, she had not been displeased. And then there had been the visit to the villa—and her accident.

That had put Lawrence Kelsall out quite a bit. He didn't like leaving her with Owen about. Well, that was just too bad. He had served his turn—and anyway, a bit of opposition would not do any harm, any more than it had done Owen any harm to see all the gorgeous flowers Lawrence had sent her.

But from then on, nothing had turned out as she had anticipated it would. Owen simply avoided her. She wondered if she had overdone it a bit. Was he jealous of Lawrence to the point where he was sulking? It didn't really seem like Owen, but you never could tell. She'd wondered a little about Lucy as well, but she was out of the way now, thank goodness, so there was no need to worry about her any more, though at one time—

No, it all came back to those two old fogies. Somehow or other, they had got such a hold over Owen that they were in a position to make him keep away from her, even when they were living under the same roof.

Marion scowled. She had laid her plans so carefully, been so sure that they would work out to her complete satisfaction, and now, to be frustrated by two old people who had lived their own lives—it was infuriating ! It made her wonder if, after all, marrying Owen was such a good idea. *She* had no wish to spend possibly years dancing to the tune they chose to pipe !

Well then, wouldn't it be wiser to cut her losses and —she gave a convulsive start. Owen had come out of the open french windows behind her and was now standing beside her.

"I want to have a talk with you, Marion," he said unsmilingly, making no attempt to apologise for having startled her.

With an effort Marion checked the desire to twit him by asking if Uncle and Auntie had given him permission to speak to her, strong though it was. Better hear what he had to say—

"In that case, you'd better sit down," she suggested. "It gives me a crick in my neck looking up at you."

Owen complied, drawing up a chair so that he was practically facing her.

"Well ?" Marion asked, realising too late that she had put a defiant note into the word that suggested she felt unsure of herself.

"I want to talk about the future," Owen went on deliberately. "Your future."

"What about it ?" Marion demanded, her eyes guarded.

Owen regarded her steadily for a moment or two before he answered.

"I'm wondering if you realise just what a pity it is that you had to cancel your German engagements," he explained.

"Well, of course it was a pity," Marion's eyes widened as if to suggest surprise that there could be any other opinion about it. "But these things do happen, you know !"

"Yes, they do," Owen agreed. "But I wonder if you realise the effect that such a cancellation has on people who are important to your future career ?"

Marion sat up suddenly.

"I don't know what you mean," she insisted angrily.

"I couldn't sing with a sore throat, could I ? Or are you insinuating that it was a put-up job so that I could accept Mr. Kelsall's invitation ?"

It was taking the war into the enemy's camp with a vengeance, but at least Marion did not lack courage. In any case, boldness quite often paid dividends—

"Because if you are, you'd better think again ! I told you that my doctor called in one of the best throat specialists there is. Do you honestly think a man like that would lend himself to trickery of that sort ?"

"No, I don't," Owen said bluntly. "He wouldn't be such a fool."

"Well then—" Marion lay back against her cushions, "what's this all about ?"

"I'll try to make myself clear," Owen altered his position slightly. "First of all, I'd like to know just what your plans are. Mr. Kelsall, I understand, is returning later today and you are rejoining *La Mouette* with him?"

"Yes," Marion said curtly. "Have you any objections ?"

Owen ignored the question.

"And the yacht then continues on her cruise," he went on. "How long will that take ?"

"Several weeks—I don't quite know," Marion shrugged.

"But long enough for it to mean that you will have to cancel your Belgian tour as well ?" Owen persisted.

"I've already done that," Marion announced sulkily.

"Rather prematurely perhaps," Owen suggested. "It might, I think, have been wiser to have delayed doing that until you had your throat examined again—"

"Why ?" Marion demanded. "I told you what Mr. Brecknock said—that I needed a rest and a holiday—"

"I'll tell you why, Marion. Because it doesn't do a singer any good to get a name for having throat trouble which requires such a long holiday to restore it," Owen explained. "No, let me finish. It may be callous, but quite frankly, the people who put engagements your way are hard-headed business folk. They build up a lot of expensive advance publicity for a well-known artist and they don't want that to go for nothing. Consequently, if you, or anyone else in your position, get the name for being unreliable, don't you see that they may become chary of engaging you in the future?"

"You're trying to frighten me," Marion declared angrily. "I don't know why, but—"

"I'll tell you why," Owen said quietly. "Because you don't appear to appreciate your own danger! There are always newcomers treading on the heels of the successful ones, you know. Yes, you *do* know that! You know how ruthlessly you had to fight to get to the top!"

"You do think I ought to have gone to Germany—and perhaps wrecked my voice permanently," Marion declared stormily. "And I don't think you believe Mr. Brecknock—"

"You're wrong on both scores," Owen said wearily. "But if you want to know exactly what I do think, it's this—I think, as I've already told you, that you should have had a second examination before backing out of the Belgian tour. As you didn't, you're giving the impression that you're determined to spin out your 'rest' just as long as it suits you to—in other words, until this cruise comes to an end—"

"You've no right to say that!" Marion protested indignantly. "You're jumping to conclusions—"

"Am I?" Owen asked deliberately. "I don't think so. You've been very indiscreet, you know, Marion!"

"Indiscreet? And what do you mean by that?"

"Le Marquand—you remember him? A very useful man! Well, le Marquand saw you in Nice on the evening of the day when we lunched on *La Mouette*. You were dining with Mr. Kelsall—"

371

"What if I was ?" Marion flashed at him. "What's indiscreet about that ?"

"According to le Marquand, you appeared to be the picture of health," Owen said tonelessly. "You were talking and laughing a great deal, and although you yourself were not smoking, the atmosphere was so smoky that he wondered it didn't make you cough—"

"And I suppose you two put your heads together and came to the conclusion that there was nothing wrong with me and never had been," Marion said furiously. "Well, you can think what you like ! I'm tired of being bullied and badgered by you or anybody else ! If I'd known what grinding hard work it meant, not only getting to the top but staying there, I'd never have let you push me into being a singer !"

Owen did not reply, and his silence stung Marion still further.

"I'm thinking of packing up my career," she declared recklessly.

"In favour of marriage ?" Owen suggested almost casually.

"Well—" Marion looked at him between half-closed lids. "Why not?"

Owen shrugged his shoulders.

"Why not, indeed ! Kelsall, I imagine ?"

"Perhaps." She laughed softly. "Or—someone else !"

"But I understood that you've never fancied any of the offers that have so far been made to you, and have turned them down," Owen said deliberately. "Is there someone I don't know about who has entered the lists?"

Her eyes fell. She knew what he was really saying— that he had not, and never had had, any intention of asking her to marry him. It was the most humiliating moment of her life. She hated him, she wanted to hurt him as he had hurt her—

But it couldn't be true. It couldn't ! Owen had never exactly made love to her, but all the same—

She put out her hand and laid it on his arm.

"Oh, Owen, what's happened to us?" she asked plaintively. "We used to be such good friends—"

"Did we?" Owen asked, taking no more notice of her hand than if it had not been there at all. "I think, perhaps, you and I have different ideas of friendship, Marion, just as I'm quite sure that we have different ideas as to the reason why two people should get married."

Marion snatched her hand away as if it had been scorched.

"Oh? And what are your ideas on that subject?" she asked ironically.

Owen hesitated momentarily.

"I would never dream of asking a girl to marry me unless I was deeply in love with her—and believed her to be the sort of girl who would not agree to marry me unless she felt the same way," he said quietly.

Marion laughed discordantly.

"Dear little Lucy, I suppose?" she suggested mockingly. "So sweet, so naïve, so innocent—what a fool you are, Owen!"

He stood up without replying, and Marion swung herself to her feet and faced him aggressively.

"Oh, you don't have to admit it, it stuck out a mile! And how she must have laughed up her sleeve at you! Did you know that she's already been engaged once—and that she was jilted on her wedding day?"

"Yes," Owen said quietly, "I knew that! I also know who the man was, if it interests you."

"But I bet there's one thing you don't know!" Marion triumphed crudely. "All that business about her going home because her father was ill—you believed it, didn't you? Well, I'll tell you what really happened! She's gone off with Dick Corbett—they left quite brazenly on the same plane—and I know that's true because Gwenda herself told me ! So now what about your precious, innocent Lucy ?"

• • •

Lucy had decided that in the meantime at least she would take temporary posts. For one thing it meant shorter hours and for another that she could, if necessary, terminate her appointment more easily or even take a week or so off between jobs. By and by she would have to get a permanent post, of course, one which, if possible, would mean a pension in the future, she decided wryly. Because now, of course, there would never be any question of her getting married.

She had thought the same thing, of course, when Dick had jilted her, but now she could look back on that young, inexperienced Lucy with amazement and the strange feeling that she had been a different girl altogether. How could she ever have believed that the tepid feeling she had felt for Dick had been true, lasting love ? But then she knew now what real, deep love meant. It was something that swept one off one's feet, that could not be killed by indifference or separation—or even the knowledge that the loved one was going to marry someone else.

At that point, Lucy tried hard to stop thinking. She thought Marion was very beautiful and that she had a lovely voice—but there was something about her that struck a false note. If Lucy was honest, she knew that she had not liked Marion from the first time they had met—and had liked her still less lately. She seemed to be so completely self-centred. And Owen was just the reverse. Well, people said that some of the happiest marriages were between opposites. Perhaps it would be so in this case—with all her heart, Lucy hoped so. Owen deserved happiness, seeing how he went out of his way to gain it for others. But she wished she knew for sure—

She never would, of course. She had cut herself off entirely from all of them. Mrs. Mayberry had acknowledged her letter briefly, though pleasantly. She had said that she quite understood how Lucy felt, and that she was not to worry about the money which had been advanced for her fare home, it was to be regarded as a gift. Apart from good wishes for Mr. Darvill's continued improvement, that was all. No reference to Owen, no suggestion that she should ever visit them as a guest by and by—which, of course, was just as well, since such an invitation would have been a temptation, though one which would have had to be withstood.

Since her return, Lucy had received another communication—a postcard, this time, from Dick. It was very brief:

"It worked ! Thanks. D.C."

She was glad about that. She had no feeling, one way or the other, for Dick now, but at least she wished him well. There was no reason why she should do anything else.

And now she had got to set to work to make still another new life for herself. It wasn't going to be easy, and this time there would be no one to help her as Owen had helped her before. She had got to stand on her own feet and learn to make something out of nothing. And what was more, she must all the time seem cheerful and content, quite a lot for her parents' sake, but also because it was the only way in which she could be sure of not being questioned. What had happened was locked away in her own heart and there it had got to stay.

There was, however, one thing about which she could be genuinely cheerful. Mr. Darvill was making excellent progress. There was even talk of him coming home in the not very distant future. In preparation for this, Lucy set to work on his beloved garden. It had been sadly neglected lately, and it meant hard work to get it back to its usual trim condition, but Lucy welcomed that. On top of a tiring day in a stuffy London office it sent her to bed so exhausted that it was easier to sleep than she had thought would be possible. And sleep meant that one did not think—though one dreamed, of course.

Dreamed of a little blue lake hidden in the mountains, of a companion who understood so well that sometimes beauty could be so overwhelming that no words could describe it—dreamed, and woke to the emptiness of reality. Despite her mother's good cooking, Lucy had no appetite these days, though, fortunately, one could put that down to the heat—

The weather broke, and Lucy, compelled to stay indoors, became restless—so restless that her mother wondered if it had been a good thing for the child to have had that taste of the luxury that money brings or whether there was something else—

It was getting on for a fortnight now since Lucy had returned home. She had completed her first week's work and the weekend loomed ahead, empty and purposeless. She helped her mother with household tasks on Saturday morning and then announced that, despite the rain, she would take Collie for a walk.

"Oh, darling, but it's pouring," Mrs. Darvill protested. "You'll get soaked! Wait for a bit, it may clear up."

"Oh, all right," Lucy said listlessly. "Can I do anything for you?"

"No, dear, but you can do something for yourself," Mrs. Darvill said briskly. "Your hair—it looks quite awful! Can't you do something about it?"

So Lucy washed her hair, dried it and combed it into its usual easy natural swirls. Then, because most of her make-up had been washed off, she tidied up her face and went downstairs.

She was half way down when the doorbell rang.

"Answer it, darling, will you?" Mrs. Darvill called from the kitchen. "I'm all over flour—I expect it's the joint."

But when Lucy opened the door it wasn't the butcher or any other tradesman who stood there.

It was Owen.

CHAPTER XII

LUCY stood very still. Wide-eyed, she stared at Owen in sheer consternation. Why had he come ? And why, since he was here, didn't he say something instead of gazing at her as if—as if—

His lips parted and Lucy held her breath.

"It's raining, Lucy. Aren't you going to ask me in ?"

Speechlessly, she turned and led the way to the sitting room. Behind her she heard a slight rustling sound as Owen took off his light raincoat and hung it up. Then they were alone in the sitting room—and the door was shut firmly behind them.

Owen stood in front of her, but he made no attempt to touch her.

"Do you know why I've come ?" he asked quietly.

"Oh, to ask how Father is, I suppose," Lucy said breathlessly. "How very kind of you ! He's improving steadily—"

"I'm delighted to hear it," Owen announced. "But it's not on your father's account that I'm here," he paused and then went on deliberately. "I came—because I want your help and advice."

"Mine ?" Lucy laughed nervously. "I don't understand !"

"Do you remember, right at the beginning of our acquaintance, you asked me if I had ever been really up against it ? And I admitted that I hadn't—but that sooner or later I would meet my Waterloo ?"

"Yes." Lucy flushed. "I was very rude, I'm afraid."

"You certainly were," Owen agreed fervently. "Well, I've come to tell you that it's happened ! I'm at my wits' end to know what to do—will you try to help me ?"

"If—if I can," Lucy said uncertainly. "After all that you've done to help me, it's the least—"

"Never mind that," Owen said curtly. "But if you'll

listen to what may seem a very dull little story—"

"Yes, of course. Wouldn't you like to sit down—?" Lucy suggested.

"No, thanks, I'd rather prowl, if you don't mind." He dug his hands deep into his jacket pockets and strode restlessly over to the window. "There was a man," he began after a moment's silence, "who met a girl. He admired her from the word 'go'—and very soon he realized that he was deeply in love with her. But there was a reason, which seemed very good to him, why he did not tell her so."

"Yes," Lucy said faintly. Marion—and her career. Owen had felt that it would be selfish to rob her of her triumph so soon—

"So he waited. To be quite honest, there was a certain amount of antagonism between them to begin with—but that went, and they became quite good friends. He even dared to think that, perhaps, she was beginning to care for him. Rather a nerve, wasn't it?"

"Perhaps—perhaps she wanted to encourage him a little," Lucy suggested. But how strange! Marion had spoken of them being deeply in love—as if they had confessed as much to one another!

"He was only too glad to persuade himself that was so," Owen admitted. "But then something went wrong. The girl seemed to drift away from him—"

Mr. Kelsall, of course, Lucy thought indignantly. How could Marion possibly have encouraged him to such a degree that Owen believed he had lost her?

"And suddenly it dawned on him that people—or perhaps one person, was making mischief between him and this girl," Owen went on, suddenly turning and striding back to face Lucy. "What ought he to do about that, Lucy?"

"What—sort of mischief?" Lucy asked uncertainly.

"Oh, that he was paying attention to another girl," Owen explained. "It was all nonsense, of course, but not an easy thing to prove—"

"She should have believed him—without proof," Lucy said hotly. "If he told her that he loved her, and that there wasn't and never had been anyone else—" She stopped short, biting her lip.

"So he felt," Owen agreed. "Particularly as this very clever person had told him a story—a beastly story, which he did not for a moment believe—that the girl he loved had run off with a married man. A man, actually, with whom she had once been in love—whom she had been on the point of marrying," he finished deliberately.

Lucy's heart turned over. He couldn't have said that! He simply couldn't mean—the familiar room swam dizzily about her.

Owen gathered her hands in his and held them close against his heart.

"Listen to me now, Lucy, for I give you my word that I'm telling you the truth ! Marion persuaded you that I was in love with her, didn't she ?"

Unable to speak, Lucy nodded.

"It was not and never has been true," Owen said steadily. "Any more than the story she told me about you running off with Dick Corbett was true. I know that—because I know you! Can you say the same about me?"

"Oh!" Lucy breathed tremulously. "Yes—if you say it's true!"

"It is true," Owen said, his lips against hers, his arms holding her close.

Lucy was lost—drowned—in a sea of happiness. This was bliss such as she had never known before. Owen loved her—it was the fulfilment of her dreams— and it was blessed reality as well. She surrendered to the passion of his kisses, responding to them with all her heart.

Then, suddenly, she drew back.

"Owen, you've got to know—I did travel back to England with Dick—" she said anxiously. "But, truth and honour, it was by chance, not design "

"I knew that, my sweet, even before Kelsall told me that you had talked to the young man like a Dutch uncle—or rather, a Dutch aunt—for his own good, as a result of which he has now got his nose to the grindstone, to the great satisfaction of his father-in-law ! Just what made you go out of your way to try to help Corbett, Lucy ?"

"Oh—" Lucy frowned. "I don't know really. I just felt I had to. That it would be a load off my mind if I did."

"That suggested you felt you owed him something," Owen suggested curiously.

"I think I did," Lucy admitted.

"But, my darling girl," Owen protested, "that's nonsense !"

"Not really," Lucy insisted earnestly. "You see, there was a time when I blamed him for what had happened —I almost hated him. And then I realised that actually he and I had done exactly the same thing."

"Indeed ?" Owen raised his dark brows. "How do you make that out ?"

"Why, don't you see, if—if I had really loved him I would have kept on loving him, no matter what he had done. One does, if it's the real thing."

"So—" Owen prompted, his arms tightening round her again.

"So—I knew that I had never been really in love with him. If I had, I simply couldn't have—fallen in love with someone else. So I can hardly blame him for changing his mind when I've done exactly the same thing, can I ?" Lucy finished triumphantly.

"No, my adorable sweet, I don't suppose you can—being you," Owen agreed, worship in his eyes. "I'm afraid I don't feel quite so benevolently disposed towards Marion, though."

"Oh—" Lucy said doubtfully. "Well, that is rather different—I mean, if she meant to—to do harm—"

"She meant to do that, all right," Owen said grimly. "But, like a fool, I didn't realise it until almost too late—"

"But it doesn't matter now, does it?" Lucy asked anxiously. "It hasn't made any difference, in the end, has it?"

"No," Owen admitted. "All the same, I hope I never see her again."

"But aren't you almost bound to? I mean, your work and hers—you can hardly avoid seeing her."

"Marion has decided to give up her career," Owen said indifferently. "She's going to marry Kelsall."

"But—" Lucy gasped.

"I know. There are a whole lot of 'buts' about it—to you and me. But not apparently to them. Let's leave it at that, shall we?"

Lucy nodded. She was more than willing to leave Marion in the past—and even more thankful that Owen would be able to.

"Yes," she agreed. "There are lots of nicer things to talk about than that."

"For instance?" he asked, running his finger along the soft line of her chin.

"Us," Lucy suggested. "For instance, when did you know you'd fallen in love with me?"

He smiled down into her upturned face. If his precious little Lucy could ask that question so confidently, then all was well. She believed in him, and she was no longer afraid of him.

"I had a shrewd suspicion very early on," he confessed. "When I realised, looking at that photograph, that it should have given me considerable pleasure to bash that young man's face in for having hurt you!"

"Oh!" Lucy looked astonished. "As soon as that! But

when did you know for sure?"

Owen laughed softly.

"Inquisitive!" he chided lovingly. "When you sang *Annie Laurie!* Remember? The last two lines? *'And for bonnie Annie Laurie, I'd lay me doon and dee!'* Then. Because I knew that there was nothing I wouldn't do for you—" He caught her close, and the moments passed.

"But why didn't you tell me?" Lucy said reproachfully at last.

"Because I was afraid of its being too soon," Owen explained. "We'd started off so badly. I not only had to wait until you could forgive me for that, little love, but I had to stand back and leave you to discover for yourself that not all men are false and fickle—though I did warn you that you must not lose faith in your own judgment or be afraid that no one could prove to be trustworthy."

"So you did," Lucy marvelled. "But it never occurred to me that you could be referring to yourself, because I knew, even at the beginning, that you could be trusted. Besides, it would have seemed too wonderful—"

"Would it?" Owen buried his face in her soft hair, lest she should be frightened by the depths of feeling her words had aroused in him. "And when did you discover that, sweetheart?"

"Coming back from the pool, that last day, when I stumbled!" How extraordinary it was that she could speak of that to him so confidently. "I think, in a way, I had known before, but then I knew for sure!"

"And I so nearly told you then!" Owen regretted. "And for that matter, on the Grande Corniche—the day you saw Corbett in Nice. What a lot of time I've wasted! And that reminds me. I'd have come to see you before, darling, but Aunt Louise has been desperately ill. So bad, in fact, that for a few days we were afraid—"

"Oh, Owen!" Anxiety swept all the happiness from her sensitive face. "But now? Is she better?"

"Pulling round nicely," Owen assured her. "In fact, she was well enough to tell me that if I could give you my love, I could give you hers as well! And Uncle Stanley sent much the same message—in the same circumstances."

"The darlings!" Lucy said affectionately. "They've both been so sweet to me!"

"And small wonder," Owen told her ardently, and took some time to explain why.

When, at last, a rosy, happy Lucy broke from his arms to say that they really must go and explain to her mother who he was, Owen laughed.

"Oh, she knew I was coming," he announced. "I telephoned to her last night asking her to do her best to see that you were in when I got here— and not to tell you I was coming in case you ran away again!"

Lucy bubbled with sudden laughter.

"She did more than that! She made me wash my hair so that I didn't look too much of a scarecrow when you arrived!"

"And that reminds me," Owen began promptly. "Your hair—"

But Lucy kept him at arms' length.

"Not any more—not yet!" she begged, but Owen, charmed by the last two words, took no notice, and in the haven of his arms Lucy found the courage to ask, softly:

"Do you remember asking me once what my world was?"

"I remember. And you were not at all sure."

"I am now," she whispered shyly. "It's *your* world, Owen. For always, whatever or wherever that world may be—"

"It was a considerable time before, at last, they went in search of Mrs. Darvill.

CHERISH THIS WAYWARD HEART

Cherish This Wayward Heart

All her life Judith had tried to make up for not being the son her father had wanted. She was determined to be as good as any man.

Now, with her father's death, Windygates Farm was hers. And right from the start she deeply resented the new estate manager, Charles Saxilby.

But, in the ensuing battle of wills between them, Charles taught Judith to be a woman!

CHAPTER ONE

CHARLES came quietly downstairs, fully expecting that his early breakfast would be a lonely one, but there were already two people at the table.

"Mary!" He dropped his hand lightly on his sister-in-law's shoulder as he passed to his own place. "You shouldn't have worried—but I admit I'm glad you have!"

"Couldn't let you go off as if we were glad to see the back of you," his half-brother Roger said gruffly from the other side of the table.

Charles's glance towards him was full of affection—and a certain amount of wonder, too. After all, it was amazing that, in these days when everybody seemed to be doing their best to loosen family ties, they, in spite of the twenty years' difference in their ages and the comparative slightness of the blood-tie, had always enjoyed each other's company so much. Mostly their mother's doing, of course. One had always known that there was room in her heart for both of them. And Mary was pretty wonderful, too. One of those rare women who could love her husband with all her heart and yet not resent his having a man friend. She'd been a good friend to him, too.

A silence fell on the three of them, as it will when one of such a tightly knit little group is going away. And nobody seemed to have the ability to break it. Until, when some of the marmalade that Charles had spread on his toast slid stickily over his fingers, he said "Confound it!" in a perfectly normal way and the tension eased.

"How long do you reckon you'll take?" Roger asked, handing up his cup for a refill of coffee.

"Oh—five, five and a half hours," Charles replied. "I want to get to Wyford about lunch-time. I don't relish an interview on an empty stomach—besides, people don't welcome an extra mouth to feed if it can be avoided these days."

Roger got up and limped to the table. His limp was always more pronounced when he was worried, Mary thought anxiously. And he was worried about Charles and this venture. In a minute he would say so—and it wasn't any good. Charles had made his mind up.

"I wish you weren't going," Roger said abruptly, just as she had known he would.

Charles unfolded his long legs from beneath the table and joined his brother at the window. For a moment they stood side by side gazing out at the sunny Sussex acres that Charles loved no less because they were Roger's and not his own. He knew every inch of them, had taken all the heavy end of the farming ever since Roger's war injury had made it impossible for him to do as much as he would have liked. Now—he was leaving it all.

"Old man, honestly, it's the right thing! No, listen! I've been thinking about it for a long time—ever since young Jerry started his last year at the Agricultural College. No, before that. We've both known this was a temporary arrangement. It was all right when Jerry was too much of a kid to take on the job, but now it's his—and I'm not going to have him feel bad because he's turning me out or resentful because he can't!"

"I'll give him something to think about if he tries that on!" Roger growled, but from his tone Charles knew that he was at least half convinced. He laughed.

"There's another side to it! I'm only rule-of-thumb trained—Jerry will be all scientific. I don't want my horrible ignorance exposed!"

"If he knows half what you do—" Roger began, and laughed. "I suppose you're right," he admitted. "And there is nothing like pitchforking a young man into his responsibilities! It's difficult to take a real interest when your hand is held in every emergency."

"Exactly!" Charles could not entirely suppress the relief in his tone, and Mary looked at him sharply. An idea that had occurred to her more than once became established as a certainty, and a little later, when they had seen the last of Charles as he and his car vanished down the drive, she tucked her arm through her husband's and said, thoughtfully:

"You know, Roger, while it's true enough that Jerry is one of the reasons why Charles is going after this job, I don't think it's the only one!"

"Oh?" Roger looked at her questioningly. He had a profound respect for Mary's intelligence and frankly admitted that she could get to the bottom of people better than he could. "Well, what else can it be?"

Mary hesitated for a moment.

"Charles is going on for thirty," she said slowly. "It's time he had his own place, his own interests——"

"You mean—you think he's looking for a wife?" Roger said in amazement. "But there are plenty of charming girls round about here! Why couldn't he have chosen one of those?"

"Because—perhaps I'm wrong, but I think Charles is the questing, adventurous type," Mary explained. "And, in any case, I don't suppose he has consciously decided that it is about time he got married. Just— what is unfamiliar has suddenly seemed attractive."

Roger considered this for a moment. Certainly it had not occurred to him before, but . . .

"You may be right," he agreed, and then, anxiously: "I hope to goodness he chooses a suitable girl!"

Mary smiled. Charles, she felt very sure, would choose exactly as he thought fit. And they would have to make the best of it.

But, as Charles drew near to Wyford, there was nothing farther from his thoughts than romance. The day that had started so promisingly in Sussex had gradually deteriorated, and now was grey and wet. None the less, he had made pretty good time. He had come by minor roads to Reading, from there through to Gloucester, and now he proposed taking minor roads again. But this part of the west country was comparatively strange to him, and he realised that if he took the wrong turning he could easily find himself miles out of his way.

At the next signpost he brought the car to a halt and got out. He grimaced a little as he caught the full impact of the chill, misty rain that had prevented him from reading the sign from the shelter of the car, and wondered if he was being a fool. He pulled the collar of his burberry closer round his throat and peered up at the signpost. Yes, he was all right. His sense of direction had held good.

He went slowly back to the car, but he did not drive on immediately. Suddenly, in spite of the weather, he was not anxious to get to the end of his journey. What had seemed like high adventure when he had started that morning now held no appeal whatsoever. For two pins he would have turned the car's head round and beat a retreat.

But no sooner had the thought taken actual shape than it was rejected. The strong, square jaw jutted forward aggressively, the fair brows were knit in a scowl. Whatever might lie ahead, he was hanged if he was going to give anyone the opportunity of saying that he couldn't take it!

He let in the clutch, put his foot down on the accelerator and, in spite of the winding road, made the best time that he had achieved all day for the rest of the trip.

In little over half an hour he was crossing the bridge, turning past the unexpectedly reddish cathedral into the town centre. And then he realised, for the first time, that he had, of all days, chosen market day.

He frowned. That might be a bit inconvenient. It meant that both car parks and and hotels would be full; on the other hand, of course, meals would be served far later than on ordinary days. He had already decided to go to an hotel in Marsh Street, since his way to Windygates lay in that direction, and, taking his turn to pass the policeman on his neat little round platform, he made his way down the narrow street. It was a slow business. Farm carts, cars of all ages and sizes, pedestrians, a puzzled, frightened calf that had contrived to escape, all blocked his way and made it difficult to turn in under the hotel archway. And when he did, it was none too easy to find parking space.

When, at last, he made enquiries about a meal, he found that his guess had been correct. The restaurant was packed. Would be, so he was assured, for the next half hour. But if he could wait . . .

Charles decided that he could and would. In the meantime he could use up the time comfortably and profitably in the bar. Nothing like a bar on market day for getting a good cross-section of the community.

The place was crowded and it took him some time to get his drink and even longer to find a quiet spot where he could observe without being too noticeable.

None the less, as he slipped into a corner, he noticed that conversation momentarily halted and, outsider though it made him feel, he had lived far too long himself in a county where a stranger is still regarded as a foreigner not to appreciate that here, in this border town, there was to this day that inherent fear of invasion that one also found in Sussex—although perhaps with less cause here.

Then they appeared to forget all about him and the talk began again. It was mainly about farming matters and of to-day's market in particular, although the few women there, he could hear, were discussing people rather than affairs. He grinned faintly. So long as there were market days, there would be gossip!

The women, he noticed, kept mainly to themselves, leaving their men to their own affairs. It was rather a pleasant picture. There was the hum of good-natured talk, an occasional laugh or so.

Then he realised that, not an arm's length from him, voices were being raised. Fairly good-temperedly as yet, but— He studied the group more closely. Four or five men and a much younger lad with dark, close-cropped hair. Like the rest of the group, he was wearing breeches and a tweed jacket, yet without knowing just why, Charles realised that there was a difference in class. And then—the lad spoke. And Charles started involuntarily. It was not a boy at all, it was a girl! And she was very angry. Moreover, her anger was amusing the men and that was making her still angrier.

"But of course I am right!" The high, arrogant young voice admitted no possibility of error. "Champion Garwin Master was the one that had to be shot! And

393

Champion Garwin Major was the bull that Sir Garwin sold to Mr. Preece! It's absurd——"

"No, Miss Judith, you've got it wrong!" If the girl was confident of being in the right, so equally was this big, black-browed man. There was obstinacy in every line of his face and grim determination in his voice. Charles felt a certain sympathy for him. Just who this girl was and how she came to be so knowledgeable he had no idea, but he was firmly of the opinion that she wanted a good spanking. She was deliberately presuming on the fact that few men will flatly contradict a woman in public, least of all when their relative social spheres were so clearly defined as now. The man was obviously a farmer who would be the last to claim, or wish to claim, gentility. The girl—for the first time Charles took a good look at her.

Small and slim and very dark. That was his first impression. His second—was of elegant, tapering hands, of the perfect carriage of the young body and the arrogant tilt of the beautifully poised head. The arrogance was all to the fore now. The dark eyes flashed, the proud nostrils flared.

Some warning bell rang in Charles's brain and an instinct even stronger than his sympathy for his own sex warned him that the girl was on the point of making a fool of herself—and that afterwards she would hate herself for having done it. He had got to do something.

"I think I can settle the discussion for you," he said pleasantly.

They turned at the sound of the alien voice, regarding him not so much suspiciously as impartially. Giving him a chance to say what he had to say before judging him. They waited in silence.

"I've worked for Sir Roger Garwin for some years," he explained. "And, actually, it was I who had to shoot—Major. It was Master that we—that Sir Roger sold."

For a moment the silence remained unbroken. Charles saw the flash of satisfaction in the big farmer's eyes, the covert grins of the other men. At the girl he was careful not to look.

"Thank you, sir," the farmer said civilly enough, and, with a nod, Charles passed on his way, wondering whether, after all, it would have been better if he had not spoken. He was not left long in doubt. As he made his way to the door he found his way barred by a furious girl who was beside herself with rage.

"I don't know," she said in a clear, contemptuous voice, "what is considered good manners in the place you come from, but here, we don't like strangers who push their way into other people's conversations unasked—particularly when they try to make bad blood between us!"

Charles regarded her dispassionately. She *did* need a spanking! And if one was going to talk about manners. . . .

"Listen, my child!" She had spoken with the deliberate intention of allowing other people to hear what she was saying. He spoke so quietly she herself only just heard. "Before you get into an argument, I advise you to make sure of your facts. Better still, since you can't keep your temper, don't argue in public at all!"

He saw the sudden puzzled look in her eyes, the slight drop of her jaw, but he had no desire to prolong the conversation and so, stepping to one side, he walked round her obstructive figure and went to see about his lunch.

After the meal was over he went straight out to the yard to get his car. Whether the girl had gone or not, at least he did not encounter her, for which he was thankful. But somewhat to his annoyance he found that he could not forget that striking young face. And even more irritating was the fact that he was blaming himself for having mishandled the situation. And yet— he had felt compelled to intervene. As if he were responsible for the girl.

He moved his shoulders irritably. Absurd! A lovely child, no doubt, but one who had never been taught either to control her temper or to appreciate the fact that there were certain basic privileges of either sex which could not be disregarded with impunity. He had seen the glances of the other women in the direction of that slim figure. They had resented her claim to equality with their men while they, however willingly, had been outside the group.

Yes, that was it. She wanted to be equal to the men—but she wanted to retain the privileges of a woman as well. He wondered how it came about that there was no older, wiser person to keep her in check. A ticklish job for someone—but not for him, thank heaven!

Before he drove out of the yard he took a letter from his pocket. It was typed, except for the signature, "H. Ravensdale," and it contained a neat pen-and-ink sketch of his route once he left the town. It was, in fact, evidence that H. Ravensdale had both an orderly mind and the ability to recognise other people's needs, two attributes which made considerable appeal to Charles.

Without difficulty he found his way to Windygates. A bigger house than he had visualised. Pinkish, as the cathedral had been, but he liked the stone better in this domestic setting. Creepers broke the austerity of its line, and the fluttering curtains at the mullioned windows had a homelike appearance.

Rather to his relief the weather had cleared now, and as he went through the gates the sun came out.

"A good omen!" he thought, and grinned at himself. He, of all men, was not superstitious, and yet he knew that his spirits rose at the sight of those rather watery beams of light.

He was evidently expected about now, for a trim, middle-aged woman, obviously on the watch for him, stopped weeding a garden bed and stood erect at the sound of the car. Charles jumped out of the car and walked towards her. Quick to make up his mind, he took an instant liking to her. Though her hair was grey, her face was fresh and unlined and her frank smile was very attractive as she took off her gardening glove and held out her hand.

"Mr. Saxilby?" she said pleasantly, and Charles was delighted to discover that her voice was as charming as her face. "I am Miss Ravensdale, with whom you have been in correspondence."

"*Miss* Ravensdale?" he repeated, making no attempt to hide his surprise. "But I was under the impression——"

"That I was a man?" she said quickly. "Oh, dear, I suppose that is because of my signature! Most women sign with their Christian names in full, don't they? But I happen to detest mine—it is Harriet—and so I always use the initial. I am so sorry!"

"Not at all," he answered mechanically. It was a good enough reason—so far as it went. But several letters had passed between them and she had made no attempt to correct his misapprehension. He looked at her with greater intensity and recognised, from the faint flush that stained her cheeks, that his guess was right. She had wanted him to think that she was a man. Possibly she realised that few men like business dealings with a woman.

For a moment their eyes met, and if he wanted confirmation, here he had it, for hers were the first to drop, and she said, hurriedly:

"Please come this way. I usually indulge myself with a cup of tea about this time, and I shall be delighted if you will join me."

He bowed slightly and followed her into the house. Without appearing to look about him, he nevertheless contrived to gain a pretty comprehensive impression of the place.

It was, he decided, essentially a home rather than a show place. The furniture was good, although it was quite evidently there for use rather than because it was old and valuable. The carpets were far from new, but age had mellowed rather than worn them. There were vases of flowers well arranged here and there, plenty of cushions, sizeable ashtrays that even the most casual hand could hardly miss. Charles liked it. The sort of home a man would think of when he was away from it and come back to relax in.

Miss Ravensdale led the way to a small room which caught the afternoon sunshine.

"Do sit down." She indicated a solid-looking arm-chair as she walked over to the mantelpiece and gave a quick, competent pull to the old-fashioned bell-pull. Charles, with more eye to detail than is perhaps usual in his sex, noted that, despite its quaintness of style, the pull itself was actually quite new. The colours of the embroidery were fresh and bright.

Until the pink-cheeked, dark-haired maid had brought in the tea, Miss Ravensdale kept the conversation competently to trivial topics, but Charles was keenly aware that for all her ease of manner, he was none the less under close observation.

"Sugar and milk?" she enquired, arching her well-drawn brows in a query.

"Please. One lump." Charles, for all her quizzing, felt completely at his ease. His first reaction, admittedly, had been one of regret and even resentment that he had not a man with whom to deal. Now he was no longer concerned over the fact, although he was still curious. After all, she *had* let him go on thinking that she was a man. It suggested to him that she was terribly anxious, for all her poise, to get him here.

"Now, Mr. Saxilby," she said briskly as she handed him his cup. "I think we have discussed matters fairly thoroughly in our letters. You know that we go in for mixed farming here. I have told you our acreage and the way in which it is divided between our various interests. You, on the other hand, have given me a complete account of your experience. It seems to me to be sufficient for you to take charge here."

She was becoming increasingly nervous! He could sense the tension in the air and became instantly the more cautious, more deliberate.

"Yes, I think it is," he agreed. "But, of course, I should like to see over the farm——"

"Yes, of course——" she agreed hurriedly.

"And also, I should like to work with your present manager for at least a month before taking over." Not unreasonable, that, surely. And yet the moment the words were out of his mouth he saw the nervous twitch of a muscle at the corner of her mouth. She set her cup and saucer down with a little jarring crash.

"That," she said with evident reluctance, "would be difficult to arrange——"

"Why?" he asked bluntly. "Have you had to sack him?"

"No——" Ever since this conversation had begun, Harriet Ravensdale knew that she had deliberately avoided looking at this astute man with his keen eyes and strong face. Now she drew a deep breath and faced him squarely. "Mr. Saxilby, I think I had better be frank with you. I find myself in an extremely difficult situation—and the difficulties are of such a personal, family nature . . ."

She paused, and Charles waited in silence. Evidently she had taken to him as he had to her, but none the less, she was finding it difficult to take him into her confidence. Not a woman who would ever wear her heart on her sleeve, he thought with approval.

Suddenly she began to speak.

"Until four months ago, Windygates belonged to my brother. Then, very unexpectedly, he died. He left everything he had to his daughter, Judith, and, until she is of age, I am her guardian and trustee. My brother ran the farm himself, with Judith's help. Now, she is running it herself and—it won't do, Mr. Saxilby. It won't do! I am determined to put a stop to it."

She got up hurriedly and stood staring down at the gently smouldering log fire, her back to Charles. It was obvious that she was very much troubled, and Charles, who had come here simply to see about a job, found himself taking command.

"I think, Miss Ravensdale," he said quietly, "that you had better tell me all about it—right from the beginning."

And, as if that was all that Harriet Ravensdale had been waiting for, she began to speak hurriedly, yet as if she knew exactly what she had to say.

"It was not until four or five years after they were married that my brother and his wife knew they were going to have a child. Elaine was glad, but mainly,

I think, because she knew how delighted Mark would be. And he was. He kept on talking about 'my son' and planning what he would do, years ahead, for the boy. He was so certain—and then Judith was born. He simply couldn't believe it. And then, when he knew that there could never be any more children! . . . When Judith was two, Elaine died. I don't think she wanted to live. You see, she adored Mark and she knew that he blamed her. And yet, in his way, he must have loved her, for he never married again. I—came back here and ran the house for him. And Judith grew up. That was where the trouble began. She had all her mother's adoration for her father and she knew that he had wanted a boy—he made no attempt to hide it from her. And she, poor child, did her best to be the son he had so wanted. At first it made him laugh. She did not take naturally to riding, for instance. She would fall off time and time again and scramble up again despite her bruises, while her father taunted her that a boy wouldn't have made such a mess of it!"

"Poor child!" Charles said softly, and Miss Ravensdale shot a grateful glance at him.

"And, after a time, he began to take a queer sort of pride in her. 'That child simply doesn't know when she is beaten' he used to say, and he'd set her harder and harder things to do. And Judith obeyed him blindly, regardless of risk or pain — it frightened me less because of any physical danger than because of the mental effect it was having on her. Her father was bringing her up as a boy, and nothing that I or any of his old friends said made any difference. She had absolutely no use for what are usually regarded as women's interests—or for women, for that matter. She is reasonably fond of me—but none the less she treats me with a sort of good-natured contempt. I suppose she has been happy enough, but while she has every intention of carrying on the management of the farm just as she did when her father was alive—and she is quite competent to—other people are beginning to take a different view of it."

"Other farmers—and their wives?" Charles suggested

softly. "And the men who have to take orders from her?"

Miss Ravensdale shot a questioning look at him.

"Yes," she said slowly. "That is it. It was one thing for her to mix with other farmers and go to stock sales when everybody knew that her father stood behind her, but now—they resent it. And Judith's is a contradictory sort of arrogance. It makes her despise her own sex—and yet she feels superior to any man she has met—yet."

There was a silence which Charles made no attempt to break.

"Now, you see," Miss Ravensdale went on at length, "why, if you come here, you can not only expect no co-operation but, on the contrary, definite opposition. And yet I am determined that, in the six months before Judith will be her own mistress, I will do my best to undo the wrong my brother has done her!"

"Mend in six months the damage of years?" Charles said softly. "I think you are taking on an impossible task, Miss Ravensdale."

Her hands—hands that were strangely familiar in their elegance—moved in a gesture of despair.

"I know," she admitted. "And yet, what can I do? Leave things as they are? Do you think that would be right?"

"No, it would be very wrong. Yet you can do little without your niece's agreement, Miss Ravensdale."

"She has agreed," she replied surprisingly. "In principle, that is. I pointed out to her that it was impossible for one person to do the work of two and that the farm must suffer in consequence. That is an argument that she cannot ignore. So, as I said, she agreed in principle. But she has done absolutely nothing to find anyone suitable. Consequently—I have. And I am convinced that when she is faced with a *fait accompli* she will keep her promise. That is one of her traditions."

"Yes, I think you are right," Charles agreed. "But—I am not the man!"

"But why—why?" Miss Ravensdale beat her hands gently together. "I admit that Judith said a man good

401

enough to trust would be farming on his own account and that she would have no one less than the best. But that does not apply to you! The reason why you are not farming your own land is easily explained—first the war and then your brother's need of you! There is nothing to which she can take exception!"

"None the less, I am not the right man," Charles insisted. "You see, Miss Ravensdale, your niece and I have already met!"

"What!"

"Yes," he nodded. "In Wyford, an hour or so ago. It must have been her. I heard her addressed as Miss Judith. A slim girl with short dark hair and very lovely hands—like your own, Miss Ravensdale!"

She nodded dumbly and he went on:

"Yes, I realised it must be, as you were speaking! Believe me, your niece would never agree that I was a suitable choice! You see—our brief encounter was—stormy, to say the least of it."

"Tell me," Miss Ravensdale asked.

As briefly as possible Charles explained just what had happened, keeping strictly to facts and making no attempt to explain why he had intervened. When he had done, his hostess nodded.

"You could not have told me anything which would so confirm my own opinion!" she said sadly. "Don't you understand, Mr. Saxilby, that in those few minutes you saw all that I have been seeing for months! It must be stopped!"

"But not by me," he insisted. He saw the disappointment in Harriet Ravensdale's face with very real regret, but he knew he must be firm. The situation would be hopeless from the very first.

"I suppose you are right," she admitted sadly. "And yet—I cannot help feeling that you are the right man, you know! It is a situation requiring both understanding and patience. And I think you are capable of being both kind—and strong."

"Soft-hearted and pig-headed, according to my sister-in-law," he said cheerfully, determined to get the conversation on to a more ordinary basis. "But—

402

no, Miss Ravensdale! I'm sorry, believe me, but that is the right answer, I am sure!"

"Certainly pig-headed!" she said with a flash of humour. "Very well, we will not discuss it any more! But do, at least, pay homage to our cook! These cakes are very good; we have our own butter and eggs, of course, which is just as well, for cook would probably leave us if she could not express her art adequately!"

He accepted the cake, admiring her ability to ease what had threatened to become an embarrassing situation and, in his turn, introduced another topic that would help to turn this into purely a pleasant social interlude.

"Furniture?" she glanced round the room with evident love. "Yes, we have some very good stuff here and, of course, it is the better for being used! There is nothing like regular elbow grease, you know! The only drawback is, of course, that there is never any need to buy anything new, and most women have an itch to do that, from time to time!"

"However, things need replacing," he remarked, indicating the embroidered bell-pull. "That is your work?"

"Yes, my work," she agreed. "But even that is a copy of the one before—and the one before that!" she sighed. "Please do not imagine I do not love all these things, but home-making is an ingrained instinct in a woman, and it cannot be denied with impunity."

"I suppose not," he agreed; then, realising that they were perilously near to getting back to their earlier conversation: "That is a Gainsborough, isn't it?" he asked, pointing to the one picture that hung in the room.

"Yes, rather a good one, so I am told," she admitted. "But it is not a family portrait. Actually, no one knows who it is—but it has always been there, so it always will be, I expect! Are you interested in paintings?"

"Yes, I suppose I am," Charles agreed. "Although I don't know much about them, I'm afraid."

"Perhaps you would like to see our collection?" she

suggested. "It is not very big, but there are several good ones."

She led the way so determinedly out of the room that he could not help but follow. Across the wide hall, up three shallow stairs.

"This is the big drawing-room," she told him. "It is rarely used now—entertaining is out of fashion these days! Wait, I will draw the curtains!"

It was a handsome, well-proportioned room, although perhaps rather too formal for homeliness. None the less, it was a good setting for the ten or so portraits that hung on the walls. Charles listened with perfectly genuine interest while his hostess told him all she knew about them.

"Here are my brother and his wife," she said at last. "Judith's parents."

He looked at the double portrait with a more personal interest than the others, however good, had been able to arouse in him.

"It was done shortly after they were married," Miss Ravensdale said softly. "They were very happy then."

A fragile wisp of a woman, a sturdy, virile man—inevitable choice, almost inevitable disaster. The attributes that made the appeal would, in time, be the very ones which grated beyond endurance. A tragedy that might have been averted if there had been a son.

"I do not think Judith will ever have the patience to give sittings," he heard Miss Ravensdale say regretfully. "This is the nearest that we have to a proper portrait of her!"

Charles took the framed photograph from her. It was obviously an enlargement of a snapshot, but it was very good. Judith, dressed just as he had seen her a short time ago, was on horseback. One hand lay on the horse's neck as if she were quieting him, yet the action was obviously mechanical, for her head was turned so that she faced the camera. And yet one felt that she must have been unaware that she was being snapped, for her eyes did not look out of the photograph. Instead, they seemed to be fixed on the distant horizon, far beyond any other human being.

Harriet Ravensdale held her breath. What would he see in it? The challenge of the arrogant head, the gentleness of the caressing hand or—something that, as far as she knew, no one but she had ever seen there, the wistful, questing look?

Charles did not speak. The only sound in the room was the soft ticking of the Louis XV clock on the mantelpiece.

Suddenly, without turning, Charles spoke.

"Miss Ravensdale, if you will allow me to, I am going to usurp a privilege that is usually supposed to be a woman's! I should like to change my mind about this job!"

CHAPTER TWO

HARRIET RAVENSDALE drew a deep, sighing breath.

"I am glad to hear you say that, Mr. Saxilby," she said quietly. "When—when will you begin?"

"Why not now?" Charles asked coolly. He had taken the first, most difficult hurdle in deciding that he would come to Windygates. Having done that, he saw no reason for delay. But, to his surprise, Miss Ravensdale apparently did. He saw that her slim fingers were twisting restlessly and that in the bright afternoon light her face was suddenly a little drawn.

"I'm not sure—" she began, and paused to start again. "I think it might be better if I were to tell Judith first."

She was afraid, she honestly was, of that attractive but troublesome niece of hers! There was no mistaking the signs, but his liking for her alone was sufficient reason for him to say firmly:

"I disagree with you, Miss Ravensdale. You tell me that Miss Judith Ravensdale has agreed in principle to someone coming here. And you believe that she will not go back on that. I think that if you present her with a *fait accompli* she is far more likely to accept the situation than if you give her time to get her second wind!"

It was not exactly what he meant, but he thought that he could read Miss Ravensdale's character sufficiently well to know that if he said what was really in his mind—that this way the brunt of the fight would fall on him, whereas the other, she would have to face Judith alone—she would rebel. Pride would make it imperative that she should.

He had, however, reckoned without her shrewdness. Her lips quivered into a little smile.

"That is very ingenious, Mr. Saxilby," she said with just a hint of dryness in her tone. "But—confess it, you don't think I shall be so able to manage Judith as you will!"

Instantly Charles's face became blank. He had no liking for having his inmost thoughts read as easily as that!

"That is the last thing that I would claim," he said coolly. "And you should never trust a man who says that he can manage a woman. He is either a liar or a braggart—which is worse! No, Miss Ravensdale, it is quite simple. If I am not here, it will be possible for your niece to raise all sorts of objections to which it may well be impossible for you to find answers. But if I am here, she can put me to the test in her own way and prove for herself whether I am satisfactory or not!"

Harriet looked at him curiously.

"And do you think, in view of what you have told me of your meeting with Judith, that she will play fair?" she asked.

"As to that, time will show," he replied discreetly. "I can tell you that *I* shall."

"Oh, dear!" Miss Ravensdale said blankly. "That *will* put you to a disadvantage!"

Charles laughed. Suddenly the situation had become exhilarating, exciting. He knew that nothing in the whole world would make him turn his back on Windygates now—least of all any opposition that Judith could put up—and that he did not underestimate. He knew quite well that he was in for a difficult time, that everything he did or said would be under constant inspection, but he was not afraid of that. It would, he believed, be a worth-while struggle and, at the end of it—involuntarily he caught his breath, but the next second his manner was entirely controlled and he said easily:

"Now, as to details. I imagine you are not prepared for me to stay. Will it be possible for me to get a room in the village?"

"There is no need for that," Miss Ravensdale said promptly. "There is rather a charming little cottage on the estate which was always used for the agent before my brother's day. It has always been kept in repair, and now it is ready for immediate occupation. You see, I was determined that if you agreed to come, accommodation should be no obstacle! You could go there at once, and I can arrange for Mrs. Parlett to keep it clean for you as she does at present. She could probably cook for you as well——"

"Who is Mrs. Parlett?" Charles asked patiently.

"The wife of our chauffeur-handyman," Miss Ravensdale explained. "They both live here, but Mrs. Parlett is not very strong, so she only helps out in a small way. But I am sure she could do this."

"That sounds admirable," Charles admitted. "Perhaps you would have a word with her while I go over to the cottage and get myself installed?"

"Yes," Miss Ravensdale agreed slowly. "Yes, very well. If you will come back to the sitting-room I will give you the key. You continue round the drive in the direction you have already come, so that, if you kept on, you would find the other entry. About three or four hundred yards before you get to those gates, you will find the cottage. It is the only one, and you cannot mistake it because the name is on the gate—Windygates Cottage. Now, if you will come . . ."

He followed her back to the room where they had had tea, and she went to a small, neat desk. From it she took rather a large, old-fashioned key and held it in her hand for a moment.

"I wonder if I am doing the right thing?" she mur-

407

mured. And then she looked Charles straight in the eyes. "Am I, Mr. Saxilby?"

Charles shook his head.

"That I cannot tell you Miss Ravensdale! But I can tell you this: it is something about which you must be very sure in your mind, because otherwise, quite certainly, I shall not last a week here!"

"But I am sure!" she said vehemently and even agitatedly. Then, as Charles did not reply, she repeated the words. But this time she spoke very quietly, very steadily. "I am quite sure, Mr. Saxilby! Here is the key!"

Charles took it from her and turned to go. As he reached the door she called him back.

"Mr. Saxilby, I appreciate your reluctance to claim any ability for managing women, but—I have a distinct feeling, none the less, that I have been very–competently managed!"

"Oh no!" Charles said imperturbably. "Surely not! Believe me, nothing was further from my mind! I think it is probable that discussing the matter with me has helped you to see the situation clearly. Thoughts that have been confusing are often clarified when they are put into words!"

"It may be that!" Miss Ravensdale agreed, gravely.

When he had gone, she stood for a long time gazing down into the log fire. At last she sighed.

"Of course, if *that* could be the ultimate outcome. . . . He's right, *I* can't undo the influence of years in a few months—but he could!"

Charles drove circumspectly to his new home with a feeling that eyes were watching him. And not only human eyes at that, but the eyes that surely every old house has been given. To Charles they seemed to be brooding, dispassionate, as if, having watched so many frail humans come and go, Windygates was willing to wait, postponing judgment until he had shown his mettle.

He squared his shoulders. This was imaginative nonsense! What was far more important was Judith's judgment, and that, he knew, would neither be post-poned nor kindly.

However, in the meantime, he had other things to think about. A slight curve in the drive and there was his new home revealed! It was a delightful little place. Built a little later than Windygates itself, he thought, but none the less missing the terrible gaudiness of the *cottage orné* of a later period. He left the car drawn well to one side of the drive and let himself into the cottage.

To his relief he found that it had been suitably modernised. There was running water, with up-to-date facilities for heating it. Apart from the well-planned kitchen, there were three other rooms, two furnished as bedrooms and one as a sitting-room. Absolutely ideal for a bachelor, Charles thought.

He decided which of the two bedrooms he would use himself and went down to the car to get his luggage. And as he did so he heard the sound of another car approaching.

He guessed who it was, and he was right. Judith, driving a small, workmanlike car which he remembered had been parked next to his own in Wyford, was now returning to her home.

Watching, though as yet unperceived, he saw her eyes widen as she noticed his car. She came to a halt and jumped out to inspect it, and as she did so, Charles approached her. He must have been quieter than he realised, for she did not hear him until he was almost up to her, and then she turned sharply.

"What are you doing here?" she demanded curtly. "This is private property; you are trespassing."

Evidently she had not realised that he had actually come out of the cottage, he thought. Well, the sooner she did, the better.

"Yes, I know," he said quietly. "But I am employed on the estate you see! This is where I am to live!"

Judith stood her ground and Charles was conscious of genuine admiration for her courage. If he had not been what he actually was, but, instead, a trespasser out for what he could get, she might have been in considerable danger, but she never seemed to give a thought to that consideration.

"Nonsense!" she said crisply. "You've chosen the wrong person to tell a tale of that sort to! You see, Windygates happens to belong to me! Consequently, I know all my employees! And you are certainly not one of them!"

"Then you are Miss Judith Ravensdale?" he asked quietly.

She stared uncomprehendingly.

"I am, though I don't know how you—" she paused and looked at him more narrowly. "Now I recognise you," she said slowly. "You are the man who was so insolent to me in Wyford——"

Charles looked at her thoughtfully. An arrogant child this! Quite deliberately, he believed, she had used the word "insolent" as if to make him realise quite clearly what a gulf was fixed between their social ranks. Of an equal she would far more likely have used the word "rude."

"Was I?" he said quietly. "That was not my intention. I thought that I saw an opportunity of preventing trouble and I took it. That was all!"

"You saw an opportunity of humiliating—" she began impetuously and stopped, evidently realising that she was only, as she probably expressed it, lowering herself to his level by arguing. She made a gesture as if dismissing the whole incident. "Now then, what is all this about being employed here? Who engaged you and in what capacity?"

"I was engaged by Miss Harriet Ravensdale." Charles was watching her face narrowly to see how she took it. "As bailiff, agent—whichever you like to call it—to run the farm."

He saw the sudden blenching of her sunburned face, the flaring of her nostrils, and braced himself for the storm.

"I prefer to call it neither!" she said cuttingly. "You must please understand that there has been some mistake! *I* am the owner of Windygates, and consequently

410

I choose my assistants. Surely you can see that for yourself?"

"But I understood from Miss Ravensdale——" Charles began.

Judith interrupted him.

"Whatever my aunt has said is beside the point. I absolutely refuse to have you here in any capacity whatsoever, so I suggest that you get into your car and take yourself off as quickly as possible!"

"But I can't do that, Miss Ravensdale," Charles protested quietly.

"Oh?" she said stonily, "and why not?"

"Well," Charles said slowly. "For one thing, I want work and this seems very suitable to me. And for another, I understand from your aunt that she is your guardian——that at present you are not of age——"

"So that's it!" Her voice was so low that he could hardly hear what she said. Without another word she went over to her car and got into it. As she was about to let the clutch in she hesitated and turned round.

"At the moment," she said clearly, "you seem to have won the first round! But don't be too pleased with yourself! And don't settle yourself in too thoroughly at the cottage! Because I am determined that you shall go."

"And I," Charles said quietly, "am just as determined to stay!"

For a moment the blue eyes and the brown clashed. And it was Judith's that fell first.

She let in the clutch with a bang and drove recklessly off up the drive.

Charles drew a long breath. He felt as if he had been swimming for a very long time against an almost overpoweringly strong current.

Half an hour later Judith drove away from the house again. But this time, in order that she might not pass the cottage, she went out by the other gates.

It had been a stormy interview between aunt and niece—and Judith had come off worst because, if she had only realised it, it was her uncontrolled rage

411

at the situation which confirmed Miss Ravensdale in her belief that what she was doing was right. And in that belief she could stand up to all Judith's onslaughts.

And, wisely, Miss Ravensdale kept to arguments that were irrefutable.

"You agreed that there was too much work for you and that we needed someone. You have taken no steps to find an agent, so I have had to. If you do not like my choice, you have only yourself to blame!"

At that, Judith had shifted her angle of attack. She questioned her aunt's right to interfere in her affairs when she was so nearly of age.

"My dear Judith," Miss Ravensdale said rather wearily. "Do you think that I have not gone into that? I consulted Mr. Bellairs not only about this, but other plans—" she checked herself, but Judith faced her resolutely.

"You'd better tell me everything that you have planned," she said stonily. "And then I shall go and see Mr. Bellairs myself!"

"A good idea!" her aunt agreed. "Well, for a month or so I want you to work with Mr. Saxilby so that he can take over from you, and then—I want you to come abroad with me for a few months!"

"The South of France?" Judith asked scornfully. "I'd rather die!"

"That's rather an extreme statement," Miss Ravensdale said mildly. "But as a matter of fact, I had not thought of France—for one thing it will be rather too hot for comfort at that time of year."

Judith scowled. She knew quite well that her aunt disagreed with the way in which she had been brought up, and that several times there had been arguments about sending her to a finishing school or at least bringing her out properly, and now she suspected Miss Ravensdale of deliberately pointing out her ignorance—as if she didn't know that it was hot along the Mediterranean shores in the summer.

"I had thought—Canada. We have got relatives there—they farm. It would be interesting for you——"

The scowl deepened.

"You're trying to marry me off, aren't you?" Judith asked bluntly. "I know you are the sort of woman who thinks no woman is happy unless she is married."

If her aunt winced Judith did not notice it, and Miss Ravensdale said quietly:

"No, I wasn't thinking of that. I certainly hope that you will marry one day——"

"Of course I shall!" Judith interrupted impatiently. "There must be someone to look after Windygates when I die. I shall have a son——"

Miss Ravensdale ignored the bland assumption and went on as if she had not heard.

"—but you are still far too young to think of that yet! No, what I want is for you to meet people of your own age and have a good time with them. I want you to have the fun of going out to parties and dressing up for dances. And more than that, I want you to have more than one thing to fill your mind. Don't you see, Judith, life is such a complex thing. It is impossible for you to be able to cope with it if you meet only one tiny corner of it. So—take this opportunity, dear. I—I wouldn't insist on it if I was not convinced that it is for your good! Now, what about it?"

She put a gentle hand on Judith's arm, but it was roughly shaken off.

"I am going to see Mr. Bellairs—now!" Judith said passionately. "If you are right—if you can do this to me, then we will talk about it. But I am going to fight every inch of the way! I won't be turned out of Windygates by a stranger!"

"But there is no question——" Miss Ravensdale stopped. There was no point in talking to the empty air, and she could already hear Judith's small but workmanlike shoes scrunching on the gravel outside. A moment or two later she heard the car go roaring off.

Judith drove as if she were possessed. If she had not been an exceptionally good driver she would almost certainly have had a spill at more than one corner, but as it was she came to a halt outside Mr. Bellair's private residence in perfect safety an incredibly short time later.

The solicitor—an elderly man who had looked after the Ravensdales' affairs for many years, as had his father before him—was at home and came almost immediately into the room to which she had been shown.

"My dear Judith," he said anxiously, taking her hand in his. "I hope there is nothing wrong?"

"But there is—something very much wrong!" she blurted out.

Mr. Bellairs looked at her intently. Yes, he could certainly believe that. The child was shaking with some sort of nervous strain.

Had she been a little older he would have offered her sherry, hoping that the brief delay would quieten her down, but for the young there was only one thing. Whatever their troubles might be, they had to get them off their chests as quickly as possible.

He indicated a chair and sat down himself in such a position that he could see her face clearly in the light of the table lamp.

"You had better tell me," he suggested.

He listened in silence to her story. Just as he had listened to Miss Ravensdale's. And when Judith had finished he said quietly:

"Yes, it is quite true. Your aunt did consult me, and I told her what it was my duty to. Namely, that if she believed it was in your interests that an agent should be brought in, then she had no choice but to take the necessary steps to bring it about."

"But it isn't in my interests—or the interests of Windygates!" Judith stormed. "Who can possibly know as well as I do how it ought to be run? Why, Daddy used to say that I was a second brain to him—and if he was willing to trust me, why can't everybody else?"

The man of experience looked at her pitifully. How these young things ran their heads against brick walls! And how sure they were that they knew best! For a moment he hesitated, then he came to a decision.

"But did he?" he asked quietly.

Judith stared at him uncomprehendingly for a moment.

"Did he—what?" she enquired. And then, as she realised what he meant she said indignantly: "Do you mean, did he trust me? Why, of course he did!"

"Your father never trusted any woman in his life!" Mr. Bellairs said bluntly, "and you were no exception! More than once he confided his anxiety about the situation in which you would be left were he to die——"

"You mean, he didn't like making Aunt Harriet my guardian?" she said eagerly.

Mr. Bellairs frowned.

"No, I mean nothing of the sort! His anxiety was because he knew just how difficult it would be for you to do a man's job with no man to back you up! That was why he was so anxious to get you married. It may be a surprise to you to know that your aunt's plan for you to go abroad is actually your father's. He and I had discussed it several times."

Judith was silent. She knew perfectly well that he was speaking the truth. For one thing, there was no reason why he should not be, and for another, there was a ring of truth in every word. She stood up.

"There doesn't seem much that I can do, does there?" she said dully. "Why didn't Aunt Harriet tell me this?"

"I advised her to," Mr. Bellairs admitted. "Because I thought that it would mean less fuss, but she was anxious to spare your feelings——"

"She need not have worried," Judith said harshly. "I haven't any! I just feel—numbed."

The solicitor got up and took her hands in his. He, like Harriet Ravensdale, had often argued with Mark about the way in which he was bringing Judith up, but he would never listen—until it occurred to him one day, not that he was doing his daughter a wrong, but that the estate might suffer. But that, as it turned out, was not very long before his unexpected death.

"Will it not make everything easier for you that you know now it was your father's wish?" he asked gently.

Judith shook her head.

"No. You see, I thought—I really did think—I had

415

come to mean as much to him as a son could have done! Now—I know I was just deceiving myself."

Mr. Bellairs was silent. He knew, as Miss Ravensdale did, that not only could Judith never really have taken the place with Mark of the son he had wanted so badly, but also that she had been robbed of the opportunity of being what a daughter should be to a father.

"Poor child," he said gently, but Judith pulled her hand from his friendly grasp.

"No!" she gasped. "Don't pity me—I—I can't bear——"

She fled out of the room and Mr. Bellairs made no attempt to follow her. Instead he went to the telephone and called up Miss Ravensdale.

"Oh Hugh, I've made such a terrible mess of it!" Miss Ravensdale said despondently. "And I'd have given all I had——"

"You don't need to tell me that!" he interrupted her sadly. "Haven't I good cause to know it?"

Judith woke the next morning with the feeling that an intolerable burden was weighing her down. She propped herself up on one elbow and gazed out of the wide open window with none of the joy that a new-born morning usually brought her. Instead, she pondered over the problems that the day would bring.

Late into the night she had turned over what she had heard from Mr. Bellairs, and she had made up her mind. No matter what it cost her, she would follow out her father's wishes—but Charles should go. Not that she would ask her aunt to send him away. Pride forbade that. But she had no such faith in him as Miss Ravensdale had, and even in such a short time as a month there would surely be time to prove that he had made mistakes too bad for him to be left in charge of Windygates.

Slowly she got out of bed and slipped into the boyish dressing-gown that lay at the foot of the bed. Then she went out to the bathroom and took the cold bath that she had been trained to have as long as she could remember. She shivered a little, and out of the past came a voice that said, as it had said so many times of so many things: "A boy would not do that!"

Stony-faced, she went downstairs. Miss Ravensdale was already seated at the table, and she looked up as the girl came in.

"Good morning, Judith!" she said cheerfully.

"Good morning," Judith responded curtly as she slipped into her seat. As usual, she was wearing riding breeches and thick stockings, with a severe, man-tailored shirt. It was, as a matter of fact, the only outfit she ever wore except on Sundays when she went to church, and in the evenings. Even then, though she was properly dressed, her clothes were of the simplest. One could not imagine Judith in frills and delicate fabrics.

Miss Ravensdale, taking the bull by the horns, said quietly:

"I have sent a message down to Mr. Saxilby asking him to come up to the office at half-past eight. You will have a lot to discuss."

"Yes," Judith said shortly. It was infuriating that, because she had stayed awake so late the previous night, she had slept in this morning. Otherwise she would have breakfasted and been out of the house long before Miss Ravensdale put in an appearance. As it was, Judith felt that she had laid herself wide open to more interference, and the knowledge that she had no one but herself to blame did not make her feel any better tempered.

Hardly eating any breakfast, she went straight to the room which had always been used as the estate office and found Charles already there. As she came in he laid down the book that he had been reading and stood up.

"Good morning, Miss Ravensdale," he said quietly.

Judith's lips parted to reply, but her eyes fell on the book he had been studying. It was hand-written—her own writing.

"You had no right to read that!" she said indignantly. "It is my diary——"

"Yes, I realised that," he admitted. "But not a personal one, is it? Otherwise I should not have read it, of course. Actually, I cannot think of anything that could so quickly put me *au fait* with the running of the farm as a day-to-day diary of events like this."

His tone expressed genuine approval, but Judith was convinced that he had read her reason for annoyance. It was perfectly true that it gave him invaluable information about the running of the farm—and that was the very reason why she had not intended that he should see it.

He left the book open on the table, his hand resting lightly on it, and the slightly possessive attitude irritated Judith beyond measure.

"Have you any particular plans of how you would like me to take over?" he asked pleasantly.

Judith's eyes dropped. He was so infuriatingly sure of himself, so certain that he would make no mistakes.

"No," she said slowly, "I have no plans. You see—I think it is better to be frank, Mr. Saxilby."

"Much better," he agreed gravely.

"Yes. Well, the situation is this. I shall not be of age for six months. Consequently it appears that I am not in a position to give orders on my own property."

He was startled at the bitterness in her voice. And realised, perhaps for the first time, just how intense was the opposition which he had to overcome. He waited in silence for her to go on.

"But in six months the situation is going to be quite different. It is only fair to warn you, Mr. Saxilby, that one of the first things I do will be to get rid of you!"

Charles, of course, had got up when Judith came in. Now he came a little closer to her, and she had a sudden sense of being overwhelmed. He towered so over her—it was one of her griefs that she was so small and unimposing—and though he was not heavily built, his lithe, easy movements suggested considerable strength. Involuntarily she took a step backwards. Charles seemed to be unaware of it. He said slowly:

"You will dismiss me—even though I make quite a success of the job?"

Once again Judith's eyes dropped. It was infuriating that this man should have the ability of making her feel at a disadvantage, but—he should learn!

"I do not think it is likely that you will," she said bluntly. "After all, I have already had some experience of how you deal with other people, and frankly, I think your manner is tactless and in doubtful taste. I cannot have you making trouble here."

The impertinence of it! If she had been a boy, at that moment she would have found herself laid across his knees, face down, while his good right hand taught her a much needed lesson. As it was, he found himself saying quietly:

"I agree that our encounter yesterday was unfortunate. None the less, I acted in good faith. I should like you to believe that."

He paused, but Judith did not reply, and Charles went on:

"I think it is probable that both of us formed opinions then which were not very accurate. I hope that is the case, anyhow."

She flashed him a sudden, questioning glance, and he saw the bright colour surge up her slim neck to stain her cheeks. He *might* have been apologising, but she knew quite well that he was doing nothing of the kind. On the contrary, he was saying quite unmistakably that she had behaved badly and he hoped that it was not an example of her usual behaviour. He was daring to criticise her.

Here was the moment where justifiably angry words should have put him in his place, but to her consternation she found herself suddenly dumb. And, to her horror, her eyes filled with tears.

She turned blindly away, making for the door, but as she reached it she heard that hateful, self-satisfied voice say:

"You have not yet told me what you would like me to do——"

"Oh—" her hand made a blind, sweeping gesture. "Do what you like—it doesn't matter."

She stumbled out into the sunshine, and a moment

419

later he heard the sound of her car. She was running away.

Charles's lean face was grim. Not a good start. She quite obviously genuinely disliked and mistrusted him and, more than that, had no intention of playing fair. And his contribution to the situation, already sufficiently explosive, had served to irritate her still further. That he had done it deliberately and achieved his purpose gave him no satisfaction at all.

He stood for a moment in thought. Then he shut up Judith's diary and went from the office down to the farm buildings, there to make the acquaintance of the men who would work under him without the proper introduction that Judith should have made. From their silence and their curious eyes, he knew that a quite unnecessary hurdle had been put in his way, but this was not a thing that worried him. Here he was dealing with men, and men, he knew, would judge him on results. He was content to leave it at that.

Judith's first foolish instinct to escape from a situation that had got completely out of hand dwindled before she had gone more than a mile or so. She drove more and more slowly, so that an ancient rattle-trap of a car coming up behind her had no difficulty in passing her. Once he had done that, the driver drew into the side of the road and stopped.

"Hi, Judith, anything wrong with the car?"

He thought that she seemed to awaken from a dream at the sound of his voice, and it flashed through his mind to wonder what—or who—had been the subject of it.

"Oh, Des, you made me jump!" she said breathlessly.

Desmond Enstone jumped out of his car and came to her side.

"So I saw. Is there anything wrong, Judith?"

Her slim hands gripped the wheel and her dark eyes rested moodily on the road ahead.

"Everything in the world, I think!" she said with something like a sob.

Desmond's eyes narrowed ever so slightly. He and Judith had been friends since their childhood days, but this was the first time that he had ever seen a trace of weakness in her. It was interesting. He wanted to find out if, by chance, it was illuminating as well. He was extremely interested in Judith.

"Here, whatever it is, we can't block up the road like this!" he pointed out as a passing car hooted indignantly at them. "I'm going to take you to Linda. You can have some of her coffee and tell us all about it. How's that?"

Judith hesitated for a moment.

"All right," she said at length, and when he went back to his car, she followed his lead to a pleasant old house which had once been a small row of cottages and now, turned into one building, advertised the fact that teas were served.

There had been a time when the Enstones, if not possessed of such wide acres as the Ravensdales, had yet been very comfortably placed. But a succession of death duties plus an attempt on the part of the father of Desmond and Linda to restore the family wealth by spectacular and entirely unjustifiable gambling on the Stock Exchange had ended all that. When the inevitable happened, Mr. Enstone, most conveniently for himself, was suddenly taken very ill with influenza and died within a few days, leaving his wife and children penniless. Mrs. Enstone followed her husband within a few weeks, for, if he had been a failure in other ways, he had certainly always been perfect in her eyes.

All that was left was the house that Desmond and Linda now used both to live in and to make their living from. Linda was the backbone of the concern, but because Desmond had no illusions that his sister would keep him if he did not work, he turned to as well, and the results were surprisingly good.

And now, as Desmond drew up before their quaint home with its heavy black timbers and whitewashed walls, Judith relaxed.

Of all the people that she knew, these were the only ones with whom she felt quite at ease. Theirs seemed to be a different standard of life from hers. More easy-going, less critical of others—Judith did not quite understand just what it was, but she knew that she had two good friends in the Enstones. And surely, she thought bitterly, no one ever needed friends more than she did at this moment!

CHAPTER THREE

LINDA was in the middle of making a batch of scones when Desmond brought Judith round to the kitchen door. He called out cheerfully:

"Judith has come for a cup of your famous coffee! I wouldn't mind one myself, either!"

"Then you can see to it yourself!" Linda suggested amiably, and turned to greet Judith, her hands still in the mixing bowl.

There was little likeness of appearance between the brother and sister. Even their colouring was different. Desmond's hair was simply straw colour while Linda's was a rich, tawny brown. As a matter of fact, an impartial observer might have said that the colour of their hair was as typical of their different characters as anything could be.

For there was no doubt about it, Desmond lacked drive and initiative. Left to his own devices he would always take the easier course, the tempting short cut.

Linda was different. There was something tiger-like in her ruthless determination to make life surrender to her. She could bide her time, even as a tiger can lurk patiently for its victim, but she knew what her goal was, and, sooner or later, there was little chance but that she would reach it. In the meantime she was quite willing to work hard for her living, and she was, in fact, doing that. For a girl who had been brought up in considerable luxury with the comfort of a good domestic staff it was something of an achievement that she not only cooked superlatively well but contrived to keep the house spotless into the bargain, although admittedly with Desmond's help.

Her brown eyes that could smoulder so provocatively at times were shrewd now as they rested on the younger girl—Linda was twenty-six.

It was easy to see that something was wrong with Judith, and after she had popped her batch of scones into the oven Linda sat down on the chintz-covered window seat beside her visitor.

"What's wrong, Judith?" she asked sympathetically.

Judith shook her head.

"It isn't fair to bother you with my affairs," she said. "After all, you must have enough worries of your own!"

"Not so many as you'd think," Linda said rather cryptically. "Come on, let's hear about it! After all, what is the good of friends if they aren't interested in your troubles?"

Encouraged by that, Judith told her story simply and, in the main, quite truthfully. If she told it from her own point of view, that was natural, and in any case the Enstones knew Judith well enough to assess what they heard pretty accurately.

But if they had any criticism of her, they kept it to themselves.

Linda said commiseratingly:

"Poor old Judith, you have had a time of it! I must say, it seems rather absurd that your wishes can be over-ridden when it is only such a short time to your birthday! But I'm afraid if Mr. Bellairs says so he is right! He always errs on the cautious side, you know!"

"I know," Judith agreed. Her fingers twisted restlessly in her lap. "In any case, it isn't that so much. It's knowing that Father was worried. That he didn't think I was capable—I've tried so hard. But now I don't feel safe. I suppose I've lost my confidence."

Linda hesitated. Privately she thought that Judith was rather a fool. Why on earth should she ever have exerted herself as she had in order to please a father who never put himself out in the least for her sake? Much better, according to Linda's theories, to accept the facts as they were, sit back and let the men get on with the hard work. After all, what difference would it have made? Judith would have found herself mistress of Windygates just the same, and as pleasantly placed an heiress as she was would surely have no difficulty in finding a husband who would run things for her.

But it appeared that Judith had other ideas.

"Of course, I shall have to get married," she said flatly. "Only—I don't think I am the sort of girl that men like very much!"

For the first time for some while, Desmond spoke.

"That's just plain nonsense!" he insisted stoutly. "If you didn't behave like a prickly little hedgehog and frighten a chap out of his senses, you'd have so many suitors that Windygates would be cluttered up with them and you'd have to sweep them up with a brush and pan!" It was, of course, an absurd exaggeration, but it amused Judith, as Desmond's watchful eyes told him. He went on: "I remember, for instance, what happened the only time I tried to kiss you!" and he rubbed his jaw feelingly.

Judith laughed.

"It served you right!" she told him unrepentantly. "It was at the gymkhana and I was competing in the next event! Fancy choosing a time like that to start kissing!" There was all the scorn in the world in her voice. "Besides, I was only sixteen," she added.

"Meaning that you look at such things differently now?" Desmond asked, moving a little closer.

Judith laughed and shook her head, but Desmond saw the colour creep into her cheeks and was not displeased.

"I must go," Judith said rather hastily. "Thank you for listening and for bucking me up! I expect it will be all right in the end, but—I can't bear the thought of leaving Windygates! I'd do anything to avoid that!"

Desmond went out to her car with her, and just as she was about to drive off, he leaned his arms on the edge of it and looked down at her.

"Judith, don't worry too much," he said softly. "You see, I've got the glimmerings of an idea that might help you out!"

"Have you, Des?" she said eagerly. "Tell me what it is!"

But he shook his head.

"No, it's too soon yet. I'll only say—it depends partly on you."

Judith regarded him gravely.

"When I said that I would do anything so that I need not leave Windygates, I meant it," she told him.

Desmond nodded.

"I know. I'm relying on that." He stood up. "Well—be seeing you, Judith!"

When she had gone he strolled slowly back into the kitchen and slumped down on the window seat, his hands in his pockets. Linda had finished preparing her baking now and was clearing up the table. She glanced across at Desmond and said bluntly:

"It's no good your deciding to marry Judith, because she'd never have you! After all, you don't know half as much about farming as she does, and she'd never marry a man who wasn't at least her match."

Desmond did not attempt to deny that she had read his thoughts, for the simple reason that, whatever other dissimilarities there were between them, their brains worked in the same way. They did not of a necessity, however, come to the same conclusion. This was a case in point.

"That is just where you are wrong," Desmond retorted negligently. "Don't you know that Judith would absolutely hate being married to anyone who could put her in the wrong or even knew enough to argue with her! No, she'll always want to be the boss where the farm is concerned, and that's all right by me!"

Linda regarded him thoughtfully. There was something in that, she reflected, and it was admittedly quite clever of Desmond to have seen it. None the less. . . .

"I know," Desmond's mouth twisted in a smile that held cynicism as well as genuine amusement. "What sort of a man is it that permits his wife to wear the trousers? Well, I'll tell you. One that isn't afraid of the truth. I know you think I'm a slacker, and perhaps

I am—but not when it pays me to be energetic! And, married to Judith, it would pay me to see that we got the utmost penny out of Windygates!"

"I thought you said—" Linda began, but he disregarded her interruption.

"To begin with, as a matter of fact, I know quite a lot about farming—and I could easily learn more. Also, I've a name for being pretty shrewd. I'd see to it that Judith didn't get done, as I'm pretty sure she does at present. And in addition to that, I should take particular interest in one special line—rotation of crops, the strain of the sheep—it wouldn't matter what, and there is plenty to choose from in a mixed farm like that. The point would be that, being an expert on one subject, no one would regard me as a parasite, and yet Judith would have the last word in almost every case, so everybody would be happy!" He leaned back against the window frame, hugging his knees and grinning with maddening confidence at his sister.

"You think you're mighty clever, don't you?" she said tartly.

"I know I am. And so do you," he retorted.

Linda shrugged her shoulders.

"I gather you've been thinking of this for some time, haven't you?" she suggested.

"I have," he admitted.

She sniffed disparagingly.

"You don't seem to have made much headway!"

"No? Well, you tell me any other man that Judith knows to whom she would have given her confidence as she has to me!" Desmond challenged. "But you know what Judith is. She's been so immersed in the farm that she's never looked at a man! She's neither mercenary nor romantic minded. In fact, if you can bear with my being somewhat poetical for a moment, I would suggest that the word 'unawakened' is the best description of Judith that one could find. I would also point out that I am the first man to know that she is thinking of marriage now, and to whom would it be more natural that she should turn than her old friend, Desmond? She isn't afraid of me, you see."

Linda had to admit that there was a lot in what he said. And privately, she was determined to give him all the support that lay in her power. None the less, a desire to irritate him as well as genuine curiosity prompted her to say:

"What about this Saxilby man? He's on the spot, remember!"

Desmond made a gesture of derision.

"From what Judith says, he's one of those appallingly dominant males that treat women as if they are dirt! No, he's too much like her father to attract Judith!"

As to that, Linda was not so sure. Many women, for all their talk of emancipation and individuality, still preferred a man who asked nothing more of them than to look charming, be the mistress of his house and the mother of his children. And to such a woman, a man who was willing to shoulder all the responsibilities was absolutely essential. Judith, unawakened, to use Desmond's word, was not such a woman, but—who knew? Many a woman in love is a very different being from what she was before. However, to argue with Desmond was quite pointless and, besides, there was something else occupying her mind.

"Saxilby. It's a queer name, isn't it? Uncommon. And yet I have the feeling that I have heard it before— I've an idea that it was linked up with something very important. The same way that if you hear the name Churchill—only in this case I can't remember what was important about it!"

"It all sounds rather vague," Desmond commented, lounging to his feet. "In any case, if it was important I should hardly think it was anything connected with this chap. From what we know, he must be a bit of a rolling stone or he wouldn't be wanting a job like this: he'd be farming on his own. Well, I'm going into Wyford now. I wish to heaven you'd let me know sooner that you were getting low in flour! It's an awful bind making a trip just for one thing like this when I was in earlier in the week anyhow."

427

Linda made no reply to his complaint. Desmond always had got something to grouse about, and though in this case she had to admit that it was bad management on her part not to have let him know before, one got into the way of ignoring complaints when they were such frequent occurrences. And, in any case, her mind was still occupied with that half memory of hers.

Saxilby. Saxilby. It was a queer name and, as she had said, an unusual one. It was not very recently that she had heard it.

And then, suddenly, she remembered. Nearly two years ago she had gone to stay with some friends in Sussex. They had taken her to a point-to-point and Charles had been there. They had told her that he was the best rider in the county. She wondered how she could have forgotten, for Charles, tall, fair and bronzed, had made quite an impression on her. He had, she remembered, been with a man who limped and a small, quiet woman. His brother and sister-in-law. A man with a title.

"But," she had been told, "Charles is the man that has got the money! His grandfather was Andrew Saxilby—an American, practically a millionaire! Charles's parents were killed in an air crash, so Charles——"

No wonder she had thought that it was important! The grandson of a dead millionaire may well be important! Linda drew a deep breath. For a moment she hesitated. Should she tell Desmond what she had remembered? Or keep her own counsel? She decided on the latter. First of all, she wanted to make sure that it was the same man. In the meantime she would write to her friends and find out a little more about him. The name of his relations, something of his background, perhaps even a little about his likes and dislikes. It all helped when one was—was planning a campaign.

For the moment, however, that must wait. A bell summoned her to the little room in which she served coffees and teas. A big, prosperous-looking man, obviously an American, was sitting alone at a table. Through the window she could see his large, shining car. Well, whatever the future might hold of golden

428

promise, she needed money now! She smiled politely and took the order. And later, when her customer made enquiries about the age of the house, she obligingly showed him all over it. But her mind was still on Charles Saxilby, and her manner, though pleasant enough, was a little distrait. It was a new experience for the man who followed her eagerly from one oak-beamed room to another. He was not used to women being indifferent to his presence. The new sensation was not, perhaps, a very gratifying one—but it was certainly intriguing.

By the end of a week Charles felt that he had a fairly good picture in his mind of the layout of the farm and the use to which the ground was put. As Harriet had told him, they went in for mixed farming, and with considerable success. Hereford cattle were the primary product, and, as Charles quickly found out, were also Judith's chief interest. In addition there was a not very large flock of ewes. The bulk of the arable land was under wheat, with smaller areas devoted to potatoes, sugar beet and various roots. It said a lot for the standard of management that in addition to himself and Judith there were only five permanent men and one boy. Incidentally, after a day or so, Charles came to the conclusion that the boy was going to be more trouble than all the men put together. Nor did his judgment turn out to be incorrect.

His first act had been to go to the stables. Here he found a mare so obviously meant as a lady's mount that he knew she must be Judith's. In addition, there were a sturdy little cob and a big, handsome horse who gazed at him with mournful, questioning eyes. Charles immediately laid a caressing hand on his neck.

"This is a splendid chap," he commented to Joe, the boy, who had followed him like a shadow. "I suppose it was Mr. Ravensdale's mount?"

"That's right, sir," Joe agreed eagerly. "Always out together they were. Darky don't seem to be able to understand what's happened now he doesn't get out so much."

"Do you mean he is not exercised sufficiently?" Charles asked sharply.

Joe shrugged his shoulders.

"Well, I take him out every day, sir, but it ain't the same. And he's too big for Miss Judith, you see."

"Yes, right. Well, saddle him, will you?"

Joe looked doubtful.

"Miss Judith said——"

"That's all right, Joe," Charles said casually. "I will see Miss Judith about it."

Joe looked up at him from under a sandy thatch of hair with eyes that were just so small and close together as to give him rather an unpleasantly sly look, but he made no comment and got on with the job.

It was perhaps unfortunate that Charles had hardly left the stable yard before he encountered Judith—a Judith whose eyes flamed and who stood deliberately in his path.

"Get off!" she ordered furiously.

Charles swung down with the ease of long experience.

"Yes, Miss Ravensdale?" he asked pleasantly, as if there was nothing remarkable in her manner.

"How dare you—how dare you!" she stammered and then took hold of herself. "That is my father's horse! I've given orders——"

"That no one but the boy who exercises him is to ride him?" Charles said quietly. "Yes, so I understand. But I also understand that Darky was in the habit of being out a great deal with your father. Have you thought how cruel it is to a horse to cut down the exercise it is used to? And, what is more, the human companionship it has grown to need?"

"The only companionship he has ever wanted was my father's!" Judith said belligerently. "He will do what you tell him to because he is well trained, but you will never gain his affection!"

And at that moment, Darky, who had possibly grown a little tired of waiting, gently nuzzled Charles's ear and blew down his neck. Before Charles's eyes Judith's face crumpled up like that of a child which has been

430

disappointed or hurt, and without a word she turned on her heel and went swiftly away.

Charles pushed his head against that of the horse. "Did you have to do that at just that minute, you mutt?" he enquired. "Don't you know you've earned me another bad mark?"

But Darky, superbly indifferent to everything but the desire to stretch his legs, suggested unmistakably that Charles should stop talking nonsense and get into the saddle.

And Charles, with a shrug, did so because there was nothing else to do. But in his mind's eye he was following Judith and wondering, as he had done more than once, whether, after all, Miss Ravensdale had been right in her determination to alter Judith's life. After all, wasn't the trouble that she was having with local farmers and their wives due to nothing more than stupid prejudice which ought to be ignored? What could be worse than compelling a human being to live what seemed to them an unnatural life? After all, he had seen the cruelty of it quickly enough where Darky was concerned. Surely what was unfair to an animal was at least equally hard on Judith?

And yet—Darky tossed his head impatiently and Charles found all his attention required to quietening the beautiful, highly strung creature. He thought no more about Judith—for the time being.

In the days that followed he found Judith hardly co-operative, but at least she answered any questions he asked her, though she never volunteered information. It seemed that she had accepted the situation, however grudgingly, and no one but Judith knew how heavily time hung on her hands.

But what else could she do? Charles must go. She was determined on that, and the only way to see that he did was to give him sufficient rope to hang himself.

The worst of it was that he had such a trick of making it appear that he was in the right. Over Darky, for instance. Her conscience had told her that the horse ought to have more exercising, and that to allow him to spend so much time at grass could only be bad for him. Yet Charles had had no right to use him without her permission—in her heart of hearts she knew quite well that his fault would have been easier to forgive if it had not been for that confident nuzzling of Darky's. She had seen him do that so many times to her father.

There was to be another clash over Darky. Judith, relieved of an increasing amount of work, spent more and more time riding her mare, Truda. More than once she met Desmond out in his old car, and they would stop and have a talk. In the old days they had frequently ridden together and Judith spoke of that, regretting that his time was so fully occupied now that they could not go out together.

Desmond grimaced.

"It isn't only the time, my child. I haven't a mount these days! We're not doing too badly, but—it doesn't run to luxuries yet!"

"Oh, Des!" Judith said self-reproachfully. "I ought to have thought of it before! I'd mount you! You can have Darky—that is, if you'd like to!"

Desmond noticed that sudden diffidence with satisfaction. There had been a time when Judith took their friendship just for granted. Now she was not quite sure of herself—or him. It meant a subtle change in their relationship that could imply quite a lot.

For a fleeting second he laid his hand gently over hers, removing it before she had a chance to withdraw.

"Surely you know, Judith," he said quietly, "that there is nothing that I should enjoy more than riding—with you?"

Judith fumbled with her reins and flashed him a quick, unsure look. She saw that he was smiling and—just the same familiar Desmond as ever. She found herself smiling in return, completely reassured.

"That's settled then!" she said gaily. "When? Would next Tuesday suit you?"

"Marvellous!" he declared. "How about the early afternoon?"

"Splendid!" Judith sparkled, and left him, in higher spirits than she had known for some time.

For she knew perfectly well that Charles had planned

to be out riding most of that afternoon. He had spoken of his intention of going over to a near-by farm to inspect some stock and he, like her father, usually did his travelling on horseback, except when the distance was too great.

Well, for once he would have to change his habits! He could either have the cob or go by car. Desmond was going to have Darky. She was determined on that.

And yet, she made no mention of her plans to Charles. Only on the Tuesday morning she strolled down to the stables and, in front of Charles, told Joe that she would want both horses saddled for half-past two.

"A friend of mine is riding with me," she explained to Charles, her eyes limpid and innocent.

Of course Charles knew perfectly well that she was deliberately trying to provoke him. She wanted him to protest so that she had the opportunity of pointing out that, after all, he had never really been given permission to ride Darky, and it was hardly reasonable that he, her employee, should have the monopoly of the horse when she required it. It was not as if there was not the cob— grimly Charles pictured himself on that useful little animal and decided that he would use his car. The cob was quite up to his weight, but with his long legs he would not only look extremely funny but would be uncommonly uncomfortable as well. So he made no other comment than:

"It should be a good afternoon for a ride!" and had proof of what Judith's intentions had been by the disappointment in her expressive face.

Desmond, for all her profession of pleasure at his appearance, found her an extremely silent companion that afternoon.

Linda heard from her friends in Sussex. They gave her all the information she had asked for and more besides. For instance, that he was not engaged and, so far as they knew, was not likely to be.

Linda folded the letter up and smiled to herself as she put it safely away in one of her private drawers to which she knew there was no likelihood of Desmond going. She had no intention whatever of sharing her information with anyone yet. She wanted to use it herself to the best advantage, and she had no desire to see it explode prematurely.

Rather to her surprise, a few days later, she and Desmond had an invitation to dine at Windygates. There had been very little entertaining done by Judith's father for many years, and her and Desmond's visits there had been informal and latterly infrequent. They were both usually too tired to want to turn out in the evening. But this was rather different. True, knowing that Desmond would be eager to accept, she pretended to be rather reluctant, but in the end she gave way.

"It means dressing, though!" she reminded him. "Mr. Bellairs is going to be there, and he still clings to convention!"

"Oh well, only dinner jacket," Desmond commented. "Now if it were a boiled shirt I might jib, this weather!"

"Oh, I wasn't thinking about you!" Linda said with sisterly candour. "I was wondering what on earth I've got that is fit to wear! You're lucky. Men's clothes never date. Ours do! And they wear out more quickly."

"Wear that red thing of yours," Desmond suggested. "I've always liked you in that!"

Linda cast despairing eyes to the ceiling.

"Don't you know that that is one of the remarks you should never make to a woman?" she asked. "It is as good as calling it an old rag!"

Desmond laughed.

"I suppose, whatever a woman wears, a mere man ought to exclaim that he has never seen her look more marvellous and why has she never let him see that dress before!"

"Well, it would be an improvement," Linda admitted, her mind more concerned with her own dress than with abstract discussions like this. "Of course, she might tell you that it just showed you never really noticed what she wore and she'd had it for years!"

Desmond groaned.

"I give up!" he declared.

But if Linda was concerned about what to wear, Judith had no such problems. Dress had never interested her very much. She liked to look neat and tidy, but style and cut meant absolutely nothing to her. Consequently, there was only one dress in her wardrobe that she could wear on such an occasion, and it was utterly uninspired. Not only was the material unexciting and the colour, a tired blue, utterly unsuitable, but somehow or other the slim loveliness of her figure was masked and blurred. And, as she squirmed and wriggled to reach all the down-the-back buttons that fastened it, she grimaced at her reflection and wished that Mr. Bellairs wasn't such a stickler for customs that were long since out of date. It was not that she cared how she looked, but it was all such a nuisance. She would much rather have worn her usual work-a-day breeches or one of the plain cotton frocks that she wore most evenings in the summer.

Linda's toilette that night took such a long time that Desmond began to shout warnings up the narrow, twisted staircase. And when at last his sister did appear, he gave an expressive whistle.

"Got up to kill, aren't you?" he suggested. Linda shrugged her shoulders. Fortunately for her, Mrs. Enstone had made almost a hobby of buying up lengths of beautiful materials that caught her eye, and necessity had forced Linda to find out how to make the best of them. For this dress she had chosen a green and bronze shot taffeta. The well-fitting bodice showed her figure to perfection, while the deep swathe of almost carelessly folded material round her shoulders drew attention to their whiteness. The skirt, close fitting at the hips, flared out into wide, graceful lines and, for the finishing touch, she rustled softly like a summer breeze as she walked.

"Don't be silly," she said lightly in response to Desmond's remark. "It's only polite——"

"Do you know what I'd call that rig if I were a *couturier* giving a show?" Desmond interrupted. Linda shook her head indifferently. "Tiger's lair! Yes, I mean it! The changing colours of the material suggest the depths of a jungle, and your hair—you know, I believe I was right! You are out to kill! What interests me is—who is the prey? Somehow, I hardly think Bellairs fills the bill. So it must be Saxilby. Is it?"

"Don't be a fool, Desmond!" Linda said coolly. "According to Judith he is neither attractive nor well-to-do. Is that the sort of man I should be interested in?"

"No," he admitted promptly. "But all the same, *you* are the sort of woman who believes in first impressions. I'm not sure you altogether trust Judith's opinion—and you are taking no chances!"

"You are altogether too clever," Linda told him. And with the obvious intention of changing the subject went on rather sharply: "I suppose you *did* give the car a clean up inside? I've no desire to arrive with smears of oil all over me."

"You won't," he promised.

After all, they were not late, for Mr. Bellairs had still to arrive when they got to Windygates, and so had Charles.

It struck Linda afresh as Miss Ravensdale greeted her that the older woman did not really like her—or, for that matter, Desmond, and not for the first time she wondered what had prompted the invitation.

"What a charming dress!" Miss Ravensdale commented pleasantly. "And a very beautiful material!"

"It is some that Mother had stored away," Linda said rather shortly. In view of the simplicity of Miss Ravensdale's own silver-grey dress, she felt that the remark was in the nature of a criticism, and she resented it.

They were sitting on the terrace enjoying the cool of the early evening, and almost immediately Mr. Bellairs joined them, followed closely by Charles.

Both the Enstones knew the solicitor, of course, for, so long as the family had had any affairs he had dealt with them. They greeted him politely, and then Miss Ravensdale introduced Charles to Linda.

Linda paid him the compliment that few men can resist of giving him all her attention at that moment. She smiled up at him not only with her lips but with her eyes as she offered Charles her hand and he, taking it, bowed over it with an ease and grace which recalled to her the fact that he was, after all, half-American by birth and consequently far more a squire of dames than a man entirely English usually admits to being.

And then, as he stood erect again, their eyes met for a moment and Linda found herself thinking:

"Judith is a fool! The man is amazingly attractive! Good-looking and intelligent. You can see it at a glance. Something else, as well! Exciting."

But, from her cool, possessed manner, no one would ever have guessed her thoughts—or her deep interest as he turned to greet Judith—Judith looking, so Linda had decided when they met, like a sack tied in the middle. She *was* a fool! With a man like this about.

But it was very evident that Judith simply did not see him in that light. As a matter of fact, she was very much annoyed that Miss Ravensdale had invited him at all, and she vented her anger on Charles by ignoring him as far as possible. So that, Linda realised, was why she and Desmond had been asked. For some reason or other, Miss Ravensdale was determined that Charles should be entertained and, knowing Judith's prejudices, had taken care that they need not be thrown together too much.

And when it was time to go into dinner she found that her guess was correct. The dining-table was round, and Judith had been carefully placed between Mr. Bellairs and Desmond, although that meant that brother and sister were next to each other. However, it soon appeared that Miss Ravensdale knew what she was doing. She, naturally, after a few words with Charles, turned to her contemporary, Mr. Bellairs, while Desmond devoted all his attention to Judith. Evidently, Linda thought drily, Charles had been as much of a surprise to him as to her and, consequently, he was working hard to keep all Judith's interest for himself.

He need not have been quite so assiduous, Linda thought complacently. For Charles, apparently, had no eyes at all for Judith. And really, was it any wonder? Why should a man like that, who obviously must know his own attractions, be bothered to pay attention to a badly dressed girl with no manners or charm of any sort when he could talk to herself? Fortunately for her self-confidence it did not occur to her to wonder why a man who worked from choice and not necessity should stay on in what must be very uncomfortable conditions.

Of course, what Judith in her prejudice had missed entirely, was the fact that he was a man of considerable education and culture. Or if she did realise it, it only served to strengthen her opinion that Charles must be a waster to need such a job. Linda, with her greater knowledge of the truth, could appreciate the fact that it betokened considerable character in a man to work hard when he did not have to.

Nor did her first impression of him change. Definitely exciting. The sort of man who, however unconsciously, makes women aware of his presence. And, Linda judged, who was able to find considerable pleasure in the companionship of an attractive woman.

She was intensely conscious of the fact that he was deliberately assessing her, weighing up her attractions, deciding what she was really like, and Linda felt completely unperturbed. She knew perfectly well that she could stand any amount of scrutiny that night, and if anything was needed to add a finishing touch to her charms it was that she was on trial. It was like a spark to tinder, and she was by turns a sparkling raconteur or an absorbed listener as the moment demanded.

But Charles could not help noticing that more than once there was a puzzled look in her eyes, and, man-like, he naturally wondered what it was all about.

Not until they were out on the terrace again drinking their coffee did she give vent to an exclamation of triumph. Charles looked up, smiling an enquiry.

"You know, ever since Miss Ravensdale introduced us, I was sure that I had seen you before!" she explained. "And now I remember where it was! The year before last I attended a point-to-point with some friends in Sussex, and you were riding!"

"I don't remember," Charles said apologetically.

"Oh, we weren't introduced," Linda explained. "As a matter of fact, you were talking with some other people. I think my friends said your brother and his wife. Sir Roger—something. I'm afraid I've forgotten what!"

It was so naturally done that inevitably Charles replied:

"Garwin. Yes, we'd driven over."

Suddenly there was an abrupt movement and Judith was standing there.

"Do you mean to say—is it true that Sir Roger is your brother?" she demanded fiercely.

Charles stood up.

"My half-brother," he corrected. "Yes, it is quite true!"

Judith's laugh was almost hysterical in its triumph.

"It isn't any wonder then that your references were so marvellous!" she said viciously. "Or that, right from the beginning, I was convinced that they were worthless!"

CHAPTER FOUR

FOR a second there was a silence so intense that it could be felt. Then Miss Ravensdale gave a little gasp and Mr. Bellairs clicked his tongue disapprovingly.

"I suppose it might seem like that," Charles admitted. "But one day I hope you will meet my brother. Then you will realise how unjust such a thought is."

For a moment Judith's lips moved silently and her hands clenched and unclenched. Then, without another word, she turned abruptly and fled into the house.

Mr. Bellairs laid a hand on Miss Ravensdale's arm as she half rose in her chair.

"No!" he said authoritatively. "Leave her alone! She is in no mood to listen to common sense!"

Miss Ravensdale sank back, troubled, yet seeing that he was right.

Linda caught Desmond's eye and made a slight movement of her head to which he, as cautiously, replied.

Linda stood up.

"I am sure you will forgive us if we go now, Miss Ravensdale," she said pleasantly. "We are working people, you know, and we keep early hours!"

It was charmingly done and even Miss Ravensdale, who, as Linda had suspected, did not like her very much, had to admit it. If, too, there occurred to her the thought that it was a pity Linda's good manners showed Judith up to even greater disadvantage, perhaps that was natural enough.

When the Enstones had gone, Mr. Bellairs got slowly to his feet.

"Oh, you're not going as well, are you, Hugh?" Miss Ravensdale asked forlornly.

He smiled reassuringly.

"No, my dear. But I promised that I would spare the Parletts a little time this evening, with your permission. They are a bit worried about that young nephew of theirs—he will certainly get himself into trouble one day—and I may be able to help!"

He went slowly into the house, and Charles saw that Miss Ravensdale's fine eyes followed him until he was out of sight. Then she turned to Charles.

"I am very sorry," she said simply, and he did not attempt to misunderstand her.

"How was it she did not know?" he asked.

"When you first came, I suggested that she should read the letters which you wrote to me, but she did not do so," Miss Ravensdale explained, and then, apologetically: "I must admit that I wasn't sorry because, knowing Judith's prejudice about having anyone, I realised that she would say something like that! After all, she was on the look-out for something—anything—that would——" she stopped abruptly.

"That would get rid of me," Charles finished. "Yes, I know." He paused and went on more slowly. "You know, Miss Ravensdale, I have come to the conclusion that my first decision was the right one. I am not the man for this job!"

Miss Ravensdale turned and searched his face with grave, penetrating eyes.

"But you are not going!" she stated rather than asked.

"I am not going," he repeated. "If only because—I am rather an obstinate man."

"Yes, I think you are," she agreed candidly. "But you can't be finding it easy——"

"I'm not," he admitted. "But—never mind about that, Miss Ravensdale. Will it hurt you to tell me more about your brother? I have a feeling that it will help me to get to the bottom of something I heard the other day. Otherwise, I would not probe."

"It's all right," she assured him quietly. "What is it that you want to know?"

He hesitated, less because he did not know what to say than because he wanted to make it very clear to her.

"The thing I heard was this," he said slowly. "I was having a look at Shawbury's bull with him—a magnificent animal. And I asked him if he was showing it at the local Agricultural Show. He looked at me sideways and instead of answering me, he asked me another question. It was: 'Is Windygates showing Trumpeter?' When I said that we were, he said: 'No, mister, I'm not showing!' Of course, I tried to get to the bottom of it, but all he would say was that it didn't always pay a tenant farmer to win prizes."

"I don't understand," Miss Ravensdale said slowly.

"Nor did I at first. Then I got it. Shawbury's farm actually belongs to Judith, doesn't it? And Shawbury rents it? Well, I gather that he is not the only one of your brother's tenants who realised that he was not the sort of man who could brook opposition. In other words, a Windygates bull carried off the cup year after year because there was no serious competition."

"Mr. Saxilby!" Miss Ravensdale gasped.

"I know. Not pretty, is it? But I didn't leave it there. I looked up records. The last time another farmer had

441

the prize-winning bull was in 1946. A man named Heriot. His farm is now in the hands of a man named Williams. Heriot left the district within a year of the show. It seems that one disaster after another befell him. His ricks were burned, his hens refused to lay, his pigs sickened and died. He left the district practically a ruined man!"

"But you are not suggesting——"

Charles rubbed his chin meditatively.

"People don't talk nowadays about the evil eye," he said thoughtfully. "But I suspect they still believe in it! But leaving superstition out of it, there are quite a lot of people about here who feel that they owed your brother a grudge. Doubtless they came to lay every catastrophe at his door, but—there must have been some foundation to it. I want to know—how much?"

Miss Ravensdale hesitated.

"Quite a lot, I am afraid. You—and they—are quite right. He could not bear to be opposed, and defeat simply infuriated him. Of course, witchcraft is sheer nonsense! But I remember the occasion. I remember hearing my brother say that Heriot must be taught his place! Of course, what chiefly annoyed him was that Heriot really was a bad farmer. Lazy and ignorant. That bull was sheer luck! His disasters were due to his own carelessness and mismanagement. But—they all have had sufficient reason for *some* complaint. An incident like Heriot's farm adds fuel to the fire."

"Yes," Charles agreed. "Now, Miss Ravensdale, is it any use telling Judith this?"

In their absorption, neither of them noticed his use of Judith's Christian name. Miss Ravensdale pondered.

"What are you afraid of?" she asked.

"I've come to the conclusion," he said slowly, "that the feeling against Judith is not entirely because she is a girl. Rather it is that, though some of them at least had a grudge against her father, he was too strong a man for them to hit back at. But it is a different story now. Judith is genuinely competent where farming is concerned. Her opinions are well worth listening to. But in the nature of things, she cannot dominate them as a man could do. And yet she behaves as though she could. Do you understand, Miss Ravensdale?"

She leaned forward, her face strained and white.

"Just what is it you are afraid of, Mr. Saxilby?" she asked again in a whisper.

"I am afraid," he said deliberately, "that sooner or later someone will pay off to Judith the grudges they owe her father. And that is why I say, is it any good telling her?"

"No!" her aunt said decisively. "Not yet! Even if it is a risk, you must wait until you have more proof! She would just not listen!"

Charles got up, a dim, looming shadow in the twilight.

"I was afraid you would say that," he admitted. "Certain, in fact, after to-night. Well, I'll just have to keep my eyes skinned, that's all!" He kicked a stone moodily with his shoe. "By the way, there is just one other thing. I wonder if your brother ever realised how lucky he was to have a daughter and not a son!"

"Lucky!"

"Yes. Don't you see—no rivalry! If Judith had been a boy, there would have come a time when your brother would have realised that his son was quicker-witted, more virile than he. I doubt if he would have liked it! Inevitably, there would have been clashes—the more so if the son had been like his father! As it was, a girl could be made to feel that she was inferior clay! And her adoration for her father tended to keep her young. That sort of unreasoning love does, you know. Many a man has discovered that there is no stronger rival than the father of the girl he wants to marry. You see, a very strong love for parents is a looking-backwards to childhood all the time. The other sort of love is looking forwards, usurping for oneself the rank of parenthood. Yes, your brother was lucky!"

Miss Ravensdale sighed.

"It sounds only too true. But—what about Judith? Can things ever come right for her?"

A subtle change came into Charles's voice. It became guarded, impersonal.

"Time will show!" And with a quick nod he strolled off into the darkness.

Miss Ravensdale was left to await Mr. Bellairs' return alone, but with a great deal about which to think.

And Judith? She had rushed into the house up to her own room and had flung herself down on her bed.

He had done it again! Somehow or other he had twisted her words so that he had put her in the wrong! And, at the same time, he had at least given the impression that there was nothing for which he himself could be blamed. Judith's strong little hands clenched and unclenched as her anger mounted. If only he would meet her openly and fairly, but he was so evasive— it gave her a sense of impotence that she could not get at grips with this man whom she disliked and mistrusted so much. Suddenly she sat up. Had Aunt Harriet known about this relationship? Had she deliberately kept quiet about it—that was rather horrible to think of, because of course it meant that she had not really got the well-being either of Judith herself or Windygates at heart.

Everybody seemed to be siding with the Saxilby man. Even Linda. She had seemed to enjoy talking to him. Had gone out of her way to be charming. And her dress—

Judith got up slowly from the bed and went over to the long mirror that she so rarely consulted. It was rather a shock to see the reflection of herself with the picture of Linda still so fresh in her mind.

She scowled heavily. For the first time she realised that there was something wrong with the dress. But even her new perception could not tell her what it was. She put her hand behind and gathered lumps of material together in it so that, for the moment it was a better fit. That, she supposed, improved things. At least she looked a better shape. But there was still something wrong. Disparagingly she tore off the offending garment and then went over to her dressing-table. From a drawer she took a big silk square that Linda had given her last Christmas. She had never worn it because she felt that its bright scarlet just didn't fit in with any of her other clothes. But now she folded it cornerwise and draped it round her slim shoulders, knotting it in front so that it was like a fichu. Then she went slowly over to the glass again and examined the result. Her eyes widened. Whether you liked it or not, you had to admit that it was striking in its effect, particularly as she was wearing a white silk slip which suddenly looked rather like a well-tailored dress.

Perhaps that was what was wrong, Judith thought. Perhaps she ought to wear bright colours and sharp contrasts. Perhaps, if she dressed differently, people would treat her differently.

Suddenly, with an expression of repugnance, she tore off the scarf and threw it on to the floor with the blue frock. It lay there, glowing, vital, like newly spilled blood.

Turning her back on it, Judith began to dress hurriedly in her working clothes. She felt more comfortable in them—and somehow safer.

After all, why should one trouble to dress up just for the sake of other people? They ought to accept one for what one was, not because one flattered them and asked in return for flattery. If people really cared for one another, that was the way it would be. And if they didn't care, what did clothes matter?

She went quietly down the back staircase and out into the silent night. She had heard the Enstones drive off—it was impossible not to hear Desmond's car if one was anywhere near, or to mistake it for any other. Mr. Bellairs' gentle, precise voice she could hear as she went past the Parletts' sitting-room, and Charles—.

Her chin jutted out belligerently. Better for Charles if he were to keep out of the way!

She circled the house stealthily, taking advantage of every bush and shadow, and at last she was sufficiently far away for it not to matter if anyone did see or hear her. As hard as she could, she raced down the drive, to turn off at a little by-path which led into the woods.

Suddenly she heard a voice—and knew that it was Charles's.

"Who's that?" he asked sharply. And she heard footsteps crunching over last year's leaves.

Holding her breath, Judith melted into the shadows and waited, still and silent. For a time she heard Charles beating about in the undergrowth, and once he passed so near to her that if she had put out her hand she could have touched him. Then he evidently concluded that there was no one there, for he turned and walked slowly to the drive again.

And after a while, Judith ventured out. She made her way so surely that it was obvious she had some particular destination in mind, and that was the case.

For in the very heart of the little wood, she came to a clearing into which the moonlight poured, making it an enchanted spot. Across the ground lay a section of a tree-trunk which made such a comfortable support if one sat on the ground just in front of it that Judith had come to the conclusion that someone else must have found this sanctuary and come to it many times. It gave her a feeling of happiness such as one gets in sharing some beloved object with someone who also appreciates it. She never felt lonely here—or at odds with the world.

So now, confidently, she sat down and leaned back against the trunk, her face turned up to the moon. To herself she had called it Lob's wood, for surely here, if anywhere, one could forget old mistakes and make new beginnings.

But to-night, for the first time, the charm failed. Everything was just the same. The moon, the dark shadows around her, the mournful hoot of owls and the little squeakings and scurryings of small night creatures. All the same. Only she was different. Not part of the picture or the paradise.

She waited awhile, her eyes closed, but it was no use. The restlessness, the unanswered question in her heart, did not lessen. If anything, the beauty of the night only served to make them worse, until at last, with a sigh, she got up and slowly retraced her steps.

Charles, of course, had gone home long ago. She was perfectly safe from interception now! So, confidently, she stepped out into the drive—and, too late, saw him.

He was standing in the shadow of a tree resting his back against it, his arms folded, his eyes on the moon, even as hers had been.

But as he heard her step he straightened up, and for a moment, panic-stricken, she thought that he was coming towards her. Almost she slipped back into the protecting woods, but now that he knew she was there, they would be no protection. Yet she must avoid a conversation at all costs! In this mood of uncertainty and disillusion she would be at such a disadvantage.

Then she realised that he had obviously no intention of coming nearer to her.

She heard his voice, deep and oddly musical.

"Good night, dryad!"

Then he turned and strolled quietly away.

In the morning Judith said carelessly:

"I suppose I shall be wanting more clothes for this holiday you insist on?"

Miss Harriet, startled but unwilling to let her niece see it, carefully folded the letter she was reading and put it back into its envelope before she answered.

"Yes, I suppose you will. Why not consult Linda about it?"

Judith's dark lashes swept her cheek.

"Oh, Linda is too busy," she replied. "It would not be fair to ask her."

"No," Miss Harriet replied judicially. "Perhaps not. Although she has very good taste. What will you do, then?"

Judith did not seem to find it very easy to reply.

"I thought you and I might go up to town for a few days. You will need some new things as well, I expect."

"I do," Miss Harriet agreed. "All right. When shall we go?"

"At once!" Judith said recklessly. "Well—the day after to-morrow?" as she saw how doubtful her aunt looked. "I mean, it isn't any good wasting time—and though I expect a lot of the things can be bought ready made, I want a new suit."

Well, Miss Harriet thought drily, if this was the result of Linda's wearing that spectacular, elegant frock, one could only regard it as a miracle and accept it with gratitude!

"I'll make a hotel reservation and so on," Miss Harriet promised. "Train or car?"

Judith thought.

"Car, I think. We can bring things back more easily, and, besides, it won't be so sticky and dirty!"

And if Charles, when he heard about it, wondered whether he was not being given an additional bit of rope in order that he might hang himself as rapidly as possible, perhaps he should be forgiven.

Anyhow, as a result of it, he wrote a long letter to his sister-in-law and had one back by return of post which evidently gave him considerable pleasure.

It was the first time that Judith had left Windygates for more than a year and, to her surprise, she experienced a strange sense of freedom when they had left the well-known scene behind and were on the open road. She and Miss Harriet took it in turns to drive and, even with a stop for lunch, found themselves on the outskirts of London some four and a half hours after they had started.

It was a hot day, but tempered with a soft little breeze—which was just as well, otherwise a country girl like Judith would probably have felt too tired to take any interest in her surroundings. As it was, she found plenty to interest her, although, as she told her aunt in all sincerity, she could not understand how anybody could possibly live in London.

"It seems awful," she said seriously. "Here it was all fields that used to provide food for the Londoners and now the houses have swallowed up the land and the food has to come from miles away! They can't ever know what it is like to have a lettuce that is just crisp from the earth or tomatoes that taste like they smell because they are so fresh!"

"Oh yes, they can," Miss Harriet said promptly. "Most people have gardens, you know, and they grow things for themselves. It must be just as wonderful for them to go out and pick their own produce as it is for you. More, perhaps, because it's all so personal."

"Yes," Judith said doubtfully as if she did not quite understand, and left it at that. It occurred to her aunt that there had been a time, not so very long ago, when she would have argued about a thing like that.

They had a double bedroom in a hotel which overlooked the Park, and Judith, leaning out of the window, said over her shoulder:

"I'm glad about the trees!"

Miss Harriet, knowing that they would arrive too late to do any shopping, had got tickets for a theatre, and Judith, in spite of her dislike for being shut in when she could be out of doors, made no protest. Actually, when she got there, she became so absorbed in it that during the intervals she could not talk. It was all so real, so important, that she could only wait, bemused and entranced, until the next act began. And when it was all over she followed her aunt, still in a dream, to the real world with feet that seemed reluctant to leave fantasy behind.

Miss Harriet, seeing her starry eyes, felt it in her heart to pity her dead brother. He had had it in his power to bring that light to his girl's eyes. And he had never thought it worth while. Rather, he had bent her to his own whims, ignoring her needs and thinking only of his own pleasure and satisfaction.

Perhaps, Miss Harriet thought sadly, it was because she herself had never had any children that she could wonder in amazement how casually people took the responsibility of other human beings who were dependent on them. Few people would deliberately neglect a child's physical needs, but what a terrible lot there were who were completely indifferent to their mental ones! Strange how often one heard about the duty of children towards their parents, but how rarely that uncomfortable word was used the other way round. And yet, surely, that was how it ought to be. One had a child and one did the best possible for it. And if you had given your child the right ideas, in its turn it passed on what you had done for it to the next generation. Looking forward all the time, not backward. Surely that was the right way!

She realised that Judith was speaking to her. Was it too late to go down to the Embankment and see what the river looked like?

Miss Harriet, herself reluctant to go indoors on such a night, led the way through narrow lanes until they came to the river that glittered just as bravely in the light of the moon as it would in its upper reaches where trees were reflected in its changing mirror instead of the harsh outlines of the buildings which only the night made beautiful.

For a long while Judith gazed, and her aunt did not interrupt her thoughts, though, to herself, she admitted that she was curious to know what they were.

A little launch belonging to the River Police shot downstream, disturbing the silver path of the moon and shattering the smooth water into a thousand sparkling sequins. When it had passed and everything had grown still again, Judith gave a little sigh and turned away.

"Shall we go back now?" she asked in a voice that was suddenly tired.

They got back to their hotel to find that, during their absence, Mr. Bellairs had called and left his card.

"Do you think there is anything wrong?" Judith asked anxiously. "It seems odd that he should come here specially."

"Oh, he hasn't just come up from Wyford," Miss Harriet told her. "He came yesterday, on business. He said he would call, but I did not quite know when."

"All the same, why should he call?" Judith worried. "Unless there was something he needed to tell us."

"He probably called because he wanted to see me," her aunt said pleasantly. She hesitated for a moment, and then went on: "It is probably news to you that Hugh Bellairs and I were engaged at one time. We have always remained friends!"

"But—" Judith stared at her uncomprehendingly. "If you were engaged, why didn't you get married?"

Again Miss Harriet hesitated, but at length she said, slowly:

"The wedding was two months off when—your mother died, Judith. Your father needed me—and so did you. So I postponed the wedding, as I thought, temporarily. But, somehow——" she shook her head. Even now she could not understand how it was that she had ever been so foolish. She ought to have *made* Mark understand.

But Judith understood. Deep down in her heart she had always known that her father never troubled to see anything from any other point of view than his own. He had needed a housekeeper, so Aunt Harriet had to give up the idea of having a home of her own. Judith shook her head.

"I did not know, I'm sorry." Her voice trailed off inconclusively. "I think I will go to bed!"

She went to her room, but her aunt lingered for a moment, thinking over the last few moments. And in particular, over Judith's last words. Probably it had never entered her head before to wonder just how it had come about that her aunt had taken over the running of the house. But if it had, surely it would not have been surprising if she had taken the attitude that anyone was lucky to have a chance of living at Windygates. Now, even though she might, at heart, still think that, it had at least been clear to her that evidently Miss Ravensdale did not share that feeling. She might even go so far as realising that some people would say she had been unfairly treated.

But with her own feelings Miss Harriet was not concerned. What interested her was that this was the first indication she had ever had that Judith was growing away from her father's influence. It sent her to bed refreshed and hopeful.

The following evening Judith dined alone at the hotel. Mr. Bellairs had come round earlier in the evening and had firmly removed Miss Harriet without at the same time suggesting that Judith should join them. Not that Judith minded. She was used to her own company and, besides, she had acquired various farming papers during the day and wanted to go through them. So, after she had dined, she settled herself in a remote corner of the hotel lounge and became absorbed in her papers. But not for long. She had chosen her secluded corner because she did not want people to start talking to her. But by chance there was no one else in the room, and after a while it seemed to become increasingly big and unfriendly. She sneezed, and the small sound seemed positively to echo through the empty room. The papers lay in a heap beside her as she sat gazing rather fixedly at a portrait of an incredibly smug-faced child, wondering what was happening at Windygates.

But thinking of home only made her feel more lonely, and it was a relief even when one of the hotel reception staff came in, obviously looking for someone. Suddenly the man caught sight of her and came hurrying up.

"Miss Ravensdale? A lady and gentleman are asking for you—Sir Roger and Lady Garwin."

"Oh!" Judith jumped to her feet. Charles's half-brother and his wife! She felt that it was rather an embarrassing situation and wished with all her heart that her aunt was there. But she was not, and Judith had no choice but to see them—supposing Charles had written to them telling them what she had said.

"I will come," she said quickly, and followed the man out of the room.

They were sitting together on a small settee, talking, and without in the least being able to explain why, Judith knew that though they were the sort of people who were bound to have a great many friends, they would always enjoy one another's company more than any other. It must be rather wonderful, she thought, when two people did feel like that—but most unusual, she decided with the dogmatism of youth.

Then Mary saw her and smiled, and that horrible little feeling of being out in the cold vanished. Roger stood up to greet her and said pleasantly:

"Charles knew that we were to be in town and asked us to call."

"But please tell us if it is not convenient," **Mary** added gently.

What a lovely child! she was thinking. But how very young and defenceless! Was Charles attracted by that? One could never tell what attracted a man, but Charles was one of the two nicest men she knew, and he might be able to see past the proud tilt of the little head and the chin and mouth that could obviously be so aggressive.

"It is quite convenient," Judith said with unconscious eagerness. "I was all alone! Will you come into the lounge? We shall have it all to ourselves."

She led the way, and Mary and Roger followed her. At the door of the room Judith stood aside for them to pass and then, for the first time, realised that Roger limped. Judith's heart filled with pity. She had hardly known a day's illness in her life, and to see a man who was still far from old and otherwise healthy condemned to take nothing but halting steps for the rest of his life seemed terrible to her. Mary, seeing the expression on her face, felt reassured. If Charles did care for the child, it was good to know that she was capable of such tender pity.

"Would you like some coffee—or something to drink?" Judith asked anxiously. It suddenly occurred to her that this was the first time that she had ever been hostess entirely on her own. Her interest was all with the farm and it had suited her, as it had suited her father, to leave the house management to her aunt. Now she wished that she knew a little more about such situations as this. Had she said the right thing! She had taught herself to drink shandy, but even that she did not really enjoy. And now, she would have to have more or less what they did, she supposed.

"A cup of coffee would be very nice," Mary said gently. She was, of course, unable to read what was running through the child's mind, but obviously she was nervous, and pouring out coffee would give her something to do with her hands, which would be helpful. And judging by the fact that Judith gave an unconscious little sigh of relief, she had said the right thing.

All the same, conversation lagged a little until Roger brought up Charles's name by saying:

"Charles tells me that you have a remarkably good herd of Herefords—and he knows what he is talking about! We go in a lot for sheep in our part of the country, but he has built up a very good herd for me."

"You've had some champions, haven't you?" Judith said eagerly, and then, as the words left her lips, she remembered that first encounter with Charles in Wyford, and her cheeks flushed ever so little. Perhaps he *had* meant to be helpful.

Mary, sitting a little aside, listened to their conversation but did not join in it very much. Her knowledge of farm matters was extremely good, but Roger had got the child talking naturally and it was a good chance to study her.

"Beautiful and intelligent," she decided. "But far too highly strung! Living on her nerves—yes, of course, Charles said that! He knows what he is talking about! But there is more than a hint of obstinacy! It will be difficult ever to make her relax—far more likely she would collapse first!"

A little later Miss Harriet came back with Mr. Bellairs, who only stayed for a moment or two. Miss Harriet found herself talking very comfortably with Roger while Mary chatted with Judith.

Deliberately she kept the conversation to impersonal topics, but when it became obvious that they would be leaving shortly, she leaned a little nearer to Judith and said quietly:

"I wonder whether you would do something for me?"

"Yes, of course," Judith agreed, wondering what was coming.

"It is just a message I want Charles to have," Mary explained. "We are up in town because my husband has to pay a six-monthly visit to a specialist about his leg. We have been waiting a long time, during which he has had constant treatment. Now they say that they can operate, and—this is the point—they are convinced that it will be successful. Roger may still limp a little, but there will be no pain as there is at present. I want you to convince Charles of that because otherwise he will worry, and it is time that he was free to think only of his own affairs without bothering about us. He has done so much already!"

"Has he?" Judith was completely unaware of the eager note in her voice.

"He has indeed," Mary replied, affection for Charles very evident in her tone. "He has been loyalty itself while Roger has been so handicapped. And perhaps the most loyal thing he has ever done has been to leave us now that our son is old enough to take over. You see, he did not want Jerry to feel either that he had been robbed of his rightful place or that he must push his uncle out to get it. We are very fond—and proud—of Charles."

"Yes," Judith said quickly, and then with evident sincerity, even if she were anxious to change the subject: "I am *very* glad your husband is going to be better, Lady Garwin."

Mary smiled. Yes, Charles might certainly do worse!

They went a little later, and Miss Harriet, who had found the situation to which she had come home surprising, to say the least of it, merely remarked casually:

"What very pleasant people! I am glad I was in time to meet them!"

"Yes," Judith agreed and then, quickly: "Did you enjoy yourself?"

"Very much, thank you—" Miss Harriet began, and turned as one of the hotel staff approached her. "Yes?"

"A trunk call for Miss Judith Ravensdale," the man announced. "If you will come this way, madam."

Judith followed him, conscious of a feeling of suppressed excitement. A trunk call could only be from Windygates. There was no one else who would think of telephoning.

"Judith Ravensdale," she said clearly, and a man's voice answered her. It was Desmond!

"Hallo, darling!" he said cheerfully. "I had to know how you were getting on."

"Oh—marvellously," Judith said mechanically. She felt suddenly at a loss, but she made an effort to pull herself together. "How—how nice of you to telephone, Des!"

"Nice to myself!" he assured her. "I wish I were up there; I'd love to be the one that trots you about instead of the horde of men you must have met by now who are clamouring for your favours!"

"But they're not!" Judith protested laughingly. "Truly, we've been far too busy."

"That's good!" Desmond said lightly and yet in a way that somehow suggested he really meant it. There was a little pause.

"Des—is everything all right at Windygates—the farm, I mean?"

"I suppose so," Desmond replied. "Here wait a minute, I'll call Saxilby—he's only in the other room."

"Oh!" Judith said with unconscious sharpness. "Where are you speaking from?"

"Home. Linda and Saxilby have been out to a dance. They are just back. Hold on!"

"No!" Judith said quickly. "No, it's quite all right. He would not have gone out if anything had been wrong—I must go now, Des. Give Linda my love!"

She rang off abruptly before Desmond could reply, but that did not worry him. He stood smiling thoughtfully at the dumb instrument for several moments before he rejoined his sister and Charles.

CHAPTER FIVE

TWO days later Judith and Miss Harriet returned. They had shopped intensively and almost everything they had set out to do had been accomplished.

It had interested Miss Harriet considerably to watch Judith making her purchases. The tailored suit was a simple business. Measurements were taken and material and style chosen very quickly. Another fitting was arranged, for which Judith would have to come up specially, and then they turned to the question of dresses. For a girl of Judith's slim figure it presented little difficulty to buy these ready made. Most of them needed a little shortening, but this was an easy matter, and the articles could be posted home to her. This sort of arrangement, Miss Harriet knew, was simple for Judith, long since trained in thoroughly business-like methods by her father. But colour and style—Miss Harriet had made up her mind that while this shopping must be a success, it would be infinitely better for Judith to do her own choosing. For one thing it would be an education for her, and for another, she would like what she got better if she did not feel that anything had been forced on her.

So Miss Harriet sat back, and Judith, realising that it was up to her, coped with it by finding out who was the head saleswoman and then being perfectly frank with her. (Miss Harriet could hear the echo of her brother's voice: "Always deal with the man at the top. He knows!")

"I am going to Canada by sea shortly and I shall be there several months." Judith's clear young voice was very businesslike. "I want quite a lot of clothes, but I have very little idea what colours would suit me best. Will you help me?"

The subtle flattery of being consulted worked even greater wonders than the promise of a substantial order. One assistant in particular proved to be exceptionally helpful.

She regarded Judith through narrowed eyes, asked her age and delivered her judgment.

"Your own colouring is sufficiently decisive for you to wear white and cream to advantage. I should suggest several tailored linen dresses in either of those colours with vivid belts and other accessories to match—scarlet, emerald, hyacinth blue. For slightly more formal wear, patterned materials—yes, I think so. Although I strongly advise you to avoid frills and meaningless bows. It does not seem your style to have anything which is not simple in line. For the evening—well, we will get on with the day gowns first!"

But it was an informal evening gown that really won Judith's heart, although her pride, which made her treat this whole expedition in such a casual way, would not allow her to admit it. It was a crisp little white dress of *broderie anglaise,* and apart from the very good fit and the simple lines of it, the chief attraction was the way in which round the neck, sleeves and hem the material had been cut to the design of the embroidery.

It had a particularly charming effect round the neck, where the cut outline of little leaves made a softly broken line and served to show up Judith's peachy skin to delightful advantage. But Judith did not analyse her liking for the dress. She just knew that she felt happy in it—and that was a new experience for a girl who had always regarded anything but breeches and a shirt as rather silly and useless.

They saw no more of Roger and Mary, for they had returned to Sussex, but the memory of their visit remained with Judith, and more than once she found herself thinking of the relationship between the two of them. Although it was so obviously something that nobody else could really share, it had not made Judith feel shut out in the cold. On the contrary, because it was something so obviously stable and enduring, it had given her a feeling of security and confidence. She found herself wondering how people could know that it was going to turn out like that. Or didn't you? Was it just a gamble? Judging by some people she knew, a gamble that did not come off. And yet they must have thought that it would, otherwise they would not have gone into it. So was it just a question of luck? She remembered hearing someone say that the question about those who expected least being least disappointed was obviously made about marriage. Yet Roger and Mary were not disappointed. Quite evidently they expected a tremendous lot of marriage—and somehow they had achieved it. Well, how?

It had never occurred to Judith to wonder very much about marriage before. It was just something vaguely looming in the future. Now, suddenly, to understand all that it meant became urgent, vital. And Judith knew that she would never be able to ask anybody's guidance. Aunt Harriet, for instance. The thought of marriage could not have meant a tremendous lot to her, otherwise she would never have allowed any obstacles to get in the way of marrying Mr. Bellairs. She did not stop to think it might perhaps be ungenerous to dismiss Miss Harriet's sacrifice so casually as her thoughts passed on to other women she knew. Linda? No, she decided hastily, it was not a subject that she could discuss with Linda. Besides, she knew so well what Linda would say—had said many times: "People talk about love as if it is the most important thing in the world and then do their utmost to make sure it won't last! Don't talk to me about love in a cottage! A man whose wife is a dowdy drudge because he cannot afford to keep a maid for her is always being reminded that he is a failure. And he doesn't like that. So he blames his wife—and that is the end of that! No, maybe one shouldn't marry for money, but heaven protect me from loving where it isn't!"

That was Linda's solution. And, of course, the Garwins were probably not worried with money problems. But it was more than that.

The problem was beyond her, but as soon as she got home she sought Charles out and delivered Mary's message. Charles listened in attentive silence, and when she had finished he sighed in evident relief.

"That is the best news I have had for a long time," he said simply. "Thank you for bringing it!"

He smiled, and Judith found herself smiling in response.

"I liked them," she found herself saying, and then, in a little rush: "You were quite right. Your brother would not tell lies to get you a job—even if you asked him to!"

Charles ignored the final slur on his own character and even grinned a little, mentally, at it.

"Thank you for saying that!" he said, and added: "I always feel that my relations are the best recommendations I could possibly have! The only bother is that they take a bit of living up to!"

Judith nodded silently, and since she had obviously something more to say, Charles did not interrupt whatever train of thought it was which was occupying her. At last she said slowly:

"They are very happy together, aren't they?"

Charles's blue eyes became both more alert and intent. So she had seen that, had she? Well, after all, one could hardly miss it unless one was absolutely blind to such things. The only thing was, he had thought Judith *was* blind.

"Very happy," he agreed. "So happy that—" he broke off abruptly and wheeled sharply. Judith had come down to the farm buildings to deliver her message and now, suddenly, he heard a furtive sound.

"Yes?" he said sharply and from round the corner of the barn young Joe Sellars put in a sheepish appearance.

Charles's eyes narrowed. How long had the boy been there? And how much had he heard? It was not that anything had been said which really mattered, but the Sellars family were noted for their gift of manufacturing gossip if it did not actually exist and, in any case, the fact that the two of them were talking alone together would be quite enough—after all, he knew perfectly well that his name and Judith's had already been linked together in the village. With the feeling that there was against Judith it needed very little to turn ordinary village curiosity into a scandal.

"Why aren't you down in the Five Acre?" Charles demanded. "It isn't your time yet, you know!"

Joe grinned sheepishly and held up a large oil can he was carrying.

"Must be a leak," he explained. "Tom sent me back to get more because there's a squeak in the tractor!"

"Right!" Charles said shortly. "Well, don't use the same can or we'll lose more oil! And get a move on!"

"Yessir!" Joe said more smartly, and touched his forehead ingratiatingly to Judith. "Glad to see you back, miss!" he said and shot a sly look at Charles as if to say: "I expect you are too!" But Charles took a step in the direction of the boy and he scuttled off about his business.

Judith was frowning faintly. She had realised that

there was more than a hint of tension in the situation, but she could not understand what it was all about. She was not particularly partial to the Sellars family, but young Joe did not work too badly and that was something to be thankful for these days.

"Weren't you rather down on him?" she suggested, but far more mildly than she would have done a very short while back.

"Yes!" Charles agreed without hesitation. "He needs to know that he can't take liberties!"

"But has he?" Judith asked.

Charles looked at her thoughtfully. What a child she was in so many ways, in spite of her undoubted ability. Didn't she realise—no, he was sure she did not, and he certainly was not going to open her eyes to what existed only in the unpleasant minds of other people.

"He has been turning up a bit late every morning and pushing off early, no doubt to make up for it!" he explained quite truthfully. "We can't allow that, you know!"

"No," Judith admitted, evidently relieved at the simplicity of the explanation. "We can't have that!"

"Now," Charles said briskly, determined to get away from the subject before he could be asked any more awkward explanations, "I expect you would like to know all that has gone on while you have been away. Shall we go up to the office?"

They spent an intensive hour going over everything that had happened, the dark head and the fair one bent close together over books and papers.

"Oh, by the way, are you going to enter Trumpeter for the Show?" he asked when they had gone through everything.

"Yes, of course," Judith said promptly. "Why not?"

Charles shrugged his shoulders.

"Only that—he rather swept the board last year, didn't he?" he suggested mildly.

"He's an extremely good bull," Judith pointed out promptly. "Why shouldn't he?"

"Yes," Charles said slowly. "Only—don't you think

that very fact is rather discouraging for other people who can't hope to beat you?"

"Not a bit," Judith said promptly, all her old arrogance returning at the suggestion. "If other farmers took as much care as has always been taken here, they would stand a chance just as I do! But if I withdrew, someone else would win with an inferior beast and standards would drop. Surely you must see that?"

Charles was silent, and Judith frowned.

"You do see it, don't you?" she demanded.

"I think there is a feeling that you have greater opportunities—that you have more money behind you," he explained.

Judith's eyes flashed.

"That isn't true!" she said forcefully. "My farm pays, as you know! It is true that I have got other means besides, but I live on what the farm makes and maintain a far more expensive house than most of them have got!"

"Yes," he admitted. "But all the same, you have the knowledge that, if there is a bad year, you have got other money to see you through. Consequently, too, you can afford to lock up more capital in good buildings and fertilisers and so on!"

Judith stood up.

"Of course, you are a newcomer here, but I should have thought you would have realised by now that the whole essence of a show like this is that everybody enters—no matter what their social position. Don't you see that though they may think Windygates wins because there is more money behind it, if I didn't enter for the various competitions they would be sure to say that I thought too much of myself! They always find something to criticise, you know!"

So she realised that, did she! Evidently she was not so oblivious to village ways as he had imagined. Or perhaps it was that she had a blind spot where her own personal affairs were concerned.

"Surely your brother shows locally, doesn't he?" she went on and he had to admit that it was so. "Well, then!"

And Charles knew that, short of telling her the truth as he believed it to be, he would never convince her. Probably he wouldn't even if he did try to explain, for there was still no proof; his suspicions were certainties only in his own mind.

"I'll fill up the form for you to sign," he said slowly, and went back to his work a rather troubled man. He could not convince her without proof, but finding that proof would mean that the trouble was coming to a head. And that was the last thing that he wanted.

Desmond came in the same evening and stayed for an hour or so. He was amusing and entertaining and had no reason to complain of unresponsiveness in Judith. Indeed, her frequent laughter and the amount of interest she showed in their visitor put an idea into Miss Harriet's head that made her grow silent and thoughtful.

Linda was quite right in thinking that Miss Harriet did not like her, but in fact it was Desmond whom she really mistrusted most. He was far too charming and easy-going ever to make his way in the world without assistance, and Miss Harriet had no wish for Judith to be the one who provided that assistance. Some women might not suffer by being the leading spirit in a marriage, but Judith would. Inevitably she would grow more and more aggressive, less her true self. No, what she wanted was a man sufficiently strong not to be a bully, who would allow her to have a personality of her own yet would not let her deny him the same right. It was a lot to ask of a human being, but supposing one did find such a man, he would certainly not be Desmond's type.

However, there was nothing that she could do about it. Judith had been friendly with the Enstones all her life, and to suggest that Desmond would not make the best sort of husband might be putting ideas into Judith's head that were not there so far. But that they were in Desmond's she had little doubt. She as well as Judith had known both brother and sister since they were little children, and had noticed that trick of theirs of regarding, through narrowed eyes, anything which was the subject of more than usual interest to them. Their father had had the same trick—and he had looked at a youthful Harriet like that, too. It was too deliberate, too calculating to be pleasant. She remembered shivering when Laurence Enstone had looked at her in just that way. He had proposed to her shortly after, and she had refused him—odd to think that Desmond and Linda might have been her children, and to wonder whether she would have been strong enough to give them the something that they lacked. With half an ear, now, she listened to what Desmond was saying.

"Linda was sorry that she could not come with me, but she is very busy. I told her it served her right. A working girl ought not to go gadding about to dances night after night."

"Night after——" Judith began rather blankly, when Miss Harriet interrupted her.

"On the contrary, Linda needs more amusement than she gets!" she said briskly. "All work and no play is as bad for Jill as it is for Jack, you know!"

She collected up her needlework and went out of the room, leaving rather a silent couple behind her. Desmond stared moodily at the door through which she had vanished.

"That was one in the eye for me!" he commented. "It isn't the first one either! Most people seem to think that I am living on Linda—she thinks so as well, so probably it is true. But what the deuce can I do? Women always seem to be able to turn their hand to something, but most worthwhile jobs for men need specialised training, and that I've never had. Of course I know a bit about farming, and it interests me, but not enough really to take charge, and who wants to be bothered with training a wastrel like me?"

Judith looked troubled. It was not like her old friend to be so introspective and glum, and it hurt her. Des was always so gay, so able to convey something of his light-heartedness to those he was with.

"No, Des, not a waster. Things have never quite gone your way, have they?"

He smiled ruefully and took one of her small, capable hands in his.

"That's the way I tell myself it is," he admitted. "And it is sweet of you to do the same! None the less, it never occurred to anyone that I should take over for you instead of Saxilby, and why? For the simple reason that I'm not only ignorant but indolent!"

"No!" Judith said sharply. "You mustn't talk like that! People are what they believe they are! Let me think, Des!"

He was silent, noting with satisfaction that she allowed her hand to remain in his.

"Would you like to come and work here?" she said at length, slowly. "No, not in charge, I'm afraid," as she saw his look of surprise. "But to learn. I could have a word with Mr. Saxilby about it—you could learn a lot from him!"

Desmond's eyes narrowed speculatively.

"Your opinion of him has changed, hasn't it?" he asked.

Judith shrugged her shoulders.

"I suppose it has," she admitted. "I admit that I was suspicious of his ability when he came, but—I'm beginning to realise he does know his job!"

"But you still don't like him personally?" he suggested softly.

Judith hesitated.

"I still think he is too aggressive and autocratic," she said at length. "I don't think people like him very much." She made a gesture that dismissed the subject. "But how about it, Des? Would you like to come?"

Now it was his turn to hesitate. There were quite a lot of things to be said in favour of the idea, but one very strong one against it. It altered the relationship between Judith and himself, and he did not think it would be for the better. True, he could convince her of his real interest in Windygates, but on the other hand, it was one thing to visualise working there as husband of its owner, quite another to be the pupil of her agent.

"I'll think it over, Judith, if you don't mind," he said at length, adding hastily: "And I'm not hesitating because I don't like the idea. It's just—there is more to be thought of than appears on the surface."

"What?" Judith asked, uncomprehendingly.

Desmond regarded her thoughtfully.

"Well—gossip, for one thing," he pointed out. "I mean, if your father were still alive, I wouldn't hesitate at all, Judith. But—it is rather different now, isn't it?"

"I don't see why," Judith said stubbornly. "You mean that they will start linking our names together immediately? Well, why should we worry? They have to have something to talk about, and you know as well as I do that they soon tire of it if one takes no notice! Besides, we're such old friends and we've been about so much together that I expect they've long since given up trying to marry us off!"

Desmond could have kicked himself for ever having introduced the idea at all, for Judith's matter-of-fact reactions were not in the least what he had wanted. He would, he realised, have to use more definite tactics to suggest to her the new relationship which he had in mind. But for the present the sooner he terminated this visit the better, he decided, and a little later he got up.

But just as he was getting into his car, he halted.

"Heavens, I nearly forgot, and Linda would have given me what for! She's organising a scavenger hunt on Sunday in aid of the Red Cross, and she told me I wasn't to let you refuse! You will come, won't you?"

"Oh—" Judith hesitated. "Des, I'm not awfully good at that sort of thing! I mean—of course, I know all the people here, but—I've never really been great friends with any of them. You see—I suppose it sounds rather nasty of me to say it, but the girls always seem so empty-headed and giggly, and the men—I think they find me too bossy and—critical. Am I, Des?"

He laughed and ruffled her hair.

"Sometimes," he admitted. "But not as much as you used to be," he added, seeing her troubled face. "Anyway, you and I will be partners, so it won't matter about anyone else. So you will come, won't you?"

"All right," Judith promised, and then, just as he was about to start: "Des?"

He turned with a smile, but Judith shook her head.

"No, never mind," she said harshly. "It's nothing."

She had been on the point of asking him if Charles was taking part in the hunt and who was to be his partner. And then, all at once, she had known that she would die rather than show any interest at all in Charles's affairs.

"Yes, of course I'm taking part," Linda said as she slit open the sealed envelope. "I've no more idea than the rest of you what we've got to find, because I got Mrs. Hannay to make up the list! Here you are!"

She handed round the sheets of paper, one to each couple, who read them avidly amid a chorus of groans and laughter.

"Heavens above, where on earth can one find a beadwork antimacassar these days?" protested one entrant.

"I know where there's one!" a girl said eagerly, only to be hastily suppressed by her partner.

"Well, there you are!" Linda declared. "Ordinary rules—no fetching things from your own houses and no paying more than sixpence for any article! We start in two minutes—eight o'clock—and report back here at ten-thirty. We'll use the church clock, then there's no arguing! Wait for it!"

They waited for the striking of the clock on the church tower, and watches were set. Then they were off.

In spite of the age of his car, Desmond was off to a racing start, with Judith beside him. He said complacently:

"That ought to do us a bit of good! Now then, read out the exact description of the place where we've got to clock in first. Something about a tower on a hill, isn't it?"

Judith did not reply immediately. She was looking back over her shoulder. Charles was following them closely and beside him—Linda. Desmond, looking into his driving-mirror, knew what she had seen, and his jaw set rather grimly. He wished to heaven Linda wasn't quite so obvious! Many a girl had found a man interesting only when she realised that another girl was attracted to him. And Judith was an odd girl—he had been right when he had said that the right description of her was 'unawakened.' But he wanted to be the one that did the waking up—not Saxilby.

They reached the check-point ahead of all the others, thanks to Desmond's knowledge of a short cut that no one else would think of putting a car to. But, as Desmond said quite cheerfully, there was something to be said for having an old car. It couldn't be battered much more than it was and, having no false ideas about its own importance, would submit to rough-and-ready repairs at which another car would turn up its nose.

"Full marks!" Desmond reported as he got back into the car after having had his instruction sheet initialled by the man at the check-point. "Wanted to see my driving licence—got another ten points for having it with me. Come on! Read out the list."

It was an amusing list and one likely to test the ingenuity of the entrants to the utmost. And, in this case, Desmond, it appeared, had far more notion of where they might be able to borrow the necessary articles than Judith had.

"I thought the lady of the manor always knew everybody and all about their belongings," Desmond commented, evidently slightly surprised. "You know, going round with good nourishing soup and red flannel petticoats!"

"Oh!" Judith said with rather forced lightness, "that sort of thing has gone out of fashion now! People would regard it as being impudence. They like to keep their cottages to themselves. Besides—I've never had time for that sort of thing. Whatever has been necessary, Aunt Harriet has done."

Desmond looked at her quizzically.

"You don't have to apologise to me, love!" he commented. "And, anyway, I expect you are quite right. Times have changed! Now then—a pair of *pince-nez*—hang it, we've got some at home, but that's against the rules. I know, how about the Rector?"

From the Rectory they not only got *pince-nez* but also the bead antimacassar and an artificial rose, somewhat battered but none the less authentic. A Coronation mug was unearthed with some difficulty and reluctance by the woman who sold mineral waters on the Common, and then their luck failed them with twenty articles still to be found.

"A last year's calendar, a stuffed bird and a pair of kippers!" Desmond moaned. "It just isn't possible!"

"It is, you know," Judith said thoughtfully, thoroughly excited now by the chase. "Because one of the conditions is that whoever made out the list knew that everything could be found—if one looked in the right place! Oh—the only way the person who made out the list could know about the kippers would be if they had some in their own house!"

"The Hannay's house, then," Desmond said, letting in the clutch.

"No!" Judith shook her head. "They haven't got a refrigerator, and this weather—her best friend, Mrs. Dallas!"

"That's inspired!" Desmond declared, and they were off.

But Judith's inspiration was never put to the test. They had hardly gone more than a few hundred yards when, without warning, a lorry turned out of a narrow lane just ahead of them. If Desmond had not reacted instinctively to the danger, they must have crashed into the back of it. As it was, he slewed the wheel over sharply and they shot across to the other side of the road. But the road was narrow, and before he had time to straighten out they had mounted the low grass verge and had dipped into the ditch. Fortunately it was not a very deep one and fortunately, too, the brakes on Desmond's car were in good order, if nothing else was. None the less, they were both shot forward and Judith's head hit the wind-screen with considerable violence.

She gave a little cry, and as soon as Desmond could extricate himself from behind the wheel he helped her out.

"Here, sit down on the grass," he suggested, realising that she was clinging dizzily to him. "That was something of a bump you got. Let me see!"

She turned her face up to him, and already a large lump was coming up on her forehead.

"I say, I am sorry!" he said with genuine regret.

"It wasn't your fault——" Judith began, and swayed towards him again. "Desmond, I think I'm going to faint."

It was not quite as bad as that, but it was some little time before she felt well enough to smile wanly at him.

"I'm sorry," she began, but Desmond interrupted her.

"No need to be. If it weren't for the fact that you are in pain, I'd be getting quite a kick out of being the strong supporting male!"

Instantly Judith stiffened.

"Girls are just as strong as men!" she insisted defensively.

"I expect they are, love," he agreed pacifically. "Stronger, perhaps! But anybody, male or female, who has had a crump like that is likely to be a bit woozly, so you had better let me look after you!"

And, indeed, Judith was not sorry to let him. It was, of course, only because of the accident that it was suddenly pleasant to feel the strength of Desmond's arm round her and to lean her head against his shoulder.

It was very quiet, for they were some distance from any houses and no more traffic passed. Judith, content just to remain still, did not look up at Desmond's face, or she would have seen an unusual look of determination gradually increase as if he were coming to some decision. And suddenly he spoke.

"Judith!"

She looked up instantly, startled by the queer, broken note in his voice.

"Oh, Des!" she said anxiously. "Are you hurt? You should have said——"

His arm tightened.

"No, it isn't that. It's something I've been wanting to ask you for a long time."

"Ask me?" she said, puzzled. "But why ever did you put it off? What is it?"

"It's something that may—surprise you," he said slowly, wondering even now if he was making a mistake. "It's this—will you marry me, Judith?"

She turned in his grasp so that she could look into his face and he saw with a sinking heart that he had no chance of a favourable reply. There was utter surprise and consternation written all over the expressive little face.

"But why?" she gasped. "I don't understand."

She was very sweet and very appealing at that moment in her youth and inexperience, and Desmond was stirred as he had never been before by her nearness. He had always been fond of Judith, and marriage to her had seemed an easy way out of all his troubles. But now, quite genuinely, he wanted to be the man who awakened her, who taught her what love and life meant.

His arm tightened round her, and with his other hand he turned her face up to his.

"Because I love you," he said hoarsely.

She did not stir, and that alone told Desmond the degree of his failure. To her he was still the old friend whom she had known and trusted all her life and whom she need never fear.

A soft sigh fluttered between her parted lips and her eyes grew troubled.

"Oh, Des, I didn't know!" she said pitifully. "I'm sorry."

He let her go so abruptly that she stumbled a little and had to clutch at his arm again.

"Sorry, Judith," he said mechanically. And then, "Is it—quite hopeless?"

Regretfully she nodded.

"I've just never thought," she faltered.

He managed to smile reassuringly.

"Never mind!" he said with an effort. "And don't look so worried! It isn't your fault, you know!"

471

"No, but—but—won't it make a difference?" she asked anxiously.

"To us being friends?" He shook his head. "No, it isn't going to do that, Judith! But—tell me one thing. Have you turned me down because there is someone else?"

"No!" she said vehemently. "Oh no—who could there be?"

"I wouldn't know," Desmond said rather drily. "But if that is so, then—I'm not going to give up hoping!"

"Oh, but you mustn't—" Judith began, and then suddenly became aware that a car was stopping just by them.

It was Charles and Linda.

Charles was out in a moment.

"Anything serious?" he asked, gripping her shoulders.

"No!" Judith said quickly. "Just a bump that made me silly for a little while!"

With a nod Charles turned to Desmond.

"What happened?" he demanded, and feeling uncomfortably like a small boy who has been caught out by a master, Desmond explained.

"Perhaps we can get it back on to the road," Charles suggested. "Judith, go and sit in my car until we see what we can do about it!"

Judith went slowly over to Charles's two-seater and got in beside Linda. Linda looked at her critically.

"That will be black and blue by the morning!" she commented without much sympathy.

Judith flushed.

"I expect so," she agreed, and lapsed into silence.

With the help of a passing farm hand the men succeeded in getting Desmond's car back on to the road. Apart from a crumpled fender and a lamp that was bent up at an angle, it did not seem to have sustained much damage.

"Good!" Charles said briefly, dusting off his hands. "Well, Enstone, you'd better carry on with your sister. I'll take Judith back home. The sooner she is resting the better!"

"But I'm quite all right," Judith protested.

472

Charles did not reply. He opened the door for Linda to get out and, to her intense annoyance, she found herself meekly obeying.

But when Charles had driven off with Judith, she turned to her brother and worked her spleen off on him.

"You've made a nice mess of it!" she said vindictively.

Desmond said nothing. He was rather of the same opinion himself.

For the first time in her life Judith had to give in. By the time they reached Windygates her head was throbbing unbearably. She felt sick, too, and when Miss Harriet suggested that she should go to bed for a time, she had no fight left in her.

Except that, just as he was leaving, she turned to Charles and said rather grudgingly:

"I suppose I ought to thank you."

Charles grinned in genuine amusement.

"I shouldn't, if it hurts you," he said, and strolled off before she had time to reply.

CHAPTER SIX

JUDITH passed the strangest night that she had ever experienced. Miss Harriet had insisted that she should take two aspirins, and for once Judith, who had inherited all of her father's scorn for even the mildest of drugs, did not refuse. But though the effect of them was to send her off to sleep very quickly, she woke an hour or so later and after that found it difficult to go properly off again. She lay in a semi-stupor through which waking dreams passed in a ceaseless procession. Sometimes she lived over again things that had actually happened and sometimes she seemed to be puzzling over the problems of a stranger who was yet herself.

In her mind she heard Desmond's proposal all over again and came to greater consciousness to hear herself muttering regrets that she could not give him the answer that he wanted. But mainly it was Charles's face—and Linda's—which floated nebulously in the queer, half-lit world she was in. Again she heard Linda's gay "Yes, of course, I'm taking part!" as if she was quite determined not to be left out. And then, later: "That will be black and blue by the morning!" as she regarded the bump on Judith's forehead. Judith stirred restlessly on her hot pillow. Suddenly, it seemed that Linda was a different person from the one whom she had known so long. Unfriendly, grasping—no, that was nonsense! Why should she be unfriendly to a girl who could never possibly rival her own charm and beauty? Or feel that Judith had something which she wanted to possess? And yet, with that strange clear-sightedness that comes in a wakeful night, Judith knew that it was so.

Or perhaps it was that Linda had resented Charles's insisting on being the one who took control and ordered her into her brother's car while he himself took Judith home. Perhaps she had misinterpreted that, whereas actually, of course, it had only been because it was necessary for her to get home as quickly as possible and Desmond's car might easily have broken down on the way—one could not tell what damage had been done with nothing more than a cursory look.

Charles had been very helpful, even kind, and she had been grateful and yet, when it came to thanking him, she had found it difficult. She must have sounded ungracious—and Charles had been amused. He had made allowances for her, treated her like a child as he so often did. She hated that. It robbed her of her self-confidence and left her feeling puzzled and muddled in her mind.

So often she had felt like that lately. As if everything that had been familiar was vanishing, and with it something of herself. And in the place of the old personality with whom she had been on such good terms a stranger was intruding. A stranger who seemed to take control and make her do things that, only a little while ago, she would never have done. Like buying all those dresses—a thing she had never wanted to do before. And, being almost painfully honest, she admitted to herself that she had wanted to get them. She had made the excuse of her forthcoming travels, but actually she had been conscious of some almost primitive urge to buy fine feathers.

And then she stopped puzzling about herself any more and thought of what she had bought. Those plain linen dresses that had suited her so well, the soft, flowery silk dresses and above all, that lovely white dress. She indulged in what is perhaps the most feminine day-dream of all—she saw herself in her pretty dress. But whereas another girl who had had a more natural upbringing would have dreamed also of a perfect companion who looked at her with adoration in his eyes, Judith was conscious only of a knowledge that, when she wore that dress, everything would be all right.

Shortly after, she fell into a deep sleep. But though she woke late she did not feel particularly refreshed, and when she went downstairs she experienced a lethargy which was entirely foreign to her. Miss Harriet looked up as she came in but made no comment. She poured out a cup of coffee as Judith sat down at the table, but did not offer any food, for which Judith was thankful. She had no desire at all to eat, but she would have done so rather than enter into an argument about it.

After a while Miss Harriet said:

"Charles came up to enquire after you. I told him that you were still sleeping and he left a message for you. He said that there was no need for you to worry about anything if you were feeling under the weather, but he would send Joe up later for any orders you might want to give."

Judith frowned, and was all the more annoyed with Charles because the action made her headache worse. Perhaps it was the headache which made it impossible for her to know for sure whether she was most irritated by the calm way in which he made it quite clear that he could do without her, or by his assumption that she would never be content if she could not give orders.

"I'll go down later," she said shortly, and Miss Harriet, who had doubted the wisdom of Charles's message, made no comment.

It was unusual for Judith to be in the house at this time of day, and she wandered restlessly from one room to another looking at her possessions with eyes that were perhaps more seeing than usual. There were many examples of her aunt's handiwork about the place. Embroidered cushions, *gros-point* chair covers, long embroidered bell-pulls. Things that Ravensdale women of every generation had always done. Things that she never had. But then, of course, they were not really Ravensdales. It was only that they had married into the family. And yet, she realised for the first time, she had their blood in her veins as well as that of her father's family. And even her father was not entirely Ravensdale. His mother had been a Grandon and neither of her parents, of course, had been Ravensdales. Odd that when there was all that family pride, actually one owed only a small amount of one's personality to the family whose name one bore. That must be so, and yet it was something that she had never thought of before. She walked slowly round the big drawing-room looking intently at the portraits. Her father and mother—she could not remember her mother, but she had picked up some of her father's scorn for the woman who had disappointed him so much. Now she looked with deeper vision and saw that her mother had a mouth that was made for laughter—and that her eyes were bitterly sad. She sighed and passed a generation back to her grandfather and his wife. Edwardians. Her grandfather, rather too stout and immensely complacent. Her grandmother—with a sense of shock, she looked closer. Strange she had never realised before what a dominating face it was. Slightly full in the lips as—she glanced across the room —her father had been. There was the same obstinate line to the chin as well.

Judith turned at the sound of the door opening and saw her aunt standing there.

"Aunt Harriet, what sort of a woman was your mother?" she asked, turning back to the picture.

Her aunt came and stood beside her.

"A woman who could not brook opposition in any form," she said slowly. "Surely you can see that. She got that from *her* mother—a Blackwood. The Blackwood men were noted for their unwillingness to accept any sort of authority over them. They were the sort that insisted on fighting duels after the law against them was passed, simply because they would not tolerate any interference with what they believed were their rightful privileges. One of them was killed that way. Of course Mother, being a woman, had no rights or privileges to speak of, and it must have been very galling to her. So, as marriage was the only escape for a girl of her position, she decided to make an early marriage. But one that suited herself. That was why she turned down an attractive young ruffian who was boon companion to her brother's, although she loved him, and married Father. And though he was my father, I always knew that he had very little strength of character. But he did not. Mother never let him guess. She was very clever, you see, and her head always ruled her, not her heart. Of course, if she had been in love with him she would never have made such a success of what could have been a hopeless situation. Emotion has a way of robbing a woman of judgment just at the time when she needs it most."

Her voice was very sad, and Judith, without turning, looked again at the portrait of her own parents.

"Did—did my mother love my father too much?" she asked in a low tone.

Miss Harriet linked her arm through Judith's.

"Yes, my dear, she did. Too much for her own good—and his. A woman who had cared a little less might have been less sensitive. There is not the same temptation to hurt someone who gives no sign to show that your shaft has gone home!"

Judith did not reply, but a moment later she gently disengaged her arm and said casually:

"I'll go down to the farm now!"

Miss Harriet did not attempt to dissuade her, but when the door had closed behind the girl, she turned back to the portraits and dared let herself hope, for the first time, that at last Judith was escaping from the bondage in which she had been for so long.

Judith went slowly down to the farm buildings, her head full of thoughts utterly alien to those which usually occupied her. The day and the work it provided were more than enough as a rule. But now it was people and the way they reacted on those around them that she thought about. To realise that one might inherit characteristics which had belonged to someone dead many years before one was born——it gave an odd feeling of insecurity. She must find out more about the women who had married past and gone Ravensdales——perhaps she might understand herself better then.

Suddenly, as she came nearer to the farm buildings, she realised that there was an odd sound going on—— the heavy pounding of feet, an occasional gasping breath——strange thuds.

Forgetting all her other puzzles, Judith hurried round the cow house in the direction from which the sounds were coming and stopped abruptly, gasping at what she saw.

For in the field behind the shed were two figures, Charles and young Joe Sellars. And they were fighting. Leaning over the fence were one or two of the farm hands, apparently completely indifferent to the fact that Joe was getting the worst of it——as he was bound to, seeing their relative ages and strength.

"Stop it at once!" she shouted, and the men at the fence turned sheepishly and began to edge away. But Charles took no notice. Methodically he countered every one of Joe's blind rushes and then scientifically planted his own blow with as little inconvenience to himself as possible.

"Stop it!" she shouted again, beating her fist on the top rail of the fence.

But at that moment Joe rushed at Charles with arms that flailed like a windmill, and Charles, neatly side-stepping, caught the boy on the chin and that was the end of it.

For a moment Charles stood, looking down thoughtfully at the boy. Then he bent and picked him up.

For the first time he appeared to notice Judith, and he nodded towards the latched gate.

"Open that, will you?" he asked coolly.

To her own amazement Judith found herself complying. Still carrying the inert form of the boy, Charles strode in the direction of the old pump. He put Joe down, soaked his own handkerchief under the pump and began to wipe the boy's face. After a moment Joe stirred and looked about him with dazed eyes. Then they fixed on Charles's, and a slow grin broke over his face.

"That was a peach, that was!" he said admiringly. "You don't half know your stuff, sir!"

"Yes. Well, I'll give you some coaching if you like," Charles offered, standing erect. "Now clear off and—don't forget!"

Joe scrambled to his feet, grinned, and ran off little the worse. Charles turned to Judith.

"Now then!" he said as if she were a troublesome child who was interrupting his work.

Judith, infuriated at his coolness, suddenly lost control of her temper.

"How dare you! How dare you!" she fumed.

Charles, his hands on his hips, stared down at her from the superiority of his great height.

"How dare I what?" he asked coolly.

"Fight like that—on my land!" she said furiously.

"I wasn't fighting," he told her with a patience that infuriated her still more. "I was giving young Joe a much-needed lesson—one that he won't forget in a hurry!"

"Nothing justified such brutality," she insisted.

"Brutality?" He shook his head. "Oh no. I could

have smashed Joe to pulp if I had wanted to. I have both more strength and more knowledge than he has. But you saw for yourself that I didn't—and that Joe himself owes me no grudge. He knew perfectly well that he has been asking for this ever since I came here, and that to-day was just the last straw."

"To-day?" she said sharply. "What has he done specially to-day?"

"Oh, that's between Joe and me," he said with maddening calm. "Don't you worry, though, there's no harm done. Except that Joe will probably indulge in a bit of hero-worship, which will be rather a bother."

"Hero-worship—because you knocked him out?" Judith said scornfully.

"Yes—it goes that way. A kid of Joe's age always has a weak spot for someone who can get the better of him by fair means—particularly when it is in the realms of physical strength."

"I don't believe it!" Judith said impatiently. "Why should anybody——"

"Ah—not anybody. A boy of that age. And it is something that I can understand and you can't because I experienced the same thing years ago, and you never have. Women see things differently."

"I don't want a lecture on psychology," Judith blazed. "Tell me at once what you were fighting about!"

And then, for the first time, she realised that Charles had a very strong chin. It jutted obstinately now and he said quietly:

"I am sorry, but—no!" and turned away.

Judith watched him go. She felt frustrated and humiliated. There was absolutely nothing that she could do about it, but at least she was determined on one thing. She *would* find out why he had fought young Joe.

She looked about her. The farm hands who had been watching had melted away, but she knew who they were and went in search of one of them.

"Tom, what had Joe done that annoyed Mr. Saxilby?" she asked curtly.

The man took off his battered old Panama hat and scratched his head.

"Well," he said slowly. "I reckon Mr. Saxilby could tell you better'n I could!"

So he was teaching her employees to defy her, was he? Judith set her teeth.

"Tom, you'll either tell me or—" she made a gesture with her head in the direction of the village—"you can find another job!"

"Well," he said slowly. "it was this way. Young Joe he mentioned a lady's name the way Mr. Saxilby didn't like, so he up and gave Joe a trouncing. Which is what he's been asking for. You don't need to worry, miss. Mr. Saxilby knew what he was doing and there won't be no more trouble with Joe now, miss!"

The man touched his hat respectfully and turned to get on with his work, but Judith did not move.

A lady! Linda, of course! Suddenly she remembered things that Desmond had said—"A working girl ought not to go out gadding to dances night after night!" With Charles, of course. She had known that subconsciously right from the beginning. And things Linda had done— that lovely dress she had worn. Of course it had been for Charles. The way they had paired off for the scavenger hunt.

Suddenly tears stung her eyes. Whichever way she turned, there was Charles making things difficult, robbing her of her self-confidence.

Charles must have been criticising her to Linda and that was why Linda was so unfriendly now. Charles had so won round her own employees that he had undermined her authority. He had tried to make out that people resented Windygates winning prizes at the local Agricultural Show.

Charles—Charles—Charles. And she could not get rid of him. She would be going away and he would be left here in charge. When she came back it would be even more difficult to get rid of him, because he would have dug himself in completely during her absence and have turned everybody even more against her so that she simply could not run the place without him.

The old Judith would have known what to do. There had been odd little bits of trouble in the past and she had dealt faithfully with them. But now——

The new Judith walked slowly back to the house. Her house. Her farm. And yet she felt lonely and an outcast, as if she were a stranger and Charles the master of Windygates.

Desmond rang up later in the day to ask how Judith was and seemed reassured when she told him that, except for the bruise, she was completely fit. None the less, he did not suggest a meeting, and Judith rang off with the feeling that in spite of Desmond's insistence that her refusal to marry him would not make any difference, actually it was bound to. In her simplicity it never occurred to her that Desmond might be deliberately trying to make her miss him. Nor did she attempt to analyse why she had said "no." For when Desmond had pointed out to Linda that there was no other man to whom Judith would give her confidence as she had done to him, he had been quite correct. Consequently, once she had got over her surprise at his suggestion, there was no reason at all why she should not turn to him. And if he had seen the advantage that it would be to him to be married to Judith for some time, that little glimpse he had had of something he had never seen in her before had increased his determination many times over. But he must not rush his fences.

The days passed. All Judith's pretty clothes had come down from London, but in spite of Miss Harriet's suggestion that she might wear at least some of them before they started on their journeyings, Judith simply packed them all away and seemed to forget all about them. All her eagerness to possess them seemed to have gone, and she was devoting as much time as ever to farm work, just as if they were not going away at all. It was a month now since Charles had come—the length of time that Miss Harriet had originally suggested he and Judith should work together—but it had proved to be impossible to book their passages as quickly as that and there was still another fortnight before they would sail. As Miss Harriet put both their passports away in her desk she felt suddenly discouraged, for a conviction came to her that they would not go at all.

She said as much to Mr. Bellairs, and he was silent.

"You think the same thing, don't you?" she insisted, and he nodded slowly.

"I do. Although I cannot tell you what makes me think so," he admitted. "But whether you go or whether you stay, there is one thing about which I am determined!"

"What?" she asked rather breathlessly.

He looked at her with tender, gently mocking eyes.

"You know perfectly well, my dear," he told her. "None the less, I will tell you so that you are under no misapprehension. As soon as Judith is twenty-one, you are going to marry me. What is more, you are going to live in my house and I am not going to live at Windygates. Do you quite understand?"

She dimpled bewitchingly, and laughed.

"It doesn't look as if I shall have much choice, does it?" she asked demurely.

"None at all, my darling," he told her firmly and took her into his arms. "This is what I ought to have done years ago, only——"

"Only I've got a lot of the same obstinacy that is Judith's curse!" she sighed. "Oh, Hugh, it does seem unfair that there should be such a thing as inherited tendencies! Surely everybody ought to start off with a clean sheet."

"Even then, environment would play its part," he pointed out. "And we should probably all be very simple and very dull souls, incapable of experiencing any very strong emotion at all! Do you think you would like a sort of jelly-fish existence?"

"How do you know jelly-fish aren't perfectly happy being jelly-fish?" she asked mutinously, and Hugh Bellairs laughed. Anything less like a jelly-fish than Harriet he could not well imagine, and knowing, as he did, that the richness of her personality owed no little to the sacrifice of years which she had made, he felt that he could even forgive Mark Ravensdale and his selfishness.

"I don't know," he admitted. "But some instinct tells me that I prefer to remain as I am! Are you going to tell Judith now that we are going to get married, or wait until after her birthday?"

Miss Harriet pondered.

"If you had asked me that when we were up in London I would have said 'now.' I felt I got closer to Judith in that short time than I ever have done before."

"Or since?" he asked, watching her closely.

She sighed.

"Or since. Hugh, I really did see signs of development and change in Judith then. Or I persuaded myself I did. But since we came back it seems to me that she has shut herself away not only from me but from everybody. She rarely goes to see the Enstones now, and they were her closest friends."

"Well, you're not sorry about that, are you?" he asked quizzically.

"No-o," she admitted. "You know how I've always felt about them. But at least it was an outlet for her, and I don't *think* she would ever marry Desmond."

"I sincerely hope not!" Mr. Bellairs said, evidently somewhat alarmed. "He's not a bad fellow really, but——" he shook his head. "I don't as a rule listen to gossip, but I have heard what I can only describe as circumstantial evidence about his habits which was not at all reassuring. He has been seen more than once at horse-race meetings, and it appears that he is neither lucky nor knowledgeable. My informant personally heard him make a bet of twenty-five pounds on a horse which was not placed. And neither he nor his sister has the money to be able to stand losses like that! The boy wants someone to take him in hand."

"But not Judith!" Miss Harriet said quickly.

"No, not Judith. Not any woman. Some man whom he respects and likes. You know, Harriet, respect sounds a chilly sentiment, but actually it's a basic need in any relationship that is to last. And perhaps, after all, it isn't so chilly! For it implies trust and confidence, and love itself without those would be torment!"

"Yes," Miss Harriet said softly, thinking of her brother and his wife. "They are the things Judith must be able to find in the man she marries if she is to be happy! It must be someone whom she knows will always play fair—oh!" Her hand flew up to her mouth. From the back of her mind came the memory of her first meeting with Charles. She had asked him if he thought that Judith would play fair, and he had said that whether she did or not, he would.

Mr. Bellairs looked at her thoughtfully.

"I see that you have remembered something interesting but that you have no intention of telling me," he commented. "That is one of the things I respect in *you*, Harriet. So many women are totally incapable of keeping their own counsel, but you have a discretion which, if you will forgive my saying so, is far more often found in my sex than your own."

"I expect so," Miss Harriet admitted meekly, and laughed. "Oh, Hugh, I was just bursting to tell you, but you are quite right, some things are better not said!"

He pulled her gently to him.

"You are a woman in a million," he declared. "You can not only accept a word of warning graciously, but you have a sense of humour which is just as acute if the point is against you as not! Listen, my dear, don't worry too much about Judith! You have the same blood in you and she has lived with you for a good many years. She cannot help having learned something from you!"

And Miss Harriet's eyes thanked him as much for the reassurance as for the compliment he had paid her.

For several days there was, if not actual peace at Windygates, at least no open conflict. Indeed, it seemed to Judith that Charles was going out of his way to be civil now. Possibly, she thought scornfully, he had suddenly realised how soon she would really be mistress of Windygates and, if he did intend marrying Linda, he would do his best to keep his job.

Anyhow, after having rather arbitrarily taken so much into his own hands, he now began to consult her on every point. And that, as it turned out, was the cause of the worst difference they had yet had.

That spring the young calves had shown a far greater proportion of bull calves than heifers and, as Charles knew from the records and from what Judith had said, she intended buying several more cows to make up for this. The question now arose as to where these should be purchased. Charles secretly wished that she would approach his brother on the subject, but felt that such a suggestion must come from her. And, it appeared, such an idea had never entered her head, for she announced her intention of buying locally.

"It does a cow no good to travel," she said with some truth. "Besides, I know more about local stock. For instance, Shawbury has some very good cows— they are the same strain as the bull that his brother-in-law, Heriot, won the prize with."

"Shawbury," Charles said slowly. That was the name of the farmer with whom Judith had argued that first day in Wyford. A civil enough man, but—if Charles had had to pick on any one man who believed that he owed Windygates and its owner a grudge, it was Shawbury. Shawbury and Heriot were, as Judith had said, brothers-in-law, but there was an even closer bond than that. Heriot had owed Shawbury a considerable amount of money. If, as was locally believed, Heriot owed his failure to Mark Ravensdale's enmity, then it followed that Shawbury blamed the Ravensdales for the fact that he had never been able to get his money back from Heriot.

"Well?" Judith said sharply.

Charles hesitated. There was another reason why he was troubled, but that he did not feel he could speak of yet to Judith in her present frame of mind.

"When had you thought of making the deal?" he asked.

Judith's brows lifted.

"It is made already," she said shortly. "I have been in touch with Shawbury for some time. This morning I telephoned to him and confirmed the deal."

"I see," Charles said slowly. He could have told her that, for the sake of the farm, it would be wiser to present at least a semblance of unity towards the rest of the farming fraternity, and that, in fact, she had treated him most unfairly. However, such an attitude would have done no good, so he merely said rather earnestly: "I would be glad if you would defer the actual delivery for a few days."

"But why?" she asked belligerently.

"Because—" he began and stopped, shaking his head. He was up against the same trouble as he had been before. Lack of proof. Without that, it would be worse than useless to present mere suspicion to Judith. "It would be more convenient if you were to delay a day or two," he said, knowing, as he spoke, how unconvincing it must sound to her.

"On the contrary," Judith said briskly, "I intend going over to-day to have a look at the herd. I want four cows. I shall probably bring a couple back with me!"

Suddenly she realised that Charles was breathing very heavily as if he had been running a great distance. His lips were pressed closely together and his nostrils flared ever so slightly. He was really angry, Judith saw, and with sudden recklessness she knew that she wanted to make him still more angry.

"You can come as well, if you like," she said indifferently. "I am sure you would like to give me the advantage of your great knowledge!"

For a moment he stared down at her with eyes that hardly seemed to see her. Then he shook his head.

"No, I have another job to do!" and turned on his heel.

For a moment she debated whether she should not call him back and insist on his accompanying her. Then she decided not to. He had said he would not come and she knew him well enough to know that he would not retreat from that.

"See that the cattle van is ready for me in half an hour!" she ordered curtly as she passed one of the men.

He touched his forehead and Judith went back to the house to tell Miss Harriet what were, actually, somewhat altered plans. She had not intended going over until the following day—if Charles had not interfered. But he should, he must, learn who gave orders at Windygates. She telephoned through to Shawbury to tell him of her intentions, and there was a little silence at the other end.

"Is that all right?" she asked sharply, and could have declared she heard a slight chuckle from the other end.

"Suits me very well," Shawbury assured her smoothly. "Very well indeed!"

"Very well, then, I'll be over in about an hour!"

But when she got down to the yard she found that, instead of the van being ready, Charles and another man were bending over its open bonnet, poking into the engine.

"What's the matter?" Judith asked sharply.

Charles spoke without turning.

"Not quite sure," he said in a muffled voice. "She was coughing a bit—might be a choked jet."

Judith bit her lip, impatient of the delay.

"Is it anything you can do, or must it go to the garage?"

Charles turned his head slightly.

"I can do it," he said with exaggerated patience, or so it seemed to Judith. "But it will take me some little time—twenty minutes, probably."

Judith nodded and climbed into the driver's seat to wait. She would have liked to watch Charles more closely, suspecting him of using a time-worn ruse to delay her, but with the other man standing there, there was little that she could see and, from the way in which Charles was giving the man orders, it looked as if he really needed his help. At last Charles stood erect.

"Will you start her up?" he requested.

Judith pulled out the self-starter and the car started up instantly.

"Now rev her up." Charles stood listening with his

488

head on one side. "That sounds better!" he declared. "I think you will be all right now!"

Without a word Judith drove off and Charles watched her go, but no sooner was she out of sight than he raced for his own car, and was out on to the main road in time to see Judith vanish round her first corner. He did not follow her. He needed to get to Shawbury's farm, almost twenty miles away, before her without her seeing him. And the only way that he could do that was to take narrow lanes at a speed which would beat hers on the more direct main road. He only hoped to heaven that the man he had got to meet there would do his part, otherwise—he grimaced at the thought, and his foot came hard down on the accelerator.

Judith admitted to herself that she did not really like Shawbury. More than once he had gone out of his way to annoy her, but that, she considered, was beside the point. He had something that she wanted and intended to have. He was perfectly willing to deal with her at a reasonable price—far more reasonable than she had thought likely. Nothing that Charles or anyone else said was going to stand in her way. None the less, there was something about his dark eyes that she disliked. They were insolent and amused although his words were civil enough.

She made her selection, wrote her cheque and decided which of the cows she would take with her. Shawbury, with the aid of one of his sons, separated them from the herd and drove them, protesting, to the yard where Judith had left her van.

"Now, if you'll open her up——" Shawbury began, and stopped, a scowl bringing his heavy black brows into one straight line. "Now what——" he began.

For the first time Judith realised that two cars had driven up. From one a man got out whom she recognised as the local Government vet. From the other—Charles.

Mr. Trent came straight to the point.

"You can't move those cows, Shawbury," he said curtly. "Take them back!"

"And why?" the big man asked belligerently.

"Because that cow you've so carefully segrated in the shack by the wood has got foot-and-mouth!" Mr. Trent told him. "Nothing must be moved from the farm— you've got yourself into a nice bit of trouble now, Shawbury! You know as well as I do that you ought to have reported——"

"I wasn't sure!" the man said surlily. "There's many a thing can ail a cow and it isn't foot-and-mouth."

"There's absolutely no doubt about it in this case," the vet declared. "It's well advanced—go on, back with those cows."

For a moment Shawbury hesitated. Then, with a baleful glance at Charles, whom he evidently regarded as the author of all his troubles, he turned away, driving the animals before him.

Judith, suddenly sick and trembling, sat down rather abruptly on a wooden bench.

"You've had a lucky escape, Miss Ravensdale," Mr. Trent said cheerfully. "Thanks to Mr. Saxilby here! If you'd once got those cows on to your land—well, you might have had an outbreak as well. At the least, you'd have been included in the quarantine. As it is, you're outside the radius. But I'll have to ask you to leave your van here. I'll see to it that the tyres and the underside are properly disinfected, and I'll have it run to Windygates. Don't forget your boots, either. I'll see to them as well if you like to take them off. Make doubly sure. Saxilby will drive you home."

In an incredibly short time they were on the return journey. Charles, his face set and sphinx-like, stared straight ahead and drove in complete silence. Judith, crouching by his side, did not speak either until—

"Stop, please, will you?" she asked, and Charles, with a nod, ran off the road into a little wood, dappled with sunlight.

Judith drew a deep breath.

"He did know?" she asked.

Charles nodded.

"Must have," he said shortly.

"Yet he was deliberately allowing me to take animals

that would more than likely have infected our herd—possibly others as well."

"Yes," Charles agreed heavily. "Just that!"

"But why?" She brought her clenched fist down on the edge of the door. "Why, why, why! People don't do things like that! But he has! And I must know why?"

Charles looked into her flushed, troubled face. This was it, he thought grimly. There was no hiding the truth any longer, and he, of all men, had got to be the one who shattered the last bastion of her old, familiar world.

CHAPTER SEVEN

STARING straight ahead, Charles told Judith all that he knew and she listened in silence, neither questioning the reliability of his information nor attempting to contradict it. Charles had the satisfaction, if satisfaction it was, of knowing that he was carrying conviction.

At last the whole miserable story was finished, but still she did not speak, and at last Charles turned to her. He knew that what he had told her must be a terrible shock, but he was not prepared for the white bleakness of her face or the misery in the dark eyes that met his.

Slowly her lips parted and a long shuddering sigh passed them.

"I wish—I were dead!" she said in a muted, exhausted voice.

Charles put a warm, protecting arm round her and drew her close. She was shivering violently and made no resistance.

"No, child, no!" he said vigorously. "You wish nothing of the sort! This is a bad time for you—there is nothing so horrible as to lose one's faith. But we are not gods, you know. Only blundering humans who see things from our own point of view only and so make mistakes. Can't you see that all that has happened is due to that? Both your father and Shawbury——"

"Does that excuse it?" she asked broodingly. "Does it? Not even trying to play fair—no, nothing excuses that," as Charles did not reply. "And I am as bad as any of them—ever since you came here you've been trying to make me see that, haven't you?"

"It was like my confounded impertinence!" Charles said angrily. "Who am I——"

Judith shook her head.

"At the back of my mind I knew all the time that you were right," she admitted. "I knew that you were playing fair—and trying to make me. That's why I've been so beastly. It—it is so difficult to admit that you are in the wrong!"

"The most difficult thing in the world," he agreed emphatically. "And, in any case, it was not anything like all your fault. You've been taught not to see the other man's point of view."

Judith did not reply. She only sighed again and leaned forward, her elbows on her knees, her face buried in her hands.

"I can't go on!" she said in a muffled voice. "I can't! Everybody hates me—I shall never be able to trust anyone again!"

"Yes, you will," he contradicted firmly. "I imagine that there has been quite a lot of sympathy for Shawbury in the past, but that is all finished. He has put himself completely in the wrong now. The man must have been mad to do a thing like that—he knows perfectly well what the penalties are. But quite apart from the legal aspect of it, he's made every man his enemy! Don't you realise all the sympathy will be for you now—admittedly because the other farmers will see themselves as potential victims along with you! It's a chance, Judith, to make a new start! Don't bear malice—don't lose courage! Take the lead now with all the precautions that are necessary. Stand by your fellow farmers and lend them a hand. They will never forget it, and the past will stay where it belongs—in the past!"

"What must I do?" she asked wearily.

"See to it that instructions are properly carried out so that we stamp this out as quickly as possible. Make them all understand that we are in this together even though, as it happens, we are just outside the radius. And if it comes to the worst and herds have to be destroyed, tell them—your tenants, at least—that you will help them financially to get started again. Don't you see, Judith, it *is* your chance."

She was very still, and he waited with bated breath. Had she courage to seize this chance? Could she find the strength to turn the evil of the past into the good of the future? He had done his best, but the final decision must be with her.

Suddenly she leaned back in her seat, her eyes closed.

"I can't," she whispered. "I can't! They wouldn't trust me. Why should they expect to get anything good from a Ravensdale? They've never trusted me, partly because of that and partly because I am a girl—if I had been the boy my father wanted——"

"No!" he said positively. "You cannot tell what would have happened if you had been a boy! It might well be that you would have clashed so badly with your father that you would have felt compelled to leave home. You must accept things as they are, Judith!"

She hesitated, evidently thinking this over.

"Yes, that is all one can do," she agreed. "I must see this through—or you must for me, for I shall be away. But, when I come back——" she drew a deep sigh, "I shall sell Windygates!"

"No"' he said sternly. "You cannot do that! It is running away!"

"No," she said dully. "Just—facing up to things as they are! The way you said."

Charles could find nothing to say. Only the hand that still lay on the steering wheel clenched so that the knuckles showed white and shining. Judith was too immersed in her own thoughts to notice how strained his face was, that twice his lips parted as if he were going to speak, only to be closed again in an even firmer line.

At last he said deliberately:

"Judith, at least take no definite steps yet about selling."

She laughed drearily.

"I can't" she pointed out. "I'm still under age!"

There was no bitterness in the remark, but not for

the first time he realised how hard his advent had been on her. His teeth gritted.

"I think when you get away you will see your problems more clearly from a distance than you can now close at hand. And when you come back, I promise you that things will be a lot easier than they are now—they will have sorted themselves out. And I will do everything that lies in my power to see that they do. But if, when you come back, you still say you cannot go on, then——"

She turned and looked at him gravely.

"Then?" she asked.

Charles bit his lip.

"Then—will you give me the first refusal of Windygates?" he asked quietly.

"You?" She was alert in an instant. "But—you could not afford to buy Windygates, could you?"

"Yes, I could—provided you are willing to take a fair price for it," he explained.

"But I thought—you didn't tell me—I thought you had to work——" she stammered.

"People are disinclined to take a man seriously if he does not have to work. I think they are wrong. At least in my own case. Because I have been able to choose the job I really want to do I can put my whole heart into it."

She nodded as if she agreed.

"Oh, I wish I had known!" she said earnestly. "I wish you had told me!"

His eyes were curious.

"Would it have made so much difference?" he asked.

"Of course it would!" Her emphasis left no doubt of her sincerity. "Don't you see, if I had realised that you really loved farming, that you had no—no——"

"No axe to grind?" he suggested. "Yes, I see what you mean, but it is a point of view that never occurred to me. Besides, can you think of any occasion in our rather stormy joint history when I could have said, casually: 'By the way, I'm quite well off, I don't have to work for you or anyone else!' Can you imagine what would have happened?"

The faintest of smiles curved Judith's lips. Then they grew grave again.

"No, I suppose you couldn't," she agreed. "All the same——" she stopped abruptly. "Does anyone else know, Charles?"

He knew that she was completely unconscious of the fact that, for the first time, she had called him by his Christian name, and he made no comment on it, although he realised that it implied a trust in him which had been so flagrantly missing before.

"You mean round here?" he asked. "I should think it is most unlikely. I certainly have not spoken of it. And surely, if anyone did know, it would have got back to you?"

"Yes, I suppose so," she agreed, but as he drove the car on to the road again and turned for home, she was very silent.

He wondered what she was thinking about—Shawbury, her father, her own aching desire to cut loose and start fresh. Poor child, she had plenty with which to occupy her mind!

But it was none of these things which was troubling Judith. She had remembered that evening on which Linda had revealed the fact that she already knew Charles by sight when he came to Windygates. Her friends in Sussex had pointed him out to her. They had told her who his brother was, so surely they had passed on some facts about Charles himself. That he was rich? Surely that was more than likely!

"Maybe one shouldn't marry for money, but heaven protect me from loving where it isn't!"

She could hear the echo of Linda's voice. Was it just Linda's luck that she had fallen in love with a wealthy man? Or—could you make yourself love to suit?

"I couldn't!" Judith told herself positively. "But——"

And hated herself for her suspicion of her friend.

Even before nightfall it was evident that Charles was right. Urgent telephoning on the part of Mr. Trent had spread the news, and all movement of cattle in the prescribed area was forbidden. He must have explained

495

the circumstances pretty clearly, for before long, calls began to come through to Windygates. Either Charles or Judith seemed to be answering the telephone all the evening, and it became quite clear that personal indignation against Shawbury was blended with genuine feeling against the way in which he had tried to injure her.

More than once, when Charles was speaking, he called Judith over and insisted on a repetition of what had been said. And each time, in addition to the sympathy that she gave, Judith added:

"We are in this together, you know, and I will do every possible thing I can to help. While I am away, Mr. Saxilby will have complete authority to act on my behalf."

At last, well past eleven, it seemed probable that there would be no more calls. Charles stretched and yawned.

"Well, that's that!" he said with a certain amount of satisfaction. "I don't think there is anything else that can be done. If you can cope for a day or two I'd like to go round with Trent. I'll take all the necessary precautions, of course, in case there is going to be a really bad outbreak, but I've hopes that it is going to be limited. After all, Shawbury's farm is fairly well isolated, and there have been no movements of animals from it for a good many weeks. Heavens, the man must be mad—of course, he will stick to it that he didn't think it was foot-and-mouth, but—he's for it!"

"Yes," Judith said soberly. "Poor Mrs. Shawbury."

"H'm," Charles said thoughtfully. "I don't know. I have an idea she was in it as much as he was—still, there it is. I had to tell Trent—although I was by no means sure. It was a risk. If I had been wrong, Shawbury would have been very awkward."

"That was why you wanted me to wait," Judith said slowly. "Why didn't you tell me—no, I know. I wouldn't have believed it. I couldn't have, you know. I hardly can now, although I know it is true!" Suddenly she thought of something. "Charles, was there anything wrong with the cattle truck?"

"The engine? No, I'm afraid there wasn't," he admitted. "But I had been on the telephone to Trent, and it was impossible for him to get there quickly enough if you started straight away. So I had to delay you. I'm sorry!"

"You did it very cleverly," she told him gravely, and as she met his eyes, they both laughed. Charles came nearer and touched her lips with the tips of his fingers.

"Do you know, that is the first time I have seen you laugh!" he said wonderingly. "You should do it again, it suits you!"

"Does it?" Judith whispered.

"It certainly——" Charles broke off and clapped his hand to his forehead. "Good heavens, I've just remembered, I was dining with the Enstones! And I haven't even let them know that I wasn't coming! Phew! You'll have to think up some excuses for me, Judith!"

Judith turned away.

"I think your own apologies will be sufficient," she said very quietly, and vanished into the shadows.

Charles made a step as if to go after her. Then he drew back. Nor could anyone have told from his face at that moment whether his thoughts were pleasant or the reverse. There was a strange lack of expression about it which might have given the impression that he himself found it impossible to look even the shortest way into the future. That was all.

"Of all the disgusting tricks!" Desmond said hotly. "I hope Shawbury catches it hot and strong!"

"I expect he will," Linda said slowly. "But that won't do anyone much good if it really spreads. You're lucky, Judith, to be so far away from the outbreak."

"Not really so very far," Judith said soberly. "You know how easily it can spread. Still, of course, we shall do our very best. Charles is wonderful."

The eyes of brother and sister met in complete understanding. They were sitting together in the Enstones' small private sitting-room, having tea. Desmond had seen Judith pass and had insisted on her coming in, although she had protested that she really hadn't time.

"Nonsense!" he had put his arm through hers and

pulled her gently towards the house. "We see so little of you these days that the next thing will be you don't even remember who we are!"

"Silly!" she said lightly, and because she knew that she had been deliberately avoiding both him and Linda, she allowed him to persuade her.

And, of course, Shawbury and his misdeeds were the first topic of conversation.

"It was certainly fortunate that he found out about it in the nick of time," Linda agreed. "Otherwise, you would have been in it up to the neck—it wouldn't have made you any more popular either, Judith."

Judith's face clouded. It was the first time that her lack of popularity in the district had ever been spoken of so openly—it hurt rather to know that other people had realised it although she had been too blind.

"That's what I don't like about this set-up," Desmond said slowly.

Linda turned slowly towards him, her lips smiling ever so slightly.

"What do you mean, Des?" she asked softly.

He shrugged his shoulders.

"Just that Saxilby has properly got himself into everybody's good books somewhat at Judith's expense," he said promptly.

"Oh, no!" Judith said quickly. "Really, there is nothing like that about it."

Desmond shrugged his shoulders.

"Well, of course, if you are satisfied—" he said doubtfully, and then, catching his sister's warning glance, knew that he had said enough.

"Can I give you a lift?" he asked Judith as he stood up. "I'm going into Wyford."

"No, thank you," Judith said rather quickly. "I was just walking down to the village, that's all. It won't take me a minute." She stood up as well. "But I really must be going."

"No!" Linda spoke so slowly that it was almost a drawl. "Sit down a minute, Judith! I want to talk to you for a moment!"

Judith looked uncertainly from one to the other, sensitive to something almost electric in the still air of the little room.

"Well, I must be going," Desmond said hurriedly. "Be seeing you, Judith."

"Yes, of course," she agreed rather breathlessly.

Then he had gone and she was alone with Linda.

"Sit down," Linda said slowly, lighting another cigarette from the end of the previous one. "Have one?"

"No, thank you. I don't smoke," Judith said briefly.

"No, of course you don't, I forgot." Linda smiled. "Fancy forgetting a thing like that when I know you so well!"

Judith moved restlessly.

"Linda, really, I am in a hurry," she said.

"I shan't be long," Linda assured her. Her eyes narrowed. "Judith, do you think that two women ever know one another sufficiently well to be completely frank with one another?"

Judith laughed nervously.

"Yes, I suppose they do," she said uncertainly.

"And you and I have known each other almost all our lives," Linda mused. "That ought to be enough, surely! Well, Judith, what I want to say is quite brief and simple. It's just this—don't lose your heart to Charles, however wonderful he is!"

"Linda!" Judith was so obviously startled that for a second Linda wondered if she had made a mistake and put an idea into her head that had not been there before. But she was never one to doubt her own actions very long, so she went on confidently:

"I know it is quite shocking of me to say such a thing, but, as I said, we are old friends, and I've no wish to see you get hurt."

"But why should I?" Judith protested. "I mean——"

Linda stubbed out her cigarette.

"I hope not. But I'm not going to take any chances! Judith, has it never seemed strange that a man in Charles's position should not only take on such a job but also should stick it in spite of the way in which you have treated him? Oh, it's no good your pretending! You've behaved outrageously and you know it! Well, isn't it ob-

499

vious then? Charles stayed on because he had something to gain by doing so!"

"What?" Judith asked with a defiance that did not even convince herself, let alone Linda.

"Windygates, of course!" Linda said coolly. "You must know that sooner or later a man of Charles's type wants roots—something permanent and established. Charles's father left him money."

"You did know that!" Judith interrupted, and it was Linda's turn to be surprised. She had no idea that Judith had learned of it. In fact, she had intended to use it as one of her most convincing arguments. However—

"Of course I did! Charles told me as soon as—" she checked herself, but Judith was insistent.

"You'd better go on!" she said stonily. "You've said too much now to stop."

Linda shrugged her shoulders.

"Perhaps I have," she agreed. "Very well, then! When he realised that there are some shrews who are untamable and that it would be better to buy the place than— get it through marriage. He is the sort of man who prefers to be master in his own home, you see!"

"By marriage!" Judith whispered. "Oh, no. I know he would like to own Windygates, but he couldn't have been so——"

"So practical?" Linda shrugged. "Why not? Really, Judith, for a girl who has never troubled to look at anything from any point of view but her own, I must say I think you expect a lot from other people! Charles knows what he wants and he intends to get it! Is he any different from you or me or any of us? A little more clever, perhaps, one has to admit that! He has the patience to approach his objective obliquely so that it is not too obvious—he will always get what he wants! You will sell!"

"But—but you speak as if it is Charles's fault that we've got a bad name," Judith said quickly. "Surely you can see that if he really wanted to make it impossible for me to stay he would not have interfered over Shawbury. He'd have left me to get into a mess that would have made everybody absolutely hate me!"

Linda laughed scornfully.

"Don't be a fool, Judith! He has every interest in keeping Windygates clear of infection! He's looking to the future, my dear, when it is his own, not worrying about you! But, as Desmond pointed out, he has achieved popularity at your expense! Oh yes, Charles is clever, he knows how to extract the last bit of advantage from a situation."

"You sound as if you admire him for it!" Judith commented.

Linda raised her brows.

"But I do, my dear!" she said with convincing earnestness. "It is one of the characteristics that I admire in any man! It is particularly desirable in a husband! These days, more than ever before, a woman wants a man who knows how to look after his own interests—and hers. And I've always wanted Windygates! I think it is delightful—although you have never made the most of it! I shall use the big drawing-room far more, for instance. I tell you one thing, Judith—" She got up, flicking an odd piece of cigarette from her dress, "you will have the satisfaction of knowing that the place is in the hands of people who really value it and know how to look after it!"

Judith did not reply. Her lips were pressed very tightly together, her eyes burning. For a moment she faced Linda scornfully and the older girl's eyes fell. But she covered that by saying rather impatiently:

"Really, Judith, you must try to take a more realistic view of life! After all, you're not a child any more."

But she was talking to the empty air. Judith had turned on her heel and gone out of reach of her tongue. Linda shrugged her shoulders. Really, it had been too easy! Judith, for all her arrogance, was extraordinarily simple! Nor had she any fears either that Judith would ask for confirmation that they were going to be married or, when it came to the point, that she would refuse to sell at Charles's price. Pride would forbid the one and sheer inability to stand the strain would compel the other.

She had no compunction about what she had done.

At least in one thing she agreed with Miss Harriet—that Judith had never had a fair chance to enjoy life. Well, once she had sold Windygates, there was no reason why she should not have a marvellous time! She could marry Desmond, and if she had the sense to tie up her capital in such a way that he could not touch it, he would make a delightful husband.

Linda began to feel that she had really been something of a benefactor to Judith.

Judith lay face down among the bracken in her secret sanctuary. She was very still and her eyes were dry and burning with tears that would not be shed.

She felt as if she had touched the very depths of humiliation and disillusion. She could see no good in anything or anybody, least of all herself.

Of course, really she had always known that Linda was pretty hard, but she had never before realised just how hard. Her protestations that she was speaking for Judith's good were just nonsense. There was only one thing that prompted any action on Linda's part—her own interests. And Charles, she said, was just the same.

But Linda said that he was more clever than most, and of course she was right. He could contrive to turn black into white if it suited him. Her first impression had been right. She should never have let him persuade her to trust him. But now it was too late to think about that. And why he had wanted to gain her trust was so obvious now. He wanted her to be off her guard so that he could have a free hand to ingratiate himself with the other farmers. The more difficult he could make it for her to stay, the cheaper he could hope to get Windygates. Only, sometimes he himself was off his guard and she saw the real man. Secretly, he laughed at her and despised her. He treated her like a child—or, what was it Linda had said? A shrew that could not be tamed.

A muffled sob broke from her lips. Linda pretended that she, Judith, might be on the verge of losing her heart to Charles, but there had never been, she told herself, such a possibility, and now she hated him with all her strength. If he were here, she would tell him.

"Judith, my dear little girl, what is it?" Charles *was* there, kneeling beside her, touching her shoulder. How like him, she thought angrily, to sneak up on her and catch her at a disadvantage!

She rolled over and sat up.

"I am not your little girl and there is nothing the matter!" she said coldly. "I have just been—thinking."

He stood erect, surveying her with puzzled, troubled eyes.

"Will you tell me what about?" he asked gently.

Judith stood up, brushing bits of leaves from her.

"Certainly," she said deliberately. "I have been making plans for when I come back to England—if I do."

"If you do?" he shot back. "But——"

"I have definitely decided that I shall sell Windygates," she told him. "But—I am afraid that I shall not be able to give you the first refusal of it. You see, I really hardly think that would be fair to me!"

"What do you intend doing?" he asked quietly.

"Doing? Oh, I shall put it up to auction!" she said lightly. "One stands a much better chance of getting a good price that way, don't you think?"

"Yes—possibly," he agreed. "But you have no control over who buys it, remember! You might see it go to a man who regards it as nothing more than a commercial proposition and who will wring the last ounce out of your land instead of nursing it."

He saw the quick spasm of pain that twisted her face, and knew that he had pierced the veil of indifference that she wore so unconvincingly. Then her face hardened.

"I shall not be here to see it, so it will not matter," she told him with studied indifference.

"I wonder?" he said slowly. "Judith, at least tell me what has made you change your mind. Something has happened—something, surely, that has made you—" he shook his head and went on slowly: "If I were not afraid of making a bad situation even worse, I should say 'unhappy,' but I am sure you will deny that!"

"Of course I do!" she said promptly. "No, it is just

that I have had time to think things over now and, as I said, I don't think it would be fair to myself to take the first price offered for Windygates. If you want it enough, you will pay for it!"

"I expect I shall," he admitted. "But I must warn you that there are circumstances in which I shall not want it at all!"

"Oh!" she said blankly. "What circumstances?"

"No!" he shook his head. "I'm not going to tell you that unless—first of all—you tell me who it is that has been dribbling out some vile poison about me—and what it was!"

"You are quite mistaken—there was nothing—I told you—" Each sentence was begun but never finished. Linda had been quite right in thinking that Judith would never repeat what she had said. Pride made it impossible to tell a man that one had been suspected of falling in love with him.

"I see!" he said shortly. "Well, if you will not tell me yourself, there is only one thing for it. I shall have to find out myself! And," he leaned a little towards her, "rest assured, I shall!"

"You won't!" she said defiantly, and then, seeing that she had betrayed herself into admitting that he was right, added hastily: "There is nothing to find out!"

"No?" he asked thoughtfully. "Then why are you shaking as if you had got the ague?"

"Oh—!" Suddenly she stamped her foot. "I hate you! I wish I had never set eyes on you—everything was all right until you came."

"No," he said deliberately. "It wasn't! But one of these days I promise you that everything will be all right for you! Won't you believe me?"

"I will never trust you or anyone else so long as I live!" she declared passionately, and ran away as quickly as she could. But the ground was rough and Charles's legs longer than hers.

"No!" he said sternly. "This time you are not going to run away until you have listened to what I have to say! Because that is your trouble, Judith! You will not stand your ground when you are face to face with anything unpleasant. And until you do that you will never be on good terms with yourself! Listen, my dear!" His voice became infinitely persuasive, utterly gentle. "I asked you to give me the first refusal of Windygates because I believe that, in your present mood, you might sell it to the first comer only to regret it for the rest of your life. It is your home, Judith! There could never be another place like it to you! And I promise you this, if I buy it from you, I will sell it back to you at any time you like for three-quarters of the price I pay you for it! Judith, Judith, don't you see it's you I'm thinking of—won't you trust me?"

"Why should I?" she asked hardly. "To me it looks as if you are trying to persuade me not to auction the place so that you will get it cheap! But—if you can give me any single reason why I should trust you—well, I'll listen!"

He looked broodingly into her face as if he were searching there for something, but evidently he did not find it, for he shook his head.

"No, it wouldn't do any good," he told her. "There is a reason."

"Well, what is it?" she demanded, her hands behind her back, her arrogant young head in the air.

"You are too much of a child to understand," he said quietly. "One day, perhaps——"

Judith laughed.

"You are clever, you know! Linda said you were!"

"Linda—" he said sharply, but this time Judith had made her escape and he let her go.

Once she was sure that he had not followed her she slowed down. She was breathless, but from her encounter rather than because she had been running. She was very angry with herself, too, for having mentioned Linda's name. Not that it really mattered, of course! No doubt Linda would tell him all about their interview anyhow. Or would she? Would Charles be pleased to know just how far his plans had been revealed to her? Or had he himself dictated what Linda was to say to her so that she would realise just how impossible it was for her to stay on at Windygates? She did not know, and her brain seemed on fire as she tried to puzzle it all out.

Vaguely she realised that Linda's had been essentially a woman's approach to the situation, but what she did not realise was that in one thing at least Linda had lied. She really did admire what she believed to be Charles's cleverness, but it had been a long time before she had been able to work out to her own satisfaction just what motives activated him. But at last everything had seemed perfectly clear to her—so clear that it had hardly seemed to her that she lied when telling Judith that Charles himself had told her.

She walked slowly back to the house, and now her head was full, not of Charles and what he had said, but of her own plans.

Somehow or other she must make it quite clear to both Linda and Charles that it did not matter what they did, neither of them had the power to hurt her.

Suddenly she realised that there was a car standing outside the house which she recognised as that of the local bank manager. With a little frown she decided that she did not want to see him just then. He was an extremely good-natured man, but rather talkative and always so tremendously interested in the affairs of what he called "the young people." She would go round to the back of the house—anyway, it would not matter, because doubtless it was Aunt Harriet whom he had come to see.

But suddenly her aunt came to the door of the small living-room and called her.

"Judith—I'm so glad! Mr. Tiverton wants to see you for a moment."

There was no escape, so Judith went slowly in and greeted the bank manager. But this time there was nothing effusive in his manner. Indeed, he greeted Judith very soberly, and Miss Harriet came to his assistance, since he was obviously reluctant to come to the point.

"A cheque for a hundred pounds has been presented to the bank, Judith, and Mr. Tiverton would like to have your assurance that it really is your signature. Will you show my niece, Mr. Tiverton?"

He fumbled in his wallet.

"Of course—I am sure it is all right, but—rather a large amount, you know—and one cannot be too careful! None the less, I felt it would be more discreet if I were to ask you personally."

Judith held out her hand. Her heart was thudding uncomfortably, and for a moment she could not make herself look at it. She knew perfectly well that she had not made out a cheque for that amount at all lately.

"Pay D. Enstone, Esq.—" The words blurred. Never in her life had she made out a cheque in Desmond's favour. She realised that they were watching her, waiting for her to speak. She moistened her lips with her tongue.

"Yes," she said clearly, "I signed that! There is nothing wrong with it at all, Mr. Tiverton!"

CHAPTER EIGHT

THERE was a silence that could be felt in the sun-filled room. It was perfectly obvious that neither Miss Harriet nor Mr. Tiverton believed Judith.

Mr. Tiverton coughed uneasily.

"Miss Ravensdale, this is very difficult for me to say, for I know that you and Mr. Enstone have been friends for a very long while, but—you are quite sure that it is not just because of that very fact that you are making such a statement?"

Judith's small body stiffened and her chin grew obstinate. So like her father, Miss Harriet thought anxiously. Opposition had always had the very worst effect on them, however justified it might be.

"I don't think I understand you," Judith said coldly.

Mr. Tiverton wiped his forehead with his immaculate handkerchief and looked appealingly at Miss Harriet, but she shook her head. Only too well she knew that there was nothing she could do now.

"It is not easy to make myself clear without—" he began diffidently. "However—what I mean is this: were it not for the statement you have just made, my opinion

507

would be that this signature is a forgery—and not a very good one!"

"Oh?" Judith said indifferently, glancing down again at the cheque which she held. "I agree it isn't a very good signature, but I wrote it in rather a hurry with a different pen, so I expect that is why." She handed the cheque back to Mr. Tiverton. "Is there anything else?"

"No," he said uncertainly. "No——" and glanced again at Miss Harriet.

With a sigh, she turned to Judith. It was useless, but——

"You must understand that Mr. Tiverton only has your well-being at heart, Judith," she began.

"Quite, quite!" he agreed hurriedly.

"Consequently, although I am sure he would not insist on being told, I think he would be reassured if you would explain how it came about that you did make out such a big cheque in Desmond's favour."

Judith shrugged her shoulders. Not for a moment did she believe that Mr. Tiverton was thinking of anything but his own position as manager of the local bank. He had no intention of jeopardising that, she was perfectly sure. And, of course, he was reluctant to offend her, his biggest client, so he was getting Aunt Harriet to ask questions that he did not like to.

"I don't mind in the least," she said coolly. "Desmond and I are engaged. We intend getting married as soon as I am of age. In the meantime, during my absence, I want him to do some shopping for me. That cheque is to cover his purchases. Now are you satisfied, Mr. Tiverton?"

"Yes, of course, Miss Ravensdale," he said hurriedly, obviously torn between relief and the fear that he had offended. "That is a perfectly reasonable explanation. You must allow me to congratulate you."

"Thank you," Judith said shortly. "I should like to make it clear to you, though, that this is a private matter and one which would not have been spoken of but for your—your reluctance to accept my unsupported word!" She looked straight at him with hard, unfriendly eyes, and the bank manager looked uncomfortable.

"I am sure no one regrets more than I—of course you can rely on me not to let your confidence go any farther," he said hurriedly.

"I hope so," Judith said with a nod that carried dismissal with it.

Hurriedly Mr. Tiverton said good-bye to Miss Harriet and left the two women together.

Judith shrugged her shoulders.

"What a silly, interfering old man he is!" she said irritably.

"No, he's nothing of the sort," Miss Harriet said quietly. "He performed a difficult, thankless task as well as possible, in the circumstances. You did not make it easier for him, you know."

"Why should I?" Judith asked. "He annoyed me!"

"That was perfectly obvious," Miss Harriet commented. "However, never mind Mr. Tiverton for a moment! You were not telling the truth, Judith!"

Judith did not reply, and her aunt went on:

"You neither made out that cheque, nor are you engaged to Desmond!"

For answer, Judith walked slowly over to the telephone and asked for the Enstones' number.

"Des?" she asked. "Oh, Des, the silliest thing! You know the cheque for a hundred pounds I gave you? Yes, well, Mr. Tiverton got it into his head that you had forged it! I tried to convince him that he was wrong, but the only way I could get him to believe it was to explain that we were engaged! He accepted that all right, but now Aunt Harriet refuses to believe it! Could you possibly come over and help me convince her? It's really too silly, but——"

She had heard the quick intake of his breath as she started speaking. Then there had been utter silence, as if Desmond was listening with agonising intentness.

"Hallo?" she said sharply.

"Yes, I heard," he said slowly. "I'll be over right away, and—I'll do just as you say!"

Judith hung up the telephone. Until that moment she

had hoped against hope that it was not true. That it must have been someone else—there must be some other explanation. But Desmond, her old friend, had deliberately attempted to defraud her. She turned to her aunt.

"Des will be over at once," she announced. "Between us we ought to convince you!"

Miss Harriet, more troubled than ever, came over to the girl and pulled her down beside her on the couch.

"Judith, my dear, I suppose I am convinced. But—why did you do it without telling me?"

Gently but firmly Judith disengaged her hands.

"Because," she said clearly, "I am very tired of having my affairs interfered with! If we had made an announcement in the ordinary way, I am quite sure you would have made a fuss! You would probably have insisted that we did not say anything about it until after my return! Well, that is just what we are doing, so what is there for you to say? I know you don't like Des, but—it is I who propose marrying him, not you!"

Miss Harriet sat very still. At this moment she knew that she was farther away from Judith than she had ever been, and that the gulf between them was not one that was ever likely to be bridged. And what was there that she could say? Nothing, she felt, that would not drive them still farther apart. So she waited.

"Now that Mr. Tiverton has had to be told," Judith went on in that hard, determined voice, "I am afraid that it will have to be announced at once. I absolutely refuse to have any gossip about it!"

"Mr. Tiverton gave you his promise—" Miss Harriet began.

Judith's hands moved in an impatient gesture.

"Oh, he won't tell anyone outright!" she agreed. "But if I know him he will hint—give people the impression that if only he would, he could tell them something about me! No, Aunt Harriet, I am sorry, but surely you must see for yourself."

And Miss Harriet, knowing the village, did see, only too well.

"I think," went on that young, arrogant voice, "that

the best thing will be for us to give a party just before we sail—the night before will be best. It can be a sort of farewell party and an engagement party as well."

"Surely——" Miss Harriet began, but Judith interrupted her.

"There is something else I have to tell you," she said slowly, and now, avoiding her aunt's eyes, she picked nervously at a loose piece of wool on a tapestry cushion. "As soon as I am of age, I am going to sell Windygates!"

"Sell——!" Miss Harriet gasped. "Judith—you can't——"

Judith stood up.

"I can—and I will," she said resolutely. "It is mine—to do with as I like. And that—is what I choose."

"Is this Desmond's idea——?" Miss Harriet began, but Judith shook her head. Suddenly, she felt very tired, as if all the spirit had gone out of her.

"No," she said wearily. "I haven't told Des yet. But I think he will be quite pleased. After all, we are both young. Is it unnatural that we should want some fun out of life instead of working so hard that there is never any time for anything else?"

"There could be——" Miss Harriet began, but again Judith interrupted her.

"If I would consent to your friend Charles Saxilby staying on?" she asked scornfully. "No, that is the last thing I would agree to! Unless, of course, he buys Windygates! He wants to, you know. He wanted me to give him the first refusal of it, but I had to make it clear to him that he could not expect to get it cheap. He must bid when it is auctioned, the same as anyone else! Listen! That's Des, I think!" She went to the window and leaned out. "Des, come in here, will you? The door is open!"

He came slowly in, and it seemed to Miss Harriet that if she wanted confirmation of her belief that Judith had lied to her, she had it in his manner. Usually so full of self-confidence, now he had none at all. His eyes went from Judith's face to her own and back again. He did not know what to say, and he waited for Judith to give him a lead.

She slipped her arm through his.

"Des, I am sorry! Was it a nuisance coming just now?"

"Well—a bit," he said hesitatingly. "But, of course, I couldn't let you shoulder this alone."

Judith smiled at her aunt.

"You see?" she said almost too patiently. "Des is as annoyed as I am! Look, Des, will you just confirm what I've told Aunt Harriet—that we are engaged, but we wanted it to be a secret until I came back so that there was no fuss."

She felt her arm being crushed against his side, felt the deep intake of his breath.

"That is quite true, Miss Ravensdale," he said steadily. "I am sorry if you are not pleased about it, but—after all that has happened, you can hardly blame us!"

"I blame no one but myself," Miss Harriet said quietly, her face suddenly old and tired. She walked over to the door. "If you will prepare a list of the guests you propose asking, Judith, I will make arrangements for your party!"

"Very well," Judith said indifferently.

The door shut behind Miss Harriet and Desmond turned to Judith eagerly.

"Judith, what——" he began, but she silenced him.

"Not now!" she said quickly. "Take me out somewhere in your car—if you can spare the time?"

He looked at her with a peculiar expression on his good-looking face.

"My time is completely at your disposal, Judith," he told her quietly.

Judith flushed, and for the first time since she had come into the room to see Mr. Tiverton, her eyes were troubled.

They drove for the best part of three miles before Desmond drew up at the side of the road. He drew a deep breath.

"Now!" he said quietly, and with an access of dignity strange to his happy-go-lucky nature.

"Now what?" Judith asked carelessly.

Desmond shook his head.

"No, Judith, that won't do!" he told her resolutely. "It is all very well for us to lie to other people, but not to one another! We've got to be honest—" He stopped, his mouth twitching uneasily.

Judith leaned back. Her eyes were on the summer glory of the woods and fields and sky but she, who had loved them so much all her life, did not even see them now.

"Suppose you start," she suggested.

"Yes," he said slowly. "It's rather up to me, isn't it? Well, I was desperate——"

"Yes, I suppose so," she said wearily. "Otherwise you wouldn't have taken such a risk. Or was it such a risk? You knew I would not prosecute you, didn't you?"

His eyes dropped.

"Yes," he muttered, "that's what is so foul about it! Judith, I'm sorry."

"Are you?" she looked at him with eyes that held cynical amusement. "But why? You were in difficulties and you saw a way out—just as I did! Oh, Desmond, if we are to be honest with one another, why not admit it? It is the most natural instinct in the world for people to look after themselves! That's all you did—and you took the least possible risk in doing it!"

Desmond shook his head as he stared incredulously at her.

"That doesn't sound like you, Judith!" he said slowly. "When have you ever——"

"All my life!" she told him, her hands moving restlessly in her lap. "Only I've never admitted it before. Perhaps I never saw it that way before! But now that I do, believe me, I intend to go on just the same way!"

"You *are* changed, Judith," Desmond insisted. "And I'm not sure——"

"Of course I have changed!" she said impatiently. "I've grown up, that's all! It had to happen sooner or later! Now that it has, you don't appear to like it! Perhaps you would rather we didn't get married?"

He looked at her for a long, brooding minute. Then he shook his head.

"If you are content, so am I!" he averred. "But—I would like to know your reason, Judith, if you don't mind? You see—" he smiled deprecatingly—"I haven't the cheek to imagine that you love me!"

"Love?" she said slowly. "No, I suppose not. But does that matter? From what one hears, romantic love never lasts. Surely it is better to build on a friendship that has lasted for a good many years? After all, we shall not expect too much."

"You still haven't told me why you have changed your mind about marrying me," Desmond interrupted.

"Well—" Judith said slowly. "Partly realising how much I am disliked about here——"

"Not nearly so much as Saxilby makes out, I'll swear to that!" he said quickly. "Besides, what difference——"

"I haven't explained everything yet," Judith said hurriedly. "You see, Des, when we get married, we shan't live here!"

"Not live—!" He stared at her incredulously.

Judith's eyes dropped.

"No, I want to get right away from here—never come back!" she explained in a tight, brittle little voice. "I thought we might travel—I expect I shall get a taste for it in the next few months, and you would enjoy getting out of England, wouldn't you?"

He nodded slowly.

"It has been one of my greatest ambitions," he admitted. "But——"

"Well?" she asked coolly.

"I would never have believed that you— Judith, is that your only reason? I suppose—" he hesitated—"you aren't in love with someone else, are you? Someone that isn't—that doesn't——"

"That isn't in love with me?" she asked hardly, and laughed. "My dear Des, whatever made you think of such a thing! No, I'm completely fancy free!"

"I'm glad of that!" Desmond said quickly, and suddenly his arms were round her. "You think I want to marry you for the sake of your money, don't you? No, don't deny it! It's so obvious. And I don't blame you. I admit that it was my reason for proposing to you! But—something happened to me that day when I asked you—I'd tell you that I had fallen in love with you, only I don't suppose for a moment——"

"That I should believe you?" she finished. "No, I shouldn't! And you did say we had better be honest."

He stared down into her cool, impersonal eyes.

"This is honest!" he said in a thick, hurried voice that she had never heard before. "I do love you, Judith! And I swear I'll teach you——"

His lips came down hard on hers, and at their touch Judith's heart seemed to die in her. Perhaps Desmond did love her—a little. But however much it was, she knew that he would never be able to stir a like emotion in her.

And perhaps Desmond knew it as well. Against the warmth of his lips her own lay cold and unresponsive. It was true that she did not shrink from him, but neither did she quicken to his touch.

Unwillingly, and yet with a curious tenderness, he let her go and turned away.

"I'll take you home now," he said quietly. "Make whatever arrangements you think best—you can rely on me to fall in with them!"

"Very well," she agreed lifelessly. "I suppose you told Linda before you came up to Windygates, didn't you?"

"Yes," he admitted. "I was a bit taken aback, you see."

"It doesn't matter in the least," Judith assured him. "After all, she is one of the family, isn't she? And I told Aunt Harriet, so——"

He turned impetuously to her.

"Judith——" he began. And stopped.

"Yes?" she asked indifferently.

"No, nothing!" he said shortly, and turned the car in a homeward direction.

It was no good. In her present mood he knew that he could not reach Judith. There was a barrier between them, one that had put an end even to their friendship.

Judith was a stranger to him. It was as if she were under a spell—and one that, in his heart of hearts, he knew that he would never be able to break.

Linda looked up curiously as her brother came in.

"Well?" she asked.

He flung himself down in a chair which creaked violently.

"What do you mean; 'Well'?" he asked irritably.

Linda remained completely unperturbed by his display of bad temper.

"You know perfectly well what I mean," she said calmly, lighting a cigarette. "And be careful with that chair! The worst of these antiques is that though they may look good, they have to be treated with respect. Now tell me what happened!"

Desmond knew perfectly well what she meant, but he found himself wishing that he had not been surprised into displaying his astonishment when Judith had rung up.

"Not much to tell you. I proposed to Judith that day we had the scavenger hunt. At the time it took her so much by surprise that she turned me down. But I told her that so long as there was no one else, I wasn't going to take that as final, and I should keep on hoping. Well, now she's changed her mind and she has told me so, as I asked her to. We are going to get married. That's all!"

"Is it?" she asked, and had her brother been less immersed in his own affairs he might have realised that her curiosity was more than touched with anxiety.

"Oh—she's getting rid of Windygates," Desmond added, far more casually than he felt the news really deserved.

"Is she, though!" Linda said softly. "That's news indeed!"

Desmond suddenly awoke to the fact that there was some meaning in her words which for the moment evaded him.

"Did you know that she was going to?" he asked sharply.

Linda shrugged her shoulders gracefully.

"I had an idea she might," she admitted thoughtfully. "Well, isn't that nice for you! You won't have to go to all the trouble of pretending to be interested in the farm!"

"It wouldn't have been pretence," Desmond said shortly. "I expect it seems a bit odd to you, but as a matter of fact, I'd have liked it. Still——"

"Still, if Judith decides otherwise, you are in no position to object, are you?" Linda spoke softly. It was not that she had any particular desire to annoy him, but she did want to get to the bottom of it all. The more one knew, the fewer mistakes one was likely to make, and she was neither too vain nor too dense to realise that she was as yet far from accomplishing all she had set out to do. "Des, I wish for once in your life you'd be straightforward with me! Why did Judith suddenly change her mind?"

"How do you know it was sudden?" he asked.

"Because, for one thing, it was such an odd time that she rang you up!" Linda retorted. "She knew perfectly well that it must be inconvenient for you—particularly racing up to Windygates then and there. Besides, you were as surprised as I was!"

Desmond regarded her thoughtfully.

"Anyone would think, from the way you speak, that you know something yourself!" he told her. "Wait a minute! Of course, she was down here earlier in the day! All that has happened since had put it out of my mind! And you very obviously wanted me out of the way! What did you say to her after I had gone, Linda?"

His sister smiled mockingly at him.

"You know, Des, there are times when I begin to feel really hopeful about you! You are not such a fool as I had feared!"

"Never mind the bouquets," he said roughly, standing up and towering over her. "What did you say?"

Linda laughed softly.

"I helped on your cause quite a bit, if you must know," she announced. "You see, it became rather painfully evident that somehow or other Charles had contrived to get into her good books! He's certainly tried hard enough!"

"Is he in love with her?" Desmond asked sharply.

"We-ll," Linda deliberated, "I wouldn't call it just that. But I should say that Charles is not a man who has ever come up against much opposition where women are concerned. He is—attractive in more ways than one."

"One, of course, being money. At least, as far as you are concerned," Desmond remarked.

"Quite. After all, you and I are akin, Des. We see eye to eye in so many things! You wouldn't call Judith exactly poverty-stricken, would you?"

"Never mind that," he said brusquely. "Get on with it!"

"Judith, on the other hand, has obviously had no use for him at all! She has, as I told her, been extremely rude to him. But he has taken it from her. Ask yourself why!"

Desmond went over to the window and stared out at the quiet little High Street.

"I suppose you mean that she had intrigued him— that his vanity won't be satisfied until he has got the mastery over her," he said slowly. "All right, suppose that is true. Where do you come in?"

Linda laughed softly.

"Really, Des, you're not so bright as I had thought!" she told him. "Think for yourself! I'm not the only person who thinks that he has been after Judith. Well, now she is engaged to you! Do you think he is going to give people the chance to laugh at him? Oh no, he'll get engaged himself—and it will be to someone that people know he has been friendly with. Otherwise, it would not seem natural!"

"In other words, you?"

"Exactly!"

"H'm!" Desmond pondered. "You've been uncommonly clever," he said at length. "And I'm perfectly willing to admit that you probably started things off! But I'm equally sure you have had a tremendous lot of luck as well!"

"I have!" she admitted unhesitatingly. After all, it had only been a guess on her part that Charles would like Windygates for his own. Nor had she imagined for a moment that he had admitted as much to Judith, and it still puzzled her just how that had come about. There were other things as well. The way in which Judith had suddenly turned to Desmond.

"So have I!" she heard him say fervently, and his tone caught her attention.

"You've been up to something!" she insisted. "You'd better tell me—oh, you needn't be afraid! Am I in any position to tell tales on you? If I did, I admit that I'd give myself away as well!"

"Well—" he said reluctantly. "I've been a bit of a fool at the horse-races. I knew it wasn't any good trying to get anything out of you."

"I'm glad you've got that much sense," she observed drily. "Go on! What did you do? Confess all to Judith and appeal to her womanly sweetness?"

He moved impatiently as if her cynicism grated, but he made no comment about it.

"No. I—if you must know, I forged her name to a cheque.

"Des, you fool!" Linda said vehemently.

"Knave is the proper word," he said drearily. "Anyway, old Tiverton picked it up and took it to Judith for confirmation. She, for some reason or other, didn't give me away. Instead, she rang me up, explained what had happened—except that she spoke as if she *had* signed the cheque, and asked me to come and confirm the fact that we were engaged. I told you that part."

"You did indeed!" Linda said abstractedly. So, in spite of her denials, Judith was in love with Charles! And she had turned to Des for exactly the same motive as would, if all went well, bring Charles to her, Linda! What a useful thing vanity was! People so hated to look small, and if one had a little bit of ingenuity, one could make such use of the fact!

Suddenly she laughed. Triumphantly, exultantly.

"You know, Des, it was a bit steep of me to criticise you for gambling! If ever there were two of a sort, it is you and I! I suppose we get it from Father—only I think we have more nerve than he had!"

Desmond regarded her thoughtfully.

"You have," he admitted. "You would go right through to the bitter end with anything that you started."

"Wouldn't you?" she retorted. He hesitated, then he shook his head.

"Maybe. I don't know. I say, here *is* Charles!" There was a certain reluctant admiration in his voice as he went on: "Well, I'll say this for you, you're a good psychologist! I'd better clear out, hadn't I?"

"You had!" she agreed energetically. "As far and fast as you possibly can! And I hope to goodness no one comes in wanting tea for the next half-hour! Wait a moment until I see which way he is coming in, and then you had better make yourself scarce the other way! Oh—he's going to the back! Out you go, Des, and don't come back until you see that Charles's car has gone!"

She went out into the kitchen, a song on her lips, a welcome in her eyes.

"Charles! How lovely!" she said warmly. "It is so rarely that my friends turn up when I am free, but there isn't a soul in yet for tea. Let's have some together and pretend that you are the only guest I am likely to have this afternoon. Come along!"

Charles came slowly into the kitchen, and involuntarily Linda took a step away from him. As he had stood in the open doorway she had been blinded by the glare of the sun behind him. Now, for the first time, she saw his face clearly. There was no answering smile on it, no gratification at her welcome. Instead, it was stern and—threatening. Linda felt her heart begin to pound.

"Charles!" she faltered. "Charles!"

He came near to her. So near that she could have laid her hands on his shoulders and turned her face up to his—if she had dared!

"I want to know what lies you have been telling Judith about me!" he said without preamble.

"I?" She tried to laugh naturally, but the sound

strangled in her throat. "Charles, how absurd! What on earth makes you say a thing like that?"

"You don't deny that you saw her this morning, do you?" he demanded.

"No, I don't," she said readily. "Judith came in to see Des—and I was about. Of course I saw her."

"And talked to her?" he wanted to know.

"Naturally! I'll tell you what we talked about if you like!" she offered.

"Do!" he said curtly.

"We were talking about the wedding," she said calmly.

"Whose wedding?" he enquired sharply.

"Whose?" she arched her slender brows. "Why, hers and Desmond's of course."

Suddenly his hand fell on her shoulder. He did not grip it, but she felt as if the weight of it would press her to the ground.

"You are lying again!" he gritted.

"Really, Charles!" she said with an indignation that was not all put on. Like so many people, her lies, once uttered, became almost the truth to her simply because she wanted them to be. "Well, if you don't believe me, ask Des! Or, if you don't trust him, Judith—or Miss Harriet!"

She saw that he was less sure of himself, and for the first time since he had come into the house she found herself breathing more naturally.

"There hasn't been time," he muttered.

"Time?" she said curiously. "I don't understand! They've known each other for years—and actually, they have been secretly engaged for some time. Only now, for reasons of their own which they have not even told me, they have suddenly decided to announce it. I can't tell you any more than that!"

"Was there nothing else you spoke of?" he asked urgently.

Linda's eyes narrowed. The most convincing lies, she had long since decided, were those that had at least a grain of truth in them.

"Yes! We were talking about Windygates—and you!" she told him.

"But you said——"

"You asked me what lies I had told her," Linda said calmly, turning aside to take a cigarette out of a box. "And I denied that I had done any such thing! I still do! If you like, I will tell you what was said. Wait a minute! With a suspicious sort of person like you, one wants to be exact! I know they told me about this announcement, and Judith said that she was going to sell Windygates. Des asked her if she had really thought it over, because it was a pretty big step. And she said that it had been in her head some time. Ever since she had realised that it was a saleable thing. I think you put that idea into her head, didn't you?" she asked curiously.

"If so, she had not had very long to think it over!" he said grimly.

"No? Well, then she said that you wanted to have the first refusal if she did sell."

"And your precious brother pointed out to her that she would probably make more out of it if she auctioned it!" Charles said, breathing heavily.

"Well—" she shrugged her shoulders. "If you come to think of it, that was natural enough! After all, as her future husband, he has got to look after her interests!"

Charles was silent. He had come here absolutely convinced that at last he was going to be able to get things sorted out—that Linda would admit the truth when confronted with his suspicions that had seemed so like convictions until now, and that he would be able to prove to Judith that he had never tried to cheat her or get the better of her. Now he felt farther away from the truth than ever.

He said slowly, as if to convince himself:

"When I came here, Judith hated and mistrusted me. But with the business of the foot-and-mouth disease, she was beginning to trust me—she did trust me! And then, quite suddenly, to-day, all that old mistrust returned. She hated me as she has never hated me before. And there must be some reason for it!"

"Possibly," Linda agreed indifferently. "But I can't tell you what it was! Why don't you ask her?"

"I have done already," he said heavily. "She swears there is nothing wrong."

"Oh dear, Charles, you do take a lot of convincing, don't you?" Linda said distractedly. "Ask her again! Only—do remember one thing!"

"What?"

"Well—just this. It was never Judith's idea that you should come in the first place. You know that. Surely, in the circumstances, it would be better to accept the situation as it is for the few days that are left! Judith sails on Friday. This is Tuesday. Does it matter so very much what she thinks of you?"

Charles's hand dropped to his side.

"More than anything else in the world," he said quietly. "It always has!"

"Always!" Linda spoke sharply. "Do you mean you never——"

She stopped abruptly, but it was too late. Charles had read the rest of her sentence in her face. She saw the sudden loathing in it and hated him with an intensity that even Judith had never known.

"I mean," he said deliberately, "that Judith is the only woman I have ever loved or wanted to marry. And I think you are clever enough to have known it all the time—though she never has!"

And then he was gone.

Linda clutched the back of a kitchen chair, swaying a little. That—was that! Charles might never marry Judith, but he would certainly never marry her, Linda. All her schemes had come to nothing.

Slowly she became conscious that a bell was ringing. It was the one that hung in the tea-room for visitors to summon her. Holding on to first one piece of furniture and then another, she made her way to the front of the house.

There was just one customer there. It was the American who had been so interested in seeing over the house the day that Judith had told them about Charles. She had seen him several times since—in church, in the

High Street and twice when he had come in for tea. He had always been pleasant and friendly but now his face was very grave. Linda stiffened.

"How long—" she began, and stopped. Suddenly it did not matter. Nothing mattered—and the room was getting oddly dark.

She heard an exclamation. The next moment strong arms were helping her into a chair and someone was telling her to take it easy—then a glass of water was held to her lips and she drank avidly. The room cleared.

"That's better!" a pleasant voice said cheerfully. "No, sit still! This is where I take command! I've shut the front door—a liberty, I'm afraid, but necessary. You are in no state to wait on people. Besides," he sat down beside her and took her hands in his, "you are going to tell me just what is wrong—everything, right from the beginning!"

CHAPTER NINE

LINDA jumped to her feet, her face white with anger.

"How dare you!" she gasped. "You're outrageous! Please go—at once!"

The American shook his head.

"I can't do that," he said gently. "You're in no condition to be left. I think you've got to the end of your tether, you know. And—you need someone to lend you a hand. Someone who is a bit stronger than you are, perhaps."

The strength seemed to go out of Linda's legs and she sat down suddenly. It was so true. She had worked very hard and, with Desmond's not too efficient help, made some sort of a living for both of them. But the years stretched ahead with no hope of relief—it would always just be hard work for very little gain. And she was very tired. More tired than she ever let herself acknowledge. Slowly she buried her face in her hands.

There was silence in the quaint little room. Then her visitor sat down beside her and suddenly, in spite of the fact that he was a stranger, his nearness brought reassurance and comfort.

"I want to tell you a bit about myself," he began quietly. "You've a right to know that. My name is Carl Brand and I'm over here partly on business and partly pleasure. As far as the pleasure is concerned, I meant to tour about seeing some of your old towns—well, this is the only one I've seen. You see, I found something here that wouldn't be anywhere else."

Linda looked at him quickly.

"Yes, I mean you," he admitted. "You're different from any other women I've ever met. I just knew——"

"Please," Linda begged, but he shook his head.

"I'll be grateful if you'll hear me out," he told her, and not entirely against her will, Linda found herself listening.

"I suppose," he went on slowly, "in this country you'd call me a self-made man. If by that you mean I started out with nothing, you'd be right. But it wasn't all my doing. It was my mother who fought for me before I was old enough to fight myself. She was left a widow with a family of four to bring up. There was hardly any money at all, but she was determined that we should have a fair chance. Can you guess what that meant?"

"I suppose she went without things herself," Linda said, interested in spite of herself.

"She did that," he agreed. "But more—much more besides. She worked—she didn't mind what she turned her hand to or how long the hours were. Sometimes she had to do things that she would have despised herself for doing if it had been just for her own gain. But it wasn't. It was for us kids. That's why I can never find it in my heart to blame a woman, no matter what weapons she uses to fight with. You see, the odds against her are always so heavy."

Again Linda looked at him in that quick, enquiring way, and saw nothing but compassion and understanding in the strong, rugged face.

"I don't suppose you are aware of it," he went on, "but since that first visit I paid to you I've been living in the district. I didn't come back to see you again before because I didn't want to embarrass you. Besides—I wanted to find out something about you."

Linda laughed bitterly.

"I don't suppose you heard much to my advantage!" she remarked. "We've always been what I suppose you would feel are parasites—we've lived on the money that our ancestors earned, and now that is gone we squeal about our hard luck!" He did not reply immediately, and she went on savagely: "Well, go on, say it! Tell me that if we had worked half as hard as you have we'd not have been in this mess! It's true, you know!"

He shook his head.

"No. You have had hard luck! You know," he said slowly, "I can't think of anything that would have felt so stable, so permanent as life did to people of your sort before the war—and even more before the first one. A big, well-built house. Well-cared-for grounds—yes, I've had a look at your old home. It was very easy to imagine you in that setting. And I suppose that there was an income that came in steadily. An existence that must have seemed to have the most solid foundations one could want. And then, suddenly, it was all different. I don't suppose you ever had a moment's anxiety until right at the end, when you found out just how bad things were?"

"Not until after my father's death," she admitted in a low voice. Her eyes dilated as the memory of that terrifying time came back to her. "We knew things were tight, that we should have to get rid of Brierly sooner or later. But we had no idea the house was mortgaged to the last penny. And all the money that had been raised on that and everything else besides had gone. All that we had was a few hundred pounds and this house that an old aunt had left to Mother."

"You couldn't have known which way to turn!" he said softly.

"We didn't—and Mother was ill. I think, really, she began to die when Father did. It wasn't very long, you know."

"So then you looked round to see what you could do." He took on the story so confidently that Linda looked amazed. He certainly had found out about her! "You, a girl who had never had to do any hard work in her life, decided to start this tea-room. And from what I hear it is a success."

"It is," she admitted half proudly, half anxiously. "But this is the summer, you know. There are a lot of tourists—it is mainly cars which stop here that bring us trade. I get very little support from local people. And we are making our way—doing a bit more than that, actually. But it won't keep on. As soon as the bad weather comes—it's inevitable that our takings will drop. And I don't know—I can't see—" she stopped, biting her lip, and found, to her surprise, that her hand was being held in a warm, comforting clasp.

"Easy!" said a reassuring voice. "Easy! It hasn't happened yet!"

"But it will, it will!" she insisted, the panic that she had shut up within her for so long getting the upper hand. "And there is nobody to whom it really matters! Why should it? I never worried about other people when we had money! So that's why—" she stopped suddenly, but once again Carl Brand finished her sentence for her.

"That's why you decided to marry the first rich man you came across. Saxilby."

"Oh—" the colour flamed into her face. "How did you know?"

"That you meant to marry him?" he enquired coolly. "Or that he was rich? Well, that wasn't difficult. You see, it isn't a common name, and yet I knew it very well. His grandfather's name was a household word in the States, and when I met him casually one day he told me that his father was an American. The old man's younger son who didn't carry on with the family business. All the same, there was plenty of money for him. And it's come to this young man. I liked him. A good type. Maybe it's a good blend, English and American. You'd say, first go, that he is a perfect English gentleman. But then, talking, you realise that there is something more. A bit more punch, perhaps."

527

"You mean because, in spite of his money, he works?" Linda asked.

"Partly that," he admitted. "Although I can't claim that all our young men with money see things the same way. But what I was thinking was—he's a man that knows what he wants—and will get it."

Linda was silent. She knew now perfectly well what Charles wanted. To be honest, she had to admit that she had known all along. Just as Charles had said. Only one woman whom he had ever loved or wanted to marry— Judith.

"And now," went on the quiet voice, "you are going to tell me just what you did say to that little girl— Judith, isn't it? The one who is going about looking as if her heart were broken."

"Why should it be?" Linda asked bitterly. "She's got everything one could want."

"Has she?" Carl asked thoughtfully. "Now, from what I've pieced together, I've doubts about that. Her father seems to have done his best to wreck her life."

Linda was silent. That was true, as she knew perhaps better than anyone else.

"Tell me!" he said again, and now, in spite of the kindness that was still in his voice, there was a note of command as well. And to her own surprise, Linda found herself beginning to speak.

At last it was all told. Linda made no attempt to spare herself, and when it was all done, she sat huddled up in her chair, waiting for the verdict of a man who was almost a stranger and yet whose opinion seemed to matter more than that of any other human being she knew.

And all Carl Brand did was to nod and say quietly: "You'll feel better now you've got that off your chest!"

She looked up quickly, her lips parted, incredulous.

"And now," he went on cheerfully, "I'm going to get a cup of tea for both of us! That's one thing I've learned over here—both to enjoy tea and to make it properly! You just sit still and leave it to me!"

Linda laughed uncertainly.

"It's absurd," she said, but she did as she was told. She heard Carl moving about in her little kitchen, and for the first time in a very long while, so it seemed to her, she relaxed in body and mind. Someone else had taken charge, someone she could trust.

She took the opportunity of his absence to repair the damage to her make-up that her tears had caused, and when he came back into the room she was sitting at her ease in a big old Windsor chair, smiling up at him.

For a moment he paused in the doorway. His eyes were full of longing—and hope.

"That's what a man wants when he comes home," he said slowly. "A woman waiting for him—smiling!"

But that was the only glimpse of emotion that he showed. The next moment he was pouring out tea competently and neatly and entertaining her with amusing stories of his experiences and the mistakes he had made during his visit to England.

"But you like it?" she asked, suddenly anxious that he should.

He nodded.

"Very much indeed! I had never imagined there were such things to see. And I've still got a month to go!"

"You'll be able to see a lot in that time," Linda suggested.

Carl smiled.

"I'd like to see as much of you as possible," he said simply.

Linda turned away.

"In spite of what you know about me?" she asked bitterly.

He met her eyes fairly.

"Because of it, perhaps," he told her. "You surely need looking after—and I hope to prove to you that it is my job!"

"But—" Linda protested, only to be silenced.

"I've not asked anything of you—yet, have I? Only to be allowed to see you!" he pointed out.

There was a long silence. A rose tapped softly at the open window pane, the birds were singing.

Linda sighed deeply and shook her head.

"I suppose the next thing will be that you try to persuade me to confess my sins to Judith," she said, half resentfully, half wistfully.

Carl laughed in genuine amusement.

"There will be no need for me to persuade you," he told her very positively. "You will do that off your own bat! You're not nearly so tough as you imagine!"

He went away a little later, after he had helped Linda wash up the crockery they had used. The last memory she had of him was his reassuring smile as he turned at the gate for a last look at her.

She went slowly back into the house and sat in the chair he had just vacated, trying to sort out her thoughts.

She felt a completely different person. Less sure of herself than she had ever been in her life, but strangely content.

The weather, which had been unbrokenly fine for weeks, had changed in the last few days and was now sultry and oppressive. More than one person foretold a storm, and indeed, it did not take very much weather-wisdom to believe that they were right.

Miss Harriet looked apprehensively at the sky and reconsidered the arrangements that she had made for the party on which Judith had insisted.

"I had thought that we might have dancing on the lawn," she said to Judith. "But now it looks as if we may have to stay indoors. I think I had better get the big drawing-room ready for dancing."

"Just as you like," Judith said indifferently.

And, indeed, indifference was the keynote to her mood now. She had shown it when the question of guests had been raised.

"Oh—everybody," she had said. "You know better than I do."

That was perfectly true, but Miss Harriet was not content to leave it there.

"I would like you to look at the list I have made out," she said, and handed it to Judith.

Judith shrugged her shoulders as she took it, but for the sake of peace she ran her eyes down it. It included all the people of their own standing in the neighbourhood, and at the end was Charles's name.

"That looks all right," she said casually as she passed it back to her aunt.

"You have no objection to Charles's coming?" Miss Harriet asked bluntly.

Judith regarded her with a completely expressionless face.

"No. Why should I?" she asked.

Miss Harriet hesitated.

"You have shown your dislike for him pretty obviously," she pointed out. "It would be awkward if there was any unpleasantness at the party."

Judith kicked idly at a loose stone—they were out on the terrace—and said positively:

"There won't be!" And then, as her aunt did not speak, she went on: "You see, Aunt Harriet, you used the wrong word. It isn't so much a question of dislike. It is just that I am—completely indifferent. I can afford to be—now."

Miss Harriet found nothing to say in reply, but afterwards she repeated the conversation to Mr. Bellairs. He listened in silence and then nodded as she finished.

"Very reassuring," he commented.

"Reassuring!" Miss Harriet said. "That's the last word I should have used."

"But don't you see, my dear," he explained, "this makes it perfectly obvious that there is little depth to Judith's engagement. She is using young Enstone to blind herself to the fact that Charles matters. I am more sure that she is in love with Charles than I have ever been before."

Miss Harriet shook her head.

"I'm not," she sighed. "Or, if she is, it will take a miracle to convince her of it."

"Well, miracles do happen," Mr. Bellairs said encouragingly. "And never more frequently than when love affairs are concerned. After all, one has been worked for us. In spite of all the years that have passed, we still love one another."

Miss Harriet gave him a grateful glance and, for the time being, forgot Judith's troubles as she planned her own future with the man who had loved her so faithfully for so many years.

To Charles the days seemed both to drag—and yet to pass like lightning. He never seemed to find time to seek Judith out, and yet, at the end of the day, it seemed as if it had been going on for ever.

Judith was avoiding him. That he knew perfectly well. Believing what she did about him, that was not surprising. It was perfectly obvious that nothing he could say would convince her that he and not Linda had spoken the truth. Neither was it in the least possible for him to speak of his love. In her present mood she would simply have thought that he was lying in order to get round her. He felt as near to helpless as a man of his type will ever allow himself to be. There seemed nothing that he could do—he had no illusions after his interview with Linda that she would ever admit to having lied about him, although he was more convinced than ever that she had.

There was only one gleam of light. Judith was not planning to marry Desmond because she loved him. If Charles had heard Carl describe Judith as a broken-hearted little girl, he would have agreed absolutely. Her face was too tanned by her open-air life for unhappiness to make her lose her colour, but there was a pinched look about her face, a blank look in her eyes that wrenched at Charles's heart. Sometimes he wondered whether it was because of her obvious unhappiness that she avoided him, and decided that possibly it was—but not because she cared for him and was hurt because she thought he was completely mercenary. It was that everything stable in her old life had vanished and nothing had taken its place. She felt insecure and life was a wounding, unfamiliar thing. Because he had contributed to that feeling, pride compelled her to hide her hurt, so far as possible, from him. If, as he believed, Linda had also hurt her, then Judith would try to keep up appearances with her as well. And when he heard that he and Linda were both invited to this farewell party of Judith's he was convinced that he was right. To the last moment she would keep up appearances. Then she would run away—and she would not come back again to Windygates.

Charles's face grew grim. He had told Linda the truth when he had said that Judith was the only woman he had ever loved or wished to marry. Admittedly his first impression of her had been that she was an arrogant young person who should be taught a good lesson. But later, when he had heard her story from Miss Harriet, when he had seen that revealing photograph of her, he had realised that, right from the beginning, she had made an impression on him that no other woman ever had. He knew that he would do anything in his power to give her happiness—and there seemed no way.

His work that afternoon took him some distance from Windygates and, coming home, he stopped on a high ridge and, leaving the car, climbed still higher up the sloping ground that rose steeply from the roadside.

From this vantage-point he could see miles across the surrounding countryside, and although he was a comparative newcomer to the district, he could understand how Judith felt about it. She would tear her heart out by the roots if she were to leave it. For her own sake as well as his, she must be compelled to see the madness of her present course.

He had gone straight back to Windygates after his interview with Linda to find out if it was true about the engagement. Judith had been out but he had seen Miss Harriet. Her distress was obvious, and it was evident that she at least believed this story about it being of some weeks' standing. But Charles could not make himself believe that, though he could have given no clear reason why. Had he known of the incident of the cheque, it might have helped, but Miss Harriet had not told him of that. Indeed, it was hardly possible that she should. Since Judith had stated so categorically that she had signed it, though she might not believe it, to have passed on any information about the incident could do no good. If he had made use of it in arguing with Judith it would only have added to her conviction that no one was trustworthy.

So Charles puzzled.

"I hope I'm not intruding?" said a pleasant voice.

Charles turned sharply. The American whom he had met once or twice in the village was standing there regarding him rather diffidently. Convention forbade that Charles should tell him that he certainly was and that the sooner he cleared out the better, so he got up from the boulder on which he had been sitting and put his pipe back into his pocket.

"Not at all," he said with impersonal politeness. "I was just going."

"Don't do that!" the man said. "I saw your car down below and I thought I'd like to have a talk."

"With me?" Charles said sharply.

Carl shrugged his shoulders.

"With whoever the car belonged to," he explained. "You see, there come times when, if I don't let off steam about this country of yours, I just about explode. I like it—but I can't get the hang of it."

Charles's eyes wandered over the broad acres.

"What's odd about it?" he asked uncomprehendingly.

"With the land? Nothing—barring its pocket size to my eyes. No, the people, I mean."

"What's wrong with us?" And, despite himself, a hostile note crept into his voice.

" 'Us'?" Carl asked. "You count yourself one of them?"

"I was born in England. I've lived here all my life. That goes for something," Charles retorted.

"Yes, it certainly does. Come to think of it, maybe you're the right person to ask. You ought to see it from both sides."

"Maybe," Charles said shortly. Or, on the other hand, perhaps he could see neither side's point of view very clearly because he could not bring a double vision into focus? Was he able to see the question but not the answer? Could he understand Judith's problems yet be unable to find a solution for them?

"Right! Well, first, why is it that you regard one another with such suspicion? Why does an Englishman clash temperamentally with a Welshman? Why are your social barriers so difficult to overcome for any of you born out of them—and yet, a foreigner like me you just accept. No one says to me, 'Who was your father?'"

"They wouldn't," Charles said promptly. "Just because you are a foreigner. You're not expected to conform to our rules. Besides, haven't the worst rows you've ever known been between relatives rather than acquaintances?"

"That's right," Carl agreed. "So you think that's it?"

"Partly. But what a man is goes for something. In spite of regimentation and all the limitations over here, we're still individualists. Consequently, though we may be suspicious, we do let a man speak for himself."

"You're a newcomer here, aren't you?" pursued Carl thoughtfully.

"Yes. I've only been here about six weeks," Charles explained. "I've lived in Sussex most of my life."

"People know you're half a foreigner?"

Suddenly Charles became really interested in his companion. The man wasn't just asking aimless questions, he was really trying to work something out. He himself became curious to know what it was.

"No, as a matter of fact, they don't," he confessed. "You see, as I said, I was born in this country and I've lived here all my life. That means I had the right when I came of age to choose my nationality. I decided to stick to the country I've known all my life. Sometimes I forget that my father was an American—maybe you'll have heard of our family?"

"Yes," Carl said thoughtfully. "I knew your grandfather."

"Did you?" Charles said with interest. "He was a grand old chap. I only saw him once or twice, but I've never forgotten him! Some time you must tell me more about him!"

"Oh, I didn't visit him socially!" Carl said drily. "I was the boy he bought his afternoon paper from. But you're right, he was a grand old man. Gave me a couple of dollars one Christmas. Seemed more of a fortune to me then than what I've got does now."

"Yes—I can believe that," Charles said slowly. "I remember a golden half-sovereign he gave me when I was ten. It was the realest money I've ever touched."

There was a silence for a moment, and then Carl said slowly:

"How come if you're not a foreigner to them, if you're English like themselves—and yet a stranger, they trust you round here?"

"Who?" Charles asked sharply.

"The farmers—the village people."

"Do they trust me?" Charles asked slowly.

"Yes. They do. They think you've got something, the way you dropped on that farmer with the sick cow."

"Shawbury?" Charles said slowly. "That was luck."

"More than luck!" Carl insisted. "At least, they say so. Well?"

Charles drew a long breath. Only too well he knew that he had gained their trust—but that his gain had been Judith's loss.

"I've tried to play fair, that's all!" he said shortly.

He glanced down at his watch.

"I must be going." He turned to his companion with a smile. "I hope I've made things a bit clearer to you?"

"So far as you've gone," Carl admitted. "But the thing that gets me most——"

"Yes?" Charles said rather impatiently.

"Yes," Carl said slowly. "I want to know why you always leave action until so late it's almost too late!"

"What!" Charles said sharply.

"It's true. You ask yourself. Time and again. You ask any American—any foreigner for that matter. He'll tell you the British always start out by being haughty as if they don't care a damn for what anyone else thinks because they know they are right. Then they start explaining. They use all the words in the book. Then they use them all over again. When the rest of the world is decided that there's nothing to it but words, then, bing! they go into action!"

"Do we?" In spite of himself Charles laughed.

"You do!" Carl insisted. "Now with us, we scramble to get the first word in! So long as you get the last one, you don't worry. And," he finished explosively, "your way works!"

"Does it?" Suddenly Charles's eyes glinted with excitement. "Does it? Are you sure?"

"I'm sure!" Carl said laconically.

Suddenly Charles grinned.

"Thanks," he said warmly. "That was what I was wanting to know."

He ran down the steep incline, and Carl Brand watched him with a peculiar smile on his lips.

"I wish the storm would break," Judith said impatiently.

She and Desmond had been playing tennis on the Windygates court. Now they were sitting on the terrace watching the sunset, a fiery, ominous thing.

Desmond did not reply.

Judith had been strung up all the afternoon, and more than once he had been at a loss to know what to do or say to her. Several times he had spoken to her and she had not seemed to hear. Now, sitting beside him, she was restless and ill at ease.

Suddenly she seemed to realise how difficult she was being, and she turned to him impetuously.

"Sorry, Des, I'm being a pest," she said contritely.

He smiled at her.

"I feel rather like exploding myself," he admitted. "I expect it is the storm. Let's try to forget it! What have you been doing all day?"

"Oh—nothing much," Judith said indifferently. "You see, there isn't much point in putting myself out now, is there?"

Desmond hesitated.

"Judith, are you really sure you want to sell Windygates?"

"Absolutely certain!" she said promptly. "That is quite settled, Des. You don't have to worry about that! I've made up my mind."

That silenced him. Judith had made up her mind, and it was not for him to try to dissuade her. It stung a little, but there was nothing he could say, he knew, that would change her mind. She had always been like that, just as her father had. He could either accept it or——

With forced brightness she said:

"Tell me what you have been doing."

"I?" he laughed. "Nothing that would interest you very much! Helping Linda clear out the cellar. Going into Wyford to buy stores, peeling potatoes for our dinner this evening—not much of a day's work for a man, is it?"

Judith was silent.

"Des, do you wish I wasn't selling Windygates?" she asked at length. "I mean, it isn't as if you could really take over, could you?"

He laughed shortly.

"No, you're quite right; I'm not much use. I wonder you bother with me!"

"Oh, Des!" she protested. And then, hesitatingly: "Des, I know it can't be easy for you. Me being the one——"

"That has got the money?" he finished. "No, it isn't. I never thought I was so thin-skinned."

"I thought—" she went on slowly, "that when we are married we could make some arrangement so that you didn't feel you had got to ask——"

He got up and went to the wide stone balustrade at the edge of the terrace. He had been right when he had said that he did not know that he was so thin-skinned. He had thought that it would be quite easy to take from a rich wife, but Judith was being so decent. In trying to make it easy for him she was making it all the harder.

Suddenly he turned. He was being a fool. Judith had not agreed to marry him just to please him. She was getting something out of it herself—escape, companionship—he did not know. But he need not feel guilty about it. After all, he really cared for her.

He fumbled in his pocket.

"Judith—I've got something here—it was Mother's,

but I thought in the meantime—I'll have the stones reset or something while you are away."

A diamond ring sparkled in the palm of his hand. He took Judith's small brown hand in his and slipped the ring on to her engagement finger. She let him do it without protest, and when he drew her to him and gently kissed her, she still yielded unquestioningly. He even thought that he felt her lips move under his, but if so, it was the passionless kiss of a child.

He let her go and stood up.

"I'll be getting off now," he said somewhat uncertainly. "Be seeing you to-morrow evening!"

"Yes," she said mechanically. "To-morrow evening!"

When he got home, one glance told Linda that he was in a bad mood. And knowing where he had been, it was not difficult to guess what was the matter. For a time she did not speak. Then, at last, she could restrain herself no more.

"Des, why don't you call it off?" she asked.

He started at the sound of her voice.

"Call what off?" he demanded.

"The engagement," she said impatiently. "You know as well as I do that it won't work out."

Desmond stared at her.

"Do you know what you are saying?" he asked.

"The last thing you ever expected to hear me say," she nodded. "Well, you ought to take all the more notice because of that."

"Well, I'm not going to!" he said loudly. "Understand that? I don't know what tricks you are up to now, but—don't interfere with my affairs! Understand? Judith and I are engaged and we are going to get married. Nothing is going to alter that!"

And leaving Linda to her thoughts, he swung angrily out of the little room.

CHAPTER TEN

WHEN Judith dressed on the night of the party the storm had still not broken. Both the previous night and now there was a grumble of thunder in the distance, but still nothing really came of it.

Both up here and downstairs all the windows and doors were open, but in spite of that there was no movement of the air.

For a long time Judith sat at the window in her dressing-gown, hardly conscious of actual thought but feeling herself part of the heavy air and the threatening sky. Soon something must happen, otherwise even mere existence would be impossible.

Vaguely she was aware that the stable clock struck the half-hour and the three-quarters. Then it chimed the hour and she knew that she could delay no longer. The guests—the last ones that she would ever entertain at Windygates—would begin to arrive in another half-hour and she must be ready to receive them.

She slipped off her severe dressing-gown and put on a set of the undies that she and her aunt had selected when they were in town. They had been absurdly expensive, but perhaps justifiably so, for they were exquisitely fragile and beautifully made. But to-night, for all the pleasure they gave Judith, they might as well have been sackcloth. Sheer nylons, high-heeled white shoes—they gave her an unfamiliar feeling of being tipped forward, for usually she wore very flat heels. Then the pretty white *broderie anglaise* dress that she had so enjoyed buying. As she slipped it over her head she remembered that she had told herself once that when she was wearing this, everything would be all right. It was that sort of dress. Her mouth twisted in a mirthless smile. How silly she had been, how childish. As if clothes could make any difference.

She ran a comb carelessly through her dark curls and regarded the result in the mirror. She supposed she ought to wear make-up—other girls did. But the only time she had ever powdered her nose her father had laughed at her. She had never done it again. Now she wished that she knew all about that sort of thing. It would be a sort of mask behind which one could hide. But she was too much afraid of her own ignorance to risk it. To make a mess of it would be worse than not having any on at all. Then suddenly she changed her mind. From a drawer she took out a lipstick that she had bought in town but never used. Carefully she performed the unfamiliar task and observed the result in the glass. It seemed to make her mouth stand out with unfamiliar clarity, but it was rather striking. It made her look quite different.

From a side-table she took a spray of red roses that Desmond had sent to her. She laid them against her shoulder and saw that they matched the lipstick. It was just luck, of course, but probably people would think that she was rather clever to have thought of it. Carefully she pinned the flowers into place, and shivered a little. Against the whiteness of her dress they looked like great drops of blood.

Abruptly she turned away from the dressing-table. That was all. She was ready to go downstairs now. Miss Harriet had suggested that she should have her mother's pearls out of the bank vaults, but she had decided not to. They would be starting so early the following day that it would be a nuisance to get them back to the bank before leaving. She certainly had no wish to be burdened by the care of them while she was travelling.

At the door she turned abruptly and came back into the room. She had forgotten Desmond's ring.

From the top of the stairs she could hear Miss Harriet's voice as she and the housekeeper discussed the final arrangements. Then she went slowly downstairs. She had no inclination to hurry, but in any case it would have been impossible to do so. Those heels had been difficult enough to manage on a level floor. On the stairs they felt downright dangerous.

She hesitated as she came to the door of the big drawing-room. With the carpets rolled up and most of the furniture moved to the sides of the room it looked unfamiliar and vast. Miss Harriet looked up and saw her. She herself was wearing a silvery-grey dress, and pinned to it were delicate pink roses that had been Mr. Bellairs' gift. She had felt pleasantly excited as she had dressed, for it was not often that occasion arose for wearing formal evening dress nowadays, and with all the excitement of a girl in her teens she had dressed with the knowledge of how she would look to the man she loved.

But now, looking at Judith's unsmiling face, her heart sank. Nothing was to be gained though by commenting on it, so she said as naturally as she was able:

"The dress looks delightful," and turned back to her tasks.

Soon the guests began to arrive, and among the first were Desmond and Linda. Desmond, of course, in conventional evening dress, Linda in a midnight blue dress that had the strange effect of making her seem part of the background, and Miss Harriet found herself wondering if the girl realised it. If so, it indicated a most unusual state of mind in a girl who so persistently stole the limelight as a rule.

Gravely and correctly Judith received congratulations. She and Desmond stood side by side, and it was a far less difficult situation than she had anticipated, for everyone said the same sort of thing and it became almost mechanical to reply adequately. Only Charles's good wishes were different. He bent over her hand as if he were going to kiss it and involuntarily she drew it back a little. Then he straightened up and said so quietly that even Desmond did not hear:

"I hope that the future will hold far more happiness for you than you imagine to be possible!"

Then he turned away to speak to Miss Harriet, and Desmond had to touch Judith gently on the arm to remind her that there were other guests to greet.

At last the dancing began and Judith led off with Desmond. It was something of an ordeal to her to be the first on the floor, for she was painfully conscious that she was not a good dancer. It was a form of entertainment that had never appealed to her particularly and she had just not bothered about it. Desmond, on the other hand, was a good dancer, but not so good that he could make up for the deficiencies in his partner. He was rather inclined to introduce difficult steps, and more than once Judith stumbled. He murmured the

542

usual polite "Sorry," but Judith became increasingly conscious that he was finding the situation difficult, and it was something of a relief when the dance came to an end. After that there were duty dances for both of them and it was not until some time later that they were together again.

Desmond was mopping his forehead.

"Goodness, it's hot! What about going out on to the terrace?"

Judith went out silently with him, but when they had found two empty chairs she blurted out uncomfortably:

"I'm sorry I am so clumsy. I expect I could take lessons, couldn't I?"

"Darling Judith!" He took her hand in his and pressed it gently. "That's a lovely idea. We'll both take lessons. It's the only way to keep up to date. How would you like, when you come back, to spend a while in London? You enjoyed the little you saw of it with Miss Harriet, didn't you?"

"Yes," Judith admitted. "I did—though it was very stuffy after living here." She caught herself up. She was not coming back to Windygates, so that was a silly thing to say. "I expect I shall soon get used to that, though." she finished quickly.

Desmond laughed.

"I want you to do more than get used to it," he told her. "I want you to have the time of your life! We'll go over to Paris as well, shall we? And some time or other we'll do the winter sports—you've no idea how marvellous it is to be surrounded by miles and miles of crisp white snow; it never seems to get muddy there as it does in this country, with the sun shining on it and making it sparkle like diamonds. You'll like that, Judith!"

"Go on," she said almost in a whisper.

"About the things we will do?" he asked. "Well— how about going to Palm Beach? You can swim, can't you?"

"Yes," she said briefly. It was one of the things that her father had insisted on her learning. She had been terrified, but greater than her fear of the water had been her fear of his sarcasm.

"We'll go just where the spirit moves us," he went on softly. "You and I, Judith."

She leaned forward a little, peering into the gathering darkness. There was something white gleaming out there in the garden. A man's white shirt-front—faintly she could hear the sound of two voices, but the woman was strangely invisible. Then there was the little rasp of a cigarette-lighter and Linda's face sprang momentarily into sharp relief. The man was Charles, of course. She could tell him by his height. Besides, what more natural than that they should seek one another's company?

She turned to Desmond and laid her hand on his arm.

"Yes, we *will* have a good time, Des! And nothing and nobody shall stop us, shall they?"

For a second he paused, then:

"Nothing and nobody," he echoed, an oddly sober note in his voice.

Suddenly Judith stood up.

"It's not very polite of me to stay out here too long, Des. After all, I suppose I am really the hostess."

"Of course you are," he said promptly, and went in with her.

Out in the garden Charles was saying coldly:

"If you will excuse me, I must look for my partner for the next dance."

Linda laughed. She was in an oddly contradictory mood.

"How useful conventionality is," she said mockingly. "You would just love to wring my neck, wouldn't you? Only because we are both guests in someone else's house you behave like the perfect English gentleman I have heard you described as."

"I don't know who called me that," Charles said bitterly. "But if they could read my thoughts at the moment that is the last description they would use."

He turned abruptly and left her. It was no wish of his that they had danced together, but she had made it impossible for him to do anything else but ask her to. Now, manners or not, he could not tolerate her company another second. He had seen Desmond and Judith on the terrace, their heads together, deep, no doubt, in plans.

Momentarily Judith was without a partner. She stood half hidden by a slender column, watching the other dancers, and Charles came quietly up behind her.

"Will you dance this with me?" he asked quietly.

She started at the sound of his voice, and he saw her small hands clench.

"Forgive me, but—I have danced such a lot," she said without turning.

Suddenly Charles was filled with sheer, primitive fury. Linda had jibed at him for observing the conventions. Now he flung them from him.

"I wonder if that is your real reason?" he asked deliberately. "Or—are you afraid to dance with me?"

"Afraid!" she swirled round on him. "Of course not! Why should I be?"

"I can't think," he admitted. "I—I just wondered."

"As a matter of fact," Judith said coldly. "I am perfectly well aware that I am not a good dancer and I sought to spare you. But if you like to take the risk."

The next second she was in his arms. And instantly she knew that dancing with Charles was a very different thing from dancing with Desmond. Admittedly she had had a tango with Desmond, which was very different from the sweet lilting rhythm of the waltz they were playing now, but that was not the only difference.

She felt as if she had melted into his arms so that they were moving as one person. Her feet were obeying no conscious directions of her brain and yet they moved in perfect accord with his. They were moving in a world from which everyone else was shut out, and she was strangely content to have it so. It was so peaceful— and then, abruptly, the peace was shattered.

Against her own slender body she could feel the throbbing of his heart, and she caught her breath as his arm tightened.

"Judith, Judith!" She heard his hoarse whisper in her ear, half believed that she felt his lips on her hair.

Suddenly, it seemed that her heart was beating in unison with his and she was conscious of a rising tide of emotion that had little or nothing to do with the dance or the sweetness of the music. It was Charles—his nearness, the sheer intoxication of being in his arms.

She realised that he was steering her to the doors that led to the terrace and she was powerless to resist him, but even as they passed out into the darkness the spell was shattered.

Someone already out there gave a shout.

"There's a fire somewhere down at the farm! There—look—the flames shot up then——"

"The ricks!" Charles shouted, flinging off his coat. "Judith, tell someone to ring for the fire brigade." Then he was gone.

Over her shoulder Judith gasped:

"Aunt Harriet!"

Then she was running, stumbling, falling over the uneven ground in her high heels with half her guests behind her.

By the time they reached the farm buildings Charles had already fixed a long hose to the hydrant that Judith had had put in just that summer, and was unrolling it.

"It won't stretch!" Judith gasped. "We'll have to wait until the brigade comes!"

"There'll be nothing left for them to put out by then," Charles said grimly. "No, this will take the water as near as possible, and we'll have to go at it with a string of buckets. Get out as many as we've got and get everybody that's fit to lend a hand. Hurry—there isn't much time."

A glance was sufficient to see that he was quite right. One rick was well alight and a gusty wind had risen. It was lifting flaming shreds of hay from the burning rick and blowing them on to the next one. Unless they acted very quickly that must blaze up, and then the next.

Fortunately the wind was blowing away from the farm buildings so they were in no danger, and despite their party attire most of Judith's guests were working like Trojans. For the rest of her life she was to have little pictures like cameos stamped on her mind of Mr. Bellairs in his shirt-sleeves filling buckets that were instantly grabbed up by both men and women to be flung into the burning mass; of Charles standing on the top of the second rick pitchforking down the burning wisps as they were blown over; of Desmond beating them out with a sack as they fell to the ground.

She heard someone speak, and turned. Above the noise of the flames and the shouting young Joe Sellars bawled in her ear:

"Mr. Saxilby—he would be doing the most dangerous job, he would. I'm going up with him."

"No, Joe," she began quickly, but he had gone, and she saw the comradely grin with which Charles greeted him. Her heart seemed to swell with something that was oddly like pride. It was so true. Charles would be where there was most danger.

She saw her aunt hurry into the field and speak to Mr. Bellairs, and in the glare of the fire saw the consternation on his face. She did not need to go over to ask what was wrong—it was only too obvious. The fire brigade was already out. It just depended on their own efforts. That meant that there was no hope of saving anything of the rick that had started all the trouble. All that they could do would be to stand by and see that it did not spread, and that was growing more and more difficult as the fire got a greater hold and sparks leaped madly into the air. Charles was in increasing danger, and before long he turned to Joe, the sweat running down his blackened face.

"Get down!" he gasped. "We shan't be able to hold it off much longer."

"I'll get down when you do," Joe said stubbornly, and even at such a moment Charles's heart lifted. There had been many times when he had doubted the wisdom of his presence at Windygates, but whatever the future might hold he could at least have the satisfaction of knowing that he had won both the affection and trust of this tough youngster. It was something.

"You'll get down now—when I tell you!" he ordered. "Go on—hop it!"

Reluctantly Joe obeyed. Even he had to admit that despite his hero's efforts the flames were gaining the upper hand. He, as many others of them had done, glanced up at the sky. If only the clouds gathered up there would break——if only the rain would come. It couldn't be long delayed now, in fact, more than one heavy drop had already fallen, but reluctantly, isolated, useless.

"We want it turned on like a tap!" Joe muttered, and looked back to see Charles scrambling down and the second rick alight.

"Can't we do nothing?" Joe asked, and Charles, even at such a moment, found himself heartened at that "we."

" 'Fraid not, Joe," he admitted regretfully. "We may be able to hold it off the third rick until the rain comes, but that's the best we can hope for now." He passed his hand across his dry lips. "Get me something to drink, there's a good chap."

Joe turned eagerly to run off, but Judith was already standing there with a big mug of cold water.

"Aunt Harriet has organised supplies," she said gravely. "I expect you can do with this."

His fingers touched hers as he took it from her, and as he drank, his eyes were fixed on her face.

"That was good," he said, handing it back to her. "I'm sorry about this, Judith."

"So am I," she admitted. "But I don't think it is anybody's fault, least of all yours! Probably it was the heat that started it off. I don't suppose we are the only ones that are in trouble, you know."

He grinned ruefully at her.

"And the insurance is paid up, so why should we worry," he finished. "You know as well as I do that we're both sick at heart over it——the waste, the labour that has gone for nothing."

Judith nodded silently, and Charles laid his hand heavily on her shoulder.

"At least we're in it together," he said, and for a moment his hand gripped. Then he was gone again into the thick of the fight.

For a moment Judith stood rooted to the ground, still feeling the pressure of his hand; then her attention was caught by a sound that seemed to rise above all other sounds.

In the field next to that in which the ricks were burning was a large herd of bullocks. They were in no danger whatever, for the wind was blowing in the opposite direction, but there was no doubt that they were becoming increasingly nervous with the noise and leaping flames. A little more and they might stampede, possibly even break through the hedges. Any animal in the clutches of mass fear can perform what would at other times be impossibilities.

Obviously the best thing to do was to get them into an adjacent field where they would not only be farther off from all the noise, but because of a drop in the ground would in effect have a much higher hedge to protect them from the sight of those terrifying flames.

She slipped away quietly without bothering to tell anyone of her intentions and climbed over the gate rather than open it. Already several animals were careering about sowing the seeds of panic, and one of these caught sight of Judith. Probably to its terrified mind and dazed eyes the sight of the small white figure was so unusual that it was the last straw. And, unlike those other terrifying things that could not be inspected at close quarters, this thing could.

Suddenly Judith, rather foolishly taking the shortest cut possible to the farther gate instead of working round the edge of the field, was conscious of heavy hoof-beats behind her, and turned. With a gasp she recognised her danger. Only one steer was taking much notice of her, but other heads were lowered as they watched the bellowing, over-wrought creature. At any moment, she knew perfectly well, mass hysteria might cause them to follow a leader, any leader, so long as he seemed to know what he was up to.

Sheer panic surged up in Judith's heart. If she continued walking steadily they might decide to take her for granted, but she would lose valuable time. On the other hand, if she were to run, they would almost certainly stampede.

With her hands clenched by her side she tried to make herself walk on, but for her as well as for the animals that watched her, it had been an unnerving evening. Suddenly she began to run—and knew as she did that she had done the wrong thing.

In real earnest now they were chasing her, and the gate that meant safety seemed farther off than ever. She was getting breathless too, and the unfamiliar high-heeled shoes were slowing her down considerably. Terrifyingly they were on her. She redoubled her efforts and tripped full length over a thick tussock of grass. As she fell, she knew that only in seconds now they would trample over her.

And at that instant she heard a shout. Strong arms caught her up and she was running again, running desperately, forced on by a strength and determination greater than her own.

"I can't!" she gasped, but she had no choice. Charles —she knew that it was Charles although there was no time to look up at him—was forcing her relentlessly on, and from his strong grip there was no escape.

Fortunately for Judith, he had seen her almost as soon as she had entered the field, guessing her intention but realising the danger she was exposed to more accurately than she did. He had shouted to her, but above the other noises she had not heard him and there had been only one thing for it. He had abandoned the ricks to their fate and raced after her.

Actually, he had reached the gate before she was in any immediate danger, and for a moment or two he had stood there knowing that if he went after her he might precipitate the very panic in the herd of which he was so apprehensive. Then Judith had begun to run.

He had vaulted the gate and was running like a mad-man in almost no time at all, but he had to skirt the fringe of the herd to get to her, and his heart almost failed him. If only he had not wasted time—then he saw her stumble, and fear lent wings to his feet.

He caught her up in his arms and knew grimly that

their chance was not a good one. Into his mind there flashed a picture of her small, beloved body crushed by mad, heedless hooves.

Then the gate seemed to rise up suddenly before them, and with a sob of relief, he knew that he could save her.

Judith felt herself picked up bodily in his arms and the next instant he had almost thrown her over the gate into the safety of the field beyond.

She stumbled forward on to her hands and knees, her hands grasping at the rough grass. A stinging-nettle slashed at her face but she did not feel it as she scrambled to her feet and rushed to the gate.

"Charles! Charles!" she screamed and saw him throw up his arms. Then he was submerged in a wave of heavy, blundering bodies and she could not see him any more.

Great sobs tore at her. He had saved her, but at what a price!

And then it seemed as if the herd had run the fear out of themselves, for they turned quietly away, completely uninterested in the still form on the ground.

Judith scrambled back over the gate to him and knelt down beside him.

"Charles! Charles!" she bent over him and saw that the blood was welling from a deep cut on his head, that his shirt was torn and bloodstained, and to Judith the world went suddenly black.

She put her hand to her mouth, biting the soft flesh in an effort to remain conscious. Charles had saved her, she must not faint now when he was lying there so badly injured—or—or dead.

She did not know whether to drag him to safety first in the other field before she went for help, or to leave him where he was lest in moving him she should work more damage. Then she heard a shout and saw that a group of men were hurrying across the field through the herd of now quietly grazing steers. And as she waited for them, crouching over Charles as she pressed the edges of the wound in his head together in an effort to minimise the bleeding, she felt the sudden lash of rain on her back. The storm had broken at last.

Very carefully, on an improvised stretcher, they carried Charles to the house. Miss Harriet and Mr. Bellairs quietly took command. The doctor was already on the way, they told Judith—would be there any moment. And the ambulance would not be long after.

Their voices seemed to come from a great distance, and Judith found that someone was holding a glass to her lips. She drank its contents because it would have been too difficult to refuse, and the mist that had surrounded her cleared away.

"Is he—is he———" she whispered, and could not finish the sentence.

"He is alive," said Mr. Bellairs' grave, gentle voice. "But he is very badly injured. You will have to be brave, Judith."

She turned away, her lips quivering.

"If only I could do something," she muttered.

Almost instantly the doctor arrived, approved of Miss Harriet's temporary bandaging and the fact that they had moved Charles as little as possible.

To Judith he was cheerful and reassuring.

"A chap like Saxilby is too tough to let a little thing like that put him out," he told her.

Judith shook her head.

"Please, please, Doctor," she begged.

He looked down at the strained, anxious face and cleared his throat. There were some women you could lie to and some you couldn't. This was one of those who had to know the truth.

"He's in a nasty mess," he admitted. "But I can't tell how bad until I get him to the hospital. You'd better come along as well. And Miss Harriet."

They followed the ambulance in Mr. Bellairs' car, and Desmond, a silent spectator standing a little apart from the other watching guests, made no attempt to hinder Judith.

Linda, from the other side of the room, came quietly over to her brother and slipped her arm through his. They were not usually a demonstrative couple, but now she felt him hug her arm against him.

"We'd better get home," he said gruffly. "There's no point in our staying here."

To Judith the next hour or so seemed an eternity. She sat very still in an armchair in the waiting-room, her hands loosely linked in her lap, her eyes staring unseeingly before her.

In her mind's eye she could still see Charles's still figure on the ground, was still bruised with that agonising fear that he was dead.

And even now, he still might die.

All the warmth seemed to drain out of her body and her heart was frozen with fear. If Charles were to die— it would be the end of the world for her.

And, as she sat there, in a moment of blinding vision she understood why.

She loved Charles. Had, so it seemed to her, loved him for a long, long while.

CHAPTER ELEVEN

HOW could one love a person and yet believe all the time that one hated him? Judith was too inexperienced to realise what a thin line there can be between the two emotions—or that hatred can be engendered of fear—fear of the unknown, fear of being hurt.

But one thing she did at least understand. Whether she would share the future with Charles or not, whether he died now or lived—to marry Linda—she would always love him.

And in that knowledge she found something that stabilised life and taught her a woman's true place in it. Men and women were different. Had and ought to have a different outlook on life so that each was not the same as the other but complementary. Right from the beginning it had been impossible for her to take the place of the son that her father had wanted so fervently, and she should never have been allowed to try. Life had always been frustrating because she had attempted to live it in a way that was foreign to a woman's nature, only she had been too stubborn to see that or admit it if she had.

And that, of all reasons, was the real one why she had hated Charles. He, with the normal man's approach, had taken it for granted that she would rely on him—that she would need to, just because he was a man and she a woman. And he had compelled her to admit it to herself, if no one else. He had always been there when she needed help—and she *had* needed it. But besides that, he had made her conscious of himself as a man. He had stirred some chord in her so unfamiliar that she had denied its existence until last night when they had danced together.

Subconsciously, she had known then. Later, when she had seen him lying unconscious and injured, she knew that she would never be able to deny it again.

And Charles? Why, Charles loved Linda, of course. They had planned to get married. So he could not possibly love her, Judith. It had just been a trick of her imagination, wishful thinking, that had persuaded her that he, too, had been stirred last night. Or perhaps she had shown too clearly that she was so supremely conscious of his nearness and he, pitying her, had responded ever so slightly to save her pride—she sighed. She understood so little about her own sex, had despised it for the very things that now she would have given the world to. be able to put into their correct perspective.

Miss Harriet, hearing the sigh looked tenderly at the girl with whom she was keeping this vigil. She had seen Judith's tortured face as she had walked beside the hurdle on which they had placed Charles and had read its message only too well. She blamed herself quite unreasonably that such a thing should have happened. If only I had not interfered, if I had not chosen Charles —but it was no use thinking things like that now, still less saying them.

The door opened and both women turned expectantly, but it was only an attendant with a pot of tea and two cups.

"Thought you might like it," he said sympathetically. "It passes the time, like."

Judith stirred herself. The last thing she felt she wanted was to eat or drink, but it was a kind thought.

"Thank you," she said gently. "You are one of the Sellars boys, aren't you? I am afraid I don't remember your name."

"Chris," he said eagerly. "I came three above young Joe.—I've got him outside. Thinks the world of Mr. Saxilby, he does. Been a different boy since he came down here. He was a real handful, and Mum didn't know what to do with him, but butter wouldn't melt in his mouth now! Mr. Saxilby gave him a good tanning for saying something rude about you, didn't he, Miss?"

"About me!" she echoed in amazement. "No, I don't think so—about someone else, though."

"No, it was you, Miss," he persisted. "Because I made young Joe tell me what he'd said. And it was about you being boss at Windygates. Said he wasn't going to take orders from a woman—least of all one that no man had ever looked at twice. If you'll excuse me for repeating it, Miss," he added diffidently.

The quick colour rushed to Judith's face. She had been so sure that he had fought for Linda—and all the time it had been on her account. Not, of course, she told herself firmly, that it meant anything. Naturally Charles could not allow the boy to say things like that without taking notice of it; it did not mean that he disagreed with Joe. And, after all, it was true no man had ever looked at her. Except Des, and that had probably surprised other people as much as it had her.

Des. She had forgotten all about him. And he had not attempted to stop her coming here, though he certainly must have known that she had done so. She would have to see him as soon as possible and tell him that she could not marry him—that she had nothing to give him and that it was not fair.

And Linda. How strange that she had not come to the hospital as well. But perhaps she had and was waiting somewhere else.

"Is there anyone else waiting for news of Mr. Saxilby?" she asked Chris Sellars, and he shook his head.

"Only Joe. Another cup, Miss? No? Well, by and by, p'raps, if they keep you waiting much longer."

He went out, and Judith said suddenly:

"If he dies, it will be my fault. I asked for trouble—and it all fell upon Charles. I shall never forgive myself."

Miss Harriet got up and walked over to her. She sat down on the arm of the chair and took Judith's cold hands in hers.

"Judith, dear—" she began, and then the door opened for a second time and the doctor came in with a flourish that in itself spoke of good news.

"Well," he began cheerfully. "It's not so bad as we thought! That young man certainly must have been born under a lucky star. Two ribs gone and rather a nasty cut on his head. A little bit of concussion, of course, but I wonder his skull wasn't battered in. Oh, and one hand is burnt a bit. Of course, he's pretty badly bruised, but apart from being very sorry for himself for a while, that isn't important. Yes, he's been very lucky. Now don't you start fainting all over the place, Judith. Isn't that a woman all over. Keeps going quite all right until she gets good news and then keels over. Stick her head between her knees, Miss Harriet. She'll be all right in a moment."

"I'm all right now," Judith gasped, gripping the arms of the chair. "It's only——"

"I know. Reaction. Don't try to teach me my job," he said calmly. "I'm only relieved that you aren't as tough as you've always thought you were. Now then, Miss Harriet." He turned his back on Judith, for which she was grateful, and addressed himself to the older woman. "This boy is unconscious and probably will be for quite a while. When he starts coming round I shall give him something to keep him quiet for a bit. He needs rest—loads of it—and he won't get it with that smack on the head and his bruises. Now then, the point is this. We're so full up here that we don't know which way to turn. Any more emergencies and they'll have to have a bed made up on the floor. Is there anywhere that young Saxilby can be taken—to-morrow morning say?"

Miss Harriet heard the catch of Judith's breath and made up her mind.

"Certainly," she said calmly. "He must come to Windygates."

The doctor shot a look at Judith, and then cocked a curious eye at Miss Harriet.

"Oh!" he said mildly. "I was under the impression—however, if you are sure. You can have a nurse in night and morning to dress the wounds. Can you cope with the rest of it?"

"I can," Miss Harriet said tranquilly. "Judith will help me, you see."

The doctor looked again at Judith, but though his glance was still curious it was very kind as well.

"All right, then. Provided there have been no adverse developments, you can expect the ambulance at about ten. And," he added, "you've let yourself in for something this time. Oh, he'll be grateful enough while he feels bad, but just wait until he is convalescent. These men who have never had a day's illness are always the worst to deal with."

Miss Harriet smiled but made no comment, and she and Judith prepared to go.

"I'll run you home if you like," the doctor offered.

"That is very kind of you," Miss Harriet said gratefully. "But I think we may find—Mr. Bellairs."

He nodded understandingly.

"Yes, of course," he said. "Well, we'll see."

But Mr. Bellairs was waiting. He jumped out of the car as soon as they approached, and it was evident from his face that he had heard the news. But a glance at Judith told him that this was no time for talking. The sooner she was home and in her own bed the better.

He opened the door for them and drove them back in silence, and if, as he said good-bye, his hand held Miss Harriet's very closely, that was the only thought that they had for themselves. Their one desire was to help the girl who had, all unconsciously, kept them apart for so long.

Suddenly Judith began to shiver, and with her arm

round the slim shoulders, Miss Harriet took her upstairs to her own room and helped her into bed.

"Aunt Harriet," Judith said suddenly from the depths of the big four-poster bed in which she looked so very small. *"Shall* I be able to help you? I—I don't know anything about nursing, you know," she added wistfully.

Miss Harriet sat down on the edge of the bed and took her hand in a reassuring clasp.

"You can, if you are willing to learn," she said gently. "Of course, you will be very busy on the farm without Charles, but I shall be grateful for your help in the evening."

"Will you really?" Judith said eagerly, her face suddenly alight.

Her aunt smiled.

"Really and truly," she insisted. "And now, darling, you must try to get some sleep. Would you like some aspirin?"

"No, I don't think so. They make me feel so odd," Judith told her. "I will try to be sensible."

And just at that moment the stable clock struck two.

Judith sat up abruptly.

"Aunt Harriet, we were to have started in six hours' time!" she exclaimed.

"Yes, but——"

"Aunt Harriet—" Judith caught feverishly at her aunt's hands. "We can't go—you said we'd have Charles—we—I can't leave him."

Miss Harriet took the girl in her arms and held her close.

"I know, darling," she soothed. "I know! In the morning I will telephone through to the steamship line and cancel our sailing. We shall have to forfeit our fares but—that can't be helped. I must cable to Canada as well."

Gently Judith released herself.

"You must go to bed, too. There will be a lot to do in the morning—getting ready for Charles, and I expect a lot of people will ring up."

"Sure to," Miss Judith agreed. "We must get in

touch with Charles's brother as well. I wonder if I can find the number on one of the letters Charles wrote to me before he came?"

"Aunt Harriet—if you don't mind, I would like to ring Sir Roger up," Judith said thoughtfully. "I—I think I ought to. You see, after all, it is my responsibility, isn't it? As Charles works here."

"And you are mistress of Windygates," Miss Harriet said understandingly. "Yes, I think you are quite right. And now I must go. You're sure you wouldn't like me to sleep with you?"

"No, I shall be all right," Judith promised.

For a moment the eyes of the two women met, and although Judith's lips were quivering she managed to give Miss Harriet an answering smile.

As the older woman went along the corridor to her room she had to admit that she felt thankful for one thing at least. Out of the night's events a better understanding between the two of them had grown up than there had ever been before. Whatever the future held for Judith, her aunt would be able to help her to some extent at least.

Actually Judith did not go to sleep for a long time, but her thoughts that night were her own property and it was a long time before she ever spoke of what they had been.

With the morning came activity. As early as was reasonable, Judith made the call to Sussex. Sir Roger, she was told, was out riding, but Lady Garvin——

So Mary came to the telephone and took the message.

"He should be quite all right," Judith said earnestly. "I spoke to the matron about ten minutes ago and she says his condition is quite satisfactory. I know they always say that, but I don't think she would try to put me off with silly reassurances if they weren't justified," she explained, unconscious of the quiet note of assurance which her position locally gave to her voice.

"I am quite sure she wouldn't," Mary agreed. "Judith —you'll look after him, won't you?"

"I'll do anything—everything—" Judith began, and stopped because a sob was choking her.

"I know you will," Mary said gently. "You'll keep in touch with us, won't you?"

"Of course," Judith promised. "And if you and Sir Roger would like to come here, I shall be very pleased."

"Well," Mary deliberated. "We'll see! I'll speak to my husband about it and ring you back if he decides he would like to be there."

As she rang off, Mary's face was thoughtful. She was quite sure that Roger would want to dash straight off, but——

"I'm not sure that we should," she said when, as she had expected, Roger reacted in just that way. "I don't see what we could do that isn't being done already. And—we might spoil everything."

"Spoil everything?" Roger asked blankly. "I don't see——"

Mary slipped her arm through his.

"I think," she said softly, "that very soon Charles will have everything in the world that he wants—if we don't interfere."

Miss Harriet had been right in saying that Judith would be busy about the farm. The insurance company would, of course, have to be notified about the fire and would certainly want to inspect the scene of it. Judith herself was satisfied that the excessive heat had been the cause of it, but it would be wiser for her not to disturb the sodden, blackened ricks, leaving that to the insurance inspector. So, in gumboots and heavy mackintosh, she supervised the covering of the two ricks with heavy tarpaulins, tethering the corners firmly with well-driven pegs.

The rain, now that it had started, seemed as if it would go on indefinitely. Little brown streams meandered through some of the drenched fields, but there was no danger of flooding. The ground was too well drained for that, as well as being slightly on the slope.

She took a roundabout route to go to the gate over which Charles had tossed her to safety the night before.

On the other side of it was the place where his inert body had lain. As for the herd that had caused the trouble, they were so quiet that it seemed impossible that they had ever been so menacing. They were sheltering under trees, gently chewing the cud, utterly indifferent to everything but their own comfort.

But she had little time to think. There was the day's routine to superintend, the milk returns to make up, letters to write and answer—all the hundred and one tasks that make life on a farm.

She had visitors, too. Farmers from round about who came to sympathise about the fire and enquire about Charles, a possible new hand whom Charles had made an appointment to see. And Joe Sellars, red-eyed with lack of sleep but talking nineteen to the dozen about Charles. To him he attributed so many amazing escapades that Judith's hair nearly stood on end until she realised that most of them must be culled from the weekly thrillers that were always sticking out of Joe's pocket. But she fully sympathised with his feelings. If Charles had got into the situations which his fiction heroes did, there was no doubt but that he would have coped with the whole lot of them.

When she got back to Windygates she found Miss Harriet on the telephone. When she hung up, she turned to Judith with a gusty sigh.

"The only time that bell has stopped ringing was when I was already talking to someone else on the telephone," she commented. "Oh, by the way, Desmond rang up. He asked me to tell you that he was coming to see you this afternoon. And Linda," she added rather reluctantly.

Judith, with her back to her aunt, said quietly:

"Yes—of course." And then: "Have they brought Charles?"

Miss Harriet nodded.

"The doctor came with him, and is quite satisfied that the journey has done him no harm. He is in the room next to mine."

"That is a good arrangement," Judith said quietly. "He is still unconscious, of course?"

"Yes—though he muttered a little as they carried him in."

Judith nodded and went slowly upstairs. She hesitated for a moment at the door of Charles's room and then she went quietly in.

The curtains were drawn and she had to wait a moment before she became accustomed to the dimmer light. Charles lay very still, and for a moment the shadow of the fear she had felt the previous night caught at Judith's heart. But he was breathing steadily, and although colour had not entirely returned to his face, there was a suggestion of latent strength and health that was reassuring.

Slowly she came closer until she stood beside the bed. It was a more modern one than her own four-poster and it would be easier, she realised, for nursing. Probably Aunt Harriet had thought of that, as well as the wisdom of having him near her own room in case he stirred in the night.

A little sob forced itself between Judith's lips because she herself could do so little for Charles. It was such a soft sound that it could hardly have disturbed him, yet he moved restlessly, and instantly Judith drew back, waiting breathlessly. But he did not stir again and, greatly daring, she leant over him and softly touched his crisp fair hair with her lips.

Then she went to her own room and, sitting by the open window, looked out on to the broad acres that had once meant so much to her and now meant nothing at all in comparison with Charles.

Slow tears forced themselves from her wistful brown eyes, but when, later on, she was told that Linda was downstairs, she was completely composed and gravely welcoming. Desmond had not come with his sister, as she had imagined would be the case. Instead, there was a man whose face seemed vaguely familiar to Judith, although she could not remember that she had ever met him. Linda, without explanation as to his presence, introduced him as Carl Brand.

"I've been staying in the village," he explained when

he saw the expression on Judith's face. "You may have seen me about."

"That must be it," she agreed, and turned to Linda. "Charles is still unconscious," she said quietly. "But I expect you would like to see him. Will you come up?"

To her surprise, Linda shook her head.

"No, thank you," she said firmly, and then, seeing Judith's surprise, she added: "He might come round, and I should be the last person that he would want to set eyes on."

"But——" Judith began uncomprehendingly.

Carl Brand, who had been watching the two girls with considerable interest, suddenly took a step or two nearer to Linda and gripped her hand firmly in his.

"Linda has something she wants to tell you, Miss Ravensdale," he announced. "When you're heard it, you'll understand why she says that." He looked at Linda expectantly.

Linda drew a long, sighing breath and seemed suddenly to find courage from his sustaining clasp.

"I've played you a pretty beastly trick," she began precipitately. "I'd better put it as briefly as I can. It's this: Charles has never made love to me and never so much as hinted that he wanted to marry me. I made all that up because I thought that you were beginning to be attracted to him and I intended marrying him myself. Because he has got plenty of money," she added.

Wide-eyed, Judith stared at her. It couldn't be true. Linda's story had been so convincing—and who could help preferring Linda to her? Linda had all the charms, all the graces that men like, while she was just a hobbledehoy—and an unpleasantly arrogant one at that.

Linda turned to Carl.

"She doesn't believe me," she said anxiously. "That's what I was afraid of."

"Tell her the rest of it," Carl advised confidently.

"Yes, of course. Judith, you know the day I told you all about Charles? Well, something you said must have made him guess that there was some specific reason why your attitude towards him had suddenly changed. And what is more, he seems to have connected it up with me immediately, because he came straight down to see me. He told me that you had begun to trust him and then, it had all gone and you were back where you had been at the beginning. He wanted to know what I had said. I—I told him half-truths, but I didn't convince him. And then he guessed what my motive for lying had been, for he told me—" her voice shook a little at the memory of that humiliating moment for which she had only herself to thank—"that you mattered more to him than anything else in the world, that you were the only woman he had ever loved or wanted to marry, though you had no idea of it."

Judith's hand pressed against her throat.

"It can't be true," she whispered. "It can't be——"

"It is true," Carl Brand said gently. "I heard him say it, Miss Ravensdale."

"Don't you see," Linda said eagerly, "how everything fits? I told you that Charles stayed here in spite of the fact that you gave him such a rough time because he wanted to get hold of Windygates. But it wasn't that. Charles wanted to stay because he loved you and he had to have time to teach you." Suddenly she dropped Carl's hand and caught Judith by the shoulders. "Wake up, Judith!" she said urgently. "You've got to believe it! It's true! And you can't deny that you want it to be! You love Charles, don't you?"

Suddenly a beautiful wave of colour stained Judith's cheeks.

"Yes" she admitted softly. "I love him!"

"Well, then," Linda said impatiently. "Don't you understand? Everything is all right?"

Judith did not reply for a moment. Suddenly she had realised that what Linda had said was true, it did all fit in. Charles's regretful "There is a reason, but you are too much of a child to understand" when she had demanded that he should tell her why she should trust him. The way, in spite of the difficulties that she herself had put in his way, he had always stood by her —had even fought for her and finally saved her life. She had been so blind, so incredibly blind. She had even tried to explain away the moved tone in which he had said her name just last night, that soft touch on her hair.

It was incredible—so unbelievable that it left her dazed with happiness—but it was true. Charles loved her.

She heard Linda give a sigh of relief, and suddenly she could smile at the girl who had been her friend and yet who had behaved so meanly to her only to regret it.

"That's all right," she heard Linda say as if it were suddenly difficult to speak. "I—I suppose you couldn't find it in your heart to forgive me, Judith? I know it's a lot to ask."

For answer, Judith caught her in warm, friendly arms.

"It's over—and forgotten," she declared firmly. "So don't think about it ever again."

Linda looked at her with eyes that glinted with tears.

"I shall, you know," she said. "It's one thing for you to forgive me, but I'm not going to forgive myself in a hurry."

Judith looked troubled. In her new-found happiness she wanted everybody else to be happy, and with instinctive knowledge she turned to Carl Brand.

"You mustn't let her feel like that," she said earnestly. "Promise you won't."

Carl put an arm round Linda's shoulders.

"I'll do my best," he promised, and led Linda out of the open french windows. Judith heard a car start up.

She stood very still in the quiet room, gazing at her own reflection in a mirror that must, in its time, have reflected so many Ravensdale women. And in its quiet depths she saw the face of a woman made happy by beauty.

"I'm glad," she whispered. "To be beautiful—for Charles," and gazed on, though her eyes were dreamy and she saw, not her own face, but the future, shared with Charles.

That was how Desmond saw her as he came quietly to the window. For a long moment he watched, his lips twitching at the sight, and then, though he had not consciously made any sound, she must have become aware that she was being watched, for she turned. And instantly all the joy, all the tender anticipation of the future faded.

Desmond, with a wordless exclamation, crossed the space that separated them in a couple of strides. He took Judith by the shoulders and shook her.

"Do you think I am such a rotter as to keep you to your promise after all this?" he asked roughly. "Particularly when I've known right from the first that I could never make you happy."

Judith's sensitive face grew troubled. She knew that it was true, but she had given her word and—Desmond had trusted her.

"But you?" she asked wistfully. "You—you did want to marry me, didn't you?"

Desmond smiled crookedly.

"Little silly," he said, gently rocking her backwards and forwards. "Of course I did! But—I shall get over it. Oh yes, I shall! You see, although I love you, I know perfectly well that I should not have been happy either. It takes two to make a love story that lasts, you know. So it is better this way. At least we shall always be good friends."

"I think you are trying to make things easier for me," Judith insisted, very near tears.

Desmond bent his head and kissed her gently on the tip of her nose.

"Stop that," he commanded firmly. "I never could stand having a tearful woman on my hands! So damp and depressing."

Judith laughed rather uncertainly.

"That's better," Desmond told her approvingly. "Now, listen to me. There is nothing for you to worry about. I've got a job—a good one—in America. That chap who came here with Linda offered it to me. And Linda is coming too. She will housekeep for me. Now are you satisfied?"

"Well—quite a lot," Judith admitted and then, as a question that had been in her mind earlier occurred to her, she asked curiously: "Des, who *is* Carl Brand?"

Desmond grinned cheerfully.

"My future brother-in-law, I imagine. And I rather fancy that I shall be looking for a new housekeeper in the not very distant future. Now then, I really must go."

Just for a moment Judith clung to him. After all, he represented the past, had been one of her few friends.

And Desmond, recognising the gesture for what it was, gave her a warm, brotherly hug and kissed her soundly.

"That's for good-bye," he told her. "I am going to be very busy for the short time that is left before we go, and I may not have time to come again," his voice broke suddenly. "Bless you, darling," he said, and hurried out of the room.

Judith took a few steps as if to follow him, but, with an understanding that she would not have had a short while ago, she halted. Unless she could have gone to Des and told him that she loved him, it was better to let him go like this, keeping his chin up, pretending, for her sake, that everything was all right.

Yet she waited a little while before, slowly, she went up to Charles's room.

He was sleeping peacefully now, and instead of lying so quiet and straight, had turned on one side and was hunched up as a small boy might be.

Judith's lips curved tenderly. He was so strong, and yet, at this moment, his face was so young, so vulnerable. She bent nearer, tracing each beloved feature of his sleeping face with love-filled eyes.

She dared to believe now that Charles loved her, and yet she knew that she wanted to hear him say it, that nothing else would carry that last little fortress of doubt. Anything so wonderful could not be true.

And as if, even in his sleep, Charles knew of her need, he suddenly stirred and opened his eyes. For a moment they wandered vaguely and then they centred on her face.

His lips parted.

"Hallo, my darling," he said weakly and put up his hand to find hers.

Very gently Judith laid it in his, and with a little sigh of satisfaction Charles went to sleep again, a smile on his lips.

CHAPTER TWELVE

CHARLES'S progress was reassuringly steady and, contrary to the doctor's prophecy, he proved an extremely amenable convalescent.

He was, in fact, completely docile and very patient, and Miss Harriet, waiting on him, had difficulty in keeping from smiling. There was, however, a twinkle in her eye that defied all her control, but this Charles, usually so observant, failed to notice.

Nor did it appear to worry her that in spite of her request to help her aunt, Judith showed positive reluctance to go into Charles's room. To Judith's immense relief, Miss Harriet did not even comment on the fact.

But the truth of the matter was that Judith, madly happy though she was, was suddenly shy in Charles's presence. While he had been completely helpless it had been a different matter, but now that he was sitting propped up in bed he looked so much like his usual self, so fit and so essentially masculine that Judith found it difficult to talk naturally. And she had to, for since that one tender greeting when, for all she knew, he might have mistaken her for Linda, he had not said another word to suggest that he cared for her.

It was not that she disbelieved Linda or the evidence of her own ears, but—but—why did he say nothing? The old Judith, had she wanted an answer to a question, would have asked for it straight out, but this was different. Ignorant though she was of the ways of a woman, instinct told her that the first move must come from him. Until he chose to speak, she must wait as patiently as she could, the prey to changing moods of utter bliss or black despair.

She found refuge in talking to him of matters connected with the farm. The local Agricultural Show was, of course, indefinitely postponed with foot-and-mouth in the district, but so far reports showed that the outbreak was confined to Shawbury's farm, thanks more to the fact of its isolation than any care of his. He was, of course, as they had expected, in trouble both for not having reported the outbreak and also, knowing it, for having intended moving cattle to another farm. Both Charles and Judith would have to give evidence, but the case would not come up for some time. In the meantime Judith plunged into masses of information about the day-to-day work, spoke approvingly of the new hand, and told Charles that she thought Joe was sufficiently responsible now to be promoted to work that, only a short time ago, she would have hesitated to entrust to him. To all this Charles listened with interest, making a suggestion here and there, giving a word of commendation that brought the colour to Judith's cheeks. But as to more personal matters, he said nothing.

"I think I shall persuade the doctor to allow me up pretty soon," he told her one day. "Then at least I can give you a hand in the office."

Judith caught her breath. To have him so near, to be so constantly with him—it would be difficult, almost impossible to hide her feelings.

"Oh, but you mustn't," she said quickly. "I can manage . . ."

Charles looked at her quizzically, his head on one side.

"Anyone would think that you don't want me about," he commented. "I suppose—you're not thinking of sacking me yet, are you, Judith? Not until you are twenty-one! I am going to keep you to that."

"Oh, don't be absurd. You know perfectly well—" she began incoherently.

"What do I know, Judith?" he asked softly, touching her hand with gentle fingers. "Tell me."

But Judith had taken sudden alarm. She backed away from the bedside, saying breathlessly:

"You must excuse me—I think I heard Aunt Harriet calling," and scuttled out of the room. Charles, strange to say, did not seem in the least bit put out. Indeed, his lips were curved in a smile and his eyes were very tender.

After that, she definitely made excuses not to be alone with Charles until there came a day when, as Miss Harriet was just about to go upstairs with his tea-tray, the telephone bell rang. She thrust the tray into Judith's hands just as she was going to answer it and said in a way that was uncommonly fussy and flurried for her:

"Dear, dear, that will be Mrs. Gabbett. I expected her to call, but I asked her particularly to leave it until after six o'clock. Take the tray up, Judith, or the boy's tea will be cold! Have a cup with him—I was going to, but goodness knows when I'll get rid of this woman."

So Judith had no choice. She went slowly upstairs and knocked at Charles's door. A cheerful voice told her to come in and, balancing the tray on one hand, she obeyed. With her eyes lowered to the level of her burden she said a little breathlessly:

"Aunt Harriet got caught on the telephone so I had to bring it. Oh!"

For suddenly she had realised that Charles was no longer in bed. He was sitting in a chair by the window dressed in grey flannels and a white shirt, and he was smiling—smiling in a way that made Judith's heart suddenly pound.

"I didn't know——" she gasped.

"I thought it would be a surprise for you," he said easily. "I've had orders not to do anything or I'd pull the little table up." He made a movement as if it irked him to sit still and, orders or no, he intended helping her, but Judith shook her head. He must sit still. If he got up, towering above her, she would drop the tray and run away.

"I can manage," she insisted. She set the tray on the foot of the bed while she pulled up the table close to him and then began to pour out the tea. She was acutely conscious of his watchful eyes and, meeting them, found that her own dropped. Hastily she picked up the sugar tongs and lifted a lump to put into his cup, only to feel his hand descend on hers.

"Not again, Judith," he told her, and when she so obviously did not understand what he meant, added:

"You sugared it before you poured out."

"Did I?" she asked in quick confusion. "I had forgotten."

They sipped tea in silence until Judith realised that he was not eating anything. And very primly and rather reproachfully, in the way that a good nurse might speak, Judith called his attention to it.

"M'm?" he said as if his thoughts had been miles away. "Oh, yes, of course. Only it's a little bit difficult, you know. Men never do have an adequate lap for afternoon tea, and with these wretched bandages, I'm even more left-handed than usual. I suppose," he said doubtfully, "you couldn't be an angel and help me, could you? Your aunt always does."

"Yes—of course," Judith began hurriedly. "If I cut everything up small."

"And pop the bits into my mouth," he suggested, and then, seeing the doubt in her face, he sighed and added wistfully: "They say that one always feels stronger in bed than one actually is. Perhaps I ought not——"

Instantly Judith was on her knees beside him, cutting his scone and butter into tiny pieces and feeding him as one would a child.

One—two—three—four mouthfuls. Judith felt the colour in her cheeks betraying her. It seemed to mount and retreat with every beat of her heart. So close to him, actually feeling the touch of his lips on her fingers.

Very gently Judith felt the plate being taken away from her and then Charles's hand was under her chin, forcing her face up so that he could look into it. Her long lashes swept her cheeks.

"Judith!" he whispered, "Judith! Look at me!"

Slowly yet not unwillingly, her lids lifted and her eyes met his.

Charles gave a little exclamation in which triumph and impatience were blended. Then he stood up, gently lifting her to her feet, and took her into his arms. And Judith found that it did not need words for him to convince her of his love.

It was a long time before, suddenly, Judith remembered that, after all, he was still an invalid.

"Please, please, my darling!" she begged as he refused to let her go. "You must sit down, I couldn't bear that anything should go wrong—now."

He laughed ruefully.

"I suppose you are right. I have an idea, you know, young woman, that I am going to be a completely hen-pecked husband."

"No!" she said, fervently. "Never that. I promise you. But please, please——!"

Charles looked down into the anxious, loving little face and his heart seemed suddenly too big for his body. She was his, all his, and for nobody else would she ever look like that. He held her to him closely and tasted again the sweetness of her surrender. Then he sat down, but he did not let go of her hand.

"Sit on the arm," he suggested. "And put your arm round my shoulders—that's it." His head made a slight, confident movement and came to rest against the curve of her shoulder and throat. For a time silence was all-sufficient; then Charles said masterfully:

"You are going to marry me, not Desmond."

"Yes," Judith said in a small voice, and added: "Desmond is going to America—and Linda!"

"Are they?" he said in surprise. "That's sudden, isn't it? What are they planning to do there?"

"Desmond has got a job and Linda is going to keep house for him—until she gets married," Judith explained and waited, holding her breath, to see how he took that.

"Married, eh?" Charles said calmly, and then, with more interest: "Wait a minute, I bet I can tell you his name! Carl Brand—American, rather a rugged sort of face but extremely good-natured."

"Yes," Judith admitted. "I—I think he is very fond of her. And," she added with an odd little assumption of authority that made Charles smile, "that will make all the difference to Linda. Nobody has minded very much before what happened to her, and so—she got hard. But she is different now."

"I'm glad," Charles said, and meant it—for Judith's sake. For his own, he was frankly glad that Linda would not be living in the district. It would simplify life considerably, however much she had altered for the better. "And—Desmond?"

"Desmond—" Judith began, and paused. It was tempting to tell Charles everything—especially her own feeling of guilt because she did not love Desmond as he loved her. Then she remembered that she had told Desmond she believed that he was trying to make things easier for her. It was true, of course. But he was saving his own pride as well in releasing her of his own free will. And the least that she could do was back him up. "Desmond is very glad to be making a fresh start," she said quietly. "And—we parted good friends."

Charles took her hand in his and lifted it to his lips.

"You adorable child," he said softly, exactly as if he could read between the lines, but Judith stiffened ever so slightly.

"I am *not* a child!" she said firmly.

"Aren't you?" Charles asked teasingly. "What are you, then?"

A delicious smile curved Judith's lips and something sparkled in her eyes—coquetry, the knowledge that she was loved.

"Suppose you tell me," she suggested demurely.

Startled, Charles sat up so that he could look into her face, and what he saw there sent the blood tingling through his veins.

"I will!" he vowed and pulled her down on to his knees. "No, you're not such a heavy weight, nor am I so frail that I shall hurt myself. Be quiet—and listen."

And breathlessly, Judith waited.

"You are the only woman I have ever loved," he said adoringly, using, perhaps unknowingly, the very words that Linda had repeated to Judith. "The only one I have ever wanted to marry."

For a moment his eyes lingered on the small face so close to his. Then his lips met hers tenderly and yet with a passion that was unmistakable for all its restraint.

There was no room left now for any doubt. Judith, no longer scorning her sex, knew that she had found the crowning glory of a woman.

She loved—and she was loved.